MRS HUMPHRY WARD

(1851–1920) was born in Hobart, Tasmania, granddaughter of Thomas Arnold of Rugby and niece of Matthew Arnold. Her father's conversion to Roman Catholicism in 1856 effected a return to England where he joined Newman at Edgbaston, and Mary was looked after by her grandmother at Fox How, near Grasmere, and educated at boarding school. In 1865 her family—she was one of eight children—moved to Oxford, following her father's temporary return to the Anglican Church. Here Mary began her rigorous self-education: under the guidance of such men as T. H. Green, Walter Pater, Jowett ánd Mark Pattison she became a formidable scholar.

In 1872 she married T. Humphry Ward, Fellow of Brasenose College, Oxford, moving to London in 1881 when he became a member of *The Times* staff. They had a son and two daughters, the younger of whom married George Macaulay Trevelyan, and entertained the Trevelyans, the Huxleys (Julian Huxley was her nephew), the Asquiths, Henry James and Lord Haldane at their home 'Stocks' in Hertfordshire. Her first novel, *Miss Bretherton*, was published in 1884. Earlier research on Spanish ecclesiastical history for the *Dictionary of Christian Biography* led her to question certain aspects of contemporary Christianity, ideas she expressed in her second novel, *Robert Elsmere* (1888). Quoted in pulpits, reviewed by Gladstone, denounced by Marie Corelli, translated into dozens of languages, it became a best-seller in both England and America.

Mrs Humphry Ward was a prodigious social worker, establishing the Passmore Edwards Settlement (now bea̶r̶i̶ ̶ her name), campaigning to better conditions fo̶r̶ ̶ ̶ ̶ ̶ ̶ ̶ ̶ ̶ ̶ ̶ ̶ ac-tories, and working for women's h̶i̶ ̶ ̶ ̶ ̶ ̶ ̶ ̶ ̶ ̶ ̶ ̶ ̶ ̶ ̶ ̶ ite this, she was vehemently o̶ ̶ ̶ ̶ ̶ ̶ ̶ ̶ ̶ ̶ ̶ ̶ ̶ d was president of the An̶t̶ ̶ ̶ ̶ ̶ ̶ ̶ ̶ ̶ ̶ ̶ ̶ ̶ r final year Mrs Humphry ̶ ̶ ̶ ̶ ̶ ̶ ̶ ̶ ̶ ̶ ̶ ̶ having written twenty-five ̶ ̶ ̶ ̶ ̶ ̶ ̶ ̶ ̶ ̶ ̶ are *Marcella* (1894), *Helbeck ̶ ̶ ̶ ̶ ̶ ̶ ̶ ̶ ̶ ̶ ̶ ̶ ̶ ̶ y Rose's Daughter* (1903), and *The M̶ ̶ ̶ ̶ ̶ ̶ ̶ ̶ ̶m Ashe* (1905).

MARCELLA

MRS HUMPHRY WARD

With a New Introduction by
TAMIE WATTERS

PENGUIN BOOKS—VIRAGO PRESS

TO MY FATHER
I inscribe this book
in Love and Gratitude

PENGUIN BOOKS
Viking Penguin Inc., 40 West 23rd Street,
New York, New York 10010, U.S.A.
Penguin Books Ltd, Harmondsworth,
Middlesex, England
Penguin Books Australia Ltd, Ringwood,
Victoria, Australia
Penguin Books Canada Limited, 2801 John Street,
Markham, Ontario, Canada L3R 1B4
Penguin Books (N.Z.) Ltd, 182–190 Wairau Road,
Auckland 10, New Zealand

First published in Great Britain by Smith, Elder and Co. 1894
First published in the United States of America by Macmillan 1894
This edition first published in Great Britain by
Virago Press Limited 1984
Published in Penguin Books 1985

Introduction copyright © Tamie Watters, 1984
All rights reserved

ISBN 0 14 016.103 1

Printed in the United States of America by
R. R. Donnelley & Sons Company, Harrisonburg, Virginia

CONTENTS

INTRODUCTION

Mrs Humphry Ward recalled the publication in April 1894 of *Marcella* (3 vols) as 'probably the happiest date in my literary life'. She was half in love with her heroine Marcella Boyce—mad keen on socialism but as imperial a beauty as the ancestral Italian heiress whose name she bore. In 1888 *Robert Elsmere* had been a dark horse. Neither she nor her publisher George Smith were prepared for its astonishing success. But *Marcella*, a favourite from the start, was celebrated on its publication by notices placarding Piccadilly, and in Rome where she had fled to escape publicity, Marcella's name emblazoned the Spanish Steps, thanks to the English papers.

In a two-column *Times* review, she was congratulated for again thrusting

> her hand into the hot fire of living interests—this time not into the burning controversies menacing man's innermost convictions, but those that surge round property, capital, landowners, and employers, and all our economical institutions . . . Everywhere is fresh, bright actuality . . . Beneath the crust of discussions of often debated questions flows one of the old stories of humanity . . . Two or three chapters . . . almost touch the high water mark of English fiction . . . It is not a faultless piece of art . . . But many a generous-minded woman laying down *Marcella* will say, 'This is for me. Here is written what I have experienced or desired.'

Mrs Ward's fourth novel was generally heralded as an advance over *Robert Elsmere* and *David Grieve*. 'Artistically beyond all dispute, her best novel,' declared the *Manchester Guardian*. Within a month of its publication, *Marcella* went into its third edition, and before long its overwhelming popularity demanded a sequel; hence *Sir George Tressady* (1896), in one volume: the format the rest of her twenty novels were to take. In it

Marcella stages a behind-scenes war for parliamentary legislation against the sweatshops.

The reception accorded *Marcella* becomes credible when viewed against Henry James' early tribute to Mrs Ward in *The English Illustrated Magazine* (Feb. 1892). Noting two things that made the present 'completely different from yesterday . . . the immensely greater conspicuity of the novel and . . . the immensely greater conspicuity of the attitude of women', he saw their union 'represented . . . in the high distinction of Mrs Humphry Ward, who is at once the author of the work of fiction [*Robert Elsmere*] that has in our hour been most widely circulated, and the most striking example of the unprecedented *kind* of attention which the feminine mind is now at liberty to excite.' From Mrs Ward, not a man, had come 'the most deliberate and most comprehensive attempt made in England, in this later time, to hold the mirror of prose fiction up to life . . . She gave it . . . charm, and she accomplished the feat, unique, so far as I remember, in the long annals of the novel with a purpose, of carrying out her purpose without spoiling her novel. *Robert Elsmere*, James reminds us, was 'a momentous public event,' after which any work from the same pen was 'as impatiently awaited as the birth of an heir to great possessions'.

The author was thirty-seven when fame overtook her, the mother of three children and wife to Humphry Ward, *The Times'* art critic. She was born Mary Augusta Arnold in Hobart during the year of England's Great Exhibition. Her father—Thomas Arnold, son of Rugby's Arnold, had married beautiful Julia Sorell, granddaughter of a past Governor of Tasmania, while a school inspector in the province.

James made no mention of her possible debt to her uncle Matthew Arnold, as an encapsulator of culture. But in her *Recollections of a Writer* (1918), she affirmed that his *Essays in Criticism*, read at seventeen, 'set for me the currents of life'. In both scepticism and religious intensity mingle, a quality also characteristic of the Swiss philosopher Amiel whose *Journal Intime* she translated in 1885. Steeped like her uncle in European and classical literature, she had a far-ranging intelligence and would cite Cervantes, Goethe, and George Sand as precedents for her novel of ideas. Just as Matthew Arnold thought of poetry as a criticism of life, so she thought of the novel.

Though he dismissed her first novel *Miss Bretherton* (inspired by the American actress Mary Anderson) with the remark that no Arnold could write a novel, he could not be so cavalier about the second. The story of Oxford-educated Elsmere who broke with the established church to form a humanistic Christian Brotherhood in London's East End, claimed within weeks of its publication Britain's vast readership. Before his sudden death in 1888, Arnold like everyone else was wrapt in *Robert Elsmere*.

The book set off a tidal wave of reviews, debates, and sermons, including Gladstone's review in *The Nineteenth Century*. Though the then Prime Minister deplored Robert's heresy, he, like T. H. Huxley, praised the author's sympathetic portrait of the devout Evangelical Catherine Elsmere—wife and foil to the hero. Mrs Ward's tolerance received short shrift from the young Rebecca West, who, in a savage attack on the ageing author, recommended that saintly Catherine (reappearing in a 1911 novel would be better off behind the local bar struggling for a livelihood.

In America the sale of *Robert Elsmere*, mainly in pirated editions, was said to be second only to *Uncle Tom's Cabin*. So began a transatlantic reputation which grew to such outlandish proportions that in 1910 Yale professor William Lyon Phelps felt compelled to tell fellow Americans that Mrs Ward was not another Shakespeare, not England's greatest living novelist, and not even, in his opinion, a successor to George Eliot (*Essays on Modern Novelists*). Nevertheless, Theodore Roosevelt turned to Mrs Ward when he wanted Britain's cause in World War I given a hearing by the American people. So in spite of years and a malady of the leg from which she had suffered since 1892, she inspected trenches and factories and hobbled aboard the Admiral's flagship in order to produce *England's Effort* (1916) and thereby perhaps hasten America's entry into the war.

As James anticipated, Mrs Ward's distinction was confirmed by *Robert Elsmere's* successor—*The History of David Grieve* (1892), another three decker. Across a vast canvas, she follows bookish David from humble beginnings on Derbyshire moors to a northern town where he becomes a bookseller with a profit-sharing printing press for his workers, as well as an intellectual and moral force in the North, though he almost loses his way in a torrid love affair with a

Parisian artist who rejects him for art. Mrs Ward popped her nephew Julian Huxley into the novel as Grieve's whimsical baby son. Her sister Julia was married to Leonard Huxley, and Aldous, born in 1894, took the name of *Marcella's* hero.

Marcella is the last of a trio of three-volume blockbusters, which in themselves earn Mrs Ward a niche in literary history, though much is to be said for her more linear novels to come, such as *Helbeck of Bannisdale* and *Lady Rose's Daughter*. With its technical ease, *Marcella* best demonstrates her unique talent for marshalling a host of characters, events, scenes, and facts into the service of her narrative of ideas. Underriding this novel as its predecessors is the Victorian quest for betterment and spiritual fulfilment, but in addressing an ailing economy and offering a human rights protester for a heroine, it has a particular fascination for the modern reader. Equally, it is the novel which best justifies Conan Doyle's claim that Mrs Humphry Ward along with Trollope pictured the Victorian age for posterity.

At a dinner of the male Authors' Club honouring Mrs Ward in 1901, Doyle spoke on the permanent value of a work which is 'a true picture of the age in which it is produced . . . broad in conception, accurate in detail, and philosophical in spirit'. Commending Trollope for best conveying the rather soulless period of the earlier Victorian era, he then asked the company, 'And if we wish to give an idea of the later Victorian era with its transition period, its mental unrest, its groping after new truths, its sharp contrasts between old conditions and new problems, where could the student of 2000 find it more clearly set forth, with great dignity of language and thought than' in Mrs Ward.

Marcella shows a nation in social, economic, and political ferment. Bad harvests and foreign competition have brought a depression. Employers blame the loss of markets to Belgium and Germany on high wages. Workers, faced with wage cuts, strike in the Midlands. Out of such a climate socialism has risen like a Leviathan threatening the very structure of society—in mind if not in fact. 21-year-old Marcella has read Marx, a seer poet sounding like William Morris, and become a Venturist (Fabian).

The actual voices and organs raised on socialism's behalf were not so numerous as they were powerful in this period of British history.

Rivalling *Marcella* in sales in 1894 was the socialist Robert Blatchford's *Merrie England*, an edition of letters to the worker in the actual *Clarion* of the day. The articulate Fabians— Shaw, the Webbs, Annie Besant—had made their impact as had such works as H. M. Hyndman's *England for All*, Morris' *The Dream of John Ball* and *News from Nowhere*, and Henry George's *Progress and Poverty*. Under such a barrage, upper-class certainties were crumbling. As that 'moral epicure' Lady Winterbourne says, 'It is no laughing matter to feel that your *heart* and *conscience* have gone over to the enemy.' The remark gains point if Janet Trevelyan were right in thinking the model for this *grande dame* Lady Wemyss, wife of the Chairman of the Liberty and Property Defence League.

The old hierarchical society in Brookshire (Buckinghamshire) where the novel opens (and closes) is very much intact. *Marcella* fresh from art studies and Venturist companions in London feels the charm of historic Mellor to which her father's inheritance has brought her, but chafes under the constraints and inequalities. Harry Wharton, running on the Liberal ticket for West Brookshire, preaches graduated income tax and nationalisation of the land with an opportunistic eye toward the leadership of the newly-formed Labour party. For upper-class landowners like himself 'the land is mined' since '84 (agricultural labourers' franchise). Aldous Raeburn, Tory candidate for East Brookshire and heir to Lord Maxwell's estate (making up half the county), wishes he could unking himself. He jokes about preserving stately Maxwell Court until the commune takes over, but knows that 'to dogmatise about any subject under heaven, at the present day . . . was the act of an idiot'. Shortly, he sees his Cambridge mentor Edward Hallin (modelled on the Christian Economist Arnold Toynbee), one time darling of the workers he championed, cruelly ditched for militant trade unionists and their mammonish lures.

The dramatic poaching episode at the heart of the book drives home to the reader the intolerable conditions of the poor. Marcella's eloquent rage sees to that. Mrs Ward found the materials for this high drama (belying any charge that she could not write such scenes) in her own neighbourhood of Stocks, the great pile she bought in 1892 with earnings pouring in subsequent to the change in American copyright law. Shortly before the Wards moved into their Hertfordshire house, two Pendley gamekeepers were found murdered in a field near by. The death penalty passed on the culpable poachers aroused controversy not only in the local village of Aldbury but throughout the country.

Though Mrs Ward undoubtedly agreed with Aldous in think-ing the law must be upheld until changed, she makes us tingle with the excitement of the little Celt Jim Hurd, as he sets forth on his nightly forays to lay snares on the land which he has worked and known as a boy. The question is not just that of a needed change in the game laws, though *Marcella* denounces 'the wrack and waste of human life . . . for the protection of a hateful sport which demoralised the rich and their agents, no less than it tempted and provoked the poor'. The novel anticipates upheaval, an overdue redressing of the balance—hence the appraisal of the socialist panacea. Marcella recognised upon first sight of her father's neglected labourers, relegated to insanitary and leaky cottages, that 'It *is* too great a risk to let the individual alone when all these lives depend on him.' At the peak of her revolt, she contemplates revolution, for when asked to consider the poacher's victim, she retorts, 'So when a Czar of Russia is blown up, do you expect one to think only of his children. No! I will think of the tyranny and the revolt.'

With a scene shift to London where we are made as familiar with Belgravia salons and gin alleys as we were with country cottages and great houses, the novel takes on needed scope and provides a moral testing ground for the major characters. Raeburn and Wharton are at the centre of power in Parliament, while Marcella seeks power over her own destiny as a District nurse. The wild womanish desires aroused in her by Wharton's brilliance threaten self-betrayal for vanity and sex. In wanting to love, to be happy, she faces the career girl's dilemma, Wharton who has bought the *Labour Clarion* to win over the workers encounters the seductive appeal of high society. His opinions, we learn, as much as his curls and wit gain him entry, for 'few people . . . were more in demand among the great than those who gave it out that they would, if they could, abolish the great'. Wharton with his showmanship and intrigue may have pricked contemporary interest by a likeness to the prominent upper-class Marxist H. M. Hyndman, to whose alleged opportunism, conspiracies, and theatrical ways, William Morris laid the split in the Socialist Democratic Federation in 1884.

Beside his foil Wharton, the best of Mrs Ward's stock charmers, and a descendant of Jane Austen's Henry Crawford, Aldous Raeburn fades, as modesty must always do before glamour. Awkward, physically nondescript, he nonetheless wears well with his endearing sensibility and loyalty, and as his knowledge of political economy and 'I am my brother's keeper' dedication win him the regard of fellow M.P.s, he shines as the proper hero of a Victorian novel of ideas.

But what of the source and literary antecedents of the heroine who storms through the novel, looking never more beautiful than in revolt, 'with that knit brow—that tragic scorn for a base world— that royal gait'? In shunning 'the squaw theory of matrimony', she follows the path lighted by Meredith's *Diana of the Crossways* (which Mrs Ward reviewed with such enthusiasm for the *Athenaeum*) and by Nora in Ibsen's *The Doll's House*, as well as by the heroines of George Sand, who also have Marcella's broader social concerns. Very much the modern woman in her sense of autonomy and flouting of social decorum, she exerts an independence denied the earlier heroines in Virago's Victorian Classic Series—Miss Braddon's Aurora Floyd, Rhoda Broughton's Belinda, and Mrs Oliphant's Hester. Yet she has a closer kinship with those other would-be shapers and rescuers of mankind— Isabel Archer in James' *Portrait of a Lady*, Dorothea Brooke in George Eliot's *Middlemarch*, and even Jane Austen's *Emma*—than she does with the heroines of the popular New Woman novels of the day and their narrower feminist concerns (e.g. the wife with the syphilitic husband in Sarah Grand's *Heavenly Twins* (1893) or the sexually frigid woman in Iota's *Yellow Aster* (1894). Like Dorothea and Isabel she errs through vanity and ignorance (treating Aldous 'like a piece of furniture in my play'), ripens in wisdom, and undergoes a mystical spiritual experience through suffering. But she gets off lightly compared to the other two with their miserable marriages, and we can quite see Mrs Oliphant's point in chiding Mrs Ward for calling upon us 'to surrender all our convictions' to 23-year-old Marcella, adding that 'there is no girl of intelligence or imagination who has not planned a new incarnation of her'. (The Anti-Marriage League', *Blackwoods*, Jan. 1896)

In the arresting image of Marcella sick in bed at school, 'a wild mass of black hair and roving, defiant eyes in a pale face,' making-up stories in which she was always the heroine, we find a clue to the deeper origin of the novel's heroine and perhaps to the impetus behind Mrs Ward's

enormous ouput—literary and social. This is certainly little Mary
Arnold packed away to Annie Clough's Eller How school at the age of
seven. (A schoolmate confirmed the storytelling.) Mary or Polly as she
was called was as surely estranged from her roots and parental hearth
by her father's conversion to Rome in 1856, as Marcella was by Mr
Boyce's embezzlement. When Tom Arnold returned to England with
his disconsolate Protestant wife in order to join Newman at Edgbaston,
five-year-old Mary—a little black-haired wildcat like Marcella with
volatile Latin blood (from the Sorell line)—was taken in charge by
Arnold's relatives. Her grandmother's home Fox How near Grasmere
became effectively the home of her childhood and the youngest of her
aunts tamed her ('I like Aunt Fan—she's the master of me!'); but the
better part of those years was spent at boarding schools.

From the Arnolds, as her daughter and biographer Janet Trevelyan
points out, "she learnt the art of living, the art of harnessing her
daemon', but from the Sorells, she inherited 'those wilder springs of
energy and courage which impelled her . . . to be up and doing in life's
race'. She had like Marcella 'the mixed blood' needed to fuse the
English parts. She also had reason to feel with Marcella that she had
made herself.

When Thomas Arnold's temporary return to the Anglican church
established his family (numbering eight children) at Oxford, sixteen-
year-old Mary set out to educate herself under the guidance of
Jowett, T. H. Green, and Mark Pattison and eventually became a
formidable intellect. If she owed her spiritual thrust to Green, she
owed her scholarship to Pattison. Following Pattison's advice to get
to the bottom of something, she became an authority on early
Spanish ecclesiastical history, with accompanying modern German
criticism, thus paving the way to her challenge to orthodox Christianity in *Robert Elsmere* and the requisite knowledge to become the
first woman to examine at Oxford. She was also instrumental in
establishing education for women at Oxford, suggesting the name for
Somerville College and becoming its first Secretary.

The tremendous drive could be seen as a demand for recognition
from the outsider—the foreign born, the child farmed out to relatives at five, the school girl bereft of the usual parental attentions. In
Marcella's distress at her mother's indifference, we sense an un-
requited yearning for maternal love. Like memorable heroines to

INTRODUCTION

come—Laura Fountain of *Helbeck of Bannisdale* and Julie Le Breton of *Lady Rose's Daughter*, Marcella is essentially motherless.

Always ready to befriend or help, whether it was campaigning for better factory conditions, writing on infant feeding, or producing diagnostic novels, Mrs Ward became for a while the heroine Marcella dreamt of being. Somewhat the victim of her own success, she was taken up by the Establishment and lured into dreams of Empire. But what really cast a shadow over her life was her presidency of the Anti-Suffrage League. Why should she who championed free thought and created stunning Laura Fountain, who gives up her life rather than forfeit her mental freedom, so box herself in? She acted from the belief that suffragettes were wasting energies better used in women's education, social work, and local government, and that men as the managers of the Empire should also control parliament. In her suffragette novel *Delia Blanchflower* (1914), the gifted teacher Gertrude Marvell destroys herself and a national treasure in militant action.

Mrs Ward paid dearly for her stand in reputation and emotional stress. It is now time her achievement was recognised—not just the prodigious literary output of novels, translations, reviews, and articles, but the imaginative social work—the first playschools, the first vacation schools, and the first school for handicapped children in London, all emanating from the Passmore Edwards Settlement (now bearing her name), which she founded to serve the spiritual, educational, and recreational needs of the working class.

The novels are due for a reassessment, and one cannot help agreeing with Somerset Maugham, 'How unjust it is that Mrs Humphry Ward with her well-stored mind and her command of language, with her solid gifts, her conscientiousness and seriousness, should be so forgotten that even her name will be unknown to most readers today.' The novels with their purposefulness and bias of an age past, fell out of favour during the war years and came under attack by Bloomsbury and the young Rebecca West. But as she would plead, 'What authority bars the way' to the novel of purpose if it is done with art? She recommended a greater indulgence for one another, admiring what we cannot do—as George Sand and Balzac admired each other's differing gifts. She after all was the woman novelist most read and admired at the turn of the century. Today she is the Victorian novelist most deserving a revival.

As an introduction to her work, *Marcella* offers a well-told and moving love story, as well as the treasure-packed cargo ship Henry James declared her early novels to be. *The Bookman* found in it a 'liberal education' on the Labour question, while a fellow novelist Margaret Woods saw its charm in the mellow beauty of the old-world civilisation depicted. Far from being thesis ridden, the pictures of village life with irrepressible survivors like Mrs Jellison and old Patton have the vitality of Flora Thompson's *Lark Rise to Candleford*. For the modern reader, the novel unloads issues and problems still to the fore in the late twentieth century—women's battle for self-realisation, personal liberty versus a welfare state, law and order versus progress, and even the plight of the stately home in an egalitarian headed society. The novel's considered view, 'Socialism will not bring in a new order but make the old one sound', still gives a glimmer of hope in a jaded Western society. What astonishes is *Marcella*'s sense of urgency, prophetic warnings of vast changes to come, and unheeded as England fell into its deceptive Edwardian summer.

Tamie Watters, Mapledurham Village, Oxfordshire 1983

BOOK I

'If Nature put not forth her power
About the opening of the flower,
Who is it that could live an hour?'

CHAPTER I

'THE mists—and the sun—and the first streaks of yellow in the beeches—beautiful !—*beautiful* !'

And with a long breath of delight Marcella Boyce threw herself on her knees by the window she had just opened, and, propping her face upon her hands, devoured the scene before her with that passionate intensity of pleasure which had been her gift and heritage through life.

She looked out upon a broad and level lawn, smoothed by the care of centuries, flanked on either side by groups of old trees—some Scotch firs, some beeches, a cedar or two—groups where the slow selective hand of time had been at work for generations, developing here the delightful roundness of quiet mass and shade, and there the bold caprice of bare fir trunks and ragged branches, standing black against the sky. Beyond the lawn stretched a green descent indefinitely long, carrying the eye indeed almost to the limit of the view, and becoming from the lawn onwards a wide irregular avenue, bordered by beeches of a splendid maturity, ending at last in a far distant gap where a gate—and a gate of some importance—clearly should have been, yet was not. The size of the trees, the wide uplands of the falling valley to the left of the avenue, now rich in the tints of harvest, the autumn sun pouring steadily through the vanishing mists, the green breadth of the vast lawn, the unbroken peace of wood and cultivated ground, all carried with them a confused general impression of well-being and of dignity. Marcella drew it in—this impression—with avidity. Yet at the same moment she noticed involuntarily the gateless gap at the end of the avenue, the choked condition of the garden paths on either side of the lawn, and the unsightly tufts of grass spotting the broad gravel terrace beneath her window.

'It *is* a heavenly place, all said and done,' she protested to herself with a little frown. 'But no doubt it would have been better still if Uncle Robert had looked after it, and we could afford to keep the garden decent. Still——'

She dropped on a stool beside the open window, and as her eyes steeped themselves afresh in what they saw, the frown disappeared again in the former look of glowing content—that content of youth which is never merely passive, nay, rather, contains an invariable element of covetous eagerness.

It was but three months or so since Marcella's father, Mr. Richard Boyce, had succeeded to the ownership of Mellor Park, the old home of the Boyces, and it was little more than six weeks since Marcella had received her summons home from the students' boarding-house in Kensington where she had been lately living. She had ardently wished to assist in the June 'settling-in,' having not been able to apply her mind to the music or painting she was supposed to be studying, nor indeed to any other subject whatever, since the news of their inheritance had reached her. But her mother in a dry little note had let it be known that she preferred to manage the move for herself. Marcella had better go on with her studies as long as possible.

Yet Marcella was here at last. And as she looked round her large bare room, with its old dilapidated furniture, and then out again to woods and lawns, it seemed to her that all was now well, and that her childhood with its squalors and miseries was blotted out—atoned for by this last kind sudden stroke of fate, which might have been delayed so deplorably !—since no one could have reasonably expected that an apparently sound man of sixty would have succumbed in three days to the sort of common chill a hunter and sportsman must have resisted successfully a score of times before.

Her great desire now was to put the past—the greater part of it at any rate—behind her altogether. Its shabby worries were surely done with, poor as she and her parents still were, relatively to their present position. At least she was no longer the self-conscious schoolgirl, paid for at a lower rate than her companions, stinted in dress, pocket-money, and education, and fiercely resentful at every turn of some real or fancied slur ; she was no longer even the half-Bohemian student of these past two years, enjoying herself in London so far as the iron necessity of keeping her boarding-house expenses down to the lowest possible figure would allow. She was something altogether different. She was Marcella Boyce, a 'finished' and grown-up young woman of twenty-one, the only daughter and child of Mr. Boyce of Mellor Park, inheritress of one of the most ancient names in Midland England, and just entering on a life which, to her own fancy and will at any rate, promised the highest possible degree of interest and novelty.

Yet, in the very act of putting her past away from her, she only succeeded, so it seemed, in inviting it to repossess her.

For against her will, she fell straightway—in this quiet of the autumn morning—into a riot of memory, setting her past self

against her present more consciously than she had done yet,
recalling scene after scene and stage after stage with feelings of
sarcasm, or amusement, or disgust, which showed themselves freely
as they came and went, in the fine plastic face turned to the
September woods.

She had been at school since she was nine years old—there was
the dominant fact in these motley uncomfortable years behind her,
which, in her young ignorance of the irrevocableness of living, she
wished so impatiently to forget. As to the time before her school
life, she had a dim memory of seemly and pleasant things, of a
house in London, of a large and bright nursery, of a smiling mother
who took constant notice of her, of games, little friends, and
birthday parties. What had led to the complete disappearance of
this earliest ' set,' to use a theatrical phrase, from the scenery of
her childhood, Marcella did not yet adequately know, though she
had some theories and many suspicions in the background of her
mind. But at any rate this first image of memory was succeeded
by another precise as the first was vague—the image of a tall
white house, set against a white chalk cliff rising in terraces behind
it and alongside it, where she had spent the years from nine to
fourteen, and where, if she were set down blindfold, now, at
twenty-one, she could have found her way to every room and door
and cupboard and stair with a perfect and fascinated familiarity.

When she entered that house she was a lanky, black-eyed
creature, tall for her age, and endowed or, as she herself would
have put it, cursed with an abundance of curly unmanageable hair,
whereof the brushing and tending soon became to a nervous
clumsy child, not long parted from her nurse, one of the worst
plagues of her existence. During her home life she had been an
average child of the quick and clever type, with average faults.
But something in the bare, ugly rooms, the discipline, the teaching,
the companionship of Miss Frederick's Cliff House School for
Young Ladies, transformed little Marcella Boyce, for the time
being, into a demon. She hated her lessons, though, when she
chose, she could do them in a hundredth part of the time taken by
her companions ; she hated getting up in the wintry dark, and her
cold ablutions with some dozen others in the comfortless lavatory ;
she hated the meals in the long schoolroom, where, because twice
meat was forbidden and twice pudding allowed, she invariably
hungered fiercely for more mutton and scorned her second course,
making a sort of dramatic story to herself out of Miss Frederick's
tyranny and her own thwarted appetite as she sat black-browed
and brooding in her place. She was not a favourite with her
companions, and she was a perpetual difficulty and trouble to her

perfectly well-intentioned schoolmistress. The whole of her first
year was one continual series of sulks, quarrels, and revolts.

Perhaps her blackest days were the days she spent occasionally
in bed, when Miss Frederick, at her wit's end, would take advantage
of one of the child's perpetual colds to try the effects of a day's
seclusion and solitary confinement, administered in such a form
that it could do her charge no harm, and might, she hoped, do her
good. 'For I do believe a great part of it's liver or nerves ! No
child in her right senses could behave so,' she would declare to the
mild and stout French lady who had been her partner for years,
and who was more inclined to befriend and excuse Marcella than
anyone else in the house—no one exactly knew why.

Now the rule of the house when any girl was ordered to bed
with a cold was, in the first place, that she should not put her arms
outside the bedclothes—for if you were allowed to read and amuse
yourself in bed you might as well be up ; that the housemaid should
visit the patient in the early morning with a cup of senna-tea, and
at long and regular intervals throughout the day with beef-tea and
gruel ; and that no one should come to see and talk with her,
unless, indeed, it were the doctor, quiet being in all cases of sickness the first condition of recovery, and the natural schoolgirl in
Miss Frederick's persuasion being more or less inclined to complain
without cause if illness were made agreeable.

For some fourteen hours, therefore, on these days of durance
Marcella was left almost wholly alone, nothing but a wild mass of
black hair and a pair of roving, defiant eyes in a pale face showing
above the bedclothes whenever the housemaid chose to visit her—
a pitiable morsel, in truth, of rather forlorn humanity. For though
she had her movements of fierce revolt, when she was within an
ace of throwing the senna-tea in Martha's face, and rushing downstairs in her night-gown to denounce Miss Frederick in the midst
of an astonished schoolroom, something generally interposed ; not
conscience, it is to be feared, or any wish 'to be good,' but only an
aching, inmost sense of childish loneliness and helplessness ; a
perception that she had indeed tried everybody's patience to the
limit, and that these days in bed represented crises which must be
borne with even by such a rebel as Marcie Boyce.

So she submitted, and presently learnt, under dire stress of
boredom, to amuse herself a good deal by developing a natural
capacity for dreaming awake. Hour by hour she followed out an
endless story of which she was always the heroine. Before the
annoyance of her afternoon gruel, which she loathed, was well
forgotten, she was in full fairy-land again, figuring generally as the
trusted friend and companion of the Princess of Wales—of that

beautiful Alexandra, the top and model of English society, whose portrait in the window of the little stationer's shop at Marswell— the small country town near Cliff House—had attracted the child's attention once, on a dreary walk, and had ever since governed her dreams. Marcella had no fairy-tales, but she spun a whole cycle for herself around the lovely Princess who came to seem to her before long her own particular property. She had only to shut her eyes and she had caught her idol's attention—either by some look or act of passionate yet unobtrusive homage as she passed the royal carriage in the street—or by throwing herself in front of the divinity's runaway horses—or by a series of social steps easily devised by an imaginative child, well aware, in spite of appearances, that she was of an old family and had aristocratic relations. Then, when the Princess had held out a gracious hand and smiled, all was delight! Marcella grew up on the instant : she was beautiful, of course ; she had, so people said, the ' Boyce eyes and hair ;' she had sweeping gowns, generally of white muslin with cherry-coloured ribbons ; she went here and there with the Princess, laughing and talking quite calmly with the greatest people in the land, her romantic friendship with the adored of England making her all the time the observed of all observers, bringing her a thousand delicate flatteries and attentions.

Then, when she was at the very top of ecstasy, floating in the softest summer sea of fancy, some little noise would startle her into opening her eyes, and there beside her in the deepening dusk would be the bare white beds of her two dormitory companions, the ugly wall-paper opposite, and the uncovered boards with their frugal strips of carpet stretching away on either hand. The tea-bell would ring perhaps in the depths far below, and the sound would complete the transformation of the Princess's maid-of-honour into Marcie Boyce, the plain naughty child, whom nobody cared about, whose mother never wrote to her, who in contrast to every other girl in the school had not a single ' party frock,' and who would have to choose next morning between another dumb day of senna-tea and gruel, supposing she chose to plead that her cold was still obstinate, or getting up at half-past six to repeat half a page of Ince's ' Outlines of English History ' in the chilly school-room, at seven.

Looking back now as from another world on that unkempt frac-tious Marcie of Cliff House, the Marcella of the present saw with a mixture of amusement and self-pity that one great aggravation of that child's daily miseries had been a certain injured, irritable sense of social difference between herself and her companions. Some proportion of the girls at Cliff House were drawn from the

tradesman class of two or three neighbouring towns. Their trades-
men papas were sometimes ready to deal on favourable terms with
Miss Frederick for the supply of her establishment ; in which case
the young ladies concerned evidently felt themselves very much at
home, and occasionally gave themselves airs which alternately
mystified and enraged a little spitfire outsider like Marcella Boyce.
Even at ten years old she perfectly understood that she was one of
the Boyces of Brookshire, and that her great-uncle had been a
famous Speaker of the House of Commons. The portrait of this
great-uncle had hung in the dining-room of that pretty London
house which now seemed so far away ; her father had again and
again pointed it out to the child, and taught her to be proud of it ;
and more than once her childish eye had been caught by the likeness between it and an old grey-haired gentleman who occasionally
came to see them, and whom she called ' Grandpapa.' Through
one influence and another she had drawn the glory of it, and the
dignity of her race generally, into her childish blood. There they
were now—the glory and the dignity—a feverish leaven, driving
her perpetually into the most crude and ridiculous outbreaks, which
could lead to nothing but humiliation.

' I wish my great-uncle were here ! *He'd* make you remember
—you great—you great—big bully you !'—she shrieked on one
occasion when she had been defying a big girl in authority, and
the big girl—the stout and comely daughter of a local ironmonger
—had been successfully asserting herself.

The big girl opened her eyes wide and laughed.

' *Your* great-uncle ! Upon my word ! And who may he be,
miss ? If it comes to that, I'd like to show *my* great-uncle David
how you've scratched my wrist. He'd give it you. He's almost
as strong as father, though he is so old. You get along with you,
and behave yourself, and don't talk stuff to me.'

Whereupon Marcella, choking with rage and tears, found
herself pushed out of the schoolroom and the door shut upon her.
She rushed up to the top terrace which was the school playground,
and sat there in a hidden niche of the wall, shaking and crying,—
now planning vengeance on her conqueror, and now hot all over
with the recollection of her own ill-bred and impotent folly.

No—during those first two years the only pleasures, so memory
declared, were three : the visits of the cake-woman on Saturday—
Marcella sitting in her window could still taste the three-cornered
puffs and small sweet pears on which, as much from a fierce sense
of freedom and self-assertion as anything else, she had lavished
her tiny weekly allowance ; the mad games of ' tig,' which she led
and organised in the top playground ; and the kindnesses of fat

Mademoiselle Rénier, Miss Frederick's partner, who saw a likeness in Marcella to a long-dead small sister of her own, and surreptitiously indulged 'the little wild-cat,' as the school generally dubbed the Speaker's great-niece, whenever she could.

But with the third year fresh elements and interests had entered in. Romance awoke, and with it certain sentimental affections. In the first place, a taste for reading had rooted itself—reading of the adventurous and poetical kind. There were two or three books which Marcella had absorbed in a way it now made her envious to remember. For at twenty-one people who take interest in many things, and are in a hurry to have opinions, must skim and 'turn over' books rather than read them, must use indeed as best they may a scattered and distracted mind, and suffer occasional pangs of conscience as pretenders. But at thirteen—what concentration ! what devotion ! what joy ! One of these precious volumes was Bulwer's 'Rienzi ;' another was Miss Porter's 'Scottish Chiefs ;' a third was a little red volume of 'Marmion' which an aunt had given her. She probably never read any of them through—she had not a particle of industry or method in her composition—but she lived in them. The parts which it bored her to read she easily invented for herself, but the scenes and passages which thrilled her she knew by heart ; she had no gift for verse-making, but she laboriously wrote a long poem on the death of Rienzi, and she tried again and again with a not inapt hand to illustrate for herself in pen and ink the execution of Wallace.

But all these loves for things and ideas were soon as nothing in comparison with a friendship, and an adoration.

To take the adoration first. When Marcella came to Cliff House she was recommended by the same relation who gave her ' Marmion' to the kind offices of the clergyman of the parish, who happened to be known to some of the Boyce family. He and his wife—they had no children—did their duty amply by the odd undisciplined child. They asked her to tea once or twice ; they invited her to the school-treat, where she was only self-conscious and miserably shy ; and Mr. Ellerton had at least one friendly and pastoral talk with Miss Frederick as to the difficulties of her pupil's character. For a long time little came of it. Marcella was hard to tame, and when she went to tea at the Rectory Mrs. Ellerton, who was refined and sensible, did not know what to make of her, though in some unaccountable way she was drawn to and interested by the child. But with the expansion of her thirteenth year there suddenly developed in Marcie's stormy breast an overmastering absorbing passion for these two persons. She did not show it to them much, but for herself it raised her to another plane of existence, gave her new objects and new standards. She who had hated going to church now counted time entirely by Sundays. To see the pulpit occupied by any other form and face than those of the rector was a calamity hardly to be borne ; if the exit of the school party were delayed by any accident so that Mr. and Mrs. Ellerton overtook them in the churchyard, Marcella would walk home on air, quivering with a passionate delight, and in the dreary afternoon of the school Sunday she would spend her time happily in trying to write down the heads of Mr. Ellerton's sermon. In the natural course of things she would, at this time, have taken no interest in such things at all, but whatever had been spoken by him had grace, thrill, meaning.

Nor was the week quite barren of similar delights. She was generally sent to practise on an old square piano in one of the top rooms. The window in front of her overlooked the long white drive and the distant high road into which it ran. Three times a week on an average Mrs. Ellerton's pony carriage might be expected to pass along that road. Every day Marcella watched for it, alive with expectation, her fingers strumming as they pleased. Then with the first gleam of the white pony in the distance, over would go the music stool, and the child leapt to the window, remaining fixed there, breathing quick and eagerly till the trees on the left had hidden from her the graceful erect figure of Mrs. Ellerton. Then her moment of Paradise was over ; but the after-glow of it lasted for the day.

So much for romance, for feelings as much like love as child-hood can know them, full of kindling charm and mystery. Her friendship had been of course different, but it also left deep mark. A tall, consumptive girl among the Cliff House pupils, the mother-less daughter of a clergyman-friend of Miss Frederick's, had for some time taken notice of Marcella, and at length won her by nothing else, in the first instance, than a remarkable gift for story-telling. She was a parlour-boarder, had a room to herself, and a fire in it when the weather was cold. She was not held strictly to lesson hours ; many delicacies in the way of food were provided for her, and Miss Frederick watched over her with a quite maternal solicitude. When winter came she developed a troublesome cough, and the doctor recommended that a little suite of rooms looking south and leading out on the middle terrace of the garden should be given up to her. There was a bedroom, an intermediate dressing-room, and then a little sitting-room built out upon the terrace, with a window-door opening upon it.

Here Mary Lant spent week after week. Whenever lesson hours were done she clamoured for Marcie Boyce, and Marcella was always eager to go to her. She would fly up stairs and passages, knock at the bedroom door, run down the steps to the queer little dressing-room where the roof nearly came on your head, and down more steps again to the sitting-room. Then when the door was shut, and she was crooning over the fire with her friend, she was entirely happy. The tiny room was built on the edge of the terrace, the ground fell rapidly below it, and the west window commanded a broad expanse of tame arable country, of square fields and hedges, and scattered wood. Marcella, looking back upon that room, seemed always to see it flooded with the rays of wintry sunset, a kettle boiling on the fire, her pale friend in a shawl crouching over the warmth, and the branches of a snowberry tree, driven by the wind, beating against the terrace door.

But what a story-teller was Mary Lant! She was the inventor of a story called 'John and Julia,' which went on for weeks and months without ever producing the smallest satiety in Marcella. Unlike her books of adventure, this was a domestic drama of the purest sort ; it was extremely moral and evangelical, designed indeed by its sensitively religious author for Marcie's correction and improvement. There was in it a sublime hero, who set everybody's faults to rights and lectured the heroine. In real life Marcella would probably before long have been found trying to kick his shins—a mode of warfare of which in her demon moods she was past mistress. But as Mary Lant described him, she not only bore with and trembled before him—she adored him. The taste for him and his like, as well as for the story-teller herself—a girl of a tremulous, melancholy fibre, sweet-natured, possessed by a Calvinist faith, and already prescient of death—grew upon her. Soon her absorbing desire was to be altogether shut up with Mary, except on Sundays and at practising times. For this purpose she gave herself the worst cold she could achieve, and cherished diligently what she proudly considered to be a racking cough. But Miss Frederick was deaf to the latter, and only threatened the usual upstairs seclusion and senna-tea for the former, whereupon Marcella in alarm declared that her cold was much better and gave up the cough in despair. It was her first sorrow and cost her some days of pale brooding and silence, and some nights of stifled tears, when during an Easter holiday a letter from Miss Frederick to her mother announced the sudden death of Mary Lant.

CHAPTER II

FRIENDSHIP and love are humanising things, and by her four-teenth year Marcella was no longer a clever little imp, but a fast-maturing and in some ways remarkable girl, with much of the woman in her already. She had begun even to feel an interest in her dress, to speculate occasionally on her appearance. At the fourth breaking-up party after her arrival at Cliff House, Marcella, who had usually figured on these occasions in a linsey-woolsey high to the throat, amid the frilled and sashed splendours of her companions, found lying on her bed, when she went up with the others to dress, a plain white muslin dress with blue ribbons. It was the gift of old Mademoiselle Rénier, who affectionately wished her queer, neglected favourite to look well. Marcella examined it and fingered it with an excited mixture of feelings. First of all there was the sore and swelling bitterness that she should owe such things to the kindness of the French governess, whereas finery for the occasion had been freely sent to all the other girls from 'home.' She very nearly turned her back upon the bed and its pretty burden. But then the mere snowy whiteness of the muslin and freshness of the ribbons, and the burning curiosity to see herself decked therein, overcame a nature which, in the midst of its penury, had been always really possessed by a more than common hunger for sensuous beauty and seemliness. Marcella wore it, was stormily happy in it, and kissed Mademoiselle Rénier for it at night with an effusion, nay, some tears, which no one at Cliff House had ever witnessed in her before except with the ac-companiments of rage and fury.

A little later her father came to see her, the first and only visit he paid to her at school. Marcella, to whom he was by now almost a stranger, received him demurely, making no confidences, and took him over the house and gardens. When he was about to leave her a sudden upswell of paternal sentiment made him ask her if she was happy and if she wanted anything.

'Yes!' said Marcella, her large eyes gleaming; 'tell mamma I want a "fringe." Every other girl in the school has got one.'

And she pointed disdainfully to her plainly parted hair. Her father, astonished by her unexpected vehemence, put up his eye-glass and studied the child's appearance. Three days later, by her mother's permission, Marcella was taken to the hairdresser at Marswell by Mademoiselle Rénier, returned in all the glories of a 'fringe,' and, in acknowledgment thereof, wrote her mother a letter which for the first time had something else than formal news in it.

Meanwhile new destinies were preparing for her. For a variety of small reasons Mr. Boyce, who had never yet troubled himself about the matter from a distance, was not, upon personal inspection, very favourably struck with his daughter's surroundings. His wife remarked shortly, when he complained to her, that Marcella seemed to her as well off as the daughter of persons of their means could expect to be. But Mr. Boyce stuck to his point. He had just learnt that Harold, the only son of his widowed brother Robert, of Mellor Park, had recently developed a deadly disease, which might be long, but must in the end be sure. If the young man died and he outlived Robert, Mellor Park would be his; they would and must return, in spite of certain obstacles, to their natural rank in society, and Marcella must of course be produced as his daughter and heiress. When his wife repulsed him, he went to his eldest sister, an old maid with a small income of her own, who happened to be staying with them, and was the only member of his family with whom he was now on terms. She was struck with his remarks, which bore on family pride, a commodity not always to be reckoned on in the Boyces, but which she herself possessed in abundance; and when he paused she slowly said that if an ideal school of another type could be found for Marcella, she would be responsible for what it might cost over and above the present arrangement. Marcella's manners were certainly rough; it was difficult to say what she was learning, or with whom she was associating; accomplishments she appeared to have none. Something should certainly be done for her—considering the family contingencies. But being a strong evangelical, the aunt stipulated for 'religious influences,' and said she would write to a friend.

The result was that a month or two later Marcella, now close on her fourteenth birthday, was transferred from Cliff House to the charge of a lady who managed a small but much-sought-after school for young ladies at Solesby, a watering place on the east coast.

But when in the course of reminiscence Marcella found herself once more at Solesby, memory began to halt and wander, to choose another tone and method. At Solesby the rough surroundings and primitive teaching of Cliff House, together with her own burning sense of inferiority and disadvantage, had troubled her no more. She was well taught there, and developed quickly from the troublesome child into the young lady duly broken in to all social proprieties. But it was not her lessons or her dancing-masters that she remembered. She had made for herself agitations at Cliff House, but what were they as compared to the agitations of Solesby ! Life there had been one long Wertherish romance in which there were few incidents, only feelings, which were themselves events. It contained humiliations and pleasures, but they had been all matters of spiritual relation, connected with one figure only—the figure of her schoolmistress, Miss Pemberton ; and with one emotion only—a passion, an adoration, akin to that she had lavished on the Ellertons, but now much more expressive and mature. A tall slender woman, with brown, grey-besprinkled hair falling in light curls after the fashion of our grandmothers on either cheek, and braided into a classic knot behind—the face of a saint, an enthusiast—eyes overflowing with feeling above a thin firm mouth—the mouth of the obstinate saint, yet sweet also : this delicate significant picture was stamped on Marcella's heart. What tremors of fear and joy could she not remember in connection with it ? what night-vigils when a tired girl kept herself through long hours awake that she might see at last the door open and a figure with a night-lamp standing an instant in the doorway?—for Miss Pemberton, who slept little and read late, never went to rest without softly going the rounds of her pupils' rooms. What storms of contest, mainly provoked by Marcella for the sake of the emotions, first of combat, then of reconciliation to which they led ! What a strange development on the pupil's side of a certain histrionic gift, a turn for imaginative intrigue, for endless small contrivances such as might rouse or heighten the recurrent excitements of feeling ! What agitated moments of religious talk ! What golden days in the holidays, when long-looked-for letters arrived full of religious admonition, letters which were carried about and wept over till they fell to pieces under the stress of such a worship —what terrors and agonies of a stimulated conscience—what remorse for sins committed at school—what zeal to confess them in letters of a passionate eloquence—and what indifference meanwhile to anything of the same sort that might have happened at home !

Strange faculty that women have for thus lavishing their heart's blood from their very cradles ! Marcella could hardly look back now, in the quiet of thought, to her five years with Miss Pemberton without a shiver of agitation. Yet now she never saw her. It was two years since they parted ; the school was broken up ; her idol had gone to India to join a widowed brother. It was all over— for ever. Those precious letters had worn themselves away ; so, too, had Marcella's religious feelings ; she was once more another being.

But these two years since she had said good-bye to Solesby

and her schooldays ? Once set thinking of bygones by the stimulus
of Mellor and its novelty, Marcella must needs think, too, of her
London life, of all that it had opened to her, and meant for her.
Fresh agitations !—fresh passions !—but this time impersonal,
passions of the mind and sympathies.

At the time she left Solesby her father and mother were abroad,
and it was apparently not convenient that she should join them.
Marcella, looking back, could not remember that she had ever
been much desired at home. No doubt she had been often moody
and tiresome in the holidays ; but she suspected—nay, was certain
—that there had been other and more permanent reasons why her
parents felt her presence with them a burden. At any rate, when
the moment came for her to leave Miss Pemberton, her mother
wrote from abroad that, as Marcella had of late shown decided
aptitude both for music and painting, it would be well that she
should cultivate both gifts for a while more seriously than would
be possible at home. Mrs. Boyce had made inquiries, and was
quite willing that her daughter should go, for a time, to a lady
whose address she enclosed, and to whom she herself had written
—a lady who received girl-students working at the South Kensington art classes.

So began an experience, as novel as it was strenuous. Marcella
soon developed all the airs of independence and all the jargon of
two professions. Working with consuming energy and ambition,
she pushed her gifts so far as to become at least a very intelligent,
eager, and confident critic of the art of other people—which is
much. But though art stirred and trained her, gave her new
horizons and new standards, it was not in art that she found ultimately the chief excitement and motive-power of her new life—not
in art, but in the birth of social and philanthropic ardour, the sense
of a hitherto unsuspected social power.

One of her girl-friends and fellow-students had two brothers in
London, both at work at South Kensington, and living not far from
their sister. The three were orphans. They sprang from a nervous, artistic stock, and Marcella had never before come near anyone capable of crowding so much living into the twenty-four hours.
The two brothers. both of them skilful and artistic designers in
different lines, and hard at work all day, were members of a rising
Socialist society, and spent their evenings almost entirely on
various forms of social effort and Socialist propaganda. They
seemed to Marcella's young eyes absolutely sincere and quite
unworldly. They lived as workmen ; and both the luxuries and
the charities of the rich were equally odious to them. That there
could be any ' right ' in private property or private wealth had

become incredible to them ; their minds were full of lurid images or resentments drawn from the existing state of London ; and though one was humorous and handsome, the other short, sickly, and pedantic, neither could discuss the Socialist ideal without passion, nor hear it attacked without anger.   And in milder measure their sister, who possessed more artistic gift than either of them, was like unto them.

Marcella saw much of these three persons, and something of their friends.   She went with them to Socialist lectures, or to the public evenings of the Venturist Society, to which the brothers belonged.   Edie, the sister, assaulted the imagination of her friend, made her read the books of a certain eminent poet and artist, once the poet of love and dreamland, ' the idle singer of an empty day,' now seer and prophet, the herald of an age to come, in which none shall possess, though all shall enjoy.   The brothers, more ambitious, attacked her through the reason, brought her popular translations and selections from Marx and Lassalle, together with each Venturist pamphlet and essay as it appeared ; they flattered her with technical talk ; they were full of the im-portance of women to the new doctrine and the new era.

The handsome brother was certainly in love with her; the other, probably.   Marcella was not in love with either of them, but she was deeply interested in all three, and for the sickly brother she felt at that time a profound admiration—nay, rever-ence—which influenced her vitally at a critical moment of life. ' Blessed are the poor '—' Woe unto you, rich men '—these were the only articles of his scanty creed, but they were held with a fervour, and acted upon with a conviction, which our modern religion seldom commands.   His influence made Marcella a rent-collector under a lady friend of his in the East End ; because of it, she worked herself beyond her strength in a joint attempt made by some members of the Venturist Society to organise a Tailor-esses' Union ; and, to please him, she read articles and blue-books on Sweating and Overcrowding.   It was all very moving and very dramatic ; so, too, was the persuasion Marcella divined in her friends, that she was destined in time, with work and experience, to great things and high place in the movement.

The wholly unexpected news of Mr. Boyce's accession to Mellor had very various effects upon this little band of comrades. It revived in Marcella ambitions, instincts and tastes wholly different from those of her companions, but natural to her by temperament and inheritance.   The elder brother, Anthony Craven, always melancholy and suspicious, divined her imme-diately.

'How glad you are to be done with Bohemia!' he said to her ironically one day, when he had just discovered her with the photographs of Mellor about her. 'And how rapidly it works!'

'What works?' she asked him angrily.

'The poison of possession. And what a mean end it puts to things! A week ago you were all given to causes not your own; now, how long will it take you to think of us as " poor fanatics!" —and to be ashamed you ever knew us?'

'You mean to say that I am a mean hypocrite!' she cried. 'Do you think that because I delight in—in pretty things and old associations, I must give up all my convictions? Shall I find no poor at Mellor—no work to do? It is unkind—unfair. It is the way all reform breaks down—through mutual distrust!'

He looked at her with a cold smile in his dark, sunken eyes, and she turned from him indignantly.

When they bade her good-bye at the station, she begged them to write to her.

'No, no!' said Louis, the handsome younger brother. 'If ever you want us, we are there. If you write, we will answer. But you won't need to think about us yet awhile. Good-bye!'

And he pressed her hand with a smile.

The good fellow had put all his own dreams and hopes out of sight with a firm hand since the arrival of her great news. Indeed, Marcella realised in them all that she was renounced. Louis and Edith spoke with affection and regret. As to Anthony, from the moment that he set eyes upon the maid sent to escort her to Mellor, and the first-class ticket that had been purchased for her, Marcella perfectly understood that she had become to him as an enemy.

'They shall see—I will show them!' she said to herself with angry energy, as the train whirled her away. And her sense of their unwarrantable injustice kept her tense and silent till she was roused to a childish and passionate pleasure by a first sight of the wide lawns and time-stained front of Mellor

Of such elements, such memories of persons, things, and events, was Marcella's reverie by the window made up. One thing, however, which, clearly, this report of it has not explained, is that spirit of energetic discontent with her past in which she had entered on her musings. Why such soreness of spirit? Her childhood had been pinched and loveless; but, after all, it could well bear comparison with that of many another child of impoverished parents. There had been compensations all through—

and was not the great passion of her Solesby days, together
with the interest and novelty of her London experience, enough
to give zest and glow to the whole retrospect ?

Ah ! but it will be observed that in this sketch of Marcella's
schooldays nothing has been said of Marcella's holidays. In this
omission the narrative has but followed the hasty, half-conscious
gaps and slurs of the girl's own thought. For Marcella never
thought of those holidays and all that was connected with them *in
detail*, if she could possibly avoid it. But it was with them, in
truth, and with what they implied, that she was so irritably anxious
to be done when she first began to be reflective by the window ;
and it was to them she returned with vague, but still intense consciousness when the rush of active reminiscence died away.

That surely was the breakfast bell ringing, and with the dignified
ancestral sound which was still so novel and attractive to Marcella's
ear. Recalled to Mellor Park and its circumstances, she went
thoughtfully downstairs, pondering a little on the shallow steps of
the beautiful Jacobean staircase. *Could* she ever turn her back
upon those holidays ? Was she not rather, so to speak, just
embarked upon their sequel, or second volume ?

But let us go downstairs also.

CHAPTER III

BREAKFAST was laid in the ' Chinese room,' a room which formed
part of the stately ' garden front,' added to the original structure of
the house in the eighteenth century by a Boyce whose wife had
money. The decorations, especially of the domed and vaulted
roof, were supposed by their eighteenth-century designer to be
'Oriental ;' they were, at any rate, intricate and overladen ; and
the figures of mandarins on the worn and discoloured wall-paper
had, at least, top-knots, pig-tails, and petticoats to distinguish them
from the ordinary Englishmen of 1760, besides a charming mellow-
ness of colour and general effect bestowed on them by time and
dilapidation. The marble mantelpiece was elaborately carved in
Chinamen and pagodas. There were Chinese curiosities of a miscellaneous kind on the tables, and the beautiful remains of an
Indian carpet underfoot. Unluckily, some later Boyce had thrust
a crudely Gothic sideboard, with an arched and pillared front,
adapted to the purposes of a warming apparatus, into the midst of
the mandarins, which disturbed the general effect. But with all its

original absurdities, and its modern defacements, the room was a beautiful and stately one. Marcella stepped into it with a slight unconscious straightening of her tall form. It seemed to her that she had never breathed easily till now, in the ample space of these rooms and gardens.

Her father and mother were already at table, together with Mrs. Boyce's brown spaniel Lynn.

Mr. Boyce was employed in ordering about the tall boy in a worn and greasy livery coat, who represented the men-service of the establishment; his wife was talking to her dog, but from the lift of her eyebrows, and the twitching of her thin lips, it was plain to Marcella that her mother was as usual of opinion that her father was behaving foolishly.

'There, for goodness' sake, cut some bread on the sideboard,' said the angry master, 'and hand it round instead of staring about you like a stuck pig. What they taught you at Sir William Jute's I can't conceive. *I* didn't undertake to make a man-servant of you, sir.'

The pale, harassed lad flew at the bread, cut it with a vast scattering of crumbs, handed it clumsily round, and then took glad advantage of a short supply of coffee to bolt from the room to order more.

'Idiot!' said Mr. Boyce, with an angry frown, as he disappeared.

'If you would allow Ann to do her proper parlour work again,' said his wife blandly, 'you would, I think, be less annoyed. And as I believe William was boot boy at the Jutes', it is not surprising that he did not learn waiting.'

'I tell you, Evelyn, that our position *demands* a man-servant!' was the hot reply. 'None of my family have ever attempted to run this house with women only. It would be unseemly—unfitting —incon——'

'Oh, I am no judge of course of what a Boyce may do,' said his wife, carelessly. 'I leave that to you and the neighbourhood.'

Mr. Boyce looked uncomfortable, cooled down, and presently when the coffee came back asked his wife for a fresh supply in tones from which all bellicosity had for the time departed. He was a small and singularly thin man, with blue wandering eyes under the blackest possible eyebrows and hair. The cheeks were hollow, the complexion as yellow as that of the typical Anglo-Indian. The special character of the mouth was hidden by a fine black moustache, but his prevailing expression varied between irritability and a kind of plaintiveness. The conspicuous blue eyes were as a rule melancholy; but they could be childishly bright

and self-assertive. There was a general air of breeding about
Richard Boyce, of that air at any rate which our common generalisations connect with the pride of old family ; his dress was careful and correct to the last detail ; and his hands with their long
fingers were of an excessive delicacy, though marred as to beauty
by a thinness which nearly amounted to emaciation.

'The servants say they must leave unless the ghost does,
Marcella,' said Mrs. Boyce, suddenly, laying a morsel of toast as
she spoke on Lynn's nose. 'Someone from the village of course
has been talking—the cook says she heard *something* last night,
though she will not condescend to particulars—and in general it
seems to me that you and I may be left before long to do the house-
work.'

'What do they say in the village?' asked Marcella eagerly.

'Oh ! they say there was a Boyce two hundred years ago who
fled down here from London after doing something he shouldn't—
I really forget what. The sheriff's officers were advancing on the
house. Their approach displeased him, and he put an end to
himself at the head of the little staircase leading from the tapestry-
room down to my sitting-room. Why did he choose the *staircase*?'
said Mrs. Boyce with light reflectiveness.

'It won't do,' said Marcella, shaking her head. 'I know the
Boyce they mean. He was a ruffian, but he shot himself in London ; and, any way, he was dead long before that staircase was
built.'

'Dear me, how well up you are !' said her mother. 'Suppose
you give a little lecture on the family in the servants' hall. Though
I never knew a ghost yet that was undone by dates.'

There was a satiric detachment in her tone which contrasted
sharply with Marcella's amused but sympathetic interest. *Detachment* was perhaps the characteristic note of Mrs. Boyce's manner,
—a curious separateness, as it were, from all the things and human
beings immediately about her.

Marcella pondered.

'I shall ask Mr. Harden about the stories,' she said presently.
'He will have heard them in the village. I am going to the church
this morning.'

Her mother looked at her—a look of quiet examination—and
smiled. The Lady Bountiful airs that Marcella had already assumed
during the six weeks she had been in the house entertained Mrs.
Boyce exceedingly.

'Harden !' said Mr. Boyce, catching the name. 'I wish that
man would leave me alone. What have I got to do with a water-
supply for the village? It will be as much as ever I can manage

to keep a watertight roof over our heads during the winter after the way in which Robert has behaved.'

Marcella's cheek flushed.

'The village water-supply is a *disgrace*,' she said with low emphasis. 'I never saw such a crew of unhealthy, wretched-looking children in my life as swarm about those cottages. We take the rent, and we ought to look after them. I believe you could be *forced* to do something, papa—if the local authority were of any use.'

She looked at him defiantly.

'Nonsense !' said Mr. Boyce testily. 'They got along in your Uncle Robert's days, and they can get along now. Charity indeed ! Why, the state of this house and the pinch for money altogether are enough, I should think, to take a man's mind. Don't you go talking to Mr. Harden in the way you do, Marcella. I don't like it, and I won't have it. You have the interests of your family and your home to think of first.'

'Poor starved things !' said Marcella sarcastically—'living in such a *den* !'

And she swept her white hand round, as though calling to witness the room in which they sat.

'I tell you,' said Mr. Boyce, rising and standing before the fire, whence he angrily surveyed the handsome daughter who was in truth so little known to him, and whose nature and aims during the close contact of the last few weeks had become something of a perplexity and disturbance to him—'I tell you our great effort, the effort of us all, must be to keep up the family position !—*our* position. Look at that library, and its condition ; look at the state of these wall-papers ; look at the garden ; look at the estate books, if it comes to that. Why, it will be years before, even with all my knowledge of affairs, I can pull the thing through—years !'

Mrs. Boyce gave a slight cough—she had pushed back her chair, and was alternately studying her husband and daughter. They might have been actors performing for her amusement. And yet, amusement is not precisely the word. For that hazel eye, with its frequent smile, had not a spark of geniality. After a time those about her found something scathing in its dry light.

Now, as soon as her husband became aware that she was watching him, his look wavered, and his mood collapsed. He threw her a curious furtive glance, and fell silent.

'I suppose Mr. Harden and his sister remind you of your London Socialist friends, Marcella ?' asked Mrs. Boyce lightly, in the pause that followed. 'You have, I see, taken a great liking for them.'

'Oh ! well—I don't know,' said Marcella, with a shrug, and

something of a proud reticence. 'Mr. Harden is very kind—but —he doesn't seem to have thought much about things.'

She never talked about her London friends to her mother, if she could help it. The sentiments of life generally avoided Mrs. Boyce when they could. Marcella, being all sentiment and impulse, was constantly her mother's victim, do what she would. But in her quiet moments she stood on the defensive.

'So the Socialists are the only people who think?' said Mrs. Boyce, who was now standing by the window, pressing her dog's head against her dress as he pushed up against her. 'Well, I am sorry for the Hardens. They tell me they give all their substance away—already—and everyone says it is going to be a particularly bad winter. The living, I hear, is worth nothing. All the same, I should wish them to look more cheerful. It is the first duty of martyrs.'

Marcella looked at her mother indignantly. It seemed to her often that she said the most heartless things imaginable.

'Cheerful!' she said—'in a village like this—with all the young men drifting off to London, and all the well-to-do people dissenters —no one to stand by him—no money and no helpers—the people always ill—wages eleven and twelve shillings a week—and only the old wrecks of men left to do the work! He might, I think, expect the people in *this* house to back him up a little. All he asks is that papa should go and satisfy himself with his own eyes as to the difference between our property and Lord Maxwell's——'

'Lord Maxwell's!' cried Mr. Boyce, rousing himself from a state of half-melancholy, half-sleepy reverie by the fire, and throwing away his cigarette—'Lord Maxwell! Difference! I should think so. Thirty thousand a year, if he has a penny. By the way, I wish he would just have the civility to answer my note about those coverts over by Willow Scrubs!'

He had hardly said the words when the door opened to admit William the footman, in his usual tremor of nervousness, carrying a salver and a note.

'The man says, please sir, is there any answer, sir?'

'Well, that's odd!' said Mr. Boyce, his look brightening. 'Here *is* Lord Maxwell's answer, just as I was talking of it.'

His wife turned sharply and watched him take it; her lips parted, a strange expectancy in her whole attitude. He tore it open, read it, and then threw it angrily under the grate.

'No answer. Shut the door.' The lad retreated. Mr. Boyce sat down and began carefully to put the fire together. His thin left hand shook upon his knee.

There was a moment's pause of complete silence. Mrs. Boyce's face might have been seen by a close observer to quiver and then stiffen as she stood in the light of the window, a tall and queenly figure in her sweeping black. But she said not a word, and presently left the room.

Marcella watched her father.

'Papa—*was* that a note from Lord Maxwell?'

Mr. Boyce looked round with a start, as though surprised that anyone was still there. It struck Marcella that he looked yellow and shrunken—years older than her mother. An impulse of tenderness, joined with anger and a sudden sick depression—she was conscious of them all as she got up and went across to him, determined to speak out. Her parents were not her friends, and did not possess her confidence ; but her constant separation from them since her childhood had now sometimes the result of giving her the boldness with them that a stranger might have had. She had no habitual deference to break through, and the hindering restraints of memory, though strong, were still less strong than they would have been if she had lived with them day by day and year by year, and had known their lives in close detail instead of guessing at them, as was now so often the case with her.

'Papa, is Lord Maxwell's note an uncivil one ?'

Mr. Boyce stooped forward and began to rub his chilly hand over the blaze.

'Why, that man's only son and I used to loaf and shoot and play cricket together from morning till night when we were boys. Henry Raeburn was a bit older than I, and he lent me the gun with which I shot my first rabbit. It was in one of the fields over by Soleyhurst, just where the two estates join. After that we were always companions—we used to go out at night with the keepers after poachers ; we spent hours in the snow watching for woodpigeons ; we shot that pair of kestrels over the inner hall door, in the Windmill Hill fields—at least I did—I was a better shot than he by that time. He didn't like Robert—he always wanted me.'

'Well, papa ; but what does he say ?' asked Marcella, impatiently. She laid her hand, however, as she spoke, on her father's shoulder.

Mr. Boyce winced and looked up at her. He and her mother had originally sent their daughter away from home that they might avoid the daily worry of her awakening curiosities, and one of his resolutions in coming to Mellor Park had been to keep up his dignity with her. But the sight of her dark face bent upon him, softened by a quick and womanly compassion, seemed to set free a new impulse in him.

'He writes in the third person, if you want to know, my dear,

and refers me to his agent, very much as though I were some
London grocer who had just bought the place. Oh, it is quite
evident what he means. They were here without moving all
through June and July, and it is now three weeks at least since he
and Miss Raeburn came back from Scotland, and not a card nor
a word from either of them ! Nor from the Winterbournes, nor
the Levens. Pleasant ! Well, my dear, you must make up your
mind to it. I did think—I was fool enough to think—that when
I came back to the old place, my father's old friends would let
bygones be bygones. I never did *them* any harm. Let them "gang
their gait," confound them !'—the little dark man straightened
himself fiercely—'I can get my pleasure out of the land ; and as
for your mother, she'd not lift a finger to propitiate one of them !'

In the last words, however, there was not a fraction of that
sympathetic pride which the ear expected, but rather fresh bitterness and grievance.

Marcella stood thinking, her mind travelling hither and thither
with lightning speed, now over the social events of the last six
weeks—now over incidents of those long-past holidays. Was
this, indeed, the second volume beginning—the natural sequel to
those old mysterious histories of shrinking, disillusion, and re-
pulse ?

'What was it you wanted about those coverts, papa?' she
asked presently, with a quick decision.

'What the deuce does it matter? If you want to know, I
proposed to him to exchange my coverts over by the Scrubs, which
work in with his shooting, for the wood down by the Home Farm.
It was an exchange made year after year in my father's time.
When I spoke to the keeper, I found it had been allowed to lapse.
Your uncle let the shooting go to rack and ruin after Harold's
death. It gave me something to write about, and I was determined
to know where I stood—— Well ! the old Pharisee can go his
way : I'll go mine.'

And with a spasmodic attempt to play the squire of Mellor on
his native heath, Richard Boyce rose, drew his emaciated frame to
its full height, and stood looking out drearily to his ancestral
lawns—a picturesque and elegant figure, for all its weakness and
pitiableness.

'I shall ask Mr. Aldous Raeburn about it, if I see him in the
village to-day,' said Marcella quietly.

Her father started, and looked at her with some attention.

'What have you seen of Aldous Raeburn?' he inquired. 'I
remember hearing that you had come across him.'

'Certainly I have come across him. I have met him once or

twice at the Vicarage—and—oh ! on one or two other occasions,'
said Marcella, carelessly. 'He has always made himself agreeable.
Mr. Harden says his grandfather is devoted to him, and will hardly
ever let him go away from home. He does a great deal for Lord
Maxwell now : writes for him, and helps to manage the estate ;
and next year, when the Tories come back and Lord Maxwell is
in office again——'

'Why, of course, there'll be plums for the grandson,' said
Mr. Boyce with a sneer. 'That goes without saying—though we
are such a virtuous lot.'

'Oh yes, he'll get on—everybody says so. And he'll deserve it
too !' she added, her eye kindling combatively as she surveyed her
father. 'He takes a lot of trouble down here about the cottages
and the board of guardians and the farms. The Hardens like him
very much, but he is not exactly popular, according to them. His
manners are sometimes shy and awkward, and the poor people
think he's proud.'

'Ah ! a prig I dare say—like some of his uncles before him,'
said Mr. Boyce irritably. 'But he was civil to you, you say ?'

And again he turned a quick considering eye on his daughter.

'Oh dear ! yes,' said Marcella, with a little proud smile. There
was a pause ; then she spoke again. 'I must go off to the church ;
the Hardens have hard work just now with the harvest festival, and
I promised to take them some flowers.'

'Well '—said her father grudgingly, 'so long as you don't
promise anything on my account ! I tell you, I haven't got
sixpence to spend on subscriptions to anything or anybody. By
the way, if you see Reynolds anywhere about the drive, you can
send him to me. He and I are going round the Home Farm to
pick up a few birds if we can, and see what the coverts look like.
The stock has all run down, and the place has been poached to
death. But he thinks if we take on an extra man in the spring,
and spend a little on rearing, we shall do pretty decently next year.'

The colour leapt to Marcella's cheek as she tied on her hat.

'You will set up another keeper, and you won't do anything for
the village ?' she cried, her black eyes lightening, and without
another word she opened the French window and walked rapidly
away along the terrace, leaving her father both angered and amazed.

A man like Richard Boyce cannot get comfortably through life
without a good deal of masquerading, in which those in his
immediate neighbourhood are expected to join. His wife had long
since consented to play the game, on condition of making it plain
the whole time that she was no dupe. As to what Marcella's part
in the affair might be going to be, her father was as yet uneasily

in the dark. What constantly astonished him, as she moved and talked under his eye, was the girl's beauty. Surely she had been a plain child, though a striking one. But now she had not only beauty, but the air of beauty. The self-confidence given by the possession of good looks was very evident in her behaviour. She was very accomplished, too, and more clever than was always quite agreeable to a father whose self-conceit was one of the few compensations left him by misfortune. Such a girl was sure to be admired. She would have lovers—friends of her own. It seemed that already, while Lord Maxwell was preparing to insult the father, his grandson had discovered that the daughter was handsome. Richard Boyce fell into a miserable reverie, wherein the Raeburns' behaviour and Marcella's unexpected gifts played about equal parts.

Meanwhile Marcella was gathering flowers in the 'Cedar garden,' the most adorable corner of Mellor Park, where the original Tudor house, grey, mullioned and ivy-covered, ran at right angles into the later 'garden front,' which projected beyond it to the south, making thereby a sunny and sheltered corner where roses, clematis, hollyhocks, and sunflowers grew with a more lavish height and blossom than elsewhere, as though conscious they must do their part in a whole of beauty. The grass indeed wanted mowing, and the first autumn leaves lay thickly drifted upon it ; the flowers were untied and untrimmed. But under the condition of two gardeners to ten acres of garden, nature does very much as she pleases, and Mr. Boyce when he came that way grumbled in vain.

As for Marcella, she was alternately moved to revolt and tenderness by the ragged charm of the old place.

On the one hand it angered her that anything so plainly meant for beauty and dignity should go so neglected and unkempt. On the other, if house and gardens had been spick and span like the other houses of the neighbourhood, if there had been sound roofs, a modern water-supply, shutters, greenhouses, and weedless paths, —in short, the general self-complacent air of a well-kept country house,—where would have been that thrilling intimate appeal, as of something forlornly lovely, which the old place so constantly made upon her? It seemed to depend even upon *her*, the latest born of all its children—to ask for tendance and cherishing even from *her*. She was always planning how—with a minimum of money to spend—it could be comforted and healed, and in the planning had grown in these few weeks to love it as though she had been bred there.

But this morning Marcella picked her roses and sunflowers in tumult and depression of spirit. What *was* this past which in these new surroundings was like some vainly fled tyrant clutching at them again? She energetically decided that the time had come for her to demand the truth. Yet, of whom? Marcella knew very well that to force her mother to any line of action Mrs. Boyce was unwilling to follow, was beyond her power. And it was not easy to go to her father directly and say, 'Tell me exactly how and why it is that society has turned its back upon you.' All the same, it *was* due to them all, due to herself especially, now that she was grown up and at home, that she should not be kept in the dark any longer like a baby, that she should be put in possession of the facts which, after all, threatened to stand here at Mellor Park, as untowardly in their, in *her* way, as they had done in the shabby school and lodging-house existence of all those bygone years.

Perhaps the secret of her impatience was that she did not, and could not, believe that the facts, if faced, would turn out to be insurmountable. Her instinct told her as she looked back that their relation toward society in the past, though full of discomforts and humiliations, had not been the relation of outcasts. Their poverty and the shifts to which poverty drives people had brought them the disrespect of one class; and as to the acquaintances and friends of their own rank, what had been mainly shown them had been a sort of cool distaste for their company, an insulting readiness to forget the existence of people who had so to speak lost their social bloom, and laid themselves open to the contemptuous disapproval or pity of the world. Everybody, it seemed, knew their affairs, and knowing them saw no personal advantage and distinction in the Boyces' acquaintance, but rather the contrary.

As she put the facts together a little, she realised, however, that the breach had always been deepest between her father and his relations, or his oldest friends. A little shiver passed through her as she reflected that here, in his own country, where his history was best known, the feeling towards him, whatever it rested upon, might very probably be strongest. Well, it *was* hard upon them! —hard upon her mother—hard upon her. In her first ecstasy over the old ancestral house and the dignities of her new position, how little she had thought of these things! And there they were all the time—dogging and thwarting.

She walked slowly along, with her burden of flowers, through a laurel path which led straight to the drive, and so, across it, to the little church. The church stood all alone there under the great limes of the Park, far away from parsonage and village—the property, it seemed, of the big house. When Marcella entered, the doors on the north and south sides were both standing open, for the vicar and his sister had been already at work there, and had but gone back to the parsonage for a bit of necessary business, meaning to return in half an hour.

It was the unpretending church of a hamlet, girt outside by the humble graves of toiling and forgotten generations, and adorned, or, at any rate, diversified within by a group of mural monuments, of various styles and dates, but all of them bearing, in some way or another, the name of Boyce—conspicuous amongst them a florid cherub-crowned tomb in the chancel, marking the remains of that Parliamentarian Boyce who fought side by side with Hampden, his boyish friend, at Chalgrove Field, lived to be driven out of Westminster by Colonel Pryde, and to spend his later years at Mellor, in disgrace, first with the Protector, and then with the Restoration. From these monuments alone a tolerably faithful idea of the Boyce family could have been gathered. Clearly not a family of any very great pretensions—a race for the most part of frugal, upright country gentlemen—to be found, with scarcely an exception, on the side of political liberty, and of a Whiggish religion ; men who had given their sons to die at Quebec, and Plassy, and Trafalgar, for the making of England's Empire ; who would have voted with Fox, but that the terrors of Burke, and a dogged sense that the country must be carried on, drove them into supporting Pitt ; who, at home, dispensed alternate justice and doles, and when their wives died put up inscriptions to them intended to bear witness at once to the Latinity of a Boyce's education, and the pious strength of his legitimate affections—a tedious race perhaps and pig-headed, tyrannical too here and there, but on the whole honourable English stuff—the stuff which has made, and still in new forms sustains, the fabric of a great state.

Only once was there a break in the uniform character of the monuments—a break corresponding to the highest moment of the Boyce fortunes, a moment when the respectability of the family rose suddenly into brilliance, and the prose of generations broke into a few years of poetry. Somewhere in the last century an earlier Richard Boyce went abroad to make the grand tour. He was a man of parts, the friend of Horace Walpole and of Gray, and his introductions opened to him whatever doors he might wish to enter, at a time when the upper classes of the leading European nations were far more intimately and familiarly acquainted with each other than they are now. He married at Rome an Italian lady of high birth and large fortune. Then he brought her home to Mellor, where straightway the garden front was built with all its fantastic and beautiful decoration, the great avenue was planted, pictures began to invade the house, and a musical library was collected whereof the innumerable faded volumes, bearing each of them the entwined names of Richard and Marcella Boyce, had been during the last few weeks mines of delight and curiosity to the Marcella of to-day.

The Italian wife bore her lord two sons, and then in early middle life she died—much loved and passionately mourned. Her tomb bore no long-winded panegyric. Her name only, her parentage and birthplace—for she was Italian to the last, and her husband loved her the better for it—the dates of her birth and death, and then two lines from Dante's *Vita Nuova*.

The portrait of this earlier Marcella hung still in the room where her music-books survived,—a dark blurred picture by an inferior hand ; but the Marcella of to-day had long since eagerly decided that her own physique and her father's were to be traced to its original, as well, no doubt, as the artistic aptitudes of both— aptitudes not hitherto conspicuous in her respectable race.

In reality, however, she loved every one of them—these Jacobean and Georgian squires with their interminable epitaphs. Now, as she stood in the church, looking about her, her flowers lying beside her in a tumbled heap on the chancel step, cheerful- ness, delight, nay, the indomitable pride and exultation of her youth, came back upon her in one great lifting wave. The de- pression of her father's repentances and trepidations fell away ; she felt herself in her place, under the shelter of her forefathers, incorporated and redeemed, as it were, into their guild of honour.

There were difficulties in her path, no doubt—but she had her vantage-ground, and would use it for her own profit and that of others. *She* had no cause for shame ; and in these days of the developed individual the old solidarity of the family has become injustice and wrong. Her mind filled tumultuously with the evidence these last two years had brought her of her natural power over men and things. She knew perfectly well that she could do and dare what other girls of her age could never venture —that she had fascination, resource, brain.

Already, in these few weeks—— Smiles played about her lips as she thought of that quiet grave gentleman of thirty she had been meeting at the Hardens. His grandfather might write what he pleased. It did not alter the fact that during the last few weeks Mr. Aldous Raeburn, clearly one of the *partis* most coveted, and one of the men most observed, in the neighbourhood, had taken and shown a very marked interest in Mr. Boyce's daughter—all the more marked because of the reserved manner with which it had to contend.

No! whatever happened, she would carve her path, make her own way, and her parents' too. At twenty-one, nothing looks irrevocable. A woman's charm, a woman's energy should do it all.

Ay, and something else too. She looked quickly round the church, her mind swelling with the sense of the Cravens' injustice and distrust. Never could she be more conscious than here—on this very spot—of mission, of an urging call to the service of man. In front of her was the Boyces' family pew, carved and becushioned, but behind it stretched bench after bench of plain and humble oak, on which the village sat when it came to church. Here, for the first time, had Marcella been brought face to face with the agricultural world as it is—no stage ruralism, but the bare fact in one of its most pitiful aspects. Men of sixty and upwards, grey and furrowed like the chalk soil into which they had worked their lives ; not old as age goes, but already the refuse of their genera-tion, and paid for at the rate of refuse ; with no prospect but the workhouse, if the grave should be delayed, yet quiet, impassive, resigned, now showing a furtive childish amusement if a schoolboy misbehaved, or a dog strayed into church, now joining with a stolid unconsciousness in the tremendous sayings of the Psalms ; women coarse, or worn, or hopeless; girls and boys and young children already blanched and emaciated beyond even the normal Londoner from the effects of insanitary cottages, bad water, and starvation food—these figures and types had been a ghastly and quickening revelation to Marcella. In London the agricultural labourer, of whom she had heard much, had been to her as a pawn in the game of discussion. Here he was in the flesh ; and she was called upon to live with him, and not only to talk about him. Under circumstances of peculiar responsibility too. For it was very clear that upon the owner of Mellor depended, and had always depended, the labourer of Mellor.

Well, she had tried to live with them ever since she came—had gone in and out of their cottages in flat horror and amazement at them and their lives and their surroundings ; alternately pleased and repelled by their cringing ; now enjoying her position among them with the natural aristocratic instinct of women, now grinding her teeth over her father's and uncle's behaviour and the little good she saw any prospect of doing for her new subjects.

What, *their* friend and champion, and ultimately their redeemer too? Well, and why not? Weak women have done greater things in the world. As she stood on the chancel step, vowing herself to these great things, she was conscious of a dramatic moment—would not have been sorry, perhaps, if some admiring eye could have seen and understood her.

But there was a saving sincerity at the root of her, and her strained mood sank naturally into a girlish excitement.

'We shall see!—We shall see!' she said aloud, and was startled to hear her words quite plainly in the silent church. As she spoke she stooped to separate her flowers and see what quantities she had of each.

But while she did so a sound of distant voices made her raise herself again. She walked down the church and stood at the open south door, looking and waiting. Before her stretched a green field path leading across the park to the village. The vicar and his sister were coming along it towards the church, both flower-laden, and beside walked a tall man in a brown shooting suit, with his gun in his hand and his dog beside him.

The excitement in Marcella's eyes leapt up afresh for a moment as she saw the group, and then subsided into a luminous and steady glow. She waited quietly for them, hardly responding to the affectionate signals of the vicar's sister; but inwardly she was not quiet at all. For the tall man in the brown shooting coat was Mr. Aldous Raeburn.

CHAPTER IV

'How kind of you !' said the rector's sister, enthusiastically ; ' but I thought you would come and help us.'

And as Marcella took some of her burdens from her, Miss Harden kissed Marcella's cheek with a sort of timid eagerness. She had fallen in love with Miss Boyce from the beginning, was now just advanced to this privilege of kissing, and being entirely convinced that her new friend possessed all virtues and all knowledge, found it not difficult to hold that she had been divinely sent to sustain her brother and herself in the disheartening task of civilising Mellor. Mary Harden was naturally a short, roundly made girl, neither pretty nor plain, with grey-blue eyes, a shy manner, and a heart all goodness. Her brother was like unto her—also short, round, and full-faced, with the same attractive eyes. Both were singularly young in aspect—a boy and girl pair. Both had the worn, pinched look which Mrs. Boyce complained of, and which, indeed, went oddly with their whole physique. It was as though creatures built for a normal life of easy give and take with their fellows had fallen upon some unfitting and jarring experience. One striking difference, indeed, there was between them, for amid the brother's timidity and sweetness there lay, clearly to be felt and seen, the consciousness of the priest—nascent and immature, but already urging and characteristic.

Only one face of the three showed any other emotion than quick pleasure at the sight of Marcella Boyce. Aldous Raeburn was clearly embarrassed thereby. Indeed, as he laid down his gun outside the low churchyard wall, while Marcella and the Hardens were greeting, that generally self-possessed though modest person was conscious of a quite disabling perturbation of mind. Why in the name of all good manners and decency had he allowed himself to be discovered in shooting trim, on that particular morning, by Mr. Boyce's daughter on her father's land, and within a stone's throw of her father's house? Was he not perfectly well aware of the curt note which his grandfather had that morning despatched to the new owner of Mellor? Had he not ineffectually tried to delay execution the night before, thereby puzzling and half-offending his grandfather? Had not the incident weighed on him ever since, wounding an admiration and sympathy which seemed to have stolen upon him in the dark, during these few weeks since he had made Miss Boyce's acquaintance, so strong and startling did he all in a moment feel them to be?

And then to intrude upon her thus, out of nothing apparently but sheer moth-like incapacity to keep away! The church footpath indeed was public property, and Miss Harden's burdens had cried aloud to any passing male to help her. But why in this neighbourhood at all?—why not rather on the other side of the county? He could have scourged himself on the spot for an unpardonable breach of manners and feeling.

However, Miss Boyce certainly made no sign. She received him without any *empressement*, but also without the smallest symptom of offence. They all moved into the church together, Mr. Raeburn carrying a vast bundle of ivy and fern, the rector and his sister laden with closely-packed baskets of cut flowers. Everything was laid down on the chancel steps beside Marcella's contribution, and then the Hardens began to plan out operations. Miss Harden ran over on her fingers the contributions which had been sent in to the rectory, or were presently coming over to the church in a hand-cart. 'Lord Maxwell has sent the most *beautiful* pots for the chancel,' she said, with a grateful look at young Raeburn. 'It will be quite a show.' To which the young rector assented warmly. It was very good, indeed, of Lord Maxwell to remember them always so liberally at times like these, when they had so little direct claim upon him. They were not his church or his parish, but he never forgot them all the same, and Mellor was grateful. The rector had all his sister's gentle effusiveness, but a professional dignity besides, even in his thanks, which made itself felt.

Marcella flushed as he was speaking.

'I went to see what I could get in the way of greenhouse things,' she said in a sudden proud voice. 'But we have nothing. There are the houses, but there is nothing in them. But you shall have all our out-of-door flowers, and I think a good deal might be done with autumn leaves and wild things if you will let me try.'

A speech which brought a flush to Mr. Raeburn's cheek as he stood in the background, and led Mary Harden into an eager asking of Marcella's counsels, and an eager praising of her flowers.

Aldous Raeburn said nothing, but his discomfort increased with every moment. Why had his grandfather been so officious in this matter of the flowers? All very well when Mellor was empty, or in the days of a miser and eccentric, without womankind, like Robert Boyce. But now—the act began to seem to him offensive, a fresh affront offered to an unprotected girl, whose quivering sensitive look as she stood talking to the Hardens touched him profoundly. Mellor church might almost be regarded as the Boyces' private chapel, so bound up was it with the family and the house. He realised painfully that he ought to be gone—yet could not tear himself away. Her passionate willingness to spend herself for the place and people she had made her own at first sight, checked every now and then by a proud and sore reserve— it was too pretty, too sad. It stung and spurred him as he watched her ; one moment his foot moved for departure, the next he was resolving that somehow or other he must make speech with her— excuse—explain. Ridiculous ! How was it possible that he should do either !

He had met her—perhaps had tried to meet her—tolerably often since their first chance encounter weeks ago in the vicarage drawing-room. All through there had been on his side the uncomfortable knowledge of his grandfather's antipathy to Richard Boyce, and of the social steps to which that antipathy would inevitably lead. But Miss Boyce had never shown the smallest consciousness, so far, of anything untoward or unusual in her position. She had been clearly taken up with the interest and pleasure of this new spectacle upon which she had entered. The old house, its associations, its history, the beautiful country in which it lay, the speech and characteristics of rural labour as compared with those of the town,—he had heard her talk of all these things with a freshness, a human sympathy, a freedom from conventional phrase, and, no doubt, a touch of egotism and extravagance, which rivetted attention. The egotism and extravagance, however, after a first moment of critical discomfort on his part, had not in the end repelled him at all. The girl's vivid beauty glorified them ; made them seem to him a mere special fulness of

life. So that in his new preoccupation with herself, and by contact
with her frank self-confidence, he had almost forgotten her position, and his own indirect relation to it. Then had come that
unlucky note from Mellor ; his grandfather's prompt reply to it ;
his own ineffective protest ; and now this tongue-tiedness—this
clumsy intrusion—which she must feel to be an indelicacy—an
outrage.

Suddenly he heard Miss Harden saying, with penitent emphasis, ' I *am* stupid ! I have left the scissors and the wire on
the table at home ; we can't get on without them ; it is really too
bad of me.'

' I will go for them,' said Marcella promptly. ' Here is the
hand-cart just arrived and some people come to help ; you can't
be spared. I will be back directly.'

And, gathering up her black skirt in a slim white hand, she
sped down the church, and was out of the south door before the
Hardens had time to protest, or Aldous Raeburn understood what
she was doing.

A vexed word from Miss Harden enlightened him, and he
went after the fugitive, overtaking her just where his gun and dog
lay, outside the churchyard.

' Let me go, Miss Boyce,' he said, as he caught her up. ' My
dog and I will run there and back.'

But Marcella hardly looked at him, or paused.

' Oh no ! ' she said quickly, ' I should like the walk.'

He hesitated ; then, with a flush which altered his usually quiet,
self-contained expression, he moved on beside her.

' Allow me to go with you then. You are sure to find fresh
loads to bring back. If it's like our harvest festival, the things
keep dropping in all day.'

Marcella's eyes were still on the ground.

' I thought you were on your way to shoot, Mr. Raeburn ? '

' So I was, but there is no hurry ; if I can be useful. Both the
birds and the keeper can wait.'

' Where are you going ? '

' To some outlying fields of ours on the Windmill Hill. There
is a tenant there who wants to see me. He is a prosy person with
a host of grievances. I took my gun as a possible means of
escape from him.'

' Windmill Hill ? I know the name. Oh ! I remember : it
was there—my father has just been telling me—that your father
and he shot the pair of kestrels, when they were boys together.'

Her tone was quite light, but somehow it had an accent, an
emphasis, which made Aldous Raeburn supremely uncomfortable.

In his disquiet, he thought of various things to say ; but he was not ready, nor naturally effusive ; the turn of them did not please him ; and he remained silent.

Meantime Marcella's heart was beating fast. She was medita-ting a *coup*.

'Mr. Raeburn !'

'Yes !'

'Will you think me a very extraordinary person if I ask you a question ? Your father and mine were great friends, weren't they, as boys ?—your family and mine were friends, altogether ?'

'I believe so—I have always heard so,' said her companion, flushing still redder.

'You knew Uncle Robert—Lord Maxwell did ?'

'Yes—as much as anybody knew him—but——'

'Oh, I know : he shut himself up and hated his neighbours. Still you knew him, and papa and your father were boys together. Well then, if you won't mind telling me—I know it's bold to ask, but I have reasons—why does Lord Maxwell write to papa in the third person, and why has your aunt, Miss Raeburn, never found time in all these weeks to call on mamma ?'

She turned and faced him, her splendid eyes one challenge. The glow and fire of the whole gesture—the daring of it, and yet the suggestion of womanish weakness in the hand which trembled against her dress and in the twitching lip—if it had been fine acting, it could not have been more complete. And, in a sense, acting there was in it. Marcella's emotions were real, but her mind seldom deserted her. One half of her was impulsive and passionate ; the other half looked on and put in finishing touches.

Acting or no, the surprise of her outburst swept the man beside her off his feet. He found himself floundering in a sea of excuses —not for his relations, but for himself. He ought never to have intruded ; it was odious, unpardonable ; he had no business what-ever to put himself in her way ! Would she please understand that it was an accident ? It should not happen again. He quite understood that she could not regard him with friendliness. And so on. He had never so lost his self-possession.

Meanwhile Marcella's brows contracted. She took his excuses as a fresh offence.

'You mean, I suppose, that I have no rignt to ask such ques-tions !' she cried ; 'that I am not behaving like a lady—as one of your relations would ? Well, I dare say ! I was not brought up like that. I was not brought up at all ; I have had to make my-self. So you must avoid me if you like. Of course you will. But I resolved there—in the church—that I would make just one effort, before everything crystallises, to break through. If we must live on here hating our neighbours and being cut by them, I thought I would just ask you why, first. There is no one else to ask. Hardly anybody has called, except the Hardens, and a few new people that don't matter. And *I* have nothing to be ashamed of,' said the girl passionately, 'nor has mamma. Papa, I suppose, did some bad things long ago. I have never known—I don't know now—what they were. But I should like to understand. Is everybody going to cut us because of that?'

With a great effort Aldous Raeburn pulled himself together, certain fine instincts both of race and conduct coming to his help. He met her excited look by one which had both dignity and friend-liness.

'I will tell you what I can, Miss Boyce. If you ask me, it is right I should. You must forgive me if I say anything that hurts you. I will try not—I will try not!' he repeated earnestly. 'In the first place, I know hardly anything in detail. I do not re-member that I have ever wished to know. But I gather that some years ago—when I was still a lad—something in Mr. Boyce's life —some financial matters, I believe—during the time that he was a member of Parliament, made a scandal, and especially among his family and old friends. It was the effect upon his old father, I think, who, as you know, died soon afterwards——'

Marcella started.

'I didn't know,' she said quickly.

Aldous Raeburn's distress grew.

'I really oughtn't to speak of these things,' he said, 'for I don't know them accurately. But I want to answer what you said—I do indeed. It was that, I think, chiefly. Everybody here respected and loved your grandfather—my grandfather did—and there was great feeling for him——'

'I see! I see!' said Marcella, her chest heaving; 'and against papa.'

She walked on quickly, hardly seeing where she was going, her eyes dim with tears. There was a wretched pause. Then Aldous Raeburn broke out—

'But after all it is very long ago. And there may have been some harsh judgment. My grandfather may have been misin-formed as to some of the facts. And I——'

He hesitated, struck with the awkwardness of what he was going to say. But Marcella understood him.

'And you will try to make him alter his mind?' she said, not ungratefully, but still with a touch of sarcasm in her tone. 'No, Mr. Raeburn, I don't think that will succeed.'

They walked on in silence for a little while. At last he said, turning upon her a face in which she could not but see the true feeling of a just and kindly man—

'I meant that if my grandfather could be led to express himself in a way which Mr. Boyce could accept, even if there were no great friendship as there used to be, there might be something better than this—this, which—which—is so painful. And any way, Miss Boyce, whatever happens, will you let me say this once, that there is no word, no feeling in this neighbourhood—how could there be?—towards you and your mother, but one of respect and admiration? Do believe that, even if you feel that you can never be friendly towards me and mine again—or forget the things I have said!'

'Respect and admiration!' said Marcella wondering, and still scornful. 'Pity, perhaps. There might be that. But any way mamma goes with papa. She always has done. She always will. So shall I, of course. But I am sorry—*horribly* sore and sorry! I was so delighted to come here. I have been very little at home, and understood hardly anything about this worry—not how serious it was, nor what it meant. Oh! I *am* sorry—there was so much I wanted to do here—if anybody could only understand what it means to me to come to this place!'

They had reached the brow of a little rising ground. Just below them, beyond a stubble field in which there were a few bent forms of gleaners, lay the small scattered village, hardly seen amid its trees, the curls of its blue smoke ascending steadily on this calm September morning against a great belt of distant beechwood which begirt the hamlet and the common along which it lay. The stubble field was a feast of shade and tint, of apricots and golds shot with the subtlest purples and browns; the flame of the wild-cherry leaf and the deeper crimson of the haws made every hedge a wonder; the apples gleamed in the cottage garden; and a cloudless sun poured down on field and hedge, and on the half-hidden medley of tiled roofs, sharp gables, and jutting dormers which made the village.

Instinctively both stopped. Marcella locked her hands behind her in a gesture familiar to her in moments of excitement; the light wind blew back her dress in soft, eddying folds; for the moment, in her tall grace, she had the air of some young Victory poised upon a height, till you looked at her face, which was, indeed, not exultant at all, but tragic, extravagantly tragic, as Aldous Raeburn, in his English reserve, would perhaps have thought in the case of any woman with tamer eyes and a less winning mouth.

'I don't want to talk about myself,' she began. 'But you know, Mr. Raeburn—you must know—what a state of things there is here—you know what a *disgrace* that village is. Oh I one reads books, but I never thought people could actually *live* like that— here in the wide country, with room for all. It makes me lie awake at night. We are not rich—we are very poor—the house is all out of repair, and the estate, as of course you know, is in a wretched condition. But when I see these cottages, and the water, and the children, I ask what right we have to anythivg we get. I had some friends in London who were Socialists, and I followed and agreed with them, but here one *sees* I Yes, indeed I— it *is* too great a risk to let the individual alone when all these lives depend upon him. Uncle Robert was an eccentric and a miser; and look at the death-rate of the village—look at the children; you can see how it has crushed the Hardens already. No, we have no right to it I—it ought to be taken from us; some day it will be taken from us I'

Aldous Raeburn smiled, and was himself again. A woman's speculations were easier to deal with than a woman's distress.

'It is not so hopeless as that, I think,' he said kindly. 'The Mellor cottages are in a bad state certainly. But you have no idea how soon a little energy and money and thought set things to rights.'

'But we have no money I' cried Marcella. 'And if he is miserable here, my father will have no energy to do anything. He will not care what happens. He will defy everybody, and just spend what he has on himself. And it will make me wretched— *wretched*. Look at that cottage to the right, Mr. Raeburn. It is Jim Hurd's—a man who works mainly on the Church Farm, when he is in work. But he is deformed, and not so strong as others. The farmers too seem to be cutting down labour everywhere—of course I don't understand—I am so new to it. Hurd and his family had an *awful* winter, last winter—hardly kept body and soul together. And now he is out of work already—the man at the Church Farm turned him off directly after harvest. He sees no prospect of getting work by the winter. He spends his days tramping to look for it; but nothing turns up. Last winter they parted with all they could sell. This winter it must be the work- house I It's *heart-breaking*. And he has a mind; he can *feel* I I lend him the Labour paper I take in, and get him to talk. He has more education than most, and oh I the *bitterness* at the bottom of him. But not against persons—individuals. It is like a sort of blind patience when you come to that—they make excuses even for Uncle Robert, to whom they have paid rent all these years for a cottage which is a crime—yes, a *crime*! The woman must have been such a pretty creature—and refined too. She is consumptive, of course—what else could you expect with that cottage and that food? So is the eldest boy—a little white atomy! And the other children. Talk of London—I never saw such sickly objects as there are in this village. Twelve shillings a week, and work about half the year! Oh! they *ought* to hate us!—I try to make them,' cried Marcella, her eyes gleaming. 'They ought to hate all of us landowners, and the whole wicked system. It keeps them from the land which they ought to be sharing with us; it makes one man master, instead of all men brothers. And who is fit to be master? Which of us? Everybody is so ready to take the charge of other people's lives, and then look at the result!'

'Well, the result, even in rural England, is not always so bad,' said Aldous Raeburn, smiling a little, but more coldly. Marcella, glancing at him, understood in a moment that she had roused a certain family and class pride in him—a pride which was not going to assert itself, but none the less implied the sudden opening of a gulf between herself and him. In an instant her quick imagination realised herself as the daughter and niece of two discredited members of a great class. When she attacked the class, or the system, the man beside her—any man in similar circumstances—must naturally think: 'Ah, well, poor girl—Dick Boyce's daughter—what can you expect?' Whereas—Aldous Raeburn!—she thought of the dignity of the Maxwell name, of the width of the Maxwell possessions, balanced only by the high reputation of the family for honourable, just and Christian living, whether as amongst themselves or towards their neighbours and dependents. A shiver of passionate vanity, wrath, and longing passed through her as her tall frame stiffened.

'There are model squires, of course,' she said slowly, striving at least for a personal dignity which should match his. 'There are plenty of landowners who do their duty as they understand it—no one denies that. But that does not affect the system; the grandson of the best man may be the worst, but his one-man power remains the same. No! the time has come for a wider basis. Paternal government and charity were very well in their way—democratic self-government will manage to do without them!'

She flung him a gay, quivering, defiant look. It delighted her to pit these wide and threatening generalisations against the Maxwell power—to show the heir of it that she at least—father or no father—was no hereditary subject of his, and bound to no blind admiration of the Maxwell methods and position.

Aldous Raeburn took her onslaught very calmly, smiling frankly back at her indeed all the time. Miss Boyce's opinions could hardly matter to him intellectually, whatever charm and stimulus he might find in her talk. This subject of the duties, rights, and prospects of his class went, as it happened, very deep with him—too deep for chance discussion. What she said, if he ever stopped to think of it in itself, seemed to him a compound of elements derived partly from her personal history, partly from the random opinions that young people of a generous type pick up from newspapers and magazines. She had touched his family pride for an instant; but only for an instant. What he was abidingly conscious of, was of a beautiful wild creature struggling with difficulties in which he was somehow himself concerned, and out of which, in some way or other, he was becoming more and more determined—absurdly determined—to help her.

'Oh! no doubt the world will do very well without us some day,' he said lightly, in answer to her tirade; 'no one is indispensable. But are you so sure, Miss Boyce, you believe in your own creed? I thought I had observed—pardon me for saying it—on the two or three occasions we have met, some degenerate signs of individualism. You take pleasure in the old place, you say; you were delighted to come and live where your ancestors lived before you; you are full of desires to pull these poor people out of the mire in your own way. No! I don't feel that you are thoroughgoing!'

Marcella paused a frowning moment, then broke suddenly into a delightful laugh—a laugh of humorous confession, which changed her whole look and mood.

'Is that all you have noticed? If you wish to know, Mr. Raeburn, I love the labourers for touching their hats to me. I love the school children for bobbing to me. I love my very self—ridiculous as you may think it—for being Miss Boyce of Mellor!'

'Don't say things like that, please!' he interrupted; 'I think I have not deserved them.'

His tone made her repent her gibe. 'No, indeed, you have been most kind to me,' she cried. 'I don't know how it is. I am bitter and personal in a moment—when I don't mean to be. Yes! you are quite right. I am proud of it all. If nobody comes to see us, and we are left all alone out in the cold, I shall still have room enough to be proud in—proud of the old house and our few bits of pictures, and the family papers, and the beeches! How absurd it would seem to other people, who have so much more! But I have had so little—so little!' Her voice had a hungry lingering note. 'And as for the people, yes, I am proud too that they like me, and that already I can influence them. Oh, I will do my best for them, my *very best*! But it will be hard, very hard, if there is no one to help me!'

She heaved a long sigh. In spite of the words, what she had said did not seem to be an appeal for his pity. Rather there was in it a sweet self-dedicating note as of one going sadly alone to a painful task, a note which once more left Aldous Raeburn's self-restraint tottering. She was walking gently beside him, her pretty dress trailing lightly over the dry stubble, her hand in its white ruffles hanging so close beside him—after all her prophetess airs a pensive womanly thing, that must surely hear how his strong man's heart was beginning to beat!

He bent over to her.

'Don't talk of there being no one to help! There may be many ways out of present difficulties. Meanwhile, however things go, could you be large-minded enough to count one person here your friend?'

She looked up at him. Tall as she was, he was taller—she liked that; she liked too the quiet cautious strength of his English expression and bearing. She did not think him handsome, and she was conscious of no thrill. But inwardly her quick dramatising imagination was already constructing her own future and his. The ambition to rule leapt in her, and the delight in conquest. It was with a delicious sense of her own power, and of the general fulness of her new life, that she said, 'I *am* large-minded enough! You have been very kind, and I have been very wild and indiscreet. But I don't regret: I am sure, if you can help me, you will.'

There was a little pause. They were standing at the last gate before the miry village road began, and almost in sight of the little vicarage. Aldous Raeburn, with his hand on the gate, suddenly gathered a spray of travellers'-joy out of the hedge beside him.

'That was a promise, I think, and I keep the pledge of it,' he said, and with a smile put the cluster of white seed-tufts and green leaves into one of the pockets of his shooting jacket.

'Oh, don't tie me down!' said Marcella, laughing, but flushing also. 'And don't you think, Mr. Raeburn, that you might open that gate? At least, we can't get the scissors and the wire unless you do.'

CHAPTER V

THE autumn evening was far advanced when Aldous Raeburn, after his day's shooting, passed again by the gates of Mellor Park on his road home. He glanced up the ill-kept drive, with its fine over-hanging limes, caught a glimpse to the left of the little church, and, to the right, of the long eastern front of the house ; lingered a moment to watch the sunset light streaming through the level branches of two distant cedars, standing black and sharp against the fiery west, and then walked briskly forwards in the mood of a man going as fast as may be to an appointment he both desires and dreads.

He had given his gun to the keeper, who had already sped far ahead of him, in the shooting-cart which his master had declined. His dog, a black retriever, was at his heels, and both dog and man were somewhat weary and stiff with exercise. But for the privilege of solitude, Aldous Raeburn would at that moment have faced a good deal more than the two miles of extra walking which now lay between him and Maxwell Court.

About him, as he trudged on, lay a beautiful world of English woodland. After he had passed through the hamlet of Mellor, with its three-cornered piece of open common, and its patches of arable —representing the original forest-clearing made centuries ago by the primitive fathers of the village in this corner of the Chiltern uplands—the beech woods closed thickly round him. Beech woods of all kinds—from forest slopes, where majestic trees, grey and soaring pillars of the woodland roof, stood in stately isolation on the dead-leaf carpet woven by the years about their carved and polished bases, to the close plantations of young trees, where the saplings crowded on each other, and here and there amid the airless tangle of leaf and branch some long pheasant-drive, cut straight through the green heart of the wood, refreshed the seeking eye with its arched and far-receding path. Two or three times on his walk Aldous heard from far within the trees the sounds of hatchet and turner's wheel, which told him he was passing one of the wood-cutter's huts that in the hilly parts of this district supply the first simple steps of the chairmaking industry, carried on in the little factory towns of the more populous valleys. And two or three times also he passed a string of the great timber carts which haunt the Chiltern lanes ; the patient team of brown horses straining at the weight behind them, the vast prostrate trunks rattling in their chains, and the smoke from the carters' pipes rising slowly into the damp sunset air. But for the most part the road along which he walked was utterly forsaken of human kind. Nor were there

any signs of habitation—no cottages, no farms. He was scarcely
more than thirty miles from London ; yet in this solemn evening
glow it would have been hardly possible to find a remoter, lonelier
nature than that through which he was passing.

And presently the solitude took a grander note   He was nearing the edge of the high upland along which he had been walking.
In front of him the long road with its gleaming pools bent sharply
to the left, showing pale and distinct against a darkening heaven
and the wide grey fields which had now, on one side of his path,
replaced the serried growth of young plantations.   Night was fast
advancing from south and east over the upland. But straight in
front of him and on his right, the forest trees, still flooded with sunset, fell in sharp steeps towards the plain.   Through their straight
stems glowed the blues and purples of that lower world ; and when
the slopes broke and opened here and there, above the rounded
masses of their red and golden leaf the level distances of the plain
could be seen stretching away, illimitable in the evening dusk, to a
west of glory, just vacant of the sun.   The golden ball had sunk
into the mists awaiting it, but the splendour of its last rays was still
on all the western front of the hills, bathing the beech woods as
they rose and fell with the large undulations of the ground.

Insensibly Raeburn, filled as he was with a new and surging
emotion, drew the solemnity of the forest glades and of the rolling
distances into his heart. When he reached the point where the
road diverged to the left, he mounted a little grassy ridge, whence
he commanded the whole sweep of the hill rampart from north to
west, and the whole expanse of the low country beneath, and there
stood gazing for some minutes, lost in many thoughts, while the
night fell.

He looked over the central plain of England—the plain which
stretches westward to the Thames and the Berkshire hills, and
northward through the Buckinghamshire and Bedfordshire lowlands
to the basin of the Trent.   An historic plain—symbolic, all of it, to
an English eye.   There in the western distance, amid the light-
filled mists, lay Oxford ; in front of him was the site of Chalgrove
Field, where Hampden got his clumsy death-wound, and Thame
where he died ; and far away, to his right, where the hills swept to
the north, he could just discern, gleaming against the face of the
down, the vast scoured cross, whereby a Saxon king had blazoned
his victory over his Danish foes to all the plain beneath.

Aldous Raeburn was a man to feel these things. He had seldom
stood on this high point, in such an evening calm, without the expansion in him of all that was most manly, most English, most strenuous. If it had not been so, indeed, he must have been singularly

dull of soul. For the great view had an interest for him personally it could hardly have possessed to the same degree for any
other man.   On his left hand Maxwell Court rose among its woods
on the brow of the hill—a splendid pile which some day would be
his.   Behind him ; through all the upland he had just traversed ;
beneath the point where he stood ; along the sides of the hills, and
far into the plain, stretched the land which also would be his—
which, indeed, practically was already his—for his grandfather was
an old man with a boundless trust in the heir on whom his affections
and hopes were centred.   The dim churches scattered over the
immediate plain below ; the villages clustered round them, where
dwelt the toilers in these endless fields ; the farms amid their trees ;
the cottages showing here and there on the fringes of the wood—
all the equipment and organisation of popular life over an appreciable part of the English midland at his feet, depended to an extent
hardly to be exaggerated, under the conditions of the England of
to-day, upon him—-upon his one man's brain and conscience, the
degree of his mental and moral capacity.

In his first youth, of course, the thought had often roused a
boy's tremulous elation and sense of romance.   Since his Cambridge days, and of late years, any more acute or dramatic perception than usual of his lot in life had been wont to bring with it
rather a consciousness of weight than of inspiration.   Sensitive,
fastidious, reflective, he was disturbed by remorses and scruples
which had never plagued his forefathers.   During his college days,
the special circumstances of a great friendship had drawn him
into the full tide of a social speculation which, as it happened, was
destined to go deeper with him than with most men.   The responsibilities of the rich, the disadvantages of the poor, the relation
of the State to the individual—of the old Radical dogma of free
contract to the thwarting facts of social inequality ; the Tory ideal
of paternal government by the few as compared with the Liberal
ideal of self-government by the many : these commonplaces of
economical and political discussion had very early become living
and often sore realities in Aldous Raeburn's mind, because of the
long conflict in him, dating from his Cambridge life, between the
influences of birth and early education and the influences of an
admiring and profound affection which had opened to him the
gates of a new moral world.

Towards the close of his first year at Trinity, a young man
joined the college who rapidly became, in spite of various practical
disadvantages, a leader among the best and keenest of his fellows.
He was poor and held a small scholarship ; but it was soon plain
that his health was not equal to the Tripos routine, and that the

prizes of the place, brilliant as was his intellectual endowment, were not for him. After an inward struggle, of which none perhaps but Aldous Raeburn had any exact knowledge, he laid aside his first ambitions and turned himself to another career. A couple of hours' serious brainwork in the day was all that was ever possible to him henceforward. He spent it, as well as the thoughts and conversation of his less strenuous moments, on the study of history and sociology, with a view to joining the staff of lecturers for the manufacturing and country towns which the two great Universities, touched by new and popular sympathies, were then beginning to organise. He came of a stock which promised well for such a pioneer's task. His father had been an able factory inspector, well known for his share in the inauguration and revision of certain important factory reforms ; the son inherited a passionate humanity of soul ; and added to it a magnetic and personal charm which soon made him a remarkable power, not only in his own college, but among the finer spirits of the University generally. He had the gift which enables a man, sitting perhaps after dinner in a mixed society of his college contemporaries, to lead the way imperceptibly from the casual subjects of the hour—the river, the dons, the schools—to arguments 'of great pith and moment,' discussions that search the moral and intellectual powers of the men concerned to the utmost, without exciting distrust or any but an argumentative opposition. Edward Hallin could do this without a pose, without a false note, nay, rather by the natural force of a boyish intensity and simplicity. To many a Trinity man in after life the memory of his slight figure and fair head, of the eager slightly parted mouth, of the eyes glowing with some inward vision, and of the gesture with which he would spring up at some critical point to deliver himself, standing amid his seated and often dissentient auditors, came back vivid and ineffaceable as only youth can make the image of its prophets.

Upon Aldous Raeburn, Edward Hallin produced from the first a deep impression. The interests to which Hallin's mind soon became exclusively devoted—such as the systematic study of English poverty, or of the relation of religion to social life, reforms of the land and of the Church—overflowed upon Raeburn with a kindling and disturbing force. Edward Hallin was his gad-fly ; and he had no resource, because he loved his tormentor.

Fundamentally, the two men were widely different. Raeburn was a true son of his fathers, possessed by natural inheritance of the finer instincts of aristocratic rule, including a deep contempt for mob-reason and all the vulgarities of popular rhetoric ; steeped, too, in a number of subtle prejudices, and in a silent but intense pride of family of the nobler sort. He followed with disquiet and distrust the quick motions and conclusions of Hallin's intellect. Temperament and the Cambridge discipline made him a fastidious thinker and a fine scholar ; his mind worked slowly, yet with a delicate precision ; and his generally cold manner was the natural protection of feelings which had never yet, except in the case of his friendship with Edward Hallin, led him to much personal happiness.

Hallin left Cambridge after a pass degree to become lecturer on industrial and economical questions in the northern English towns. Raeburn stayed on a year longer, found himself third classic and the winner of a Greek verse prize, and then, sacrificing the idea of a fellowship, returned to Maxwell Court to be his grandfather's companion and helper in the work of the estate, his family proposing that, after a few years' practical experience of the life and occupations of a country gentleman, he should enter Parliament and make a career in politics. Since then five or six years had passed, during which he had learned to know the estate thoroughly, and to take his normal share in the business and pleasures of the neighbourhood. For the last two years he had been his grandfather's sole agent, a poor-law guardian and magistrate besides, and a member of most of the various committees for social and educational purposes in the county. He was a sufficiently keen sportsman to save appearances with his class ; enjoyed a walk after the partridges indeed, with a friend or two, as much as most men ; and played the host at the two or three great battues of the year with a propriety which his grandfather however no longer mistook for enthusiasm. There was nothing much to distinguish him from any other able man of his rank. His neighbours felt him to be a personality, but thought him reserved and difficult ; he was respected, but he was not popular like his grandfather ; people speculated as to how he would get on in Parliament, or whom he was to marry ; but, except to the dwellers in Maxwell Court itself, or of late to the farmers and labourers on the estate, it would not have mattered much to anybody if he had not been there. Nobody ever connected any romantic thought with him. There was something in his strong build, pale but healthy aquiline face, his inconspicuous brown eyes and hair, which seemed from the beginning to mark him out as the ordinary earthy dweller in an earthy world.

Nevertheless, these years had been to Aldous Raeburn years marked by an expansion and deepening of the whole man, such as few are capable of. Edward Hallin's visits to the Court, the walking tours which brought the two friends together almost every year in Switzerland or the Highlands, the course of a full and intimate correspondence, and the various calls made for public purposes by the enthusiast and pioneer upon the pocket and social power of the rich man—these things and influences, together, of course, with the pressure of an environing world, ever more real, and, on the whole, ever more oppressive, as it was better understood, had confronted Aldous Raeburn before now with a good many teasing problems of conduct and experience. His tastes, his sympathies, his affinities were all with the old order; but the old faiths—economical, social, religious—were fermenting within him in different stages of disintegration and reconstruction; and his reserved habit and often solitary life tended to scrupulosity and over-refinement. His future career as a landowner and politician was by no means clear to him. One thing only was clear to him —that to dogmatise about any subject under heaven, at the present day, more than the immediate practical occasion absolutely demanded, was the act of an idiot.

So that Aldous Raeburn's moments of reflection had been constantly mixed with struggle of different kinds. And the particular point of view where he stood on this September evening had been often associated in his memory with flashes of self-realisation which were, on the whole, more of a torment to him than a joy. If he had not been Aldous Raeburn, or any other person, tied to a particular individuality, with a particular place and label in the world, the task of the analytic mind, in face of the spectacle of what is, would have been a more possible one !—so it had often seemed to him.

But to-night all this cumbering consciousness, all these self-made doubts and worries, had for the moment dropped clean away ! A transfigured man it was that lingered at the old spot—a man once more young, divining with enchantment the approach of passion, feeling at last through all his being the ecstasy of a self-surrender, long missed, long hungered for.

Six weeks was it since he had first seen her—this tall, straight Marcella Boyce ? He shut his eyes impatiently against the disturbing golds and purples of the sunset, and tried to see her again as she had walked beside him across the church fields, in that thin black dress, with the shadow of the hat across her brow and eyes —the small white teeth flashing as she talked and smiled, the hand so ready with its gesture, so restless, so alive ! What a presence —how absorbing, troubling, preoccupying ! No one in her company could forget her—nay, could fail to observe her. What ease and daring, and yet no hardness with it—rather deep on deep of womanly weakness, softness, passion beneath it all !

How straight she had flung her questions at him !—her most
awkward embarrassing questions. What other woman would have
dared such candour—unless perhaps as a stroke of fine art—he had
known women indeed who could have done it so. But where
could be the art, the policy, he asked himself indignantly, in the
sudden outburst of a young girl pleading with her companion's
sense of truth and good feeling in behalf of those nearest to
her ?

As to her dilemma itself, in his excitement he thought of it
with nothing but the purest pleasure ! She had let him see that
she did not expect him to be able to do much for her, though she
was ready to believe him her friend. Ah !—well—he drew a long
breath. For once, Raeburn, strange compound that he was of the
man of rank and the philosopher, remembered his own social
power and position with an exultant satisfaction. No doubt Dick
Boyce had misbehaved himself badly—the strength of Lord Maxwell's feeling was sufficient proof thereof. No doubt the ' county,'
as Raeburn himself knew, in some detail, were disposed to leave
Mellor Park severely alone. What of that ? Was it for nothing
that the Maxwells had been for generations at the head of the
' county,' i.e. of that circle of neighbouring families connected by
the ties of ancestral friendship, or of intermarriage, on whom in
this purely agricultural and rural district the social pleasure and
comfort of Miss Boyce and her mother must depend?

He, like Marcella, did not believe that Richard Boyce's offences
were of the quite unpardonable order ; although, owing to a certain
absent and preoccupied temper, he had never yet taken the trouble
to inquire into them in detail. As to any real restoration of cordiality between the owner of Mellor and his father's old friends
and connections, that of course was not to be looked for ; but
there should be decent social recognition, and—in the case of
Mrs. Boyce and her daughter—there should be homage and warm
welcome, simply because she wished it, and it was absurd she
should not have it ! Raeburn, whose mind was ordinarily destitute
of the most elementary capacity for social intrigue, began to plot
in detail how it should be done. He relied first upon winning his
grandfather—his popular distinguished grandfather, whose lightest
word had weight in Brookshire. And then, he himself had two
or three women friends in the county—not more, for women had
not occupied much place in his thoughts till now. But they were
good friends, and, from the social point of view, important. He
would set them to work at once. These things should be chiefly
managed by women.

But no patronage ! She would never bear that, the glancing

proud creature. She must guess, indeed, let him tread as delicately as he might, that he and others were at work for her. But oh ! she should be softly handled ; as far as he could achieve it, she should, in a very little while, live and breathe compassed with warm airs of good-will and consideration.

He felt himself happy, amazingly happy, that at the very beginning of his love it should thus be open to him, in these trivial, foolish ways, to please and befriend her. Her social dilemma and discomfort one moment, indeed, made him sore for her ; the next, they were a kind of joy, since it was they gave him this opportunity to put out a strong right arm.

Everything about her at this moment was divine and lovely to him ; all the qualities of her rich uneven youth which she had shown in their short intercourse—her rashness, her impulsiveness, her generosity. Let her but trust herself to him, and she should try her social experiments as she pleased—she should plan Utopias, and he would be her hodman to build them. The man perplexed with too much thinking remembered the girl's innocent, ignorant readiness to stamp the world's stuff anew after the forms of her own pitying thought, with a positive thirst of sympathy. The deep poetry and ideality at the root of him under all the weight of intellectual and critical debate leapt towards her. He thought of the rapid talk she had poured out upon him, after their compact of friendship, in their walk back to the church, of her enthusiasm for her Socialist friends and their ideals,—with a momentary madness of self-suppression and tender humility. In reality, a man like Aldous Raeburn is born to be the judge and touchstone of natures like Marcella Boyce. But the illusion of passion may deal as disturbingly with moral rank as with social.

It was his first love. Years before, in the vacation before he went to college, his boyish mind had been crossed by a fancy for a pretty cousin a little older than himself, who had been very kind indeed to Lord Maxwell's heir. But then came Cambridge, the flow of a new mental life, his friendship for Edward Hallin, and the beginnings of a moral storm and stress. When he and the cousin next met, he was quite cold to her. She seemed to him a pretty piece of millinery, endowed with a trick of parrot phrases. She, on her part, thought him detestable ; she married shortly afterwards, and often spoke to her husband in private of her 'escape' from that queer fellow Aldous Raeburn.

Since then he had known plenty of pretty and charming women, both in London and in the country, and had made friends with some of them in his quiet serious way. But none of them had roused in him even a passing thrill of passion. He had despised himself for it ; had told himself again and again that he was but half a man——

Ah ! he had done himself injustice—he had done himselt injustice !

His heart was light as air. When at last the sound of a clock striking in the plain roused him with a start, and he sprang up from the heap of stones where he had been sitting in the dusk, he bent down a moment to give a gay caress to his dog, and then trudged orf briskly home, whistling under the emerging stars.

CHAPTER VI

By the time, however, that Aldous Raeburn came within sight of the windows of Maxwell Court his first exaltation had sobered down. The lover had fallen, for the time, into the background, and the capable, serious man of thirty, with a considerable experience of the world behind him, was perfectly conscious that there were many difficulties in his path. He could not induce his grandfather to move in the matter of Richard Boyce without a statement of his own feelings and aims. Nor would he have avoided frankness if he could. On every ground it was his grandfather's due. The Raeburns were reserved towards the rest of the world, but amongst themselves there had always been a fine tradition of mutual trust ; and Lord Maxwell amply deserved that at this particular moment his grandson should maintain it.

But Raeburn could not and did not flatter himself that his grandfather would, to begin with, receive his news even with toleration. The grim satisfaction with which that note about the shooting had been despatched, was very clear in the grandson's memory. At the same time it said much for the history of those long years during which the old man and his heir had been left to console each other for the terrible bereavements which had thrown them together, that Aldous Raeburn never for an instant feared the kind of violent outburst and opposition that other men in similar circumstances might have looked forward to. The just living of a life-time makes a man incapable of any mere selfish handling of another's interests—a fact on which the bystander may reckon.

It was quite dark by the time he entered the large open-roofed hall of the Court.

' Is his lordship in ?' he asked of a passing footman.

' Yes, sir—in the library. He has been asking for you, sir.'

Aldous turned to the right along the fine corridor lighted with

Tudor windows to an inner quadrangle, and filled with Græco-Roman statuary and sarcophagi, which made one of the piincipal features of the Court. The great house was warm and scer.ted, and the various open doors which he passed on his way to the library disclosed large fire-lit rooms, with panelling, tapestry, pictures, books everywhere. The colour of the whole was dim and rich; antiquity, refinement reigned, together with an exquisite quiet and order. No one was to be seen, and not a voice was to be heard; but there was no impression of solitude. These warm, darkly-glowing rooms seemed to be waiting for the return of guests just gone out of them; not one of them but had an air of cheerful company. For once, as he walked through it, Aldous Raeburn spared the old house an affectionate possessive thought. Its size and wealth, with all that both implied, had often weighed upon him. To-night his breath quickened as he passed the range of family portraits leading to the library door. There was a vacant space here and there—'room for your missus, too, my boy, when you get her!' as his grandfather had once put it.

'Why, you've had a long day, Aldous, all by yourself,' said Lord Maxwell, turning sharply round at the sound of the opening door. 'What's kept you so late?'

His spectacles fell forward as he spoke, and the old man shut them in his hand, peering at his grandson through the shadows of the room. He was sitting by a huge fire, an 'Edinburgh Review' open on his knee. Lamp and fire-light showed a finely-carried head, with a high wave of snowy hair thrown back, a long face delicately sharp in the lines, and an attitude instinct with the alertness of an unimpaired bodily vigour.

'The birds were scarce, and we followed them a good way,' said Aldous, as he came up to the fire. 'Rickman kept me on the farm, too, a good while, with interminable screeds about the things he wants done for him.'

'Oh, there is no end to Rickman,' said Lord Maxwell good-humouredly. 'He pays his rent for the amusement of getting it back again. Landowning will soon be the most disinterested form of philanthropy known to mankind. But I have some news for you! Here is a letter from Barton by the second post'—he named an old friend of his own, and a Cabinet Minister of the day. 'Look at it. You will see he says they can't possibly carry on beyond January. Half their men are becoming unmanageable, and S——'s bill, to which they are committed, will certainly dish them. Parliament will meet in January, and he thinks an amendment to the Address will finish it. All this confidential, of course; but he saw no harm in letting me know. So now, my boy, you

will have your work cut out for you this winter! Two or three
evenings a week—you'll not get off with less. Nobody's plum
drops into his mouth nowadays. Barton tells me, too, that he
hears young Wharton will certainly stand for the Durnford division,
and will be down upon us directly. He will make himself as disagreeable to us and the Levens as he can—that we may be sure of.
We may be thankful for one small mercy, that his mother has
departed this life! otherwise you and I would have known *furens
quid femina posset!*'

The old man looked up at his grandson with a humorous eye.
Aldous was standing absently before the fire, and did not reply
immediately.

'Come, come, Aldous!' said Lord Maxwell with a touch of
impatience, 'don't overdo the philosopher. Though I am getting
old, the next Government can't deny me a finger in the pie. You
and I between us will be able to pull through two or three of the
things we care about in the next House, with ordinary luck. It is
my firm belief that the next election will give our side the best
chance we have had for half a generation. Throw up your cap,
sir! The world may be made of green cheese, but we have got to
live in it!'

Aldous smiled suddenly—uncontrollably—with a look which
left his grandfather staring. He had been appealing to the man
of maturity standing on the threshold of a possibly considerable
career, and, as he did so, it was as though he saw the boy of
eighteen reappear!

'*Je ne demande pas mieux!*' said Aldous with a quick lift of the
voice above its ordinary key. 'The fact is, grandfather, I have
come home with something in my mind very different from politics
—and you must give me time to change the focus. I did not come
home as straight as I might—for I wanted to be sure of myself
before I spoke to you. During the last few weeks——'

'Go on!' cried Lord Maxwell.

But Aldous did not find it easy to go on. It suddenly struck
him that it was after all absurd that he should be confiding in any
one at such a stage, and his tongue stumbled.

But he had gone too far for retreat. Lord Maxwell sprang up
and seized him by the arms.

'You are in love, sir! Out with it!'

'I have seen the only woman in the world I have ever wished
to marry,' said Aldous, flushing, but with deliberation. 'Whether
she will ever have me, I have no idea. But I can conceive no
greater happiness than to win her. And as I want *you*, grandfather, to do something for her and for me, it seemed to me I had

no right to keep my feelings to myself. Besides, I am not accustomed to—to——' His voice wavered a little. 'You have treated me as more than a son !'

Lord Maxwell pressed his arm affectionately.

'My dear boy ! But don't keep me on tenterhooks like this— tell me the name !—the name !'

And two or three long meditated possibilities flashed through the old man's mind.

Aldous replied with a certain slow stiffness—

'Marcella Boyce !—Richard Boyce's daughter. I saw her first six weeks ago.'

'God bless my soul !' exclaimed Lord Maxwell, falling back a step or two, and staring at his companion. Aldous watched him with anxiety.

'You know that fellow's history, Aldous ?'

'Richard Boyce ? Not in detail. If you will tell me now all you know, it will be a help. Of course, I see that you and the neighbourhood mean to cut him,—and—for the sake of—of Miss Boyce and her mother, I should be glad to find a way out.'

'Good heavens !' said Lord Maxwell, beginning to pace the room, hands pressed behind him, head bent. 'Good heavens ! what a business ! what an extraordinary business !'

He stopped short in front of Aldous. 'Where have you been meeting her—this young lady ?'

'At the Hardens—sometimes in Mellor village. She goes about among the cottages a great deal.'

'You have not proposed to her ?'

'I was not certain of myself till to-day. Besides it would have been presumption so far. She has shown me nothing but the merest friendliness.'

'What, you can suppose she would refuse you !' cried Lord Maxwell, and could not for the life of him keep the sarcastic intonation out of his voice.

Aldous's look showed distress. 'You have not seen her, grandfather,' he said quietly.

Lord Maxwell began to pace again, trying to restrain the painful emotion that filled him. Of course, Aldous had been entrapped ; the girl had played upon his pity, his chivalry—for obvious reasons.

Aldous tried to soothe him, to explain, but Lord Maxwell hardly listened. At last he threw himself into his chair again with a long breath.

'Give me time, Aldous—give me time. The thought of marrying my heir to that man's daughter knocks me over a little.'

There was silence again. Then Lord Maxwell looked at his watch with old-fashioned precision.

'There is half an hour before dinner. Sit down, and let us talk this thing out.'

The conversation thus started, however, was only begun by dinner-time; was resumed after Miss Raeburn—the small, shrewd, bright-eyed person who governed Lord Maxwell's household—had withdrawn; and was continued in the library some time beyond his lordship's usual retiring hour. It was for the most part a monologue on the part of the grandfather, broken by occasional words from his companion; and for some time Marcella Boyce herself— the woman whom Aldous desired to marry—was hardly mentioned in it. Oppressed and tormented by a surprise which struck, or seemed to strike, at some of his most cherished ideals and just resentments, Lord Maxwell was bent upon letting his grandson know, in all their fulness, the reasons why no daughter of Richard Boyce could ever be, in the true sense, fit wife for a Raeburn.

Aldous was, of course, perfectly familiar with the creed implied in it all. A Maxwell should give himself no airs whatever, should indeed feel no pride whatever, towards 'men of goodwill,' whether peasant, professional, or noble. Such airs or such feeling would be both vulgar and unchristian. But when it came to *marriage*, then it behoved him to see that 'the family'—that carefully grafted and selected stock to which he owed so much—should suffer no loss or deterioration through him. Marriage with the fit woman meant for a Raeburn the preservation of a pure blood, of a dignified and honourable family habit, and moreover the securing to his children such an atmosphere of self-respect within, and of consideration from without, as he had himself grown up in. And a woman could not be fit, in this sense, who came either of an insignificant stock, untrained to large uses and opportunities, or of a stock which had degenerated, and lost its right of equal mating with the vigorous owners of unblemished names. Money was of course important and not to be despised, but the present Lord Maxwell, at any rate, large-minded and conscious of wealth he could never spend, laid comparatively little stress upon it; whereas, in his old age, the other instinct had but grown the stronger with him, as the world waxed more democratic, and the influence of the great families waned.

Nor could Aldous pretend to be insensible to such feelings and beliefs. Supposing the daughter could be won, there was no doubt whatever that Richard Boyce would be a cross and burden to a Raeburn son-in-law. But then! After all! Love for once made philosophy easy—made class tradition sit light. Impatience grew ; a readiness to believe Richard Boyce as black as Erebus and be done with it,—so that one might get to the point—the real point.

As to the story, it came to this. In his youth, Richard Boyce had been the younger and favourite son of his father. He possessed some ability, some good looks, some manners, all of which were wanting in his loutish elder brother. Sacrifices were accordingly made for him. He was sent to the bar. When he stood for Parliament his election expenses were jubilantly paid, and his father afterwards maintained him with as generous a hand as the estate could possibly bear, often in the teeth of the grudging resentment of Robert his firstborn. Richard showed signs of making a rapid success, at any rate on the political platform. He spoke with facility, and grappled with the drudgery of committees during his first two years at Westminster in a way to win him the favourable attention of the Tory whips. He had a gift for modern languages, and spoke chiefly on foreign affairs, so that when an important Eastern Commission had to be appointed, in connection with some troubles in the Balkan States, his merits and his father's exertions with certain old family friends, sufficed to place him upon it.

The Commission was headed by a remarkable man, and was able to do valuable work at a moment of great public interest, under the eyes of Europe. Its members came back covered with distinction, and were much fêted through the London season. Old Mr. Boyce came up from Mellor to see Dick's success for himself, and his rubicund country gentleman's face and white head might have been observed at many a London party beside the small Italianate physique of his son.

And love, as he is wont, came in the wake of fortune. A certain fresh west-country girl, Miss Evelyn Merritt, who had shown her stately beauty at one of the earliest drawing-rooms of the season, fell across Mr. Richard Boyce at this moment when he was most at ease with the world, and the world was giving him every opportunity. She was very young, as unspoilt as the daffodils of her Somersetshire valleys, and her character—a character of much complexity and stoical strength—was little more known to herself than it was to others. She saw Dick Boyce through a mist of romance ; forgot herself absolutely in idealising him, and could have thanked him on her knees when he asked her to marry him.

Five years of Parliament and marriage followed, and then—a

crash. It was a common and sordid story, made tragic by the
quality of the wife, and the disappointment of the father, if not by
the ruined possibilities of Dick Boyce himself. First, the desire to
maintain a 'position,' to make play in society with a pretty wife,
and, in the City, with a marketable reputation ; then company-
promoting of a more and more doubtful kind ; and, finally, a
swindle more energetic and less skilful than the rest, which bomb-
like went to pieces in the face of the public, filling the air with
noise, lamentations, and unsavoury odours. Nor was this all. A
man has many warnings of ruin, and when things were going
badly in the stock market, Richard Boyce, who on his return from
the East had been elected by acclamation a member of several
fashionable clubs, tried to retrieve himself at the gaming-table.
Lastly, when money matters at home and abroad, when the
anxieties of his wife and the altered manners of his acquaintance
in and out of the House of Commons grew more than usually disagreeable, a certain little chorus girl came upon the scene and served
to make both money and repentance scarcer even than they were
before. No story could be more commonplace or more detestable.

'Ah, how well I remember that poor old fellow—old John
Boyce,' said Lord Maxwell slowly, shaking his stately white head
over it, as he leant talking and musing against the mantelpiece.
'I saw him the day he came back from the attempt to hush up
the company business. I met him in the road, and could not help
pulling up to speak to him. I was so sorry for him. We had
been friends for many years, he and I. "Oh, good God !" he
said, when he saw me. "Don't stop me—don't speak to me !"
And he lashed his horse up—as white as a sheet—fat, fresh-
coloured man that he was in general—and was off. I never saw
him again till after his death. First came the trial, and Dick
Boyce got three months' imprisonment on a minor count, while
several others of the precious lot he was mixed up with came in
for penal servitude. There was some technical flaw in the evidence
with regard to him, and the clever lawyers they put on made the
most of it ; but we all thought, and society thought, that Dick was
morally as bad as any of them. Then the papers got hold of the
gambling debts and the woman. She made a disturbance at his
club, I believe, during the trial, while he was out on bail—anyway
it all came out. Two or three other people were implicated in the
gambling business—men of good family. Altogether it was one
of the biggest scandals I remember in my time.'

The old man paused, the long frowning face sternly set.
Aldous gazed at him in silence. It was certainly pretty bad—
worse than he had thought

'And the wife and child?' he said presently.

'Oh, poor things!'—said Lord Maxwell, forgetting everything for the moment but his story—'when Boyce's imprisonment was up they disappeared with him. His constituents held indignation meetings, of course. He gave up his seat, and his father allowed him a small fixed income—she had besides some little money of her own—which was secured him afterwards, I believe, on the estate during his brother's lifetime. Some of her people would have gladly persuaded her to leave him, for his behaviour towards her had been particularly odious,—and they were afraid, too, I think, that he might come to worse grief yet and make her life unbearable. But she wouldn't. And she would have no sympathy and no talk. I never saw her after the first year of their marriage, when she was a most radiant and beautiful creature. But, by all accounts of her behaviour at the time, she must be a remarkable woman. One of her family told me that she broke with all of them. She would know nobody who would not know him. Nor would she take money, though they were wretchedly poor; and Dick Boyce was not squeamish. She went off to little lodgings in the country or abroad with him without a word. At the same time, it was plain that her life was withered. She could make one great effort; but, according to my informant, she had no energy left for anything else—not even to take interest in her little girl——'

Aldous made a movement.

'Suppose we talk about her?' he said rather shortly.

Lord Maxwell started and recollected himself. After a pause he said, looking down under his spectacles at his grandson with an expression in which discomfort strove with humour—

'I see. You think we are beating about the bush. Perhaps we are. It is the difference between being old and being young, Aldous, my boy. Well—now then—for Miss Boyce. How much have you seen of her?—how deep has it gone? You can't wonder that I am knocked over. To bring that man amongst us! Why, the hound!' cried the old man suddenly, 'we could not even get him to come and see his father when he was dying. John had lost his memory mostly—had forgotten, any way, to be angry—and just *craved* for Dick, for the only creature he had ever loved. With great difficulty I traced the man, and tried my utmost. No good! He came when his father no longer knew him, an hour before the end. His nerves, I understood, were delicate—not so delicate, however, as to prevent his being present at the reading of the will! I have never forgiven him that cruelty to the old man, and never will!'

And Lord Maxwell began to pace the library again, by way of working off memory and indignation.

Aldous watched him rather gloomily. They had now been discussing Boyce's criminalities in great detail for a considerable time, and nothing else seemed to have any power to touch—or, at any rate, to hold—Lord Maxwell's attention. A certain deep pride in Aldous — the pride of intimate affection — felt itself wounded.

' I see that you have grave cause to think badly of her father,' he said at last, rising as he spoke. ' I must think how it concerns me. And to-morrow you must let me tell you something about her. After all, she has done none of these things. But I ought not to keep you up like this. You will remember Clarke was very emphatic about your not exhausting yourself at night, last time he was here.'

Lord Maxwell turned and stared.

' Why—why, what is the matter with you, Aldous ? Offended ? Well—well—— There—— I *am* an old fool ! '

And, walking up to his grandson, he laid an affectionate and rather shaking hand on the younger's shoulder.

' You have a great charge upon you, Aldous—a charge for the future. It has upset me—I shall be calmer to-morrow. But as to any quarrel between us ! Are you a youth, or am I a three-tailed bashaw ? As to money, you know, I care nothing. But it goes against me, my boy, it goes against me, that *your* wife should bring such a story as that with her into this house ! '

' I understand,' said Aldous, wincing. ' But you must see her, grandfather. Only, let me say it again—don't for one moment take it for granted that she will marry me. I never saw anyone so free, so unspoilt, so unconventional.'

His eyes glowed with the pleasure of remembering her looks, her tones.

Lord Maxwell withdrew his hand and shook his head slowly.

' You have a great deal to offer. No woman, unless she were either foolish or totally unexperienced, could overlook that. Is she about twenty ? '

' About twenty.'

Lord Maxwell waited a moment, then, bending over the fire, shrugged his shoulders in mock despair.

' It is evident you are out of love with me, Aldous. Why, I don't know yet whether she is dark or fair ! '

The conversation jarred on both sides. Aldous made an effort.

' She is very dark,' he said ; ' like her mother in many ways, only quite different in colour. To me she seems the most beautiful—the only beautiful woman I have ever seen. I should think she was very clever in some ways—and very unformed—childish almost—in others. The Hardens say she has done everything she could—of course it isn't much—for that miserable village in the time she has been there. Oh! by the way, she is a Socialist. She thinks that all we landowners should be done away with.'

Aldous looked round at his grandfather, so soon probably to be one of the lights of a Tory Cabinet, and laughed. So, to his relief, did Lord Maxwell.

'Well, don't let her fall into young Wharton's clutches, Aldous, or he will be setting her to canvass. So, she is beautiful and she is clever—and *good*, my boy? If she comes here, she will have to fill your mother's and your grandmother's place.'

Aldous tried to reply once or twice, but failed.

'If I did not feel that she were everything in herself to be loved and respected'—he said at last with some formality—'I should not long, as I do, to bring you and her together.'

Silence fell again. But instinctively Aldous felt that his grandfather's mood had grown gentler—his own task easier. He seized on the moment at once.

'In the whole business,' he said, half smiling, 'there is only one thing clear, grandfather, and that is, that, if you will, you can do me a great service with Miss Boyce.'

Lord Maxwell turned quickly and was all sharp attention, the keen commanding eyes under their fine brows absorbing, as it were, expression and life from the rest of the blanched and wrinkled face.

'You could, if you would, make matters easy for her and her mother in the county,' said Aldous, anxious to carry it off lightly. 'You could, if you would, without committing yourself to any personal contact with Boyce himself, make it possible for me to bring her here, so that you and my aunt might see her and judge.'

The old man's expression darkened.

'What, take back that note, Aldous! I never wrote anything with greater satisfaction in my life!'

'Well,—more or less,' said Aldous quietly. 'A very little would do it. A man in Richard Boyce's position will naturally not claim very much—will take what he can get.'

'And you mean besides,' said his grandfather, interrupting him, 'that I must send your aunt to call?'

'It will hardly be possible to ask Miss Boyce here unless she does!' said Aldous.

'And you reckon that I am not likely to go to Mellor, even to see her ? And you want me to say a word to other people—to the Winterbournes and the Levens, for instance?'

'Precisely,' said Aldous.

Lord Maxwell meditated ; then rose.

' Let me now appease the memory of Clarke by going to bed !' (Clarke was his lordship's medical attendant and autocrat.) 'I must sleep upon this, Aldous.'

' I only hope I shall not have tired you out.'

Aldous moved to extinguish a lamp standing on a table near. Suddenly his grandfather called him.

'Aldous !'

' Yes.'

But, as no words followed, Aldous turned. He saw his grandfather standing erect before the fire, and was startled by the emotion he instantly perceived in eye and mouth.

'You understand, Aldous, that for twenty years—it is twenty years last month since your father died—you have been the blessing of my life? Oh! don't say anything, my boy ; I don't want any more agitation. I have spoken strongly ; it was hardly possible but that on such a matter I should feel strongly. But don't go away misunderstanding me—don't imagine for one instant that there is anything in the world that really matters to me in comparison with your happiness and your future !'

The venerable old man wrung the hand he held, walked quickly to the door, and shut it behind him.

An hour later, Aldous was writing in his own sitting-room, a room on the first floor, at the western corner of the house, and commanding by daylight the falling slopes of wood below the Court, and all the wide expanses of the plain. To-night, too, the blinds were up, and the great view drawn in black and pearl, streaked with white mists in the ground hollows and overarched by a wide sky holding a haloed moon, lay spread before the windows. On a clear night Aldous felt himself stifled by blinds and curtains, and would often sit late, reading and writing, with a lamp so screened that it threw light upon his book or paper, while not interfering with the full range of his eye over the night-world without. He secretly believed that human beings see far too little of the night, and so lose a host of august or beautiful impressions, which might be honestly theirs if they pleased, without borrowing or stealing from anybody, poet or painter.

The room was lined with books, partly temporary visitors from the great library downstairs, partly his old college books and prizes, and partly representing small collections for special studies. Here were a large number of volumes, blue books, and pamphlets, bearing on the condition of agriculture and the rural poor in England and abroad ; there were some shelves devoted to general economics, and on a little table by the fire lay the recent numbers of various economic journals, English and foreign. Between the windows stood a small philosophical bookcase, the volumes of it full of small reference slips, and marked from end to end ; and on the other side of the room was a revolving book-table crowded with miscellaneous volumes of poets, critics, and novelists—mainly, however, with the first two. Aldous Raeburn read few novels, and those with a certain impatience. His mind was mostly engaged in a slow wrestle with difficult and unmanageable fact ; and for that transformation and illumination of fact in which the man of idealist temper must sometimes take refuge and comfort, he went easily and eagerly to the poets and to natural beauty. Hardly any novel writing, or reading, seemed to him worth while. A man, he thought, might be much better employed than in doing either.

Above the mantelpiece was his mother's picture—the picture of a young woman in a low dress and muslin scarf, trivial and empty in point of art, yet linked in Aldous's mind with a hundred touching recollections, buried all of them in the silence of an unbroken reserve. She had died in childbirth when he was nine ; her baby had died with her, and her husband, Lord Maxwell's only son and surviving child, fell a victim two years later to a deadly form of throat disease, one of those ills which come upon strong men by surprise, and excite in the dying a sense of helpless wrong which even religious faith can only partially soothe.

Aldous remembered his mother's death ; still more his father's, that father who could speak no last message to his son, could only lie dumb upon his pillows, with those eyes full of incommunicable pain, and the hand now restlessly seeking, now restlessly putting aside the small and trembling hand of the son. His boyhood had been spent under the shadow of these events, which had aged his grandfather, and made him too early realise himself as standing alone in the gap of loss, the only hope left to affection and to ambition. This premature development, amid the most melancholy surroundings, of the sense of personal importance—not in any egotistical sense, but as a sheer matter of fact—had robbed a nervous and sensitive temperament of natural stores of gaiety and elasticity which it could ill do without. Aldous Raeburn had been too much thought for and too painfully loved. But for Edward Hallin he might well have acquiesced at manhood in a certain impaired vitality, in the scholar's range of pleasures, and the landowner's customary round of duties.

It was to Edward Hallin he was writing to-night, for the stress
and stir of feeling caused by the events of the day, and not least
by his grandfather's outburst, seemed to put sleep far off. On the
table before him stood a photograph of Hallin, besides a miniature
of his mother as a girl. He had drawn the miniature closer to
him, finding sympathy and joy in its youth, in the bright expectancy
of the eyes, and so wrote, as it were, having both her and his friend
in mind and sight.

To Hallin he had already spoken of Miss Boyce, drawing her
in light, casual, and yet sympathetic strokes as the pretty girl in a
difficult position whom one would watch with curiosity and some
pity. To-night his letter, which should have discussed a home
colonisation scheme of Hallin's, had but one topic, and his pen
flew.

'Would you call her beautiful? I ask myself again and again,
trying to put myself behind your eyes. She has nothing, at any
rate, in common with the beauties we have down here, or with
those my aunt bade me admire in London last May. The face has
a strong Italian look, but not Italian of to-day. Do you remember
the Ghirlandajo frescoes in Santa Maria Novella, or the side groups
in Andrea's frescoes at the Annunziata? Among them, among the
beautiful tall women of them, there are, I am sure, noble, freely-
poised, suggestive heads like hers—hair, black wavy hair, folded
like hers in large simple lines, and faces with the same long, subtle
curves. It is a face of the Renaissance, extraordinarily beautiful,
as it seems to me, in colour and expression ; imperfect in line, as
the beauty which marks the meeting point between antique perfection and modern character must always be. It has *morbidezza*—
unquiet melancholy charm, then passionate gaiety—everything
that is most modern grafted on things Greek and old. I am told
that Burne Jones drew her several times while she was in London,
with delight. It is the most *artistic* beauty, having both the har-
monies and the dissonances that a full-grown art loves.

'She may be twenty, or rather more. The mind has all sorts
of ability ; comes to the right conclusion by a divine instinct,
ignoring the how and why. What does such a being want with
the drudgery of learning? to such keenness life will be master
enough. Yet she has evidently read a good deal—much poetry,
some scattered political economy, some modern socialistic books,
Matthew Arnold, Ruskin, Carlyle. She takes everything dramatically, imaginatively, goes straight from it to life, and back again.
Among the young people with whom she made acquaintance while
she was boarding in London and working at South Kensington,
there seem to have been two brothers, both artists, and both

Socialists; ardent young fellows, giving all their spare time to good works, who must have influenced her a great deal. She is full of angers and revolts, which you would delight in. And first of all, she is applying herself to her father's wretched village, which will keep her hands full. A large and passionate humanity plays about her. What she says often seems to me foolish—in the ear; but the inner sense, the heart of it, command me.

'Stare as you please, Ned! Only write to me, and come down here as soon as you can. I can and will hide nothing from you, so you will believe me when I say that all is uncertain, that I know nothing, and, though I hope everything, may just as well fear everything too. But somehow I am another man, and the world shines and glows for me by day and night.'

Aldous Raeburn rose from his chair and, going to the window, stood looking out at the splendour of the autumn moon. Marcella moved across the whiteness of the grass; her voice was still speaking to his inward ear. His lips smiled; his heart was in a wild whirl of happiness.

Then he walked to the table, took up his letter, read it, tore it across, and locked the fragments in a drawer.

'Not yet, Ned—not yet, dear old fellow, even to you,' he said to himself, as he put out his lamp.

CHAPTER VII

THREE days passed. On the fourth Marcella returned late in the afternoon from a round of parish visits with Mary Harden. As she opened the oak doors which shut off the central hall of Mellor from the outer vestibule, she saw something white lying on the old cut and disused billiard table, which still occupied the middle of the floor till Richard Boyce, in the course of his economies and improvements, could replace it by a new one.

She ran forward and took up a sheaf of cards, turning them over in a smiling excitement. 'Viscount Maxwell,' 'Mr. Raeburn,' 'Miss Raeburn,' 'Lady Winterbourne and the Misses Winterbourne,' two cards of Lord Winterbourne's—all perfectly in form.

Then a thought flashed upon her. 'Of course it is his doing—and I asked him!'

The cards dropped from her hand on the billiard table, and she stood looking at them, her pride fighting with her pleasure. There was something else in her feeling too—the exultation of proved power over a person not, as she guessed, easily influenced, especially by women.

'Marcella, is that you?'

It was her mother's voice. Mrs. Boyce had come in from the garden through the drawing-room, and was standing at the inner door of the hall, trying with shortsighted eyes to distinguish her daughter among the shadows of the great bare place. A dark day was drawing to its close, and there was little light left in the hall, except in one corner where a rainy sunset gleam struck a grim contemporary portrait of Mary Tudor, bringing out the obstinate mouth and the white hand holding a jewelled glove.

Marcella turned, and by the same gleam her mother saw her flushed and animated look.

'Any letters?' she asked.

'No; but there are some cards. Oh yes, there is a note,' and she pounced upon an envelope she had overlooked. 'It is for you, mother—from the Court.'

Mrs. Boyce came up and took note and cards from her daughter's hand. Marcella watched her with quick breath.

Her mother looked through the cards, slowly putting them down one by one without remark.

'Oh, mother! do read the note!' Marcella could not help entreating.

Mrs. Boyce drew herself together with a quick movement as though her daughter jarred upon her and opened the note. Marcella dared not look over her. There was a dignity about her mother's lightest action, about every movement of her slender fingers and fine fair head, which had always held the daughter in check, even while she rebelled.

Mrs. Boyce read it, and then handed it to Marcella.

'I must go and make the tea,' she said, in a light, cold tone, and turning, she went back to the drawing-room, whither afternoon tea had just been carried.

Marcella followed, reading. The note was from Miss Raeburn, and it contained an invitation to Mrs. Boyce and her daughter to take luncheon at the Court on the following Friday. The note was courteously and kindly worded. 'We should be so glad,' said the writer, 'to show you and Miss Boyce our beautiful woods while they are still at their best, in the way of autumn colour.'

'How will mamma take it?' thought Marcella anxiously. 'There is not a word of papa!'

When she entered the drawing-room, she caught her mother standing absently at the tea-table. The little silver caddy was still in her hand as though she had forgotten to put it down; and her eyes, which evidently saw nothing, were turned to the window, the brows frowning. The look of suffering for an instant was unmistakeable ; then she started at the sound of Marcella's step, and put down the caddy amid the delicate china crowded on the tray, with all the quiet precision of her ordinary manner.

'You will have to wait for your tea,' she said, ' the water doesn't nearly boil.'

Marcella went up to the fire and, kneeling before it, put the logs with which it was piled together. But she could not contain herself for long.

'Will you go to the Court, mamma ?' she asked quickly, without turning round.

There was a pause. Then Mrs. Boyce said drily—

'Miss Raeburn's proceedings are a little unexpected. We have been here four months, within two miles of her, and it has never occurred to her to call. Now she calls and asks us to luncheon in the same afternoon. Either she took too little notice of us before, or she takes too much now—don't you think so ?'

Marcella was silent a moment. Should she confess ? It began to occur to her for the first time that in her wild independence she had been taking liberties with her mother.

'Mamma !'

'Yes.'

'I asked Mr. Aldous Raeburn the other day whether everybody here was going to cut us ! Papa told me that Lord Maxwell had written him an uncivil letter, and——'

'You—asked—Mr. Raeburn—' said Mrs. Boyce quickly. 'What do you mean ?'

Marcella turned round and met the flash of her mother's eyes.

'I couldn't help it,' she said in a low hurried voice. ' It seemed so horrid to feel everybody standing aloof—we were walking together—he was very kind and friendly—and I asked him to explain.'

'I see !' said Mrs. Boyce. ' And he went to his aunt—and she went to Lady Winterbourne—they were compassionate—and there are the cards. You have certainly taken us all in hand, Marcella!'

Marcella felt an instant's fear—fear of the ironic power in the sparkling look so keenly fixed on her offending self ; she shrank before the proud reserve expressed in every line of her mother's fragile imperious beauty. Then a cry of nature broke from the girl.

'You have got used to it, mamma ! I feel as if it would kill me to live here, shut off from everybody—joining with nobody—with no friendly feelings or society. It was bad enough in the old lodging-house days ; but here—why *should* we ?'

Mrs. Boyce had certainly grown pale.

'I supposed you would ask sooner or later,' she said in a low determined voice, with what to Marcella was a quite new note of reality in it. 'Probably Mr. Raeburn told you—but you must of course have guessed it long ago—that society does not look kindly on us—and has its reasons. I do not deny in the least that it has its reasons. I do not accuse anybody, and resent nothing. But the question with me has always been, Shall I accept pity? I have always been able to meet it with a No! You are very different from me—but for you also I believe it would be the happiest answer.'

The eyes of both met—the mother's full of an indomitable fire which had for once wholly swept away her satiric calm of every day; the daughter's troubled and miserable.

'I want friends!' said Marcella slowly. 'There are so many things I want to do here, and one can do nothing if everyone is against you. People would be friends with you and me—and with papa too,—through us. Some of them wish to be kind'—she added insistently, thinking of Aldous Raeburn's words and expression as he bent to her at the gate—'I know they do. And if we can't hold our heads high because—because of things in the past—ought we to be so proud that we won't take their hands when they stretch them out—when they write so kindly and nicely as this?'

And she laid her fingers almost piteously on the note upon her knee.

Mrs. Boyce tilted the silver urn and replenished the tea-pot. Then with a delicate handkerchief she rubbed away a spot from the handle of a spoon near her.

'You shall go,' she said presently—'you wish it—then go—go by all means. I will write to Miss Raeburn and send you over in the carriage. One can put a great deal on health—mine is quite serviceable in the way of excuses. I will try to do you no harm, Marcella. If you have chosen your line and wish to make friends here—very well—I will do what I can for you so long as you do not expect me to change my life—for which, my dear, I am grown too crotchety and too old.'

Marcella looked at her with dismay and a yearning she had never felt before.

'And you will never go out with me, mamma?'

There was something child-like and touching in the voice, something which for once suggested the normal filial relation. But Mrs. Boyce did not waver. She had long learnt perhaps to regard Marcella as a girl singularly well able to take care of herself; and had recognised the fact with relief.

'I will not go to the Court with you anyway,' she said, daintily sipping her tea—' in your interests as well as mine. You will make all the greater impression, my dear, for I have really forgotten how to behave. Those cards shall be properly returned, of course. For the rest—let none disturb themselves till they must. And if I were you, Marcella, I would hardly discuss the family affairs any more— with Mr. Raeburn or anybody else.'

And again her keen glance disconcerted the tall handsome girl, whose power over the world about her had never extended to her mother. Marcella flushed and played with the fire.

'You see, mamma,' she said after a moment, still looking at the logs and the shower of sparks they made as she moved them about, ' you never let me discuss them with you.'

'Heaven forbid !' said Mrs. Boyce quickly ; then, after a pause : ' You will find your own line in a little while, Marcella, and you will see, if you so choose it, that there will be nothing unsurmountable in your way. One piece of advice let me give you. Don't be too *grateful* to Miss Raeburn, or anybody else ! You take great interest in your Boyce belongings, I perceive. You may remember too, perhaps, that there is other blood in you—and that no Merritt has ever submitted quietly to either patronage or pity.'

Marcella started. Her mother had never named her own kindred to her before that she could remember. She had known for many years that there was a breach between the Merritts and themselves. The newspapers had told her something at intervals of her Merritt relations, for they were fashionable and important folk, but no one of them had crossed the Boyces' threshold since the old London days, wherein Marcella could still dimly remember the tall forms of certain Merritt uncles, and even a stately lady in a white cap whom she knew to have been her mother's mother. The stately lady had died while she was still a child at her first school ; she could recollect her own mourning frock ; but that was almost the last personal remembrance she had, connected with the Merritts.

And now this note of intense personal and family pride, under which Mrs. Boyce's voice had for the first time quivered a little ! Marcella had never heard it before, and it thrilled her. She sat on by the fire, drinking her tea and every now and then watching her companion with a new and painful curiosity. The tacit assumption of many years with her had been that her mother was a dry limited person, clever and determined in small ways, that affected her own family, but on the whole characterless as compared with other people of strong feelings and responsive susceptibilities. But her own character had been rapidly maturing of late, and her insight sharpening. During these recent weeks of close contact.

her mother's singularity had risen in her mind to the dignity at least of a problem, an enigma.

Presently Mrs. Boyce rose and put the scones down by the fire.

'Your father will be in, I suppose. Yes, I hear the front door.'

As she spoke she took off her velvet cloak, put it carefully aside on a sofa, and sat down again, still in her bonnet, at the tea table. Her dress was very different from Marcella's, which, when they were not in mourning, was in general of the ample 'æsthetic' type, and gave her a good deal of trouble out of doors. Marcella wore 'art serges' and velveteens; Mrs. Boyce attired herself in soft and costly silks, generally black, closely and fashionably made, and completed by various fanciful and distinguished trifles— rings, an old chatelaine, a diamond brooch—which Marcella remembered, the same, and worn in the same way, since her child-hood. Mrs. Boyce, however, wore her clothes so daintily, and took such scrupulous and ingenious care of them, that her dress cost, in truth, extremely little—certainly less than Marcella's.

There were sounds first of footsteps in the hall, then of some scolding of William, and finally Mr. Boyce entered, tired and splashed from shooting, and evidently in a bad temper.

'Well, what are you going to do about those cards?' he asked his wife abruptly when she had supplied him with tea, and he was beginning to dry by the fire. He was feeling ill and reckless; too tired anyway to trouble himself to keep up appearances with Marcella.

'Return them,' said Mrs. Boyce calmly, blowing out the flame of her silver kettle.

'*I* don't want any of their precious society,' he said irritably. 'They should have done their calling long ago. There's no grace in it now; I don't know that one isn't inclined to think it an intrusion.'

But the women were silent. Marcella's attention was diverted from her mother to the father's small dark head and thin face. There was a great repulsion and impatience in her heart, an angry straining against circumstance and fate; yet at the same time a mounting voice of natural affection, an understanding at once sad and new, which paralysed and silenced her. He stood in her way —terribly in her way—and yet it strangely seemed to her, that never before till these last few weeks had she felt herself a daughter.

'You are very wet, papa,' she said to him as she took his cup: 'don't you think you had better go at once and change?'

'I'm all right,' he said shortly—'as right as I'm likely to be, anyway. As for the shooting, it's nothing but waste of time and shoe leather. I shan't go out any more. The place has been clean swept by some of those brutes in the village—your friends, Marcella. By the way, Evelyn, I came across young Wharton in the road just now.'

'Wharton?' said his wife interrogatively. 'I don't remember —ought I?'

'Why, the Liberal candidate for the division, of course,' he said testily. 'I wish you would inform yourself of what goes on. He is working like a horse, he tells me. Dodgson, the Raeburns' candidate, has got a great start; this young man will want all his time to catch him up. I like him. I won't vote for him; but I'll see fair play. I've asked him to come to tea here on Saturday, Evelyn. He'll be back again by the end of the week. He stays at Dell's farm when he comes—pretty bad accommodation, I should think. We must show him some civility.'

He rose and stood with his back to the fire, his spare frame stiffening under his nervous determination to assert himself—to hold up his head physically and morally against those who would repress him.

Richard Boyce took his social punishment badly. He had passed his first weeks at Mellor in a tremble of desire that his father's old family and country friends should recognise him again and condone his 'irregularities.' All sorts of conciliatory ideas had passed through his head. He meant to let people see that he would be a good neighbour if they would give him the chance— not like that miserly fool, his brother Robert. The past was so much past; who now was more respectable or more well intentioned than he? He was an impressionable imaginative man in delicate health; and the tears sometimes came into his eyes as he pictured himself restored to society—partly by his own efforts, partly, no doubt, by the charms and good looks of his wife and daughter—forgiven for their sake, and for the sake also of that store of virtue he had so laboriously accumulated since that long-past catastrophe. Would not most men have gone to the bad altogether, after such a lapse? He, on the contrary, had recovered himself, had neither drunk nor squandered, nor deserted his wife and child. These things, if the truth were known, were indeed due rather to a certain lack of physical energy and vitality, which age had developed in him, than to self-conquest; but he was no doubt entitled to make the most of them. There were signs indeed that his forecast had been not at all unreasonable. His women-kind *were* making their way. At the very moment when Lord Maxwell had written him a quelling letter, he had become aware that Marcella was on good terms with Lord Maxwell's heir. Had he not also been stopped that morning in a remote lane by Lord Winterbourne and Lord Maxwell on their way back from the meet, and had not both recognised and shaken hands with him? And now there were these cards.

Unfortunately, in spite of Raeburn's opinion to the contrary, no man in such a position and with such a temperament ever gets something without claiming more—and more than he can conceivably or possibly get. Startled and pleased at first by the salutation which Lord Maxwell and his companion had bestowed upon him, Richard Boyce had passed his afternoon in resenting and brooding over the cold civility of it. So these were the terms he was to be on with them—the deuce take them and their pharisaical airs! If all the truth were known, most men would look foolish; and the men who thanked God that they were not as other men, soonest of all. He wished he had not been taken by surprise; he wished he had not answered them; he would show them in the future that he would eat no dirt for them or anybody else.

So on the way home there had been a particular zest in his chance encounter with the young man who was likely to give the Raeburns and their candidate—so all the world said—a very great deal of trouble. The seat had been held to be an entirely safe one for the Maxwell nominee. Young Wharton, on the contrary, was making way every day, and, what with securing Aldous's own seat in the next division, and helping old Dodgson in this, Lord Maxwell and his grandson had their hands full. Dick Boyce was glad of it. He was a Tory; but all the same he wished every success to this handsome, agreeable young man, whose deferential manners to him at the end of the day had come like ointment to a wound.

The three sat on together for a little while in silence. Marcella kept her seat by the fire on the old gilt fender-stool, conscious in a dreamlike way of the room in front of her—the stately room with its stucco ceiling, its tall windows, its Prussian-blue wall-paper behind the old cabinets and faded pictures, and the chair covers in Turkey-red twill against the blue, which still remained to bear witness at once to the domestic economies and the decorative ideas of old Robert Boyce—conscious also of the figures on either side of her, and of her own quick-beating youth betwixt them. She was sore and unhappy; yet, on the whole, what she was thinking most about was Aldous Raeburn. What had he said to Lord Maxwell? —and to the Winterbournes? She wished she could know. She wished with leaping pulse that she could see him again quickly. Yet it would be awkward too.

Presently she got up and went away to take off her things. As the door closed behind her, Mrs. Boyce held out Miss Raeburn's note, which Marcella had returned to her, to her husband.

'They have asked Marcella and me to lunch,' she said. 'I am not going, but I shall send her.'

He read the note by the firelight, and it produced the most contradictory effects upon him.

'Why don't you go?' he asked her aggressively, rousing himself for a moment to attack her, and so vent some of his ill-humour.

'I have lost the habit of going out,' she said quietly, 'and am too old to begin again.'

'What! you mean to say,' he asked her angrily, raising his voice, 'that you have never *meant* to do your duties here—the duties of your position?'

'I did not foresee many, outside this house and land. Why should we change our ways? We have done very well of late. I have no mind to risk what I have got.'

He glanced round at her in a quick nervous way, and then looked back again at the fire. The sight of her delicate blanched face had in some respects a more and more poignant power with him as the years went on. His anger sank into moroseness.

'Then why do you let Marcella go? What good will it do her to go about without her parents? People will only despise her for a girl of no spirit—as they ought.'

'It depends upon how it is done. I can arrange it, I think,' said Mrs. Boyce. 'A woman has always convenient limitations to plead in the way of health. She need never give offence if she has decent wits. It will be understood that I do not go out, and then someone—Miss Raeburn or Lady Winterbourne—will take up Marcella and mother her.'

She spoke with her usual light gentleness, but he was not appeased.

'If you were to talk of *my* health, it would be more to the purpose,' he said, with grim inconsequence. And raising his heavy lids he looked at her full.

She got up and went over to him.

'Do you feel worse again? Why will you not change your things directly you come in? Would you like Dr. Clarke sent for?'

She was standing close beside him; her beautiful hand, for which in their young days it had pleased his pride to give her rings, almost touched him. A passionate hunger leapt within him. She would stoop and kiss him if he asked her; he knew that. But

he would not ask her; he did not want it; he wanted something
that never on this earth would she give him again.

Then moral discomfort lost itself in physical.

'Clarke does me no good—not an atom,' he said, rising.
'There—don't you come. I can look after myself.'

He went, and Mrs. Boyce remained alone in the great fire-lit
room. She put her hands on the mantelpiece, and dropped her
head upon them, and so stood silent for long. There was no
sound audible in the room, or from the house outside. And in the
silence a proud and broken heart once more nerved itself to an
endurance that brought it peace with neither man nor God.

'I shall go, for all our sakes,' thought Marcella, as she stood
late that night brushing her hair before her dimly lighted and
rickety dressing-table. 'We have, it seems, no right to be proud.'

A rush of pain and bitterness filled her heart—pain, new-born
and insistent, for her mother, her father, and herself. Ever since
Aldous Raeburn's hesitating revelations, she had been liable to
this sudden invasion of a hot and shamed misery. And to-night,
after her talk with her mother, it could not but overtake her afresh.

But her strong personality, her passionate sense of a moral
independence not to be undone by the acts of another, even a
father, made her soon impatient of her own distress, and she flung
it from her with decision.

'No, we have no right to be proud,' she repeated to herself.
'It must be all true what Mr. Raeburn said—probably a great deal
more. Poor, poor mamma! But, all the same, there is nothing to
be got out of empty quarrelling and standing alone. And it was
so long ago.'

Her hand fell, and she stood absently looking at her own black
and white reflection in the old flawed glass.

She was thinking, of course, of Mr. Raeburn. He had been
very prompt in her service. There could be no question but that
he was specially interested in her.

And he was not a man to be lightly played upon—nay, rather
a singularly reserved and scrupulous person. So, at least, it had
been always held concerning him. Marcella was triumphantly
conscious that he had not from the beginning given *her* much
trouble. But the common report of him made his recent manner
towards her, this last action of his, the more significant. Even the
Hardens—so Marcella gathered from her friend and admirer Mary
—unworldly dreamy folk, wrapt up in good works, and in the hasten-
ing of Christ's kingdom, were on the alert and beginning to take
note.

It was not as though he were in the dark as to her antecedents. He knew all—at any rate, more than she did—and yet it might end in his asking her to marry him. What then?

Scarcely a quiver in the young form before the glass ! *Love*, at such a thought, must have sunk upon its knees and hid its face for tender humbleness and requital. Marcella only looked quietly at the beauty which might easily prove to be so important an arrow in her quiver.

What was stirring in her was really a passionate ambition— ambition to be the queen and arbitress of human lives—to be believed in by her friends, to make a mark for herself among women, and to make it in the most romantic and yet natural way, without what had always seemed to her the sordid and unpleasant drudge- ries of the platform, of a tiresome co-operation with or subordina- tion to others who could not understand your ideas.

Of course, if it happened, people would say that she had tried to capture Aldous Raeburn for his money and position's sake. Let them say it. People with base minds must think basely ; there was no help for it. Those whom she would make her friends would know very well for what purpose she wanted money, power, and the support of such a man, and such a marriage. Her modern realism played with the thought quite freely ; her maidenliness, proud and pure as it was, being nowise ashamed. Oh ! for something to carry her *deep* into life ; into the heart of its widest and most splendid opportunities !

She threw up her hands, clasping them above her head amid her clouds of curly hair—a girlish excited gesture.

'I could revive the straw-plaiting ; give them better teaching and better models. The cottages should be rebuilt. Papa would willingly hand the village over to me if I found the money ! We would have a parish committee to deal with the charities—oh ! the Hardens would come in. The old people should have their pen- sions as of right. No hopeless old age, no cringing dependence ! We would try co-operation on the land, and pull it through. And not in Mellor only. One might be the ruler, the regenerator of half a county ! '

Memory brought to mind in vivid sequence the figures and inci- dents of the afternoon, of her village round with Mary Harden.

'*As the eyes of servants towards the hand of their mistress*'— the old words occurred to her as she thought of herself stepping in and out of the cottages. Then she was ashamed of herself and rejected the image with vehemence. Dependence was the curse of the poor. Her whole aim of course should be to teach them to stand on their own feet, to know themselves as men. But naturally they would be grateful, they would let themselves be led. Intelligence and enthusiasm give power, and ought to give it—power for good. No doubt, under Socialism, there will be less scope for either, because there will be less need. But Socialism, as a system, will not come in our generation. What we have to think for is the transition period. The Cravens had never seen that, but Marcella saw it. She began to feel herself a person of larger experience than they.

As she undressed, it seemed to her as though she still felt the clinging hands of the Hurd children round her knees, and through them, symbolised by them, the suppliant touch of hundreds of other helpless creatures.

She was just dropping to sleep when her own words to Aldous Raeburn flashed across her,—

' Everybody is so ready to take charge of other people's lives, and look at the result !'

She must needs laugh at herself, but it made little matter. She fell asleep cradled in dreams. Aldous Raeburn's final part in them was not great !

CHAPTER VIII

MRS. BOYCE wrote her note to Miss Raeburn, a note containing cold though civil excuses as to herself, while accepting the invitation for Marcella, who should be sent to the Court, either in the carriage or under the escort of a maid who could bring her back. Marcella found her mother inclined to insist punctiliously on conventions of this kind. It amused her, in submitting to them, to remember the free and easy ways of her London life. But she submitted—and not unwillingly.

On the afternoon of the day which intervened between the Maxwells' call and her introduction to the Court, Marcella walked as usual down to the village. She was teeming with plans for her new kingdom, and could not keep herself out of it. And an entry in one of the local papers had suggested to her that Hurd might possibly find work in a parish some miles from Mellor. She must go and send him off there.

When Mrs. Hurd opened the door to her, Marcella was astonished to perceive behind her the forms of several other persons filling up the narrow space of the usually solitary cottage—in fact, a tea-party.

' Oh, come in, miss,' said Mrs. Hurd, with some embarrassment, as though it occurred to her that her visitor might legitimately

wonder to find a person of her penury entertaining company.
Then, lowering her voice, she hurriedly explained : 'There's Mrs.
Brunt come in this afternoon to help me wi the washin while I
finished my score of plait for the woman who takes 'em into town
to-morrow. And there's old Patton an' his wife—you know 'em,
miss?—them as lives in the parish houses top o' the common.
He's walked out a few steps to-day. It's not often he's able, and
when I see him through the door I said to 'em, " if you'll come in
an' take a cheer, I dessay them tea-leaves 'ull stan another wettin.
I haven't got nothink else." And there's Mrs. Jellison, she came
in along o' the Pattons. You can't say her no, she's a queer one.
Do you know her, miss?'

'Oh, bless yer, yes. She knows me!' said a high, jocular
voice, making Mrs. Hurd start ; 'she couldn't be long hereabouts
without makkin eëaste to know me. You coom in, miss. We're
not afraid o' you—Lor' bless you !'

Mrs. Hurd stood aside for her visitor to pass in, looking round
her the while, in some perplexity, to see whether there was a spare
chair and room to place it. She was a delicate, willowy woman,
still young in figure, with a fresh colour, belied by the grey circles
under the eyes and the pinched sharpness of the features. The
upper lip, which was pretty and childish, was raised a little over
the teeth ; the whole expression of the slightly open mouth was
unusually soft and sensitive. On the whole, Minta Hurd was liked
in the village, though she was thought a trifle ' fine.' The whole
family, indeed, ' kept theirsels to theirsels,' and to find Mrs. Hurd
with company was unusual. Her name, of course, was short for
Araminta.

Marcella laughed as she caught Mrs. Jellison's remarks, and
made her way in, delighted. For the present, these village people
affected her like figures in poetry or drama. She saw them with
the eye of the imagination through a medium provided by Socialist
discussion, or by certain phases of modern art ; and the little scene
of Mrs. Hurd's tea-party took for her in an instant the dramatic
zest and glamour.

' Look here, Mrs. Jellison,' she said, going up to her ; ' I was
just going to leave these apples for your grandson. Perhaps you'll
take them, now you're here. They're quite sweet, though they look
green. They're the best we've got, the gardener says.'

' Oh, they are, are they ?' said Mrs. Jellison composedly, looking up at her. 'Well, put 'em down, miss. I dare say he'll eat
'em. He eats most things, and don't want no doctor's stuff nayther,
though his mother do keep on at me for spoilin his stummuck.'

' You are just fond of that boy, aren't you, Mrs. Jellison ?' said

Marcella, taking a wooden stool, the only piece of furniture left in
the tiny cottage on which it was possible to sit, and squeezing herself into a corner by the fire, whence she commanded the whole
group. 'No! don't you turn Mr. Patton out of that chair, Mrs.
Hurd, or I shall have to go away.'

For Mrs. Hurd, in her anxiety, was whispering in old Patton's
ear that it might be well for him to give up her one wooden arm-
chair in which he was established to Miss Boyce. But he, being
old, deaf, and rheumatic, was slow to move, and Marcella's peremptory gesture bade her leave him in peace.

'Well, it's you that's the young 'un, ain't it, miss?' said Mrs.
Jellison, cheerfully. 'Poor old Patton, he do get slow on his legs,
don't you, Patton? But there, there's no helpin it when you're
turned of eighty.'

And she turned upon him a bright, philosophic eye, being herself a young thing not much over seventy, and energetic accordingly. Mrs. Jellison passed for the village wit, and was at least
talkative and excitable beyond her fellows.

'Well, *you* don't seem to mind getting old, Mrs. Jellison,' said
Marcella, smiling at her.

The eyes of all the old people round their tea-table were by
now drawn irresistibly to Miss Boyce in the chimney corner, to her
slim grace, and the splendour of her large black hat and feathers.
The new squire's daughter had so far taken them by surprise.
Some of them, however, were by now in the second stage of critical
observation—none the less critical because furtive and inarticulate.

'Ah?' said Mrs. Jellison interrogatively, with a high, long-
drawn note peculiar to her. 'Well, I've never found you get forrarder wi snarlin over what you can't help. And there's mercies.
When you've had a husband in his bed for fower year, miss, and
he's took at last, you'll *know*.'

She nodded emphatically. Marcella laughed.

'I know you were very fond of him, Mrs. Jellison, and looked
after him very well too.'

'Oh, I don't say nothin about that,' said Mrs. Jellison hastily.
'But all the same you kin reckon it up, and see for yoursen. Fower
year—an' fire upstairs, an' fire downstairs, an' fire all night, an'
soomthin allus wanted. An' he such an objeck afore he died!
It do seem like a holiday now to sit a bit.'

And she crossed her hands on her lap with a long breath of
content. A lock of grey hair had escaped from her bonnet, across
her wrinkled forehead, and gave her a half-careless, rakish air.
Her youth of long ago—a youth of mad spirits, and of an extraordinary capacity for physical enjoyment—seemed at times to pierce

to the surface again, even through her load of years. But in general she had a dreamy, sunny look, as of one fed with humorous fancies, but disinclined often to the trouble of communicating them.

'Well, I missed my daughter, I kin tell you,' said Mrs. Brunt, with a sigh, 'though she took a deal more lookin after nor your good man, Mrs. Jellison.'

Mrs. Brunt was a gentle, pretty old woman, who lived in another of the village almshouses, next door to the Pattons, and was always ready to help her neighbours in their domestic toils. Her last remaining daughter, the victim of a horrible spinal disease, had died some nine or ten months before the Boyces arrived at Mellor. Marcella had already heard the story several times, but it was part of her social gift that she was a good listener to such things even at the twentieth hearing.

'You wouldn't have her back though,' she said gently, turning towards the speaker.

'No, I wouldn't have her back, miss,' said Mrs. Brunt, raising her hand to brush away a tear, partly the result of feeling, partly of a long-established habit. 'But I do miss her nights terrible ! "Mother, ain't it ten o'clock ?—mother, look at the clock, do, mother—ain't it time for my stuff, mother?—oh, I do *hope* it is." That was her stuff, miss, to make her sleep. And when she'd got it, she'd *groan*—you'd think she couldn't be asleep, and yet she was, dead-like—for two hours. I didn't get no rest with her, and now I don't seem to get no rest without her.'

And again Mrs. Brunt put her hand up to her eyes.

'Ah, you were allus one for toilin an' frettin,' said Mrs. Jellison calmly. 'A body must get through wi it when it's there, but I don't hold wi thinkin about it when it's done.'

'I know one,' said old Patton slily, 'that fretted about *her* darter when it didn't do her no good.'

He had not spoken so far, but had sat with his hands on his stick, a spectator of the women's humours. He was a little hunched man, twisted and bent double with rheumatic gout, the fruit of seventy years of field work. His small face was almost lost, dog-like, under shaggy hair and overgrown eyebrows, both snow-white. He had a look of irritable eagerness, seldom, however, expressed in words. A sudden passion in the faded blue eyes ; a quick spot of red in his old cheeks ; these Marcella had often noticed in him, as though the flame of some inner furnace leapt. He had been a Radical and a rebel once in old rick-burning days, long before he lost the power in his limbs and came down to be thankful for one of the parish almshouses. To his social betters he was now a quiet and peaceable old man, well aware of the cakes and ale to be got

by good manners; but in the depths of him there were reminis-
cences and the ghosts of passions, which were still stirred sometimes
by causes not always intelligible to the bystander.

He had rarely, however, physical energy enough to bring any
emotion—even of mere worry at his physical ills—to the birth.
The pathetic silence of age enwrapped him more and more. Still
he could gibe the women sometimes, especially Mrs. Jellison, who
was in general too clever for her company.

'Oh, you may talk, Patton!' said Mrs. Jellison, with a little
flash of excitement. 'You do like to have your talk, don't you?
Well, I dare say I *was* orkard with Isabella. I won't go for to say
I *wasn't* orkard, for I *was*. She should ha used me to 't before, if
she wor took that way. She and I had just settled down comfortable after my old man went, and I didn't see no sense in it, an'
I don't now. She might ha let the men alone. She'd seen enough
o' the worrit ov 'em.'

'Well, she did well for hersen,' said Mrs. Brunt, with the same
gentle melancholy. 'She married a stiddy man as 'ull keep her
well all her time, and never let her want for nothink.'

'A sour, wooden-faced chap as iver I knew,' said Mrs. Jellison,
grudgingly. 'I don't have nothink to say to him, nor he to me.
He thinks hissen the Grand Turk, he do, since they gi'en him his
uniform, and made him full keeper. A nassty, domineerin sort, I
calls him. He's allus makin bad blood wi the yoong fellers when
he don't need. It's the way he's got wi 'im. But *I* don't make no
account of 'im, an' I let 'im see't.'

All the tea-party grinned except Mrs. Hurd. The village was
well acquainted with the feud between Mrs. Jellison and her son-
in-law, George Westall, who had persuaded Isabella Jellison at the
mature age of thirty-five to leave her mother and marry him, and
was now one of Lord Maxwell's keepers, with good pay, and an
excellent cottage some little way out of the village. Mrs. Jellison
had never forgiven her daughter for deserting her, and was on
lively terms of hostility with her son-in-law; but their only child,
little Johnnie, had found the soft spot in his grandmother, and her
favourite excitement in life, now that he was four years old, was to
steal him from his parents and feed him on the things of which
Isabella most vigorously disapproved.

Mrs. Hurd, as has been said, did not smile. At the mention of
Westall, she got up hastily, and began to put away the tea things.

Marcella meanwhile had been sitting thoughtful.

'You say Westall makes bad blood with the young men, Mrs.
Jellison,' she said, looking up. 'Is there much poaching in this
village now, do you think?'

There was a dead silence. Mrs. Hurd was at the other end of
the cottage with her back to Marcella ; at the question, her hands
paused an instant in their work. The eyes of all the old people—
of Patton and his wife, of Mrs. Jellison, and pretty Mrs. Brunt—
were fixed on the speaker, but nobody said a word, not even Mrs.
Jellison. Marcella coloured.

'Oh, you needn't suppose——' she said, throwing her beautiful
head back, 'you needn't suppose that *I* care about the game, or
that I would ever be mean enough to tell anything that was told
me. I know it *does* cause a great deal of quarrelling and bad
blood. I believe it does here—and I should like to know more
about it. I want to make up my mind what to think. Of course,
my father has got his land and his own opinions. And Lord
Maxwell has too. But I am not bound to think like either of them—I
should like you to understand that. It seems to me right about all
such things that people should inquire and find out for themselves.'

Still silence. Mrs. Jellison's mouth twitched, and she threw a
sly provocative glance at old Patton, as though she would have
liked to poke him in the ribs. But she was not going to help him
out ; and at last the one male in the company found himself
obliged to clear his throat for reply.

'We're old folks, most on us, miss, 'cept Mrs. Hurd. We don't
hear talk o' things now like as we did when we were younger. If
you ast Mr. Harden he'll tell you, I dessay.'

Patton allowed himself an inward chuckle. Even Mrs. Jellison,
he thought, must admit that he knew a thing or two as to the best
way of dealing with the gentry.

But Marcella fixed him with her bright frank eyes.

'I had rather ask in the village,' she said. 'If you don't know
how it is now, Mr. Patton, tell me how it used to be when you were
young. Was the preserving very strict about here ? Were there
often fights with the keepers—long ago ?—in my grandfather's
days ?—and do you think men poached because they were hungry,
or because they wanted sport ? '

Patton looked at her fixedly a moment undecided, then her
strong nervous youth seemed to exercise a kind of compulsion on
him ; perhaps, too, the pretty courtesy of her manner. He cleared
his throat again, and tried to forget Mrs. Jellison, who would be
sure to let him hear of it again, whatever he said.

'Well, I can't answer for 'em, miss, I'm sure ; but if you ast *me*,
I b'lieve ther's a bit o' boath in it. Yer see it's not in human
natur, when a man's young and 's got his blood up, as he shouldn't
want ter have 'is sport with the wild creeturs. Perhaps he see 'em
when ee's going to the wood with a wood cart—or he cooms across

'em in the turnips—wounded birds, you understan, miss, perhaps
the day after the gentry 'as been bangin at 'em all day. An' ee
don't see, not for the life of 'im, why ee shouldn't have 'em. Ther's
bin lots an' lots for the rich folks, an' he don't see why *ee* shouldn't
have a few arter they've enjoyed theirselves. And mebbe he's
eleven shillin a week—an' two-threy little chillen—you understan,
miss ? '

'Of course I understand ! ' said Marcella, eagerly, her dark
cheek flushing. 'Of course I do ! But there's a good deal of
game given away in these parts, isn't there ? I know Lord Maxwell does, and they say Lord Winterbourne gives all his labourers
rabbits, almost as many as they want.'

Her questions wound old Patton up as though he had been a
disused clock. He began to feel a whirr among his creaking
wheels, a shaking of all his rusty mind.

'Perhaps they do, miss,' he said, and his wife saw that he was
beginning to tremble. 'I dessay they do—I don't say nothink
agen it—though theer's none of it cooms my way. But that isn't
all the rights on it nayther—no, that it ain't. The labourin man
ee's glad enough to get a hare or a rabbit for 'is eatin—but ther's
more in it nor that, miss. Ee's allus in the fields, that's where it
is—ee can't help seein the hares and the rabbits a-comin in and out
o' the woods, if it were iver so. Ee knows ivery run ov ivery one on
'em ; if a hare's started furthest corner o' t' field, he can tell yer
whar she'll git in by, because he's allus there, you see, miss, an'
it's the only thing he's got to take his mind off like. And then he
sets a snare or two—an' ee gits very sharp at settin on 'em—an'
ee'll go out nights for the sport of it. Ther isn't many things *ee's*
got to liven him up ; an' ee takes 'is chances o' goin to jail—it's
wuth it, ee thinks.'

The old man's hands on his stick shook more and more visibly.
Bygones of his youth had come back to him.

'Oh, I know ! I know ! ' cried Marcella with an accent half of
indignation, half of despair. 'It's the whole wretched system. It
spoils those who've got, and those who haven't got. And there'll
be no mending it till the *people* get the land back again, and till
the rights on it are common to all.'

'My ! she do speak up, don't she ? ' said Mrs. Jellison, grinning again at her companions. Then, stooping forward with one
of her wild movements, she caught Marcella's arm—'I'd like to
hear yer tell that to Lord Maxwell, miss. I likes a roompus, I do.'

Marcella flushed and laughed.

'I wouldn't mind saying that or anything else to Lord Maxwell,' she said proudly. 'I'm not ashamed of anything I think.'

'No, I'll bet you ain't,' said Mrs. Jellison, withdrawing her hand. 'Now then, Patton, you say what *you* thinks. You ain't got no vote now you're in the parish houses—I minds that. The quality don't trouble *you* at 'lection times. This yoong man, Muster Wharton, as is goin round so free, promisin yer the sun out o' the sky, iv yer'll only vote for 'im, so th' men say—*ee* don't coom an' set down along o' you an' me, an' cocker of us up as ee do Joe Simmons or Jim Hurd here. But that don't matter. Yur thinkin's yur own, any way.'

But she nudged him in vain. Patton had suddenly run down, and there was no more to be got out of him.

Not only had nerves and speech failed him as they were wont, but in his cloudy soul there had risen, even while Marcella was speaking, the inevitable suspicion which dogs the relations of the poor towards the richer class. This young lady, with her strange talk, was the new Squire's daughter. And the village had already made up its mind that Richard Boyce was 'a poor sort,' and 'a hard sort' too, in his landlord capacity. He wasn't going to be any improvement on his brother—not a haporth! What was the good of this young woman talking, as she did, when there were three summonses as he, Patton, heard tell, just taken out by the sanitary inspector against Mr. Boyce for bad cottages? And not a farthing given away in the village neither, except perhaps the bits of food that the young lady herself brought down to the village now and then, for which no one, in truth, felt any cause to be particularly grateful. Besides, what did she mean by asking questions about the poaching? Old Patton knew as well as anybody else in the village, that during Robert Boyce's last days, and after the death of his sportsman son, the Mellor estate had become the haunt of poachers from far and near, and that the trouble had long since spread into the neighbouring properties, so that the Winterbourne and Maxwell keepers regarded it as their most arduous business to keep watch on the men of Mellor. Of course the young woman knew it all, and she and her father wanted to know more. That was why she talked. Patton hardened himself against the creeping ways of the quality.

'I don't think nought,' he said roughly in answer to Mrs. Jellison. 'Thinkin won't come atwixt me and the parish coffin when I'm took. I've no call to think, I tell yer.'

Marcella's chest heaved with indignant feeling.

'Oh, but, Mr. Patton!' she cried, leaning forward to him, 'won't it comfort you a bit, even if you can't live to see it, to think there's a better time coming? There must be. People can't go on like this always—hating each other and trampling on each other.

They're beginning to see it now, they are! When I was living in London, the persons I was with talked and thought of it all day. Some day, whenever the people choose—for they've got the power now they've got the vote—there'll be land for everybody, and in every village there'll be a council to manage things, and the labourer will count for just as much as the squire and the parson, and he'll be better educated and better fed, and care for many things he doesn't care for now. But all the same, if he wants sport and shooting, it will be there for him to get. For everybody will have a chance and a turn, and there'll be no bitterness between classes, and no hopeless pining and misery as there is now!'

The girl broke off catching her breath. It excited her to say these things to these people, to these poor tottering old things who had lived out their lives to the end under the pressure of an iron system, and had no lien on the future, whatever Paradise it might bring. Again the situation had something foreseen and dramatic in it. She saw herself, as the preacher, sitting on her stool beside the poor grate—she realised as a spectator the figures of the women and the old man played on by the firelight—the white, bare, damp-stained walls of the cottage, and in the background the fragile though still comely form of Minta Hurd, who was standing with her back to the dresser, and her head bent forward, listening to the talk while her fingers twisted the straw she plaited eternally from morning till night, for a wage of about one and threepence a week.

Her mind was all aflame with excitement and defiance—defiance of her father, Lord Maxwell, Aldous Raeburn. Let him come, her friend, and see for himself what she thought it right to do and say in this miserable village. Her soul challenged him, longed to provoke him! Well, she was soon to meet him, and in a new and more significant relation and environment. The fact made her perception of the whole situation the more rich and vibrant.

Patton, while these broken thoughts and sensations were coursing through Marcella's head, was slowly revolving what she had been saying, and the others were waiting for him.

At last he rolled his tongue round his dry lips and delivered himself by a final effort.

'Them as likes, miss, may believe as how things are going to happen that way, but yer won't ketch me! Them as have got 'ull *keep*'—he let his stick sharply down on the floor—' an' them as 'aven't got 'ull 'ave to go without and *lump it*—as long as you're alive, miss, you mark my words!'

'Oh, Lor, you wor allus one for makin a poor mouth, Patton!' said Mrs. Jellison. She had been sitting with her arms folded across her chest, part absent, part amused, part malicious. 'The young lady speaks beautiful, just like a book she do. An' she's likely to know a deal better nor poor persons like you and me. All *I* kin say is,—if there's goin to be dividin up of other folks' property, when I'm gone, I hope George Westall won't get nothink ov it! He's bad enough as 'tis. Isabella 'ud have a fine time if *ee* took to drivin ov his carriage.'

The others laughed out, Marcella at their head, and Mrs. Jellison subsided, the corners of her mouth still twitching, and her eyes shining as though a host of entertaining notions were trooping through her—which, however, she preferred to amuse herself with rather than the public. Marcella looked at Patton thoughtfully.

'You've been all your life in this village, haven't you, Mr. Patton?' she asked him.

'Born top o' Witchett's Hill, miss. An' my wife here, she wor born just a house or two further along, an' we two bin married sixty-one year come next March.'

He had resumed his usual almshouse tone, civil and a little plaintive. His wife behind him smiled gently at being spoken of. She had a long fair face, and white hair surmounted by a battered black bonnet, a mouth set rather on one side, and a more observant and refined air than most of her neighbours. She sighed while she talked, and spoke in a delicate quaver.

'D'ye know, miss,' said Mrs. Jellison, pointing to Mrs. Patton, ' as she kep school when she was young?'

'Did you, Mrs. Patton?' asked Marcella in her tone of sympathetic interest. 'The school wasn't very big then, I suppose?'

'About forty, miss,' said. Mrs. Patton, with a sigh. 'There was eighteen the Rector paid for, and eighteen Mr. Boyce paid for, and the rest paid for themselves.'

Her voice dropped gently, and she sighed again like one weighted with an eternal fatigue.

'And what did you teach them?'

'Well, I taught them the plaitin, miss, and as much readin and writin as I knew myself. It wasn't as high as it is now, you see, miss,' and a delicate flush dawned on the old cheek as Mrs. Patton threw a glance round her companions as though appealing to them not to tell stories of her.

But Mrs. Jellison was implacable. 'It wor she taught *me*,' she said, nodding at Marcella and pointing sideways to Mrs. Patton. 'She had a queer way wi the hard words, I can tell yer, miss. When she couldn't tell 'em herself she'd never own up to it. 'Say Jerusalem, my dear, and pass on.' That's what she'd say, she would, sure as you're alive! I've heard her do it times. An' when Isabella an' me used to read the Bible, nights, I'd allus rayther do't than be beholden to me own darter. It gets yer through, any way.'

'Well, it wor a good word,' said Mrs. Patton, blushing and mildly defending herself. ' It didn't do none of yer any harm.'

' Oh, an' before her, miss, I went to a school to another woman, as lived up Shepherd's Row. You remember her, Betsy Brunt?'

Mrs. Brunt's worn eyes began already to gleam and sparkle.

'Yis, I recolleck very well, Mrs. Jellison. She wor Mercy Moss, an' a goodish deal of trouble you'd use to get me into wi Mercy Moss, all along o' your tricks.'

Mrs. Jellison, still with folded arms, began to rock herself gently up and down as though to stimulate memory.

' My word, but Muster Maurice—he wor the clergyman here then, miss—wor set on Mercy Moss. He and his wife they flat- tered and cockered her up. Ther wor nobody like her for keepin school, not in their eyes—till one midsummer—she—well she—I don't want to say nothink onpleasant—*but she transgressed,*' said Mrs. Jellison, nodding mysteriously, triumphant however in the unimpeachable delicacy of her language, and looking round the circle for approval.

'What do you say?' asked Marcella innocently. 'What did Mercy Moss do?'

Mrs. Jellison's eyes danced with malice and mischief, but her mouth shut like a vice. Patton leaned forward on his stick, shaken with a sort of inward explosion ; his plaintive wife laughed under her breath till she must needs sigh because laughter tired her old bones. Mrs. Brunt gurgled gently. And finally Mrs. Jellison was carried away.

' Oh, my goodness me, don't you make me tell tales o' Mercy Moss !' she said at last, dashing the water out of her eyes with an excited tremulous hand. ' She's bin dead and gone these forty year—married and buried mos respeckable—it 'ud be a burnin shame to bring up tales agen her now. Them as tittle-tattles about dead folks needn't look to lie quiet theirselves in their graves. I've said it times, and I'll say it again. What are you lookin at me for, Betsy Brunt?'

And Mrs. Jellison drew up suddenly with a fierce glance at Mrs. Brunt.

'Why, Mrs. Jellison, I niver meant no offence,' said Mrs. Brunt hastily.

' I won't stand no insinooatin,' said Mrs. Jellison with energy. ' If you've got soomthink agen me, you may out wi 't an' niver mind the young lady.'

But Mrs. Brunt, much flurried, retreated amid a shower of excuses, pursued by her enemy, who was soon worrying the whole little company, as a dog worries a flock of sheep, snapping here and teasing there, chattering at the top of her voice in broad dialect, as she got more and more excited, and quite as ready to break her wit on Marcella as on anybody else. As for the others, most of them had known little else for weeks than alternations of toil and sickness ; they were as much amused and excited to-night by Mrs. Jellison's audacities as a Londoner is by his favourite low comedian at his favourite music-hall. They played chorus to her, laughed, baited her ; even old Patton was drawn against his will into a caustic sociability.

Marcella meanwhile sat on her stool, her chin upon her hand, and her full glowing eyes turned upon the little spectacle, absorbing it all with a covetous curiosity.

The light-heartedness, the power of enjoyment left in these old folk struck her dumb. Mrs. Brunt had an income of two-and-sixpence a week, *plus* two loaves from the parish, and one of the parish or ' charity' houses, a hovel, that is to say, of one room, scarcely fit for human habitation at all. She had lost five children, was allowed two shillings a week by two labourer sons, and earned sixpence a week—about—by continuous work at 'the plait.' Her husband had been run over by a farm-cart and killed ; up to the time of his death his earnings averaged about twenty-eight pounds a year. Much the same with the Pattons. They had lost eight children out of ten, and were now mainly supported by the wages of a daughter in service. Mrs. Patton had of late years suffered agonies and humiliations indescribable, from a terrible illness which the parish doctor was quite incompetent to treat, being all through a singularly sensitive woman, with a natural instinct for the decorous and the beautiful.

Amazing ! Starvation wages ; hardships of sickness and pain ; horrors of birth and horrors of death ; wholesale losses of kindred and friends ; the meanest surroundings ; the most sordid cares—of this mingled cup of village fate every person in the room had drunk, and drunk deep. Yet here in this autumn twilight they laughed and chattered and joked—weird, wrinkled children, enjoying an hour's rough play in a clearing of the storm ! Dependent from birth to death on squire, parson, parish, crushed often, and ill-treated, according to their own ideas, but bearing so little ill-will ; amusing themselves with their own tragedies even, if they could but sit by a fire and drink a neighbour's cup of tea.

Her heart swelled and burned within her. Yes, the old people were past hoping for ; mere wreck and driftwood on the shore, the

spring-tide of death would soon have swept them all into unremem-
bered graves. But the young men and women, the children, were
they too to grow up, and grow old like these—the same smiling,
stunted, ignobly submissive creatures? One woman at least would
do her best with her one poor life to rouse. some of them to discontent and revolt !

CHAPTER IX

THE fire sank, and Mrs. Hurd made no haste to light her lamp.
Soon the old people were dim chattering shapes in a red darkness
Mrs. Hurd still plaited, silent and upright, lifting her head every
now and then at each sound upon the road.

At last there was a knock at the door. Mrs. Hurd ran to
open it.

'Mother, I'm going your way,' said a strident voice. 'I'll help
you home if you've a mind.'

On the threshold stood Mrs. Jellison's daughter, Mrs. Westall,
with her little boy beside her, the woman's broad shoulders and
harsh striking head standing out against the pale sky behind.
Marcella noticed that she greeted none of the old people, nor they
her. And as for Mrs. Hurd, as soon as she saw the keeper's wife,
she turned her back abruptly on her visitor, and walked to the
other end of the kitchen.

'Are you comin, mother?' repeated Isabella.

Mrs. Jellison grumbled, gibed at her, and made long leave-
takings, while the daughter stood silent, waiting, and every now
and then peering at Marcella, who had never seen her before.

'I don know where yur manners is,' said Mrs. Jellison sharply
to her, as though she had been a child of ten, 'that you don't say
good evenin to the young lady.'

Mrs. Westall curtsied low, and hoped she might be excused,
as it had grown so dark. Her tone was smooth and servile, and
Marcella disliked her as she shook hands with her.

The other old people, including Mrs. Brunt, departed a minute
or two after the mother and daughter, and Marcella was left an
instant with Mrs. Hurd.

'Oh, thank you, thank you kindly, miss,' said Mrs. Hurd,
raising her apron to her eyes to staunch some irrepressible tears,
as Marcella showed her the advertisement which it might possibly
be worth Hurd's while to answer. 'He'll try, you may be sure.
But I can't think as how anythink 'ull come ov it.'

And then suddenly, as though something unexplained had upset her self-control, the poor patient creature utterly broke down. Leaning against the bare shelves which held their few pots and pans, she threw her apron over her head and burst into the forlornest weeping. 'I wish I was dead; I wish I was dead, an' the chillen too!'

Marcella hung over her, one flame of passionate pity, comforting, soothing, promising help. Mrs. Hurd presently recovered enough to tell her that Hurd had gone off that morning before it was light to a farm near Thame, where it had been told him he might possibly find a job.

'But he'll not find it, miss, he'll not find it,' she said, twisting her hands in a sort of restless misery ; 'there's nothing good happens to such as us. An' he wor allus a one to work if he could get it.'

There was a sound outside. Mrs. Hurd flew to the door, and a short, deformed man, with a large head and red hair, stumbled in blindly, splashed with mud up to his waist, and evidently spent with long walking.

He stopped on the threshold, straining his eyes to see through the fire-lit gloom.

'It's Miss Boyce, Jim,' said his wife. 'Did you hear of anythink?'

'They're turnin off hands instead of takin ov 'em on,' he said briefly, and fell into a chair by the grate.

He had hardly greeted Marcella, who had certainly looked to be greeted. Ever since her arrival in August, as she had told Aldous Raeburn, she had taken a warm interest in this man and his family. There was something about them which marked them out a bit from their fellows—whether it was the husband's strange but not repulsive deformity, contrasted with the touch of plaintive grace in the wife, or the charm of the elfish children, with their tiny stick-like arms and legs, and the glancing wildness of their blue eyes, under the frizzle of red hair, which shone round their little sickly faces. Very soon she had begun to haunt them in her eager way, to try and penetrate their peasant lives, which were so full of enigma and attraction to her, mainly because of their very defectiveness, their closeness to an animal simplicity, never to be reached by anyone of her sort. She soon discovered, or imagined, that Hurd had more education than his neighbours. At any rate, he would sit listening to her—and smoking, as she made him do—while she talked politics and socialism to him ; and though he said little in return, she made the most of it, and was sure anyway that he was glad to see her come in, and must some time read the labour newspapers and Venturist leaflets she brought him, for they were always well thumbed before they came back to her.

But to-night his sullen weariness would make no effort, and the hunted restless glances he threw from side to side as he sat crouching over the fire—the large mouth tight shut, the nostrils working —showed her that he would be glad when she went away.

Her young exacting temper was piqued. She had been for some time trying to arrange their lives for them. So, in spite of his dumb resistance, she lingered on, questioning and suggesting. As to the advertisement she had brought down, he put it aside almost without looking at it. 'There ud be a hun'erd men after it before ever he could get there,' was all he would say to it. Then she inquired if he had been to ask the steward of the Maxwell Court estate for work. He did not answer, but Mrs. Hurd said timidly that she heard tell a new drive was to be made that winter for the sake of giving employment. But their own men on the estate would come first, and there were plenty of them out of work.

'Well, but there is the game,' persisted Marcella. 'Isn't it possible they might want some extra men now the pheasant shooting has begun ? I might go and inquire of Westall—I know him a little.'

The wife made a startled movement, and Hurd raised his misshapen form with a jerk.

'Thank yer, miss, but I'll not trouble yer. I don't want nothing to do with Westall.'

And taking up a bit of half-burnt wood which lay on the hearth, he threw it violently back into the grate. Marcella looked from one to the other with surprise. Mrs. Hurd's expression was one of miserable discomfort, and she kept twisting her apron in her gnarled hands.

'Yes, I *shall* tell, Jim !' she broke out. 'I shall. I know Miss Boyce is one as ull understand——'

Hurd turned round and looked at his wife full. But she persisted.

'You see, miss, they don't speak, don't Jim and George Westall. When Jim was quite a lad he was employed at Mellor, under old Westall, George's father as was. Jim was watcher, and young George he was assistant. That was in Mr. Robert's days, you understand, miss—when Master Harold was alive ; and they took a deal o' trouble about the game. An' George Westall, he was allays leadin the others a life—tale-bearin an' spyin, an' settin his father against any of 'em as didn't give in to him. An', oh, he behaved *fearful* to Jim ! Jim ull tell you.   Now, Jim, what's wrong with you—why shouldn't I tell ?'

For Hurd had risen, and as he and his wife looked at each other a sort of mute conversation seemed to pass between them. Then he turned angrily, and went out of the cottage by the back door into the garden.

The wife sat in some agitation a moment, then she resumed. ' He can't bear no talk about Westall—it seems to drive him silly. But I say as how people *should* know.'

Her wavering eye seemed to interrogate her companion. Marcella was puzzled by her manner—it was so far from simple.

' But that was long ago, surely,' she said.

' Yes, it wor long ago, but you don't forget them things, miss ! An' Westall, he's just the same sort as he was then, so folks say,' she added hurriedly.   ' You see Jim, miss, how he's made ?   His back was twisted that way when he was a little un.   His father was a good old man—everybody spoke well of 'im—but his mother, she was a queer mad body, with red hair, just like Jim and the children, and a temper ! my word.   They do say she was an Irish girl, out of a gang as used to work near here—an' she let him drop one day when she was in liquor, an' never took no trouble about him after-wards.   He was a poor sickly lad, he was ! you'd wonder how he grew up at all.   And oh ! George Westall he treated him *cruel*. He'd kick and swear at him ; then he'd dare him to fight, an' thrash him till the others came in, an' got him away.   Then he'd carry tales to his father, and one day old Westall beat Jim within an inch of 'is life, with a strap end, because of a lie George told 'im.   The poor chap lay in a ditch under Disley Wood all day, because he was that knocked about he couldn't walk, and at night he crawled home on his hands and knees.   He's shown me the place many a time ! Then he told his father, and next morning he told me, as he couldn't stand it no longer, an' he never went back no more.'

' And he told no one else ?—he never complained ?' asked Marcella indignantly.

' What ud ha been the good o' that, miss ?' Mrs. Hurd said, wondering.   ' Nobody ud ha' taken his word agen old Westall's. But he come and told me.   I was housemaid at Lady Leven's then, an' he and his father were old friends of ourn.   And I knew George Westall too.   He used to walk out with me of a Sunday, just as civil as could be, and give my mother rabbits now and again, and do anything I'd ask him.   An' I up and told him he was a brute to go ill-treatin a sickly fellow as couldn't pay him back.   That made him as cross as vinegar, an' when Jim began to be about with me ov a Sunday sometimes, instead of him, he got madder

and madder. An' Jim asked me to marry him—he begged of me
—an' I didn't know what to say.   For Westall had asked me
twice ; an' I was afeard of Jim's health, an' the low wages he'd get,
an' of not bein strong myself.   But one day I was going up a lane
into Tudley End woods, an' I heard George Westall on t'other
side of the hedge with a young dog he was trainin.   Somethin
crossed him, an' he flew into a passion with it.   It turned me *sick*.
I ran away and I took against him there and then.   I was
frightened of him.   I dursen't trust myself, and I said to Jim I'd
take him.   So you can understan, miss, can't you, as Jim don't
want to have nothin to do with Westall ?   Thank you kindly, all
the same,' she added, breaking off her narrative with the same uncertainty of manner, the same timid scrutiny of her visitor that
Marcella had noticed before.

Marcella replied that she could certainly understand.

'But I suppose they've not got in each other's way of late
years,' she said as she rose to go.

'Oh ! no, miss, no,' said Mrs. Hurd as she went hurriedly to
fetch a fur tippet which her visitor had laid down on the dresser.

'There is *one* person I can speak to,' said Marcella as she put
on the wrap.   'And I will.'   Against her will she reddened a little ;
but she had not been able to help throwing out the promise.   'And
now, you won't despair, will you ?   You'll trust me ?   I could
always do something.'

She took Mrs. Hurd's hand with a sweet look and gesture.
Standing there in her tall vigorous youth, her furs wrapped about
her, she had the air of protecting and guiding this poverty that
could not help itself.   The mother and wife felt herself shy, in-
timidated.   The tears came back to her brown eyes.

When Miss Boyce had gone, Minta Hurd went to the fire and
out it together, sighing all the time, her face still red and miserable.

The door opened and her husband came in.   He carried some
potatoes in his great earth-stained hands.

'You're goin to put that bit of hare on ?   Well, make eëaste, do,
for I'm starvin.   What did she want to stay all that time for ?   You
go and get it.   I'll blow the fire up—damn these sticks !—they're
as wet as Dugnall pond.'

Nevertheless, as she sadly came and went, preparing the supper,
she saw that he was appeased, in a better temper than before.

'What did you tell 'er ?' he asked abruptly.

'What do you spose I'd tell her ?   I acted for the best.   I'm
always thinkin for you !' she said as though with a little cry, ' or

we'd soon be in trouble—worse trouble than we are!' she added miserably.

He stopped working the old bellows for a moment, and, holding his long chin, stared into the flames. With his deformity, his earth-stains, his blue eyes, his brown wrinkled skin, and his shock of red hair, he had the look of some strange gnome crouching there.

'I don't know what you're at, I'll swear,' he said after a pause. 'I ain't in any pertickler trouble just now—if yer wouldn't send a fellow stumpin the country for nothink. If you'll just let me alone I'll get a livin for you and the chillen right enough. Don't you trouble yourself—an' hold your tongue!'

She threw down her apron with a gesture of despair as she stood beside him, in front of the fire, watching the pan.

'What am I to do, Jim, an' them chillen—when you're took to prison?' she asked him vehemently.

'I shan't get took to prison, I tell yer. All the same, Westall got holt o' me this mornin. I thought praps you'd better know.'

Her exclamation of terror, her wild look at him, were exactly what he had expected; nevertheless, he flinched before them. His brutality was mostly assumed. He had adopted it as a mask for more than a year past, because he *must* go his way, and she worried him.

'Now look here,' he said resolutely, 'it don't matter. I'm not goin to be took by Westall. I'd kill him or myself first. But he caught me lookin at a snare this mornin—it wor misty, and I didn't see no one comin. It wor close to the footpath, an it worn't my snare.'

'"Jim, my chap," says he, mockin, "I'm sorry for it, but I'm going to search yer, so take it quietly," says he. He had young Dynes with him—so I didn't say nought—I kep as still as a mouse, an sure enough he put his ugly hans into all my pockets. An' what do yer think he foun?'

'What?' she said, breathlessly.

'Nothink!' he laughed out. 'Nary an end o' string, nor a kink o' wire—nothink. I'd hidden the two rabbits I got las' night, and all my bits o' things in a ditch far enough out o' his way. I just laughed at the look ov im. "I'll have the law on yer for assault an' battery, yer damned miscalculatin brute!" says I to him—"why don't yer get that boy there to teach yer your business?" An' off I walked. Don't you be afeard—ee'll never lay hands on me!'

But Minta was sore afraid, and went on talking and lamenting while she made the tea. He took little heed of her. He sat by the fire quivering and thinking. In a public-house two nights before this one, overtures had been made to him on behalf of a well-known gang of poachers with head-quarters in a neighbouring county town, who had their eyes on the pheasant preserves in Westall's particular beat—the Tudley End beat—and wanted a local watcher and accomplice. He had thought the matter at first too dangerous to touch. Moreover, he was at that moment in a period of transition, pestered by Minta to give up 'the poachin,' and yet drawn back to it after his spring and summer of field work by instincts only recently revived, after long dormancy, but now hard to resist.

Presently he turned with anger upon one of Minta's wails which happened to reach him.

'Look ere !' said he to her, 'where ud you an' the chillen be this night if I 'adn't done it ? 'Adn't we got rid of every stick o' stuff we iver 'ad ? Ere's a well-furnished place for a chap to sit in !'—he glanced bitterly round the bare kitchen, which had none of the little properties of the country poor, no chest, no set of mahogany drawers, no comfortable chair, nothing, but the dresser and the few rush chairs and the table, and a few odds and ends of crockery and household stuff—'wouldn't we all a bin on the parish, if we 'adn't starved fust—*wouldn't* we ?—jes answer me that ! *Didn't* we sit here an' starve, till the bones was comin' through the chillen's skin ?—didn't we ?'

That he could still argue the point with her showed the inner vulnerableness, the inner need of her affection and of peace with her, which he still felt, far as certain new habits were beginning to sweep him from her.

'It's Westall or Jenkins' (Jenkins was the village policeman) 'havin the *law* on yer, Jim,' she said with emphasis, putting down a cup and looking at him—'it's the thought of *that* makes me cold in my back. None o' *my* people was ever in prison—an' if it appened to you I should just die of shame !'

'Then yer'd better take and read them papers there as *she* brought,' he said impatiently, first jerking his finger over his shoulder in the direction of Mellor to indicate Miss Boyce, and then pointing to a heap of newspapers which lay on the floor in a corner, 'they'd tell yer summat about the shame o' *makin* them game-laws—not o' breakin ov 'em. But I'm sick o' this ! Where's them chillen ? Why do yer let that boy out so late ?'

And opening the door he stood on the threshold looking up and down the village street, while Minta once more gave up the struggle, dried her eyes, and told herself to be cheerful. But it was hard. She was far better born and better educated than her husband. Her father had been a small master chair-maker in Wycombe, and her mother, a lackadaisical silly woman, had given her her 'fine' name by way of additional proof that she and her children were something out of the common. Moreover, she had the conforming law-abiding instincts of the well-treated domestic servant, who has lived on kindly terms with the gentry and shared their standards. And for years after their marriage Hurd had allowed her to govern him. He had been so patient, so hard-working, such a kind husband and father, so full of a dumb wish to show her he was grateful to her for marrying such a fellow as he. The quarrel with Westall seemed to have sunk out of his mind. He never spoke to or of him. Low wages, the burden of quick-coming children, the bad sanitary conditions of their wretched cottage, and poor health, had made their lives one long and sordid struggle. But for years he had borne his load with extraordinary patience. He and his could just exist, and the man who had been in youth the lonely victim of his neighbours' scorn had found a woman to give him all herself and children to love. Hence years of submission, a hidden flowering time for both of them.

Till that last awful winter !—the winter before Richard Boyce's succession to Mellor—when the farmers had been mostly ruined, and half the able-bodied men of Mellor had tramped 'up into the smoke,' as the village put it, in search of London work—then, out of actual sheer starvation—that very rare excuse of the poacher ! —Hurd had gone one night and snared a hare on the Mellor land. Would the wife and mother ever forget the pure animal satisfaction of that meal, or the fearful joy of the next night, when he got three shillings from a local publican for a hare and two rabbits ?

But after the first relief Minta had gone in fear and trembling. For the old woodcraft revived in Hurd, and the old passion for the fields and their chances which he had felt as a lad before his 'watcher's' place had been made intolerable to him by George Westall's bullying. He became excited, unmanageable. Very soon he was no longer content with Mellor, where, since the death of young Harold, the heir, the keepers had been dismissed, and what remained of a once numerous head of game lay open to the wiles of all the bold spirits of the neighbourhood. He must needs go on to those woods of Lord Maxwell's, which girdled the Mellor estate on three sides. And here he came once more across his enemy. For George Westall was now in the far better-paid service of the Court—and a very clever keeper, with designs on the head keeper's post whenever it might be vacant. In the case of a poacher he had the scent of one of his own hares. It was known to him in an incredibly short time that that 'low caselty fellow Hurd' was attacking 'his' game.

Hurd, notwithstanding, was cunning itself, and Westall lay in wait for him in vain. Meanwhile, all the old hatred between the two men revived. Hurd drank this winter more than he had ever drunk yet. It was necessary to keep on good terms with one or two publicans who acted as 'receivers' of the poached game of the neighbourhood. And it seemed to him that Westall pursued him into these low dens. The keeper—big, burly, prosperous—would speak to him with insolent patronage, watching him all the time, or with the old brutality, which Hurd dared not resent. Only in his excitable dwarf's sense hate grew and throve, very soon to monstrous proportions. Westall's menacing figure darkened all his sky for him. His poaching, besides a means of livelihood, became more and more a silent duel between him and his boyhood's tyrant.

And now, after seven months of regular field-work and respectable living, it was all to begin again with the new winter ! The same shudders and terrors, the same shames before the gentry and Mr. Harden !—the soft, timid woman with her conscience could not endure the prospect. For some weeks after the harvest was over she struggled. He had begun to go out again at nights. But she drove him to look for employment, and lived in tears when he failed.

As for him, she knew that he was glad to fail ; there was a certain ease and jauntiness in his air to-night as he stood calling the children :

'Will !—you come in at once ! Daisy !—Nellie !'

Two little figures came pattering up the street in the moist October dusk, a third panted behind. The girls ran in to their mother chattering and laughing. Hurd lifted the boy in his arm.

'Where you bin, Will ? What were yo out for in this nasty damp ? I've brought yo a whole pocket full o' chestnuts, and summat else too.'

He carried him in to the fire and sat him on his knees. The little emaciated creature, flushed with the pleasure of his father's company, played contentedly in the intervals of coughing with the shining chestnuts, or ate his slice of the fine pear—the gift of a friend in Thame—which proved to be the ' summat else ' of promise. The curtains were close-drawn ; the paraffin lamp flared on the table, and as the savoury smell of the hare and onions on the fire filled the kitchen, the whole family gathered round watching for the moment of eating. The fire played on the thin legs and pinched faces of the children ; on the baby's cradle in the further corner ; on the mother, red-eyed still, but able to smile and talk again ; on the strange Celtic face and matted hair of the dwarf. Family affection

—and the satisfaction of the simpler physical needs—these things make the happiness of the poor.   For this hour, to-night, the Hurds were happy.

Meanwhile, in the lane outside, Marcella, as she walked home, passed a tall, broad-shouldered man in a velveteen suit and gaiters, his gun over his shoulder and two dogs behind him, his pockets bulging on either side.   He walked with a kind of military air, and touched his cap to her as he passed.

Marcella barely nodded.

'Tyrant and bully!' she thought to herself with Mrs. Hurd's story in her mind.   'Yet no doubt he is a valuable keeper; Lord Maxwell would be sorry to lose him!   It is the system makes such men—and must have them.'

The clatter of a pony-carriage disturbed her thoughts.   A small, elderly lady, in a very large mushroom hat, drove past her in the dusk and bowed stiffly.   Marcella was so taken by surprise that she barely returned the bow.   Then she looked after the carriage. That was Miss Raeburn.

To-morrow!

CHAPTER X

'WON'T you sit nearer to the window?   We are rather proud of our view at this time of year,' said Miss Raeburn to Marcella, taking her visitor's jacket from her as she spoke, and laying it aside.   'Lady Winterbourne is late, but she will come, I am sure. She is very precise about engagements.'

Marcella moved her chair nearer to the great bow-window, and looked out over the sloping gardens of the Court, and the autumn splendour of the woods girdling them in on all sides.   She held her head nervously erect, was not apparently much inclined to talk, and Miss Raeburn, who had resumed her knitting within a few paces of her guest, said to herself presently after a few minutes' conversation on the weather and the walk from Mellor : 'Difficult —decidedly difficult—and too much manner for a young girl.   But the most picturesque creature I ever set eyes on!'

Lord Maxwell's sister was an excellent woman, the inquisitive, benevolent despot of all the Maxwell villages ; and one of the soundest Tories still left to a degenerate party and a changing time.   Her brother and her great-nephew represented to her the flower of human kind ; she had never been capable, and probably never would be capable, of quarrelling with either of them on any subject whatever.   At the same time she had her rights with them.

She was at any rate their natural guardian in those matters, relating
to womankind, where men are confessedly given to folly. She had
accordingly kept a shrewd eye in Aldous's interest on all the young
ladies of the neighbourhood for many years past ; knew perfectly
well all that he might have done, and sighed over all that he had
so far left undone.

At the present moment, in spite of the even good-breeding with
which she knitted and chattered beside Marcella, she was in truth
consumed with curiosity, conjecture, and alarm on the subject of
this Miss Boyce. Profoundly as they trusted each other, the Raeburns were not on the surface a communicative family. Neither
her brother nor Aldous had so far bestowed any direct confidence
upon her ; but the course of affairs had, notwithstanding, aroused
her very keenest attention. In the first place, as we know, the
mistress of Maxwell Court had left Mellor and its new occupants
unvisited ; she had plainly understood it to be her brother's wish
that she should do so. How, indeed, could you know the women
without knowing Richard Boyce ? which, according to Lord Maxwell, was impossible. And now it was Lord Maxwell who had
suggested not only that after all it would be kind to call upon the
poor things, who were heavily weighted enough already with Dick
Boyce for husband and father, but that it would be a graceful act
on his sister's part to ask the girl and her mother to luncheon.
Dick Boyce of course must be made to keep his distance, but the
resources of civilisation were perhaps not unequal to the task of
discriminating, if it were prudently set about. At any rate Miss
Raeburn gathered that she was expected to try, and instead of
pressing her brother for explanations she held her tongue, paid her
call forthwith, and wrote her note.

But although Aldous, thinking no doubt that he had been
already sufficiently premature, had said nothing at all as to his own
feelings to his great-aunt, she knew perfectly well that he had said
a great deal on the subject of Miss Boyce and her mother to Lady
Winterbourne, the only woman in the neighbourhood with whom
he was ever really confidential. No woman, of course, in Miss
Raeburn's position, and with Miss Raeburn's general interest in
her kind, could have been ignorant for any appreciable number of
days after the Boyces' arrival at Mellor that they possessed a
handsome daughter, of whom the Hardens in particular gave striking but, as Miss Raeburn privately thought, by no means wholly
attractive accounts. And now, after all these somewhat agitating
preliminaries, here was the girl established in the Court drawing-
room, Aldous more nervous and preoccupied than she had ever
seen him, and Lord Maxwell expressing a particular anxiety to

return from his Board meeting in good time for luncheon, to which he had specially desired that Lady Winterbourne should be bidden, and no one else ! It may well be supposed that Miss Raeburn was on the alert.

As for Marcella, she was on her side keenly conscious of being observed, of having her way to make. Here she was alone among these formidable people, whose acquaintance she had in a manner compelled. Well—what blame? What was to prevent her from doing the same thing again to-morrow? Her conscience was absolutely clear. If they were not ready to meet her in the same spirit in which through Mr. Raeburn she had approached them, she would know perfectly well how to protect herself !—above all, how to live out her life in the future without troubling them.

Meanwhile, in spite of her dignity and those inward propitiations it from time to time demanded, she was, in her human vivid way, full of an excitement and curiosity she could hardly conceal as perfectly as she desired—curiosity as to the great house and the life in it, especially as to Aldous Raeburn's part therein. She knew very little indeed of the class to which by birth she belonged ; great houses and great people were strange to her. She brought her artist's and student's eyes to look at them with ; she was determined not to be dazzled or taken in by them. At the same time, as she glanced every now and then round the splendid room in which they sat, with its Tudor ceiling, its fine pictures, its combination of every luxury with every refinement, she was distinctly conscious of a certain thrill, a romantic drawing towards the stateliness and power which it all implied, together with a proud and careless sense of equality, of kinship so to speak, which she made light of, but would not in reality have been without for the world.

In birth and blood she had nothing to yield to the Raeburns—so her mother assured her. If things were to be vulgarly measured, this fact too must come in. But they should not be vulgarly measured. She did not believe in class or wealth—not at all. Only—as her mother had told her—she must hold her head up. An inward temper, which no doubt led to that excess of manner of which Miss Raeburn was meanwhile conscious.

Where were the gentlemen? Marcella was beginning to resent and tire of the innumerable questions as to her likes and dislikes, her accomplishments, her friends, her opinions of Mellor and the neighbourhood, which this knitting lady beside her poured out upon her so briskly, when to her great relief the door opened and a footman announced 'Lady Winterbourne.'

A very tall thin lady in black entered the room at the words. 'My dear !' she said to Miss Raeburn, 'I am very late, but the roads are abominable, and those horses Edward has just given me have to be taken such tiresome care of. I told the coachman next time he might wrap them in shawls and put them to bed, and *I* should walk.'

'You are quite capable of it, my dear,' said Miss Raeburn, kissing her. 'We know you! Miss Boyce—Lady Winterbourne.'

Lady Winterbourne shook hands with a shy awkwardness which belied her height and stateliness. As she sat down beside Miss Raeburn the contrast between her and Lord Maxwell's sister was sufficiently striking. Miss Raeburn was short, inclined to be stout, and to a certain gay profusion in her attire. Her cap was made of a bright silk handkerchief edged with lace; round her neck were hung a number of small trinkets on various gold chains; she abounded too in bracelets, most of which were clearly old-fashioned mementoes of departed relatives or friends. Her dress was a cheerful red verging on crimson; and her general air suggested energy, bustle, and a good-humoured common sense.

Lady Winterbourne, on the other hand, was not only dressed from head to foot in severe black without an ornament; her head and face belonged also to the same impression, as of some strong and forcible study in black and white. The attitude was rigidly erect; the very dark eyes, under the snowy and abundant hair, had a trick of absent staring; in certain aspects the whole figure had a tragic, nay, formidable dignity, from which one expected, and sometimes got, the tone and gesture of tragic acting. Yet at the same time, mixed in therewith, a curious strain of womanish, nay childish, weakness, appealingness. Altogether, a great lady, and a personality—yet something else too—something ill-assured, timid, incongruous—hard to be defined.

'I believe you have not been at Mellor long?' the new-comer asked, in a deep contralto voice which she dragged a little.

'About seven weeks. My father and mother have been there since May.'

'You must of course think it a very interesting old place?'

'Of course I do; I love it,' said Marcella, disconcerted by the odd habit Lady Winterbourne had of fixing her eyes upon a person, and then, as it were, forgetting what she had done with them.

'Oh, I haven't been there, Agneta,' said the new-comer, turning after a pause to Miss Raeburn, 'since that summer—you remember?—that party when the Palmerstons came over—so long ago—twenty years!'

Marcella sat stiffly upright. Lady Winterbourne grew a little nervous and flurried.

'I don't think I ever saw your mother, Miss Boyce—I was much away from home about then.   Oh, yes, I did once——'

The speaker stopped, a sudden red suffusing her pale cheeks. She had felt certain somehow, at sight of Marcella, that she should say or do something untoward, and she had promptly justified her own prevision.   The only time she had ever seen Mrs. Boyce had been in court, on the last day of the famous trial in which Richard Boyce was concerned, when she had made out the wife sitting closely veiled as near to her husband as possible, waiting for the verdict.   As she had already confided this reminiscence to Miss Raeburn, and had forgotten she had done so, both ladies had a moment of embarrassment.

'Mrs. Boyce, I am sorry to say, does not seem to be strong,' said Miss Raeburn, bending over the heel of her stocking.   ' I wish we could have had the pleasure of seeing her to-day.'

There was a pause.   Lady Winterbourne's tragic eyes were once more considering Marcella.

'I hope you will come and see me,' she said at last abruptly— 'and Mrs. Boyce too.'

The voice was very soft and refined though so deep, and Marcella looking up was suddenly magnetised.

'Yes, I will,' she said, all her face melting into sensitive life. ' Mamma won't go anywhere, but I will come, if you will ask me.'

'Will you come next Tuesday?' said Lady Winterbourne quickly—'come to tea, and I will drive you back.   Mr. Raeburn told me about you.   He says—you read a great deal.'

The solemnity of the last words, the fixedness of the tragic look, were not to be resisted.   Marcella laughed out, and both ladies simultaneously thought her extraordinarily radiant and handsome.

'How can he know?   Why, I have hardly talked about books to him at all.'

'Well ! here he comes,' said Lady Winterbourne, smiling suddenly ; ' so I can ask him.   But I am sure he did say so.'

It was now Marcella's turn to colour.   Aldous Raeburn crossed the room, greeted Lady Winterbourne, and next moment she felt her hand in his.

'You did tell me, Aldous, didn't you?' said Lady Winterbourne, ' that Miss Boyce was a great reader?'

The speaker had known Aldous Raeburn as a boy, and was, moreover, a sort of cousin, which explained the Christian name.

Aldous smiled.

'I said I thought Miss Boyce was like you and me, and had a weakness that way, Lady Winterbourne.   But I won't be cross-examined !'

'I don't think I am a great reader,' said Marcella bluntly—'at least I read a great deal, but I hardly ever read a book through. I haven't patience.'

'You want to get at everything so quickly?' said Miss Raeburn, looking up sharply.

'I suppose so!' said Marcella. 'There seems to be always a hundred things tearing one different ways, and no time for any of them.'

'Yes, when one is young one feels like that,' said Lady Winterbourne, sighing. 'When one is old one accepts one's limitations. When I was twenty I never thought that I should be still an ignorant and discontented woman at nearly seventy.'

'It is because you are so young still, Lady Winterbourne, that you feel so,' said Aldous, laughing at her, as one does at an old friend. 'Why, you are younger than any of us! I feel all brushed and stirred up—a boy at school again—after I have been to see you!'

'Well, I don't know what you mean, I'm sure,' said Lady Winterbourne, sighing again. Then she looked at the pair beside her—at the alert brightness in the man's strong and quiet face as he sat stooping forward, with his hands upon his knees, hardly able to keep his eyes for an instant from the dark apparition beside him—at the girl's evident shyness and pride.

'My dear!' she said, turning suddenly to Miss Raeburn, 'have you heard what a monstrosity Alice has produced this last time in the way of a baby? It was born with four teeth!'

Miss Raeburn's astonishment fitted the provocation, and the two old friends fell into a gossip on the subject of Lady Winterbourne's numerous family, which was clearly meant for a *tête-à-tête*.

'Will you come and look at our tapestry?' said Aldous to his neighbour, after a few nothings had passed between them. 'I think you would admire it, and I am afraid my grandfather will be a few minutes yet. He hoped to get home earlier than this, but his Board meeting was very long and important, and has kept him an unconscionable time.'

Marcella rose, and they moved together towards the south end of the room where a famous piece of Italian Renaissance tapestry entirely filled the wall from side to side.

'How beautiful!' cried the girl, her eyes filling with delight. 'What a delicious thing to live with.'

And, indeed, it was the most adorable medley of forms, tints, suggestions, of gods and goddesses, nymphs and shepherds, standing in flowery grass under fruit-laden trees and wreathed about with roses. Both colour and subject were of fairyland. The golds and browns and pinks of it, the greens and ivory whites had been mellowed and pearled and warmed by age into a most glowing, delicate, and fanciful beauty.   It was Italy at the great moment—subtle, rich, exuberant.

Aldous enjoyed her pleasure.

'I thought you would like it ; I hoped you would.   It has been my special delight since I was a child, when my mother first routed it out of a garret.   I am not sure that I don't in my heart prefer it to any of the pictures.'

'The flowers !' said Marcella, absorbed in it—'look at them—the irises, the cyclamens, the lilies !   It reminds one of the dreams one used to have when one was small of what it would be like to have *flowers enough*. I was at school, you know, in a part of England where one seemed always cheated out of them !   We walked two and two along the straight roads, and I found one here and one there—but such a beggarly, wretched few, for all one's trouble.   I used to hate the hard dry soil, and console myself by imagining countries where the flowers grew like this—yes, just like this, in a gold and pink and blue mass, so that one might thrust one's hands in and gather and gather till one was really *satisfied* ! That is the worst of being at school when you are poor ! You never get enough of anything.   One day it's flowers—but the next day it is pudding—and the next frocks.'

Her eye was sparkling, her tongue loosened.   Not only was it pleasant to feel herself beside him, enwrapped in such an atmosphere of admiration and deference, but the artistic sensitive chord in her had been struck, and vibrated happily.

'Well, only wait till May, and the cowslips in your own fields will make up to you !' he said, smiling at her.   'But now, I have been wondering to myself in my room upstairs what you would like to see.   There are a good many treasures in this house, and you will care for them, because you are an artist.   But you shall not be bored with them !   You shall see what and as much as you like.   You had about a quarter of an hour's talk with my aunt, did you not?' he asked, in a quite different tone.

So all the time while she and Miss Raeburn had been making acquaintance, he had known that she was in the house, and he had kept away for his own purposes !   Marcella felt a colour she could not restrain leap into her cheek.

'Miss Raeburn was very kind,' she said, with a return of shyness, which passed however the next moment, by reaction, into her usual daring.   'Yes, she was very kind !—but all the same she doesn't like me—I don't think she is going to like me—I am not her sort.'

'Have you been talking Socialism to her?' he asked her smiling.

'No, not yet—not yet,' she said emphatically. 'But I am dreadfully uncertain—I can't always hold my tongue—I am afraid you will be sorry you took me up.'

'Are you so aggressive? But Aunt Neta is so mild!—she wouldn't hurt a fly. She mothers every one in the house and out of it. The only people she is hard upon are the little servant girls, who will wear feathers in their hats!'

'There!' cried Marcella, indignantly. 'Why shouldn't they wear feathers in their hats? It is their form of beauty—their tapestry!'

'But if one can't have both feathers and boots?' he asked her humbly, a twinkle in his grey eye. 'If one hasn't boots, one may catch a cold and die of it—which is, after all, worse than going featherless.'

'But why *can't* they have feathers and boots? It is because you—we—have got too much. You have the tapestry—and—and the pictures'—she turned and looked round the room—'and this wonderful house—and the park. Oh, no—I think it is Miss Raeburn has too many feathers!'

'Perhaps it is,' he admitted, in a different tone, his look changing and saddening as though some habitual struggle of thought were recalled to him. 'You see I am in a difficulty. I want to show you our feathers. I think they would please you—and you make me ashamed of them.'

'How absurd!' cried Marcella, 'when I told you how I liked the school children bobbing to me!'

They laughed, and then Aldous looked round with a start—'Ah, here is my grandfather!'

Then he stood back, watching the look with which Lord Maxwell, after greeting Lady Winterbourne, approached Miss Boyce. He saw the old man's somewhat formal approach, the sudden kindle in the blue eyes which marked the first effect of Marcella's form and presence, the bow, the stately shake of the hand. The lover hearing his own heart beat, realised that his beautiful lady had so far done well.

'You must let me say that I see a decided likeness in you to your grandfather,' said Lord Maxwell, when they were all seated at lunch, Marcella on his left hand, opposite to Lady Winterbourne. 'He was one of my dearest friends.'

'I'm afraid I don't know much about him,' said Marcella, rather bluntly, 'except what I have got out of old letters. I never saw him that I remember.'

Lord Maxwell left the subject, of course, at once, but showed a great wish to talk to her, and make her talk. He had pleasant things to say about Mellor and its past, which could be said without offence ; and some conversation about the Boyce monuments in Mellor church led to a discussion of the part played by the different local families in the Civil Wars, in which it seemed to Aldous that his grandfather tried in various shrewd and courteous ways to make Marcella feel at ease with herself and her race, accepted, as it were, of right into the local brotherhood, and so to soothe and heal those bruised feelings he could not but divine.

The girl carried herself a little loftily, answering with an independence and freedom beyond her age and born of her London life. She was not in the least abashed or shy. Yet it was clear that Lord Maxwell's first impressions were favourable. Aldous caught every now and then his quick, judging look sweeping over her and instantly withdrawn—comparing, as the grandson very well knew, every point, and tone, and gesture with some inner ideal of what a Raeburn's wife should be. How dreamlike the whole scene was to Aldous, yet how exquisitely real ! The room, with its carved and gilt cedar-wood panels, its Vandykes, its tall windows opening on the park, the autumn sun flooding the gold and purple fruit on the table, and sparkling on the glass and silver, the figures of his aunt and Lady Winterbourne, the moving servants, and dominant of it all, interpreting it all for him anew, the dark, lithe creature beside his grandfather, so quick, sensitive, extravagant, so much a woman, yet, to his lover's sense, so utterly unlike any other woman he had ever seen—every detail of it was charged to him with a thousand new meanings, now oppressive, now delightful.

For he was passing out of the first stage of passion, in which it is, almost, its own satisfaction, so new and enriching is it to the whole nature, into the second stage—the stage of anxiety, incredulity. Marcella, sitting there on his own ground, after all his planning, seemed to him not nearer, but further from him. She was terribly on her dignity ! Where was all that girlish abandonment gone which she had shown him on that walk, beside the gate ? There had been a touch of it, a divine touch, before luncheon. How could he get her to himself again ?

Meanwhile the conversation passed to the prevailing local topic —the badness of the harvest, the low prices of everything, the consequent depression among the farmers, and stagnation in the villages.

' I don't know what is to be done for the people this winter,' said Lord Maxwell, ' without pauperising them, I mean. To give money is easy enough. Our grandfathers would have doled out coal and blankets, and thought no more of it. We don't get through so easily.'

'No,' said Lady Winterbourne, sighing. 'It weighs one down. Last winter was a nightmare. The tales one heard, and the faces one saw!—though we seemed to be always giving. And in the middle of it Edward would buy me a new set of sables. I begged him not, but he laughed at me.'

'Well, my dear,' said Miss Raeburn cheerfully, 'if nobody bought sables, there'd be other poor people up in Russia, isn't it?—or Hudson's Bay?—badly off. One has to think of that. Oh, you needn't talk, Aldous! I know you say it's a fallacy. *I* call it common sense.'

She got, however, only a slight smile from Aldous, who had long ago left his great-aunt to work out her own economics. And, anyway, she saw that he was wholly absorbed from his seat beside Lady Winterbourne in watching Miss Boyce.

'It's precisely as Lord Maxwell says,' replied Lady Winterbourne: 'that kind of thing used to satisfy everybody. And our grandmothers were very good women. I don't know why we, who give ourselves so much more trouble than they did, should carry these thorns about with us, while they went free.'

She drew herself up, a cloud over her fine eyes. Miss Raeburn, looking round, was glad to see the servants had left the room.

'Miss Boyce thinks we are all in a very bad way, I'm sure. I have heard tales of Miss Boyce's opinions!' said Lord Maxwell, smiling at her, with an old man's indulgence, as though provoking her to talk.

Her slim fingers were nervously crumbling some bread beside her; her head was drooped a little. At his challenge she looked up with a start. She was perfectly conscious of him, as both the great magnate on his native heath, and as the trained man of affairs condescending to a girl's fancies. But she had made up her mind not to be afraid.

'What tales have you heard?' she asked him.

'You alarm us, you know,' he said gallantly, waiving her question. 'We can't afford a prophetess to the other side, just now.'

Miss Raeburn drew herself up, with a sharp dry look at Miss Boyce, which escaped everyone but Lady Winterbourne.

'Oh! I am not a Radical!' said Marcella, half scornfully. 'We Socialists don't fight for either political party as such. We take what we can get out of both.'

'So you call yourself a Socialist? A real full-blown one?'

Lord Maxwell's pleasant tone masked the mood of a man who after a morning of hard work thinks himself entitled to some amusement at luncheon.

'Yes, I am a Socialist,' she said slowly, looking at him. 'At least I ought to be—I am in my conscience.'

'But not in your judgment?' he said, laughing. 'Isn't that the condition of most of us?'

'No, not at all!' she exclaimed, both her vanity and her enthusiasm roused by his manner. 'Both my judgment and my conscience make me a Socialist. It's only one's wretched love for one's own little luxuries and precedences—the worst part of one—that makes me waver, makes me a traitor! The people I worked with in London would think me a traitor often, I know.'

'And you really think that the world ought to be "hatched over again and hatched different"? That it ought to be, if it could be?'

'I think that things are intolerable as they are,' she broke out, after a pause. 'The London poor were bad enough; the country poor seem to me worse! How can any one believe that such serfdom and poverty—such mutilation of mind and body—were meant to go on for ever!'

Lord Maxwell's brows lifted. But it certainly was no wonder that Aldous should find those eyes of hers superb?

'Can you really imagine, my dear young lady,' he asked her mildly, 'that if all property were divided to-morrow the force of natural inequality would not have undone all the work the day after, and given us back our poor?'

The 'newspaper cant' of this remark, as the Cravens would have put it, brought a contemptuous look for an instant into the girl's face. She began to talk eagerly and cleverly, showing a very fair training in the catchwords of the school, and a good memory —as one uncomfortable person at the table soon perceived—for some of the leading arguments and illustrations of a book of Venturist Essays which had lately been much read and talked of in London.

Then, irritated more and more by Lord Maxwell's gentle attention, and the interjections he threw in from time to time, she plunged into history, attacked the landowning class, spoke of the Statute of Labourers, the Law of Settlement, the New Poor Law, and other great matters, all in the same quick flow of glancing, picturesque speech, and all with the same utter oblivion—so it seemed to her stiff indignant hostess at the other end of the table —of the manners and modesty proper to a young girl in a strange house, and that young girl Richard Boyce's daughter!

Aldous struck in now and then, trying to soothe her by supporting her to a certain extent, and so divert the conversation. But Marcella was soon too excited to be managed; and she had her say; a very strong say often as far as language went : there could be no doubt of that.

'Ah, well,' said Lord Maxwell, wincing at last under some of her phrases, in spite of his courteous *savoir-faire*, 'I see you are of the same opinion as a good man whose book I took up yesterday : " The landlords of England have always shown a mean and malignant passion for profiting by the miseries of others ! " Well, Aldous, my boy, we are judged, you and I—no help for it !'

The man whose temper and rule had made the prosperity of a whole countryside for nearly forty years, looked at his grandson with twinkling eyes. Miss Raeburn was speechless. Lady Winterbourne was absently staring at Marcella, a spot of red on each pale cheek.

Then Marcella suddenly wavered, looked across at Aldous, and broke down.

'Of course, you think me very ridiculous,' she said, with a tremulous change of tone. 'I suppose I am. And I am as inconsistent as anybody—I hate myself for it. Very often when anybody talks to me on the other side, I am almost as much persuaded as I am by the Socialists ; they always told me in London I was the prey of the last speaker. But it can't make any difference to one's *feeling* : nothing touches that.'

She turned to Lord Maxwell, half appealing—

'It is when I go down from our house to the village ; when I see the places the people live in ; when one is comfortable in the carriage, and one passes some woman in the rain, ragged and dirty and tired, trudging back from her work ; when one realises that they have no *rights* when they come to be old, nothing to look to but charity, for which *we*—we who have everything—expect them to be grateful ; and when I know that every one of them has done more useful work in a year of their life than I shall ever do in the whole of mine, then I feel that the whole state of things is *somehow* wrong and topsy-turvy and *wicked*.' Her voice rose a little, every emphasis grew more passionate. 'And if I don't do something —the little such a person as I can—to alter it before I die, I might as well never have lived.'

Everybody at table started. Lord Maxwell looked at Miss Raeburn, his mouth twitching over the humour of his sister's dismay. Well ! this was a forcible young woman : was Aldous the kind of man to be able to deal conveniently with such eyes, such emotions, such a personality ?

Suddenly Lady Winterbourne's deep voice broke in :

'I never could say it half so well as that, Miss Boyce ; but I agree with you. I may say that I have agreed with you all my life.'

The girl turned to her, grateful and quivering.

'At the same time,' said Lady Winterbourne, relapsing with a long breath from tragic emphasis into a fluttering indecision equally characteristic, 'as you say, one is inconsistent. I was poor once, before Edward came to the title, and I did not at all like it—not at all. And I don't wish my daughters to marry poor men; and what I should do without a maid or a carriage when I wanted it, I cannot imagine. Edward makes the most of these things. He tells me I have to choose between things as they are, and a graduated income tax which would leave nobody—not even the richest —more than four hundred a year.'

'Just enough for one of those little houses on your station road,' said Lord Maxwell, laughing at her. 'I think you might still have a maid.'

'There, you laugh,' said Lady Winterbourne vehemently : 'the men do. But I tell you it is no laughing matter to feel that your *heart* and *conscience* have gone over to the enemy. You want to feel with your class, and you can't. Think of what used to happen in old days. My grandmother, who was as good and kind a woman as ever lived, was driving home through our village one evening, and a man passed her, a labourer who was a little drunk, and who did not take off his hat to her. She stopped, made her men get down and had him put in the stocks there and then—the old stocks were still standing on the village green. Then she drove home to her dinner, and said her prayers no doubt that night with more consciousness than usual of having done her duty. But if the power of the stocks still remained to us, my dear friend'—and she laid her thin old woman's hand, flashing with diamonds, on Lord Maxwell's arm—'we could no longer do it, you or I. We have lost the sense of *right* in our place and position—at least I find I have. In the old days if there was social disturbance the upper class could put it down with a strong hand.'

'So they would still,' said Lord Maxwell drily, 'if there were violence. Once let it come to any real attack on property, and you will see where all these Socialist theories will be. And of course it will not be *we*—not the landowners or the capitalists— who will put it down. It will be the hundreds and thousands of people with something to lose—a few pounds in a joint-stock mill, a house of their own built through a co-operative store, an acre or two of land stocked by their own savings—it is they, I am afraid, who will put Miss Boyce's friends down so far as they represent any real attack on property—and brutally, too, I fear, if need be.'

'I dare say,' exclaimed Marcella, her colour rising again. 'I never can see how we Socialists are to succeed. But how can any

one *rejoice* in it ?   How can any one *wish* that the present state of
things should go on ?   Oh ! the horrors one sees in London.   And
down here, the cottages, and the starvation wages, and the ridiculous worship of game, and then, of course, the poaching——'

Miss Raeburn pushed back her chair with a sharp noise.   But
her brother was still peeling his pear, and no one else moved.   Why
did he let such talk go on ?   It was too unseemly.

Lord Maxwell only laughed.   ' My dear young lady,' he said,
much amused, ' are you even in the frame of mind to make a hero
of a poacher?   Disillusion lies that way !—it does indeed.   Why—
Aldous !—I have been hearing such tales from Westall this morning.   I stopped at Corbett's farm a minute or two on the way
home, and met Westall at the gate coming out.   He says he and
his men are being harried to death round about Tudley End by a
gang of men that come, he thinks, from Oxford, a driving gang
with a gig, who come at night or in the early morning—the smartest
rascals out, impossible to catch.   But he says he thinks he will
soon have his hand on the local accomplice—a Mellor man—a
man named Hurd : not one of our labourers, I think.'

' Hurd !' cried Marcella in dismay.   ' Oh no, it *can't* be —
impossible !'

Lord Maxwell looked at her in astonishment.

' Do you know any Hurds ?   I am afraid your father will find
that Mellor is a bad place for poaching.'

' If it is, it is because they are so starved and miserable,' said
Marcella, trying hard to speak coolly, but excited almost beyond
bounds by the conversation and all that it implied.   ' And the Hurds
—I don't believe it a bit !   But if it were true—oh ! they have
been in such straits—they were out of work most of last winter ;
they are out of work now.   No one *could* grudge them.   I told you
about them, didn't I ?' she said, suddenly glancing at Aldous.   ' I
was going to ask you to-day, if you could help them?'   Her prophetess air had altogether left her.   She felt ready to cry ; and
nothing could have been more womanish than her tone.

He bent across to her.   Miss Raeburn, invaded by a new and
intolerable sense of calamity, could have beaten him for what she
read in his shining eyes, and in the flush on his usually pale
cheek.

' Is he still out of work?' he said.   ' And you are unhappy about
it ?   But I am sure we can find him work : I am just now planning
improvements at the north end of the park.   We can take him on ;
I am certain of it.   You must give me his full name and address.'

' And let him beware of Westall,' said Lord Maxwell, kindly.
' Give him a hint, Miss Boyce, and nobody will rake up bygones.

There is nothing I dislike so much as rows about the shooting.   All the keepers know that.'

'And of course,' said Miss Raeburn, coldly, 'if the family are in real distress there are plenty of people at hand to assist them. The man need not steal.'

'Oh, charity !' cried Marcella, her lip curling.

'A worse crime than poaching, you think,' said Lord Maxwell, laughing. 'Well, these are big subjects. I confess, after my morning with the lunatics, I am half inclined, like Horace Walpole, to think everything serious ridiculous. At any rate shall we see what light a cup of coffee throws upon it. Agneta, shall we adjourn ?'

CHAPTER XI

LORD MAXWELL closed the drawing-room door behind Aldous and Marcella. Aldous had proposed to take their guest to see the picture gallery, which was on the first floor, and had found her willing.

The old man came back to the two other women, running his hand nervously through his shock of white hair—a gesture which Miss Raeburn well knew to show some disturbance of mind.

'I should like to have your opinion of that young lady,' he said deliberately, taking a chair immediately in front of them.

'I like her,' said Lady Winterbourne instantly. 'Of course she is crude and extravagant, and does not know quite what she may say. But all that will improve. I like her, and shall make friends with her.'

Miss Raeburn threw up her hands in angry amazement.

'Most forward, conceited, and ill-mannered,' she said with energy. 'I am certain she has no proper principles, and as to what her religious views may be, I dread to think of them ! If *that* is a specimen of the girls of the present day——'

'My dear,' interrupted Lord Maxwell, laying a hand on her knee, 'Lady Winterbourne is an old friend, a very old friend. I think we may be frank before her, and I don't wish you to say things you may regret. Aldous has made up his mind to get that girl to marry him, if he can.'

Lady Winterbourne was silent, having in fact been forewarned by that odd little interview with Aldous in her own drawing-room, when he had suddenly asked her to call on Mrs. Boyce. But she looked at Miss Raeburn. That lady took up her knitting, laid it down again, resumed it, then broke out—

'How did it come about? Where have they been meeting?'

'At the Hardens mostly. He seems to have been struck from the beginning, and now there is no question as to his determination. But she may not have him ; he professes to be still entirely in the dark.'

'Oh !' cried Miss Raeburn, with a scornful shrug, meant to express all possible incredulity. Then she began to knit fast and furiously, and presently said in great agitation,—

'What can he be thinking of? She is very handsome, of course, but——' then her words failed her. 'When Aldous remembers his mother, how can he?—undisciplined ! self-willed ! Why, she laid down the law to *you*, Henry, as though you had nothing to do but to take your opinions from a chit of a girl like her. Oh ! no, no ; I really can't ; you must give me time. And her father—the disgrace and trouble of it ! I tell you, Henry, it will bring misfortune !'

Lord Maxwell was much troubled. Certainly he should have talked to Agneta beforehand. But the fact was he had his cowardice, like other men, and he had been trusting to the girl herself, to this beauty he had heard so much of, to soften the first shock of the matter to the present mistress of the Court.

'We will hope not, Agneta,' he said, gravely. 'We will hope not. But you must remember Aldous is no boy. I cannot coerce him. I see the difficulties, and I have put them before him. But I am more favourably struck with the girl than you are. And any way, if it comes about, we must make the best of it.'

Miss Raeburn made no answer, but pretended to set her heel, her needles shaking. Lady Winterbourne was very sorry for her two old friends.

'Wait a little,' she said, laying her hand lightly on Miss Raeburn's. 'No doubt with her opinions she felt specially drawn to assert herself to-day. One can imagine it very well of a girl, and a generous girl in her position. You will see other sides of her, I am sure you will. And you would never—you could never—make a breach with Aldous.'

'We must all remember,' said Lord Maxwell, getting up and beginning to walk up and down beside them, 'that Aldous is in no way dependent upon me. He has his own resources. He could leave us to-morrow. Dependent on me ! It is the other way, I think, Agneta—don't you?'

He stopped and looked at her, and she returned his look in spite of herself. A tear dropped on her stocking which she hastily brushed away.

'Come, now,' said Lord Maxwell, seating himself ; 'let us talk it over rationally. Don't go, Lady Winterbourne.'

'Why, they may be settling it at this moment,' cried Miss Raeburn, half-choked, and feeling as though 'the skies were impious not to fall.'

'No, no!' he said smiling. 'Not yet, I think. But let us prepare ourselves.'

Meanwhile the cause of all this agitation was sitting languidly in a great Louis-Quinze chair in the picture gallery upstairs, with Aldous beside her. She had taken off her big hat as though it oppressed her, and her black head lay against a corner of the chair in fine contrast to its mellowed golds and crimsons. Opposite to her were two famous Holbein portraits, at which she looked from time to time as though attracted to them in spite of herself, by some trained sense which could not be silenced. But she was not communicative, and Aldous was anxious.

'Do you think I was rude to your grandfather?' she asked him at last abruptly, cutting dead short some information she had stiffly asked him for just before, as to the date of the gallery and its collection.

'Rude!' he said, startled. 'Not at all. Not in the least. Do you suppose we are made of such brittle stuff, we poor landowners, that we can't stand an argument now and then?'

'Your aunt thought I was rude,' she said unheeding. 'I think I was. But a house like this excites me.' And with a little reckless gesture she turned her head over her shoulder and looked down the gallery. A Velasquez was beside her; a great Titian over the way; a priceless Rembrandt beside it. On her right hand stood a chair of carved steel, presented by a German town to a German emperor, which had not its equal in Europe; the brocade draping the deep windows in front of her had been specially made to grace a state visit to the house of Charles II.

'At Mellor,' she went on, 'we are old and tumbledown. The rain comes in; there are no shutters to the big hall, and we can't afford to put them—we can't afford even to have the pictures cleaned. I can pity the house and nurse it, as I do the village. But here——'

And looking about her, she gave a significant shrug.

'What—our feathers again!' he said, laughing. 'But consider. Even you allow that Socialism cannot begin to-morrow. There must be a transition time, and clearly till the State is ready to take over the historical houses and their contents, the present nominal owners of them are bound, if they can, to take care of them. Otherwise the State will be some day defrauded.'

She could not be insensible to the charm of his manner towards her. There was in it, no doubt, the natural force and weight of the man older and better informed than his companion, and amused every now and then by her extravagance. But even her irritable pride could not take offence. For the intellectual dissent she felt at bottom was tempered by a moral sympathy of which the gentleness and warmth touched and moved her in spite of herself. And now that they were alone he could express himself. So long as they had been in company he had seemed to her, as often before, shy, hesitating, and ineffective. But with the disappearance of spectators, who represented to him, no doubt, the harassing claim of the critical judgment, all was freer, more assured, more natural.

She leant her chin on her hand, considering his plea.

'Supposing you live long enough to see the State take it, shall you be able to reconcile yourself to it? Or shall you feel it a wrong, and go out a rebel?'

A delightful smile was beginning to dance in the dark eyes. She was recovering the tension of her talk with Lord Maxwell.

'All must depend, you see, on the conditions—on how you and your friends are going to manage the transition. You may persuade me—conceivably—or you may eject me with violence.'

'Oh, no!' she interposed, quickly. 'There will be no violence. Only we shall gradually reduce your wages. Of course, we can't do without leaders—we don't want to do away with the captains of any industry, agricultural or manufacturing. Only we think you overpaid. You must be content with less.'

'Don't linger out the process,' he said, laughing, 'otherwise it will be painful. The people who are condemned to live in these houses before the Commune takes to them, while your graduated land and income taxes are slowly starving them out, will have a bad time of it.'

'Well, it will be your first bad time! Think of the labourer now, with five children, of school age, on twelve shillings a week—think of the sweated women in London.'

'Ah, think of them,' he said in a different tone.

There was a pause of silence.

'No!' said Marcella, springing up. 'Don't let's think of them. I get to believe the whole thing a *pose* in myself and other people. Let's go back to the pictures. Do you think Titian "sweated" his drapery men—paid them starvation rates, and grew rich on their labour? Very likely. All the same, that blue woman'—she pointed to a bending Magdalen—'will be a joy to all time.'

They wandered through the gallery, and she was now all curiosity, pleasure, and intelligent interest, as though she had thrown off an oppression. Then they emerged into the upper corridor answering to the corridor of the antiques below. This also was hung with pictures, principally family portraits of the second order, dating back to the Tudors—a fine series of berobed and bejewelled personages, wherein clothes predominated and character was unimportant.

Marcella's eye was glancing along the brilliant colour of the wall, taking rapid note of jewelled necks surmounting stiff embroidered dresses, of the whiteness of lace ruffs, or the love-locks and gleaming satin of the Caroline beauties, when it suddenly occurred to her,—

'I shall be their successor. This is already potentially mine. In a few months, if I please, I shall be walking this house as mistress—its future mistress, at any rate !'

She was conscious of a quickening in the blood, a momentary blurring of the vision. A whirlwind of fancies swept across her. She thought of herself as the young peeress—Lord Maxwell after all was over seventy—her own white neck blazing with diamonds, the historic jewels of a great family—her will making law in this splendid house—in the great domain surrounding it. What power !—what a position !—what a romance ! She, the out-at-elbows Marcella, the Socialist, the friend of the people ! What new lines of social action and endeavour she might strike out ! Miss Raeburn should not stop her. She caressed the thought of the scandals in store for that lady. Only it annoyed her that her dream of large things should be constantly crossed by this foolish delight, making her feet dance—in this mere prospect of satin gowns and fine jewels—of young and fêted beauty holding its brilliant court. If she made such a marriage, it should be, it must be, on public grounds. Her friends must have no right to blame her.

Then she stole a glance at the tall, quiet gentleman beside her. A man to be proud of from the beginning, and surely to be very fond of in time. ' He would always be my friend,' she thought. ' I could lead him. He is very clever, one can see, and knows a great deal. But he admires what I like. His position hampers him—but I could help him to get beyond it. We might show the way to many !'

'Will you come and see this room here ?' he said, stopping suddenly, yet with a certain hesitation in the voice. 'It is my own sitting-room. There are one or two portraits I should like to show you if you would let me.'

She followed him with a rosy cheek, and they were presently standing in front of the portrait of his mother. He spoke of his recollections of his parents, quietly and simply, yet she felt through every nerve that he was not the man to speak of such things to anybody in whom he did not feel a very strong and peculiar interest. As he was talking a rush of liking towards him came across her. How good he was—how affectionate beneath his reserve—a woman might securely trust him with her future.

So with every minute she grew softer, her eye gentler, and with each step and word he seemed to himself to be carried deeper into the current of joy. Intoxication was mounting within him, as her slim, warm youth moved and breathed beside him ; and it was natural that he should read her changing behaviour for something other than it was. A man of his type asks for no advance from the woman ; the woman he loves does not make them ; but at the same time he has a natural self-esteem, and believes readily in his power to win the return he is certain he will deserve.

'And this?' she said, moving restlessly towards his table, and taking up the photograph of Edward Hallin.

'Ah ! that is the greatest friend I have in the world. But I am sure you know the name. Mr. Hallin—Edward Hallin.'

She paused bewildered.

'What ! *the* Mr. Hallin—*that* was Edward Hallin—who settled the Nottingham strike last month—who lectures so much in the East-End, and in the North?'

'The same. We are old college friends. I owe him much, and in all his excitements he does not forget old friends. There, you see—' and he opened a blotting book and pointed smiling to some closely written sheets lying within it—'is my last letter to him. I often write two of those in the week, and he to me. We don't agree on a number of things, but that doesn't matter.'

'What can you find to write about?' she said, wondering. 'I thought nobody wrote letters nowadays, only notes. Is it books, or people?'

'Both, when it pleases us !' How soon, oh ! ye favouring gods, might he reveal to her the part she herself played in those closely-covered sheets? 'But he writes to me on social matters chiefly. His whole heart, as you probably know, is in certain experiments and reforms in which he sometimes asks me to help him.'

Marcella opened her eyes. These were new lights. She began to recall all that she had heard of young Hallin's position in the Labour movement ; his personal magnetism and prestige ; his power as a speaker. Her Socialist friends, she remembered, thought him in the way—a force, but a dangerous one. He was for the follies of compromise—could not be got to disavow the principle of private property, while ready to go great lengths in

certain directions towards collective action and corporate control.
The 'stalwarts' of *her* sect would have none of him as a leader,
while admitting his charm as a human being—a charm she
remembered to have heard discussed with some anxiety among her
Venturist friends. But for ordinary people he went far enough.
Her father, she remembered, had dubbed him an 'Anarchist' in
connection with the terms he had been able to secure for the
Nottingham strikers, as reported in the newspapers. It astonished
her to come across the man again as Mr. Raeburn's friend.

They talked about Hallin a little, and about Aldous's Cambridge
acquaintance with him. Then Marcella, still nervous, went to look
at the bookshelves and found herself in front of that working
collection of books on economics which Aldous kept in his own
room under his hand, by way of guide to the very fine special
collection he was gradually making in the library down stairs.

Here again were surprises for her. Aldous had never made
the smallest claim to special knowledge on all those subjects she
had so often insisted on making him discuss. He had been
always tentative and diffident, deferential even so far as her own
opinions were concerned. And here already was the library of
a student. All the books she had ever read or heard discussed
were here—and as few among many. The condition of them,
moreover, the signs of close and careful reading she noticed in
them, as she took them out, abashed her : *she* had never learnt
to read in this way. It was her first contact with an exact
and arduous culture. She thought of how she had instructed
Lord Maxwell at luncheon. No doubt he shared his grandson's
interests. Her cheek burned anew ; this time because it seemed
to her that she had been ridiculous.

'I don't know why you never told me you took a particular interest in these subjects,' she said suddenly, turning round upon him
resentfully—she had just laid down, of all things, a volume of
Venturist essays. 'You must have thought I talked a great deal
of nonsense at luncheon.'

'Why !—I have always been delighted to find you cared for
such things and took an interest in them. How few women do !'
he said quite simply, opening his eyes. 'Do you know these
three pamphlets? They were privately printed, and are very
rare.'

He took out a book and showed it to her as one does to a
comrade and equal—as he might have done to Edward Hallin.
But something was jarred in her—conscience, or self-esteem—and
she could not recover her sense of heroineship. She answered
absently, and when he returned the book to the shelf she said that

it was time for her to go, and would he kindly ask for her maid, who was to walk with her?

'I will ring for her directly,' he said. 'But you will let me take you home?' Then he added hurriedly, 'I have some business this afternoon with a man who lives in your direction.'

She assented a little stiffly—but with an inward thrill. His words and manner seemed suddenly to make the situation unmistakable. Among the books it had been for the moment obscured.

He rang for his own servant, and gave directions about the maid. Then they went down stairs that Marcella might say goodbye.

Miss Raeburn bade her guest farewell, with a dignity which her small person could sometimes assume, not unbecomingly Lady Winterbourne held the girl's hand a little, looked her out of countenance, and insisted on her promising again to come to Winterbourne Park the following Tuesday. Then Lord Maxwell, with old-fashioned politeness, made Marcella take his arm through the hall.

'You must come and see us again,' he said, smiling; 'though we are such belated old Tories, we are not so bad as we sound.'

And under cover of his mild banter he fixed a penetrating attentive look upon her. Flushed and embarrassed! Had it indeed been done already? or would Aldous settle it on this walk? To judge from his manner and hers, the thing was going with rapidity. Well, well, there was nothing for it but to hope for the best.

On their way through the hall she stopped him, her hand still in his arm. Aldous was in front, at the door, looking for a light shawl she had brought with her.

'I should like to thank you,' she said shyly, 'about the Hurds. It will be very kind of you and Mr. Raeburn to find them work.'

Lord Maxwell was pleased; and with the usual unfair advantage of beauty her eyes and curving lips gave her little advance a charm infinitely beyond what any plainer woman could have commanded.

'Oh, don't thank me!' he said cheerily. 'Thank Aldous. He does all that kind of thing. And if in your good works you want any help we can give, ask it, my dear young lady. My old comrade's granddaughter will always find friends in this house.'

Lord Maxwell would have been very much astonished to hear himself making this speech six weeks before. As it was, he handed her over gallantly to Aldous, and stood on the steps looking after them in a stir of mind not unnoted by the confidential butler who held the door open behind him. Would Aldous insist on carrying his wife off to the dower house on the other side of the estate? or would they be content to stay in the old place with the old people? And if so, how were that girl and his sister to get on? As for himself, he was of a naturally optimist temper, and ever since the night of his first interview with Aldous on the subject, he had been more and more inclining to take a cheerful view. He liked to see a young creature of such evident character and cleverness holding opinions and lines of her own. It was infinitely better than mere nonentity. Of course, she was now extravagant and foolish, perhaps vain too. But that would mend with time— mend, above all, with her position as Aldous's wife. Aldous was a strong man—how strong, Lord Maxwell suspected that this impetuous young lady hardly knew. No, he thought the family might be trusted to cope with her when once they got her among them. And she would certainly be an ornament to the old house.

Her father of course was, and would be, the real difficulty, and the blight which had descended on the once honoured name. But a man so conscious of many kinds of power as Lord Maxwell could not feel much doubt as to his own and his grandson's competence to keep so poor a specimen of humanity as Richard Boyce in his place. How wretchedly ill, how feeble, both in body and soul, the fellow had looked when he and Winterbourne met him!

The white-haired owner of the Court walked back slowly to his library, his hands in his pockets, his head bent in cogitation. Impossible to settle to the various important political letters lying on his table, and bearing all of them on that approaching crisis in the spring which must put Lord Maxwell and his friends in power. He was over seventy, but his old blood quickened within him as he thought of those two on this golden afternoon, among the beech woods. How late Aldous had left all these experiences! His grandfather, by twenty, could have shown him the way.

Meanwhile the two in question were walking along the edge of the hill rampart overlooking the plain, with the road on one side of them, and the falling beech woods on the other. They were on a woodland path, just within the trees, sheltered, and to all intents and purposes alone. The maid, with leisurely discretion, was following far behind them on the high road.

Marcella, who felt at moments as though she could hardly breathe, by reason of a certain tumult of nerve, was yet apparently bent on maintaining a conversation without breaks. As they diverged from the road into the wood-path, she plunged into the subject of her companion's election prospects. How many meetings did he find that he must hold in the month? What places did he regard as his principal strongholds? She was told that certain villages, which she named, were certain to go Radical, whatever might be the Tory promises. As to a well-known Conservative League, which was very strong in the country, and to which all the great ladies, including Lady Winterbourne, belonged, was he actually going to demean himself by accepting its support? How was it possible to defend the bribery, buns, and beer by which it won its corrupting way?

Altogether, a quick fire of questions, remarks, and sallies, which Aldous met and parried as best he might, comforting himself all the time by thought of those deeper and lonelier parts of the wood which lay before them. At last she dropped out, half laughing, half defiant, words which arrested him,—

' Well, I shall know what the other side think of their prospects very soon. Mr. Wharton is coming to lunch with us to-morrow.'

' Harry Wharton!' he said, astonished. ' But Mr. Boyce is not supporting him. Your father, I think, is Conservative?'

One of Dick Boyce's first acts as owner of Mellor, when social rehabilitation had still looked probable to him, had been to send a contribution to the funds of the League aforesaid, so that Aldous had public and conspicuous grounds for his remark.

' Need one measure everything by politics?' she asked him a little disdainfully. ' Mayn't one even feed a Radical?'

He winced visibly a moment, touched in his philosopher's pride.

' You remind me,' he said, laughing and reddening—' and justly—that an election perverts all one's standards and besmirches all one's morals. Then I suppose Mr. Wharton is an old friend?'

' Papa never saw him before last week,' she said carelessly. ' Now he talks of asking him to stay some time, and says that, although he won't vote for him, he hopes that he will make a good fight.'

Raeburn's brow contracted in a puzzled frown.

' He will make an excellent fight,' he said rather shortly. ' Dodgson hardly hopes to get in. Harry Wharton is a most taking speaker, a very clever fellow, and sticks at nothing in the way of promises. Ah, you will find him interesting, Miss Boyce ! He has a co-operative farm on his Lincolnshire property. Last year he started a Labour paper—which I believe you read. I have heard you quote it. He believes in all that you hope for— great increase in local government and communal control—the land for the people—graduated income tax—the extinction of landlord and capitalist as soon as may be—*e tutti quanti*. He talks with great eloquence and ability. In our villages I find he is making way every week. The people think his manners perfect.

"Ee '*as* a way wi' un," said an old labourer to me last week. " If ee wor to coe the wild birds, I do believe, Muster Raeburn, they'd coom to un !" '

'Yet you dislike him !' said Marcella, a daring smile dancing on the dark face she turned to him. 'One can hear it in every word you say.'

He hesitated, trying, even at the moment that an impulse of jealous alarm which astonished himself had taken possession of him, to find the moderate and measured phrase.

'I have known him from a boy,' he said. 'He is a connection of the Levens, and used to be always there in old days. He is very brilliant and very gifted——'

'Your "but" must be very bad,' she threw in, 'it is so long in coming.'

'Then I will say, whatever opening it gives you,' he replied with spirit, 'that I admire him without respecting him.'

'Whoever thought otherwise of a clever opponent?' she cried. 'It is the stock formula.'

The remark stung, all the more because Aldous was perfectly conscious that there was much truth in her implied charge of prejudice. He had never been very capable of seeing this particular man in the dry light of reason, and was certainly less so than before, since it had been revealed to him that Wharton and Mr. Boyce's daughter were to be brought, before long, into close neighbourhood.

'I am sorry that I seem to you such a Pharisee,' he said, turning upon her a look which had both pain and excitement in it.

She was silent, and they walked on a few yards without speaking. The wood had thickened around them. The high road was no longer visible. No sound of wheels or footsteps reached them. The sun struck freely through the beech-trees, already half bared, whitening the grey trunks at intervals to an arrowy distinctness and majesty, or kindling the slopes of red and freshly fallen leaves below into great patches of light and flame. Through the stems, as always, the girdling blues of the plain, and in their faces a gay and buoyant breeze, speaking rather of spring than autumn. Robins, 'yellow autumn's nightingales,' sang in the hedge to their right. In the pause between them, sun, wind, birds made their charm felt. Nature, perpetual chorus as she is to man, stole in, urging, wooing, defining. Aldous's heart leapt to the spur of a sudden resolve.

Instinctively she turned to him at the same moment as he to her, and seeing his look she paled a little.

'Do you guess at all why it hurts me to jar with you?' he

said—finding his words in a rush, he did not know how—'Why every syllable of yours matters to me? It is because I have hopes —dreams—which have become my life! If you could accept this —this—feeling—this devotion—which has grown up in me—if you could trust yourself to me—you should have no cause, I think— ever—to think me hard or narrow towards any person, any enthusiasm for which you had sympathy. May I say to you all that is in my mind—or—or—am I presuming?'

She looked away from him, crimson again. A great wave of exultation—boundless, intoxicating—swept through her. Then it was checked by a nobler feeling—a quick, penitent sense of his nobleness.

'You don't know me,' she said hurriedly: 'you think you do. But I am all odds and ends. I should annoy—wound—disappoint you.'

His quiet grey eyes flamed.

'Come and sit down here, on these dry roots,' he said, taking already joyous command of her. 'We shall be undisturbed. I have so much to say!'

She obeyed trembling. She felt no passion, but the strong thrill of something momentous and irreparable, together with a swelling pride—pride in such homage from such a man.

He led her a few steps down the slope, found a place for her against a sheltering trunk, and threw himself down beside her. As he looked up at the picture she made amid the autumn branches, at her bent head, her shy moved look, her white hand lying ungloved on her black dress, happiness overcame him. He took her hand, found she did not resist, drew it to him, and clasping it in both his, bent his brow, his lips upon it. It shook in his hold, but she was passive. The mixture of emotion and self-control she showed touched him deeply. In his chivalrous modesty he asked for nothing else, dreamt of nothing more.

Half an hour later they were still in the same spot. There had been much talk between them, most of it earnest, but some of it quite gay, broken especially by her smiles. Her teasing mood, however, had passed away. She was instead composed and dignified, like one conscious that life had opened before her to great issues.

Yet she had flinched often before that quiet tone of eager joy in which he had described his first impressions of her, his surprise at finding in her ideals, revolts, passions, quite unknown to him, so far, in the women of his own class. Naturally he suppressed, perhaps he had even forgotten, the critical amusement and irrita-

tion she had often excited in him. He remembered, he spoke
only of sympathy, delight, pleasure—of his sense, as it were, of
slaking some long-felt moral thirst at the well of her fresh feeling.
So she had attracted him first,—by a certain strangeness and
daring—by what she *said*—

' Now—and above all by what you *are* !' he broke out suddenly,
moved out of his even speech. ' Oh ! it is too much to believe—to
dream of ! Put your hand in mine, and say again that it is really
true that we two are to go forward together—that you will be
always there to inspire—to help——'

And as she gave him the hand, she must also let him—in this
first tremor of a pure passion—take the kiss which was now his by
right. That she should flush and draw away from him as she did,
seemed to him the most natural thing in the world, and the most
maidenly.

Then, as their talk wandered on, bit by bit, he gave her all his
confidence, and she had felt herself honoured in receiving it. She
understood now at least something—a first fraction—of that inner
life, masked so well beneath his quiet English capacity and un-
assuming manner. He had spoken of his Cambridge years, of
his friend, of the desire of his heart to make his landowner's power
and position contribute something towards that new and better
social order, which he too, like Hallin—though more faintly and
intermittently—believed to be approaching. The difficulties of
any really new departure were tremendous ; he saw them more
plainly and more anxiously than Hallin. Yet he believed that he
had thought his way to some effective reform on his grandfather's
large estate, and to some useful work as one of a group of like-
minded men in Parliament. She must have often thought him
careless and apathetic towards his great trust. But he was not so
—not careless—but paralysed often by intellectual difficulty, by
the claims of conflicting truths.

She, too, explained herself most freely, most frankly. She
would have nothing on her conscience.

' They will say, of course,' she said with sudden nervous abrupt-
ness, ' that I am marrying you for wealth and position. And in a
sense I shall be. No ! don't stop me ! I should not marry you if
—if—I did not like you. But you can give me—you have—great
opportunities. I tell you frankly, I shall enjoy them and use them.
Oh ! do think well before you do it. I shall *never* be a meek,
dependent wife. A woman, to my mind, is bound to cherish her
own individuality sacredly, married or not married. Have you
thought that I may often think it right to do things you disagree
with, that may scandalise your relations ?'

You shall be free,' he said steadily. 'I have thought of it all.'

'Then there is my father,' she said, turning her head away. 'He is ill—he wants pity, affection. I will accept no bond that forces me to disown him.'

'Pity and affection are to me the most sacred things in the world,' he said, kissing her hand gently. 'Be content—be at rest —my beautiful lady !'

There was again silence, full of thought on her side, of heavenly happiness on his. The sun had sunk almost to the verge of the plain, the wind had freshened.

'We *must* go home,' she. said, springing up. 'Taylor must have got there an hour ago. Mother will be anxious, and I must —I must tell them.'

'I will leave you at the gate,' he suggested as they walked briskly ; 'and you will ask your father, will you not, if I may see him to-night after dinner ?'

The trees thinned again in front of them, and the path curved inward to the front. Suddenly a man, walking on the road, diverged into the path and came towards them. He was swinging a stick and humming. His head was uncovered, and his light chestnut curls were blown about his forehead by the wind. Marcella, looking up at the sound of the steps, had a sudden impression of something young and radiant, and Aldous stopped with an exclamation.

The new-comer perceived them, and at sight of Aldous smiled, and approached holding out his hand.

'Why, Raeburn, I seem to have missed you twenty times a day this last fortnight. We have been always on each other's tracks without meeting. Yet I think, if we had met, we could have kept our tempers.'

'Miss Boyce, I think you do not know Mr. Wharton,' said Aldous stiffly. 'May I introduce you ?'

The young man's blue eyes, all alert and curious at the mention of Marcella's name, ran over the girl's face and form. Then he bowed with a certain charming exaggeration—like an eighteenth-century beau with his hand upon his heart—and turned back with them a step or two towards the road.

BOOK II

'A woman has enough to govern wisely
Her own demeanours, passions and divisions.'

CHAPTER I

ON a certain night in the December following the engagement of
Marcella Boyce to Aldous Raeburn, the woods and fields of Mellor,
and all the bare rampart of chalk down which divides the Buckinghamshire plain from the forest upland of the Chilterns lay steeped
in moonlight, and in the silence which belongs to intense frost.

Winter had set in before the leaf had fallen from the last oaks ;
already there had been a fortnight or more of severe cold, with
hardly any snow.   The pastures were delicately white ; the ditches
and the wet furrows in the ploughed land, the ponds on Mellor
common, and the stagnant pool in the midst of the village, whence
it drew its main water supply, were frozen hard.   But the ploughed
chalk land itself lay a dull grey beside the glitter of the pastures,
and the woods under the bright sun of the days dropped their rime
only to pass once more with the deadly cold of the night under the
fantastic empire of the frost.   Every day the veil of morning mist
rose lightly from the woods, uncurtaining the wintry spectacle, and
melting into the brilliant azure of an unflecked sky ; every night
the moon rose without a breath of wind, without a cloud ; and all
the branch-work of the trees, where they stood in the open fields,
lay reflected clean and sharp on the whitened ground.   The bitter
cold stole into the cottages, marking the old and feeble with the
touch of Azrael ; while without, in the field solitudes, bird and
beast cowered benumbed and starving in hole and roosting place.

How still it was—this midnight—on the fringe of the woods !
Two men sitting concealed among some bushes at the edge of Mr.
Boyce's largest cover, and bent upon a common errand, hardly
spoke to each other, so strange and oppressive was the silence.
One was Jim Hurd ; the other was a labourer, a son of old Patton
of the almshouses, himself a man of nearly sixty, with a small
wizened face showing sharp and white to-night under his slouched
hat.

They looked out over a shallow cup of treeless land to a further
bound of wooded hill, ending towards the north in a bare bluff of
down shining steep under the moon.   They were in shadow, and
so was most of the wide dip of land before them ; but through a

gap to their right, beyond the wood, the moonbeams poured, and the farms nestling under the opposite ridge, the plantations ranging along it, and the bald beacon hill in which it broke to the plain, were all in radiant light.

Not a stir of life anywhere. Hurd put up his hand to his ear, and leaning forward listened intently. Suddenly—a vibration, a dull thumping sound in the soil of the bank immediately beside him. He started, dropped his hand, and, stooping, laid his ear to the ground.

'Gi us the bag,' he said to his companion, drawing himself upright. 'You can hear 'em turnin and creepin as plain as anything. Now then, you take these and go t' other side.'

He handed over a bundle of rabbit nets. Patton, crawling on hands and knees, climbed over the low overgrown bank on which the hedge stood into the precincts of the wood itself. The state of the hedge, leaving the cover practically open and defenceless along its whole boundary, showed plainly enough that it belonged to the Mellor estate. But the field beyond was Lord Maxwell's.

Hurd applied himself to netting the holes on his own side, pushing the brambles and undergrowth aside with the sure hand of one who had already reconnoitred the ground. Then he crept over to Patton to see that all was right on the other side, came back, and went for the ferrets, of whom he had four in a closely tied bag.

A quarter of an hour of intense excitement followed. In all, five rabbits bolted—three on Hurd's side, two on Patton's. It was all the two men could do to secure their prey, manage the ferrets, and keep a watch on the holes. Hurd's great hands—now fixing the pegs that held the nets, now dealing death to the entangled rabbit, whose neck he broke in an instant by a turn of the thumb, now winding up the line that held the ferret—seemed to be everywhere.

At last a ferret 'laid up,' the string attached to him having either slipped or broken, greatly to the disgust of the men, who did not want to be driven either to dig, which made a noise and took time, or to lose their animal. The rabbits made no more sign, and it was tolerably evident that they had got as much as they were likely to get out of that particular 'bury.'

Hurd thrust his arm deep into the hole where he had put the ferret. 'Ther's summat in the way,' he declared at last. 'Mos likely a dead un. Gi me the spade.'

He dug away the mouth of the hole, making as little noise as possible, and tried again.

'Ere ee be,' he cried, clutching at something, drew it out, exclaimed in disgust, flung it away, and pounced upon a rabbit which on the removal of the obstacle followed like a flash, pursued by the lost ferret. Hurd caught the rabbit by the neck, held it by main force, and killed it ; then put the ferret into his pocket. 'Lord !' he said, wiping his brow, 'they do come suddent.'

What he had pulled out was a dead cat ; a wretched puss, who on some happy hunt had got itself wedged in the hole, and so perished there miserably. He and Patton stooped over it wondering ; then Hurd walked some paces along the bank, looking warily out to the right of him across the open country all the time. He threw the poor malodorous thing far into the wood and returned.

The two men lit their pipes under the shelter of the bushes, and rested a bit, well hidden, but able to see out through a break in the bit of thicket.

'Six on 'em,' said Hurd, looking at the stark creatures beside him. 'I be too done to try another bury. I'll set a snare or two, an' be off home.'

Patton puffed silently. He was wondering whether Hurd would give him one rabbit or two. Hurd had both 'plant' and skill, and Patton would have been glad enough to come for one. Still he was a plaintive man with a perpetual grievance, and had already made up his mind that Hurd would treat him shabbily to-night, in spite of many past demonstrations that his companion was on the whole of a liberal disposition.

'You bin out workin a day's work already, han't yer?' he said presently. He himself was out of work, like half the village, and had been presented by his wife with boiled swede for supper. But he knew that Hurd had been taken on at the works at the Court, where the new drive was being made, and a piece of ornamental water enlarged and improved—mainly for the sake of giving employment in bad times. He, Patton, and some of his mates had tried to get a job there. But the steward had turned them back. The men off the estate had first claim, and there was not room for all of them. Yet Hurd had been taken on, which had set people talking.

Hurd nodded, and said nothing. He was not disposed to be communicative on the subject of his employment at the Court.

'An' it be true as *she* be goin to marry Muster Raeburn?'

Patton jerked his head towards the right, where above a sloping hedge the chimneys of Mellor and the tops of the Mellor cedars, some two or three fields away, showed distinct against the deep night blue.

Hurd nodded again, and smoked diligently. Patton, nettled by this parsimony of speech, made the inward comment that his companion was 'a deep un.' The village was perfectly aware of the particular friendship shown by Miss Boyce to the Hurds. He was goaded into ⁀ying a more stinging topic.

'Westall wor braggin last night at Bradsell's'—(Bradsell was the landlord of 'The Green Man' at Mellor)—'ee said as how they 'd taken you on at the Court—but that didn't prevent 'em knowin as you was a bad lot. Ee said *ee* 'ad 'is eye on yer—ee 'ad warned yer twoice last year——'

'That's a lie!' said Hurd, removing his pipe an instant and putting it back again.

Patton looked more cheerful.

'Well, ee spoke cru'l. Ee was certain, ee said, as you could tell a thing or two about them coverts at Tudley End, if the treuth were known. You wor allus a loafer, an' a loafer you'd be. Yer might go snivellin to Miss Boyce, ee said, but yer wouldn't do no honest work—ee said—not if yer could help it—that's what ee said.'

'Devil!' said Hurd between his teeth, with a quick lift of all his great misshapen chest. He took his pipe out of his mouth, rammed it down fiercely with his thumb, and put it in his pocket.

'Look out!' exclaimed Patton with a start.

A whistle!—clear and distinct—from the opposite side of the hollow. Then a man's figure, black and motionless an instant on the whitened down, with a black speck beside it ; lastly, another figure higher up along the hill, in quick motion towards the first, with other specks behind it. The poachers instantly understood that it was Westall—whose particular beat lay in this part of the estate—signalling to his night watcher, Charlie Dynes, and that the two men would be on them in no time. It was the work of a few seconds to efface as far as possible the traces of their raid, to drag some thick and trailing brambles which hung near over the mouth of the hole where there had been digging, to catch up the ferrets and game, and to bid Hurd's lurcher to come to heel. The two men crawled up the ditch with their burdens, as far away to leeward as they could get from the track by which the keepers would cross the field. The ditch was deeply overgrown, and when the approaching voices warned them to lie close, they crouched under a dense thicket of brambles and overhanging bushes, afraid of nothing but the noses of the keepers' dogs.

Dogs and men, however, passed unsuspecting.

'Hold still!' said Hurd, checking Patton's first attempt to move. 'Ee'll be back again mos like. It's 'is dodge.'

And sure enough in twenty minutes or so the men reappeared. They retraced their steps from the further corner of the field, where some preserves of Lord Maxwell's approached very closely to the big Mellor wood, and came back again along the diagonal path within fifty yards or so of the men in the ditch.

In the stillness the poachers could hear Westall's harsh and peremptory voice giving some orders to his underling, or calling to the dogs, who had scattered a little in the stubble. Hurd's own dog quivered beside him once or twice.

Then steps and voices faded into the distance and all was safe. The poachers crept out grinning, and watched the keepers' progress along the hill-face, till they disappeared into the Maxwell woods.

'*Ee* be sold again—blast 'im !' said Hurd, with a note of quite disproportionate exultation in his queer, cracked voice. ' Now I'll set them snares. But you'd better git home.'

Patton took the hint, gave a grunt of thanks as his companion handed him two rabbits, which he stowed away in the capacious pockets of his poacher's coat, and slouched off home by as sheltered and roundabout a way as possible.

Hurd, left to himself, stowed his nets and other apparatus in a hidden crevice of the bank, and strolled along to set his snares in three hare-runs, well known to him, round the further side of the wood.

Then he waited impatiently for the striking of the clock in Mellor church. The cold was bitter, but his night's work was not over yet, and he had had very good reasons for getting rid of Patton.

Almost immediately the bell rang out, the echo rolling round the bend of the hills in the frosty silence. Half-past twelve Hurd scrambled over the ditch, pushed his way through the dilapidated hedge, and began to climb the ascent of the wood. The outskirts of it were filled with a thin mixed growth of sapling and under-wood, but the high centre of it was crowned by a grove of full-grown beeches, through which the moon, now at its height, was playing freely, as Hurd clambered upwards amid the dead leaves just freshly strown, as though in yearly festival, about their polished trunks. Such infinite grace and strength in the line work of the branches !—branches not bent into gnarled and unexpected fantasies, like those of the oak, but gathered into every conceivable harmony of upward curve and sweep, rising all together, black against the silvery light, each tree related to and completing its neighbour, as though the whole wood, so finely rounded on itself and to the hill, were but one majestic conception of a master artist.

But Hurd saw nothing of this as he plunged through the leaves. He was thinking that it was extremely likely a man would be on the look-out for him to-night under the big beeches—a man with some business to propose to him. A few words dropped in his

ear at a certain public-house the night before had seemed to him
to mean this, and he had accordingly sent Patton out of the way.

But when he got to the top of the hill no one was to be seen or
heard, and he sat him down on a fallen log to smoke and wait
awhile.

He had no sooner, however, taken his seat than he shifted it
uneasily, turning himself round so as to look in the other direction.
For in front of him, as he was first placed, there was a gap in the
trees, and over the lower wood, plainly visible and challenging
attention, rose the dark mass of Mellor House. And the sight of
Mellor suggested reflections just now that were not particularly
agreeable to Jim Hurd.

He had just been poaching Mr. Boyce's rabbits without any
sort of scruple. But the thought of *Miss* Boyce was not pleasant
to him when he was out on these nightly raids.

Why had she meddled? He bore her a queer sort of grudge
for it. He had just settled down to the bit of cobbling which,
together with his wife's plait, served him for a blind, and was full
of a secret excitement as to various plans he had in hand for
'doing' Westall, combining a maximum of gain for the winter
with a maximum of safety, when Miss Boyce walked in, radiant
with the news that there was employment for him at the Court, on
the new works, whenever he liked to go and ask for it.

And then she had given him an odd look.

'And I was to pass you on a message from Lord Maxwell,
Hurd,' she had said : ' "You tell him to keep out of Westall's way
for the future, and bygones shall be bygones." Now, I'm not
going to ask what that means. If you've been breaking some of
our landlords' law, I'm not going to say I'm shocked. I'd alter the
law to-morrow, if I could !—you know I would. But I do say
you're a fool if you go on with it, now you've got good work for
the winter ; you must please remember your wife and children.'

And there he had sat like a log, staring at her—both he and
Minta not knowing where to look, or how to speak. Then at last
his wife had broken out, crying :—

'Oh, miss ! we should ha starved——'

And Miss Boyce had stopped her in a moment, catching her by
the hand. Didn't she know it? Was she there to preach to
them? Only Hurd must promise not to do it any more, for his
wife's sake.

And he—stammering—left without excuse or resource, either
against her charge, or the work she offered him—had promised
her, and promised her, moreover—in his trepidation—with more
fervency than he at all liked to remember.

For about a fortnight, perhaps, he had gone to the Court by day, and had kept indoors by night. Then, just as the vagabond passions, the Celtic instincts, so long repressed, so lately roused, were goading at him again, he met Westall in the road—Westall, who looked him over from top to toe with an insolent smile, as much as to say, 'Well, my man, we've got the whip hand of you now!' That same night he crept out again in the dark and the early morning, in spite of all Minta's tears and scolding.

Well, what matter? As towards the rich and the law, he had the morals of the slave, who does not feel that he has had any part in making the rules he is expected to keep, and breaks them when he can with glee. It made him uncomfortable, certainly, that Miss Boyce should come in and out of their place as she did, should be teaching Willie to read, and bringing her old dresses to make up for Daisy and Nellie, while he was making a fool of her in this way. Still he took it all as it came. One sensation wiped out another.

Besides, Miss Boyce had, after all, much part in this double life of his. Whenever he was at home, sitting over the fire with a pipe, he read those papers and things she had brought him in the summer. He had not taken much notice of them at first. Now he spelled them out again and again. He had always thought 'them rich people took advantage of yer.' But he had never supposed, somehow, they were such thieves, such mean thieves, as it appeared they were. A curious ferment filled his restless, inconsequent brain. The poor were downtrodden, but they were coming to their rights. The land and its creatures were for the people ! not for the idle rich. Above all, Westall was a devil, and must be put down. For the rest, if he could have given words to experience, he would have said that since he began to go out poaching he had burst his prison and found himself. A life which was not merely endurance pulsed in him. The scent of the night woods, the keenness of the night air, the tracks and ways of the wild creatures, the wiles by which he slew them, the talents and charms of his dog Bruno—these things had developed in him new aptitudes both of mind and body, which were in themselves exhilaration. He carried his dwarf's frame more erect, breathed from an ampler chest. As for his work at the Court, he thought of it often with impatience and disgust. It was a more useful blind than his cobbling, or he would have shammed illness and got quit of it.

'Them were sharp uns that managed that business at Tudley End !' He fell thinking about it and chuckling over it as he smoked. Two of Westall's best coverts swept almost clear just before the big shoot in November!—and all done so quick and quiet, before you could say ' Jack Robinson.' Well, there was plenty more yet, more woods, and more birds. There were those coverts down there, on the Mellor side of the hollow—they had been kept for the last shoot in January. Hang him ! why wasn't that fellow up to time ?

But no one came, and he must sit on, shivering and smoking, a sack across his shoulders. As the stir of nerve and blood caused by the ferreting subsided, his spirits began to sink. Mists of Celtic melancholy, perhaps of Celtic superstition, gained upon him. He found himself glancing from side to side, troubled by the noises in the wood. A sad light wind crept about the trunks like a whisper ; the owls called overhead ; sometimes there was a sudden sharp rustle or fall of a branch that startled him. Yet he knew every track, every tree in that wood. Up and down that field outside he had followed his father at the plough, a little sickly object of a lad, yet seldom unhappy, so long as childhood lasted, and his mother's temper could be fled from, either at school or in the fields. Under that boundary hedge to the right he had lain stunned and bleeding all a summer afternoon, after old Westall had thrashed him, his heart scorched within him by the sense of wrong and the craving for revenge. On that dim path leading down the slope of the wood, George Westall had once knocked him down for disturbing a sitting pheasant. He could see himself falling—the tall, powerful lad standing over him with a grin.

Then, inconsequently, he began to think of his father's death. He made a good end did the old man. ' Jim, my lad, the Lord's verra merciful,' or ' Jim, you'll look after Ann.' Ann was the only daughter. Then a sigh or two, and a bit of sleep, and it was done.

And everybody must go the same way, must come to the same stopping of the breath, the same awfulness—in a life of blind habit —of a moment that never had been before and never could be again ? He did not put it to these words, but the shudder that is in the thought for all of us, seized him. He was very apt to think of dying, to ponder in his secret heart *how* it would be, and when. And always it made him very soft towards Minta and the children. Not only did the *life* instinct cling to them, to the warm human hands and faces hemming him in and protecting him from that darkness beyond with its shapes of terror. But to think of himself as sick, and gasping to his end, like his father, was to put himself back in his old relation to his wife, when they were first married. He might cross Minta now, but if he came to lie sick, he could see himself there, in the future, following her about with his eyes, and thanking her, and doing all she told him, just as he'd used to do. He couldn't die without her to help him through. The very idea of her being taken first, roused in him a kind of spasm—a fierceness, a clenching of the hands. But all the same, in this poaching matter, he must have his way, and she must just get used to it.

Ah! a low whistle from the further side of the wood. He replied, and was almost instantly joined by a tall slouching youth, by day a blacksmith's apprentice at Gairsley, the Maxwells' village, who had often brought him information before.

The two sat talking for ten minutes or so on the log. Then they parted; Hurd went back to the ditch where he had left the game, put two rabbits into his pockets, left the other two to be removed in the morning when he came to look at his snares and went off home, keeping as much as possible in the shelter of the hedges. On one occasion he braved the moonlight and the open field, rather than pass through a woody corner where an old farmer had been found dead some six years before. Then he reached a deep lane leading to the village, and was soon at his own door.

As he climbed the wooden ladder leading to the one bedroom where he, his wife, and his four children slept, his wife sprang up in bed.

'Jim, you must be perished—such a night as 't is. Oh, Jim—where ha you bin?'

She was a miserable figure in her coarse nightgown, with her grizzling hair wild about her, and her thin arms nervously outstretched along the bed. The room was freezing cold, and the moonlight stealing through the scanty bits of curtains brought into dismal clearness the squalid bed, the stained walls, and bare uneven floor. On an iron bedstead, at the foot of the large bed, lay Willie, restless and coughing, with the elder girl beside him fast asleep; the other girl lay beside her mother, and the wooden box with rockers, which held the baby, stood within reach of Mrs. Hurd's arm.

He made her no answer, but went to look at the coughing boy, who had been in bed for a week with bronchitis.

'You've never been and got in Westall's way again?' she said anxiously. 'It's no good my tryin to get a wink o' sleep when you're out like this.'

'Don't you worrit yourself,' he said to her, not roughly, but decidedly. 'I'm all right. This boy 's bad, Minta.'

'Yes, an' I kep up the fire an' put the spout on the kettle, too.' She pointed to the grate and to the thin line of steam, which was doing its powerless best against the arctic cold of the room.

Hurd bent over the boy and tried to put him comfortable. The child, weak and feverish, only began to cry—a hoarse bronchial crying, which threatened to wake the baby. He could not be stopped, so Hurd made haste to take off his own coat and boots, and then lifted the poor soul in his arms.

'You'll be quiet, Will, and go sleep, won't yer, if daddy takes keer on you?'

He wrapped his own coat round the little fellow, and lying down beside his wife, took him on his arm and drew the thin brown blankets over himself and his charge. He himself was warm with exercise, and in a little while the huddling creatures on either side of him were warm too. The quick, panting breath of the boy soon showed that he was asleep. His father, too, sank almost instantly into deep gulfs of sleep. Only the wife—nervous, overdone, and possessed by a thousand fears—lay tossing and wakeful hour after hour, while the still glory of the winter night passed by.

CHAPTER II

'WELL, Marcella, have you and Lady Winterbourne arranged your classes?'

Mrs. Boyce was stooping over a piece of needlework beside a window in the Mellor drawing-room, trying to catch the rapidly failing light. It was one of the last days of December. Marcella had just come in from the village rather early, for they were expecting a visitor to arrive about tea-time, and had thrown herself, tired, into a chair near her mother.

'We have got about ten or eleven of the younger women to join; none of the old ones will come,' said Marcella. 'Lady Winterbourne has heard of a capital teacher from Dunstable, and we hope to get started next week. There is money enough to pay wages for three months.'

In spite of her fatigue, her eye was bright and restless. The energy of thought and action from which she had just emerged still breathed from every limb and feature.

'Where have you got the money?'

'Mr. Raeburn has managed it,' said Marcella, briefly.

Mrs. Boyce gave a slight shrug of the shoulders.

'And afterwards—what is to become of your product?'

'There is a London shop Lady Winterbourne knows will take what we make if it turns out well. Of course, we don't expect to pay our way.'

Marcella gave her explanations with a certain stiffness of self-defence. She and Lady Winterbourne had evolved a scheme for reviving and improving the local industry of straw-plaiting, which after years of decay seemed now on the brink of final disappearance. The village women who could at present earn a few pence a week by the coarser kinds of work were to be instructed, not only in the finer and better paid sorts, but also in the making up of the plait when done, and the 'blocking' of hats and bonnets—processes hitherto carried on exclusively at one or two large local centres.

'You don't expect to pay your way?' repeated Mrs. Boyce. 'What, never?'

'Well, we shall give twelve to fourteen shillings a week wages. We shall find the materials, and the room—and prices are very low, the whole trade depressed.'

Mrs. Boyce laughed.

'I see. How many workers do you expect to get together?'

'Oh! eventually, about two hundred in the three villages. It will regenerate the whole life !' said Marcella, a sudden ray from the inner warmth escaping her, against her will.

Mrs. Boyce smiled again, and turned her work so as to see it better.

'Does Aldous understand what you are letting him in for?'

Marcella flushed.

'Perfectly. It is "ransom"—that's all.'

'And he is ready to take your view of it?'

'Oh, he thinks us economically unsound, of course,' said Marcella impatiently. 'So we are. All care for the human being under the present state of things is economically unsound. But he likes it no more than I do.'

'Well, lucky for you he has a long purse,' said Mrs. Boyce, lightly. 'But I gather, Marcella, you don't insist upon his spending it *all* on straw-plaiting. He told me yesterday he had taken the Hertford Street house.'

'We shall live quite simply,' said Marcella quickly.

'What, no carriage?'

Marcella hesitated.

'A carriage saves time. And if one goes about much, it does not cost so much more than cabs.'

'So you mean to go about much? Lady Winterbourne talks to me of presenting you in May.'

'That's Miss Raeburn,' cried Marcella. 'She says I must, and all the family would be scandalised if I didn't go. But you can't imagine——'

She stopped and took off her hat, pushing the hair back from her forehead. A look of worry and excitement had replaced the radiant glow of her first resting moments.

'That you like it?' said Mrs. Boyce, bluntly. 'Well, I don't know. Most young women like pretty gowns, and great functions, and prominent positions. I don't call you an ascetic, Marcella.'

Marcella winced.

'One has to fit oneself to circumstances,' she said proudly. 'One may hate the circumstances, but one can't escape them.'

'Oh, I don't think you will hate your circumstances, my dear! You would be very foolish if you did. Have you heard finally how much the settlement is to be?'

'No,' said Marcella shortly. 'I have not asked papa, nor anybody.'

'It was only settled this morning. Your father told me hurriedly as he went out. You are to have two thousand a year of your own.'

The tone was dry, and the speaker's look as she turned towards her daughter had in it a curious hostility; but Marcella did not notice her mother's manner.

'It is too much,' she said in a low voice.

She had thrown back her head against the chair in which she sat, and her half-troubled eyes were wandering over the darkening expanse of lawn and avenue.

'He said he wished you to feel perfectly free to live your own life, and to follow out your own projects. Oh, for a person of projects, my dear, it is not so much. You will do well to husband it. Keep it for yourself. Get what *you* want out of it : not what other people want.'

Again Marcella's attention missed the note of agitation in her mother's sharp manner. A soft look—a look of compunction— passed across her face. Mrs. Boyce began to put her working things away, finding it too dark to do any more.

'By the way,' said the mother suddenly, 'I suppose you will be going over to help him in his canvassing this next few weeks? Your father says the election will be certainly in February.'

Marcella moved uneasily.

'He knows,' she said at last, 'that I don't agree with him in so many things. He is so full of this Peasant Proprietors Bill. And I hate peasant properties. They are nothing but a step back-wards.'

Mrs. Boyce lifted her eyebrows.

'That's unlucky. He tells me it is likely to be his chief work in the new Parliament. Isn't it, on the whole, probable that he knows more about the country than you do, Marcella?'

Marcella sat up with sudden energy and gathered her walking things together.

'It isn't knowledge that's the question, mamma; it's the principle of the thing. *I* mayn't know anything, but the people whom I follow know. There are the two sides of thought—the two ways of looking at things. I warned Aldous when he asked me to marry him which I belonged to. And he accepted it.'

Mrs. Boyce's thin fine mouth curled a little.

'So you suppose that Aldous had his wits about him on that great occasion as much as you had?'

Marcella first started, then quivered with nervous indignation.

'Mother,' she said, 'I can't bear it. It's not the first time that you have talked as though I had taken some unfair advantage—made an unworthy bargain. It is too hard too. Other people may think what they like, but that you——'

Her voice failed her, and the tears came into her eyes. She was tired and over-excited, and the contrast between the atmosphere of flattery and consideration which surrounded her in Aldous's company, in the village, or at the Winterbournes, and this tone which her mother so often took with her when they were alone, was at the moment hardly to be endured.

Mrs. Boyce looked up more gravely.

'You misunderstand me, my dear,' she said quietly. 'I allow myself to wonder at you a little, but I think no hard things of you ever. I believe you like Aldous.'

'Really, mamma!' cried Marcella, half hysterically.

Mrs. Boyce had by now rolled up her work and shut her workbasket.

'If you are going to take off your things,' she said, 'please tell William that there will be six or seven at tea. You said, I think, that Mr. Raeburn was going to bring Mr. Hallin?'

'Yes, and Frank Leven is coming. When will Mr. Wharton be here?'

'Oh, in ten minutes or so, if his train is punctual. I hear your father just coming in.'

Marcella went away, and Mrs. Boyce was left a few minutes alone. Her thin hands lay idle a moment on her lap, and leaning towards the window beside her, she looked out an instant into the snowy twilight. Her mind was full of its usual calm scorn for those—her daughter included—who supposed that the human lot was to be mended by a rise in weekly wages, or that suffering has any necessary dependence on the amount of commodities of which a man disposes. What hardship is there in starving and scrubbing and toiling? Had she ever seen a labourer's wife scrubbing her cottage floor without envy, without moral thirst? Is it these things that kill, or any of the great simple griefs and burdens? Doth man live by bread alone? The whole language of social and charitable enthusiasm often raised in her a kind of exasperation.

So Marcella would be rich, excessively rich, even now. Outside the amount settled upon her, the figures of Aldous Raeburn's present income, irrespective of the inheritance which would come to him on his grandfather's death, were a good deal beyond what even Mr. Boyce—upon whom the daily spectacle of the Maxwell wealth exercised a certain angering effect—had supposed.

Mrs. Boyce had received the news of the engagement with astonishment, but her after-acceptance of the situation had been marked by all her usual philosophy. Probably behind the philosophy there was much secret relief. Marcella was provided for. Not the fondest or most contriving mother could have done more for her than she had at one stroke done for herself. During the early autumn Mrs. Boyce had experienced some moments of sharp prevision as to what her future relations might be towards this strong and restless daughter, so determined to conquer a world her mother had renounced. Now all was clear, and a very shrewd observer could allow her mind to play freely with the ironies of the situation.

As to Aldous Raeburn, she had barely spoken to him before the day when Marcella announced the engagement, and the lover a few hours later had claimed her daughter at the mother's hands with an emotion to which Mrs. Boyce found her usual difficulty in responding. She had done her best, however, to be gracious and to mask her surprise that he should have proposed, that Lord Maxwell should have consented, and that Marcella should have so lightly fallen a victim. One surprise, however, had to be confessed, at least to herself. After her interview with her future son-in-law, Mrs. Boyce realised that for the first time for fifteen years she was likely to admit a new friend. The impression made upon him by her own singular personality had translated itself in feelings and language which, against her will as it were, established an understanding, an affinity. That she had involuntarily aroused in him the profoundest and most chivalrous pity was plain to her. Yet for the first time in her life she did not resent it; and Marcella watched her mother's attitude with a mixture of curiosity and relief.

Then followed talk of an early wedding, communications from Lord Maxwell to Mr. Boyce of a civil and formal kind, a good deal more notice from the 'county,' and finally this definite statement from Aldous Raeburn as to the settlement he proposed to make upon his wife, and the joint income which he and she would have immediately at their disposal.

Under all these growing and palpable evidences of Marcella's

future wealth and position, Mrs. Boyce had shown her usual restless and ironic spirit.   But of late, and especially to-day, restlessness had become oppression.   While Marcella was so speedily to
become the rich and independent woman, they themselves, Marcella's mother and father, were very poor, in difficulties even. and
likely to remain so.   She gathered from her husband's grumbling
that the provision of a suitable trousseau for Marcella would tax
his resources to their utmost.   How long would it be before they
were dipping in Marcella's purse?   Mrs. Boyce's self-tormenting
soul was possessed by one of those nightmares her pride had
brought upon her in grim succession during these fifteen years.
And this pride, strong towards all the world, was nowhere so strong
or so indomitable, at this moment, as towards her own daughter.
They were practically strangers to each other ; and they jarred.
To inquire where the fault lay would have seemed to Mrs. Boyce
futile.

Darkness had come on fast, and Mrs. Boyce was in the act of
ringing for lights when her husband entered.

'Where's Marcella?' he asked as he threw himself into a chair
with the air of irritable fatigue which was now habitual to him.

'Only gone to take off her things and tell William about tea.
She will be down directly.'

'Does she know about that settlement?'

'Yes, I told her.   She thought it generous, but not—I think—
unsuitable.   The world cannot be reformed on nothing.'

'Reformed !—fiddlesticks !' said Mr. Boyce angrily.   'I never
saw a girl with a head so full of nonsense in my life.   Where does
she get it from?   Why did you let her go about in London with
those people?   She may be spoilt for good.   Ten to one she'll
make a laughing stock of herself and everybody belonging to her,
before she's done.'

'Well, that is Mr. Raeburn's affair.   I think I should take him
into account more than Marcella does, if I were she.   But probably
she knows best.'

'Of course she does.   He has lost his head ; anyone can see
that.   While she is in the room, he is like a man possessed.   It
doesn't sit well on that kind of fellow.   It makes him ridiculous.
I told him half the settlement would be ample.   She would only
spend the rest on nonsense.'

'You told him that?'

'Yes, I did.   Oh !'—with an angry look at her—'I suppose
you thought I should want to sponge upon her?   I am as much
obliged to you as usual !'

A red spot rose in his wife's thin cheek. But she turned and answered him gently, so gently that he had the rare sensation of having triumphed over her. He allowed himself to be mollified. and she stood there over the fire, chatting with him for some time, a friendly natural note in her voice which was rare and, insensibly, soothed him like an opiate. She chatted about Marcella's trousseau gowns, detailing her own contrivances for economy ; about the probable day of the wedding, the latest gossip of the election, and so on. He sat shading his eyes from the firelight, and now and then throwing in a word or two. The inmost soul of him was very piteous, harrowed often by a new dread—the dread of dying. The woman beside him held him in the hollow of her hand. In the long wrestle between her nature and his, she had conquered. His fear of her and his need of her had even come to supply the place of a dozen ethical instincts he was naturally without.

Some discomfort, probably physical, seemed at last to break up his moment of rest.

' Well, I tell you, I often wish it were the other man,' he said, with some impatience. ' Raeburn's so d——d superior. I suppose I offended him by what I said of Marcella's whims, and the risk of letting her control so much money at her age, and with her ideas. You never saw such an air !—all very quiet, of course. He buttoned his coat and got up to go, as though I were no more worth considering than the table. Neither he nor his precious grandfather need alarm himself : I shan't trouble them as a visitor. If I shock them, they bore me—so we're quits. Marcella 'll have to come here if she wants to see her father. But owing to your charming system of keeping her away from us all her childhood, she's not likely to want.'

' You mean Mr. Wharton by the other man ?' said Mrs. Boyce, not defending herself or Aldous.

' Yes, of course. But he came on the scene just too late, worse luck ! Why wouldn't he have done just as well? He's as mad as she—madder. He believes all the rubbish she does—talks such *rot*, the people tell me, in his meetings. But then he's good company—he amuses you—you don't need to be on your p's and q's with *him*. Why wouldn't she have taken up with him ? As far as money goes they could have rubbed along. *He's* not the man to starve when there are game-pies going. It's just bad luck.'

Mrs. Boyce smiled a little.

' What there is to make you suppose that she would have inclined to him, I don't exactly see. She has been taken up with Mr. Raeburn, really, from the first week of her arrival here.'

'Well, I dare say—there was no one else,' said her husband testily. 'That's natural enough. It's just what I say. All I know is, Wharton shall be free to use this house just as he pleases during his canvassing, whatever the Raeburns may say.'

He bent forward and poked the somewhat sluggish fire with a violence which hindered rather than helped it. Mrs. Boyce's smile had quite vanished. She perfectly understood all that was implied, whether in his instinctive dislike of Aldous Raeburn, or in his cordiality towards young Wharton.

After a minute's silence, he got up again and left the room, walking, as she observed, with difficulty. She stopped a minute or so in the same place after he had gone, turning her rings absently on her thin fingers. She was thinking of some remarks which Dr. Clarke, the excellent and experienced local doctor, had made to her on the occasion of his last visit. With all the force of her strong will she had set herself to disbelieve them. But they had had subtle effects already. Finally she too went upstairs, bidding Marcella, whom she met coming down, hurry William with the tea, as Mr. Wharton might arrive any moment.

Marcella saw the room shut up—the large, shabby, beautiful room—the lamps brought in, fresh wood thrown on the fire to make it blaze, and the tea-table set out. Then she sat herself down on a low chair by the fire, leaning forward with her elbows on her knees and her hands clasped in front of her. Her black dress revealed her fine full throat and her white wrists, for she had an impatience of restraint anywhere, and wore frills and falls of black lace where other people would have followed the fashion in high collars and close wristbands. What must have struck anyone with an observant eye, as she sat thus, thrown into beautiful light and shade by the blaze of the wood fire, w; s the massiveness of the head compared with the nervous delicacy of much of the face, the thinness of the wrist, and of the long and slender foot raised on the fender. It was perhaps the great thickness and full wave of the hair which gave the head its breadth; but the effect was singular, and would have been heavy but for the glow of the eyes, which balanced it.

She was thinking, as a *fiancée* should, of Aldous and their marriage, which had been fixed for the end of February. Yet not apparently with any rapturous absorption. There was a great deal to plan, and her mind was full of business. Who was to look after her various village schemes while she and Lady Winterbourne were away in London? Mary Harden had hardly brains enough, dear little thing as she was. They must find some capable woman and pay her. The Cravens would tell her, of course, that she was on the high road to the most degrading of *rôles*—the *rôle* of Lady Bountiful. But there were Lady Bountifuls and Lady Bountifuls. And the *rôle* itself was inevitable. It all depended upon how it was managed—in the interest of what ideas.

She must somehow renew her relations with the Cravens in town. It would certainly be in her power now to help them and their projects forward a little. Of course they would distrust her, but that she would get over.

All the time she was listening mechanically for the hall door bell, which, however, across the distances of the great rambling house it was not easy to hear. Their coming guest was not much in her mind. She tacitly assumed that her father would look after him. On the two or three occasions when they had met during the last three months, including his luncheon at Mellor on the day after her engagement, her thoughts had been too full to allow her to take much notice of him—picturesque and amusing as he seemed to be. Of late he had not been much in the neighbourhood. There had been a slack time for both candidates, which was now to give way to a fresh period of hard canvassing in view of the election which everybody expected at the end of February.

But Aldous was to bring Edward Hallin! That interested her. She felt an intense curiosity to see and know Hallin, coupled with a certain nervousness. The impression she might be able to make on him would be in some sense an earnest of her future.

Suddenly, something undefinable—a slight sound, a current of air—made her turn her head. To her amazement she saw a young man in the doorway looking at her with smiling eyes, and quietly drawing off his gloves.

She sprang up with a feeling of annoyance.

'Mr. Wharton!'

'Oh!—must you?'—he said, with a movement of one hand, as though to stop her. 'Couldn't you stay like that? At first I thought there was nobody in the room. Your servant is grappling with my bags, which are as the sand of the sea for multitude, so I wandered in by myself. Then I saw you—and the fire—and the room. It was like a bit of music. It was mere wanton waste to interrupt it.'

Marcella flushed, as she very stiffly shook hands with him.

'I did not hear the front door,' she said coldly. 'My mother will be here directly. May I give you some tea?'

'Thanks. No, I knew you did not hear me. That delighted me. It showed what charming things there are in the world that have no spectators! What a *delicious* place this is!—what a heavenly old place—especially in these half lights ! There was a raw sun when I was here before, but now——'

He stood in front of the fire, looking round the great room, and at the few small lamps making their scanty light amid the flame-lit darkness. His hands were loosely crossed behind his back, and his boyish face, in its setting of curls, shone with content and self-possession.

'Well,' said Marcella bluntly, 'I should prefer a little more light to live by. Perhaps, when you have fallen downstairs here in the dark as often as I have, you may too.'

He laughed.

'But how much better, after all—don't you think so ?—to have too little of anything than too much !'

He flung himself into a chair beside the tea-table, looking up with gay interrogation as Marcella handed him his cup. She was a good deal surprised by him. On the few occasions of their previous meetings, these bright eyes, and this pronounced manner, had been—at any rate as towards herself—much less free and evident. She began to recover the start he had given her, and to study him with a half-unwilling curiosity.

'Then Mellor will please you,' she said drily, in answer to his remark, carrying her own tea meanwhile to a chair on the other side of the fire. 'My father never bought anything—my father can't. I believe we have chairs enough to sit down upon—but we have no curtains to half the windows. Can I give you anything ?'

For he had risen, and was looking over the tea-tray.

'Oh ! but I *must*,' he said discontentedly. 'I *must* have enough sugar in my tea !'

'I gave you more than the average,' she said, with a sudden little leap of laughter, as she came to his aid. 'Do all your principles break down like this ? I was going to suggest that you might like some of that fire taken away?' And she pointed to the pile of blazing logs which now filled up the great chimney.

'That fire !' he said, shivering, and moving up to it. 'Have you any idea what sort of a wind you keep up here on these hills on a night like this ? And to think that in this weather, with a barometer that laughs in your face when you try to move it, I have three meetings to-morrow night !'

'When one loves the "People," with a large P,' said Marcella, 'one mustn't mind winds.'

He flashed a smile at her, answering to the sparkle of her look, then applied himself to his tea and toasted bun again, with the dainty deliberation of one enjoying every sip and bite.

'No ; but if only the People didn't live so far apart. Some

murderous person wanted them to have only one neck. I want
them to have only one ear. Only then unfortunately everybody
would speak well—which would bring things round to dulness
again. Does Mr. Raeburn make you think very bad things of me,
Miss Boyce?'

He bent forward to her as he spoke, his blue eyes all candour
and mirth.

Marcella started.

'How can he?' she said abruptly. 'I am not a Conservative.'

'Not a Conservative?' he said joyously. 'Oh! but impossible!
Does that mean that you ever read my poor little speeches?'

He pointed to the local newspaper, freshly cut, which lay on a
table at Marcella's elbow.

'Sometimes—' said Marcella, embarrassed. 'There is so little
time.'

In truth she had hardly given his candidature a thought since
the day Aldous proposed to her. She had been far too much
taken up with her own prospects, with Lady Winterbourne's friendship, and her village schemes.

He laughed.

'Of course there is. When is the great event to be?'

'I didn't mean that,' said Marcella stiffly. 'Lady Winterbourne
and I have been trying to start some village workshops. We have
been working and talking, and writing, morning, noon, and night.'

'Oh! I know—yes, I heard of it. And you really think anything is going to come out of finicking little schemes of that sort?'

His dry change of tone drew a quick look from her. The fresh-
coloured face was transformed. In place of easy mirth and
mischief, she read an acute and half contemptuous attention.

'I don't know what you mean,' she said slowly, after a pause.
'Or rather—I do know quite well. You told papa—didn't you?—
and Mr. Raeburn says that you are a Socialist—not half-and-half, as
all the world is, but the real thing? And of course you want great
changes : you don't like anything that might strengthen the upper
class with the people. But that is nonsense. You can't get the
changes for a long *long* time. And, meanwhile, people must be
clothed and fed and kept alive.'

She lay back in her high-backed chair and looked at him
defiantly. His lip twitched, but he kept his gravity.

'You would be much better employed in forming a branch of
the Agricultural Union,' he said decidedly. 'What is the good of
playing Lady Bountiful to a decayed industry? All that is childish ;
we want *the means of revolution*. The people who are for reform
shouldn't waste money and time on fads.'

'I understand all that,' she said scornfully, her quick breath rising and falling. 'Perhaps you don't know that I was a member of the Venturist Society in London? What you say doesn't sound very new to me!'

His seriousness disappeared in laughter. He hastily put down his cup and, stepping over to her, held out his hand.

'You a Venturist? So am I. Joy! Won't you shake hands with me, as comrades should? We are a very mixed set of people, you know, and between ourselves I don't know that we are coming to much. But we can make an alderman dream of the guillotine —that is always something. Oh! but now we can talk on quite a new footing!'

She had given him her hand for an instant, withdrawing it with shy rapidity, and he had thrown himself into a chair again, with his arms behind his head, and the air of one reflecting happily on a changed situation. 'Quite a new footing,' he repeated thoughtfully. 'But it is—a little surprising. What does—what does Mr. Raeburn say to it?'

'Nothing! He cares just as much about the poor as you or I, please understand! He doesn't choose my way—but he won't interfere with it.'

'Ah! that is like him—like Aidous.'

Marcella started.

'You don't mind my calling him by his Christian name sometimes? It drops out. We used to meet as boys together at the Levens'. The Levens are my cousins. He was a big boy, and I was a little one. But he didn't like me. You see—I was a little beast!'

His air of appealing candour could not have been more engaging.

'Yes, I fear I was a little beast. And he was, even then, and always, "the good and beautiful." You don't understand Greek, do you, Miss Boyce? But he was very good to me. I got into an awful scrape once. I let out a pair of eagle owls that used to be kept in the courtyard—Sir Charles loved them a great deal more than his babies—I let them out at night for pure wickedness, and they came to fearful ends in the park. I was to have been sent home next day, in the most unnecessary and penal hurry. But Aldous interposed—said he would look after me for the rest of the holidays.'

'And then you tormented him?'

'Oh no!' he said with gentle complacency. 'Oh no! I never torment anybody. But one must enjoy oneself, you know; what else can one do? Then afterwards, when we were older—somehow

I don't know—but we didn't get on. It is very sad—I wish he thought better of me.'

The last words were said with a certain change of tone, and sitting up he laid the tips of his fingers together on his knees with a little plaintive air. Marcella's eyes danced with amusement, but she looked away from him to the fire, and would not answer.

'You don't help me out. You don't console me. It's unkind of you. Don't you think it a melancholy fate to be always admiring the people who detest you?'

'Don't admire them!' she said merrily.

His eyebrows lifted. '*That,*' he said drily, 'is disloyal. I call —I call your ancestor over the mantelpiece'—he waved his hand towards a blackened portrait in front of him—'to witness, that I am all for admiring Mr. Raeburn, and you discourage it. Well, but now—*now*' he drew his chair eagerly towards hers, the pose of a minute before thrown to the winds—'do let us understand each other a little more before people come. You know I have a labour newspaper?'

She nodded.

'You read it?'

'Is it the *Labour Clarion*? I take it in.'

'Capital!' he cried. 'Then I know now why I found a copy in the village here. You lent it to a man called Hurd?'

'I did.'

'Whose wife worships you?—whose good angel you have been? Do I know something about you, or do I not? Well, now, are you satisfied with that paper? Can you suggest to me means of improving it? It wants some fresh blood, I think—I must find it. I bought the thing last year, in a moribund condition, with the old staff. Oh! we will certainly take counsel together about it—most certainly! But first—I have been boasting of knowing something about you—but I should like to ask—do you know anything about me?'

Both laughed. Then Marcella tried to be serious.

'Well—I—I believe—you have some land?'

'Right!' he nodded—'I am a Lincolnshire landowner. I have about five thousand acres—enough to be tolerably poor on—and enough to play tricks with. I have a co-operative farm, for instance. At present I have lent them a goodish sum of money—and remitted them their first half-year's rent. Not so far a paying speculation. But it will do—some day. Meanwhile the estate wants money— and my plans and I want money—badly. I propose to make the *Labour Clarion* pay—if I can. That will give me more time for speaking and organising, for what concerns *us*—as Venturists—than the Bar.'

'The Bar?' she said, a little mystified, but following every word with a fascinated attention.

'I made myself a barrister three years ago, to please my mother. She thought I should do better in Parliament—if ever I got in. Did you ever hear of my mother?'

There was no escaping these frank, smiling questions.

'No,' said Marcella honestly.

'Well, ask Lord Maxwell,' he said, laughing. 'He and she came across each other once or twice, when he was Home Secretary years ago, and she was wild about some woman's grievance or other. She always maintains that she got the better of him—no doubt he was left with a different impression. Well—my mother —most people thought her mad—perhaps she was—but then somehow—I loved her!'

He was still smiling, but at the last words a charming vibration crept into the words, and his eyes sought hers with a young open demand for sympathy.

'Is that so rare?' she asked him, half laughing—instinctively defending her own feeling lest it should be snatched from her by any make-believe.

'Yes—as we loved each other—it is rare. My father died when I was ten. She would not send me to school, and I was always in her pocket—I shared all her interests. She was a wild woman— but she *lived*, as not one person in twenty lives.'

Then he sighed. Marcella was too shy to imitate his readiness to ask questions. But she supposed that his mother must be dead —indeed, now vaguely remembered to have heard as much.

There was a little silence.

'Please tell me,' she said suddenly, why do you attack my straw-plaiting? Is a co-operative farm any less of a stopgap?'

Instantly his face changed. He drew up his chair again beside her, as gay and keen-eyed as before.

'I can't argue it out now. There is so much to say. But do listen! I have a meeting in the village here next week to preach land nationalisation. We mean to try and form a branch of the Labourers' Union. Will you come?'

Marcella hesitated.

'I think so,' she said, slowly.

There was a pause. Then she raised her eyes and found his fixed upon her. A sudden sympathy—of youth, excitement, pleasure—seemed to rise between them. She had a quick impression of lightness, grace; of an open brow set in curls; of a look more intimate, inquisitive, commanding, than any she had yet met.

'May I speak to you, miss?' said a voice at the door.

Marcella rose hastily. Her mother's maid was standing there. She hurried across the room.

'What is the matter, Deacon?'

'Your mother says, miss,' said the maid, retreating into the hall, 'I am to tell you she can't come down. Your father is ill, and she has sent for Dr. Clarke. But you are please not to go up. Will you give the gentlemen their tea, and she will come down before they go, if she can.'

Marcella had turned pale.

'Mayn't I go, Deacon? What is it?'

'It's a bad fit of pain, your mother says, miss. Nothing can be done till the doctor comes. She begged *particular* that you wouldn't go up, miss. She doesn't want anyone put out.

At the same moment there was a ring at the outer door.

'Oh, there is Aldous,' cried Marcella with relief, and she ran out into the hall to meet him.

CHAPTER III

ALDOUS advanced into the inner hall at sight of Marcella, leaving his companions behind in the vestibule taking off their coats. Marcella ran to him.

'Papa is ill!' she said to him hastily. 'Mamma has sent for Dr. Clarke. She won't let me go up, and wants us to take no notice and have tea without her.'

'I am so sorry! Can we do anything? The dog-cart is here with a fast horse. If your messenger went on foot——'

'Oh, no! they are sure to have sent the boy on the pony I don't know why, but I have had a presentiment for a long time past that papa was going to be ill.'

She looked white and excited. She had turned back to the drawing-room, forgetting the other guests, he walking beside her. As they passed along the dim hall, Aldous had her hand close in his, and when they passed under an archway at the further end he stooped suddenly in the shadows and kissed the hand. Touch—kiss—had the clinging, the intensity of passion. They were the expression of all that had lain vibrating at the man's inmost heart during the dark drive, while he had been chatting with his two companions.

'My darling! I hope not Would you rather not see strangers?

Shall I send Hallin and young Leven away? They would understand at once.'

'Oh, no! Mr. Wharton is here anyway—staying. Where is
Mr. Hallin? I had forgotten him.'

Aldous turned and called. Mr. Hallin and young Frank Leven,
divining something unusual, were looking at the pictures in the hall.

Edward Hallin came up and took Marcella's offered hand.
Each looked at the other with a special attention and interest.
'She holds my friend's life in her hands—is she worthy of it?' was
naturally the question hanging suspended in the man's judgment.
The girl's manner was proud and shy, the manner of one anxious
to please, yet already, perhaps, on the defensive.

Aldous explained the position of affairs, and Hallin expressed
his sympathy. He had a singularly attractive voice, the voice
indeed of the orator, which can adapt itself with equal charm and
strength to the most various needs and to any pitch. As he spoke,
Marcella was conscious of a sudden impression that she already
knew him and could be herself with him at once.'

'Oh, I say,' broke in young Leven, who was standing behind;
'don't you be bothered with us, Miss Boyce. Just send us back at
once. I'm awfully sorry!'

'No; you are to come in!' she said, smiling through her
pallor, which was beginning to pass away, and putting out her
hand to him—the young Eton and Oxford athlete, just home for
his Christmas vacation, was a great favourite with her—'You must
come and have tea and cheer me up by telling me all the things
you have killed this week. Is there anything left alive? You had
come down to the fieldfares, you know, last Tuesday.'

He followed her, laughing and protesting, and she led the way
to the drawing-room. But as her fingers were on the handle she
once more caught sight of the maid, Deacon, standing on the
stairs, and ran to speak to her.

'He is better,' she said, coming back with a face of glad relief.
'The attack seems to be passing off. Mamma can't come down,
but she begs that we will all enjoy ourselves.'

'We'll endeavour,' said young Leven, rubbing his hands, 'by
the help of tea. Miss Boyce, will you please tell Aldous and Mr.
Hallin not to talk politics when they're taking me out to a party.
They should fight a man of their own size. I'm all limp and
trampled on, and want you to protect me.'

The group moved, laughing and talking, into the drawing-room.

'Jiminy!' said Leven, stopping short behind Aldous, who was
alone conscious of the lad's indignant astonishment; 'what the
deuce is *he* doing here?'

For there on the rug, with his back to the fire, stood Wharton, surveying the party with his usual smiling *aplomb*.

'Mr. Hallin, do you know Mr. Wharton?' said Marcella.

'Mr. Wharton and I have met several times on public platforms,' said Hallin, holding out his hand, which Wharton took with effusion. Aldous greeted him with the impassive manner, the 'three finger' manner, which was with him an inheritance—though not from his grandfather—and did not contribute to his popularity in the neighbourhood. As for young Leven, he barely nodded to the Radical candidate, and threw himself into a chair as far from the fire as possible.

'Frank and I have met before to-day!' said Wharton, laughing.

'Yes, I've been trying to undo some of your mischief,' said the boy bluntly. 'I found him, Miss Boyce, haranguing a lot of men at the dinner-hour at Tudley End—one of our villages, you know—cramming them like anything—all about the game laws, and our misdeeds—my father's, of course.'

Wharton raised a protesting hand.

'Oh—all very well! Of course it was us you meant! Well, when he'd driven off, I got up on a cart and had *my* say. I asked them whether they didn't all come out at our big shoots, and whether they didn't have almost as much fun as we did—why! the schoolmaster and the postman come to ask to carry cartridges, and everybody turns out, down to the cripples!—whether they didn't have rabbits given them all the year round; whether half of them hadn't brothers and sons employed somehow about the game, well-paid, and well-treated; whether any man-jack of them would be a ha'porth better off if there were no game; whether many of them wouldn't be worse off; and whether England wouldn't be a beastly dull place to live in, if people like him'—he pointed to Wharton—'had the governing of it! And I brought 'em all round too. I got them cheering and laughing. Oh! I can tell you old Dodgson 'll have to take me on. He says he'll ask me to speak for him at several places. I'm not half bad, I declare I'm not.'

'I thought they gave you a holiday task at Eton,' observed Wharton blandly.

The lad coloured hotly, then bethought himself—radiant :—

'I left Eton last half, as of course you know quite well. But if it had only been last Christmas instead of this, wouldn't I have scored—by Jove! They gave us a beastly *essay* instead of a book. "*Dem*agogues!" I sat up all night, and screwed out a page and a half. I'd have known something about it *now*.'

And as he stood beside the tea-table waiting for Marcella to entrust some tea to him for distribution, he turned and made a profound bow to his candidate cousin.

Everybody joined in the laugh, led by Wharton. Then there was a general drawing up of chairs, and Marcella applied herself to making tea, helped by Aldous. Wharton alone remained standing before the fire, observant and apart.

Hallin, whose health at this moment made all exertion, even a drive, something of a burden, sat a little away from the tea-table, resting, and glad to be silent. Yet all the time he was observing the girl presiding and the man beside her—his friend, her lover. The moment had a peculiar, perhaps a melancholy interest for him. So close had been the bond between himself and Aldous, that the lover's communication of his engagement had evoked in the friend that sense—poignant, inevitable—which in the realm of the affections always waits on something done and finished,—a leaf turned, a chapter closed. 'That sad word, Joy!' Hallin was alone and ill when Raeburn's letter reached him, and through the following day and night he was haunted by Landor's phrase, long familiar and significant to him. His letter to his friend, and the letter to Miss Boyce for which Raeburn had asked him, had cost him an invalid's contribution of sleep and ease. The girl's answer had seemed to him constrained and young, though touched here and there with a certain fineness and largeness of phrase, which, if it was to be taken as an index of character, no doubt threw light upon the matter so far as Aldous was concerned.

Her beauty, of which he had heard much, now that he was face to face with it, was certainly striking enough—all the more because of its immaturity, the sublety and uncertainty of its promise. *Immaturity—uncertainty*—these words returned upon him as he observed her manner with its occasional awkwardness, the awkwardness which goes with power not yet fully explored or mastered by its possessor. How Aldous hung upon her, following every movement, anticipating every want! After a while Hallin found himself half-inclined to Mr. Boyce's view, that men of Raeburn's type are never seen to advantage in this stage—this queer topsy-turvy stage—of first passion. He felt a certain impatience, a certain jealousy for his friend's dignity. It seemed to him too, every now and then, that she—the girl—was teased by all this absorption, this deference. He was conscious of watching for something in her that did not appear; and a first prescience of things anxious or untoward stirred in his quick sense.

'You may all say what you like,' said Marcella suddenly, putting down her cup, and letting her hand drop for emphasis on her knee; 'but you will never persuade me that game-preserving doesn't make life in the country much more difficult, and the difference between classes much wider and bitterer, than they need be.'

The remark cut across some rattling talk of Frank Leven's, who was in the first flush of the sportsman's ardour, and, though by no means without parts, could at the present moment apply his mind to little else than killing of one kind or another, unless it were to the chances of keeping his odious cousin out of Parliament.

Leven stared. Miss Boyce's speech seemed to him to have no sort of à propos. Aldous looked down upon her as he stood beside her, smiling.

'I wish you didn't trouble yourself so much about it,' he said.

'How can I help it?' she answered quickly; and then flushed, like one who has drawn attention indiscreetly to their own personal situation.

'Trouble herself!' echoed young Leven. 'Now, look here, Miss Boyce, will you come for a walk with me? I'll convince you, as I convinced those fellows over there. I know I could, and you won't give me the chance; it's too bad.'

'Oh, you!' she said, with a little shrug; 'what do you know about it? One might as well consult a gambler about gambling when he is in the middle of his first rush of luck. I have ten times more right to an opinion than you have. I can keep my head cool, and notice a hundred things that *you* would never see. I come fresh into your country life, and the first thing that strikes me is that the whole machinery of law and order seems to exist for nothing in the world but to protect your pheasants! There are policemen—to catch poachers; there are magistrates—to try them. To judge from the newspapers, at least, they have nothing else to do. And if *you* follow your sporting instincts, you are a very fine fellow, and everybody admires you. But if a shoemaker's son in Mellor follows his, he is a villain and a thief, and the policeman and the magistrate make for him at once.'

'But I don't steal his chickens!' cried the lad, choking with arguments and exasperation; 'and why should he steal my pheasants? I paid for the eggs, I paid for the hens to sit on 'em, I paid for the coops to rear them in, I paid the men to watch them, I paid for the barley to feed them with: why is he to be allowed to take my property, and I am to be sent to jail if I take his?'

'*Property!*' said Marcella scornfully. 'You can't settle everything nowadays by that big word. We are coming to put the public good before property. If the nation should decide to curtail your "right," as you call it, in the general interest, it will do it, and you will be left to scream.'

She had flung her arm round the back of her chair, and all her lithe young frame was tense with an eagerness, nay, an excitement, which drew Hallin's attention. It was more than was warranted by the conversation, he thought.

'Well, if you think the abolition of game preserving would be popular in the country, Miss Boyce, I'm certain you make a precious mistake,' cried Leven. 'Why, even you don't think it would be, do you, Mr. Hallin?' he said, appealing at random in his disgust.

'I don't know,' said Hallin, with his quiet smile. 'I rather think, on the whole, it would be. The farmers put up with it, but a great many of them don't like it. Things are mended since the Ground Game Act, but there are a good many grievances still left.'

'I should think there are!' said Marcella, eagerly, bending forward to him. 'I was talking to one of our farmers the other day whose land goes up to the edge of Lord Winterbourne's woods. "*They* don't keep their pheasants, miss," he said. "*I* do. I and my corn. If I didn't send a man up half-past five in the morning, when the ears begin to fill, there'd be nothing left for *us*." "Why don't you complain to the agent?" I said. "Complain! Lor' bless you, miss, you may complain till you're black in the face. I've allus found—an' I've been here, man and boy, thirty-two year—as how *Winterbournes generally best it*." There you have the whole thing in a nutshell. It's a tyranny—a tyranny of the rich.'

Flushed and sarcastic, she looked at Frank Leven ; but Hallin had an uncomfortable feeling that the sarcasm was not all meant for him. Aldous was sitting with his hands on his knees, and his head bent forward a little. Once, as the talk ran on, Hallin saw him raise his grey eyes to the girl beside him, who certainly did not notice it, and was not thinking of him. There was a curious pain and perplexity in the expression, but something else too—a hunger, a dependence, a yearning, that for an instant gripped the friend's heart.

'Well, I know Aldous doesn't agree with you, Miss Boyce,' cried Leven, looking about him in his indignation for some argument that should be final. 'You don't, do you, Aldous? You don't think the country would be the better, if we could do away with game to-morrow?'

'No more than I think it would be the better,' said Aldous quietly, 'if we could do away with gold plate and false hair to-morrow. There would be too many hungry goldsmiths and wig-makers on the streets.'

Marcella turned to him, half defiant, half softened.

'Of course, your point lies in *to-morrow*,' she said. 'I accept that. We can't carry reform by starving innocent people. But

the question is, what are we to work towards? Mayn't we regard
the game laws as one of the obvious crying abuses to be attacked
first—in the great campaign!—the campaign which is to bring
liberty and self-respect back to the country districts, and make the
labourer feel himself as much of a man as the squire?'

'What a head! What an attitude!' thought Hallin, half
repelled, half fascinated. 'But a girl that can talk politics—hostile
politics—to her lover, and mean them too—or am I inexperienced?
—and is it merely that she is so much interested in him that she
wants to be quarrelling with him?'

Aldous looked up. 'I am not *sure*,' he said, answering her.
'That is always my difficulty, you know,' and he smiled at her.
'Game preserving is not to me personally an attractive form of
private property, but it seems to me bound up with other forms,
and I want to see where the attack is going to lead me. But I
would protect your farmer—mind!—as zealously as you.'

Hallin caught the impatient quiver of the girl's lip. The tea
had just been taken away, and Marcella had gone to sit upon an
old sofa near the fire, whither Aldous had followed her. Wharton,
who had so far said nothing, had left his post of observation on the
hearthrug, and was sitting under the lamp balancing a paper-
knife with great attention on two fingers. In the half light Hallin
by chance saw a movement of Raeburn's hand towards Marcella's,
which lay hidden among the folds of her dress—quick resistance
on her part, then acquiescence. He felt a sudden pleasure in his
friend's small triumph.

'Aldous and I have worn these things threadbare many a
time,' he said, addressing his hostess. 'You don't know how
kind he is to my dreams. I am no sportsman and have no landowning relations, so he ought to bid me hold my tongue. But he
lets me rave. To me the simple fact is that *game preserving
creates crime*. Agricultural life is naturally simpler—might be, it
always seems to me, so much more easily moralised and fraternised
than the industrial form. And you split it up and poison it all by
the emphasis laid on this class pleasure. It is a natural pleasure,
you say. Perhaps it is—the survival, perhaps, of some primitive
instinct in our northern blood—but, if so, why should it be impossible for the rich to share it with the poor? I have little plans—
dreams. I throw them out sometimes to catch Aldous, but he
hardly rises to them!'

'Oh! I *say*,' broke in Frank Leven, who could really bear it no
longer. 'Now look here, Miss Boyce,—what do you think Mr.
Hallin wants? It is just sheer lunacy—it really is—though I
know I'm impertinent, and he's a great man. But I do declare he

wants Aldous to give up a big common there is—oh! over beyond
Girtstone, down in the plain—on Lord Maxwell's estate, and make
a *labourers'* shoot of it! Now, I ask you! And he vows he
doesn't see why they shouldn't rear pheasants if they choose to
club and pay for it. Well, I will say that much for him, Aldous
didn't see his way to *that*, though he isn't the kind of Conservative
I want to see in Parliament by a long way. Besides, it's such stuff!
They say sport brutalises *us*, and then they want to go and con-
taminate the labourer. But we won't take the responsibility.
We've got our own vices, and we'll stick to them; we're used to
them; but we won't hand them on: we'd scorn the action.'

The flushed young barbarian, driven to bay, was not to be resisted. Marcella laughed heartily, and Hallin laid an affectionate
hand on the boy's shoulder, patting him as though he were a
restive horse.

'Yes, I remember I was puzzled as to the details of Hallin's
scheme,' said Aldous, his mouth twitching. 'I wanted to know
who was to pay for the licences; how game enough for the
number of applicants was to be got without preserving; and how
men earning twelve or fourteen shillings a week were to pay a
keeper. Then I asked a clergyman who has a living near this
common what he thought would be the end of it. "Well," he
said, "the first day they'd shoot every animal on the place; the
second day they'd shoot each other. Universal carnage—I should
say that would be about the end of it." These were trifles, of
course—details.'

Hallin shook his head serenely.

'I still maintain,' he said, 'that a little practical ingenuity
might have found a way.'

'And I will support you,' said Wharton, laying down the paper-
knife and bending over to Hallin, 'with good reason. For
three years and a few months just such an idea as you describe
has been carried out on my own estate, and it has not worked
badly at all.'

'There!' cried Marcella. 'There! I knew something could
be done, if there was a will. I have always felt it.'

She half turned to Aldous, then bent forward instead as though
listening eagerly for what more Wharton might say, her face all
alive, and eloquent.

'Of course, there was nothing to shoot!' exclaimed Frank Leven.

'On the contrary,' said Wharton, smiling. 'We are in the
middle of a famous partridge country.'

'How your neighbours must dote on you!' cried the boy. But
Wharton took no notice.

'And my father preserved strictly,' he went on. 'It is quite a simple story. When I inherited three years ago I thought the whole thing detestable, and determined I wouldn't be responsible for keeping it up. So I called the estate together—farmers and labourers—and we worked out a plan. There are keepers, but they are the estate servants, not mine. Everybody has his turn according to the rules—I and my friends along with the rest. Not everybody can shoot every year, but everybody gets his chance, and, moreover, a certain percentage of all the game killed is public property, and is distributed every year according to a regular order.'

'Who pays the keepers?' interrupted Leven.

'I do,' said Wharton, smiling again. 'Mayn't I—for the present—do what I will with mine own? I return in their wages some of my ill-gotten gains as a landowner. It is all makeshift, of course.'

'I understand!' exclaimed Marcella, nodding to him—'you could not be a Venturist and keep up game preserving?'

Wharton met her bright eye with a half deprecating, reserved air.

'You are right, of course,' he said drily. 'For a Socialist to be letting his keepers run in a man earning twelve shillings a week for knocking over a rabbit would have been a little strong. No one can be consistent in my position—in any landowner's position —it is impossible ; still, thank Heaven, one can deal with the most glaring matters. As Mr. Raeburn said, however, all this game business is, of course, a mere incident of the general land and property system, as you will hear me expound when you come to that meeting you promised me to honour.'

He stooped forward, scanning her with smiling deference. Marcella felt the man's hand that held her own suddenly tighten an instant. Then Aldous released her, and rising walked towards the fire.

'You're *not* going to one of his meetings, Miss Boyce !' cried Frank in angry incredulity.

Marcella hesitated an instant, half angry with Wharton. Then she reddened and threw back her dark head with the passionate gesture Hallin had already noticed as characteristic.

'Mayn't I go where I belong?' she said—'where my convictions lead me?'

There was a moment's awkward silence. Then Hallin got up. 'Miss Boyce, may we see the house? Aldous has told me much of it.'

Presently, in the midst of their straggling progress through the half-furnished rooms of the garden front, preceded by the shy footman carrying a lamp, which served for little more than to make darkness visible, Marcella found herself left behind with Aldous. As soon as she felt that they were alone, she realised a jar between herself and him.   His manner was much as usual, but there was an underlying effort and difficulty which her sensitiveness caught at once.   A sudden wave of girlish trouble—remorse—swept over her.   In her impulsiveness she moved close to him as they were passing through her mother's little sitting-room, and put her hand on his arm.

'I don't think I was nice just now,' she said stammering.   'I didn't mean it.   I seem to be always driven into opposition—into a feeling of war—when you are so good to me—so much too good to me!'

Aldous had turned at her first word.   With a long breath, as it were of unspeakable relief, he caught her in his arms vehemently, passionately.   So far she had been very shrinking and maidenly with him in their solitary moments, and he had been all delicate chivalry and respect, tasting to the full the exquisiteness of each fresh advance towards intimacy, towards lover's privilege, adoring her, perhaps, all the more for her reserve, her sudden flights, and stiffenings.   But to-night he asked no leave, and in her astonishment she was almost passive.

'Oh, do let me go!' she cried at last, trying to disengage herself completely.

'No!' he said with emphasis, still holding her hand firmly. 'Come and sit down here.   They will look after themselves.'

He put her, whether she would or no, into an armchair and knelt beside her.

'Did you think it was hardly kind,' he said with a quiver of voice he could not repress, 'to let me hear for the first time, in public, that you had promised to go to one of that man's meetings after refusing again and again to come to any of mine?'

'Do you want to forbid me to go?' she said quickly.   There was a feeling in her which would have been almost relieved, for the moment, if he had said yes.

'By no means,' he said, steadily.   'That was not our compact. But—guess for yourself what I want!   Do you think'—he paused a moment—'do you think I put nothing of myself into my public life—into these meetings among the people who have known me from a boy?   Do you think it is all a convention—that my feeling, my conscience, remain outside?   You can't think that!   But if not, how can I bear to live what is to be so large a part of my life out of your ken and sight?   I know—I know—you warned me amply

—you can't agree with me. But there is much besides intellectual agreement possible—much that would help and teach us both—if only we are together—not separated—not holding aloof——'

He stopped, watching all the changes of her face. She was gulfed in a deep wave of half-repentant feeling, remembering all his generosity, his forbearance, his devotion.

'When are you speaking next?' she half whispered. In the dim light her softened pose, the gentle, sudden relaxation of every line, were an intoxication.

'Next week—Friday—at Gairsley. Hallin and Aunt Neta are coming.'

'Will Miss Raeburn take me?'

His grey eyes shone upon her, and he kissed her hand.

'Mr. Hallin won't speak for you!' she said, after the silence, with a return of mischief.

'Don't be so sure! He has given me untold help in the drafting of my Bill. If I didn't call myself a Conservative, he would vote for me to-morrow. That's the absurdity of it. Do you know, I hear them coming back?'

'One thing,' she said hastily, drawing him towards her, and then holding him back, as though shrinking always from the feeling she could so readily evoke. 'I must say it; you oughtn't to give me so much money; it is too much. Suppose I use it for things you don't like?'

'You won't,' he said gaily.

She tried to push the subject further, but he would not have it.

'I am all for free discussion,' he said in the same tone; 'but sometimes debate must be stifled. I am going to stifle it!'

And stooping, he kissed her, lightly, tremulously. His manner showed her once more what she was to him—how sacred, how beloved. First it touched and shook her; then she sprang up with a sudden disagreeable sense of moral disadvantage—inferiority—coming she knew not whence, and undoing for the moment all that buoyant consciousness of playing the magnanimous, disinterested part which had possessed her throughout the talk in the drawing-room.

The others reappeared, headed by their lamp: Wharton first, scanning the two who had lingered behind, with his curious eyes, so blue and brilliant under the white forehead and the curls.

'We have been making the wildest shots at your ancestors, Miss Boyce,' he said. 'Frank professed to know everything about the pictures, and turned out to know nothing. I shall ask for some special coaching to-morrow morning. May I engage you at ten o'clock?'

Marcella made some evasive answer, and they all sauntered back to the drawing-room.

Shall you be at work to-morrow, Raeburn?' said Wharton.

'Probably,' said Aldous drily. Marcella, struck by the tone, looked back, and caught an expression and bearing which were as yet new to her in the speaker. She supposed they represented the haughtiness natural in the man of birth and power towards the intruder, who is also the opponent.

Instantly the combative critical mood returned upon her, and the impulse to assert herself by protecting Wharton. His manner throughout the talk in the drawing-room had been, she declared to herself, excellent—modest, and self-restrained, comparing curiously with the boyish egotism and self-abandonment he had shown in their *tête-à-tête*.

'Why, there is Mr. Boyce,' exclaimed Wharton, hurrying forward as they entered the drawing-room.

There, indeed, on the sofa was the master of the house, more ghastly black and white than ever, and prepared to claim to the utmost the tragic pre-eminence of illness. He shook hands coldly with Aldous, who asked after his health with the kindly brevity natural to the man who wants no effusions for himself in public or personal matters, and concludes therefore that other people desire none.

'You *are* better, papa?' said Marcella, taking his hand.

'Certainly, my dear—better for morphia. Don't talk of me. I have got my death warrant, but I hope I can take it quietly. Evelyn, I *specially* asked to have that thin cushion brought down from my dressing-room. It is strange that no one pays any attention to my wants.'

Mrs. Boyce, almost as white, Marcella now saw, as her husband, moved forward from the fire, where she had been speaking to Hallin, took a cushion from a chair near, exactly similar to the one he missed, and changed his position a little.

'It is just the feather's weight of change that makes the difference, isn't it?' said Wharton softly, sitting down beside the invalid.

Mr. Boyce turned a mollified countenance upon the speaker, and being now free from pain gave himself up to the amusement of hearing his guest talk. Wharton devoted himself, employing all his best arts.

'Dr. Clarke is not anxious about him,' Mrs. Boyce said in a low voice to Marcella as they moved away. 'He does not think the attack will return for a long while, and he has given me the means of stopping it if it does come back.'

'How tired you look!' said Aldous, coming up to them, and speaking in the same undertone. 'Will you not let Marcella take you to rest?'

He was always deeply, unreasonably touched by any sign of stoicism, of defied suffering in women. Mrs. Boyce had proved it many times already. On the present occasion she put his sympathy by, but she lingered to talk with him. Hallin from a distance noticed first of all her tall thinness and fairness, and her wonderful dignity of carriage; then the cordiality of her manner to her future son-in-law. Marcella stood by listening, her young shoulders somewhat stiffly set. Her consciousness of her mother's respect and admiration for the man she was to marry was, oddly enough, never altogether pleasant to her. It brought with it a certain discomfort, a certain wish to argue things out.

Hallin and Aldous parted with Frank Leven at Mellor gate, and turned homeward together under a starry heaven already whitening to the coming moon.

'Do you know that man Wharton is getting an extraordinary hold upon the London working men?' said Hallin. 'I have heard him tell that story of the game preserving before. He was speaking for one of the Radical candidates at Hackney, and I happened to be there. It brought down the house. The *rôle* of your Socialist aristocrat, of your land-nationalising landlord, is a very telling one.'

'And comparatively easy,' said Aldous, 'when you know that neither Socialism nor land-nationalisation will come in your time!'

'Oh! so you think him altogether a windbag?'

Aldous hesitated and laughed.

'I have certainly no reason to suspect him of principles. His conscience as a boy was of pretty elastic stuff.'

'You may be unfair to him,' said Hallin quickly. Then, after a pause: 'How long is he staying at Mellor?'

'About a week, I believe,' said Aldous shortly. 'Mr. Boyce has taken a fancy to him.'

They walked on in silence, and then Aldous turned to his friend in distress.

'You know, Hallin, this wind is much too cold for you. You are the most wilful of men. Why would you walk?'

'Hold your tongue, sir, and listen to me. I think your Marcella is beautiful, and as interesting as she is beautiful. There!'

Aldous started, then turned a grateful face upon him.

'You must get to know her well,' he said, but with some constraint.

'Of course. I wonder,' said Hallin, musing, 'whom she has

got hold of among the Venturists.   Shall you persuade her to come out of that, do you think, Aldous?'

'No!' said Raeburn, cheerfully.   'Her sympathies and convictions go with them.'

Then, as they passed through the village, he began to talk of quite other things—college friends, a recent volume of philosophical essays, and so on.   Hallin, accustomed and jealously accustomed as he was to be the one person in the world with whom Raeburn talked freely, would not to-night have done or said anything to force a strong man's reserve.   But his own mind was full of anxiety.

CHAPTER IV

'I *LOVE* this dilapidation!' said Wharton, pausing for a moment with his back against the door he had just shut.   'Only it makes me long to take off my coat and practise some honest trade or other—plastering, or carpentering, or painting.   What useless drones we upper classes are !   Neither you nor I could mend that ceiling or patch this floor—to save our lives.'

They were in the disused library.   It was now the last room westwards of the garden front, but in reality it was part of the older house, and had been only adapted and rebuilt by that eighteenth-century Marcella whose money had been so gracefully and vainly lavished on giving dignity to her English husband's birthplace. The roof had been raised and domed to match the 'Chinese room,' at the expense of some small rooms on the upper floor ; and the windows and doors had been suited to eighteenth-century taste. But the old books in the old latticed shelves which the Puritan founder of the family had bought in the days of the Long Parliament were still there ; so were the chairs in which that worthy had sat to read a tract of Milton's or of Baxter's, or the table at which he had penned his letters to Hampden or Fairfax, or to his old friend—on the wrong side—Edmund Verney the standard-bearer. Only the worm-eaten shelves were dropping from their supports, and the books lay in mouldy confusion ; the roofs had great holes and gaps, whence the laths hung dismally down, and bats came flitting in the dusk ; and there were rotten places in the carpetless floor.

'I have tried my best,' said Marcella dolefully, stooping to look at a hole in the floor.   'I got a bit of board and some nails, and tried to mend some of these places myself.   But I only broke the rotten wood away ; and papa was angry, and said I did more harm than good. I did get a carpenter to mend some of the chairs; but one doesn't know where to begin. I have cleaned and mended some of the books, but——'

She looked sadly round the musty, forlorn place.

'But not so well, I am afraid, as any second-hand bookseller's apprentice could have done it,' said Wharton, shaking his head 'It's maddening to think what duffers we gentlefolks are!'

'Why do you harp on that?' said Marcella quickly. She had been taking him over the house, and was in twenty minds again as to whether and how much she liked him.

'Because I have been reading some Board of Trade reports before breakfast,' said Wharton, 'on one or two of the Birmingham industries in particular. Goodness! what an amount of knowledge and skill and resource these fellows have that I go about calling the "lower orders." I wonder how long they are going to let me rule over them!'

'I suppose brain-power and education count for something still?' said Marcella half scornfully.

'I am greatly obliged to the world for thinking so,' said Wharton with emphasis, 'and for thinking so about the particular kind of brain-power I happen to possess, which is the point. The processes by which a Birmingham jeweller makes the wonderful things which we attribute to "French taste" when we see them in the shops of the Rue de la Paix are, of course, mere imbecility—compared to my performances in Responsions. Lucky for *me*, at any rate, that the world has decided it so. I get a good time of it —and the Birmingham jeweller calls me "sir."'

'Oh! the skilled labour! that can take care of itself, and won't go on calling you "sir" much longer. But what about the unskilled —the people here for instance—the villagers? We talk of their governing themselves; we wish it, and work for it. But which of us *really* believes that they are fit for it, or that they are ever going to get along without *our* brain-power?'

'No—poor souls!' said Wharton with a peculiar vibrating emphasis. '"*By their stripes we are healed, by their death we have lived.*" Do you remember your Carlyle?'

They had entered one of the bays formed by the bookcases which on either side of the room projected from the wall at regular intervals, and were standing by one of the windows which looked out on the great avenue. Beside the window on either side hung a small portrait—in the one case of an elderly man in a wig, in the other of a young, dark-haired woman.

'Plenty in general, but nothing in particular,' said Marcella laughing. 'Quote.'

He was leaning against the angle formed by the wall and the bookcase. The half-serious, half-provocative intensity of his blue eyes under the brow which drooped forward contrasted with the careless, well-appointed ease of his general attitude and dress.

'"*Two men I honour, and no third,*"' he said, quoting in a slightly dragging, vibrating voice : '"*First, the toilworn craftsman that with earth-made implement laboriously conquers the earth and makes her man's.—Hardly-entreated Brother! For us was thy back so bent, for us were thy straight limbs and fingers so deformed; thou wert our conscript, on whom the lot fell, and fighting our battles wert so marred.*" Heavens! how the words swing! But it is great nonsense, you know, for you and me—Venturists—to be maundering like this. Charity—benevolence—that is all Carlyle is leading up to. He merely wants the cash nexus supplemented by a few good offices. But we want something much more unpleasant! "Keep your subscriptions—hand over your dividends —turn out of your land—and go to work!" Nowadays society is trying to get out of doing what *we* want, by doing what Carlyle wanted.'

'*Do* you want it?' said Marcella.

'I don't know,' he said, laughing. 'It won't come in our time.' Her lip showed her scorn.

'That's what we all think. Meanwhile you will perhaps admit that a little charity greases the wheels.'

'*You* must, because you are a woman ; and women are made for charity—and aristocracy.'

'Do you suppose you know so much about women?' she asked him, rather hotly. 'I notice it is always the assumption of the people who make most mistakes.'

'Oh! I know enough to steer by!' he said smiling, with a little inclination of his curly head, as though to propitiate her. 'How like you are to that portrait!'

Marcella started, and saw that he was pointing to the woman's portrait beside the window—looking from it to his hostess with a close considering eye.

'That was an ancestress of mine,' she said coldly, 'an Italian lady. She was rich and musical. Her money built these rooms along the garden, and these are her music books.'

She showed him that the shelves against which she was leaning were full of old music.

'Italian!' he said, lifting his eyebrows. 'Ah, that explains. Do you know—that you have all the qualities of a leader!'—and he moved away a yard from her, studying her—'mixed blood—one

must always have that to fire and fuse the English paste—and then
—but no ! that won't do—I should offend you.'

Her first instinct was one of annoyance—a wish to send him
about his business, or rather to return him to her mother who would
certainly keep him in order.   Instead, however, she found herself
saying, as she looked carelessly out of window—

'Oh ! go on.'

'Well, then,' he drew himself up suddenly and wheeled round
upon her.   'You have the gift of compromise.   That is invaluable
—that will take you far.'

'Thank you !' she said, 'thank you ! I know what that means
—from a Venturist.   You think me a mean, insincere person !'

He started, then recovered himself and came to lean against
the bookshelves beside her.

'I mean nothing of the sort,' he said, in quite a different manner, with a sort of gentle and personal emphasis.   'But—may I
explain myself, Miss Boyce, in a room with a fire ?   I can see you
shivering under your fur.'

For the frost still reigned supreme outside, and the white grass
and trees threw chill reflected lights into the forsaken library.
Marcella controlled a pulse of excitement that had begun to beat
in her, admitted that it was certainly cold, and led the way through
a side door to a little flagged parlour belonging to the oldest portion of the house, where, however, a great log-fire was burning,
and some chairs drawn up round it.   She took one and let the fur
wrap she had thrown about her for their promenade through the
disused rooms drop from her shoulders.   It lay about her in full
brown folds, giving special dignity to her slim height and proud
head.   Wharton, glancing about in his curious inquisitive way, now
at the neglected pictures, now on the walls, now at the old oak
chairs and chests, now at her, said to himself that she was a
splendid and inspiring creature.   She seemed to be on the verge
of offence with him too, half the time, which was stimulating.   She
would have liked, he thought, to play the great lady with him
already, as Aldous Raeburn's betrothed.   But he had so far
managed to keep her off that plane—and intended to go on
doing so.

'Well, I meant this,' he said, leaning against the old stone
chimney and looking down upon her ; 'only *don't* be offended with
me, please.   You are a Socialist, and you are going—some day—
to be Lady Maxwell.   Those combinations are only possible to
women.   They can sustain them, because they are imaginative—
not logical.'

She flushed.

'And you,' she said, breathing quickly, 'are a Socialist and a landlord. What is the difference?'

He laughed.

'Ah! but I have no gift—I can't ride the two horses, as you will be able to—quite honestly. There's the difference. And the consequence is that with my own class I am an outcast—they all hate me. But you will have power as Lady Maxwell—and power as a Socialist—because you will give and take. Half your time you will act as Lady Maxwell should, the other half like a Venturist. And, as I said, it will give you power—a modified power. But men are less clever at that kind of thing.'

'Do you mean to say,' she asked him abruptly, 'that you have given up the luxuries and opportunities of your class?'

He shifted his position a little.

'That is a different matter,' he said after a moment. 'We Socialists are all agreed, I think, that no man can be a Socialist by himself. Luxuries, for the present, are something personal, individual. It is only a man's "public form" that matters. And there, as I said before, I have no gift!—I have not a relation or an old friend in the world that has not turned his back upon me—as you might see for yourself yesterday! My class has renounced me already—which, after all, is a weakness.'

'So you pity yourself?' she said.

'By no means! We all choose the part in life that amuses us —that brings us most *thrill*. I get most thrill out of throwing myself into the workmen's war—much more than I could ever get, you will admit, out of dancing attendance on my very respectable cousins. My mother taught me to see everything dramatically. We have no drama in England at the present moment worth a cent; so I amuse myself with this great tragi-comedy of the working-class movement. It stirs, pricks, interests me, from morning till night. I feel the great rough elemental passions in it, and it delights me to know that every day brings us nearer to some great outburst, to scenes and struggles at any rate that will make us all look alive. I am like a child with the best of its cake to come, but with plenty in hand already. Ah!—stay still a moment, Miss Boyce!'

To her amazement he stooped suddenly towards her; and she, looking down, saw that a corner of her light black dress, which had been overhanging the low stone fender, was in flames, and that he was putting it out with his hands. She made a movement to rise, alarmed lest the flames should leap to her face—her hair. But he, releasing one hand for an instant from its task of twisting and rolling the skirt upon itself, held her heavily down.

'Don't move; I will have it out in a moment. You won't be burnt.'

And in a second more she was looking at a ragged brown hole in her dress; and at him, standing, smiling, before the fire, and wrapping a handkerchief round some of the fingers of his left hand.

'You have burnt yourself, Mr. Wharton?'

'A little.'

'I will go and get something—what would you like?'

'A little olive oil if you have some, and a bit of lint—but don't trouble yourself.'

She flew to find her mother's maid, calling and searching on her way for Mrs. Boyce herself, but in vain. Mrs. Boyce had disappeared after breakfast, and was probably helping her husband to dress.

In a minute or so Marcella ran downstairs again, bearing various medicaments. She sped to the Stone Parlour, her cheek and eye glowing.

'Let me do it for you.'

'If you please,' said Wharton meekly.

She did her best, but she was not skilful with her fingers, and this close contact with him somehow excited her.

'There,' she said, laughing and releasing him. 'Of course, if I were a work-girl I should have done it better. They are not going to be very bad, I think.'

'What, the burns? Oh, no! They will have recovered, I am afraid, long before your dress.'

'Oh, my dress! yes, it is deplorable. I will go and change it.'

She turned to go, but she lingered instead, and said, with an odd introductory laugh:

'I believe you saved my life!'

'Well, I am glad I was here. You might have lost self-possession—even *you* might, you know!—and then it would have been serious.'

'Anyway'—her voice was still uncertain—'I might have been disfigured—disfigured for life!'

'I don't know why you should dwell upon it now it's done with,' he declared, smiling.

'It would be strange, wouldn't it, if I took it quite for granted—all in the day's work?' She held out her hand: 'I am grateful—please.'

He bowed over it laughing, again with that eighteenth-century air which might have become a Chevalier des Grieux.

'May I exact a reward?'

'Ask it.'

'Will you take me down with you to your village? I know you are going. I must walk on afterwards and catch a midday train to Widrington. I have an appointment there at two o'clock. But perhaps you will introduce me to one or two of your poor people first?'

Marcella assented, went upstairs, changed her dress, and put on her walking things, more than half inclined all the time to press her mother to go with them. She was a little unstrung and tremulous, pursued by a feeling that she was somehow letting herself go, behaving disloyally and indecorously towards whom?—towards Aldous? But how, or why? She did not know. But there was a curious sense of lost bloom, lost dignity, combined with an odd wish that Mr. Wharton were not going away for the day. In the end, however, she left her mother undisturbed.

By the time they were half way to the village, Marcella's uncomfortable feelings had all passed away. Without knowing it, she was becoming too much absorbed in her companion to be self-critical, so long as they were together. It seemed to her, however, before they had gone more than a few hundred yards that he was taking advantage—presuming on what had happened. He offended her taste, her pride, her dignity, in a hundred ways, she discovered. At the same time it was *she* who was always on the defensive—protecting her dreams, her acts, her opinions, against the constant fire of his half-ironical questions, which seemed to leave her no time at all to carry the war into the enemy's country. He put her through a quick cross-examination about the village, its occupations, the incomes of the people, its local charities and institutions, what she hoped to do for it, what she would do if she could, what she thought it *possible* to do. She answered first reluctantly, then eagerly, her pride all alive to show that she was not merely ignorant and amateurish. But it was no good. In the end he made her feel as Antony Craven had constantly done—that she knew nothing exactly, that she had not mastered the conditions of any one of the social problems she was talking about; that not only was her reading of no account, but that she had not even managed to *see* these people, to interpret their lives under her very eyes, with any large degree of insight.

Especially was he merciless to all the Lady Bountiful pose, which meant so much to her imagination—not in words so much as in manner. He let her see that all the doling and shepherding and advising that still pleased her fancy looked to him the merest temporary palliative, and irretrievably tainted, even at that, with some vulgar feeling or other. All that the well-to-do could do for the poor under the present state of society was but a niggardly quit-rent ; as for any relation of 'superior' and 'inferior' in the business, or of any social desert attaching to these precious efforts of the upper class to daub the gaps in the ruinous social edifice for which they were themselves responsible, he did not attempt to conceal his scorn. If you did not do these things, so much the worse for you when the working class came to its own ; if you did do them, the burden of debt was hardly diminished, and the rope was still left on your neck.

Now Marcella herself had on one or two occasions taken a malicious pleasure in flaunting these doctrines, or some of them, under Miss Raeburn's eyes. But somehow, as applied to herself, they were disagreeable. Each of us is to himself a 'special case' ; and she saw the other side. Hence a constant soreness of feeling ; a constant recalling of the argument to the personal point of view ; and through it all a curious growth of intimacy, a rubbing away of barriers. She had felt herself of no account before, intellectually, in Aldous's company, as we know. But then how involuntary on his part, and how counterbalanced by that passionate idealism of his love, which glorified every petty impulse in her to the noblest proportions ! Under Wharton's Socratic method, she was conscious at times of the most wild and womanish desires, worthy of her childhood—to cry, to go into a passion !—and when they came to the village, and every human creature, old and young, dropped its obsequious curtsey as they passed, she could first have beaten them for so degrading her, and the next moment felt a feverish pleasure in thus parading her petty power before a man who in his doctrinaire pedantry had no sense of poetry, or of the dear old natural relations of country life.

They went first to Mrs. Jellison's, to whom Marcella wished to unfold her workshop scheme.

'Don't let me keep you,' she said to Wharton coldly, as they neared the cottage, 'I know you have to catch your train.'

Wharton consulted his watch. He had to be at a local station some two miles off within an hour.

'Oh ! I have time,' he said. 'Do take me in, Miss Boyce. I have made acquaintance with these people so far, as my constituents—now show them to me as your subjects. Besides, I am an observer. I "collect" peasants. They are my study.'

'They are not my subjects, but my friends,' she said with the same stiffness.

They found Mrs. Jellison having her dinner. The lively old woman was sitting close against her bit of fire, on her left a small deal table which held her cold potatoes and cold bacon; on her right a tiny window and window-sill whereon lay her coil of 'plait' and the simple straw-splitting machine she had just been working. When Marcella had taken the only other chair the hovel contained, nothing else remained for Wharton but to flatten himself as closely against the door as he might.

'I'm sorry I can't bid yer take a cheer,' said Mrs. Jellison to him, 'but what yer han't got yer can't give, so I don't trouble my head about nothink.'

Wharton applauded her with easy politeness, and then gave himself, with folded arms, to examining the cottage while Marcella talked. It might be ten feet broad, he thought, by six feet in one part and eight feet in another. The roof was within little more than an inch of his head. The stairway in the corner was falling to pieces; he wondered how the woman got up safely to her bed at night; custom, he supposed, can make even old bones agile.

Meanwhile Marcella was unfolding the project of the straw-plaiting workshop that she and Lady Winterbourne were about to start. Mrs. Jellison put on her spectacles apparently that she might hear the better, pushed away her dinner in spite of her visitors' civilities, and listened with a bright and beady eye.

'An' yer agoin to pay me one a' sixpence a score, where I now gits ninepence. And I'll not have to tramp it into town no more—you'll send a man round. And who is it agoin to pay me, miss, if you'll excuse me askin?'

'Lady Winterbourne and I,' said Marcella smiling. 'We're going to employ this village and two others, and make as good business of it as we can. But we're going to begin by giving the workers better wages, and in time we hope to teach them the higher kinds of work.'

'Lor!' said Mrs. Jellison. 'But I'm not one o' them as kin do with changes.' She took up her plait and looked at it thoughtfully. 'Eighteen-pence a score. It wor that rate when I wor a girl. An' it ha been dibble—dibble—iver sense; a penny off here, an' a penny off there, an' a hard job to keep a bite ov anythink in your mouth.'

'Then I may put down your name among our workers, Mrs. Jellison?' said Marcella, rising and smiling down upon her.

'Oh lor, no; I niver said that,' said Mrs. Jellison hastily. 'I don't hold wi' shilly-shallyin wi' yer means o' livin. I've took my plait to Jimmy Gedge—'im an' 'is son, fust shop on yer right hand when yer git into town—twenty-five year, summer and winter—me an' three other women, as give me a penny a journey for takin theirs. If I wor to go messin about wi' Jimmy Gedge, Lor bless yer, I should 'ear ov it—oh ! I shoulden sleep o' nights for thinkin o' how Jimmy ud serve me out when I wor least egspectin ov it. He's a queer un. No, miss, thank yer kindly ; but I think I'll bide.'

Marcella, amazed, began to argue a little, to expound the many attractions of the new scheme. Greatly to her annoyance, Wharton came forward to her help, guaranteeing the solvency and permanence of her new partnership, in glib and pleasant phrase, wherein her angry fancy suspected at once the note of irony. But Mrs. Jellison held firm, embroidering her negative, indeed, with her usual cheerful chatter, but sticking to it all the same. At last there was no way of saving dignity but to talk of something else and go—above all, to talk of something else before going, lest the would-be benefactor should be thought a petty tyrant.

'Oh, Johnnie ?—thank yer, miss—'e's an owdacious young villain as iver I seed—but *clever*—lor, you'd need 'ave eyes in yer back to look after '*im*. An' *coaxin* ! "'Aven't yer brought me no sweeties, Gran'ma ?" "No, my dear," says I. "But iv you was to *look*, Gran'ma—in both your pockets, Gran'ma—iv you was to let *me* look ?" It's a sharp un. Isabella, she don't 'old wi sweetstuff, she says, sich a pack o' nonsense. She'd stuff herself sick when she wor 'is age. Why shouldn't *ee* be 'appy, same as her ? There ain't much to make a child 'appy in *that* 'ouse. Westall, ee's that mad about them poachers over Tudley End ; ee's like a wild bull at 'ome. I told Isabella ee'd come to knockin ov her about *some* day, though ee did speak so oily when he wor a courtin. Now she knows as I kin see a thing or two,' said Mrs. Jellison, significantly. Her manner, Wharton noticed, kept always the same gay philosophy, whatever subject turned up.

'Why, that's an old story—that Tudley End business,' said Marcella, rising. 'I should have thought Westall might have got over it by now.'

'But, bless yer, ee says it's goin on as lively as iver. Ee says ee knows they're set on grabbin the birds t'other side the estate, over beyond Mellor way—ee's got wind of it—an ee's watchin night an' day to see they don't do him no bad turn *this* month, bekase o' the big shoot they allus has in January. An' lor, ee do speak drefful bad o' *soom* folks,' said Mrs. Jellison with an amused expression. 'You know some on 'em, miss, don't yer ?' And the old woman, who had begun toying with her potatoes, slanted her fork over her shoulder so as to point towards the Hurds' cottage, whereof the snow-laden roof could be seen conspicuously through the little lattice beside her, making sly eyes the while at her visitor.

'I don't believe a word of it,' said Marcella impatiently. 'Hurd has been in good work since October, and has no need to poach. Westall has a down on him. You may tell him I think so, if you like.'

'That I will,' said Mrs. Jellison cheerfully, opening the door for them. 'There's nobody makes 'im 'ear the trëuth, nobbut me. I *loves* naggin ov 'im, ee's that masterful. But ee don't master *me* !'

'A gay old thing,' said Wharton as they shut the gate behind them. 'How she does enjoy the human spectacle. And obstinate too. But you will find the younger ones more amenable.'

'Of course,' said Marcella, with dignity. 'I have a great many names already. The old people are always difficult. But Mrs Jellison will come round.'

'Are you going in here ?'

'Please.'

Wharton knocked at the Hurds' door, and Mrs. Hurd opened.

The cottage was thick with smoke. The chimney only drew when the door was left open. But the wind to-day was so bitter that mother and children preferred the smoke to the draught. Marcella soon made out the poor little bronchitic boy, sitting coughing by the fire, and Mrs. Hurd busied with some washing. She introduced Wharton, who, as before, stood for some time, hat in hand, studying the cottage. Marcella was perfectly conscious of it, and a blush rose to her cheek while she talked to Mrs. Hurd. For both this and Mrs. Jellison's hovel were her father's property and somewhat highly rented.

Minta Hurd said eagerly that she would join the new straw-plaiting, and went on to throw out a number of hurried, half-coherent remarks about the state of the trade past and present, leaning meanwhile against the table and endlessly drying her hands on the towel she had taken up when her visitors came in.

Her manner was often nervous and flighty in these days. She never looked happy ; but Marcella put it down to health or natural querulousness of character. Yet both she and the children were clearly better nourished, except Willie, in whom the tubercular tendency was fast gaining on the child's strength.

Altogether Marcella was proud of her work, and her eager interest in this little knot of people whose lives she had shaped was more possessive than ever. Hurd, indeed, was often silent and secretive ; but she put down her difficulties with him to our odious system of class differences, against which in her own way she was struggling. One thing delighted her—that he seemed to take more and more interest in the labour questions she discussed with him, and in that fervid, exuberant literature she provided him with. Moreover, he now went to all Mr. Wharton's meetings that were held within reasonable distance of Mellor ; and, as she said to Aldous with a little laugh, which, however, was not unsweet, *he* had found her man work—*she* had robbed his candidate of a vote.

Wharton listened a while to her talk with Minta, smiled a little, unperceived of Marcella, at the young mother's docilities of manner and phrase ; then turned his attention of the little hunched and coughing object by the fire.

' Are you very bad, little man ? '

The white-faced child looked up, a dreary look, revealing a patient, melancholy soul. He tried to answer, but coughed instead.

Wharton, moving towards him, saw a bit of ragged white paper lying on the ground, which had been torn from a grocery parcel.

'Would you like something to amuse you a bit—Ugh ! this smoke ! Come round here, it won't catch us so much. Now, then, what do you say to a doggie,—two doggies ? '

The child stared, let himself be lifted on the stranger's knee, and did his very utmost to stop coughing. But when he had succeeded, his quick panting breaths still shook his tiny frame and Wharton's knee.

' Hm—give him two months or thereabouts ! ' thought Wharton. 'What a beastly hole !—one room up, and one down, like the other, only a shade larger. Damp, insanitary, cold—bad water, bad drainage, I'll be bound—bad everything. That girl may well try her little best. And I go making up to that man Boyce ! What for ? Old spites ?—new spites ?—which ?—or both ! '

Meanwhile his rapid skilful fingers were tearing, pinching, and shaping ; and in a very few minutes there, upon his free knee, stood the most enticing doggie of pinched paper, a hound in full course, with long ears and stretching legs.

The child gazed at it with ravishment, put out a weird hand, touched it, stroked it, and then, as he looked back at Wharton, the most exquisite smile dawned in his saucer-blue eyes.

' What ? did you like it, grasshopper ? ' cried Wharton, enchanted by the beauty of the look, his own colour mounting. ' Then you shall have another.'

And he twisted and turned his piece of fresh paper, till there, beside the first, stood a second fairy animal—a greyhound this time, with arching neck and sharp long nose.

' There's two on 'em at Westall's ! ' cried the child hoarsely, clutching at his treasures in an ecstasy.

Mrs. Hurd, at the other end of the cottage, started as she heard the name. Marcella noticed it ; and with her eager sympathetic look began at once to talk of Hurd and the works at the Court. She understood they were doing grand things, and that the work would last all the winter. Minta answered hurriedly and with a curious choice of phrases. ' Oh! he didn't have nothing to say against it.' Mr. Brown, the steward, seemed satisfied. All that she said was somehow irrelevant ; and, to Marcella's annoyance, plaintive as usual. Wharton, with the boy inside his arm, turned his head an instant to listen.

Marcella, having thought of repeating, without names, some of Mrs. Jellison's gossip, then shrank from it. He had promised her, she thought to herself with a proud delicacy ; and she was not going to treat the word of a working man as different from anybody else's.

So she fastened her cloak again, which she had thrown open in the stifling air of the cottage, and turned both to call her companion and give a smile or two to the sick boy.

But, as she did so, she stood amazed at the spectacle of Wharton and the child. Then, moving up to them, she perceived the menagerie—for it had grown to one—on Wharton's knee.

' You didn't guess I had such tricks,' he said smiling.

' But they are so good—so artistic ! ' She took up a little galloping horse he had just fashioned and wondered at it.

' A great-aunt taught me—she was a genius—I follow her at a long distance. Will you let me go, young man ? You may keep all of them.'

But the child, with a sudden contraction of the brow, flung a tiny stick-like arm round his neck, pressing hard, and looking at him. There was a red spot in each wasted cheek, and his eyes were wide and happy. Wharton returned the look with one of quiet scrutiny—the scrutiny of the doctor or the philosopher. On Marcella's quick sense the contrast of the two heads impressed itself—the delicate youth of Wharton's with its clustering curls— the sunken contours and the helpless suffering of the other. Then Wharton kissed the little fellow, put his animals carefully on to a chair beside him, and set him down.

They walked along the snowy street again, in a different relation to each other. Marcella had been touched and charmed, and Wharton teased her no more. As they reached the door of the almshouse where the old Pattons lived, she said to him : ' I think I had rather go in here by myself, please. I have some things to give them—old Patton has been very ill this last week—but I know what you think of doles—and I know too what you think, what you must think, of my father's cottages. It makes me feel a hypocrite ; ' yet I must do these things ; we are different, you and I—I am sure you will miss your train ! '

But there was no antagonism, only painful feeling in her softened look.

Wharton put out his hand.

' Yes, it is time for me to go. You say I make you feel a hypo crite ! I wonder whether you have any idea what you make me feel ? Do you imagine I should dare to say the things I have said except to one of the *élite* ? Would it be worth my while, as a social reformer ? Are you not vowed to great destinies ? When one comes across one of the tools of the future, must one not try to sharpen it, out of one's poor resources, in spite of manners ? '

Marcella, stirred—abashed—fascinated—let him press her hand. Then he walked rapidly away towards the station, a faint smile twitching at his lip.

' An inexperienced girl,' he said to himself, composedly.

CHAPTER V

BEFORE she went home, Marcella turned into the little rectory garden to see if she could find Mary Harden for a minute or two. The intimacy between them was such that she generally found entrance to the house by going round to a garden door and knocking or calling. The house was very small, and Mary's little sitting-room was close to this door.

Her knock brought Mary instantly.

' Oh ! come in. You won't mind. We were just at dinner. Charles is going away directly. Do stay and talk to me a bit.'

Marcella hesitated, but at last went in. The meals at the rectory distressed her—the brother and sister showed the marks of them. To-day she found their usual fare carefully and prettily arranged on a spotless table ; some bread, cheese, and boiled rice— nothing else. Nor did they allow themselves any fire for meals. Marcella, sitting beside them in her fur, did not feel the cold, but Mary was clearly shivering under her shawl. They ate meat twice a week, and in the afternoon Mary lit the sitting-room fire. In the morning she contented herself with the kitchen, where, as she cooked for many sick folk, and had only a girl of fourteen whom she was training to help her with the house work, she had generally much to do.

The Rector did not stay long after her arrival. He had a distant visit to pay to a dying child, and hurried off so as to be home, if possible, before dark. Marcella admired him, but did not feel that she understood him more as they were better acquainted. He was slight and young, and not very clever ; but a certain inexpugnable dignity surrounded him, which, real as it was, sometimes irritated Marcella. It sat oddly on his round face —boyish still, in spite of its pinched and anxious look—but there it was, not to be ignored. Marcella thought him a Conservative, and very backward and ignorant in his political and social opinions. But she was perfectly conscious that she must also think him a saint ; and that the deepest things in him were probably not for her.

Mr. Harden said a few words to her now as to her straw-plaiting scheme, which had his warmest sympathy—Marcella contrasted his tone gratefully with that of Wharton, and once more fell happily in love with her own ideas—then he went off, leaving the two girls together.

'Have you seen Mrs. Hurd this morning?' said Mary.

'Yes, Willie seems very bad.'

Mary assented.

'The doctor says he will hardly get through the winter, especially if this weather goes on. But the greatest excitement of the village just now—do you know ?—is the quarrel between Hurd and Westall. Somebody told Charles yesterday that they never meet without threatening each other. Since the covers at Tudley End were raided, Westall seems to have quite lost his head. He declares Hurd knew all about that, and that he is hand and glove with the same gang still. He vows he will catch him out, and Hurd told the man who told Charles that if Westall bullies him any more he will put a knife into him. And Charles says that Hurd is not a bit like he was. He used to be such a patient, silent creature. Now——'

'He has woke up to a few more ideas and a little more life than he had, that's all,' said Marcella impatiently. 'He poached last winter, and small blame to him. But since he got work at the Court in November—is it likely? He knows that he was suspected ; and what could be his interest now, after a hard day's work, to go out again at night, and run the risk of falling into Westall's clutches, when he doesn't want either the food or the money?'

'I don't know,' said Mary, shaking her head. 'Charles says, if they once do it, they hardly ever leave it off altogether. It's the excitement and amusement of it.'

' He promised me,' said Marcella proudly.

'They promise Charles all sorts of things,' said Mary slyly ; ' but they don't keep to them.'

Warmly grateful as both she and the Rector had been from the beginning to Marcella for the passionate interest she took in the place and the people, the sister was sometimes now a trifle jealous —divinely jealous—for her brother. Marcella's unbounded confidence in her own power and right over Mellor, her growing tendency to ignore anybody else's right or power, sometimes set Mary aflame, for Charles's sake, heartily and humbly as she admired her beautiful friend.

' I shall speak to Mr. Raeburn about it,' said Marcella.

She never called him ' Aldous' to anybody—a stiffness which jarred a little upon the gentle, sentimental Mary.

' I saw you pass,' she said, ' from one of the top windows. He was with you, wasn't he ?'

A slight colour sprang to her sallow cheek, a light to her eyes. Most wonderful, most interesting was this engagement to Mary, who—strange to think !—had almost brought it about. Mr. Raeburn was to her one of the best and noblest of men, and she felt quite simply, and with a sort of Christian trembling for him, the romance of his great position. Was Marcella happy, was she proud of him, as she ought to be? Mary was often puzzled by her.

' Oh no ! ' said Marcella, with a little laugh. ' That wasn't Mr. Raeburn. I don't know where your eyes were, Mary. That was Mr. Wharton, who is staying with us. He has gone on to a meeting at Widrington.'

Mary's face fell.

' Charles says Mr. Wharton's influence in the village is very bad,' she said quickly. ' He makes everybody discontented ; sets everybody by the ears ; and, after all, what can he do for anybody ?'

' But that's just what he wants to do—to make them discontented,' cried Marcella. ' Then, if they vote for him, that's the first practical step towards improving their life.'

' But it won't give them more wages or keep them out of the public house,' said Mary, bewildered. She came of a homely middle-class stock, accustomed to a small range of thinking, and a high standard of doing. Marcella's political opinions were an amazement, and on the whole a scandal to her. She preferred generally to give them a wide berth.

Marcella did not reply. It was not worth while to talk to Mary on these topics. But Mary stuck to the subject a moment longer.

'You can't want him to get in, though?' she said in a puzzled voice, as she led the way to the little sitting-room across the passage, and took her work-basket out of the cupboard. 'It was only the week before last Mr. Raeburn was speaking at the schoolroom for Mr. Dodgson. You weren't there, Marcella?'

'No,' said Marcella, shortly. 'I thought you knew perfectly well, Mary, that Mr. Raeburn and I don't agree politically. Certainly, I hope Mr. Wharton will get in!'

Mary opened her eyes in wonderment. She stared at Marcella, forgetting the sock she had just slipped over her left hand, and the darning needle in her right.

Marcella laughed.

'I know you think that two people who are going to be married ought to say ditto to each other in everything. Don't you—you dear old goose?'

She came and stood beside Mary, a stately and beautiful creature in her loosened furs. She stroked Mary's straight sandy hair back from her forehead. Mary looked up at her with a thrill, nay, a passionate throb of envy—soon suppressed.

'I think,' she said steadily, 'it is very strange—that love should oppose and disagree with what it loves.'

Marcella went restlessly towards the fire and began to examine the things on the mantelpiece.

'Can't people agree to differ, you sentimentalist? Can't they respect each other, without echoing each other on every subject?'

'Respect!' cried Mary, with a sudden scorn, which was startling from a creature so soft.

'There, she could tear me in pieces!' said Marcella, laughing, though her lip was not steady. 'I wonder what you would be like, Mary, if you were engaged.'

Mary ran her needle in and out with lightning speed for a second or two, then she said almost under her breath—

'I shouldn't be engaged unless I were in love. And if I were in love, why, I would go anywhere—do anything—believe anything—if *he* told me!'

'Believe anything?—Mary—you wouldn't!'

'I don't mean as to religion,' said Mary, hastily. 'But everything else—I would give it all up!—governing one's self, thinking for one's self. He should do it, and I would *bless* him!'

She looked up crimson, drawing a very long breath, as though from some deep centre of painful, passionate feeling. It was Marcella's turn to stare. Never had Mary so revealed herself before.

'Did you ever love anyone like that, Mary?' she asked, quickly.

Mary dropped her head again over her work and did not answer immediately.

'Do you see—' she said at last, with a change of tone. 'Do you see that we have got our invitation?'

Marcella, about to give the rein to an eager curiosity Mary's manner had excited in her, felt herself pulled up sharply. When she chose, this little meek creature could put on the same un-approachableness as her brother. Marcella submitted.

'Yes, I see,' she said, taking up a card on the mantelpiece. 'It will be a great crush. I suppose you know. They have asked the whole county, it seems to me.'

The card bore an invitation in Miss Raeburn's name for the Rector and his sister to a dance at Maxwell Court—the date given was the twenty-fifth of January.

'What fun!' said Mary, her eye sparkling. 'You needn't suppose that I know enough of balls to be particular. I have only been to one before in my life—ever. That was at Cheltenham. An aunt took me—I didn't dance. There were hardly any men, but I enjoyed it.'

'Well, you shall dance this time,' said Marcella, 'for I will make Mr. Raeburn introduce you.'

'Nonsense, you won't have any time to think about me. You will be the queen—everybody will want to speak to you. I shall sit in a corner and look at you—that will be enough for me.'

Marcella went up to her quickly and kissed her, then she said, still holding her—

'I know you think I ought to be very happy, Mary!'

'I should think I do!' said Mary, with astonished emphasis, when the voice paused—'I should think I do!'

'I *am* happy—and I want to make him happy. But there are so many things, so many different aims and motives, that com-plicate life, that puzzle one. One doesn't know how much to give of one's self, to each——'

She stood with her hand on Mary's shoulder, looking away towards the window and the snowy garden, her brow frowning and distressed.

'Well, I don't understand,' said Mary, after a pause. 'As I said before, it seems to me so plain and easy—to be in love, and give one's self *all*—to that. But you are so much cleverer than I, Marcella, you know so much more. That makes the difference. I can't be like you. Perhaps I don't want to be!'—and she laughed. 'But I can admire you and love you, and think about you. There! Now, tell me what you are going to wear?'

'White satin, and Mr. Raeburn wants me to wear some pearls

he is going to give me, some old pearls of his mother's. I believe I shall find them at Mellor when I get back.'

There was little girlish pleasure in the tone. It was as though Marcella thought her friend would be more interested in her bit of news than she was herself, and was handing it on to her to please her.

'Isn't there a superstition against doing that—before you're married?' said Mary doubtfully.

'As if I should mind if there was! But I don't believe there is, or Miss Raeburn would have heard of it. She's a mass of such things. Well! I hope I shall behave myself to please her at this function. There are not many things I do to her satisfaction; it's a mercy we're not going to live with her. Lord Maxwell is a dear; but she and I would never get on. Every way of thinking she has rubs me up the wrong way; and as for her view of me, I am just a tare sown among her wheat. Perhaps she is right enough!'

Marcella leant her cheek pensively on one hand, and with the other played with the things on the mantelpiece.

Mary looked at her, and then half smiled, half sighed.

'I think it is a very good thing you are to be married soon,' she said, with her little air of wisdom, which offended nobody. 'Then you'll know your own mind. When is it to be?'

'The end of February—after the election.'

'Two months,' mused Mary.

'Time enough to throw it all up in, you think?' said Marcella, recklessly, putting on her gloves for departure. 'Perhaps you'll be pleased to hear that I *am* going to a meeting of Mr. Raeburn's next week?'

'I *am* glad. You ought to go to them all.'

'Really, Mary! How am I to lift you out of this squaw theory of matrimony? Allow me to inform you that the following evening I am going to one of Mr. Wharton's—here in the schoolroom!'

She enjoyed her friend's disapproval.

'By yourself, Marcella? It isn't seemly!'

'I shall take a maid. Mr. Wharton is going to tell us how the people can—get the land, and how, when they have got it, all the money that used to go in rent will go in taking off taxes and making life comfortable for the poor.' She looked at Mary with a teasing smile.

'Oh! I dare say he will make his stealing sound very pretty,' said Mary, with unwonted scorn, as she opened the front door for her friend.

Marcella flashed out.

'I know you are a saint, Mary,' she said, turning back on the path outside to deliver her last shaft. 'I am often not so sure whether you are a Christian!'

Then she hurried off without another word, leaving the flushed and shaken Mary to ponder this strange dictum.

Marcella was just turning into the straight drive which led past the church on the left to Mellor House, when she heard footsteps behind her, and, looking round, she saw Edward Hallin.

'Will you give me some lunch, Miss Boyce, in return for a message? I am here instead of Aldous, who is very sorry for himself, and will be over later. I am to tell you that he went down to the station to meet a certain box. The box did not come, but will come this afternoon; so he waits for it, and will bring it over.'

Marcella flushed, smiled, and said she understood. Hallin moved on beside her, evidently glad of the opportunity of a talk with her.

'We are all going together to the Gairsley meeting next week, aren't we? I am so glad you are coming. Aldous will do his best.'

There was something very winning in his tone to her. It implied both his old and peculiar friendship for Aldous, and his eager wish to find a new friend in her—to adopt her into their comradeship. Something very winning, too, in his whole personality—in the loosely knit, nervous figure, the irregular charm of feature, the benignant eyes and brow—even in the suggestions of physical delicacy, cheerfully concealed, yet none the less evident. The whole balance of Marcella's temper changed in some sort as she talked to him. She found herself wanting to please, instead of wanting to conquer, to make an effect.

'You have just come from the village, I think?' said Hallin. 'Aldous tells me you take a great interest in the people?'

He looked at her kindly, the look of one who saw all his fellow-creatures nobly, as it were, and to their best advantage.

'One may take an interest,' she said, in a dissatisfied voice, poking at the snow crystals on the road before her with the thorn-stick she carried, 'but one can do so little. And I don't know anything; not even what I want myself.'

'No; one can do next to nothing. And systems and theories don't matter, or, at least, very little. Yet, when you and Aldous are together, there will be more chance of *doing*, for you than for most. You will be two happy and powerful people! His power will be doubled by happiness; I have always known that.'

Marcella was seized with shyness, looked away, and did not know what to answer. At last she said abruptly—her head still turned to the woods on her left—

'Are you sure he is going to be happy?'

'Shall I produce his letter to me?' he said, bantering—'or letters? For I knew a great deal about you before the 5th of October' (their engagement-day), 'and suspected what was going to happen long before Aldous did. No; after all, no! Those letters are my last bit of the old friendship. But the new began that same day,' he hastened to add, smiling: 'It may be richer than the old; I don't know. It depends on you.'

'I don't think—I am a very satisfactory friend,' said Marcella, still awkward, and speaking with difficulty.

'Well, let me find out, won't you? I don't think Aldous would call me exacting. I believe he would give me a decent character, though I tease him a good deal. You must let me tell you some time what he did for me—what he was to me—at Cambridge? I shall always feel sorry for Aldous's wife that she did not know him at college.'

A shock went through Marcella at the word—that tremendous word—wife. As Hallin said it, there was something intolerable in the claim it made!

'I should like you to tell me,' she said, faintly. Then she added, with more energy and a sudden advance of friendliness, 'But you really must come in and rest. Aldous told me he thought the walk from the Court was too much for you. Shall we take this short way?'

And she opened a little gate leading to a door at the side of the house through the Cedar Garden. The narrow path only admitted of single file, and Hallin followed her, admiring her tall youth and the fine black and white of her head and cheek as she turned every now and then to speak to him. He realised more vividly than before the rare, exciting elements of her beauty, and the truth in Aldous's comparison of her to one of the tall women in a Florentine fresco. But he felt himself a good deal baffled by her, all the same. In some ways, so far as any man who is not the lover can understand such things, he understood why Aldous had fallen in love with her; in others, she bore no relation whatever to the woman his thoughts had been shaping all these years as his friend's fit and natural wife.

Luncheon passed as easily as any meal could be expected to do, of which Mr. Boyce was partial president. During the preceding month or two he had definitely assumed the character of an invalid, although to inexperienced eyes like Marcella's there did not seem to be very much the matter. But, whatever the facts might be, Mr. Boyce's adroit use of them had made a great difference to his position in his own household. His wife's sarcastic freedom of manner was less apparent; and he was obviously

less in awe of her.   Meanwhile he was as sore as ever towards the
Raeburns, and no more inclined to take any particular pleasure in
Marcella's prospects, or to make himself agreeable towards his
future son-in-law.   He and Mrs. Boyce had been formally asked
in Miss Raeburn's best hand to the Court ball, but he had at once
snappishly announced his intention of staying at home.   Marcella
sometimes looked back with astonishment to his eagerness for
social notice when they first came to Mellor.   Clearly the rising
irritability of illness had made it doubly unpleasant to him to owe
all that he was likely to get on that score to his own daughter ;
and, moreover, he had learnt to occupy himself more continuously
on his own land and with his own affairs.

As to the state of the village, neither Marcella's entreaties nor
reproaches had any effect upon him.   When it appeared certain
that he would be summoned for some specially flagrant piece of
neglect he would spend a few shillings on repairs ; otherwise not
a farthing.   All that filial softening towards him of which Marcella
had been conscious in the early autumn had died away in her.
She said to herself now plainly and bitterly that it was a misfortune
to belong to him ; and she would have pitied her mother most
heartily if her mother had ever allowed her the smallest expression
of such a feeling.   As it was, she was left to wonder and chafe at
her mother's new-born mildness.

In the drawing-room, after luncheon, Hallin came up to Marcella in a corner, and, smiling, drew from his pocket a folded
sheet of foolscap.

'I made Aldous give me his speech to show you, before to-
morrow night,' he said.   'He would hardly let me take it, said it
was stupid, and that you would not agree with it.   But I wanted
you to see how he does these things.   He speaks now, on an
average, two or three times a week.   Each time, even for an
audience of a score or two of village folk, he writes out what he
has to say.   Then he speaks it entirely without notes.   In this
way, though he has not much natural gift, he is making himself
gradually an effective and practical speaker.   The danger with
him, of course, is lest he should be over-subtle and over-critical—
not simple and popular enough.'

Marcella took the paper half unwillingly and glanced over it in
silence.

'You are sorry he is a Tory, is that it?' he said to her, but in
a lower voice, and sitting down beside her.

Mrs. Boyce, just catching the words from where she sat with
her work, at the further side of the room, looked up with a double
wonder—wonder at Marcella's folly, wonder still more at the

deference with which men like Aldous Raeburn and Hallin treated her. It was inevitable, of course—youth and beauty rule the world. But the mother, under no spell herself, and of keen, cool wit, resented the intellectual confusion, the lowering of standards involved.

'I suppose so,' said Marcella, stupidly, in answer to Hallin's question, fidgeting the papers under her hand. Then his curious confessor's gift, his quiet questioning look with its sensitive human interest to all before him, told upon her.

'I am sorry he does not look further ahead, to the great changes that must come,' she added hurriedly. 'This is all about details, palliatives. I want him to be more impatient.'

'Great political changes you mean ?'

She nodded ; then added—

'But only for the sake, of course, of great social changes to come after.'

He pondered a moment.

'Aldous has never believed in *great* changes coming suddenly. He constantly looks upon me as rash in the things *I* adopt and believe in. But for the contriving unceasing effort of every day to make that part of the social machine in which a man finds himself work better and more equitably, I have never seen Aldous's equal —for the steady passion, the persistence, of it.'

She looked up. His pale face had taken to itself glow and fire ; his eyes were full of strenuous, nay, severe expression. Her foolish pride rebelled a little.

'Of course, I haven't seen much of that yet,' she said slowly.

His look for a moment was indignant, incredulous, then melted into a charming eagerness.

'But you will ! naturally you will !—see everything.   I hug myself sometimes now for pure pleasure that someone besides his grandfather and I will know what Aldous is and does. Oh ! the people on the estate know ; his neighbours are beginning to know ; and now that he is going into Parliament, the country will know some day, if work and high intelligence have the power I believe. But I am impatient !   In the first place—I may say it to you, Miss Boyce !—I want Aldous to come out of that *manner* of his to strangers, which is the only bit of the true Tory in him ; *you* can get rid of it, no one else can.—How long shall I give you ?—And in the next, I want the world not to be wasting itself on baser stuff when it might be praising Aldous ! '

'Does he mean Mr. Wharton ?' thought Marcella, quickly. ' But this world—our world—hates him and runs him down.'

But she had no time to answer, for the door opened to admit

Aldous, flushed and bright-eyed, looking round the room immediately for her, and bearing a parcel in his left hand.

'Does she love him at all?' thought Hallin, with a nervous stiffening of all his lithe frame, as he walked away to talk to Mrs. Boyce; 'or, in spite of all her fine talk, is she just marrying him for his money and position?'

Meanwhile, Aldous had drawn Marcella into the Stone Parlour and was standing by the fire with his arm covetously round her.

'I have lost two hours with you I might have had, just because a tiresome man missed his train. Make up for it by liking these pretty things a little, for my sake and my mother's.'

He opened the jeweller's case, took out the fine old pearls—necklace and bracelets—it contained, and put them into her hand. They were his first considerable gift to her, and had been chosen for association's sake, seeing that his mother had also worn them before her marriage.

She flushed first of all with a natural pleasure, the girl delighting in her gaud. Then she allowed herself to be kissed, which was, indeed, inevitable. Finally she turned them over and over in her hands; and he began to be puzzled by her.

'They are much too good for me. I don't know whether you ought to give me such precious things. I am dreadfully careless and forgetful. Mamma always says so.'

'I shall want you to wear them so often that you won't have a chance of forgetting them,' he said, gaily.

'Will you? Will you want me to wear them so often?' she asked, in an odd voice. 'Anyway, I should like to have just these, and nothing else. I am glad that we know nobody, and have no friends, and that I shall have so few presents. You won't give me many jewels, will you?' she said, suddenly, insistently, turning to him. 'I shouldn't know what to do with them. I used to have a magpie's wish for them; and now—I don't know, but they don't give me pleasure. Not these, of course—not these!' she added, hurriedly, taking them up and beginning to fasten the bracelets on her wrists.

Aldous looked perplexed.

'My darling!' he said, half laughing, and in the tone of the apologist, 'You know we *have* such a lot of things. And I am afraid my grandfather will want to give them all to you. Need one think so much about it? It isn't as though they had to be bought fresh. They go with pretty gowns, don't they, and other people like to see them?'

'No, but it's what they imply—the wealth—the *having* so much while other people want so much Things begin to oppress me so !' she broke out, instinctively moving away from him that she might express herself with more energy. 'I like luxuries so desperately, and when I get them I seem to myself now the vulgarest creature alive, who has no right to an opinion or an enthusiasm, or anything else worth having. You must not let me like them—you must help me not to care about them !'

Raeburn's eye as he looked at her was tenderness itself. He could of course neither mock her, nor put what she said aside. This question she had raised, this most thorny of all the personal questions of the present—the ethical relation of the individual to the World's Fair and its vanities—was, as it happened, a question far more sternly and robustly real to him than it was to her. Every word in his few sentences, as they stood talking by the fire, bore on it for a practised ear the signs of a long wrestle of the heart.

But to Marcella it sounded tame ; her ear was haunted by the fragments of another tune which she seemed to be perpetually trying to recall and piece together. Aldous's slow minor made her impatient.

He turned presently to ask her what she had been doing with her morning—asking her with a certain precision, and observing her attentively. She replied that she had been showing Mr. Wharton the house, that he had walked down with her to the village, and was gone to a meeting at Widrington. Then she remarked that he was very good company, and very clever, but dreadfully sure of his own opinion. Finally she laughed, and said drily :

'There will be no putting him down all the same. I haven't told anybody yet, but he saved my life this morning.'

Aldous caught her wrists.

'Saved your life ! Dear—What do you mean ?'

She explained, giving the little incident all—perhaps more than —its dramatic due. He listened with evident annoyance, and stood pondering when she came to an end.

'So I shall be expected to take quite a different view of him henceforward?' he inquired at last, looking round at her, with a very forced smile.

'I am sure I don't know that it matters to him what view anybody takes of him,' she cried, flushing. 'He certainly takes the frankest views of other people, and expresses them.'

And while she played with the pearls in their box she gave a vivid account of her morning's talk with the Radical candidate for West Brookshire, and of their village expedition.

There was a certain relief in describing the scorn with which her acts and ideals had been treated ; and, underneath, a woman's curiosity as to how Aldous would take it.

'I don't know what business he had to express himself so frankly,' said Aldous, turning to the fire and carefully putting it together. 'He hardly knows you—it was, I think, an impertinence.'

He stood upright, with his back to the hearth, a strong, capable, frowning Englishman, very much on his dignity. Such a moment must surely have become him in the eyes of a girl that loved him. Marcella proved restive under it.

'No ; it's very natural,' she protested quickly. 'When people are so much in earnest they don't stop to think about impertinence ! I never met anyone who dug up one's thoughts by the roots as he does.'

Aldous was startled by her flush, her sudden attitude of opposition. His intermittent lack of readiness overtook him, and there was an awkward silence. Then, pulling himself together with a strong hand, he left the subject and began to talk of her straw-plaiting scheme, of the Gairsley meeting, and of Hallin. But in the middle Marcella unexpectedly said :—

'I wish you would tell me, seriously, what reasons you have for not liking Mr. Wharton ?—other than politics, I mean ?'

Her black eyes fixed him with a keen insistence.

He was silent a moment with surprise ; then he said :—

'I had rather not rake up old scores.'

She shrugged her shoulders, and he was roused to come and put his arm round her again, she shrinking and turning her reddened face away.

'Dearest,' he said, 'you shall put me in charity with all the world. But the worst of it is,' he added, half laughing, 'that I don't see how I am to help disliking him doubly henceforward for having had the luck to put that fire out instead of me!'

CHAPTER VI

A FEW busy and eventful weeks, days never forgotten by Marcella in after years, passed quickly by. Parliament met in the third week of January. Ministers, according to universal expectation, found themselves confronted by a damaging amendment on the Address, and were defeated by a small majority. A dissolution and appeal to the country followed immediately, and the meetings and speech-makings, already active throughout the constituencies, were carried forward with redoubled energy. In the Tudley End division, Aldous Raeburn was fighting a somewhat younger opponent of the same country-gentleman stock—a former fag indeed of his at Eton —whose zeal and fluency gave him plenty to do. Under ordinary circumstances Aldous would have thrown himself with all his heart and mind into a contest which involved for him the most stimulating of possibilities, personal and public. But, as these days went over, he found his appetite for the struggle flagging, and was harassed rather than spurred by his adversary's activity. The real truth was that he could not see enough of Marcella ! A curious uncertainty and unreality, moreover, seemed to have crept into some of their relations ; and it had begun to gall and fever him that Wharton should be staying there, week after week, beside her, in her father's house, able to spend all the free intervals of the fight in her society, strengthening an influence which Raeburn's pride and delicacy had hardly allowed him as yet, in spite of his instinctive jealousy from the beginning, to take into his thoughts at all, but which was now apparent, not only to himself but to others.

In vain did he spend every possible hour at Mellor he could snatch from a conflict in which his party, his grandfather, and his own personal fortunes were all deeply interested. In vain—with a tardy instinct that it was to Mr. Boyce's dislike of himself, and to the wilful fancy for Wharton's society which this dislike had promoted, that Wharton's long stay at Mellor was largely owing—did Aldous subdue himself to propitiations and amenities wholly foreign to a strong character long accustomed to rule without thinking about it. Mr. Boyce showed himself not a whit less partial to Wharton than before ; pressed him at least twice in Raeburn's hearing to make Mellor his head-quarters so long as it suited him, and behaved with an irritable malice with regard to some of the details of the wedding arrangements, which neither Mrs. Boyce's indignation nor Marcella's discomfort and annoyance could restrain. Clearly there was in him a strong consciousness that by his attentions to the Radical candidate he was asserting his independence of the Raeburns, and nothing for the moment seemed to be more of an object with him, even though his daughter was going to marry the Raeburns' heir. Meanwhile, Wharton was always ready to walk or chat or play billiards with his host in the intervals of his own campaign ; and his society had thus come to count considerably among the scanty daily pleasures of a sickly and disappointed man. Mrs. Boyce did not like her guest, and took no pains to disguise it, least of all from Wharton. But it seemed to be no longer possible for her to take the vigorous measures she would once have taken to get rid of him.

In vain, too, did Miss Raeburn do her best for the nephew to whom she was still devoted, in spite of his deplorable choice of a wife. She took in the situation as a whole probably sooner than anybody else, and she instantly made heroic efforts to see more of Marcella, to get her to come oftener to the Court, and in many various ways to procure the poor deluded Aldous more of his betrothed's society. She paid many chattering and fussy visits to Mellor—visits which chafed Marcella—and before long, indeed, roused a certain suspicion in the girl's wilful mind. Between Miss Raeburn and Mrs. Boyce there was a curious understanding. It was always tacit, and never amounted to friendship, still less to intimacy. But it often yielded a certain melancholy consolation to Aldous Raeburn's great-aunt. It was clear to her that this strange mother was just as much convinced as she was that Aldous was making a great mistake, and that Marcella was not worthy of him. But the engagement being there—a fact not apparently to be un-done—both ladies showed themselves disposed to take pains with it, to protect it against aggression. Mrs. Boyce found herself be-coming more of a *chaperon* than she had ever yet professed to be ; and Miss Raeburn, as we have said, made repeated efforts to cap-ture Marcella and hold her for Aldous, her lawful master.

But Marcella proved extremely difficult to manage. In the first place she was a young person of many engagements. Her village scheme absorbed a great deal of time. She was deep in a varied correspondence, in the engagement of teachers, the pro-vision of workrooms, the collecting and registering of workers, the organisation of local committees, and so forth. New sides of the girl's character, new capacities and capabilities were coming out ; new forms of her natural power over her fellows were developing ever day ; she was beginning, under the incessant stimulus of Wharton's talk, to read and think on social and economic subjects, with some system and coherence, and it was evident that she took a passionate mental pleasure in it all. And the more pleasure these activities gave her, the less she had to spare for those accom-paniments of her engagement and her position that was to be, which once, as Mrs. Boyce's sharp eyes perceived, had been quite normally attractive to her.

'Why do you take up her time so, with all these things?' said Miss Raeburn impatiently to Lady Winterbourne, who was now Marcella's obedient helper in everything she chose to initiate. 'She doesn't care for anything she *ought* to care about at this time, and Aldous sees nothing of her. As for her trousseau, Mrs. Boyce declares she has had to do it all. Marcella won't even go up to London to have her wedding-dress fitted !'

Lady Winterbourne looked up bewildered.

'But I can't make her go and have her wedding-dress fitted, Agneta! And I always feel you don't know what a fine creature she is. You don't really appreciate her. It's splendid the ideas she has about this work, and the way she throws herself into it.'

'I dare say!' said Miss Raeburn, indignantly. 'That's just what I object to. Why can't she throw herself into being in love with Aldous! That's her business, I imagine, just now—if she were a young woman like anybody else one had ever seen—instead of holding aloof from everything he does, and never being there when he wants her. Oh! I have no patience with her. But, of course, I must—' said Miss Raeburn, hastily correcting herself—'of course, I must have patience.'

'It will all come right, I am sure, when they are married,' said Lady Winterbourne, rather helplessly.

'That's just what my brother says,' cried Miss Raeburn, exasperated. 'He won't hear a word—declares she is odd and original, and that Aldous will soon know how to manage her. It's all very well; nowadays men *don't* manage their wives; that's all gone with the rest. And I am sure, my dear, if she behaves after she is married as she is doing now, with that most objectionable person Mr. Wharton—walking, and talking, and taking up his ideas, and going to his meetings—she'll be a handful for any husband.'

'Mr. Wharton!' said Lady Winterbourne, astonished. Her absent black eyes, the eyes of the dreamer, of the person who lives by a few intense affections, saw little or nothing of what was going on immediately under them. 'Oh! but that is because he is staying in the house, and he is a Socialist; she calls herself one——'

'My *dear*,' said Miss Raeburn, interrupting emphatically; 'if—you—had—now—an unmarried daughter at home—engaged or not—would you care to have Harry Wharton hanging about after her?'

'Harry Wharton?' said the other, pondering; 'he is the Levens' cousin, isn't he? he used to stay with them. I don't think I have seen him since then. But yes, I do remember; there was something—something disagreeable?'

She stopped with a hesitating, interrogative air. No one talked less scandal, no one put the uglinesses of life away from her with a hastier hand than Lady Winterbourne. She was one of the most consistent of moral epicures.

'Yes, *extremely* disagreeable,' said Miss Raeburn, sitting bolt upright. 'The man has no principles—never had any, since he was a child in petticoats. I know Aldous thinks him unscrupulous

in politics and everything else. And then, just when you are
worked to death, and have hardly a moment for your own affairs,
to have a man of that type always at hand to spend odd times with
your lady love—flattering her, engaging her in his ridiculous
schemes, encouraging her in all the extravagances she has got her
head twice too full of already, setting her against your own ideas
and the life she will have to live—you will admit that it is not
exactly soothing !'

'Poor Aldous !' said Lady Winterbourne thoughtfully, looking
far ahead with her odd look of absent rigidity, which had in reality
so little to do with a character essentially soft ; 'but you see he *did*
know all about her opinions. And I don't think—no, I really don't
think—I could speak to her.'

In truth, this woman of nearly seventy—old in years, but wholly
young in temperament—was altogether under Marcella's spell—
more at ease with her already than with most of her own children,
finding in her satisfaction for a hundred instincts, suppressed or
starved by her own environment, fascinated by the girl's friendship,
and eagerly grateful for her visits. Miss Raeburn thought it all
both incomprehensible and silly.

'Apparently no one can !' cried that lady in answer to her
friend's demurrer ; 'is all the world afraid of her ?'

And she departed in wrath. But she knew, nevertheless, that
she was just as much afraid of Marcella as anybody else. In her
own sphere at the Court, or in points connected with what was
due to the family, or to Lord Maxwell especially, as the head of it,
this short, capable old lady could hold her own amply with Aldous's
betrothed, could maintain, indeed, a sharp and caustic dignity,
which kept Marcella very much in order. Miss Raeburn on the
defensive was strong ; but when it came to attacking Marcella's
own ideas and proceedings, Lord Maxwell's sister became shrewdly
conscious of her own weaknesses. She had no wish to measure
her wits on any general field with Marcella's. She said to herself
that the girl was too clever, and would talk you down.

Meanwhile, things went untowardly in various ways. Marcella
disciplined herself before the Gairsley meeting, and went thither
resolved to give Aldous as much sympathy as she could. But the
performance only repelled a mind over which Wharton was every
day gaining more influence. There was a portly baronet in the
chair ; there were various Primrose dames on the platform and
among the audience ; there was a considerable representation of
clergy ; and the labourers present seemed to Marcella the most
obsequious of their kind. Aldous spoke well—or so the audience
seemed to think ; but she could feel no enthusiasm for anything

that he said. She gathered that he advocated a Government
inspection of cottages, more stringent precautions against cattle
disease, better technical instruction, a more abundant provision of
allotments and small freeholds, &c. ; and he said many cordial
and wise-sounding things in praise of a progress which should go
safely and wisely from step to step, and run no risks of dangerous
reaction. But the assumptions on which, as she told herself
rebelliously, it all went—that the rich and the educated must rule,
and the poor obey ; that existing classes and rights, the forces of
individualism and competition, must and would go on pretty much
as they were ; that great houses and great people, the English
land and game system, and all the rest of our odious class para-
phernalia were in the order of the universe ; these ideas, conceived
as the furniture of Aldous's mind, threw her again into a ferment
of passionate opposition. And when the noble baronet in the chair
—to her eye, a pompous, frock-coated stick, sacrificing his after-
dinner sleep for once, that he might the more effectually secure it
in the future—proposed a vote of confidence in the Conservative
candidate ; when the vote was carried with much cheering and
rattling of feet ; when the Primrose dames on the platform smiled
graciously down upon the meeting as one smiles at good children
in their moments of pretty behaviour ; and when, finally, scores of
toil-stained labourers, young and old, went up to have a word and
a hand-shake with ' Muster Raeburn,' Marcella held herself aloof
and cold, with a look that threatened sarcasm should she be
spoken to. Miss Raeburn, glancing furtively round at her, was
outraged anew by her expression.

'She will be a thorn in all our sides,' thought that lady.
'Aldous is a fool !—a poor dear noble misguided fool !'

Then on the way home, she and Aldous drove together.
Marcella tried to argue, grew vehement, and said bitter things for
the sake of victory, till at last Aldous, tired, worried, and deeply
wounded, could bear it no longer.

'Let it be, dear, let it be !' he entreated, snatching at her hand
as they rolled along through a stormy night. 'We grope in a dark
world—you see some points of light in it, I see others—won't you
give me credit for doing what I can—seeing what I can? I am
sure—*sure*—you will find it easier to bear with differences when
we are quite together—when there are no longer all these hateful
duties and engagements—and persons—between us.'

'Persons ! I don't know what you mean !' said Marcella.

Aldous only just restrained himself in time. Out of sheer
fatigue and slackness of nerve he had been all but betrayed into
some angry speech on the subject of Wharton, the echoes of whose

fantastic talk, as it seemed to him, were always hanging about
Mellor when he went there. But he did refrain, and was thankful.
That he was indeed jealous and disturbed, that he had been jealous
and disturbed from the moment Harry Wharton had set foot in
Mellor, he himself knew quite well. But to play the jealous part
in public was more than the Raeburn pride could bear. There
was the dread, too, of defining the situation—of striking some
vulgar irrevocable note.

So he parried Marcella's exclamation by asking her whether
she had any idea how many human hands a parliamentary
candidate had to shake between breakfast and bed; and then,
having so slipped into another tone, he tried to amuse himself and
her by some of the daily humours of the contest. She lent herself
to it and laughed, her look mostly turned away from him, as though
she were following the light of the carriage lamps as it slipped along
the snow-laden hedges, her hand lying limply in his. But neither
was really gay. His soreness of mind grew as in the pauses of
talk he came to realise more exactly the failure of the evening—of
his very successful and encouraging meeting—from his own private
point of view.

'Didn't you like that last speech?' he broke out suddenly—
'that labourer's speech? I thought you would. It was entirely
his own idea—nobody asked him to do it.'

In reality Gairsley represented a corner of the estate which
Aldous had specially made his own. He had spent much labour
and thought on the improvement of what had been a backward
district, and in particular he had tried a small profit-sharing experiment upon a farm there which he had taken into his own hands
for the purpose. The experiment had met with fair success, and
the labourer in question, who was one of the workers in it, had
volunteered some approving remarks upon it at the meeting.

'Oh! it was very proper and respectful!' said Marcella, hastily.

The carriage rolled on some yards before Aldous replied. Then
he spoke in a drier tone than he had ever yet used to her.

'You do it injustice, I think. The man is perfectly independent,
and an honest fellow. I was grateful to him for what he said.'

'Of course, I am no judge!' cried Marcella, quickly—repent-
antly. 'Why did you ask me? I saw everything crooked, I
suppose—it was your Primrose dames—they got upon my nerves.
Why did you have them? I didn't mean to vex and hurt you—I
didn't indeed—it was all the other way—and now I have.'

She turned upon him laughing, but also half crying, as he could
tell by the flutter of her breath.

He vowed he was not hurt, and once more changed both talk

and tone. They reached the drive's end without a word of Wharton. But Marcella went to bed, hating herself, and Aldous, after his solitary drive home, sat up long and late, feverishly pacing and thinking.

Then next evening how differently things fell !

Marcella, having spent the afternoon at the Court, hearing all the final arrangements for the ball and bearing with Miss Raeburn in a way which astonished herself, came home full of a sense of duty done, and announced to her mother that she was going to Mr. Wharton's meeting in the Baptist chapel that evening.

'Unnecessary, don't you think?' said Mrs. Boyce, lifting her eyebrows. 'However, if you go, I shall go with you.'

Most mothers, dealing with a girl of twenty-one, under the circumstances, would have said, ' I had rather you stayed at home.' Mrs. Boyce never employed locutions of this kind. She recognised with perfect calmness that Marcella's bringing up, and especially her independent years in London, had made it impossible.

Marcella fidgeted.

' I don't know why you should, mamma. Papa will be sure to want you. Of course, I shall take Deacon.'

' Please order dinner a quarter of an hour earlier, and tell Deacon to bring down my walking things to the hall,' was all Mrs. Boyce said in answer.

Marcella walked upstairs with her head very stiff. So her mother, and Miss Raeburn too, thought it necessary to keep watch on her. How preposterous ! She thought of her free and easy relations with her Kensington student-friends, and wondered when a more reasonable idea of the relations between men and women would begin to penetrate English country society.

Mr. Boyce talked recklessly of going too.

' Of course, I know he will spout seditious nonsense,' he said irritably to his wife, ' but it's the fellow's power of talk that is so astonishing. *He* isn't troubled with your Raeburn heaviness.'

Marcella came into the room as the discussion was going on.

' If papa goes,' she said in an undertone to her mother as she passed her, ' it will spoil the meeting. The labourers will turn sulky. I shouldn't wonder if they did or said something unpleasant. As it is, *you* had much better not come, mamma. They are sure to attack the cottages—and other things.'

Mrs. Boyce took no notice as far as she herself was concerned, but her quiet decision at last succeeded in leaving Mr. Boyce safely settled by the fire, provided as usual with a cigarette and a French novel.

The meeting was held in a little iron Baptist chapel, erected some few years before on the outskirts of the village, to the grief and scandal of Mr. Harden. There were about a hundred and twenty labourers present, and at the back some boys and girls, come to giggle and make a noise—nobody else. The Baptist minister, a smooth-faced young man, possessed as it turned out of opinions little short of Wharton's own in point of vigour and rigour, was already in command. A few late comers, as they slouched in, stole side looks at Marcella and the veiled lady in black beside her, sitting in the corner of the last bench ; and Marcella nodded to one or two of the audience, Jim Hurd amongst them. Otherwise no one took any notice of them. It was the first time that Mrs. Boyce had been inside any building belonging to the village.

Wharton arrived late. He had been canvassing at a distance, and neither of the Mellor ladies had seen him all day. He slipped up the bench with a bow and a smile to greet them. 'I am done !' he said to Marcella, as he took off his hat. ' My voice is gone, my mind ditto. I shall drivel for half an hour and let them go. Did you ever see such a stolid set?'

'You will rouse them,' said Marcella.

Her eyes were animated, her colour high, and she took no account at all of his plea of weariness.

'You challenge me? I must rouse them—that was what you came to see? Is that it?'

She laughed and made no answer. He left her and went up to the minister's desk, the men shuffling their feet a little, and rattling a stick here and there as he did so.

The young minister took the chair and introduced the speaker. He had a strong Yorkshire accent, and his speech was divided between the most vehement attacks, couched in the most Scriptural language, upon capital and privilege—that is to say, on landlords and the land system, on State churches and the 'idle rich,' interspersed with quavering returns upon himself, as though he were scared by his own invective. ' My brothers, let us be *calm* !' he would say after every burst of passion, with a long deep-voiced emphasis on the last word ; 'let us, above all things, be *calm* !'— and then bit by bit voice and denunciation would begin to mount again towards a fresh climax of loud-voiced attack, only to sink again to the same lamb-like refrain. Mrs. Boyce's thin lip twitched, and Marcella bore the good gentleman a grudge for providing her mother with so much unnecessary amusement.

As for Wharton, at the opening of his speech he spoke both awkwardly and flatly ; and Marcella had a momentary shock. He was, as he said, tired, and his wits were not at command. He began with the general political programme of the party to which—on its extreme left wing—he proclaimed himself to belong. This programme was, of course, by now a newspaper commonplace of the stalest sort. He himself recited it without enthusiasm, and it was received without a spark, so far as appeared, of interest or agreement. The minister gave an 'hear, hear,' of a loud official sort; the men made no sign.

'They might be a set of Dutch cheeses !' thought Marcella indignantly after a while. 'But, after all, why should they care for all this ? I shall have to get up in a minute and stop those children romping.'

But through all this, as it were, Wharton was only waiting for his second wind. There came a moment when, dropping his quasi-official and high political tone, he said suddenly with another voice and emphasis :—

'Well now, my men, I'll be bound you're thinking, " That's all pretty enough !—we haven't got anything against it—we dare say it's all right ; but we don't care a brass ha'porth about any of it ! If that's all you'd got to say to us, you might have let us bide at home. We don't have none too much time to rest our bones a bit by the fire, and talk to the missus and the kids. Why didn't you let us alone, instead of bringing us out in the cold ? "

'Well, but it *isn't* all I've got to say—and you know it—because I've spoken to you before. What I've been talking about is all true, and all important, and you'll see it some day when you're fit. But what can men in your position know about it, or care about it ? What do any of you want, but *bread*——'

—He thundered on the desk—

'—a bit of decent *comfort*—a bit of *freedom*—freedom from tyrants who call themselves your betters !—a bit of rest in your old age, a home that's something better than a dog-hole, a wage that's something better than starvation, an honest share in the wealth you are making every day and every hour for other people to gorge and plunder !'

He stopped a moment to see how *that* took. A knot of young men in a corner rattled their sticks vigorously. The older men had begun at any rate to look at the speaker. The boys on the back benches instinctively stopped scuffling.

Then he threw himself into a sort of rapid question-and-answer. What were their wages—eleven shillings a week ?

'Not they !' cried a man from the middle of the chapel. 'Yer mus reckon it wet an' dry. I wor turned back two days las week, an' two days this, *fower* shillin lost each week—that's what I call skinnin ov yer.'

Wharton nodded at him approvingly. By now he knew the majority of the men in each village by name, and never forgot a face or a biography. 'You're right there, Watkins. Eleven shillings, then, when it isn't less, never more, and precious often less ; and harvest money—the people that are kind enough to come round and ask you to vote Tory for them make a deal of that, don't they ?—and a few odds and ends here and there—precious few of them ! There that's about it for wages, isn't it ? Thirty pounds a year, somewhere about, to keep a wife and children on— and for ten hours a day work, not counting meal times—that's it, I think. Oh you *are* well off !—aren't you ?'

He dropped his arms, folded, on the desk in front of him, and paused to look at them, his bright kindling eye running over rank. after rank. A chuckle of rough laughter, bitter and jeering, ran through the benches. Then they broke out and applauded him.

Well, and about their cottages?

His glance caught Marcella, passed to her mother sitting stiffly motionless under her veil. He drew himself up, thought a moment, then threw himself far forward again over the desk as though the better to launch what he had to say, his voice taking a grinding determined note.

He had been in all parts of the division, he said ; seen every-thing, inquired into everything. No doubt, on the great properties there had been a good deal done of late years—public opinion had effected something, the landlords had been forced to disgorge some of the gains wrested from labour, to pay for the decent housing of the labourer. But did anybody suppose that *enough* had been done? Why, he had seen *dens*—ay, on the best properties—not fit for the pigs that the farmers wouldn't let the labourers keep, lest they should steal their straw for the littering of them !—where a man was bound to live the life of a beast, and his children after him.

A tall thin man of about sixty rose in his place, and pointed a long quavering finger at the speaker.

'What is it, Darwin? speak up !' said Wharton, dropping at once into the colloquial tone, and stooping forward to listen.

'My sleepin room's six foot nine by seven foot six. We have to shift our bed for the rain's comin in, an' yer may see for yoursels ther ain't much room to shift it in. An' beyont us ther's a room for the chillen, same size as ourn, an' no window, nothin but the door into us. Ov a summer night the chillen, three on em, is all of a sweat afore they're asleep. An' no garden, an' no chance o' decent ways nohow. An' if yer ask for a bit o' repairs yer get sworn at. An' that's all that most on us can get out of Squire Boyce !'

There was a hasty whisper among some of the men round him, as they glanced over their shoulders at the two ladies on the back bench. One or two of them half rose, and tried to pull him down. Wharton looked at Marcella ; it seemed to him he saw a sort of passionate satisfaction on her pale face, and in the erect carriage of her head. Then she stooped to the side and whispered to her mother. Mrs. Boyce shook her head and sat on immovable. All this took but a second or two.

'Ah, well,' said Wharton ; 'we won't have names, that'll do us no good. It's not the *men* you've got to go for so much—though we shall go for them too before long when we've got the law more on our side. It's the system. It's the whole way of dividing the wealth that *you* make, you and your children—by your work, your hard, slavish, incessant work—between you and those who *don't* work, who live on your labour and grow fat on your poverty ! What we want is *a fair division*. There *ought* to be wealth enough—there *is* wealth enough for all in this blessed country. The earth gives it ; the sun gives it ; labour extracts and piles it up. Why should one class take three-fourths of it and leave you and your fellow-workers in the cities the miserable pittance which is all you have to starve and breed on ? Why ?—*why* ? I say. Why !—because you are a set of dull, jealous, poor-spirited *cowards*, unable to pull together, to trust each other, to give up so much as a pot of beer a week for the sake of your children and your liberties and your class—there, *that*'s why it is, and I tell it you straight out !'

He drew himself up, folded his arms across his chest, and looked at them—scorn and denunciation in every line of his young frame, and the blaze of his blue eye. A murmur ran through the room. Some of the men laughed excitedly. Darwin sprang up again.

'You keep the perlice off us, an gie us the cuttin up o' their bloomin parks an we'll do it fast enough,' he cried.

'Much good that'll do you just at present,' said Wharton, contemptuously. 'Now, you just listen to me.'

And, leaning forward over the desk again, his finger pointed at the room, he went through the regular Socialist programme as it affects the country districts—the transference of authority within the villages from the few to the many, the landlords taxed more and more heavily during the transition time for the provision of house room, water, light, education and amusement for the labourer ; and ultimately land and capital at the free disposal of the State, to be supplied to the worker on demand at the most moderate terms, while the annexed rent and interest of the capitalist

class relieves him of taxes, and the disappearance of squire, State
parson, and plutocrat leaves him master in his own house, the
slave of no man, the equal of all.   And, as a first step to this new
Jerusalem—*organisation* !—self-sacrifice enough to form and maintain a union, to vote for Radical and Socialist candidates in the
teeth of the people who have coals and blankets to give away.

'Then I suppose you think you'd be turned out of your cottages,
dismissed your work, made to smart for it somehow. Just you
try !   There are people all over the country ready to back you, if
you'd only back yourselves.   But you *won't*.   You won't fight—
that's the worst of you ; that's what makes all of us *sick* when
we come down to talk to you.   You won't spare twopence half-
penny a week from boozing—not you !—to subscribe to a union,
and take the first little step towards filling your stomachs and
holding your heads up as free men.   What's the good of your
grumbling ?   I suppose you'll go on like that—grumbling and
starving and cringing—and talking big of the things you could do
if you would :—and all the time not one honest effort—not one !—
to better yourselves, to pull the yoke off your necks !   By the Lord !
I tell you it's a *damned* sort of business talking to fellows like
you !'

Marcella started as he flung the words out with a bitter, nay, a
brutal emphasis.   The smooth-faced minister coughed loudly with
a sudden movement, half got up to remonstrate, and then thought
better of it.   Mrs. Boyce for the first time showed some animation
under her veil.   Her eyes followed the speaker with a quick attention.

As for the men, as they turned clumsily to stare at, to laugh, or
talk to each other, Marcella could hardly make out whether they were
angered or fascinated.   Whichever it was, Wharton cared for none
of them.   His blood was up ; his fatigue thrown off.   Standing
there in front of them, his hands in his pockets, pale with the
excitement of speaking, his curly head thrown out against the
whitened wall of the chapel, he lashed into the men before him,
talking their language, their dialect even, laying bare their weaknesses, sensualities, indecisions, painting in the sombrest colours
the grim truths of their melancholy lives.

Marcella could hardly breathe.   It seemed to her that, among
these cottagers, she had never lived till now—under the blaze of
these eyes—within the vibration of this voice.   Never had she so
realised the power of this singular being.   He was scourging,
dissecting, the weather-beaten men before him, as, with a difference, he had scourged, dissected her.   She found herself exulting
in his powers of tyranny, in the naked thrust of his words, so

nervous, so pitiless. And then by a sudden flash she thought of him by Mrs. Hurd's fire, the dying child on his knee, against his breast. 'Here,' she thought, while her pulses leapt, 'is the leader for me—for these. Let him call, I will follow !'

It was as though he followed the ranging of her thought, for suddenly, when she and his hearers least expected it, his tone changed, his storm of speech sank. He fell into a strain of quiet sympathy, encouragement, hope ; dwelt with a good deal of homely iteration on the immediate practical steps which each man before him could if he would take towards the common end ; spoke of the help and support lying ready for the country labourers throughout democratic England if they would but put forward their own energies and quit themselves like men ; pointed forward to a time of plenty, education, social peace ; and so—with some good-tempered banter of his opponent, old Dodgson, and some precise instructions as to how and where they were to record their votes on the day of election—came to an end. Two or three other speeches followed, and among them a few stumbling words from Hurd. Marcella approved herself and applauded him, as she recognised a sentence or two taken bodily from the *Labour Clarion* of the preceding week. Then a resolution pledging the meeting to support the Liberal candidate was passed unanimously amid evident excitement. It was the first time that such a thing had ever happened in Mellor.

Mrs. Boyce treated her visitor on their way home with a new respect, mixed, however, as usual, with her prevailing irony. For one who knew her, her manner implied, not that she liked him any more, but that a man so well trained to his own profession must always hold his own.

As for Marcella, she said little or nothing. But Wharton, in the dark of the carriage, had a strange sense that her eye was often on him, that her mood marched with his, and that if he could have spoken her response would have been electric.

When he had helped her out of the carriage, and they stood in the vestibule—Mrs. Boyce having walked on into the hall—he said to her, his voice hoarse with fatigue :—

'Did I do your bidding, did I rouse them ?'

Marcella was seized with sudden shyness.

'You rated them enough.'

'Well, did you disapprove?'

'Oh, no ! it seems to be your way.'

'My proof of friendship? Well, can there be a greater? Will you show me some to-morrow?'

'How can I?'

'Will you criticise?—tell me where you thought I was a fool to-night, or a hypocrite? Your mother would.'

'I dare say I!' said Marcella, her breath quickening; 'but don't expect it from me.'

'Why?'

'Because—because, I don't pretend. I don't know whether you roused them, but you roused *me*.'

She swept on before him into the dark hall, without giving him a moment for reply, took her candle, and disappeared.

Wharton found his own staircase, and went up to bed. The light he carried showed his smiling eyes bent on the ground, his mouth still moving as though with some pleasant desire of speech.

CHAPTER VII

WHARTON was sitting alone in the big Mellor drawing-room, after dinner. He had drawn one of the few easy chairs the room possessed to the fire, and with his feet on the fender, and one of Mr. Boyce's French novels on his knee, he was intensely enjoying a moment of physical ease. The work of these weeks of canvassing and speaking had been arduous, and he was naturally indolent. Now, beside this fire and at a distance it amazed him that any motive whatever, public or private, should ever have been strong enough to take him out through the mire on these winter nights to spout himself hoarse to a parcel of rustics. 'What did I do it for?' he asked himself; 'what am I going to do it for again to-morrow?

Ten o'clock. Mr. Boyce was gone to bed. No more entertaining of *him* to be done; one might be thankful for that mercy. Miss Boyce and her mother would, he supposed, be down directly. They had gone up to dress at nine. It was the night of the Maxwell Court ball, and the carriage had been ordered for half-past ten. In a few minutes he would see Miss Boyce in her new dress, wearing Raeburn's pearls. He was extraordinarily observant, and a number of little incidents and domestic arrangements bearing on the feminine side of Marcella's life had been apparent to him from the beginning. He knew, for instance, that the trousseau was being made at home, and that during the last few weeks the lady for whom it was destined had shown an indifference to the progress of it which seemed to excite a dumb annoyance in her mother. Curious woman, Mrs. Boyce!

He found himself listening to every opening door, and already, as it were, gazing at Marcella in her white array. He was not asked to this ball. As he had early explained to Miss Boyce, he and Miss Raeburn had been 'cuts' for years, for what reason he had of course left Marcella to guess. As if Marcella found any difficulty in guessing—as if the preposterous bigotries and intolerances of the Ladies' League were not enough to account for any similar behaviour on the part of any similar high-bred spinster! As for this occasion, she was far too proud both on her own behalf and Wharton's to say anything either to Lord Maxwell or his sister on the subject of an invitation for her father's guest.

It so happened, however, that Wharton was aware of certain other reasons for his social exclusion from Maxwell Court. There was no necessity, of course, for enlightening Miss Boyce on the point. But as he sat waiting for her, Wharton's mind went back to the past connected with those reasons. In that past Raeburn had had the whip-hand of him; Raeburn had been the moral superior dictating indignant terms to a young fellow detected in flagrant misconduct. Wharton did not know that he bore him any particular grudge. But he had never liked Aldous, as a boy, that he could remember; naturally he had liked him less since that old affair. The remembrance of it had made his position at Mellor particularly sweet to him from the beginning; he was not sure that it had not determined his original acceptance of the offer made to him by the Liberal Committee to contest old Dodgson's seat. And during the past few weeks the exhilaration and interest of the general position—considering all things—had been very great. Not only was he on the point of ousting the Maxwell candidate from a seat which he had held securely for years— Wharton was perfectly well aware by now that he was trespassing on Aldous Raeburn's preserves in ways far more important, and infinitely more irritating! He and Raeburn had not met often at Mellor during these weeks of fight. Each had been too busy. But whenever they had come across each other Wharton had clearly perceived that his presence in the house, his growing intimacy with Marcella Boyce, the freemasonry of opinion between them, the interest she took in his contest, the village friendships they had in common, were all intensely galling to Aldous Raeburn.

The course of events, indeed, had lately produced in Wharton a certain excitement—recklessness even. He had come down into these parts to court 'the joy of eventful living'—politically and personally. But the situation had proved to be actually far more poignant and personal than he had expected. This proud, crude, handsome girl—to her certainly it was largely due that the days had flown as they had. He was perfectly, one might almost say gleefully, aware that at the present moment it was he and not Aldous Raeburn who was intellectually her master. His mind flew back at first with amusement, then with a thrill of something else, over their talks and quarrels. He smiled gaily as he recalled her fits of anger with him, her remonstrances, appeals—and then her awkward inevitable submissions when he had crushed her with sarcasm or with facts. Ah! she would go to this ball to-night; Aldous Raeburn would parade her as his possession; but she would go with thoughts, ambitions, ideals, which, as they developed, would make her more and more difficult for a Raeburn to deal with. And in those thoughts and ambitions the man who had been her tormentor, teacher, and companion during six rushing weeks knew well that he already counted for much. He had cherished in her all those ' divine discontents' which were already there when he first knew her; taught her to formulate them, given her better reasons for them ; so that by now she was a person with a far more defined and stormy will than she had been to begin with. Wharton did not particularly know why he should exult ; but he did exult. At any rate, he was prodigiously tickled— entertained—by the whole position.

A step, a rustle outside—he hastily shut his book and listened.

The door opened, and Marcella came in—a white vision against the heavy blue of the walls. With her came, too, a sudden strong scent of flowers, for she carried a marvellous bunch of hot-house roses, Aldous's gift, which had just arrived by special messenger.

Wharton sprang up and placed a chair for her.

' I had begun to believe the ball only existed in my own imagination !' he said gaily. ' Surely you are very late.'

Then he saw that she looked disturbed.

' It was papa,' she said, coming to the fire, and looking down into it. ' It has been another attack of pain—not serious, mamma says ; she is coming down directly. But I wonder why they come, and why he thinks himself so ill—do you know?' she added abruptly, turning to her companion.

Wharton hesitated, taken by surprise. During the past weeks, what with Mr. Boyce's confidence, and his own acuteness, he had arrived at a very shrewd notion of what was wrong with his host. But he was not going to enlighten the daughter.

' I should say your father wants a great deal of care—and is nervous about himself,' he said quietly. ' But he will get the care —and your mother knows the whole state of the case.'

' Yes, she knows,' said Marcella. ' I wish I did.'

And a sudden painful expression—of moral worry, remorse—

passed across the girl's face.   Wharton knew that she had often
been impatient of late with her father, and incredulous of his com-
plaints.   He thought he understood.

'One can often be of more use to a sick person if one is not too
well acquainted with what ails them,' he said.   'Hope and cheerfulness are everything in a case like your father's.   He will do well.'

'If he does he won't owe any of it——'

She stopped as impulsively as she had begun.   'To me,' she
meant to have said; then had retreated hastily before her own
sense of something unduly intimate and personal.   Wharton stood
quietly beside her, saying nothing, but receiving and soothing her
self-reproach just as surely as though she had put it into words.

'You are crushing your flowers, I think,' he said suddenly.

And indeed her roses were dangling against her dress, as if she
had forgotten all about them.

She raised them carelessly, but he bent to smell them, and she
held them out.

'Summer!' he said, plunging his face into them with a long
breath of sensuous enjoyment.   'How the year sweeps round in an
instant! And all the effect of a little heat and a little money.   Will
you allow me a philosopher's remark?'

He drew back from her.   His quick inquisitive but still respectful eye took in every delightful detail.

'If I don't give you leave, my experience is that you will take
it!' she said, half laughing, half resentful, as though she had old
aggressions in mind.

'You admit the strength of the temptation?   It is very simple,
no one could help making it.   To be spectator of the *height* of
anything—the best, the climax—makes any mortal's pulses run.
Beauty, success, happiness, for instance?'

He paused smiling.   She leant a thin hand on the mantelpiece
and looked away; Aldous's pearls slipped backwards along her
white arm.

'Do you suppose to-night will be the height of happiness?'
she said at last with a little scorn.   'These functions don't present
themselves to *me* in such a light.'

Wharton could have laughed out—her pedantry was so young
and unconscious.   But he restrained himself.

'I shall be with the majority to-night,' he said demurely.   'I
may as well warn you.'

Her colour rose.   No other man had ever dared to speak to
her with this assurance, this cool scrutinising air.   She told herself
to be indignant; the next moment she *was* indignant, but with herself, for remembering conventionalities.

'Tell me one thing,' said Wharton, changing his tone wholly.
'I know you went down hurriedly to the village before dinner.
Was anything wrong?'

'Old Patton is very ill,' she said, sighing. 'I went to ask after
him; he may die any moment. And the Hurds' boy too.'

He leant against the mantelpiece, talking to her about both
cases with a quick incisive common-sense—not unkind, but without
a touch of unnecessary sentiment, still less of the superior person—
which represented one of the moods she liked best in him. In
speaking of the poor he always took the tone of comradeship, of
a plain equality, and the tone was, in fact, genuine.

'Do you know,' he said presently, 'I did not tell you before,
but I am certain that Hurd's wife is afraid of you, that she has a
secret from you?'

'From me! how could she? I know every detail of their
affairs.'

'No matter. I listened to what she said that day, in the cottage
when I had the boy on my knee. I noticed her face, and I am
quite certain. She has a secret, and above all a secret from you.'

Marcella looked disturbed for a moment, then she laughed.

'Oh, no!' she said, with a little superior air. 'I assure you
I know her better than you.'

Wharton said no more.

'Marcella!' called a distant voice from the hall.

The girl gathered up her white skirts and her flowers in
haste.

'Good night!'

'Good night! I shall hear you come home and wonder how
you have sped. One word, if I may! Take your *rôle* and play it.
There is nothing subjects dislike so much as to see royalty decline
its part.'

She laughed, blushed, a little proudly and uncertainly, and
went without reply. As she shut the door behind her, a sudden
flatness fell upon her. She walked through the dark Stone Parlour
outside, seeing still the firmly-knit lightly-made figure—boyish,
middle-sized, yet never insignificant—the tumbled waves of fair
hair, the eyes so keenly blue, the face with its sharp mocking
lines, its powers of sudden charm. Then self-reproach leapt, and
possessed her. She quickened her pace, hurrying into the hall, as
though from something she was ashamed or afraid of.

In the hall a new sensation awaited her. Her mother, fully
dressed, stood waiting by the old billiard-table for her maid, who
had gone to fetch her a cloak.

Marcella stopped an instant in surprise and delight, then ran up to her. 'Mamma, how *lovely* you look ! · I haven't seen you like that, not since I was a child. I remember you then once, in a low dress, a white dress, with flowers, coming into the nursery. But that black becomes you so well, and Deacon has done your hair beautifully !'

She took her mother's hand and kissed her cheek, touched by an emotion which had many roots. There was infinate relief in this tender natural outlet ; she seemed to recover possession of herself.

Mrs. Boyce bore the kiss quietly. Her face was a little pinched and white. But the unusual display Deacon had been allowed to make of her pale golden hair, still long and abundant ; the unveiling of the shapely shoulders and neck, little less beautiful than her daughter's ; the elegant lines of the velvet dress, all these things had very nobly transformed her. Marcella could not restrain her admiration and delight. Mrs. Boyce winced, and, looking upward to the gallery, which ran round the hall, called Deacon impatiently.

'Only, mamma,' said Marcella discontentedly, 'I don't like that little chain round your neck. It is not equal to the rest, not worthy of it.'

'I have nothing else, my dear,' said Mrs. Boyce, drily. 'Now, Deacon, don't be all night !'

Nothing else? Yet, if she shut her eyes, Marcella could perfectly recall the diamonds on the neck and arms of that white figure of her childhood—could see herself as a baby playing with the treasures of her mother's jewel-box.

Nowadays, Mrs. Boyce was very secretive and reserved about her personal possessions. Marcella never went into her room unless she was asked, and would never have thought of treating it or its contents with any freedom.

The mean chain which went so ill with the costly hoarded dress—it recalled to Marcella all the inexorable silent miseries of her mother's past life, and all the sordid disadvantages and troubles of her own youth. She followed Mrs. Boyce out to the carriage in silence—once more in a tumult of sore pride and doubtful feeling.

Four weeks to her wedding-day ! The words dinned in her ears as they drove along. Yet they sounded strange to her, incredible almost. How much did she know of Aldous, of her life that was to be—above all, how much of herself? She was not happy—had not been happy or at ease for many days. Yet in her restlessness she could think nothing out. Moreover, the chain that galled and curbed her was a chain of character. In spite of

her modernness, and the complexity of many of her motives, there
were certain inherited simplicities of nature at the bottom of her.
In her wild demonic childhood you could always trust Marcie
Boyce, if she had given you her word—her schoolfellows knew
that. If her passions were half-civilised and southern, her way of
understanding the point of honour was curiously English, sober,
tenacious. So now. Her sense of bond to Aldous had never
been in the least touched by any of her dissatisfactions and revolts.
Yet it rushed upon her to-night with amazement, and that in four
weeks she was going to marry him ! Why ? how ?—what would
it really *mean* for him and for her ? It was as though in mid-
stream she were trying to pit herself for an instant against the
current which had so far carried them all on, to see what it might
be like to retrace a step, and could only realise with dismay the
force and rapidity of the water.

Yet all the time another side of her was well aware that she
was at that moment the envy of half a county, that in another
ten minutes hundreds of eager and critical eyes would be upon
her ; and her pride was rising to her part. The little incident of
the chain had somehow for the moment made the ball and her
place in it more attractive to her.

They had no sooner stepped from their carriage than Aldous,
who was waiting in the outer hall, joyously discovered them. Till
then he had been walking aimlessly amid the crowd of his own
guests, wondering when she would come, how she would like it.
This splendid function had been his grandfather's idea ; it would
never have entered his own head for a moment. Yet he understood
his grandfather's wish to present his heir's promised bride in this
public ceremonious way to the society of which she would some
day be the natural leader. He understood, too, that there was
more in the wish than met the ear ; that the occasion meant to
Lord Maxwell, whether Dick Boyce were there or no, the final
condoning of things past and done with, a final throwing of the
Maxwell shield over the Boyce weakness, and full adoption of
Marcella into her new family.

All this he understood and was grateful for. But how would
she respond ? How would she like it—this parade that was to be
made of her—these people that must be introduced to her ? He
was full of anxieties.

Yet in many ways his mind had been easier of late. During
the last week she had been very gentle and good to him—even
Miss Raeburn had been pleased with her. There had been no
quoting of Wharton when they met ; and he had done his philo-

sopher's best to forget him. He trusted her proudly, intensely ; and in four weeks she would be his wife.

'Can you bear it?' he said to her in a laughing whisper as she and her mother emerged from the cloak-room.

'Tell me what to do,' she said, flushing. 'I will do my best. What a crowd ! Must we stay very long?'

'Ah, my dear Mrs. Boyce,' cried Lord Maxwell, meeting them on the steps of the inner quadrangular corridor—'Welcome indeed! Let me take you in. Marcella ! with Aldous's permission !' he stooped his white head gallantly and kissed her on the cheek— 'Remember I am an old man ; if I choose to pay you compliments, you will have to put up with them !'

Then he offered Mrs. Boyce his arm, a stately figure in his ribbon and cross of the Bath. A delicate red had risen to that lady's thin cheek in spite of her self-possession. 'Poor thing,' said Lord Maxwell to himself as he led her along—'poor thing !— how distinguished and charming still ! One sees to-night what she was like as a girl.'

Aldous and Marcella followed. They had to pass along the great corridor which ran round the quadrangle of the house. The antique marbles which lined it were to-night masked in flowers, and seats covered in red had been fitted in wherever it was possible, and were now crowded with dancers 'sitting out.' From the ball-room ahead came waves of waltz-music ; the ancient house was alive with colour and perfume, with the sounds of laughter and talk, lightly fretting and breaking the swaying rhythms of the band. Beyond the windows of the corridor, which had been left uncurtained because of the beauty of the night, the stiff Tudor garden with its fountains, which filled up the quadrangle, was gaily illuminated under a bright moon ; and amid all the varied colour of lamps, drapery, dresses, faces, the antique heads ranged along the walls of the corridor—here Marcus Aurelius, there Trajan, there Seneca—and the marble sarcophagi which broke the line at intervals, stood in cold, whitish relief.

Marcella passed along on Aldous's arm, conscious that people were streaming into the corridor from all the rooms opening upon it, and that every eye was fixed upon her and her mother. 'Look, there she is,' she heard in an excited girl's voice as they passed Lord Maxwell's library, now abandoned to the crowd like all the rest. 'Come, quick ! There—I told you she was lovely !'

Every now and then some old friend, man or woman, rose smiling from the seats along the side, and Aldous introduced his bride.

'On her dignity !' said an old hunting squire to his daughter when they had passed. 'Shy, no doubt—very natural! But nowadays girls, when they're shy, don't giggle and blush as they used to in *my* young days; they look as if you meant to insult them, and they weren't going to allow it! Oh, very handsome—very handsome—of course. But you can see she's advanced—peculiar—or what d'ye call it?—woman's rights, I suppose, and all that kind of thing? Like to see you go in for it, Nettie, eh!'

'She's *awfully* handsome,' sighed his pink-cheeked, insignificant little daughter, still craning her neck to look—'very simply dressed too, except for those lovely pearls. She does her hair very oddly, so low down—in those plaits. Nobody does it like that nowadays.'

'That's because nobody has such a head,' said her brother, a young Hussar lieutenant, beside her, in the tone of connoisseurship. 'By George, she's ripping—she's the best-looking girl I've seen for a good long time. But she's a Tartar, I'll swear—looks it, anyway.'

'Everyone says she has the most extraordinary opinions,' said the girl eagerly. 'She'll manage him, don't you think? I'm sure he's very meek and mild.'

'Don't know that,' said the young man, twisting his moustache with the air of exhaustive information. 'Raeburn's a very good fellow—excellent fellow—see him shooting, you know—that kind of thing. I expect he's got a will when he wants it. The mother's handsome, too, and looks a lady. The father's kept out of the way, I see. Rather a blessing for the Raeburns. Can't be pleasant, you know, to get a man like that in the family. Look after your spoons—that kind of thing.'

Meanwhile Marcella was standing beside Miss Raeburn, at the head of the long ball-room, and doing her best to behave prettily. One after another she bowed to, or shook hands with, half the magnates of the county—the men in pink, the women in the new London dresses, for which this brilliant and long-expected ball had given so welcome an excuse. They knew little or nothing of her, except that she was clearly good-looking, that she was that fellow Dick Boyce's daughter, and was reported to be 'odd.' Some, mostly men, who said their conventional few words to her, felt an amused admiration for the skill and rapidity with which she had captured the *parti* of the county; some, mostly women, were already jealous of her. A few of the older people here and there, both men and women—but after all they shook hands like the rest!—knew perfectly well that the girl must be going through an ordeal, were touched by the signs of thought and storm in the face, and looked back at her with kind eyes.

But of these last Marcella realised nothing. What she was

saying to herself was that, if they knew little of her, she knew a great deal of many of them.   In their talks over the Stone Parlour fire she and Wharton had gone through most of the properties, large and small, of his division, and indeed of the divisions round, by the help of the knowledge he had gained in his canvass, together with a blue-book—one of the numberless!—recently issued, on the state of the midland labourer.   He had abounded in anecdote, sarcasm, reflection, based partly on his own experiences, partly on his endless talks with the working folk, now in the public-house, now at their own chimney-corner.   Marcella, indeed, had a large unsuspected acquaintance with the county before she met it in the flesh.   She knew that a great many of these men who came and spoke to her were doing their best according to their lights, that improvements were going on, that times were mending.   But there were abuses enough still, and the abuses were far more vividly present to her than the improvements.   In general, the people who thronged these splendid rooms were to her merely the incompetent members of a useless class.   The nation would do away with them in time!   Meanwhile it might at least be asked of them that they should practise their profession of landowning, such as it was, with greater conscience and intelligence—that they should not shirk its opportunities or idle them away.   And she could point out those who did both—scandalously, intolerably.   Once or twice she thought passionately of Minta Hurd, washing and mending all day, in her damp cottage; or of the Pattons in 'the parish house,' thankful after sixty years of toil for a hovel where the rain came through the thatch, and where the smoke choked you, unless, with the thermometer below freezing-point, you opened the door to the blast.   Why should *these* people have all the gay clothes, the flowers, the jewels, the delicate food—all the delight and all the leisure?   And those, nothing!   Her soul rose against what she saw as she stood there, going through her part.   Wharton's very words, every inflection of his voice was in her ears, playing chorus to the scene.

But when these first introductions, these little empty talks of three or four phrases apiece, and all of them alike, were nearly done with, Marcella looked eagerly round for Mary Harden.   There she was, sitting quietly against the wall in a remote corner, her plain face all smiles, her little feet dancing under the white muslin frock which she had fashioned for herself with so much pain under Marcella's directions.   Miss Raeburn was called away to find an arm-chair for some dowager of importance; Marcella took advantage of the break and of the end of a dance to hurry down the room to Mary.   Aldous, who was talking to old Sir Charles Leven,

Frank's father, a few steps off, nodded and smiled to her as he saw her move.

'Have you been dancing, Mary?' she said severely.

'I wouldn't for worlds! I never was so much amused in my life. Look at those girls—those sisters—in the huge velvet sleeves, like coloured balloons!—and that old lady in the pink tulle and diamonds.—I do so want to get her her cloak! *And* those Lancers!—I never could have imagined people danced like that. They didn't dance them—they romped them! It wasn't beautiful —was it?'

'Why do you expect an English crowd to do anything beautiful? If we could do it, we should be too ashamed.'

'But it *is* beautiful, all the same, you scornful person!' cried Mary, dragging her friend down beside her. 'How pretty the girls are! And as for the diamonds, I never saw anything so wonderful. I wish I could have made Charles come!'

'Wouldn't he?'

'No'—she looked a little troubled—'he couldn't think it would be quite right. But I don't know—a sight like this takes me off my feet, shakes me up, and does *me* a world of good!'

'You dear, simple thing!' said Marcella, slipping her hand into Mary's as it lay on the bench.

'Oh, you needn't be so superior!' cried Mary,—'not for another year at least. I don't believe you are much more used to it than I am!'

'If you mean,' said Marcella, 'that I was never at anything so big and splendid as this before, you are quite right.'

And she looked round the room with that curious, cold air of personal detachment from all she saw, which had often struck Mary, and to-night made her indignant.

'Then enjoy it!' she said, laughing and frowning at the same time. 'That's a much more plain duty for *you* than it was for Charles to stay at home—there! Haven't you been dancing?'

'No, Mr. Raeburn doesn't dance. But he thinks he can get through the next Lancers if I will steer him.'

'Then I shall find a seat where I can look at you,' said Mary decidedly. 'Ah, there is Mr. Raeburn coming to introduce somebody to you. I knew they wouldn't let you sit here long.'

Aldous brought up a young Guardsman, who boldly asked Miss Boyce for the pleasure of a dance. Marcella consented; and off they swept into a room which was only just beginning to fill for the new dance, and where, therefore, for the moment the young grace of both had free play. Marcella had been an indefatigable dancer in the old London days at those students' parties, with their dyed gloves and lemonade suppers, which were running in her head now, as she swayed to the rhythm of this perfect band. The mere delight in movement came back to her ; and while they danced, she danced with all her heart. Then in the pauses she would lean against the wall beside her partner, and rack her brain to find a word to say to him. As for anything that *he* said, every word— whether of Ascot, or the last Academy, or the new plays, or the hunting and the elections—sounded to here more vapid than the last.

Meanwhile Aldous stood near Mary Harden and watched the dancing figure. He had never seen her dance before. Mary shyly stole a look at him from time to time.

'Well,' he said at last, stooping to his neighbour, 'what are you thinking of ?'

'I think she is a dream !' said Mary, flushing with the pleasure of being able to say it. They were great friends, he and she, and to-night somehow she was not a bit afraid of him.

Aldous's eye sparkled a moment ; then he looked down at her with a kind smile.

'If you suppose I am going to let you sit here all night, you are very much mistaken. Marcella gave me precise instructions. I am going off this moment to find somebody.'

'Mr. Raeburn—don't !' cried Mary, catching at him. But he was gone, and she was left in trepidation, imagining the sort of formidable young man who was soon to be presented to her, and shaking at the thought of him.

When the dance was over Marcella returned to Miss Raeburn, who was standing at the door into the corridor and had beckoned to her. She went through a number of new introductions, and declared to herself that she was doing all she could. Miss Raeburn was not so well satisfied.

'Why can't she smile and chatter like other girls?' thought Aunt Neta impatiently. 'It's her "ideas," I suppose. What rubbish ! There, now—just see the difference !'

For at the moment Lady Winterbourne came up, and instantly Marcella was all smiles and talk, holding her friend by both hands, clinging to her almost.

'Oh, do come here !' she said, leading her into a corner. 'There's such a crowd, and I say all the wrong things. There !' with a sigh of relief. 'Now I feel myself protected.'

'I mustn't keep you,' said Lady Winterbourne, a little taken aback by her effusion. 'Everybody is wanting to talk to you.'

'Oh, I know ! There is Miss Raeburn looking at me severely already. But I must do as I like a little.'

'You ought to do as Aldous likes,' said Lady Winterbourne suddenly, in her deepest and most tragic voice. It seemed to her a moment had come for admonition, and she seized it hastily.

Marcella stared at her in surprise. She knew by now that when Lady Winterbourne looked most forbidding she was in reality most shy. But still she was taken aback.

'Why do you say that, I wonder?' she asked, half reproachfully. 'I have been behaving myself quite nicely—I have indeed; at least, as nicely as I knew how.'

Lady Winterbourne's tragic air yielded to a slow smile.

'You look very well, my dear. That white becomes you charmingly ; so do the pearls. I don't wonder that Aldous always knows where you are.'

Marcella raised her eyes and caught those of Aldous fixed upon her from the other side of the room. She blushed, smiled slightly, and looked away.

'Who is that tall man just gone up to speak to him?' she asked of her companion.

'That is Lord Wandle,' said Lady Winterbourne, 'and his plain second wife behind him. Edward always scolds me for not admiring him. He says women know nothing at all about men's looks, and that Lord Wandle was the most splendid man of his time. But I always think it an unpleasant face.'

'Lord Wandle!' exclaimed Marcella, frowning. 'Oh, *please* come with me, dear Lady Winterbourne ! I know he is asking Aldous to introduce him, and I won't—no, I will *not*—be introduced to him.'

And, laying hold of her astonished companion, she drew her hastily through a doorway near, walked quickly, still gripping her, through two connected rooms beyond, and finally landed her and herself on a sofa in Lord Maxwell's library, pursued meanwhile through all her hurried course by the curious looks of an observant throng.

'That man !—no, that would really have been *too* much !' said Marcella, using her large feather fan with stormy energy.

'What *is* the matter with you, my dear?' said Lady Winterbourne in her amazement ; 'and what is the matter with Lord Wandle?'

'You must know !' said Marcella indignantly. 'Oh, you *must* have seen that case in the paper last week—that *shocking* case ! A woman and two children died in one of his cottages of blood-poisoning—nothing in the world but his neglect—his *brutal* neglect !' Her breast heaved ; she seemed almost on the point of weeping. 'The agent was appealed to—did nothing. Then the clergyman wrote to him direct, and got an answer. The answer was published. For cruel insolence, I never saw anything like it ! He ought to be in prison for manslaughter—and he comes *here* ! And people laugh and talk with him ! '

She stopped, almost choked by her own passion. But the incident, after all, was only the spark to the mine.

Lady Winterbourne stared at her helplessly.

'Perhaps it isn't true,' she suggested. 'The newspapers put in so many lies, especially about *us*—the landlords. Edward says one ought never to believe them. Ah, here comes Aldous.'

Aldous, indeed, with some perplexity on his brow, was to be seen approaching, looking for his betrothed. Marcella dropped her fan and sat erect, her angry colour fading into whiteness.

'My darling ! I couldn't think what had become of you. May I bring Lord Wandle and introduce him to you ? He is an old friend here, and my godfather. Not that I am particularly proud of the relationship,' he said, dropping his voice as he stooped over her. 'He is a soured, disagreeable fellow, and I hate many of the things he does. But it is an old tie, and my grandfather is tender of such things. Only a word or two ; then I will get rid of him.'

'Aldous, I *can't*,' said Marcella, looking up at him. 'How could I ? I saw that case. I must be rude to him.'

Aldous looked considerably disturbed.

'It was very bad,' he said slowly. 'I didn't know you had seen it. What shall I do ? I promised to go back for him.'

'Lord Wandle—Miss Boyce !' said Miss Raeburn's sharp little voice behind Aldous. Aldous, moving aside in hasty dismay, saw his aunt, looking very determined, presenting her tall neighbour, who bowed low with old-fashioned deference to the girl on the sofa.

Lady Winterbourne looked with trepidation at Marcella. But the social instinct held, to some extent. Ninety-nine women can threaten a scene of the kind Lady Winterbourne dreaded, for one that can carry it through. Marcella wavered ; then, with her most forbidding air, she made a scarcely perceptible return of Lord Wandle's bow.

'Did you escape in here out of the heat ? ' he asked her. ' But I am afraid no one lets you escape to-night. The occasion is too interesting.'

Marcella made no reply. Lady Winterbourne threw in a nervous remark on the crowd.

'Oh, yes, a great crush,' said Lord Wandle. 'Of course, we all come to see Aldous happy. How long is it, Miss Boyce, since you settled at Mellor ? '

'Six months.'

She looked straight before her and not at him as she answered, and her tone made Miss Raeburn's blood boil.

Lord Wandle—a battered, coarsened, but still magnificent-looking man of sixty—examined the speaker an instant from half-shut eyes, then put up his hand to his moustache with a half-smile.

'You like the country?'

'Yes.'

As she spoke her reluctant monosyllable, the girl had really no conception of the degree of hostility expressed in her manner. Instead she was hating herself for her own pusillanimity.

'And the people?'

'Some of them.'

And straightway she raised her fierce black eyes to his, and the man before her understood, as plainly as anyone need understand, that, whoever else Miss Boyce might like, she did not like Lord Wandle, and wished for no more conversation with him.

Her interrogator turned to Aldous with smiling *aplomb*.

'Thank you, my dear Aldous. Now let me retire. No one must *monopolise* your charming lady.'

And again he bowed low to her, this time with an ironical emphasis not to be mistaken, and walked away.

Lady Winterbourne saw him go up to his wife, who had followed him at a distance, and speak to her roughly with a frown. They left the room, and presently, through the other door of the library which opened on the corridor, she saw them pass, as though they were going to their carriage.

Marcella rose. She looked first at Miss Raeburn—then at Aldous.

'Will you take me away?' she said, going up to him; 'I am tired—take me to your room.'

He put her hand inside his arm, and they pushed their way through the crowd. Outside in the passage they met Hallin. He had not seen her before, and he put out his hand. But there was something distant in his gentle greeting which struck at this moment like a bruise on Marcella's quivering nerves. It came across her that for some time past he had made no further advances to her; that his first eager talk of friendship between himself and her had dropped; that his *acceptance* of her into his world and Aldous's was somehow suspended—in abeyance. She bit her lip tightly and hurried Aldous along. Again the same lines of gay, chatting people along the corridor, and on either side of the wide staircase—greetings, introduction—a nightmare of publicity.

'Rather pronounced—to carry him off like that,' said a clergy-man to his wife with a kindly smile, as the two tall figures disappeared along the upper gallery. 'She will have him all to herself before long.'

Aldous shut the door of his sitting-room behind them. Marcella quickly drew her hand out of his arm, and going forward to the mantelpiece rested both elbows upon it and hid her face.

He looked at her a moment in distress and astonishment, standing a little apart. Then he saw that she was crying. The colour flooded into his face, and going up to her he took her hand, which was all she would yield him, and, holding it to his lips, said in her ear every soothing tender word that love's tutoring could bring to mind. In his emotion he told himself and her that he admired and loved her the more for the incident downstairs, for the temper she had shown! She alone among them all had had the courage to strike the true stern Christian note. As to the annoyance such courage might bring upon him and her in the future—even as to the trouble it might cause his own dear folk— what real matter? In these things she should lead.

What could love have asked better than such a moment? Yet Marcella's weeping was in truth the weeping of despair. This man's very sweetness to her, his very assumption of the right to comfort and approve her, roused in her a desperate stifled sense of bonds that should never have been made, and that now could not be broken. It was all plain to her at last. His touch had no thrill for her; his frown no terror. She had accepted him without loving him, coveting what he could give her. And now it seemed to her that she cared nothing for anything he could give !—that the life before her was to be one series of petty conflicts between her and a surrounding circumstance which must inevitably in the end be too strong for her, conflicts from which neither heart nor ambition could gain anything. She had desired a great position for what she might do with it. But what could she do with it! She would be subdued—oh! very quickly !—to great houses and great people, and all the vapid pomp and idle toil of wealth. All that picture of herself, stooping from place and power, to bind up the wounds of the people, in which she had once delighted, was to her now a mere flimsy vulgarity. She had been shown other ideals—other ways—and her pulses were still swaying under the audacity—the virile inventive force of the showman. Everything she had once desired looked flat to her; everything she was not to have, glowed and shone. Poverty, adventure, passion, the joys of self-realisation—these she gave up. She would become Lady Maxwell, make friends with Miss Raeburn, and wear the family diamonds !

Then, in the midst of her rage with herself and fate, she drew herself away, looked up, and caught full the eyes of Aldous Raeburn. Conscience stung and burned. What was this life she had dared to trifle with—this man she had dared to treat as a mere pawn in her own game? She gave way utterly, appalled at her own misdoing, and behaved like a penitent child. Aldous, astonished and alarmed by her emotion and by the wild incoherent things she said, won his way at last to some moments of divine happiness, when, leaving her trembling hand in his, she sat submissively beside him, gradually quieting down, summoning back her smiles and her beauty, and letting him call her all the fond names he would.

CHAPTER VIII

SCARCELY a word was exchanged between Marcella and her mother on the drive home. Yet under ordinary circumstances Marcella's imagination would have found some painful exercise in the effort to find out in what spirit her mother had taken the evening—the first social festivity in which Richard Boyce's wife had taken part for sixteen years. In fact, Mrs. Boyce had gone through it very quietly. After her first public entry on Lord Maxwell's arm she had sat in her corner, taking keen note of everything, enjoying probably the humours of her kind. Several old acquaintances who had seen her at Mellor as a young wife in her first married years had come up with some trepidation to speak to her. She had received them with her usual well-bred indifference, and they had gone away under the impression that she regarded herself as restored to society by this great match that her daughter was making. Lady Winterbourne had been shyly and therefore formidably kind to her ; and both Lord Maxwell and Miss Raeburn had been genuinely interested in smoothing the effort to her as much as they could. She meanwhile watched Marcella—except through the encounter with Lord Wandle, which she did not see— and found some real pleasure in talking both to Aldous and to Hallin.

Yet all through she was preoccupied, and towards the end very anxious to get home, a state of mind which prevented her from noticing Marcella's changed looks after her reappearance with Aldous in the ball-room, as closely as she otherwise might have done. Yet the mother *had* observed that the end of Marcella's progress had been somewhat different from the beginning; that the girl's greetings had been gentler, her smiles softer; and that in particular she had taken some pains, some wistful pains, to make Hallin talk to her. Lord Maxwell—ignorant of the Wandle incident—was charmed with her, and openly said so, both to the mother and Lady Winterbourne, in his hearty old man's way. Only Miss Raeburn held indignantly aloof, and would not pretend, even to Mrs. Boyce.

And now Marcella was tired—dead tired, she said to herself, both in mind and body. She lay back in the carriage, trying to sink herself in her own fatigue, to forget everything, to think of nothing. Outside the night was mild, and the moon clear. For some days past, after the break-up of the long frost, there had been heavy rain. Now the rain had cleared away, and in the air there was already an early promise of spring. As she walked home from the village that afternoon she had felt the buds and the fields stirring.

When they got home, Mrs. Boyce turned to her daughter at the head of the stairs, 'Shall I unlace your dress, Marcella?'

'Oh no, thank you. Can I help you?'

'No. Good night.'

'Mamma!' Marcella turned and ran after her. 'I should like to know how papa is. I will wait here if you will tell me.'

Mrs. Boyce looked surprised. Then she went into her room and shut the door. Marcella waited outside, leaning against the old oak gallery which ran round the hall, her candle the one spot of light and life in the great dark house.

'He seems to have slept well,' said Mrs. Boyce, reappearing, and speaking under her breath. 'He has not taken the opiate I left for him, so he cannot have been in pain. Good night.'

Marcella kissed her and went. Somehow, in her depression of nerve and will, she was loth to go away by herself. The loneliness of the night, and of her wing of the house, weighed upon her; the noises made by the old boards under her steps, the rustling draughts from the dark passages to right and left startled and troubled her; she found herself childishly fearing lest her candle should go out.

Yet, as she descended the two steps to the passage outside her door, she could have felt little practical need of it, for the moonlight was streaming in through its uncovered windows, not directly, but reflected from the Tudor front of the house which ran at right angles to this passage, and was to-night a shining silver palace, every battlement, window, and moulding in sharpest light and shade under the radiance of the night. Beneath her feet, as she looked out into the Cedar Garden, was a deep triangle of shadow, thrown by that part of the building in which she stood ; and beyond the garden the barred black masses of the cedars closing up the view lent additional magic to the glittering unsubstantial fabric of the moonlit house, which was, as it were, embosomed and framed among them. She paused a moment, struck by the strangeness and beauty of the spectacle. The Tudor front had the air of some fairy banqueting-hall lit by unearthly hands for some weird gathering of ghostly knights. Then she turned to her room, impatiently longing in her sick fatigue to be quit of her dress and ornaments and tumble into sleep.

Yet she made no hurry. She fell on the first chair that offered. Her candle behind her had little power over the glooms of the dark tapestried room, but it did serve to illuminate the lines of her own form, as she saw it reflected in the big glass of her wardrobe, straight in front of her. She sat with her hands round her knees, absently looking at herself, a white long-limbed apparition struck out of the darkness. But she was conscious of nothing save one mounting overwhelming passionate desire, almost a cry.

Mr. Wharton must go away—he *must*—or she could not bear it.

Quick alternations of insight, memory, self-recognition, self-surrender, rose and broke upon her. At last, physical weariness recalled her. She put up her hands to take off her pearls.

As she did so, she started, hearing a noise that made her turn her head. Just outside her door a little spiral staircase led down from her corridor to the one below, which ran at the back of the old library, and opened into the Cedar Garden at its further end.

Steps surely—light steps—along the corridor outside, and on the staircase. Nor did they die away. She could still hear them, —as she sat, arrested, straining her ears,—pacing slowly along the lower passage.

Her heart, after its pause, leapt into fluttering life. This room of hers, the two passages, the library, and the staircase, represented that part of the house to which the ghost stories of Mellor clung most persistently. Substantially the block of building was of early Tudor date, but the passages and the staircase had been alterations made with some clumsiness at the time of the erection of the eighteenth-century front, with a view to bringing these older rooms into the general plan. Marcella, however, might demonstrate as she pleased that the Boyce who was supposed to have stabbed himself on the staircase died at least forty years before the staircase was made. None the less, no servant would go alone, if she could help it, into either passage after dark ; and there was much excited marvelling how Miss Boyce could sleep where she did. Deacon abounded in stories of things spiritual and peripatetic, of steps, groans, lights in the library, and the rest. Marcella had consistently laughed at her.

Yet all the same she had made in secret a very diligent pursuit of this ghost, settling in the end to a certain pique with him that he would not show himself to so ardent a daughter of the house. She had sat up waiting for him ; she had lingered in the corridor outside, and on the stairs, expecting him. By the help of a favourite carpenter she had made researches into roofs, water-pipes, panelling, and old cupboards, in the hope of finding a practical clue to him. In vain.

Yet here were the steps—regular, soft, unmistakable. The colour rushed back into her cheeks ! Her eager healthy youth forgot its woes, flung off its weariness, and panted for an adventure, a discovery. Springing up, she threw her fur wrap round her again, and gently opened the door, listening.

For a minute, nothing—then a few vague sounds as of something living and moving down below—surely in the library ? Then the steps again. Impossible that it should be anyone breaking in. No burglar would walk so leisurely. She closed her door behind her, and, gathering her white satin skirts about her, she descended the staircase.

The corridor below was in radiant moonlight, chequered by the few pieces of old furniture it contained, and the black and white of the old portrait prints hanging on the walls. At first her seeking, excited eyes could make out nothing. Then in a flash they perceived the figure of Wharton at the further end near the garden door, leaning against one of the windows. He was apparently looking out at the moonlit house, and she caught the faint odour of a cigarette.

Her first instinct was to turn and fly. But Wharton had seen her. As he looked about him at the sound of her approach, the moon, which was just rounding the corner of the house, struck on her full, amid the shadows of the staircase, and she heard his exclamation.

Dignity—a natural pride—made her pause. She came forward slowly—he eagerly.

'I heard footsteps,' she said, with a coldness under which he plainly saw her embarrassment. 'I could not suppose that anybody was still up, so I came down to see.'

He was silent a moment, scanning her with laughing eyes Then he shook his head. 'Confess you took me for the ghost ? he said.

She hesitated ; then must laugh too. She herself had told him the stories, so that his guess was natural.

'Perhaps I did,' she said. 'One more disappointment ! Good night.'

He looked after her a quick undecided moment as she made a step in front of him, then at the half-burnt cigarette he held in his hand, threw the end away with a hasty gesture, overtook her and walked beside her along the corridor.

'I heard you and your mother come in,' he said, as though explaining himself. 'Then I waited till I thought you must both be asleep, and came down here to look at that wonderful effect on the old house.' He pointed to the silver palace outside. 'I have a trick of being sleepless—a trick, too, of wandering at night. My own people know it, and bear with me, but I am abashed that you should have found me out. Just tell me—in one word—how the ball went.'

He paused at the foot of the stairs, his hands on his sides, as keenly wide-awake as though it were three o'clock in the afternoon instead of three in the morning.

Womanlike, her mood instantly shaped itself to his.

'It went very well,' she said perversely, putting her satin-slippered foot on the first step. 'There were six hundred people upstairs, and four hundred coachmen and footmen downstairs, according to our man. Everybody said it was splendid.'

His piercing enigmatic gaze could not leave her. As he had often frankly warned her, he was a man in quest of sensations. Certainly, in this strange meeting with Aldous Raeburn's betrothed, in the midst of the sleep-bound house, he had found one. Her eyes were heavy, her cheek pale. But in this soft vague light—white arms and neck now hidden, now revealed by the cloak she had thrown about her glistening satin—she was more enchanting than he had ever seen her. His breath quickened.

He said to himself that he would make Miss Boyce stay and talk to him. What harm—to her or to Raeburn? Raeburn would have chances enough before long. Why admit his monopoly before the time? She was not in love with him ! As to Mrs. Grundy— absurd ! What in the true reasonableness of things was to prevent human beings from conversing by night as well as by day ?

'One moment '—he said, delaying her. 'You must be dead tired—too tired for romance. Else I should say to you, turn aside an instant and look at the library. It is a sight to remember.'

Inevitably she glanced behind her, and saw that the library door was ajar. He flung it open, and the great room showed wide, its high domed roof lost in shadow, while along the bare floor and up the latticed books crept, here streaks and fingers, and there wide breadths of light from the unshuttered and curtainless windows.

'Isn't it the very poetry of night and solitude?' he said, looking in with her. 'You love the place; but did you ever see it so lovable? The dead are here; you did right to come and seek them! Look at your namesake, in that ray. To-night she lives! She knows that is her husband opposite—those are her books beside her. And the rebel!'—he pointed smiling to the portrait of John Boyce. 'When you are gone I shall shut myself up here—sit in his chair, invoke him—and put my speech together. I am nervous about to-morrow (he was bound, as she knew, to a large Labour Congress in the Midlands, where he was to preside), and sleep will make no terms with me. Ah!—how strange! Who can that be passing the avenue?'

He made a step or two into the room, and put up his hand to his brow, looking intently. Involuntarily, yet with a thrill, Marcella followed. They walked to the window.

'It is *Hurd*!' she cried in a tone of distress, pressing her face against the glass. 'Out at this time, and with a gun! Oh, dear, dear!'

There could be no question that it was Hurd. Wharton had seen him linger in the shadowy edge of the avenue, as though reconnoitring, and now, as he stealthily crossed the moonlit grass, his slouching dwarf's figure, his large head, and the short gun under his arm, were all plainly visible.

'What do you suppose he is after?' said Wharton, still gazing, his hands in his pockets.

'I don't know; he wouldn't poach on *our* land; I'm sure he wouldn't! Besides, there is nothing to poach.'—Wharton smiled.—'He must be going, after all, to Lord Maxwell's coverts! They are just beyond the avenue, on the side of the hill. Oh! it is too disappointing! Can we do anything?'

She looked at her companion with troubled eyes. This incursion of something sadly and humanly real seemed suddenly to have made it natural to be standing beside him there at that strange hour. Her conscience was soothed.

Wharton shook his head.

'I don't see what we could do. How strong the instinct is! I told you that woman had a secret. Well, it is only one form—the squalid peasant's form—of the same instinct which sends the young fellows of our class ruffling it and chancing it all over the world. It is the instinct to take one's fling, to get out of the rut, to claim one's innings against the powers that be—Nature, or the law, or convention.'

'I know all that—I never blame them!'—cried Marcella—'but

just now it is so monstrous—so dangerous ! Westall specially alert
—and this gang about ! Besides, I got him work from Lord Maxwell, and made him promise me—for the wife and children's sake.'

Wharton shrugged his shoulders.

'I should think Westall is right, and that the gang have got
hold of him. It is what always happens. The local man is the
catspaw.—So you are sorry for him—this man ?' he said in another
tone, facing round upon her.

She looked astonished, and drew herself up nervously, turning
at the same time to leave the room. But before she could reply he
hurried on :

'He—may escape his risk. Give your pity, Miss Boyce, rather
to one—who has not escaped !'

'I don't know what you mean,' she said, unconsciously laying a
hand on one of the old chairs beside her to steady herself. 'But it
is too late to talk. Good night, Mr. Wharton.'

'Good-bye,' he said quietly, yet with a low emphasis, at the
same time moving out of her path. She stopped, hesitating. Beneath the lace and faded flowers on her breast he could see how
her heart beat.

'Not good-bye? You are coming back after the meeting ?'

'I think not. I must not inflict myself—on Mrs. Boyce—any
more. You will all be very busy during the next three weeks. It
would be an intrusion if I were to come back at such a time—
especially—considering the fact'—he spoke slowly—'that I am as
distasteful as I now know myself to be, to your future husband.
Since you all left to-night the house has been very quiet. I sat
over the fire thinking. It grew clear to me. I must go, and go at
once. Besides—a lonely man as I am must not risk his nerve.
His task is set him, and there are none to stand by him if he fails.'

She trembled all over. Weariness and excitement made normal
self-control almost impossible.

'Well, then, I must say thank you,' she said indistinctly, 'for
you have taught me a great deal.'

'You will unlearn it !' he said gaily, recovering his self-possession, so it seemed, as she lost hers. 'Besides, before many weeks
are over you will have heard hard things of me. I know that very
well. I can say nothing to meet them. Nor should I attempt anything. It may sound brazen, but that past of mine, which I can
see perpetually present in Aldous Raeburn's mind, for instance, and
which means so much to his good aunt, means to me just nothing
at all ! The doctrine of identity must be true—I must be the same
person I was then. But, all the same, what I did then does not
matter a straw to me now. To all practical purposes I am another

man. I was then a youth, idle, *désœuvré*, playing with all the keys of life in turn. I have now unlocked the path that suits me. Its quest has transformed me—as I believe, ennobled me. I do not ask Raeburn or anyone else to believe it. It is my own affair. Only, if we ever meet again in life, you and I, and you think you have reason to ask humiliation of me, do not ask it, do not expect it. The man you will have in your mind has nothing to do with me. I will not be answerable for his sins.'

As he said these things he was leaning lightly forward, looking up at her, his arms resting on the back of one of the old chairs, one foot crossed over the other. The attitude was easy calm itself. The tone—indomitable, analytic, reflective—matched it. Yet, all the same, her woman's instinct divined a hidden agitation, and, woman-like, responded to that and that only.

'Mr. Raeburn will never tell me old stories about anybody,' she said proudly. 'I asked him once, out—out of curiosity—about you, and he would tell me nothing.'

'Generous!' said Wharton, drily. 'I am grateful.'

'No!' cried Marcella, indignantly, rushing blindly at the outlet for emotion. 'No!—you are not grateful; you are always judging him harshly—criticising, despising what he does.'

Wharton was silent a moment. Even in the moonlight she could see the reddening of his cheek.

'So be it,' he said at last. 'I submit. You must know best. But you? are you always content? Does this *milieu* into which you are passing always satisfy you? To-night, did your royalty please you? Will it soon be enough for you?'

'You know it is not enough,' she broke out, hotly; 'it is insulting that you should ask in that tone. It means that you think me a hypocrite!—and I have given you no cause——'

'Good heavens, no!' he exclaimed, interrupting her, and speaking in a low, hurried voice. 'I had no motive, no reason for what I said—none—but this, that you are going—that we are parting. I spoke in gibes to make you speak—somehow to strike —to reach you. To-morrow it will be too late!'

And before, almost, she knew that he had moved, he had stooped forward, caught a fold of her dress, pressed it to his lips, and dropped it.

'Don't speak,' he said brokenly, springing up, and standing before her in her path. 'You shall forgive me—I will compel it! See! here we are on this moonlit space of floor, alone, in the night. Very probably we shall never meet again, except as strangers. Put off convention, and speak to me, soul to soul! You are not happy altogether in this marriage. I know it. You

have as good as confessed it. Yet you will go through with it.
You have given your word—your honour holds you. I recognise
that it holds you. I say nothing, not a syllable, against your
bond! But here, to-night, tell me, promise me that you will make
this marriage of yours serve *our* hopes and ends, the ends that
you and I have foreseen together—that it shall be your instrument,
not your chain. We have been six weeks together. You say you
have learnt from me; you have! you have given me your mind,
your heart to write on, and I have written. Henceforward you
will never look at life as you might have done if I had not been
here. Do you think I triumph, that I boast? Ah!' he drew in his
breath—'What if in helping you, and teaching you—for I have
helped and taught you!—I have undone myself? What if I came
here the slave of impersonal causes, of ends not my own? What
if I leave—maimed—in face of the battle? Not your fault? No,
perhaps not! but, at least, you owe me some gentleness now, in
these last words—some kindness in farewell.'

He came closer, held out his hands. With one of her own she
put his back, and lifted the other dizzily to her forehead.

'Don't come near me!' she said, tottering. 'What is it? I
cannot see. Go!'

And guiding herself, as though blindfold, to a chair, she sank
upon it, and her head dropped. It was the natural result of a
moment of intense excitement coming upon nerves already strained
and tried to their utmost. She fought desperately against her
weakness; but there was a moment when all around her swam,
and she knew nothing.

Then came a strange awakening. What was this room, this
weird light, these unfamiliar forms of things, this warm support
against which her cheek lay? She opened her eyes languidly.
They met Wharton's half in wonder. He was kneeling beside her,
holding her. But for an instant she realised nothing except his
look, to which her own helplessly replied.

'Once!' she heard him whisper. 'Once! Then nothing more
—for ever.'

And stooping, slowly, deliberately, he kissed her.

In a stinging flow, life, shame, returned upon her. She struggled
to her feet, pushing him from her.

'You dared,' she said, '*dared* such a thing!'

She could say no more; but her attitude, fiercely instinct,
through all her physical weakness, with her roused best self, was
speech enough. He did not venture to approach her. She walked
away. He heard the door close, hurrying steps on the little stairs,
then silence.

He remained where she had left him, leaning against the latticed wall for some time. When he moved it was to pick up a piece of maidenhair which had dropped from her dress.

'That was a scene!' he said, looking at it, and at the trembling of his own hand. 'It carries one back to the days of the Romantics. Was I Alfred de Musset?—and she George Sand? Did any of them ever taste a more poignant moment than I—when she—lay upon my breast? To be helpless—yet yield nothing—it challenged me! Yet I took no advantage—none. When she *looked*—when her eye, her *soul*, was, for that instant, mine, then!—Well!—the world has rushed with me since I saw her on the stairs; life can bring me nothing of such a quality again. What did I say?—how much did I mean? My God! how can I tell? I began as an actor, did I finish as a man?'

He paced up and down, thinking; gradually, by the help of an iron will quieting down each rebellious pulse.

'That poacher fellow did me a good turn. *Dare!* the word galled. But, after all, what woman could say less? And what matter? I have held her in my arms, in a setting—under a moon—worthy of her. Is not life enriched thereby beyond robbery? And what harm? Raeburn is not injured. *She* will never tell—and neither of us will ever forget. Ah!—what was that?'

He walked quickly to the window. What he had heard had been a dull report coming apparently from the woods beyond the eastern side of the avenue. As he reached the window it was followed by a second.

'That poacher's gun?—no doubt!'—he strained his eyes in vain.—'Collision perhaps—and mischief? No matter! I have nothing to do with it. The world is all lyric for me to-night. I can hear in it no other rhythm.'

The night passed away. When the winter morning broke, Marcella was lying with wide sleepless eyes, waiting and pining for it. Her candle still burnt beside her; she had had no courage for darkness, nor the smallest desire for sleep. She had gone through shame and anguish. But she would have scorned to pity herself. Was it not her natural, inevitable portion?

'I will tell Aldous everything—*everything*,' she said to herself for the hundredth time, as the light penetrated. 'Was *that* only seven striking—*seven*—impossible!'

She sat up haggard and restless, hardly able to bear the thought of the hours that must pass before she could see Aldous—put all to the touch.

Suddenly she remembered Hurd—then old Patton.

'He was dying last night,' she thought, in her moral torment —her passion to get away from herself. 'Is he gone? This is the hour when old people die—the dawn. I will go and see—go at once.'

She sprang up. To baffle this ache within her by some act of repentance, of social amends, however small, however futile—to propitiate herself, if but by a hairbreadth—this, no doubt, was the instinct at work. She dressed hastily, glad of the cold, glad of the effort she had to make against the stiffness of her own young bones —glad of her hunger and faintness, of everything physically hard that had to be fought and conquered.

In a very short time she had passed quietly downstairs and through the hall, greatly to the amazement of William, who opened the front door for her. Once in the village road the damp raw air revived her greatly. She lifted her hot temples to it, welcoming the waves of wet mist that swept along the road, feeling her youth come back to her.

Suddenly as she was nearing the end of a narrow bit of lane between high hedges, and the first houses of the village were in sight, she was stopped by a noise behind her—a strange unaccountable noise as of women's voices, calling and wailing. It startled and frightened her, and she stood in the middle of the road waiting.

Then she saw coming towards her two women running at full speed, crying and shouting, their aprons up to their faces.

'What is it? What is the matter?' she asked, going to meet them, and recognising two labourers' wives she knew.

'Oh! miss—oh! miss!' said the foremost, too wrapt up in her news to be surprised at the sight of her. 'They've just found 'im—they're bringin ov 'im home; they've got a shutter from Muster Wellin! 'im at Disley Farm. It wor close by Disley Wood they found 'em. And there's one ov 'is men they've sent off ridin for the inspector—here he come, miss! Come out o' th' way!'

They dragged her back, and a young labourer galloped past them on a farm colt, urging it on to its full pace, his face red and set.

'Who is found?' cried Marcella.—'What is it?'

'Westall, miss—Lor bless you—Shot him in the head they did —blowed his brains right out—and Charlie Dynes—oh! he's knocked about shamful—the doctor don't give no hopes of him. Oh deary—deary me! And we're goin for Muster Harden—ee must tell the widder—or Miss Mary—none on us can!'

'And who did it?' said Marcella, pale with horror, holding her.

'Why, the poachers, miss. Them as they've bin waitin for all along—and they do say as Jim Hurd's in it. Oh Lord, oh Lord !'

Marcella stood petrified, and let them hurry on.

CHAPTER IX

THE lane was still again, save for the unwonted sounds coming from the groups which had gathered round the two women, and were now moving beside them along the village street a hundred yards ahead.

Marcella stood in a horror of memory—seeing Hurd's figure cross the moonlit avenue, from dark to dark. Where was he? Had he escaped? Suddenly she set off running, stung by the thought of what might have already happened under the eyes of that unhappy wife, those wretched children.

As she entered the village, a young fellow ran up to her in breathless excitement. 'They've got 'im, miss. He'd come straight home—'adn't made no attempt to run. As soon as Jenkins'—Jenkins was the policeman—'heared of it, ee went straight across to 'is house, an' caught 'im. Ee wor going to make off—'is wife 'ad been persuadin ov 'im all night. But they've got 'im, miss, sure enough !'

The lad's exultation was horrible. Marcella waved him aside and ran on. A man on horseback appeared on the road in front of her leading from Widrington to the village. She recognised Aldous Raeburn, who had checked his horse in sudden amazement as he saw her talking to the boy.

'My darling! what are you here for ? Oh ! go home—go *home* !—out of this horrible business. They have sent for me as a magistrate. Dynes is alive—I *beg* you !—go home !'

She shook her head, out of breath and speechless with running. At the same moment she and he, looking to the right, caught sight of the crowd standing in front of Hurd's cottage.

A man ran out from it, seeing the horse and its rider.

'Muster Raeburn ! Muster Raeburn ! They've cotched 'im ; Jenkins has got 'im.'

'Ah !' said Aldous, drawing a long, stern breath ; 'he didn't try to get off then ? Marcella !—you are not going there—to that house !'

He spoke in a tone of the strongest remonstrance. Her soul rose in anger against it.

' I am going to *her*,' she said panting ; ' don't wait.'

And she left him and hurried on.

As soon as the crowd round the cottage saw her coming, they divided to let her pass.

' She's quiet now, miss,' said a woman to her significantly, nodding towards the hovel. ' Just after Jenkins got in you could hear her crying out pitiful.'

' That was when they wor a-handcuffin him,' said a man beside her.

Marcella shuddered.

' Will they let me in ?' she asked.

' They won't let none ov *us* in,' said the man. ' There's Hurd's sister,' and he pointed to a weeping woman supported by two others. ' They've kep her out. But here's the inspector, miss ; you ask him.'

The inspector, a shrewd officer of long experience, fetched in haste from a mile's distance, galloped up, and gave his horse to a boy.

Marcella went up to him.

He looked at her with sharp interrogation. ' You are Miss Boyce ? Miss Boyce of Mellor ?'

' Yes. I want to go to the wife ; I will promise not to get in your way.'

He nodded. The crowd let them pass. The inspector knocked at the door, which was cautiously unlocked by Jenkins, and the two went in together.

' She's a queer one,' said a thin, weasel-eyed man in the crowd to his neighbour. ' To think o' her bein in it—at this time o' day. You could see Muster Raeburn was a tellin of her to go 'ome. But she's allus pampered them Hurds.'

The speaker was Ned Patton, old Patton's son, and Hurd's companion on many a profitable night-walk. It was barely a week since he had been out with Hurd on another ferreting expedition, some of the proceeds of which were still hidden in Patton's out-house. But at the present moment he was one of the keenest of the crowd, watching eagerly for the moment when he should see his old comrade come out, trapped and checkmated, bound safely and surely to the gallows. The natural love of incident and change which keeps life healthy had been starved in him by his labourer's condition. This sudden excitement had made a brute of him.

The man next him grimaced, and took his pipe out of his mouth a moment.

' *She* won't be able to do nothin for 'im ! Ther isn't a man nor boy in this 'ere place as didn't know as ee hated Westall like pison, an' would be as like as not to do for 'im some day. That'll count agen 'im now terrible strong! Ee wor allus one to blab, ee wor.'

'Well, an' Westall said jus as much!' struck in another voice; 'theer wor sure to be a fight iv ever Westall got at 'im—on the job. You see—they may bring it in manslarter after all.'

''Ow does anyone know ee wor there at all? who seed him?' inquired a white-haired elderly man, raising a loud quavering voice from the middle of the crowd.

'Charlie Dynes seed 'im,' cried several together.

'How do yer know ee seed 'im?'

From the babel of voices which followed the white-haired man slowly gathered the beginnings of the matter. Charlie Dynes, Westall's assistant, had been first discovered by a horsekeeper in Farmer Wellin's employment as he was going to his work. The lad had been found under a hedge, bleeding and frightfully injured, but still alive. Close beside him was the dead body of Westall with shot-wounds in the head. On being taken to the farm and given brandy, Dynes was asked if he had recognised anybody. He had said there were five of them, 'town chaps'; and then he had named Hurd quite plainly—whether anybody else, nobody knew. It was said he would die, and that Mr. Raeburn had gone to take his deposition.

'An' them town chaps got off, eh?' said the elderly man.

'Clean!' said Patton, refilling his pipe. 'Trust them!'

Meanwhile, inside this poor cottage Marcella was putting out all the powers of the soul. As the door closed behind her and the inspector, she saw Hurd sitting handcuffed in the middle of the kitchen, watched by a man whom Jenkins, the local policeman, had got in to help him, till some more police should arrive. Jenkins was now upstairs searching the bedroom. The little bronchitic boy sat on the fender, in front of the untidy fireless grate, shivering, his emaciated face like a yellowish white mask, his eyes fixed immovably on his father. Every now and then he was shaken with coughing, but still he looked—with the dumb devoted attention of some watching animal.

Hurd, too, was sitting silent. His eyes, which seemed wider open and more brilliant than usual, wandered restlessly from thing to thing about the room; his great earth-stained hands in their fetters twitched every now and then on his knee. Haggard and dirty as he was, there was a certain aloofness, a dignity even, about the misshapen figure which struck Marcella strangely. Both criminal and victim may have it—this dignity. It means that a man feels himself set apart from his kind.

Hurd started at sight of Marcella. 'I want to speak to her,' he said, hoarsely, as the inspector approached him—'to that lady'—nodding towards her.

'Very well,' said the inspector; 'only it is my duty to warn you that anything you say now will be taken down and used as evidence at the inquest.'

Marcella came near. As she stood in front of him, one trembling ungloved hand crossed over the other, the diamond in her engagement ring catching the light from the window sparkled brightly, diverting even for the moment the eyes of the little fellow against whom her skirts were brushing.

'Ee might ha killed me just as well as I killed 'im,' said Hurd, bending over to her and speaking with difficulty from the dryness of his mouth. 'I didn't mean nothink o' what happened. He and Charley came on us round Disley Wood. He didn't take no notice o' them. It was they as beat Charlie. But he come straight on at me—all in a fury—a blackguardin ov me, with his stick up. I thought he was for beatin my brains out, an I up with my gun and fired. We was so close—that was how he got it all in the head. But ee might a killed me just as well.'

He paused, staring at her with a certain anguished intensity, as though he were watching to see how she took it—nay, trying its effect both on her and himself. He did not look afraid or cast down—nay, there was a curious buoyancy and steadiness about his manner for the moment which astonished her. She could almost have fancied that he was more alive, more of a *man* than she had ever seen him—mind and body better fused—more at command.

'Is there anything more you wish to say to me?' she asked him, after waiting.

Then suddenly his manner changed. Their eyes met. Hers, with all their subtle inheritance of various expression, their realised character, as it were, searched his, tried to understand them—those peasant eyes, so piercing to her strained sense in their animal urgency and shame. *Why* had he done this awful thing?—deceived her—wrecked his wife?—that was what her look asked. It seemed to her too *childish*—too *stupid* to be believed.

'I haven't made nobbut a poor return to *you*, miss,' he said in a shambling way, as though the words were dragged out of him. Then he threw up his head again. 'But I didn't mean nothink o' what happened,' he repeated, doggedly going off again into a rapid yet, on the whole, vivid and consecutive account of Westall's attack, to which Marcella listened, trying to remember every word.

'Keep that for your solicitor,' the inspector said at last, interrupting him ; 'you are only giving pain to Miss Boyce. You had better let her go to your wife.'

Hurd looked steadily once more at Marcella. 'It be a bad end I'm come to,' he said, after a moment. 'But I thank you kindly all the same. *They'll* want seein after.' He jerked his head towards the boy, then towards the outhouse or scullery where his wife was. 'She takes it terr'ble hard. She wanted me to run. But I said, "No, I'll stan it out." Mr. Brown at the Court 'll give you the bit wages he owes me. But they'll have to go on the Union. Everybody 'll turn their backs on them now.'

'I will look after them,' said Marcella, 'and I will do the best I can for you. Now I will go to Mrs. Hurd.'

Minta Hurd was sitting in a corner of the outhouse on the clay floor, her head leaning against the wall. The face was turned upward, the eyes shut, the mouth helplessly open. When Marcella saw her, she knew that the unhappy woman had already wept so much in the hours since her husband came back to her that she could weep no more. The two little girls in the scantiest of clothing, half-fastened, sat on the floor beside her, shivering and begrimed—watching her. They had been crying at the tops of their voices, but were now only whimpering miserably, and trying at intervals to dry their tear-stained cheeks with the skirts of their frocks. The baby, wrapped in an old shawl, lay on its mother's knee, asleep and unheeded. The little lean-to place, full of odds and ends of rubbish, and darkened overhead by a string of damp clothes—was intolerably cold in the raw February dawn. The children were blue ; the mother felt like ice as Marcella stooped to touch her. Outcast misery could go no further.

The mother moaned as she felt Marcella's hand, then started wildly forward, straining her thin neck and swollen eyes that she might see through the two open doors of the kitchen and the outhouse.

'They're not taking him away?' she said fiercely. 'Jenkins swore to me they'd give me notice.'

'No, he's still there,' said Marcella, her voice shaking. 'The inspector's come. You shall have notice.'

Mrs. Hurd recognised her voice, and looked up at her in amazement.

'You must put this on,' said Marcella, taking off the short fur cape she wore. 'You are perished. Give me the baby, and wrap yourself in it'

But Mrs. Hurd put it away from her with a vehement hand.

'I'm not cold, miss—I'm burning hot. He made me come in here. He said he'd do better if the children and I ud go away a bit. An' I couldn't go upstairs, because—because——' she hid her face on her knees.

Marcella had a sudden sick vision of the horrors this poor creature must have gone through since her husband had appeared to her, splashed with the blood of his enemy, under that same marvellous moon which——

Her mind repelled its own memories with haste. Moreover, she was aware of the inspector standing at the kitchen door and beckoning to her. She stole across to him so softly that Mrs. Hurd did not hear her.

'We have found all we want,' he said in his official tone, but under his breath—'the clothes anyway. We must now look for the gun. Jenkins is first going to take him off to Widrington. The inquest will be held to-morrow here, at "The Green Man." We shall bring him over.' Then he added in another voice, touching his hat, 'I don't like leaving you, miss, in this place. Shall Jenkins go and fetch somebody to look after that poor thing? They'll be all swarming in here as soon as we've gone.'

'No, I'll stay for a while. I'll look after her. They won't come if I'm here. Except his sister—Mrs. Mullins—she may come in, of course, if she wants.'

The inspector hesitated.

'I'm going now to meet Mr. Raeburn, miss. I'll tell him that you're here.'

'He knows,' said Marcella, briefly. 'Now are you ready?'

He signed assent, and Marcella went back to the wife.

'Mrs. Hurd,' she said, kneeling on the ground beside her, 'they're going.'

The wife sprang up with a cry and ran into the kitchen, where Hurd was already on his feet between Jenkins and another policeman, who were to convey him to the gaol at Widrington. But when she came face to face with her husband something—perhaps the nervous appeal in his strained eyes—checked her, and she controlled herself piteously. She did not even attempt to kiss him. With her eyes on the ground, she put her hand on his arm. 'They'll let me come and see you, Jim?' she said, trembling.

'Yes; you can find out the rules,' he said shortly. 'Don't let them children cry. They want their breakfast to warm them. There's plenty of coal. I brought a sack home from Jellaby's last night myself. Good-bye.'

'Now, march,' said the inspector sternly, pushing the wife back.

Marcella put her arm round the shaking woman. The door opened, and beyond the three figures as they passed out, her eye passed to the waiting crowd, then to the misty expanse of common and the dark woods behind, still wrapped in fog.

When Mrs. Hurd saw the rows of people waiting within a stone's throw of the door she shrank back. Perhaps it struck her, as it struck Marcella, that every face was the face of a foe. Marcella ran to the door as the inspector stepped out, and locked it after him. Mrs. Hurd, hiding herself behind a bit of baize curtain, watched the two policemen mount with Hurd into the fly that was waiting, and then followed it with her eyes along the bit of straight road, uttering sounds the while of low anguish, which wrung the heart in Marcella's breast. Looking back in after days it always seemed to her that for this poor soul the true parting, the true wrench be- tween life and life, came at this moment.

She went up to her, her own tears running over.

'You must come and lie down,' she said, recovering herself as quickly as possible. 'You and the children are both starved, and you will want your strength if you are to help him. I will see to things.'

She put the helpless woman on the wooden settle by the fire- place, rolling up her cloak to make a pillow.

'Now, Willie, you sit by your mother. Daisy, where's the cradle? Put the baby down and come and help me make the fire.'

The dazed children did exactly as they were told, and the mother lay like a log on the settle. Marcella found coal and wood under Daisy's guidance, and soon lit the fire, piling on the fuel with a lavish hand. Daisy brought her water, and she filled the kettle and set it on to boil, while the little girl, still sobbing at intervals like some little weeping automaton, laid the breakfast. Then the children all crouched round the warmth, while Marcella rubbed their cold hands and feet, and 'mothered' them. Shaken as she was with emotion and horror, she was yet full of a passionate joy that this pity, this tendance was allowed to her. The crushing weight of self-contempt had lifted. She felt morally free and at ease.

Already she was revolving what she could do for Hurd. It was as clear as daylight to her that there had been no murder but a free fight—an even chance between him and Westall. The vio- lence of a hard and tyrannous man had provoked his own destruc- tion—so it stood, for her passionate protesting sense. That at any rate must be the defence, and some able man must be found to press it. She thought she would write to the Cravens and consult them. Her thoughts carefully avoided the names both of Aldous Raeburn and of Wharton.

She was about to make the tea when someone knocked at the door. It proved to be Hurd's sister, a helpless woman, with a face swollen by crying, who seemed to be afraid to come into the cottage, and afraid to go near her sister-in-law. Marcella gave her money, and sent her for some eggs to the neighbouring shop, then told her to come back in half an hour and take charge. She was an incapable, but there was nothing better to be done. 'Where is Miss Harden?' she asked the woman. The answer was that ever since the news came to the village the rector and his sister had been with Mrs. Westall and Charlie Dynes' mother. Mrs. Westall had gone into fit after fit; it had taken two to hold her, and Charlie's mother, who was in bed recovering from pneumonia, had also been very bad.

Again Marcella's heart contracted with rage rather than pity. Such wrack and waste of human life, moral and physical ! for what ? For the protection of a hateful sport which demoralised the rich and their agents, no less than it tempted and provoked the poor !

When she had fed and physically comforted the children, she went and knelt down beside Mrs. Hurd, who still lay with closed eyes in heavy-breathing stupor.

'Dear Mrs. Hurd,' she said, 'I want you to drink this tea and eat something.'

The half-stupefied woman signed refusal. But Marcella insisted.

'You have got to fight for your husband's life,' she said firmly, 'and to look after your children. I must go in a very short time, and before I go you must tell me all that you can of this business. Hurd would tell you to do it. He knows and you know that I am to be trusted. I want to save him. I shall get a good lawyer to help him. But first you must take this—and then you must talk to me.'

The habit of obedience to a 'lady,' established long ago in years of domestic service, held. The miserable wife submitted to be fed, looked with forlorn wonder at the children round the fire, and then sank back with a groan. In her tension of feeling Marcella for an impatient moment thought her a poor creature. Then with quick remorse she put her arms tenderly round her, raised the dishevelled grey-streaked head on her shoulder, and, stooping, kissed the marred face, her own lips quivering.

'You are not alone,' said the girl with her whole soul. 'You shall never be alone while I live. Now tell me.'

She made the white and gasping woman sit up in a corner of the settle, and she herself got a stool and established herself a little way off, frowning, self-contained, and determined to make out the truth.

'Shall I send the children upstairs?' she asked.

'No!' said the boy suddenly, in his husky voice, shaking his head with energy, 'I'm not a goin'.'

'Oh! he's safe—is Willie,' said Mrs. Hurd, looking at him, but strangely, and as it were from a long distance, 'and the others is too little.'

Then gradually Marcella got the story out of her—first, the misery of alarm and anxiety in which she had lived ever since the Tudley End raid, owing first to her knowledge of Hurd's connection with it, and with the gang that had carried it out; then to her appreciation of the quick and ghastly growth of the hatred between him and Westall; lastly, to her sense of ingratitude towards those who had been kind to them.

'I knew we was acting bad towards you. I told Jim so. I couldn't hardly bear to see you come in. But there, miss, -I couldn't do anything. I tried, oh! the Lord knows I tried! There was never no happiness between us at last, I talked so. But I don't believe he could help himself—he's not made like other folks, isn't Jim——'

Her features became convulsed again with the struggle for speech. Marcella reached out for the toil-disfigured hand that was fingering and clutching at the edge of the settle, and held it close. Gradually she made out that although Hurd had not been able of course to conceal his night absences from his wife, he had kept his connection with the Oxford gang absolutely dark from her, till, in his wild exultation over Westall's discomfiture in the Tudley End raid, he had said things in his restless snatches of sleep which had enabled her to get the whole truth out of him by degrees. Her reproaches, her fears, had merely angered and estranged him; her nature had had somehow to accommodate itself to his, lest affection should lose its miserable all.

As to this last fatal attack on the Maxwell coverts, it was clear to Marcella, as she questioned and listened, that the wife had long foreseen it, and that she now knew much more about it than— suddenly—she would allow herself to say. For in the midst of her outpourings she drew herself together, tried to collect and calm herself, looked at Marcella with an agonised, suspicious eye, and fell silent.

'I don't know nothing about it, miss,' she stubbornly declared at last, with an inconsequent absurdity which smote Marcella's pity afresh. 'How am I to know? There was seven o' them Oxford fellows at Tudley End—that I know. Who's to say as Jim was with 'em at all last night? Who's to say as it wasn't them as——'

She stopped, shivering.   Marcella held her reluctant hand.

'You don't know,' she said quietly, 'that I saw your husband in here for a minute before I came in to you, and that he told me, as he had already told Jenkins, that it was in a struggle with him that Westall was shot, but that he had fired in self-defence because Westall was attacking him.   You don't know, too, that Charlie Dynes is alive, and says he saw Hurd——'

'Charlie Dynes!'   Mrs. Hurd gave a shriek, and then fell to weeping and trembling again, so that Marcella had need of patience.

'If you can't help me more,' she said at last in despair, 'I don't know what we shall do.   Listen to me.   Your husband will be charged with Westall's murder.   That I am sure of.   He says it was not murder—that it happened in a fight.   I believe it.   I want to get a lawyer to prove it.   I am your friend—you know I am.   But if you are not going to help me by telling me what you know of last night, I may as well go home—and get your sister-in-law to look after you and the children.'

She rose as she spoke.   Mrs. Hurd clutched at her.

'Oh, my God!' she said, looking straight before her vacantly at the children, who at once began to cry again.   '*Oh, my God!*   Look here, miss'—her voice dropped, her swollen eyes fixed themselves on Marcella—the words came out in a low, hurried stream —'It was just after four o'clock I heard that door turn ; I got up in my nightgown and ran down, and there was Jim.   "Put that light out," he says to me, sharp like.   "Oh, Jim," says I, "wherever have you been?   You'll be the death o' me and them poor children!"   "You go to bed," says he to me, "and I'll come presently."   But I could see him, 'cos of the moon, almost as plain as day, an' I couldn't take my eyes off him.   And he went about the kitchen so strange like, puttin down his hat and takin it up again, an' I saw he hadn't got his gun.   So I went up an' caught holt on him.   An' he gave me a push back.   "Can't you let me alone?" he says ; "you'll know soon enough."   An' then I looked at my sleeve where I'd touched him—oh, my God ! my God !'

Marcella, white to the lips and shuddering too, held her tight. She had the *seeing* faculty which goes with such quick, nervous natures, and she saw the scene as though she had been there—the moonlit cottage, the miserable husband and wife, the life-blood on the woman's sleeve.

Mrs. Hurd went on in a torrent of half-finished sentences and fragments of remembered talk.   She told her husband's story of the encounter with the keepers as he had told it to her, of course with additions and modifications already struck out by the agony of inventive pain ; she described how she had made him take his blood-stained clothes and hide them in a hole in the roof; then how she had urged him to strike across country at once and get a few hours' start before the ghastly business was known. But the more he talked to her the more confident he became of his own story, and the more determined to stay and brave it out. Besides, he was shrewd enough to see that escape for a man of his deformity was impossible, and he tried to make her understand it so. But she was mad and blind with fear, and at last, just as the light was coming in, he told her roughly, to end their long wrestle, that he should go to bed and get some sleep. She would make a fool of him, and he should want all his wits. She followed him up the steep ladder to their room, weeping. And there was little Willie sitting up in bed, choking with the phlegm in his throat, and half dead of fright because of the voices below.

'And when Hurd see him, he went and cuddled him up, and rubbed his legs and feet to warm them, an' I could hear him groanin. And I says to him, "Jim, if you won't go for my sake, will you go for the boy's?" For you see, miss, there was a bit of money in the house, an' I thought he'd hide himself by day and walk by night, and so get to Liverpool perhaps, and off to the States. An' it seemed as though my head would burst with listenin for people comin, and him taken up there like a rat in a trap, an' no way of provin the truth, and everybody agen him, because of the things he'd said. And he burst out a cryin, an' Willie cried. An' I came an' entreated of him. An' he kissed me ; an' at last he said he'd go. An' I made haste, the light was getting so terrible strong ; an' just as he'd got to the foot of the stairs, an' I was holding little Willie in my arms an' saying good-bye to him——'

She let her head sink against the settle. There was no more to say, and Marcella asked no more questions—she sat thinking. Willie stood, a wasted worn figure, by his mother, stroking her face; his hoarse breathing was for a time the only sound in the cottage.

Then Marcella heard a loud knock at the door. She got up and looked through the casement window. The crowd had mostly dispersed, but a few people stood about on the green, and a policeman was stationed outside the cottage. On the steps stood Aldous Raeburn, his horse held behind him by a boy.

She went and opened the door.

'I will come,' she said at once. 'There—I see Mrs. Mullins crossing the common. Now I can leave her.'

Aldous, taking off his hat, closed the door behind him, and

stood with his hand on Marcella's arm, looking at the huddled woman on the settle, at the pale children. There was a solemnity in his expression, a mixture of judgment and pity which showed that the emotion of other scenes also—scenes through which he had just passed—was entering into it.

'Poor unhappy souls,' he said slowly, under his breath. 'You say that you have got someone to see after her. She looks as though it might kill her, too.'

Marcella nodded. Now that her task, for the moment, was nearly over, she could hardly restrain herself nervously or keep herself from crying. Aldous observed her with disquiet as she put on her hat. His heart was deeply stirred. She had chosen more nobly for herself than he would have chosen for her, in thus daring an awful experience for the sake of mercy. His moral sense, exalted and awed by the sight of death, approved, worshipped her. His man's impatience pined to get her away, to cherish and comfort her. Why, she could hardly have slept three hours since they parted on the steps of the Court, amidst the crowd of carriages !

Mrs. Mullins came in still scared and weeping, and dropping frightened curtseys to 'Muster Raeburn.' Marcella spoke to her a little in a whisper, gave some counsels which filled Aldous with admiration for the girl's practical sense and thoughtfulness, and promised to come again later. Mrs. Hurd neither moved nor opened her eyes.

'Can you walk?' said Aldous, bending over her, as they stood outside the cottage. 'I can see that you are worn out. Could you sit my horse if I led him?'

'No, let us walk.'

They went on together, followed by the eyes of the village, the boy leading the horse some distance behind.

'Where have you been?' said Marcella when they had passed the village. 'Oh, *please* don't think of my being tired.' I had so much rather know it all. I must know it all.'

She was deathly pale, but her black eyes flashed impatience and excitement. She even drew her hand out of the arm where Aldous was tenderly holding it, and walked on erect by herself.

'I have been with poor Dynes,' said Aldous sadly ; 'we had to take his deposition. He died while I was there.'

'He died?'

'Yes. The fiends who killed him had left small doubt of that. But he lived long enough, thank God, to give the information which will, I think, bring them to justice !'

The tone of the magistrate and the magnate goaded Marcella's quivering nerves.

'What is justice?' she cried; 'the system that wastes human lives in protecting your tame pheasants?'

A cloud came over the stern clearness of his look. He gave a bitter sigh—the sigh of the man to whom his own position in life had been, as it were, one long scruple.

'You may well ask that!' he said. 'You cannot imagine that I did not ask it of myself a hundred times as I stood by that poor fellow's bedside.'

They walked on in silence. She was hardly appeased. There was a deep, inner excitement in her urging her towards difference, towards attack. At last he resumed :—

'But whatever the merits of our present game system may be, the present case is surely clear—horribly clear. Six men, with at least three guns among them, probably more, go out on a pheasant-stealing expedition. They come across two keepers, one a lad of seventeen, who have nothing but a light stick apiece. The boy is beaten to death, the keeper shot dead at the first brush by a man who has been his life-long enemy, and threatened several times in public to "do for him." If that is not brutal and deliberate murder, it is difficult to say what is!'

Marcella stood still in the misty road trying to command herself.

'It was *not* deliberate,' she said at last with difficulty; 'not in Hurd's case. I have heard it all from his own mouth. It was a *struggle*—he might have been killed instead of Westall—Westall attacked, Hurd defended himself.'

Aldous shook his head.

'Of course Hurd would tell you so,' he said sadly, 'and his poor wife. He is not a bad or vicious fellow, like the rest of the rascally pack. Probably when he came to himself, after the moment of rage, he could not simply believe what he had done. But that makes no difference. It was murder; no judge or jury could possibly take any other view. Dynes' evidence is clear, and the proof of motive is overwhelming.'

Then, as he saw her pallor and trembling, he broke off in deep distress. 'My dear one, if I could but have kept you out of this!'

They were alone in the misty road. The boy with the horse was out of sight. He would fain have put his arm round her, have consoled and supported her. But she would not let him.

'Please understand,' she said in a sort of gasp, as she drew herself away, 'that I do *not* believe Hurd is guilty—that I shall do my very utmost to defend him. He is to me the victim of unjust, abominable laws! If *you* will not help me to protect him—then I must look to someone else.'

Aldous felt a sudden stab of suspicion—presentiment.

'Of course he will be well defended; he will have every chance; that you may be sure of,' he said slowly.

Marcella controlled herself, and they walked on. As they entered the drive of Mellor, Aldous thought passionately of those divine moments in his sitting-room, hardly yet nine hours old. And now—*now* !—she walked beside him as an enemy.

The sound of a step on the gravel in front of them made them look up. Past, present, and future met in the girl's bewildered and stormy sense as she recognised Wharton.

CHAPTER X

THE first sitting of the Birmingham Labour Congress was just over, and the streets about the hall in which it had been held were beginning to fill with the issuing delegates. Rain was pouring down and umbrellas were plentiful.

Harry Wharton, accompanied by a group of men, left the main entrance of the hall,—releasing himself with difficulty from the friendly crowd about the doors—and crossed the street to his hotel.

'Well, I'm glad you think I did decently,' he said, as they mounted the hotel stairs. 'What a beastly day, and how stuffy that hall was ! Come in and have something to drink.'

He threw open the door of his sitting-room as he spoke. The four men with him followed him in.

'I must go back to the hall to see two or three men before everybody disperses,' said the one in front. 'No refreshment for me, thank you, Mr. Wharton. But I want to ask a question— what arrangements have you made for the reporting of your speech?'

The man who spoke was thin and dark, with a modest kindly eye. He wore a black frock coat, and had the air of a minister.

'Oh, thank you, Bennett, it's all right. The *Post*, the *Chronicle*, and the *Northern Guardian* will have full copies. I sent them off before the meeting. And my own paper, of course. As to the rest they may report it as they like. I don't care.'

'They'll all have it,' said another man bluntly. 'It's the best speech you've ever made—the best president's speech we've had yet, I say,—don't you think so?'

The speaker, a man called Casey, turned to the two men behind him. Both nodded.

' Hallin's speech last year was first-rate,' he continued, ' but somehow Hallin damps you down, at least he did me last year; what you want just now is *fight*—and, my word ! Mr. Wharton let 'em have it !'

And standing with his hands on his sides, he glanced round from one to another. His own face was flushed, partly from the effects of a crowded hall and bad air, but mostly with excitement. All the men present indeed—though it was less evident in Bennett and Wharton than in the rest—had the bright nervous look which belongs to leaders keenly conscious of standing well with the led, and of having just emerged successfully from an agitating ordeal. As they stood together they went over the speech to which they had been listening, and the scene which had followed it, in a running stream of talk, laughter, and gossip. Wharton took little part, except to make a joke occasionally at his own expense, but the pleasure on his smiling lip, and in his roving, contented eye was not to be mistaken. The speech he had just delivered had been first thought out as he paced the moonlit library and corridor at Mellor. After Marcella had left him, and he was once more in his own room, he had had the extraordinary self-control to write it out, and make two or three machine-copies of it for the press. Neither its range nor its logical order had suffered for that intervening experience. The programme of labour for the next five years had never been better presented, more boldly planned, more eloquently justified. Hallin's presidential speech of the year before, as Casey said, rang flat in the memory when compared with it. Wharton knew that he had made a mark, and knew also that his speech had given him the whip-hand of some fellows who would otherwise have stood in his way.

Casey was the first man to cease talking about the speech. He had already betrayed himself about it more than he meant. He belonged to the New Unionism, and affected a costume in character —fustian trousers, flannel shirt, a full red tie and workman's coat, all well calculated to set off a fine lion-like head and broad shoulders. He had begun life as a bricklayer's labourer, and was now the secretary of a recently formed Union. His influence had been considerable, but was said to be already on the wane ; though it was thought likely that he would win a seat in the coming Parliament.

The other two men were Molloy, secretary to the congress, short, smooth-faced and wiry, a man whose pleasant eye and manner were often misleading, since he was in truth one of the hottest fighting men of a fighting movement ; and Wilkins, a friend of Casey's, ex-iron-worker, Union official, and Labour candidate

for a Yorkshire division—an uneducated, passionate fellow, speaking
with a broad, Yorkshire accent, a bad man of affairs, but honest,
and endowed with the influence which comes of sincerity, together
with a gift for speaking and superhuman powers of physical endurance.

'Well, I'm glad it's over,' said Wharton, throwing himself into
a chair with a long breath, and at the same time stretching out his
hand to ring the bell. 'Casey, some whisky? No? Nor you,
Wilkins? nor Molloy? As for you, Bennett, I know it's no good
asking you. By George! our grandfathers would have thought
us a poor lot! Well, some coffee at any rate you must all of you
have before you go back. Waiter! coffee. By the way, I have
been seeing something of Hallin, Bennett, down in the country.'

He took out his cigarette case as he spoke, and offered it to the
others. All refused except Molloy. Casey took his half-smoked
pipe out of his pocket and lit up. He was not a teetotaler as the
others were, but he would have scorned to drink his whisky and
water at the expense of a 'gentleman' like Wharton, or to smoke
the 'gentleman's' cigarettes. His class-pride was irritably strong.
Molloy, who was by nature anybody's equal, took the cigarette
with easy good manners, which made Casey look at him askance.

Mr. Bennett drew his chair close to Wharton's. The mention
of Hallin had roused a look of anxiety in his quick dark eyes.

'How is he, Mr. Wharton? The last letter I had from him he
made light of his health. But you know he only just avoided a
breakdown in that strike business. We only pulled him through
by the skin of his teeth—Mr. Raeburn and I.'

'Oh, he's no constitution; never had, I suppose. But he
seemed much as usual. He's staying with Raeburn, you know,
and I've been staying with the father of the young lady whom
Raeburn's going to marry.'

'Ah! I've heard of that,' said Bennett, with a look of interest.
'Well, Mr. Raeburn isn't on our side, but for judgment and fair
dealing there are very few men of his class and circumstances I
would trust as I would him. The lady should be happy.'

'Of course,' said Wharton drily. 'However, neither she nor
Raeburn is very happy just at this moment. A horrible affair happened down there last night. One of Lord Maxwell's gamekeepers
and a "helper," a lad of seventeen, were killed last night in a fight
with poachers. I only just heard the outlines of it before I came
away, but I got a telegram just before going into congress, asking
me to defend the man charged with the murder.'

A quick expression of repulsion and disgust crossed Bennett's
face.

'There has been a whole crop of such cases lately,' he said. 'How shall we ever escape from the *curse* of this game system?'

'We shan't escape it,' said Wharton quietly, knocking the end off his cigarette, 'not in your lifetime or mine. When we get more Radicals on the bench we shall lighten the sentences; but that will only exasperate the sporting class into finding new ways of protecting themselves. Oh! the man will be hanged—that's quite clear to me. But it will be a good case—from the public point of view—will work up well——'

He ran his hand through his curls, considering.

'Will work up admirably,' he added in a lower tone of voice, as though to himself, his eyes keen and brilliant as ever. in spite of the marks of sleeplessness and fatigue visible in the rest of the face, though only visible there since he had allowed himself the repose of his cigarette and arm-chair.

'Are yo comin to dine at the " Peterloo " to-night, Mr. Wharton?' said Wilkins, as Wharton handed him a cup of coffee; 'but it ull be part o' your duties—I'm thinkin?'

While Molloy and Casey were deep in animated discussion of the great meeting of the afternoon he had been sitting silent against the edge of the table—a short-bearded, sombre figure, ready at any moment to make a grievance, to suspect a slight.

'I'm afraid I can't,' said Wharton, bending forward and speaking in a tone of concern; 'that was just what I was going to ask you all—if you would make my excuses to-night? I have been explaining to Bennett. I have an important piece of business in the country—a labourer has been getting into trouble for shooting a keeper; they have asked me to defend him. The assizes come on in little more than a fortnight, worse luck! so that the time is short——'

And he went on to explain that, by taking an evening train back to Widrington, he could get the following (Saturday) morning with the solicitor in charge of the case, and be back in Birmingham, thanks to the convenience of a new line lately opened, in time for the second meeting of the congress, which was fixed for the early afternoon.

He spoke with great cordiality and persuasiveness. Among the men who surrounded him, his youth, his good looks and easy breeding shone out conspicuous. In the opinion of Wilkins, indeed, who followed his every word and gesture, he was far too well dressed and too well educated. A day would soon come when the labour movement would be able to show these young aristocrats the door. Not yet, however.

'Well, I thowt you wouldn't dine with us,' he said, turning away with a blunt laugh.

Bennett's mild eye showed annoyance. 'Mr. Wharton has explained himself very fully, I think,' he said, turning to the others. 'We shall miss him at dinner—but this matter seems to be one of life and death. And we mustn't forget any way that Mr. Wharton is fulfilling this engagement at great inconvenience to himself. We none of us knew when we elected him last year that he would have to be fighting his election at the same time. Next Saturday, isn't it?'

Bennett rose as he spoke and carefully buttoned his coat. It was curious to contrast his position among his fellows—one of marked ascendency and authority—with his small, insignificant physique. He had a gentle deprecating eye, and the heart of a poet. He played the flute and possessed the gift of repeating verse—especially Ebenezer Elliott's Corn Law Rhymes—so as to stir a great audience to enthusiasm or tears. The Wesleyan community of his native Cheshire village owned no more successful class-leader, and no humbler Christian. At the same time he could hold a large business meeting sternly in check, was the secretary of one of the largest and oldest Unions in the country, had been in Parliament for years, and was generally looked upon even by the men who hated his 'moderate' policy, as a power not to be ignored.

'Next Saturday. Yes!' said Wharton, nodding in answer to his inquiry.

'Well, are you going to do it?' said Casey, looking round at him.

'Oh, yes!' said Wharton cheerfully; 'oh, yes! we shall do it We shall settle old Dodgson, I think.'

'Are the Raeburns as strong as they were?' asked Molloy, who knew Brookshire.

'What landlord is? Since '84 the ground is mined for them all—good and bad—and they know it.'

'The mine takes a long time blowing up—too long for my patience,' said Wilkins gruffly. 'How the country can go on year after year paying its tribute to these plunderers passes my comprehension. But you may attack them as you please. You will never get any forrarder so long as Parliament and the Cabinet is made up of them and their hangers on.'

Wharton looked at him brightly, but silently, making a little assenting inclination of the head. He was not surprised that anything should pass Wilkins's comprehension, and he was determined to give him no opening for holding forth.

'Well, we'll let you alone,' said Bennett. 'You'll have very little time to get off in. We'll make your excuses, Mr. Wharton. You may be sure everybody is so pleased with your speech we shall find them all in a good temper. It was grand!—let me congratulate you again. Good night—I hope you'll get your poacher off!'

The others followed suit, and they all took leave in character:—Molloy, with an eager business reference to the order of the day for Saturday,—'Give me your address at Widrington; I'll post you everything to-night, so that you may have it all under your eye;' Casey, with the off-hand patronage of the man who would not for the world have his benevolence mistaken for servility; and Wilkins with as gruff a nod and as limp a shake of the hand as possible. It might perhaps have been read in the manner of the last two, that although this young man had just made a most remarkable impression, and was clearly destined to go far, they were determined not to yield themselves to him a moment before they must. In truth, both were already jealous of him; whereas Molloy, absorbed in the business of the congress, cared for nothing except to know whether in the next two days' debates Wharton would show himself as good a chairman as he was an orator; and Bennett, while saying no word that he did not mean, was fully conscious of an inner judgment, which pronounced five minutes of Edward Hallin's company to be worth more to him than anything which this brilliant young fellow could do or say.

Wharton saw them out, then came back and threw himself again into his chair by the window. The venetian blinds were not closed, and he looked out on a wide and handsome street of tall red-brick houses and shops, crowded with people and carriages, and lit with a lavishness of gas which overcame even the February dark and damp. But he noticed nothing, and even the sensation of his triumph was passing off. He was once more in the Mellor drive; Aldous Raeburn and Marcella stood in front of him; the thrill of the moment beat once more in his pulse.

He buried his head in his hands and thought. The news of the murder had reached him from Mr. Boyce. The master of Mellor had heard the news from William, the man-servant, at half-past seven, and had instantly knocked up his guest, by way of sharing the excitement with which his own feeble frame was throbbing.

'By Gad! I never heard such an *atrocious* business,' said the invalid, his thin hand shaking against his dressing-gown. 'That's what your Radical notions bring us to! We shall have them plundering and burning the country-houses next.'

'I don't think my Radical notions have much to do with it,' said Wharton composedly.

But there was a red spot in his cheeks which belied his manner. So when he—*they*—saw Hurd cross the avenue he was on his way to this deed of blood. The shot that he, Wharton, had heard had been the shot which slew Westall? Probably. Well, what was the bearing of it? Could she keep her own counsel, or would they find themselves in the witness box? The idea quickened his pulse amazingly.

'Any clue? Any arrests?' he asked of his host.

'Why, I told you,' said Boyce testily, though as a matter of fact he had said nothing. 'They have got that man Hurd. The ruffian has been a marked man by the keepers and police, they tell me, for the last year or more. And there's my daughter has been pampering him and his wife all the time, and *preaching* to me about them! She got Raeburn even to take him on at the Court. I trust it will be a lesson to her.'

Wharton drew a breath of relief. So the man was in custody, and there was other evidence. Good! There was no saying what a woman's conscience might be capable of, even against her friends and herself.

When Mr. Boyce at last left him free to dress and make his preparations for the early train, by which the night before, after the ladies' departure for the ball, he had suddenly made up his mind to leave Mellor, it was some time before Wharton could rouse himself to action. The situation absorbed him. Miss Boyce's friend was now in imminent danger of his neck, and Miss Boyce's thoughts must be of necessity concentrated upon his plight, and that of his family. He foresaw the passion, the *sæva indignatio*, that she must ultimately throw—the general situation being what it was—into the struggle for Hurd's life. Whatever the evidence might be, he would be to her either victim, or champion—and Westall, of course, merely the Holofernes of the piece.

How would Raeburn take it? Ah, well! the situation must develop. It occurred to him, however, that he would catch an earlier train to Widrington than the one he had fixed on, and have half an hour's talk with a solicitor who was a good friend of his before going on to Birmingham. Accordingly, he rang for William—who came, all staring and dishevelled, fresh from the agitation of the servants' hall—gave orders for his luggage to be sent after him, got as much fresh information as he could from the excited lad, plunged into his bath, and finally emerged, fresh and vigorous in every nerve, showing no trace whatever of the fact that two hours of broken sleep had been his sole portion for a night, in which he had gone through emotions and sustained a travail of brain either of which would have left a mark on most men.

Then the meeting in the drive ! How plainly he saw them both —Raeburn grave and pale, Marcella in her dark serge skirt and cap, with an eye all passion and a cheek white as her hand.

'A tragic splendour enwrapped her !—a fierce heroic air. She was the embodiment of the moment—of the melancholy morning with its rain and leafless woods—of the human anguish throbbing in the little village. And I, who had seen her last in her festal dress, who had held her warm perfumed youth in my arms, who had watched in her white breast the heaving of the heart that I—*I* had troubled !—how did I find it possible to stand and face her? But I did. It rushed through me at once *how* I would make her forgive me—how I would regain possession of her. I had thought the play was closed : it was suddenly plain to me that the second act was but just beginning. She and Raeburn had already come to words—I knew it directly I saw them. This business will divide them more and more. His *conscience* will come in—and a Raeburn's conscience is the devil !

'By now he hates me ; every word I speak to him—still more every word to her—galls him. But he controlled himself when I made him tell me the story—I had no reason to complain—though every now and then I could see him wince under the knowledge I must needs show of the persons and places concerned—a knowledge I could only have got from *her*. And she stood by meanwhile like a statue. Not a word, not a look, so far, though she had been forced to touch my hand. But my instinct saved me. I roused her—I played upon her ! I took the line that I was morally certain *she* had been taking in their *tête-à-tête*. Why not a scuffle ?—a general scrimmage ?—in which it was matter of accident who fell? The man surely was inoffensive and gentle, incapable of deliberate murder. And as to the evidence of hatred, it told both ways. He stiffened and was silent. What a fine brow he has—a look sometimes, when he is moved, of antique power and probity ! But she —she trembled—animation came back. She would almost have spoken to me—but I did well not to prolong it—to hurry on.'

Then he took the telegram out of his pocket which had been put into his hands as he reached the hotel, his mouth quivering again with the exultation which he had felt when he had received it. It recalled to his ranging memory all the details of his hurried interview with the little Widrington solicitor, who had already scented a job in the matter of Hurd's defence. This man—needy, shrewd, and well equipped with local knowledge—had done work

for Wharton and the party, and asked nothing better than to stand
well with the future member for the division. 'There is a lady,'
Wharton had said, 'the daughter of Mr. Boyce of Mellor, who is
already very much interested in this fellow and his family. She
takes this business greatly to heart. I have seen her this morning,
but had no time to discuss the matter with her. She will, I have
little doubt, try to help the relations in the arrangements for the
defence. Go to her this morning—tell her that the case has my
sympathy—that, as she knows, I am a barrister, and, if she wishes
it, I will defend Hurd. I shall be hard put to it to get up the case
with the election coming on, but I will do it—for the sake of the
public interest involved. You understand? Her father is a Tory
—and she is just about to marry Mr. Raeburn. Her position,
therefore, is difficult. Nevertheless, she will feel strongly—she does
feel strongly about this case, and about the whole game system—
and I feel moved to support her. She will take her own line,
whatever happens. See her—see the wife, too, who is entirely
under Miss Boyce's influence—and wire to me at my hotel at
Birmingham. If they wish to make other arrangements, well and
good. I shall have all the more time to give to the election.'

Leaving this commission behind him, he had started on his
journey. At the end of it a telegram had been handed to him on
the stairs of his hotel :—

'Have seen the lady, also Mrs. Hurd. You are urgently asked
to undertake defence.'

He spread it out before him now, and pondered it. The bit of
flimsy paper contained for him the promise of all he most coveted
—influence, emotion, excitement. 'She will have returns upon
herself,' he thought smiling, 'when I see her again. She will be
dignified, resentful ; she will suspect everything I say or do—still
more, she will suspect herself. No matter ! The situation is in
my hands. Whether I succeed or fail, she will be forced to work
with me, to consult with me—she will owe me gratitude. What
made her consent?—she must have felt it in some sort a humiliation. Is it that Raeburn has been driving her to strong measures
—that she wants, woman-like, to win, and thought me after all her
best chance, and put her pride in her pocket? Or is it?—ah ! one
should put *that* out of one's head. It's like wine—it unsteadies one.
And for a thing like this one must go into training. Shall I write
to her—there is just time now, before I start—take the lofty tone,
the equal masculine tone, which I have noticed she likes?—ask her
pardon for an act of madness—before we go together to the rescue
of a life? It might do—it might go down. But no, I think not !
Let the situation develop itself. Action and reaction—the unex-

pected—I commit myself to that. *She*—marry Aldous Raeburn in a month? Well, she may—certainly she may. But there is no need for me, I think, to take it greatly into account. Curious ! twenty-four hours ago I thought it all done with—dead and done with. " So like Provvy," as Bentham used to say, when he heard of anything particularly unseemly in the way of natural catastrophe. Now to ·dine, and be off ! How little sleep can I do with in the next fortnight ?'

He rang, ordered his cab, and then went to the coffee-room for some hasty food. As he was passing one of the small tables with which the room was filled, a man who was dining there with a friend recognised him and gave him a cold nod. Wharton walked on to the further end of the room, and, while waiting for his meal, buried himself in the local evening paper, which already contained a report of his speech.

'Did you see that man ?' asked the stranger of his friend.

'The small young fellow with the curly hair?'

'Small young fellow, indeed ! He is the wiriest athlete I know —extraordinary physical strength for his size—and one of the cleverest rascals out as a politician. I am a neighbour of his in the country.· His property joins mine. I knew his father—a little, dried-up old chap of the old school—very elegant manners and very obstinate—worried to death by his wife—oh, my goodness ! such a woman !'

'What's the name?' said the friend interrupting.

'Wharton—H. S. Wharton. His mother was a daughter of Lord Westgate, and *her* mother was an actress whom the old lord married in his dotage. Lady Mildred Wharton was like Garrick, only natural when she was acting, which she did on every possible occasion. A preposterous woman ! Old Wharton ought to have beaten her for her handwriting, and murdered her for her gowns. Her signature took a sheet of note-paper, and as for her dress I never could get out of her way. Whatever part of the room I happened to be in I always found my feet tangled in her skirts. Somehow, I never could understand how she was able to find so much stuff of one pattern. But it was only to make you notice her, like all the rest. Every bit of her was a pose, and the maternal pose was the worst of all.'

' H. S. Wharton ?' said the other. 'Why, that's the man who has been speaking here to-day. I've just been reading the account of it in the *Evening Star*. A big meeting—called by a joint committee of the leading Birmingham trades to consider the Liberal election programme as it affects labour—that's the man—he's been at it hammer and tongs—red-hot—all the usual devices for harrying the employer out of existence, with a few trifles—graduated income-tax and land nationalisation—thrown in.   Oh! that's the man, is it? —they say he had a great reception—spoke brilliantly—and is certainly going to get into Parliament next week.'

The speaker, who had the air of a shrewd and prosperous manufacturer, put up his eyeglass to look at this young Robespierre. His *vis-à-vis*—a stout country gentleman who had been in the army and knocked about the world before coming into his estate—shrugged his shoulders.

'So I hear—he daren't show his nose as a candidate in *our* part of the world, though of course he does us all the harm he can.   I remember a good story of his mother—she quarrelled with her husband and all her relations, his and hers, and then she took to speaking in public, accompanied by her dear boy.   On one occasion she was speaking at a market town near us, and telling the farmers that as far as she was concerned she would like to see the big properties cut up to-morrow.   The sooner her father's and husband's estates were made into small holdings stocked with public capital the better.   After it was all over, a friend of mine, who was there, was coming home in a sort of omnibus that ran between the town and a neighbouring village.   He found himself between two fat farmers, and this was the conversation—broad Lincolnshire, of course : " Did tha hear Lady Mildred Wharton say them things, Willum ? "   " Aye, a did."   " What did tha think, Willum ? " " What did *tha* think, George ? "   " Wal, *aa* thowt Laady Mildred Wharton wor a graät fule, Willum, if tha asks me."   " I'll uphowd tha, George ! I'll uphowd tha ! " said the other, and then they talked no more for the rest of the journey.'

The friend laughed.

'So it was from the dear mamma that the young man got his opinions ? '

'Of course.   She dragged him into every absurdity she could from the time he was fifteen.   When the husband died she tried to get the servants to come in to meals, but the butler struck.   So did Wharton himself, who, for a Socialist, has always showed a very pretty turn for comfort.   I am bound to say he was cut up when she died.   It was the only time I ever felt like being civil to him— in those months after she departed.   I suppose she was devoted to him—which after all is something.'

'Good heavens ! ' said the other, still lazily turning over the pages of the newspaper as they sat waiting for their second course, ' here is another poaching murder—in Brookshire—the third I have noticed within a month.   On Lord Maxwell's property—you know them ? '

'I know the old man a little—fine old fellow ! They'll make him President of the Council, I suppose. He can't have much work left in him ; but it is such a popular, respectable name. Ah I I'm sorry ; the sort of thing to distress him terribly.'

'I see the grandson is standing.'

'Oh yes ; will get in too. A queer sort of man—great ability and high character. But you can't imagine him getting on in politics, unless it's by sheer weight of wealth and family influence. He'll find a scruple in every bush—never stand the rough work of the House, or get on with the *men*. My goodness ! you have to pull with some queer customers nowadays. By the way, I hear he is making an unsatisfactory marriage—a girl very handsome, but with no manners, and like nobody else—the daughter, too, of an extremely shady father. It's surprising ; you'd have thought a man like Aldous Raeburn would have looked for the pick of things.'

'Perhaps it was she looked for the pick of things !' said the other with a blunt laugh. 'Waiter, another bottle of champagne !'

CHAPTER XI

MARCELLA was lying on the sofa in the Mellor drawing-room. The February evening had just been shut out, but she had told William not to bring the lamps till they were rung for. Even the firelight seemed more than she could bear. She was utterly exhausted both in body and mind, yet, as she lay there with shut eyes, and hands clasped under her cheek, a start went through her at every sound in the house, which showed that she was not resting, but listening. She had spent the morning in the Hurds' cottage, sitting by Mrs. Hurd and nursing the little boy. Minta Hurd, always delicate and consumptive, was now generally too ill from shock and misery to be anywhere but in her bed, and Willie was growing steadily weaker, though the child's spirit was such that he would insist on dressing, on hearing and knowing everything about his father, and on moving about the house as usual. Yet every movement of his wasted bones cost him the effort of a hero, and the dumb signs in him of longing for his father increased the general impression as of some patient creature driven by Nature to monstrous and disproportionate extremity.

The plight of this handful of human beings worked in Marcella like some fevering torture. She was wholly out of gear physically and morally. Another practically sleepless night, peopled with images of horror, had decreased her stock of sane self-control, already lessened by long conflict of feeling and the pressure of self-contempt. Now, as she lay listening for Aldous Raeburn's ring and step, she hardly knew whether to be angry with him for coming so late, or miserable that he should come at all. That there was a long score to settle between herself and him she knew well. Shame for an experience which seemed to her maiden sense indelible—both a weakness and a treachery—lay like a dull weight on heart and conscience. But she would not realise it, she would not act upon it. She shook the moral debate from her impatiently. Aldous should have his due all in good time—should have ample opportunity of deciding whether he would, after all, marry such a girl as she. Meanwhile his attitude with regard to the murder exasperated her. Yet, in some strange way it relieved her to be angry and sore with him—to have a grievance she could avow, and on which she made it a merit to dwell. His gentle, yet firm difference of opinion with her on the subject struck her as something new in him. It gave her a kind of fierce pleasure to fight it. He seemed somehow to be providing her with excuses—to be coming down to her level—to be equalling wrong with wrong.

The door handle turned. At last! She sprang up. But it was only William coming in with the evening post. Mrs. Boyce followed him. She took a quiet look at her daughter, and asked if her headache was better, and then sat down near her to some needlework. During these two days she had been unusually kind to Marcella. She had none of the little feminine arts of consolation. She was incapable of fussing, and she never caressed. But from the moment that Marcella had come home from the village that morning, a pale, hollow-eyed wreck, the mother had asserted her authority. She would not hear of the girl's crossing the threshold again ; she had put her on the sofa and dosed her with sal-volatile. And Marcella was too exhausted to rebel. She had only stipulated that a note should be sent to Aldous, asking him to come on to Mellor with the news as soon as the verdict of the coroner's jury should be given. The jury had been sitting all day, and the verdict was expected in the evening.

Marcella turned over her letters till she came to one from a London firm which contained a number of cloth patterns. As she touched it she threw it aside with a sudden gesture of impatience, and sat upright.

'Mamma ! I have something to say to you.'

'Yes, my dear.'

'Mamma, the wedding must be put off !—it *must* !—for some weeks. I have been thinking about it while I have been lying here. How *can* I ?—you can see for yourself. That miserable woman depends on me altogether. How can I spend my time on clothing and dressmakers? I feel as if I could think of nothing else—nothing else in the world—but her and her children.' She spoke with difficulty, her voice high and strained. 'The assizes may be held that very week—who knows?—the very day we are married.'

She stopped, looking at her mother almost threateningly. Mrs. Boyce showed no sign of surprise. She put her work down.

'I had imagined you might say something of the kind,' she said after a pause. 'I don't know that, from your point of view, it is unreasonable. But, of course, you must understand that very few people will see it from your point of view. Aldous Raeburn may —you must know best. But his people certainly won't; and your father will think it——'

'Madness,' she was going to say, but with her usual instinct for the moderate fastidious word she corrected it to 'foolish.'

Marcella's tired eyes were all wilfulness and defiance.

'I can't help it. I couldn't do it. I will tell Aldous at once. It must be put off for a month. And even that,' she added with a shudder, 'will be bad enough.'

Mrs. Boyce could not help an unperceived shrug of the shoulders, and a movement of pity towards the future husband. Then she said drily,—

'You must always consider whether it is just to Mr. Raeburn to let a matter of this kind interfere so considerably with his wishes and his plans. He must, I suppose, be in London for Parliament within six weeks.'

Marcella did not answer. She sat with her hands round her knees lost in perplexities. The wedding, as originally fixed, was now three weeks and three days off. After it, she and Aldous were to have spent a short fortnight's honeymoon at a famous house in the north, lent them for the occasion by a Duke who was a cousin of Aldous's on the mother's side, and had more houses than he knew what to do with. Then they were to go immediately up to London for the opening of Parliament. The furnishing of the May-fair house was being pressed on. In her new-born impatience with such things, Marcella had hardly of late concerned herself with it at all, and Miss Raeburn, scandalised, yet not unwilling, had been doing the whole of it, subject to conscientious worryings of the bride, whenever she could be got hold of, on the subject of papers and curtains.

As they sat silent, the unspoken idea in the mother's mind was—'Eight weeks more will carry us past the execution   Mrs. Boyce had already possessed herself very clearly of the facts of the case, and it was her perception that Marcella was throwing herself headlong into a hopeless struggle—together with something else—a confession perhaps of a touch of greatness in the girl's temper, passionate and violent as it was, that had led to this unwonted softness of manner, this absence of sarcasm.

Very much the same thought—only treated as a nameless horror not to be recognised or admitted—was in Marcella's mind also, joined however with another, unsuspected even by Mrs. Boyce's acuteness. 'Very likely—when I tell him—he will not want to marry me at all—and of course I shall tell him.'

But not yet—certainly not yet. She had the instinctive sense that during the next few weeks she should want all her dignity with Aldous, that she could not afford to put herself at a disadvantage with him. To be troubled about her own sins at such a moment would be like the meanness of the lazy and canting Christian, who whines about saving his soul while he ought to be rather occupied with feeding the bodies of his wife and children.

A ring at the front door. Marcella rose, leaning one hand on the end of the sofa—a long slim figure in her black dress—haggard and pathetic.

When Aldous entered, her face was one question. He went up to her and took her hand.

'In the case of Westall the verdict is one of "Wilful Murder" against Hurd. In that of poor Charlie Dynes the court is adjourned. Enough evidence has been taken to justify burial. But there is news to-night that one of the Widrington gang has turned informer, and the police say they will have their hands on them all within the next two or three days.'

Marcella withdrew herself from him and fell back into the corner of the sofa. Shading her eyes with her hand, she tried to be very composed and business-like.

'Was Hurd himself examined?'

'Yes, under the new Act. He gave the account which he gave to you and to his wife. But the court——'

'Did not believe it?'

'No. The evidence of motive was too strong. It was clear from his own account that he was out for poaching purposes, that he was leading the Oxford gang, and that he had a gun while Westall was unarmed. He admitted too that Westall called on him to give up the bag of pheasants he held, and the gun. He refused. Then he says Westall came at him, and he fired. Dick Patton and one or two others gave evidence as to the language he has habitually used about Westall for months past.'

'Cowards—curs!' cried Marcella, clenching both her hands, a kind of sob in her throat.

Aldous, already white and careworn, showed, Mrs. Boyce thought, a ray of indignation for an instant. Then he resumed steadily—

'And Brown, our steward, gave evidence as to his employment since October. The coroner summed up carefully, and I think fairly, and the verdict was given about half-past six.'

'They took him back to prison?'

'Of course. He comes before the magistrates on Thursday.'

'And you will be one!'

The girl's tone was indescribable.

Aldous started. Mrs. Boyce reddened with anger, and checking her instinct to intervene, began to put away her working materials that she might leave them together. While she was still busy Aldous said :—

'You forget; no magistrate ever tries a case in which he is personally concerned. I shall take no part in the trial. My grandfather, of course, must prosecute.'

'But it will be a bench of landlords,' cried Marcella; 'of men with whom a poacher is already condemned.'

'You are unjust to us, I think,' said Aldous slowly, after a pause, during which Mrs. Boyce left the room—'to some of us, at any rate. Besides, as of course you know, the case will be simply sent on for trial at the assizes. By the way'—his tone changed—'I hear to-night that Harry Wharton undertakes the defence.'

'Yes,' said Marcella defiantly. 'Is there anything to say against it? You wouldn't wish Hurd not to be defended, I suppose?'

'Marcella!'

Even her bitter mood was pierced by the tone. She had never wounded him so deeply yet, and for a moment he felt the situation intolerable; the surging grievance and reproach, with which his heart was really full, all but found vent in an outburst which would have wholly swept away his ordinary measure and self-control. But then, as he looked at her, it struck his lover's sense painfully how pale and miserable she was. He could not scold! But it came home to him strongly that for her own sake and his it would be better there should be explanations. After all things had been going untowardly for many weeks. His nature moved slowly and with much self-doubt, but it was plain to him now that he must make a stand.

After his cry, her first instinct was to apologise. Then the words stuck in her throat. To her, as to him, they seemed to be close on a trial of strength. If she could not influence him in this matter—so obvious, as it seemed to her, and so near to her heart

—what was to become of that lead of hers in their married life, on which she had been reckoning from the beginning? All that was worst in her and all that was best rose to the struggle.

But, as he did not speak, she looked up at last.

'I was waiting,' he said in a low voice.

'What for?'

'Waiting till you should tell me you did not mean what you said.'

She saw that he was painfully moved; she also saw that he was introducing something into their relation, an element of proud self-assertion, which she had never felt in it before. Her own vanity instantly rebelled.

'I ought not to have said exactly what I did,' she said, almost stifled by her own excitement, and making great efforts not to play the mere wilful child; 'that I admit. But it has been clear to me from the beginning that—that'—her words hurried, she took up a book and restlessly lifted it and let it fall—'you have never looked at this thing justly. You have looked at the crime as anyone must who is a landowner; you have never allowed for the provocation; you have not let yourself feel pity——'

He made an exclamation.

'Do you know where I was before I went in to the inquest?'

'No,' she said defiantly, determined not to be impressed, feeling a childish irritation at the interruption.

'I was with Mrs. Westall. Harden and I went in to see her. She is a hard, silent woman. She is clearly not popular in the village, and no one comes in to her. Her'—he hesitated—'her baby is expected before long. She is in such a state of shock and excitement that Clarke thinks it quite possible she may go out of her mind. I saw her sitting by the fire, quite silent, not crying, but with a wild eye that means mischief. We have sent in a nurse to help Mrs. Jellison watch her. She seems to care nothing about her boy. Everything that that woman most desired in life has been struck from her at a blow. Why? That a man who was in no stress of poverty, who had friends and employment, should indulge himself in acts which he knew to be against the law, and had promised you and his wife to forgo, and should at the same time satisfy a wild beast's hatred against the man, who was simply defending his master's property. Have _you_ no pity for Mrs. Westall or her child?'

He spoke as calmly as he could, making his appeal to reason and moral sense; but, in reality, every word was charged with electric feeling.

'I _am_ sorry for her!' cried Marcella passionately. 'But, after all, how can one feel for the oppressor, or those connected with him, as one does for the victim?' He shook his head, protesting against the word, but she rushed on. 'You *do* know—for I told you yesterday—how under the shelter of this *hateful* game system Westall made Hurd's life a burden to him when he was a young man—how he had begun to bully him again this past year. We had the same sort of dispute the other day about that murder in Ireland. You were shocked that I would not condemn the Moon-lighters who had shot their landlord from behind a hedge, as you did. You said the man had tried to do his duty, and that the murder was brutal and unprovoked. But I thought of the *system*—of the *memories* in the minds of the murderers. There *were* excuses—he suffered for his father—I am not going to judge that as I judge other murders. So, when a Czar of Russia is blown up, do you expect one to think only of his wife and children? No! I will think of the tyranny and the revolt ; I will pray, yes, *pray* that I might have courage to do as they did ! You may think me wild and mad. I dare say. I am made so. I shall always feel so !'

She flung out her words at him, every limb quivering under the emotion of them. His cool, penetrating eye, this manner she had never yet known in him, exasperated her.

'Where was the tyranny in this case?' he asked her quietly. 'I agree with you that there are murders and murders. But I thought your point was that here was neither murder nor attack but only an act of self-defence. That is Hurd's plea.'

She hesitated and stumbled.

'I know,' she said, 'I know. I believe it. But, even if the attack had been on Hurd's part, I should still find excuses, because of the system, and because of Westall's hatefulness.'

He shook his head again.

'Because a man is harsh and masterful, and uses stinging language, is he to be shot down like a dog?'

There was a silence. Marcella was lashing herself up by thoughts of the deformed man in his cell, looking forward after the wretched, unsatisfied life, which was all society had allowed him, to the violent death by which society would get rid of him—of the wife yearning her heart away—of the boy, whom other human beings, under the name of law, were about to separate from his father for ever. At last she broke out thickly and indistinctly :—

'The terrible thing is that I cannot count upon you—that now I cannot make you feel as I do—feel with me. And by-and-by, when I shall want your help desperately, when your help might be everything—I suppose it will be no good to ask it.'

He started, and bending forward he possessed himself of both her hands—her not trembling hands—and kissed them with a passionate tenderness.

'What help will you ask of me that I cannot give? That would be hard to bear!'

Still held by him, she answered his question by another :—

'Give me your idea of what will happen. Tell me how you think it will end.'

'I shall only distress you, dear,' he said sadly.

'No; tell me. You think him guilty. You believe he will be convicted.'

'Unless some wholly fresh evidence is forthcoming,' he said reluctantly, 'I can see no other issue.'

'Very well; then he will be sentenced to death. But, after sentence—I know—that man from Widrington, that solicitor told me—if—if strong influence is brought to bear—if anybody whose word counts—if Lord Maxwell and you, were to join the move-ment to save him—— There is sure to be a movement—the Radicals will take it up. Will you do it—will you promise me now —for my sake?

He was silent

She looked at him, all her heart burning in her eyes, conscious of her woman's power too, and pressing it. 'If that man is hanged,' she said pleadingly, 'it will leave a mark on my life nothing will ever smooth out. I shall feel myself somehow responsible. I shall say to myself, if I had not been thinking about my own selfish affairs—about getting married—about the straw-plaiting—I might have seen what was going on. I might have saved these people who have been my friends—my *real* friends—from this horror.'

She drew her hands away and fell back on the sofa, pressing her handkerchief to her eyes. 'If you had seen her this morning !' she said in a strangled voice. 'She was saying, " Oh, miss, if they do find him guilty, they can't hang him—not my poor deformed Jim, that never had a chance of being like the others. Oh, we'll beg so hard. I know there's many people will speak for him. He was mad, miss, when he did it. He'd never been himself, not since last winter, when we all sat and starved, and he was driven out of his senses by thinking of me and the children. You'll get Mr. Raeburn to speak—won't you, miss?—and Lord Maxwell? It was their game. I know it was their game. But they'll forgive him. They're such great people, and so rich—and we—we've always had such a struggle. Oh, the bad times we've had, and no one know ! They'll try and get him off, miss? Oh, I'll go and *beg* of them." '

She stopped, unable to trust her voice any further. He stooped

over her and kissed her brow. There was a certain solemnity
in the moment for both of them. The pity of human fate over-
shadowed them. At last he said firmly, yet with great feeling :—

I will not prejudge anything, that I promise you. I will keep
my mind open to the last. But—I should like to say—it would
not be any easier to me to throw myself into an agitation for reprieve because this man was tempted to crime by *my* property—on
my land. I should think it right to look at it altogether from the
public point of view. The satisfaction of my own private compunctions—of my own private feelings—is not what I ought to regard.
My own share in the circumstances in the conditions which made
such an act possible does indeed concern me deeply. You cannot
imagine but that the moral problem of it has possessed me ever
since this dreadful thing happened. It troubled me much before.
Now, it has become an oppression—a torture. I have never seen
my grandfather so moved, so distressed, in all my remembrance
of him. Yet he is a man of the old school, with the old standards. As for me, if ever I come to the estate I will change
the whole system ; I will run no risks of such human wreck and
ruin as this——'

His voice faltered.

'But,' he resumed, speaking steadily again, 'I ought to warn
you that such considerations as these will not affect my judgment
of this particular case. In the first place, I have no quarrel with
capital punishment as such. I do not believe we could rightly give
it up. Your attitude properly means that wherever we can legitimately feel pity for a murderer, we should let him escape his
penalty. I, on the other hand, believe that if the murderer saw
things as they truly are, he would himself *claim* his own death, as
his best chance, his only chance—in this mysterious universe !—
of self-recovery. Then it comes to this—was the act murder ? The
English law of murder is not perfect, but it appears to me to be
substantially just, and guided by it——'

'You talk as if there were no such things as mercy and pity in
the world,' she interrupted wildly ; 'as if laws were not made and
administered by men of just the same stuff and fabric as the law-
breaker !'

He looked troubled.

'Ah, but *law* is something beyond laws or those who administer
them,' he said in a lower tone ; 'and the law—the *obligation-sense*
—of our own race and time, however imperfect it may be, is sacred,
not because it has been imposed upon us from without, but because
it has grown up to what it is, out of our own best life—ours, yet
not ours—the best proof we have, when we look back at it in the

large, when we feel its work in ourselves of some diviner power than our own will—our best clue to what that power may be !'

He spoke at first, looking away—wrestling out his thought, as it were, by himself—then turning back to her, his eyes emphasised the appeal implied, though not expressed, in what he said—intense appeal to her for sympathy, forbearance, mutual respect, through all acuteness of difference. His look both promised and implored.

He had spoken to her but very rarely or indirectly as yet of his own religious or philosophical beliefs. She was in a stage when such things interested her but little, and reticence in personal matters was so much the law of his life that even to her expansion was difficult. So that—inevitably—she was arrested, for the moment, as any quick perception must be, by the things that unveil character.

Then an upheaval of indignant feeling swept the impression away. All that he said might be ideally, profoundly true—*but*—the red blood of the common life was lacking in every word of it ! He ought to be incapable of saying it *now*. Her passionate question was, how could he *argue*—how could he hold and mark the ethical balance—when a *woman* was suffering, when *children* were to be left fatherless ? Besides—the ethical balance itself—does it not alter according to the hands that hold it—poacher or landlord, rich or poor ?

But she was too exhausted to carry on the contest in words. Both felt it would have to be renewed. But she said to herself secretly that Mr. Wharton, when he got to work, would alter the whole aspect of affairs. And she knew well that her vantage-ground as towards Aldous was strong.

Then at last he was free to turn his whole attention for a little to her and her physical state, which made him miserable. He had never imagined that anyone, vigorous and healthy as she was, could look so worn out in so short a time. She let him talk to her— lament, entreat, advise—and at last she took advantage of his anxiety and her admissions to come to the point, to plead that the marriage should be put off.

She used the same arguments that she had done to her mother.

'How can I bear to be thinking of these things ?'—she pointed a shaking finger at the dress patterns lying scattered on the table —' with this agony, this death, under my eyes ?

It was a great blow to him, and the practical inconveniences involved were great. But the fibre of him—of which she had just felt the toughness—was delicate and sensitive as her own, and after a very short recoil he met her with great chivalry and sweetness, agreeing that everything should be put off for six weeks, till Easter in fact. She would have been very grateful to him but that something—some secret thought—checked the words she tried to say.

'I must go home then,' he said, rising and trying to smile. 'I shall have to make things straight with Aunt Neta, and set a great many arrangements in train. Now, you will *try* to think of something else? Let me leave you with a book that I can imagine you will read.'

She let herself be tended and thought for. At the last, just as he was going, he said :—

'Have you seen Mr. Wharton at all since this happened?'

His manner was just as usual. She felt that her eye was guilty, but the darkness of the firelit room shielded her.

'I have not seen him since we met him in the drive. I saw the solicitor who is working up the case for him yesterday. He came over to see Mrs. Hurd and me. I had not thought of asking him, but we agreed that, if he would undertake it, it would be the best chance.'

'It *is* probably the best chance,' said Aldous thoughtfully. 'I believe Wharton has not done much at the Bar since he was called, but that, no doubt, is because he has had so much on his hands in the way of journalism and politics. His ability is enough for anything, and he will throw himself into this. I do not think Hurd could do better.'

She did not answer. She felt that he was magnanimous, but felt it coldly, without emotion.

He came and stooped over her.

'Good-night—good-night—tired child—dear heart ! When I saw you in that cottage this morning I thought of the words, "Give, and it shall be given unto you." All that my life can do to pour good measure, pressed down, running over, into yours, I vowed you then !'

When the door closed upon him, Marcella, stretched in the darkness, shed the bitterest tears that had ever yet been hers—tears which transformed her youth—which baptised her, as it were, into the fulness of our tragic life.

She was still weeping when she heard the door softly opened. She sprang up and dried her eyes, but the little figure that glided in was not one to shrink from. Mary Harden came and sat down beside her.

'I knew you would be miserable. Let me come and cry too. I have been my round—have seen them all—and I came to bring you news.'

'How has she taken—the verdict?' asked Marcella, struggling with her sobs, and succeeding at last in composing herself.

'She was prepared for it. Charlie told her when he saw her after you left this afternoon that she must expect it.

There was a pause.

'I shall soon hear, I suppose,' said Marcella in a hardening voice, her hands round her knees, 'what Mr. Wharton is doing for the defence. He will appear before the magistrates, I suppose.'

'Yes; but Charlie thinks the defence will be mainly reserved. Only a little more than a fortnight to the assizes! The time is so short. But now this man has turned informer, they say the case is quite straightforward. With all the other evidence the police have there will be no difficulty in trying them all. Marcella!'

'Yes.'

Had there been light enough to show it, Mary's face would have revealed her timidity.

'Marcella, Charlie asked me to give you a message. He begs you not to—not to make Mrs. Hurd hope too much. He himself believes there is no hope, and it is not kind.'

'Are you and he like all the rest,' cried Marcella, her passion breaking out again, 'only eager to have blood for blood?'

Mary waited an instant.

'It has almost broken Charlie's heart,' she said at last; 'but he thinks it was murder, and that Hurd will pay the penalty; nay, more'—she spoke with a kind of religious awe in her gentle voice—'that he ought to be glad to pay it. He believes it to be God's will, and I have heard him say that he would even have executions in public again—under stricter regulations, of course—that we may not escape, as we always do if we can—from all sight and thought of God's justice and God's punishments.'

Marcella shuddered and rose. She almost threw Mary's hand away from her.

'Tell your brother from me, Mary,' she said, 'that his God is to *me* just a constable in the service of the English game-laws! If He *is* such a one, I at least will fling my Everlasting No at him while I live.'

And she swept from the room, leaving Mary aghast.

Meanwhile there was consternation and wrath at Maxwell Court, where Aldous, on his return from Mellor, had first of all given his great-aunt the news of the coroner's verdict, and had then gone on to break to her the putting-off of the marriage. His championship of Marcella in the matter, and his disavowal of all grievance were so quiet and decided, that Miss Raeburn had been only able to allow herself a very modified strain of comment and remonstrance, so long as he was still there to listen. But she was all the more outspoken when he was gone, and Lady Winterbourne was sitting with her. Lady Winterbourne, who was at home alone, while her husband was with a married daughter on the Riviera, had come over to dine *tête-à-tête* with her friend, finding it impossible to remain solitary while so much was happening.

'Well, my dear,' said Miss Raeburn shortly, as her guest entered the room, 'I may as well tell you at once that Aldous's marriage is put off.'

'Put off!' exclaimed Lady Winterbourne, bewildered. 'Why it was only Thursday that I was discussing it all with Marcella, and she told me everything was settled.'

'Thursday!—I dare say!' said Miss Raeburn, stitching away with fiery energy; 'but since then a poacher has murdered one of our gamekeepers, which makes all the difference.'

'What *do* you mean, Agneta?'

'What I say, my dear. The poacher was Marcella's friend, and she cannot now distract her mind from him sufficiently to marry Aldous, though every plan he has in the world will be upset by her proceedings. And as for his election, you may depend upon it she will never ask or know whether he gets in next Monday or no. That goes without saying. She is meanwhile absorbed with the poacher's defence—*Mr. Wharton*, of course, conducting it. This is your modern young woman, my dear—typical, I should think.'

Miss Raeburn turned her buttonhole in fine style, and at light-ning speed, to show the coolness of her mind, then, with a rattling of all her lockets, looked up and waited for Lady Winterbourne's reflections.

'She has often talked to me of these people—the Hurds,' said Lady Winterbourne slowly. 'She has always made special friends with them. Don't you remember she told us about them that day she first came back to lunch?'

'Of course I remember! That day she lectured Maxwell, at first sight, on his duties. She began well. As for these people,' said Miss Raeburn more slowly, 'one is, of course, sorry for the wife and children, though I am a good deal sorrier for Mrs. Westall, and poor, poor Mrs. Dynes. The whole affair has so upset Maxwell and me, we have hardly been able to eat or sleep since. I thought it made Maxwell look dreadfully old this morning, and with all that he has got before him too! I shall insist on send-ing for Clarke to-morrow morning if he does not have a better night. And now this postponement will be one more trouble—all the engagements to alter, and the invitations. *Really*! that girl.'

And Miss Raeburn broke off short, feeling simply that the

words which were allowed to a well-bred person were wholly
inadequate to her state of mind.

'But if she feels it—as you or I might feel such a thing about
someone we knew or cared for, Agneta?'

'How can she feel it like that?' cried Miss Raeburn, exasperated. 'How can she know anyone of—of that class well enough?
It is not seemly, I tell you, Adelaide, and I don't believe it is sincere. It's just done to make herself conspicuous, and show her power
over Aldous. For other reasons too, if the truth were known!'

Miss Raeburn turned over the shirt she was making for some
charitable society and drew out some tacking threads with a loud
noise which relieved her. Lady Winterbourne's old and delicate
cheek had flushed.

'I'm sure it's sincere,' she said with emphasis. 'Do you mean
to say, Agneta, that one can't sympathise, in such an awful thing,
with people of another class, as one would with one's own flesh
and blood?'

Miss Raeburn winced. She felt for a moment the pressure of a
democratic world—a hated formidable world—through her friend's
question. Then she stood to her guns.

'I dare say you'll think it sounds bad,' she said stoutly; 'but
in my young days it would have been thought a piece of posing—of
sentimentalism—something indecorous and unfitting—if a girl had
put herself in such a position. Marcella *ought* to be absorbed in her
marriage; that is the natural thing. How Mrs. Boyce can allow
her to mix herself with such things as this murder—to *live* in that
cottage, as I hear she has been doing—passes my comprehension.'

'You mean,' said Lady Winterbourne dreamily, 'that if one had
been very fond of one's maid, and she died, one wouldn't put on
mourning for her. Marcella would.'

'I dare say,' said Miss Raeburn snappishly. 'She is capable
of anything far-fetched and theatrical.'

The door opened and Hallin came in. He had been suffering
of late, and much confined to the house. But the news of the
murder had made a deep and painful impression upon him, and he
had been eagerly acquainting himself with the facts. Miss Raeburn, whose kindness ran with unceasing flow along the channels
she allowed it, was greatly attached to him in spite of his views,
and she now threw herself upon him for sympathy in the matter of
the wedding. In any grievance that concerned Aldous she counted
upon him, and her shrewd eyes had plainly perceived that he had
made no great friendship with Marcella.

'I am very sorry for Aldous,' he said at once; 'but I understand
her perfectly. So does Aldous.'

Miss Raeburn was angrily silent. But when Lord Maxwell, who had been talking with Aldous, came in, he proved, to her final discomfiture, to be very much of the same opinion.

'My dear,' he said wearily as he dropped into his chair, his old face grey and pinched, 'this thing is too terrible—the number of widows and orphans that night's work will make before the end breaks my heart to think of. It will be a relief not to have to consider festivities while these men are actually before the courts. What I am anxious about is that Marcella should not make herself ill with excitement. The man she is interested in will be hanged, must be hanged; and with her somewhat volatile, impulsive nature——'

He spoke with old-fashioned discretion and measure. Then quickly he pulled himself up, and, with some trivial question or other, offered his arm to Lady Winterbourne, for Aldous had just come in, and dinner was ready.

CHAPTER XII

NEARLY three weeks passed—short flashing weeks, crowded with agitations, inward or outward, for all the persons of this story.

After the inquiry before the magistrates—conducted, as she passionately thought, with the most marked animus on the part of the bench and police towards the prisoners—had resulted in the committal for trial of Hurd and his five companions, Marcella wrote Aldous Raeburn a letter which hurt him sorely.

'Don't come over to see me for a little while,' it ran. 'My mind is all given over to feelings which must seem to you—which, I know, do seem to you—unreasonable and unjust. But they are my life, and when they are criticised, or even treated coldly, I cannot bear it. When you are not there to argue with, I can believe, most sincerely, that you have a right to see this matter as you do, and that it is monstrous of me to expect you to yield to me entirely in a thing that concerns your sense of public duty. But don't come now—not before the trial. I will appeal to you if I think you can help me. I *know* you will if you can. Mr. Wharton keeps me informed of everything. I enclose his last two letters, which will show you the line he means to take up with regard to some of the evidence.'

Aldous's reply cost him a prodigal amount of pain and difficulty.

'I will do anything in the world to make these days less of a

burden to you. You can hardly imagine that it is not grievous to
me to think of any trouble of yours as being made worse by my
being with you. But still I understand. One thing only I ask—
that you should not imagine the difference between us greater than
it is. The two letters you enclose have given me much to ponder.
If only the course of the trial enables me with an honest heart to
throw myself into your crusade of mercy, with what joy shall I
come and ask you to lead me, and to forgive my own slower sense
and pity !

' I should like you to know that Hallin is very much inclined to
agree with you, to think that the whole affair was a "scrimmage,"
and that Hurd at least ought to be reprieved. He would have
come to talk it over with you himself, but that Clarke forbids him
anything that interests or excites him for the present. He has
been very ill and suffering for the last fortnight, and, as you know,
when these attacks come on we try to keep everything from him
that could pain or agitate him. But I see that this whole affair is
very much on his mind, in spite of my efforts.

' . . . Oh, my darling ! I am writing late at night, with your
letter open before me and your picture close to my hand. So
many things rise in my mind to say to you. There will come a
time—there *must* !—when I may pour them all out. Meanwhile,
amid all jars and frets, remember this, that I have loved you better
each day since first we met.

' I will not come to Mellor then for a little while. My election,
little heart as I have for it, will fill up the week. The nomination-
day is fixed for Thursday, and the polling for Monday.'

Marcella read the letter with a confusion of feeling so great as
to be in itself monstrous and demoralising. Was she never to be
simple, to see her way clearly again ?

As for him, as he rode about the lanes and beech-woods in the
days that followed, alone often with that nature for which all such
temperaments as Aldous Raeburn's have so secret and so observant
an affection, he was perpetually occupied with this difficulty which
had arisen between Marcella and himself, turning it over and over
in the quiet of the morning, before the turmoil of the day began.

He had followed the whole case before the magistrates with
the most scrupulous care. And since then, he had twice run
across the Widrington solicitor for the defence, who was now instructing Wharton. This man, although a strong Radical, and employed generally by his own side, saw no objection at all to letting
Lord Maxwell's heir and representative understand how in his
opinion the case was going. Aldous Raeburn was a person whom
everybody respected ; confidences were safe with him ; and he was

himself deeply interested in the affair. **The Raeburns** being the Raeburns, with all that that implied for smaller people in Brook-shire, little Mr. Burridge was aware of no reason whatever why Westall's employers should not know that, although Mr. Wharton was working up the defence with an energy and ability which set Burridge marvelling, it was still his, Burridge's, opinion, that everything that could be advanced would be wholly unavailing with the jury ; that the evidence, as it came into final shape, looked worse for Hurd rather than better ; and that the only hope for the man lay in the after-movement for reprieve which can always be got up in a game-preserving case.

'And is as a rule political and anti-landlord,' thought Aldous, on one of these mornings, as he rode along the edge of the down. He foresaw exactly what would happen. As he envisaged the immediate future, he saw one figure as the centre of it—not Marcella, but Wharton ! Wharton was defending, Wharton would organise the petition, Wharton would apply for his own support and his grandfather's, through Marcella. To Wharton would belong not only the popular *kudos* of the matter, but much more, and above all, Marcella's gratitude.

Aldous pulled up his horse an instant, recognising that spot in the road, that downward stretching glade among the beeches, where he had asked Marcella to be his wife. The pale February sunlight was spreading from his left hand through the bare grey trunks, and over the distant shoulders of the woods, far into the white and purple of the chalk plain. Sounds of labour came from the distant fields ; sounds of winter birds from the branches round him. The place, the time, raised in him all the intensest powers of consciousness. He saw himself as the man *standing midway* in everything—speculation, politics, sympathies—as the perennially ineffective and, as it seemed to his morbid mood, the perennially defeated type, beside the Whartons of this world. Wharton ! He knew him—had read him long ago—read him afresh of late. Raeburn's lip showed the contempt, the bitterness which the phi-losopher could not repress, showed also the humiliation of the lover. Here was he, banished from Marcella ; here was Wharton, in possession of her mind and sympathies, busily forging a link—

'It shall be *broken* !' said Raeburn to himself with a sudden fierce concentration of will. 'So much I will claim—and enforce.'

But not now, nothing now, but patience, delicacy, prudence. He gathered himself together with a long breath, and went his way.

For the rest, the clash of motives and affections he felt and foresaw in this matter of the Disley murders became day by day more harassing. The moral debate was strenuous enough. The murders had roused all the humane and ethical instincts, which were in fact the man, to such a point that they pursued him constantly, in the pauses of his crowded days, like avenging Erinnyes. Hallin's remark that 'game preserving creates crime' left him no peace. Intellectually he argued it, and on the whole rejected it ; morally, and in feeling, it scourged him. He had suffered all his mature life under a too painful and scrupulous sense that he, more than other men, was called to be his brother's keeper. It was natural that, during these exhausting days, the fierce death on Westall's rugged face, the piteous agony in Dynes's young eyes and limbs, should haunt him, should make his landlord's place and responsibility often mere ashes and bitterness.

But, as Marcella has been obliged to perceive, he drew the sharpest line between the bearings of this ghastly business on his own private life and action, and its relation to public order. That the gamekeepers destroyed were his servants, or practically his servants, made no difference to him whatever in his estimate of the crime itself. If the circumstances had been such that he could honestly have held Hurd not to be a murderer, no employer's interest, no landlord's desire for vengeance, would have stood in his way. On the other hand, believing, as he emphatically did, that Hurd's slaying of Westall had been of a kind more deliberate and less capable of excuse than most murders, he would have held it a piece of moral cowardice to allow his own qualms and compunctions as to the rights and wrongs of game preserving to interfere with a duty to justice and society.

Ay ! and something infinitely dearer to him than his own qualms and compunctions.

Hallin, who watched the whole debate in his friend day by day, was conscious that he had never seen Aldous more himself, in spite of trouble of mind ; more 'in character,' so to speak, than at this moment. Spiritual dignity of mind and temper, blended with a painful personal humility, and interfused with all—determining all —elements of judgment, subtleties, prejudices, modes of looking at things, for which he was hardly responsible, so deeply ingrained were they by inheritance and custom. More than this : did not the ultimate explanation of the whole attitude of the man lie in the slow but irresistible revolt of a strong individuality against the passion which had for a time suppressed it ? The truth of certain moral relations may be for a time obscured and distorted ; none the less, *reality* wins the day. So Hallin read it.

Meanwhile, during days when both for Aldous and Wharton

the claims of a bustling, shouting public, which must be canvassed, shaken hands with, and spoken to, and the constant alternations of business meetings, committee-rooms and the rest, made it impossible, after all, for either man to spend more than the odds and ends of thought upon anything outside the clatter of politics, Marcella had been living a life of intense and monotonous feeling, shut up almost within the walls of a tiny cottage, hanging over sick-beds, and thrilling to each pulse of anguish as it beat in the miserable beings she tended.

The marriage of the season, with all its accompanying festivities and jubilations, had not been put off for seven weeks—till after Easter—without arousing a storm of critical astonishment both in village and county. And when the reason was known—that it was because Miss Boyce had taken the Disley murder so desperately to heart, that until the whole affair was over, and the men either executed or reprieved, she could spare no thought to wedding clothes or cates—there was curiously little sympathy with Marcella. Most of her own class thought it a piece of posing, if they did not say so as frankly as Miss Raeburn—something done for self-advertisement and to advance anti-social opinions; while the Mellor cottagers, with the instinctive English recoil from any touch of sentiment not, so to speak, in the bargain, gossipped and joked about it freely.

'She can't be very fond o' 'im, not of Muster Raeburn, she can't,' said old Patton, delivering himself as he sat leaning on his stick at his open door, while his wife and another woman or two chattered inside. 'Not what I'd call lover-y. She don't want to run in harness, she don't, no sooner than she need. She's a peert filly is Miss Boyce.'

'I've been a-waitin, an' a-waitin,' said his wife with her gentle sigh, 'to hear summat o' that new straw-plaitin she talk about. But nary a word. They do say as it's give up althegither.'

'No, she's took up wi' nursin Minta Hurd—wonderful took up,' said another woman. 'They do say as Ann Mullins can't abear her. When she's there nobody can open their mouth. When that kind o' thing happens in the fambly it's bad enoof without havin a lady trailin about you all day long, so that you have to be mindin yersel, an thinkin about givin her a cheer, an' the like.'

One day in the dusk, more than a fortnight after the inquest, Marcella, coming from the Hurds' cottage, overtook Mrs. Jellison, who was going home after spending the afternoon with her daughter.

Hitherto Marcella had held aloof from Isabella Westall and her relations, mainly, to do her justice, from fear lest she might somehow hurt or offend them. She had been to see Charlie Dynes's mother, but she had only brought herself to send a message of sympathy through Mary Harden to the keeper's widow.

Mrs. Jellison looked at her askance with her old wild eyes as Marcella came up with her.

'Oh, she's *puddlin* along,' she said in answer to Marcella's inquiry, using a word very familiar in the village. 'She'll not do herself a mischief while there's Nurse Ellen an' me to watch her like a pair o' cats. She's dreadful upset, is Isabella—shouldn't ha thought it of her. That fust day'—a cloud darkened the curious, dreamy face—'no, I'm not a-goin to think about that fust day, I'm not, tain't a ha'porth o' good,' she added resolutely; 'but she was all right when they'd let her get 'im 'ome, and wash and settle 'im, an put 'im comfortable like in his coffin. He wor a big man, miss, when he wor laid out! Searle, as made the coffin, told her as ee 'adn't made one such an extry size since old Harry Flood, the blacksmith, fifteen year ago. Ee'd soon a done for Jim Hurd if it 'ad been fists o' both sides. But guns is things as yer can't reckon on.'

'Why didn't he let Hurd alone,' said Marcella sadly, 'and prosecute him next day? It's attacking men when their blood is up that brings these awful things about.'

'Wal, I don't see that,' said Mrs. Jellison pugnaciously; 'he wor paid to do't—an' he had the law on his side. 'Ow's she?' she said, lowering her voice and jerking her thumb in the direction of the Hurds' cottage.

'She's very ill,' replied Marcella with a contraction of the brow. 'Dr. Clarke says she ought to stay in bed, but of course she won't.'

'They're a-goin to try 'im Thursday?' said Mrs. Jellison inquiringly.

'Yes.'

'An' Muster Wharton be a-goin to defend 'im. Muster Wharton may be cliver, ee may—they do say as ee can see the grass growin, ee's that knowin—but ee'll not get Jim Hurd off; there's nobody in the village as b'lieves for a moment as 'ow he will. They'll best 'im. Lor bless yer, they'll best 'im. I was a-sayin it to Isabella this afternoon—ee'll not save 'is neck, don't you be afeard.'

Marcella drew herself up with a shiver of repulsion.

'Will it mend your daughter's grief to see another woman's heart broken? Don't you suppose it might bring her some comfort, Mrs. Jellison, if she were to try and forgive that poor wretch? She might remember that her husband gave him provocation, and that anyway, if his life is spared, his punishment and their misery will be heavy enough !'

'Oh, lor no !' said Mrs. Jellison composedly. 'She don't want to be forgivin of 'im. Mr. Harden ee come talkin to 'er, but she isn't one o' that sort, isn't Isabella. I'm sartin sure she'll be better in 'erself when they've put 'im out o' the way. It makes her all ov a fever to think of Muster Wharton gettin 'im off. *I* don't bear Jim Hurd no pertickler malice. Isabella may talk herself black i' the face, but she an' Johnnie 'll have to come 'ome and live along o' me, whatever she may say. She can't stay in that cottage, cos they'll be wantin it for another keeper. Lord Maxwell ee's givin her a fine pension, my word ee is ! an' says ee'll look after johnnie. And what with my bit airnins—we'll do, yer know, miss—we'll do !'

The old woman looked up with a nod, her green eyes sparkling with the queer inhuman light that belonged to them.

Marcella could not bring herself to say good-night to her, and was hurrying on without a word, when Mrs. Jellison stopped her.

'An' 'ow about that straw-plaitin, miss?' she said slyly.

'I have had to put it on one side for a bit,' said Marcella coldly, hating the woman's society. ' I have had my hands full and Lady Winterbourne has been away ; but we shall, of course, take it up again later.'

She walked away quickly, and Mrs. Jellison hobbled after her, grinning to herself every now and then as she caught the straight tall figure against the red evening sky.

' I'll go in ter town termorrer,' she thought, ' an' have a crack wi' Jimmy Gedge ; *ee* needn't be afeard for 'is livin. An' them great fules as ha' bin runnin in a string arter 'er, an' cacklin about their eighteenpence a score, as I've told 'em times, I'll eat my apron the fust week as iver they get it. I don't hold wi' ladies —no, nor passons neither—not when it comes to meddlin wi' your wittles, an' dictatin to yer about forgivin them as ha' got the better ov yer. That young lady there, what do she matter ? That sort's allus gaddin about ! What'll she keer about us when she's got 'er fine husband ? Here o' Saturday, gone o' Monday—that's what she is. Now Jimmy Gedge, yer kin allus count on '*im*. Thirty-six year ee ha' set there in that 'ere shop, an' I guess ee 'll set there till they call 'im ter kingdom come. Ee's a cheatin, sweatin, greedy old skinflint is Jimmy Gedge ; but when yer wants 'im yer *kin* find 'im.'

Marcella hurried home, she was expecting a letter from Wharton, the third within a week. She had not set eyes on him since they had met that first morning in the drive, and it was plain to her that he was as unwilling as she was that there should be any meeting between them. Since the moment of his taking up the case, in spite of the pressure of innumerable engagements, he had found time to send her, almost daily, sheets covered with his small even writing, in which every detail and prospect of the legal situation, so far as it concerned James Hurd, were noted and criticised with a shrewdness and fulness which never wavered, and never lost for a moment the professional note.

'Dear Miss Boyce'—the letters began—leading up to a 'Yours faithfully,' which Marcella read as carefully as the rest. Often, as she turned them over, she asked herself whether that scene in the library had not been a mere delusion of the brain, whether the man whose wild words and act had burnt themselves into her life could possibly be writing her these letters, in this key, without a reference, without an allusion. Every day, as she opened them, she looked them through quietly with a shaking pulse ; every day she found herself proudly able to hand them on to her mother, with the satisfaction of one who has nothing to conceal, whatever the rest of the world may suspect. He was certainly doing his best to replace their friendship on that level of high comradeship in ideas and causes which, as she told herself, it had once occupied. His own wanton aggression and her weakness had toppled it down thence, and brought it to ruin. She could never speak to him, never know him again till it was re-established. Still his letters galled her. He assumed, she supposed, that such a thing could happen, and nothing more be said about it? How little he knew her, or what she had in her mind !

Now, as she walked along, wrapped in her plaid cape, her thought was one long tumultuous succession of painful or passionate images, interrupted none the less at times by those curious self-observing pauses of which she had always been capable. She had been sitting for hours beside Mrs. Hurd, with little Willie upon her knees. The mother, always anæmic and consumptive, was by now prostrate, the prey of a long-drawn agony, peopled by visions of Jim alone and in prison—Jim on the scaffold with the white cap over his eyes—Jim in the prison coffin—which would rouse her shrieking from dreams which were the rending asunder of soul and body. Minta Hurd's love for the unhappy being who had brought her to this pass had been infinitely maternal. There had been a boundless pity in it, and the secret pride of a soul, which, humble and modest towards all the rest of the world, yet knew itself to be the breath and sustenance, the indispensable aid of one other soul in the universe, and gloried accordingly. To be cut off now from all ministration, all comforting—to have to lie there like a log, imagining the moment when the neighbours should come in and say, 'It is all over—they have broken his neck—and buried him'—it was a doom beyond all even that her timid pessimist heart had ever dreamed. She had already seen him twice in prison, and she knew that she would see him again. She was to go on Monday, Miss Boyce said, before the trial began, and after—if they brought him in guilty—they would let her say good-bye. She was always thirsting to see him. But when she went, the prison surroundings paralysed her. Both she and Hurd felt themselves caught in the wheels of a great relentless machine, of which the workings filled them with a voiceless terror. He talked to her spasmodically of the most incongruous things—breaking out sometimes with a glittering eye into a string of instances bearing on Westall's bullying and tyrannous ways. He told her to return the books Miss Boyce had lent him, but when asked if he would like to see Marcella he shrank and said no. Mr. Wharton was 'doin capital' for him ; but she wasn't to count on his getting off. And he didn't know that he wanted to, neither. Once she took Willie to see him ; the child nearly died of the journey ; and the father, 'though anyone can see, miss, he's just sick for 'im,' would not hear of his coming again. Sometimes he would hardly kiss her at parting ; he sat on his chair, with his great head drooped forward over his red hands, lost in a kind of animal lethargy. Westall's name always roused him. Hate still survived. But it made *her* life faint within her to talk of the murdered man— wherein she showed her lack of the usual peasant's realism and curiosity in the presence of facts of blood and violence. When she was told it was time for her to go, and the heavy door was locked behind her, the poor creature, terrified at the warder and the bare prison silences, would hurry away as though the heavy hand of this awful Justice were laid upon her too, torn by the thought of him she left behind, and by the remembrance that he had only kissed her once, and yet impelled by mere physical instinct towards the relief of Ann Mullins's rough face waiting for her—of the outer air and the free heaven.

As for Willie, he was fast dwindling. Another week or two— the doctor said—no more. He lay on Marcella's knee on a pillow, wasted to an infant's weight, panting and staring with those strange blue eyes, but always patient, always struggling to say his painful 'thank you' when she fed him with some of the fruit constantly sent her from Maxwell Court. Everything that was said about his father he took in and understood, but he did not seem to fret.

His mother was almost divided from him by this passivity of the dying; nor could she give him or his state much attention. Her gentle, sensitive, but not profound nature was strained already beyond bearing by more gnawing griefs.

After her long sit in Mrs. Hurd's kitchen Marcella found the air of the February evening tonic and delightful. Unconsciously impressions stole upon her—the lengthening day, the celandines in the hedges, the swelling lilac buds in the cottage gardens. They spoke to her youth, and out of mere physical congruity it could not but respond. Still, her face kept the angered look with which she had parted from Mrs. Jellison. More than that—the last few weeks had visibly changed it, had graved upon it the signs of 'living.' It was more beautiful than ever in its significant black and white, but it was older—a *woman* spoke from it. Marcella had gone down into reality, and had found there the rebellion and the storm for which such souls as hers are made. Rebellion most of all. She had been living with the poor, in their stifling rooms, amid their perpetual struggle for a little food and clothes and bodily ease; she had seen this struggle, so hard in itself, combined with agonies of soul and spirit, which made the physical destitution seem to the spectator something brutally gratuitous, a piece of careless and tyrannous cruelty on the part of Nature—or God? She would hardly let herself think of Aldous—though she *must* think of him by and by! He and his fared sumptuously every hour! As for her, it was as though in her woman's arms, on her woman's breast, she carried Lazarus all day, stooping to him with a hungering pity. And Aldous stood aloof. Aldous would not help her—or not with any help worth having—in consoling this misery—binding up these sores. Her heart cried shame on him. She had a crime against him to confess—but she felt herself his superior none the less. If he cast her off—why then surely they would be quits, quits for good and all.

As she reached the front door of Mellor, she saw a little two-wheeled cart standing outside it, and William holding the pony.

Visitors were nowadays more common at Mellor than they had been, and her instinct was to escape. But as she was turning to a side door William touched his cap to her.

'Mr. Wharton's waiting to see you, miss.'

She stopped sharply.

'Where is Mrs. Boyce, William?'

'In the drawing-room, miss.'

She walked in calmly. Wharton was standing on the rug, talking; Mrs. Boyce was listening to what he had to say with the light repellent air Marcella knew so well.

When she came in Wharton stepped forward ceremoniously to shake hands, then began to speak at once, with the manner of one who is on a business errand and has no time to waste.

'I thought it best, Miss Boyce, as I had unexpectedly a couple of spare hours this evening, to come and let you know how things were going. You understand that the case comes on at the assizes next Thursday?'

Marcella assented. She had seated herself on the old sofa beside the fire, her ungloved hands on her knee. Something in her aspect made Wharton's eyes waver an instant as he looked down upon her—but it was the only sign.

'I should like to warn you,' he said gravely, 'that I entertain no hope whatever of getting James Hurd off. I shall do my best, but the verdict will certainly be murder; and the judge, I think, is sure to take a severe view. We may get a recommendation to mercy, though I believe it to be extremely unlikely. But if so, the influence of the judge, according to what I hear, will probably be against us. The prosecution have got together extremely strong evidence—as to Hurd's long connection with the gang, in spite of the Raeburns' kindness—as to his repeated threats that he would "do for" Westall if he and his friends were interrupted—and so on. His own story is wholly uncorroborated; and Dynes's deposition, so far as it goes, is all against it.'

He went on to elaborate these points with great clearness of exposition and at some length; then he paused.

'This being so,' he resumed, 'the question is, what can be done? There must be a petition. Amongst my own party I shall be, of course, able to do something, but we must have men of all sides. Without some at least of the leading Conservatives, we shall fare badly. In one word—do you imagine that you can induce Mr. Raeburn and Lord Maxwell to sign?'

Mrs. Boyce watched him keenly. Marcella sat in frozen paleness.

'I will try,' she said at last, with deliberation.

'Then'—he took up his gloves—'there may be a chance for us. If you cannot succeed, no one else can. But if Lord Maxwell and Mr. Raeburn can be secured, others will easily follow. Their names—especially under all the circumstances—will carry a peculiar weight. I may say everything, in the first instance—the weight the first effect of the petition—depends on them. Well, then, I leave it in your hands. No time should be lost after the sentence. As to the grounds of our plea, I shall, of course, lay them down in court to the best of my ability.'

'I shall be there,' she interrupted.

He started. So did Mrs. Boyce, but characteristically she made no comment.

'Well, then,' he resumed after a pause, 'I need say no more for the present. How is the wife?'

She replied, and a few other formal sentences of inquiry or comment passed between them.

'And your election?' said Mrs. Boyce, still studying him with hostile eyes, as he got up to take leave.

'To-morrow!' He threw up his hands with a little gesture of impatience. 'That at least will be one thread spun off and out of the way, whatever happens. I must get back to Widrington as fast as my pony can carry me. Good-bye, Miss Boyce.'

Marcella went slowly upstairs. The scene which had just passed was unreal, impossible; yet every limb was quivering. Then the sound of the front door shutting sent a shock through her whole nature. The first sensation was one of horrible emptiness, forlornness. The next—her mind threw itself with fresh vehemence upon the question, 'Can I, by any means, get my way with Aldous?'

CHAPTER XIII

AND may the Lord have mercy on your soul!'

The deep-pitched words fell slowly on Marcella's ears, as she sat leaning forward in the gallery of the Widrington Assize Court. Women were sobbing beside and behind her. Minta Hurd, to her left, lay in a half-swoon against her sister-in-law, her face buried in Ann's black shawl. For an instant after Hurd's death sentence had been spoken Marcella's nerves ceased to throb—the long exhaustion of feeling stopped. The harsh light and shade of the ill-lit room; the gas-lamps in front of the judge, blanching the ranged faces of the jury; the long table of reporters below, some writing, but most looking intently towards the dock; the figure of Wharton opposite, in his barrister's gown and wig—that face of his, so small, nervous, delicate—the frowning eyebrows a dark bar under the white of the wig—his look, alert and hostile, fixed upon the judge; the heads and attitudes of the condemned men, especially the form of a fair-haired youth, the principal murderer of Charlie Dynes, who stood a little in front of the line, next to Hurd, and overshadowing his dwarf's stature—these things Marcella saw indeed; for years after she could have described them point by point; but for some seconds or minutes her eyes stared at them

without conscious reaction of the mind on the immediate spectacle.

In place of it, the whole day, all these hours that she had been
sitting there, rushed before her in a synthesis of thought, replacing
the stream of impressions and images.   The crushing accumulation
of hostile evidence—witness after witness coming forward to add
to the damning weight of it ; the awful weakness of the defence—
Wharton's irritation under it—the sharpness, the useless, acrid
ability of his cross-examinations ; yet, contrasting with the legal
failure, the personal success, the mixture of grace with energy, the
technical accomplishment of the manner, as one wrestling before
his equals—nothing left here of the garrulous vigour and brutality
of the labourers' meeting !—the masterly use of all that could avail,
the few quiet words addressed at the end to the pity of the jury,
and by implication to the larger ethical sense of the community,—
all this she thought of with great intellectual clearness while the
judge's sonorous voice rolled along, sentencing each prisoner in
turn.   Horror and pity were alike weary ; the brain asserted itself.

The court was packed.   Aldous Raeburn sat on Marcella's right
hand ; and during the day the attention of everybody in the dingy
building had been largely divided between the scene below, and
that strange group in the gallery where the man who had just been
elected Conservative member for East Brookshire, who was Lord
Maxwell's heir, and Westall's employer, sat beside his betrothed,
in charge of a party which comprised not only Marcella Boyce, but
the wife, sister, and little girl of Westall's murderer.

On one occasion some blunt answer of a witness had provoked
a laugh coming no one knew whence.   The judge turned to the
gallery and looked up sternly—' I cannot conceive why men and
women—women especially—should come crowding in to hear such
a case as this ; but if I hear another laugh I shall clear the court.'
Marcella, whose whole conscious nature was by now one network
of sensitive nerve, saw Aldous flush and shrink as the words were
spoken.   Then, looking across the court, she caught the eye of an
old friend of the Raeburns, a county magistrate.   At the judge's
remark he had turned involuntarily to where she and Aldous sat ;
then, as he met Miss Boyce's face, instantly looked away again.
She perfectly—passionately—understood that Brookshire was very
sorry for Aldous Raeburn that day.

The death sentences—three in number—were over.   The judge
was a very ordinary man ; but, even for the ordinary man, such an
act carries with it a great tradition of what is befitting, which im-
poses itself on voice and gesture.   When he ceased, the deep
breath of natural emotion could be felt and heard throughout the

crowded court; loud wails of sobbing women broke from the gallery.

'Silence!' cried an official voice, and the judge resumed, amid stifled sounds that stabbed Marcella's sense, once more nakedly alive to everything around it.

The sentences to penal servitude came to an end also. Then a ghastly pause. The line of prisoners directed by the warders turned right about face towards a door in the back wall of the court. As the men filed out, the tall, fair youth, one of those condemned to death, stopped an instant and waved his hand to his sobbing sweetheart in the gallery. Hurd also turned irresolutely.

'Look!' exclaimed Ann Mullins, propping up the fainting woman beside her, 'he's goin'.'

Marcella bent forward. She, rather than the wife, caught the last look on his large dwarf's face, so white and dazed, the eyes blinking under the gas.

Aldous touched her softly on the arm.

'Yes,' she said quickly, 'yes, we must get her out. Ann, can you lift her?'

Aldous went to one side of the helpless woman ; Ann Mullins held her on the other. Marcella followed, pressing the little girl close against her long black cloak. The gallery made way for them ; everyone looked and whispered till they had passed. Below, at the foot of the stairs, they found themselves in a passage crowded with people—lawyers, witnesses, officials, mixed with the populace. Again a road was opened for Aldous and his charges.

'This way, Mr. Raeburn,' said a policeman with alacrity. 'Stand back, please! Is your carriage there, sir?'

'Let Ann Mullins take her—put them into the cab—I want to speak to Mr. Wharton,' said Marcella in Aldous's ear.

'Get me a cab at once,' he said to the policeman, 'and tell my carriage to wait.'

'Miss Boyce!'

Marcella turned hastily and saw Wharton beside her. Aldous also saw him, and the two men interchanged a few words.

'There is a private room close by,' said Wharton. 'I am to take you there, and Mr. Raeburn will join us at once.'

He led her along a corridor, and opened a door to the left. They entered a small dingy room, looking through a begrimed window on a courtyard. The gas was lit, and the table was strewn with papers.

'Never, never more beautiful!' flashed through Wharton's mind, 'with that knit, strenuous brow—that tragic scorn for a base world—that royal gait——'

Aloud he said :—

'I have done my best privately among the people I can get at, and I thought, before I go up to town to-night—you know Parliament meets on Monday ?—I would show you what I had been able to do, and ask you to take charge of a copy of the petition.' He pointed to a long envelope lying on the table. 'I have drafted it myself—I think it puts all the points we can possibly urge—but as to the names——'

He took out a folded sheet of paper from his breast pocket.

'It won't do,' he said, looking down at it, and shaking his head. 'As I said to you, it is so far political merely. There is a very strong Liberal and Radical feeling getting up about the case. But that won't carry us far. This petition with these names is a demonstration against game preserving and keepers' tyranny. What we want is the co-operation of a *neighbourhood*, especially of its leading citizens. However, I explained all this to you—there is no need to discuss it. Will you look at the list ?'

Still holding it, he ran his finger over it, commenting here and there. She stood beside him ; the sleeve of his gown brushed her black cloak ; and under his perfect composure there beat a wild exultation in his power—without any apology, any forgiveness—to hold her there, alone with him, listening—her proud head stooped to his—her eye following his with this effort of anxious attention.

She made a few hurried remarks on the names, but her knowledge of the county was naturally not very serviceable. He folded up the paper and put it back.

'I think we understand,' he said. 'You will do what you can in the only quarter'—he spoke slowly—'that can really aid, and you will communicate with me at the House of Commons ? I shall do what I can, of course, when the moment comes, in Parliament, and meanwhile I shall start the matter in the Press—our best hope The Radical papers are already taking it up.'

There was a sound of steps in the passage outside. A policeman opened the door, and Aldous Raeburn entered. His quick look ran over the two figures standing beside the table.

'I had some difficulty in finding a cab,' he explained, 'and we had to get some brandy ; but she came round, and we got her off. I sent one of our men with her. The carriage is here.'

He spoke—to Marcella—with some formality. He was very pale, but there was both authority and tension in his bearing.

'I have been consulting with Miss Boyce,' said Wharton with equal distance of manner, 'as to the petition we are sending up to the Home Office.'

Aldous made no reply.

'One word, Miss Boyce,'—Wharton quietly turned to her. 'May I ask you to read the petition carefully, before you attempt to do anything with it? It lays stress on the *only* doubt that can reasonably be felt after the evidence, and after the judge's summing up. That particular doubt I hold to be entirely untouched by the trial; but it requires careful stating—the issues may easily be confused.'

'Will you come?' said Aldous to Marcella. What she chose to think the forced patience of his tone exasperated her.

'I will do everything I can,' she said in a low, distinct voice to Wharton. 'Good-bye.'

She held out her hand. To both the moment was one of infinite meaning; to her, in her high spiritual excitement, a sacrament of pardon and gratitude—expressed once for all—by this touch—in Aldous Raeburn's presence.

The two men nodded to each other. Wharton was already busy, putting his papers together.

'We shall meet next week, I suppose, in the House?' said Wharton casually. 'Good-night.'

'Will you take me to the Court?' said Marcella to Aldous, directly the door of the carriage was shut upon them, and, amid a gaping crowd that almost filled the little market-place of Widrington, the horses moved off. 'I told mamma that, if I did not come home, I should be with you, and that I should ask you to send me back from the Court to-night.'

She still held the packet Wharton had given her in her hand. As though for air, she had thrown back the black gauze veil she had worn all through the trial, and, as they passed through the lights of the town, Aldous could see in her face the signs—the plain, startling signs—of the effect of these weeks upon her. Pale, exhausted, yet showing in every movement the nervous excitement which was driving her on—his heart sank as he looked at her—foreseeing what was to come.

As soon as the main street had been left behind, he put his head out of the window, and gave the coachman, who had been told to go to Mellor, the new order.

'Will you mind if I don't talk?' said Marcella, when he was again beside her. 'I think I am tired out, but I might rest now a little. When we get to the Court, will you ask Miss Raeburn to let me have some food in her sitting-room? Then, at nine o'clock or so, may I come down and see Lord Maxwell and you—together?'

What she said, and the manner in which she said it, could only add to his uneasiness ; but he assented, put a cushion behind her, wrapped the rugs round her, and then sat silent, train after train of close and anxious thought passing through his mind as they rolled along the dark roads.

When they arrived at Maxwell Court, the sound of the carriage brought Lord Maxwell and Miss Raeburn at once into the hall.

Aldous went forward in front of Marcella. ' I have brought Marcella,' he said hastily to his aunt. ' Will you take her upstairs to your sitting-room, and let her have some food and rest ? She is not fit for the exertion of dinner, but she wishes to speak to my grandfather afterwards.'

Lord Maxwell had already hurried to meet the black-veiled figure standing proudly in the dim light of the outer hall.

' My dear ! my dear ! ' he said, drawing her arm within his, and patting her hand in fatherly fashion. ' How worn-out you look !—Yes, certainly—Agneta, take her up and let her rest—And you wish to speak to me afterwards ? Of course, my dear, of course—at any time.'

Miss Raeburn, controlling herself absolutely, partly because of Aldous's manner, partly because of the servants, took her guest upstairs straightway, put her on the sofa in a cheerful sitting-room with a bright fire, and then, shrewdly guessing that she herself could not possibly be a congenial companion to the girl at such a moment, whatever might have happened or might be going to happen, she looked at her watch, said that she must go down to dinner, and promptly left her to the charge of a kind elderly maid, who was to do and get for her whatever she would.

Marcella made herself swallow some food and wine. Then she said that she wished to be alone and rest for an hour, and would come downstairs at nine o'clock. The maid, shocked by her pallor, was loth to leave her, but Marcella insisted.

When she was left alone she drew herself up to the fire and tried hard to get warm, as she had tried to eat. When in this way a portion of physical ease and strength had come back to her, she took out the petition from its envelope and read it carefully. As she did so her lip relaxed, her eye recovered something of its brightness. All the points that had occurred to her confusedly, amateurishly, throughout the day, were here thrown into luminous and admirable form. She had listened to them indeed, as urged by Wharton in his concluding speech to the jury, but it had not, alas ! seemed so marvellous to her then, as it did now, that, *after* such a plea, the judge should have summed up as he did.

When she had finished it and had sat thinking a while over the declining fire, an idea struck her. She took a piece of paper from Miss Raeburn's desk, and wrote on it :—

'Will you read this—and Lord Maxwell—before I come down? I forgot that you had not seen it.—M.'

A ring at the bell brought the maid.

'Will you please get this taken to Mr. Raeburn? And then, don't disturb me again for half an hour.'

And for that time she lay in Miss Raeburn's favourite chair, outwardly at rest. Inwardly she was ranging all her arguments, marshalling all her forces.

When the chiming clock in the great hall below struck nine, she got up and put the lamp for a moment on the mantelpiece, which held a mirror. She had already bathed her face and smoothed her hair. But she looked at herself again with attention, drew down the thick front waves of hair a little lower on the white brow, as she liked to have them, and once more straightened the collar and cuffs which were the only relief to her plain black dress.

The house as she stepped out into it seemed very still. Perfumed breaths of flowers and pot-pourri ascended from the hall. The pictures along the walls as she passed were those same Caroline and early Georgian beauties that had so flashingly suggested her own future rule in this domain on the day when Aldous proposed to her.

She felt suddenly very shrinking and lonely as she went downstairs. The ticking of a large clock somewhere—the short, screaming note of Miss Raeburn's parrot in one of the ground-floor rooms—these sounds and the beating of her own heart seemed to have the vast house to themselves.

No !—that was a door opening—Aldous coming to fetch her. She drew a childish breath of comfort.

He sprang up the stairs, two or three steps at a time, as he saw her coming.

'Are you rested—were they good to you? Oh ! my precious one !—how pale you are still ! Will you come and see my grandfather now ? He is quite ready.'

She let him lead her in. Lord Maxwell was standing by his writing-table, leaning over the petition which was open before him —one hand upon it. At sight of her he lifted his white head. His fine aquiline face was grave and disturbed. But nothing could have been kinder or more courtly than his manner as he came towards her.

'Sit down in that chair. Aldous, make her comfortable. Poor child, how tired she looks ! I hear you wished to speak to me on this most unhappy, most miserable business.'

Marcella, who was sitting erect on the edge of the chair into which Aldous had put her, lifted her eyes with a sudden confidence. She had always liked Lord Maxwell.

'Yes,' she said, struggling to keep down eagerness and emotion. 'Yes, I came to bring you this petition, which is to be sent up to the Home Secretary on behalf of Jim Hurd, and—and—to *beg* of you and Aldous to sign it, if in any way you can. I know it will be difficult, but I thought I might—I might be able to suggest something to you—to convince you—as I have known these people so well—and it is very important to have your signatures.'

How crude it sounded—how mechanical! She felt that she had not yet command of herself. The strange place, the stately room, the consciousness of Aldous behind her—Aldous, who should have been on her side and was not—all combined to intimidate her.

Lord Maxwell's concern was evident. In the first place, he was painfully, unexpectedly struck by the change in the speaker. Why, what had Aldous been about? So thin! so frail and willowy in her black dress—monstrous!

'My dear,' he said, walking up to her and laying a fatherly hand on her shoulder. 'My dear, I wish I could make you understand how gladly I would do this, or anything else, for you, if I honourably could. I would do it for your sake and for your grandfather's sake. But—this is a matter of conscience, of public duty, both for Aldous and myself. You will not surely *wish* even, that we should be governed in our relations to it by any private feeling or motive?'

'No, but I have had no opportunity of speaking to you about it—and I take such a different view from Aldous. He knows—everybody must know—that there is another side, another possible view from that which the judge took. You weren't in court to-day, were you, at all?'

'No. But I read all the evidence before the magistrates with great care, and I have just talked over the crucial points with Aldous, who followed everything to-day, as you know, and seems to have taken special note of Mr. Wharton's speeches.'

'Aldous!'—her voice broke irrepressibly into another note—'I thought he would have let me speak to you first!—to-night!'

Lord Maxwell, looking quickly at his grandson, was very sorry for him. Aldous bent over her chair.

'You remember,' he said, 'you sent down the petition. I thought that meant that we were to read and discuss it. I am very sorry.'

She tried to command herself, pressing her hand to her brow.

But already she felt the irrevocable, and anger and despair were rising.

'The whole point lies in this,' she said, looking up : ' *Can* we believe Hurd's own story? There is no evidence to corroborate it. I grant that—the judge did not believe it—and there is the evidence of hatred. But is it not possible and conceivable all the same? He says that he did not go out with any thought whatever of killing Westall, but that when Westall came upon him with his stick up, threatening and abusing him, as he had done often before, in a fit of wild rage he shot at him. Surely, *surely* that is conceivable? There *is*—there *must* be a doubt ; or, if it is murder, murder done in that way is quite, quite different from other kinds and degrees of murder.'

Now she possessed herself. The gift of flowing persuasive speech which was naturally hers, which the agitations, the debates of these weeks had been maturing, came to her call. She leant forward and took up the petition. One by one she went through its pleas, adding to them here and there from her own knowledge of Hurd and his peasant's life—presenting it all clearly, with great intellectual force, but in an atmosphere of emotion, of high pity, charged throughout with the 'tears of things.' To her, gradually, unconsciously, the whole matter—so sordid, commonplace, brutal in Lord Maxwell's eyes !—had become a tragic poem, a thing of fear and pity, to which her whole being vibrated. And as she conceived it, so she reproduced it. Wharton's points were there indeed, but so were Hurd's poverty, Hurd's deformity, Hurd as the boyish victim of a tyrant's insults, the miserable wife, the branded children—emphasised, all of them, by the occasional quiver, quickly steadied again, of the girl's voice.

Lord Maxwell sat by his writing-table, his head resting on his hand, one knee crossed over the other. Aldous still hung over her chair. Neither interrupted her. Once the eyes of the two men met over her head—a distressed, significant look. Aldous heard all she said, but what absorbed him mainly was the wild desire to kiss the dark hair, so close below him, alternating with the miserable certainty that for him at that moment to touch, to soothe her, was to be repulsed.

When her voice broke—when she had said all she could think of—she remained looking imploringly at Lord Maxwell.

He was silent a little ; then he stooped forward and took her hand.

'You have spoken,' he said with great feeling, 'most nobly— most well—like a good woman, with a true compassionate heart. But all these things you have said are not new to me, my dear child. Aldous warned me of this petition—he has pressed upon me, still more I am sure upon himself, all that he conceived to be your view of the case—the view of those who are now moving in the matter. But with the best will in the world I cannot, and I believe that he cannot—though he must speak for himself—I cannot take that view. In my belief Hurd's act was murder, and deserves the penalty of murder. I have paid some attention to these things. I was a practising barrister in my youth, and later I was for two years Home Secretary. I will explain to you my grounds very shortly.'

And, bending forward, he gave the reasons for his judgment of the case as carefully and as lucidly as though he were stating them to a fellow-expert, and not to an agitated girl of twenty-one. Both in words and manner there was an implied tribute, not only to Marcella, but perhaps to that altered position of the woman in our moving world which affects so many things and persons in unexpected ways.

Marcella listened, restlessly. She had drawn her hand away, and was twisting her handkerchief between her fingers. The flush that had sprung up while she was talking had died away. She grew whiter and whiter. When Lord Maxwell ceased, she said quickly, and as he thought unreasonably—

'So you will not sign?'

'No,' he replied firmly, 'I cannot sign. Holding the conviction about the matter I do, I should be giving my name to statements I do not believe ; and in order to give myself the pleasure of pleasing you, and of indulging the pity that every man must feel for every murderer's wife and children, I should be not only committing a public wrong, but I should be doing what I could to lessen the safety and security of one whole class of my servants—men who give me honourable service—and two of whom have been so cruelly, so wantonly hurried before their Maker !'

His voice gave the first sign of his own deep and painful feeling on the matter. Marcella shivered.

'Then,' she said slowly, 'Hurd will be executed.'

Lord Maxwell had a movement of impatience.

'Let me tell you,' he said, 'that that does not follow at all. There is *some* importance in signatures—or rather in the local movement that the signatures imply. It enables a case to be re-opened, which, in any event, this case is sure to be. But any Home Secretary who could decide a murder case on any other grounds whatever than those of law and his own conscience would not deserve his place a day—an hour ! Believe me, you mistake the whole situation.'

He spoke slowly, with the sharp emphasis natural to his age
and authority. Marcella did not believe him. Every nerve was
beginning to throb anew with that passionate recoil against tyranny
and prejudice, which was in itself an agony.

'And you say the same?' she said, turning to Aldous.

'I cannot sign that petition,' he said sadly. 'Won't you try
and believe what it costs me to refuse?'

It was a heavy blow to her. Amply as she had been prepared
for it, there had always been at the bottom of her mind a persuasion that in the end she would get her way. She had been
used to feel barriers go down before that ultimate power of personality of which she was abundantly conscious. Yet it had not
availed her here—not even with the man who loved her.

Lord Maxwell looked at the two—the man's face of suffering,
the girl's struggling breath.

'There, there, Aldous!' he said, rising. 'I will leave you a
minute. Do make Marcella rest—get her, for all our sakes, to
forget this a little. Bring her in presently to us for some coffee.
Above all, persuade her that we love her and admire her with all
our hearts, but that in a matter of this kind she must leave us to
do—as before God!—what we think right.'

He stood before her an instant, gazing down upon her with
dignity—nay, a certain severity. Then he turned away and left
the room.

Marcella sprang up.

'Will you order the carriage?' she said in a strangled voice.
'I will go upstairs.'

'Marcella!' cried Aldous; 'can you not be just to me, if it is
impossible for you to be generous?'

'Just!' she repeated, with a tone and gesture of repulsion,
pushing him back from her. '*You* can talk of justice!'

He tried to speak, stammered, and failed. That strange para-
lysis of the will-forces which dogs the man of reflection at the
moment when he must either take his world by storm or lose it
was upon him now. He had never loved her more passionately—
but as he stood there looking at her, something broke within him,
the first prescience of the inevitable dawned.

'*You*,' she said again, walking stormily to and fro, and catching
at her breath—'*You*, in this house, with this life—to talk of justice—the justice that comes of slaying a man like Hurd! And I
must go back to that cottage, to that woman, and tell her there
is *no* hope—none. Because *you* must follow your conscience—
you who have everything! Oh? I would not have your conscience—I wish you a heart—rather! Don't come to me, please!

Oh! I must think how it can be. Things cannot go on so. I should kill myself, and make you miserable. But now I must go to *her*—to the *poor*—to those whom I *love*, whom I carry in my heart!'

She broke off sobbing. He saw her, in her wild excitement, look round the splendid room as though she would wither it to ruin with one fiery, accusing glance.

'You are very scornful of wealth,' he said, catching her wrists, ·but one thing you have no right to scorn!—the man who has given you his inmost heart—and now only asks you to believe in this, that he is not the cruel hypocrite you are determined to make him!'

His face quivered in every feature. She was checked a moment —checked by the moral compulsion of his tone and manner, as well as by his words. But again she tore herself away.

'*Please* go and order the carriage,' she said. 'I cannot bear any more. I *must* go home and rest. Some day I will ask your pardon—oh! for this—and—and—' she was almost choked again —'other things. But now I must go away. There is someone who will help me. I must not forget that!'

The reckless words, the inflection, turned Aldous to stone. Unconsciously he drew himself proudly erect—their eyes met. Then he went up to the bell and rang it.

'The brougham at once, for Miss Boyce. Will you have a maid to go with you?' he asked, motioning the servant to stay till Miss Boyce had given her answer.

'No, thank you. I must go and put on my things. Will you explain to Miss Raeburn?'

The footman opened the door for her. She went.

CHAPTER XIV

'BUT this is unbearable!' said Aldous. 'Do you mean to say that she is at home and that she will not see me?'

Mrs. Boyce's self-possession was shaken for once by the flushed humiliation of the man before her.

'I am afraid it is so,' she said hurriedly. 'I remonstrated with Marcella, but I could do nothing. I think, if you are wise, you will not for the present attempt to see her.'

Aldous sat down, with his hat in his hand, staring at the floor. After a few moments' silence he looked up again.

'And she gave you no message for me?'

'No,' said Mrs. Boyce reluctantly. 'Only that she could not bear to see anybody from the Court, even you, while this matter was still undecided.'

Aldous's eye travelled round the Mellor drawing-room. It was arrested by a chair beside him. On it lay an envelope addressed to Miss Boyce, of which the handwriting seemed to him familiar. A needle with some black silk hanging from it had been thrust into the stuffed arm of the chair, the cushion at the back still bore the imprint of the sitter. She had been there, not three minutes ago, and had fled before him. The door into Mrs. Boyce's sitting-room was still ajar.

He looked again at the envelope on the chair, and recognised the writing. Walking across to where Mrs. Boyce sat, he took a seat beside her.

'Will you tell me,' he said steadily—'I think you will admit I have a right to know—is Marcella in constant correspondence now with Henry Wharton?'

Mrs. Boyce's start was not perceptible.

'I believe so,' she quickly replied. 'So far as I can judge, he writes to her almost every other day.'

'Does she show you his letters?'

'Very often. They are entirely concerned with his daily interviews and efforts on Hurd's behalf.'

'Would you not say,' he asked, after another pause, raising his clear grey eyes to her, 'that since his arrival here in December Marcella's whole views and thoughts have been largely—perhaps vitally—influenced by this man?'

Mrs. Boyce had long expected questions of this kind—had, indeed, often marvelled and cavilled that Aldous had not asked them weeks before. Now that they were put to her she was, first of all, anxious to treat them with common sense, and as much plain truth as might be fair to both parties. The perpetual emotion in which Marcella lived tired and oppressed the mother. For herself she asked to see things in a dry light. Yet she knew well that the moment was critical. Her feeling was more mixed than it had been. On the whole it was indignantly on Aldous's side—with qualifications and impatiences, however.

She took up her embroidery again before she answered him. In her opinion the needle is to the woman what the cigarette is to the diplomatist.

'Yes, certainly,' she said at last. 'He has done a great deal to form her opinions. He has made her both read and think on all those subjects she has so long been fond of talking about.'

She saw Aldous wince; but she had her reasons for being plain with him.

'Has there been nothing else than that in it?' said Aldous in an odd voice.

Mrs. Boyce tried no evasions. She looked at him straight, her slight, energetic head, with its pale gold hair lit up by the March sun behind her.

'I do not know,' she said calmly; 'that is the real truth. I *think* there is nothing else. But let me tell you what more I think.'

Aldous laid his hand on hers for an instant. In his pity and liking for her he had once or twice allowed himself this quasi-filial freedom.

'If you would,' he entreated.

'Leave Marcella quite alone—for the present. She is not herself—not normal, in any way. Nor will she be till this dreadful thing is over. But when it is over, and she has had time to recover a little, *then*'—her thin voice expressed all the emphasis it could—'*then* assert yourself! Ask her that question you have asked me —and get your answer.'

He understood. Her advice to him, and the tone of it, implied that she had not always thought highly of his powers of self-defence in the past. But there was a proud and sensitive instinct in him which both told him that he could not have done differently and forbade him to explain.

'You have come from London to-day?' said Mrs. Boyce, changing the subject. All intimate and personal conversation was distasteful to her, and she admitted few responsibilities. Her daughter hardly counted among them.

'Yes; London is hard at work cabinet-making,' he said, trying to smile. 'I must get back to-night.'

'I don't know how you could be spared,' said Mrs. Boyce.

He paused; then he broke out: 'When a man is in the doubt and trouble I am, he must be spared. Indeed, since the night of the trial, I feel as though I had been of very little use to any human being.'

He spoke simply, but every word touched her. What an inconceivable entanglement the whole thing was! Yet she was no longer merely contemptuous of it.

'Look!' she said, lifting a bit of black stuff from the ground beside the chair which held the envelope; 'she is already making the mourning for the children. I can see she despairs.'

He made a sound of horror.

'Can you do nothing?' he cried reproachfully. 'To think of

her dwelling upon this—nothing but this, day and night—and I, banished and powerless!'

He buried his head in his hands.

'No, I can do nothing,' said Mrs. Boyce deliberately. Then, after a pause, 'You do not imagine there is any chance of success for her?'

He looked up and shook his head.

'The Radical papers are full of it, as you know. Wharton is managing it with great ability, and has got some good supporters in the House. But I happened to see the judge the day before yesterday, and I certainly gathered from him that the Home Office was likely to stand firm. There may be some delay. The new ministry will not kiss hands till Saturday. But no doubt it will be the first business of the new Home Secretary.—By the way, I had rather Marcella did not hear of my seeing Mr. Justice Cartwright,' he added hastily—almost imploringly. 'I could not bear that she should suppose——'

Mrs. Boyce thought to herself indignantly that she never could have imagined such a man in such a plight.

'I must go,' he said, rising. 'Will you tell her from me,' he added slowly, 'that I could never have believed she would be so unkind as to let me come down from London to see her, and send me away empty—without a word?'

'Leave it to my discretion,' said Mrs. Boyce, smiling and looking up. 'Oh, by the way, she told me to thank you. Mr. Wharton, in his letter this morning, mentioned that you had given him two introductions which were important to him. She specially wished you to be thanked for it.'

His exclamation had a note of impatient contempt that Mrs. Boyce was genuinely glad to hear. In her opinion he was much too apt to forget that the world yields itself only to the 'violent.'

He walked away from the house without once looking back. Marcella, from her window, watched him go.

'How *could* she see him?' she asked herself passionately, both then and on many other occasions during these rushing, ghastly days. His turn would come, and it should be amply given him. But *now* the very thought of that half-hour in Lord Maxwell's library threw her into wild tears. The time for entreaty—for argument—was gone by, so far as he was concerned. He might have been her champion, and would not. She threw herself recklessly, madly into the encouragement and support of the man who had taken up the task which, in her eyes, should have been her lover's. It had become to her a *fight*—with society, with the law, with Aldous—in which her whole nature was absorbed. In the course of the fight she had realised Aldous's strength, and it was a bitter offence to her.

How little she could do after all? She gathered together all the newspapers that were debating the case, and feverishly read every line; she wrote to Wharton, commenting on what she read, and on his letters; she attended the meetings of the Reprieve Committee which had been started at Widrington; and she passed hours of every day with Minta Hurd and her children. She would hardly speak to Mary Harden and the rector, because they had not signed the petition, and at home her relations with her father were much strained. Mr. Boyce was awakening to a good deal of alarm as to how things might end. He might not like the Raeburns, but that anything should come in the way of his daughter's match was, notwithstanding, the very last thing in the world, as he soon discovered, that he really desired. During six months he had taken it for granted; so had the county. He, of all men, could not afford to be made ridiculous, apart from the solid, the extraordinary advantages of the matter. He thought Marcella a foolish, unreasonable girl, and was not the less in a panic because his wife let him understand that he had had a good deal to do with it. So that between him and his daughter there were now constant sparrings—sparrings which degraded Marcella in her own eyes, and contributed not a little to make her keep away from home.

The one place where she breathed freely, where the soul had full course, was in Minta Hurd's kitchen. Side by side with that piteous plaintive misery, her own fierceness dwindled. She would sit with little Willie on her knees in the dusk of the spring evenings, looking into the fire, and crying silently. She never suspected that her presence was often a burden and constraint, not only to the sulky sister-in-law but to the wife herself. While Miss Boyce was there, the village kept away; and Mrs. Hurd was sometimes athirst, without knowing it, for homelier speech and simpler consolations than any Marcella could give her.

The last week arrived. Wharton's letters grew more uncertain and despondent; the Radical press fought on with added heat as the cause became more desperate. On Monday the wife went to see the condemned man, who told her not to be so silly as to imagine there was any hope. Tuesday night, Wharton asked his last question in Parliament. Friday was the date fixed for the execution.

The question in Parliament came on late. The Home Secretary's answer, though not final in form, was final in substance

Wharton went out immediately and wrote to Marcella. 'She will not sleep if I telegraph to-night,' he thought, with that instinct for detail, especially for physical detail, which had in it something of the woman. But, knowing that his letter could not reach her by the early post with the stroke of eight next morning, he sent out his telegram, that she might not learn the news first from the papers.

Marcella had wandered out before breakfast, feeling the house an oppression, and knowing that, one way or another, the last news might reach her any hour.

She had just passed through the little wood behind and along-side of the house, and was in a field beyond, when she heard someone running behind her. William handed her the telegram, his own red face full of understanding. Marcella took it, com-manded herself till the boy was out of sight and hearing again, then sank down on the grass to read it.

'All over. The Home Secretary's official refusal to interfere with sentence sent to Widrington to-day. Accept my sorrow and sympathy.'

She crushed it in her hand, raising her head mechanically. Before her lay that same shallow cup of ploughed land stretching from her father's big wood to the downs, on the edge of which Hurd had plied his ferrets in the winter nights. But to-day the spring worked in it, and breathed upon it. The young corn was already green in the furrows; the hazel-catkins quivered in the hedge above her; larks were in the air, daisies in the grass, and the march of sunny clouds could be seen in the flying shadows they flung on the pale greens and sheeny purples of the wide treeless basin.

Human helplessness, human agony—set against the careless joy of nature—there is no new way of feeling these things. But not to have felt them, and with the mad, impotent passion and outcry which filled Marcella's heart at this moment, is never to have risen to the full stature of our kind.

'Marcella, it is my strong wish—my command—that you do *not* go out to the village to-night.'

'I must go, papa.'

It was Thursday night—the night before the Friday morning fixed for Hurd's execution. Dinner at Mellor was just over. Mr. Boyce, who was standing in front of the fire, unconsciously making the most of his own inadequate height and size, looked angrily at his stately daughter. She had not appeared at dinner, and she was now dressed in the long black cloak and black hat she had worn so constantly in the last few weeks. Mr. Boyce detested the garb.

'You are making yourself *ridiculous*, Marcella. Pity for these wretched people is all very well, but you have no business to carry it to such a point that you—and we—become the talk, the laughing-stock of the county. And I should like to see you, too, pay some attention to Aldous Raeburn's feelings and wishes.'

The admonition, in her father's mouth, would almost have made her laugh, if she could have laughed at anything. But, instead, she only repeated :—

'I must go ; I have explained to mamma.'

'Evelyn ! why do you permit it ?' cried Mr. Boyce, turning aggressively to his wife.

'Marcella explained to me, as she truly said,' replied Mrs. Boyce, looking up calmly. 'It is not her habit to ask permission of anyone.'

'Mamma,' exclaimed the girl, in her deep voice, 'you would not wish to stop me ?'

'No,' said Mrs. Boyce, after a pause. 'No. You have gone so far, I understand your wish to do this. Richard'—she got up and went to him—'don't excite yourself about it ; shall I read to you, or play a game with you ?'

He looked at her, trembling with anger. But her quiet eye warned him that he had had threatenings of pain that afternoon. His anger sank into fear. He became once more irritable and abject.

'Let her gang her gait,' he said, throwing himself into a chair. 'But I tell you I shall not put up with this kind of thing much longer, Marcella.'

'I shall not ask you, papa,' she said steadily, as she moved towards the door. Mrs. Boyce paused where she stood, and looked after her daughter, struck by her words. Mr. Boyce simply took them as referring to the marriage which would emancipate her before long from any control of his, and fumed, without finding a reply.

The maid-servant who, by Mrs. Boyce's orders, was to accompany Marcella to the village, was already at the front door. She carried a basket containing invalid food for little Willie, and a lighted lantern.

It was a dark night and raining fast. Marcella was fastening up her tweed skirt in the hall, when she saw Mrs. Boyce hurry along the gallery above, and immediately afterwards her mother came across the hall to her.

'You had better take the shawl, Marcella : it is cold and raw. If you are going to sit up most of the night you will want it.'

She put a wrap of her own across Marcella's arm.

'Your father is quite right,' she went on. 'You have had one horrible experience to-day already——'

'Don't, mamma!' exclaimed Marcella, interrupting her. Then suddenly she threw her arms round her mother.

'Kiss me, mamma! please kiss me!'

Mrs. Boyce kissed her gravely, and let herself even linger a moment in the girl's strong hold.

'You are extraordinarily wilful,' she said. 'And it is so strange to me that you think you do any good. Are you sure even that she wants to have you?'

Marcella's lip quivered. She could not speak, apparently. Waving her hand to her mother, she joined the maid waiting for her, and the two disappeared into the blackness.

'But *does* it do any good?' Mrs. Boyce repeated to herself as she went back to the drawing-room. '*Sympathy*! who was ever yet fed, warmed, comforted by *sympathy*? Marcella robs that woman of the only thing that the human being should want at such a moment—solitude. Why should we force on the poor what to us would be an outrage?'

Meanwhile Marcella battled through the wind and rain, thankful that the warm spring burst was over, and that the skies no longer mocked this horror which was beneath them.

At the entrance to the village she stopped, and took the basket from the little maid.

'Now, Ruth, you can go home. Run quick, it is so dark. Ruth!'

'Yes, miss.'

The young country girl trembled. Miss Boyce's tragic passion in this matter had to some extent infected the whole household in which she lived.

'Ruth, when you say your prayers to-night, pray God to comfort the poor,—and to punish the cruel!'

'Yes, miss,' said the girl timidly, and ready to cry. The lantern she held flashed its light on Miss Boyce's white face and tall form. Till her mistress turned away she did not dare to move; that dark eye, so wide, full, and living, roused in her a kind of terror.

On the steps of the cottage Marcella paused. She heard voices inside—or rather the rector's voice reading.

A thought of scorn rose in her heart. 'How long will the poor endure this religion—this make-believe—which preaches patience, *patience*! when it ought to be urging war?'

But she went in softly, so as not to interrupt. The rector looked up and made a grave sign of the head as she entered; her

own gesture forbade any other movement in the group ; she took a
stool beside Willie, whose makeshift bed of chairs and pillows stood
on one side of the fire ; and the reading went on.

Since Minta Hurd had returned with Marcella from Widrington
Gaol that afternoon, she had been so ill that a doctor had been sent
for.   He had bade them make up her bed downstairs in the warm ;
and accordingly a mattress had been laid on the settle, and she
was now stretched upon it.   Her huddled form, the staring whiteness of the narrow face and closed eyelids, thrown out against the
dark oak of the settle, and the disordered mass of grizzled hair,
made the centre of the cottage.

Beside her on the floor sat Mary Harden, her head bowed over
the rough hand she held, her eyes red with weeping.   Fronting
them, beside a little table, which held a small paraffin lamp, sat the
young rector, his Testament in his hand, his slight boy's figure
cast in sharp shadow on the cottage wall.   He had placed himself
so as to screen the crude light of the lamp from the wife's eyes ;
and an old skirt had been hung over a chair to keep it from little
Willie.   Between mother and child sat Ann Mullins, rocking herself to and fro over the fire, and groaning from time to time—a
shapeless sullen creature, brutalised by many children and much
poverty—of whom Marcella was often impatient.

' *And he said, Lord, remember me when Thou comest into Thy
Kingdom.   And He said unto him, Verily, I say unto thee, To-day
shalt thou be with Me in Paradise.*'

The rector's voice, in its awed monotony, dwelt insistently on
each word, then paused.   ' *To-day*,' whispered Mary, caressing
Minta's hand, while the tears streamed down her cheeks ; ' he repented, Minta, and the Lord took him to Himself—at once—forgiving all his sins.'

Mrs. Hurd gave no sign, but the dark figure on the other side
of the cottage made an involuntary movement, which threw down
a fire-iron, and sent a start through Willie's wasted body.   The
reader resumed ; but perfect spontaneity was somehow lost both
for him and for Mary.   Marcella's stormy presence worked in them
both, like a troubling leaven.

Nevertheless, the priest went steadily through his duty, dwelling on every pang of the Passion, putting together every sacred
and sublime word.   For centuries on centuries his brethren and
forerunners had held up the Man of Sorrows before the anguished
and the dying ; his turn had come, his moment and place in the
marvellous, never-ending task ; he accepted it with the meek ardour
of an undoubting faith.

' *And all the multitudes that came together to this sight, when they beheld the things that were done, returned, smiting their breasts.'*

He closed the book, and bent forward, so as to bring his voice close to the wife's ear.

'So He died—the Sinless and the Just—for you, for your husband. He has passed through death—through cruel death; and where He has gone, we poor, weak, stained sinners can follow,—holding to Him. No sin, however black, can divide us from Him, can tear us from His hand in the dark waters, if it be only repented,—thrown upon His Cross. Let us pray for your husband, let us implore the Lord's mercy this night—this hour!—upon his soul.'

A shudder of remembrance passed through Marcella. The rector knelt; Mrs. Hurd lay motionless, save for deep gasps of struggling breath at intervals; Ann Mullins sobbed loudly; and Mary Harden wept as she prayed, lost in a mystical vision of the Lord Himself among them—there on the cottage floor—stretching hands of pity over the woman beside her, showing His marred side and brow.

Marcella alone sat erect, her whole being one passionate protest against a faith which could thus heap all the crimes and responsibilities of this too real earth on the shadowy head of one far-off Redeemer. 'This very man who prays,' she thought, 'is in some sort an accomplice of those who, after tempting, are now destroying, and killing, because they know of nothing better to do with the life they themselves have made outcast.'

And she hardened her heart.

When the spoken prayer was over, Mr. Harden still knelt on silently for some minutes. So did Mary. In the midst of the hush, Marcella saw the boy's eyes unclose. He looked with a sort of remote wonder at his mother and the figures beside her. Then suddenly the gaze became eager, concrete; he sought for something. Her eye followed his, and she perceived in the shadow beside him, on a broken chair placed behind the rough screen which had been made for him, the four tiny animals of pinched paper Wharton had once fashioned. She stooped noiselessly and moved the chair a little forward that he might see them better. The child with difficulty turned his wasted head, and lay with his skeleton hand under his cheek, staring at his treasures—his little all—with just a gleam, a faint gleam, of that same exquisite content which had fascinated Wharton. Then, for the first time that day, Marcella could have wept.

At last the rector and his sister rose.

'God be with you, Mrs. Hurd,' said **Mr.** Harden, stooping to her; 'God support you!'

His voice trembled. Mrs. Hurd in bewilderment looked up.

'Oh, Mr. Harden!' she cried with a sudden wail. 'Mr. Harden!'

Mary bent over her with tears, trying to still her, speaking again with quivering lips of 'the dear Lord,' 'the Saviour.'

The rector turned to Marcella.

'You are staying the night with her?' he asked, under his breath.

'Yes. Mrs. Mullins was up all last night. I offered to come to-night.'

'You went with her to the prison to-day, I believe?'

'Yes.'

'Did you see Hurd?'

'For a very few minutes.'

'Did you hear anything of his state of mind?' he asked anxiously. 'Is he penitent?'

'He talked to me of Willie,' she said—a fierce humanness in her unfriendly eyes. 'I promised him that when the child died, he should be buried respectably—not by the parish. And I told him I would always look after the little girls.'

The rector sighed. He moved away. Then unexpectedly he came back again.

'I must say it to you,' he said, firmly, but still so low as not to be heard by anyone else in the cottage. 'You are taking a great responsibility here to-night. Let me implore you not to fill that poor woman with thoughts of bitterness and revenge at such a moment of her life. That *you* feel bitterly I know. Mary has explained to me—but ask yourself, I beg of you!—how is *she* to be helped through her misery, either now or in the future, except by patience and submission to the will of God?'

He had never made so long a speech to this formidable parishioner of his, and his young cheek glowed with the effort.

'You must leave me to do what I think best,' said Marcella coldly. She felt herself wholly set free from that sort of moral compulsion which his holiness of mind and character had once exerted upon her. That hateful opinion of his, which Mary had reported, had broken the spell once for all.

Mary did not venture to kiss her friend. They all went. Ann Mullins, who was dropping as much with sleep as grief, shuffled off last. When she was going, Mrs. Hurd seemed to rouse a little, and held her by the skirt, saying incoherent things.

'Dear Mrs. Hurd,' said Marcella, kneeling down beside her, 'won't you let Ann go? I am going to spend the night here, and take care of you and Willie.'

Mrs. Hurd gave a painful start.

'You're very good, miss,' she said, half-consciously, 'very good. I'm sure. But she's his own flesh and blood is Ann—his own flesh and blood. Ann!'

The two women clung together, the rough, ill-tempered sister-in-law muttering what soothing she could think of. When she was gone, Minta Hurd turned her face to the back of the settle and moaned, her hands clenched under her breast.

Marcella went about her preparations for the night. 'She is extremely weak,' Dr. Clarke had said; 'the heart in such a state she may die of syncope on very small provocation. If she is to spend the night in crying and exciting herself, it will go hard with her. Get her to sleep if you possibly can.'

And he had left a sleeping draught. Marcella resolved that she would persuade her to take it. 'But I will wake her before eight o'clock,' she thought. 'No human being has the right to rob her of herself through that last hour.'

And tenderly she coaxed Minta to take the doctor's 'medicine.' Minta swallowed it submissively, asking no questions. But the act of taking it roused her for the time, and she would talk. She even got up and tottered across to Willie.

'Willie!—Willie!—Oh! look, miss, he's got his animals—he don't think of nothing else. Oh, Willie! won't you think of your father?—you'll never have a father, Willie, not after to-night!'

The boy was startled by her appearance there beside him—his haggard, dishevelled mother, with the dews of perspiration standing on the face, and her black dress thrown open at the throat and breast for air. He looked at her, and a little frown lined the white brow. But he did not speak. Marcella thought he was too weak to speak, and for an instant it struck her with a thrill of girlish fear that he was dying then and there—that night—that hour. But when she had half helped, half forced Mrs. Hurd back to bed again, and had returned to him, his eyelids had fallen, he seemed asleep. The fast, whistling breath was much the same as it had been for days; she reassured herself.

And at last the wife slept too. The narcotic seized her. The aching limbs relaxed, and all was still. Marcella, stooping over her, kissed the shoulder of her dress for very joy, so grateful to every sense of the watcher was the sudden lull in the long activity of anguish.

Then she sat down on the rocking chair by the fire, yielding herself with a momentary relief to the night and the silence. The tall clock showed that it was not yet ten. She had brought a book with her, and she drew it upon her knee, but it lay unopened.

A fretting, gusty wind beat against the window, with occasional rushes of rain. Marcella shivered, though she had built up the fire, and put on her cloak.

A few distant sounds from the village street round the corner, the chiming of the church clock, the crackling of the fire close beside her—she heard everything there was to hear, with unusual sharpness of ear, and imagined more.

All at once restlessness, or some undefined impression, made her look round her. She saw that the scanty baize curtain was only half-drawn across one of the windows, and she got up to close it. Fresh from the light of the lamp, she stared through the panes into the night without at first seeing anything. Then there flashed out upon the dark the door of a public-house to the right, the last in the village road. A man came out stumbling and reeling; the light within streamed out an instant on the road and the common, then the pursuing rain and darkness fell upon him.

She was drawing back when, with sudden horror, she perceived something else close beside her, pressing against the window. A woman's face!—the powerful black and white of it— the strong aquiline features—the mad keenness of the look—were all plain to her. The eyes looked in hungrily at the prostrate form on the settle—at the sleeping child. Another figure appeared out of the dark, running up the path. There was a slight scuffle, and voices outside. Marcella drew the curtain close with a hasty hand, and sat down hardly able to breathe. The woman who had looked in was Isabella Westall. It was said that she was becoming more and more difficult to manage and to watch.

Marcella was some time in recovering herself. That look, as of a sleepless, hateful eagerness, clung to the memory. Once or twice, as it haunted her, she got up again to make sure that the door was fast.

The incident, with all it suggested, did but intensify the horror and struggle in which the girl stood, made her mood more strained, more piercingly awake and alert. Gradually, as the hours passed, as all sounds from without, even that of the wind, died away, and the silence settled round her in ever-widening circles, like deep waters sinking to repose, Marcella felt herself a naked soul, alone on a wide sea, with shapes of pain and agony and revolt. She looked at the sleeping wife. 'He, too, is probably asleep,' she thought, remembering some information which a kindly warder had given her in a few jerky, well-meant sentences, while she was waiting downstairs in the gaol for Minta Hurd. 'Incredible! only so many hours, minutes left—so far as any mortal *knows*—of living, thinking, recollecting, of all that makes us some-

thing as against the *nothing* of death—and a man wastes them in
sleep, in that which is only meant for the ease and repair of the
daily struggle. And Minta—her husband is her all—to-morrow
she will have no husband; yet she sleeps, and I have helped to
make her. Ah! Nature may well despise and trample on us;
there is no reason in us—no dignity! Oh, why are we here—
why am *I* here—to ache like this—to hate good people like Charles
Harden and Mary—to refuse all I could give—to madden myself
over pain I can never help? I cannot help it, yet I cannot
forsake it; it drives, it clings to me!'

She sat over the fire, Willie's hand clasped in hers. He alone
in this forlorn household *loved* her. Mrs. Hurd and the other
children feared and depended on her. This creature of thistle-
down—this little thread and patch of humanity—felt no fear of
her. It was as though his weakness divined through her harshness
and unripeness those maternal and protecting powers with which
her nature was in truth so richly dowered. He confided himself
to her with no misgivings. He was at ease when she was there.

Little piteous hand!—its touch was to her symbolic, imperative.

Eight months had she been at Mellor? And that Marcella,
who had been living and moving amid these woods and lanes all
this time—that foolish girl, delighting in new grandeurs, and
flattered by Aldous Raeburn's attentions—that hot, ambitious
person, who had meant to rule a county through a husband—
what had become of her? Up to the night of Hurd's death-
sentence she had still existed in some sort, with her obligations,
qualms, remorses. But since then—every day, every hour had
been grinding, scorching her away—fashioning in flame and
fever this new Marcella who sat here, looking impatiently into
another life, which should know nothing of the bonds of the old.

Ah, yes!—her *thought* could distinguish between the act and
the man, between the man and his class; but in her *feeling* all
was confounded. This awful growth of sympathy in her—strange
irony!—had made all sympathy for Aldous Raeburn impossible to
her. Marry him?—no! no!—never! But she would make it
quite easy to him to give her up. Pride should come in—he should
feel no pain in doing it. She had in her pocket the letter she had
received from him that afternoon. She had hardly been able to
read it. Ear and heart were alike dull to it.

From time to time she probably slept in her chair. Or else
it was the perpetual rush of images and sensations through the
mind that hastened the hours. Once, when the first streaks of
the March dawn were showing through the curtains Minta Hurd
sprang up with a loud cry:—

'Oh, my God! Jim, *Jim*! Oh, no!—take that off. Oh, *please*, sir, please! Oh, for God's sake, sir!'

Agony struggled with sleep. Marcella, shuddering, held and soothed her, and for a while sleep, or rather the drug in her veins, triumphed again. For another hour or two she lay restlessly tossing from side to side, but unconscious.

Willie hardly moved all night. Again and again Marcella held beef-tea or milk to his mouth, and tried to rouse him to take it, but she could make no impression on the passive lips; the sleeping serenity of the brow never changed.

At last, with a start, Marcella looked round and saw that the morning was fully there. A cold light was streaming through the curtains; the fire was still glowing; but her limbs were stiff and chilled under her shawl. She sprang up, horror descending on her. Her shaking fingers could hardly draw out the watch in her belt.

Ten minutes to eight!

For the first time the girl felt nerve and resolution fail her. She looked at Mrs. Hurd and wrung her hands. The mother was muttering and moving, but not yet fully awake; and Willie lay as before. Hardly knowing what she was doing, she drew the curtains back, as though inspiration might come with the light. The rain-clouds trailed across the common; water dripped heavily from the thatch of the cottage; and a few birds twittered from some bedraggled larches at the edge of the common. Far away, beyond and beneath those woods to the right, Widrington lay on the plain, with that high-walled stone building at its edge. She saw everything as it must now be happening as plainly as though she were bodily present there—the last meal—the pinioning—the chaplain.

Goaded by the passing seconds, she turned back at last to wake that poor sleeper behind her. But something diverted her. With a start she saw that Willie's eyes were open.

'Willie,' she said, running to him, 'how are you, dear? Shall I lift your head a little?'

He did not answer, though she thought he tried, and she was struck by the blueness under the eyes and nose. Hurriedly she felt his tiny feet. They were quite cold.

'Mrs. Hurd!' she cried, rousing her in haste; 'dear Mrs. Hurd, come and see Willie!'

The mother sprang up bewildered, and, hurrying across the room, threw herself upon him.

'Willie, what is it ails you, dear? Tell mother! Is it your feet are so cold? But we'll rub them—we'll get you warm

soon. And here's something to make you better.' Marcella
handed her some brandy. 'Drink it, dear ; drink it, sweetheart ! '
Her voice grew shrill.

'He can't,' said Marcella. 'Do not let us plague him ; it is the
end. Dr. Clarke said it would come in the morning.'

They hung over him, forgetting everything but him for the
moment—the only moment in his little life he came first even with
his mother.

There was a slight movement of the hand.

'He wants his animals,' said Marcella, the tears pouring down
her cheeks. She lifted them and put them on his breast, laying
the cold fingers over them.

Then he tried to speak.

'Daddy ! ' he whispered, looking up fully at his mother ; 'take
'em to Daddy ! '

She fell on her knees beside him with a shriek, hiding her face,
and shaking from head to foot. Marcella alone saw the slight,
mysterious smile, the gradual sinking of the lids, the shudder of
departing life that ran through the limbs.

A heavy sound swung through the air—a heavy repeated
sound. Mrs. Hurd held up her head and listened. The church
clock tolled eight. She knelt there, struck motionless by terror—
by recollection.

'Oh, Jim ! ' she said, under her breath—'my Jim ! '

The plaintive tone—as of a creature that has not even breath
and strength left wherewith to chide the fate that crushes it—
broke Marcella's heart. Sitting beside the dead son, she wrapt
the mother in her arms, and the only words that even her wild
spirit could find wherewith to sustain this woman through the
moments of her husband's death were words of prayer—the old
shuddering cries wherewith the human soul from the beginning
has thrown itself on that awful encompassing Life whence it issued,
and whither it returns.

CHAPTER XV

TWO days later, in the afternoon, Aldous Raeburn found himself
at the door of Mellor. When he entered the drawing-room, Mrs.
Boyce, who had heard his ring, was hurrying away.

'Don't go,' he said, detaining her with a certain peremptoriness.
'I want all the light on this I can get. Tell me, she has *actually*

brought herself to regard this man's death as in some sort my doing—as something which ought to separate us ?'

Mrs. Boyce saw that he held an opened letter from Marcella crushed in his hand. But she did not need the explanation. She had been expecting him at any hour throughout the day, and in just this condition of mind.

'Marcella must explain for herself,' she said, after a moment's thought. 'I have no right whatever to speak for her. Besides, frankly, I do not understand her, and when I argue with her she only makes me realise that I have no part or lot in her—that I never had. It is just enough. She was brought up away from me. And I have no natural hold. I cannot help you, or anyone else, with her.'

Aldous had been very tolerant and compassionate in the past of this strange mother's abdication of her maternal place, and of its probable causes. But it was not in human nature that he should be either to-day. He resumed his questioning, not without sharpness.

'One word, please. Tell me something of what has happened since Thursday, before I see her. I have written—but till this morning I have had not one line from her.'

They were standing by the window, he with his frowning gaze, in which agitation struggled against all his normal habits of manner and expression, fixed upon the lawn and the avenue. She told him briefly what she knew of Marcella's doings since the arrival of Wharton's telegram—of the night in the cottage, and the child's death. It was plain that he listened with a shuddering repulsion.

'Do you know,' he exclaimed, turning upon her, 'that she may never recover this? Such a strain, such a horror ! rushed upon so wantonly, so needlessly.'

'I understand. You think that I have been to blame ? I do not wonder. But it is not true—not in this particular case. And any way your view is not mine. Life—and the iron of it—has to be faced, even by women—perhaps, most of all, by women. But let me go now. Otherwise my husband will come in. And I imagine you would rather see Marcella before you see him or anyone.'

That suggestion told. He instantly gathered himself together, and nervously begged that she would send Marcella to him at once. He could think of nothing, talk of nothing, till he had seen her. She went, and Aldous was left to walk up and down the room planning what he should say. After the ghastly intermingling of public interests and private misery in which he had lived for these many weeks there was a certain relief in having reached the cleared space—the decisive moment—when he might at last give himself wholly to what truly concerned him. He would not lose her without a struggle. None the less he knew, and had known ever since the scene in the Court library, that the great disaster of his life was upon him.

The handle of the door turned. She was there.

He did not go to meet her. She had come in wrought up to face attack—reproaches, entreaties—ready to be angry or to be humble, as he should give her the lead. But he gave her no lead. She had to break through that quivering silence as best she could.

'I wanted to explain everything to you,' she said, in a low voice, as she came near to him. 'I know my note last night was very hard and abrupt. I didn't mean to be hard. But I am still so tired—and everything that one says, and feels, hurts so.'

She sank down upon a chair. This womanish appeal to his pity had not been at all in her programme. Nor did it immediately succeed. As he looked at her, he could only feel the wantonness of this eclipse into which she had plunged her youth and beauty. There was wrath, a passionate protesting wrath, under his pain.

'Marcella,' he said, sitting down beside her, 'did you read my letter that I wrote you the day before——?'

'Yes.'

'And after that, you could still believe that I was indifferent to your grief—your suffering—or to the suffering of any human being for whom you cared? You could still think it, and feel it?'

'It was not what you have said all through,' she replied, looking sombrely away from him, her chin on her hand; 'it is what you have done.'

'What have I done?' he said proudly, bending forward from his seat beside her. 'What have I ever done but claim from you that freedom you desire so passionately for others—freedom of conscience—freedom of judgment? You denied me this freedom, though I asked it of you with all my soul. And you denied me more. Through these five weeks you have refused me the commonest right of love—the right to show you myself, to prove to you that through all this misery of differing opinion—misery, much more, oh, much more to me than to you!—I was in truth bent on the same ends with you, bearing the same burden, groping towards the same goal.'

'No! no!' she cried, turning upon him, and catching at a word; 'what burden have you ever borne? I know you were sorry—that there was a struggle in your mind—that you pitied me—pitied *them*. But you judged it all *from above*—you looked down—and I could not see that you had any right. It made me mad to have such things seen from a height, when I was below—in the midst—*close* to the horror and anguish of them.'

'Whose fault was it,' he interrupted, 'that I was not with you? Did I not offer—entreat? I could not sign a statement of fact which seemed to me an untrue statement, but what prevented me—prevented us.—However, let me take that point first. Would you,'—he spoke deliberately, 'would you have had me put my name to a public statement which I, rightly or wrongly, believed to be false, because you asked me? You owe it to me to answer.'

She could not escape the penetrating fire of his eye. The man's mildness, his quiet, self-renouncing reserve, were all burnt up at last in this white heat of an accusing passion. In return she began to forget her own resolve to bear herself gently.

'You don't remember,' she cried, 'that what divided us was your—your—incapacity to put the human pity first; to think of the surrounding circumstances—of the debt that you and I and everybody like us owe to a man like Hurd—to one who had been stunted and starved by life as he had been.'

Her lip began to tremble.

'Then it comes to this,' he said steadily, 'that if I had been a poor man, you would have allowed me my conscience—my judgment of right and wrong—in such a matter. You would have let me remember that I was a citizen, and that pity is only one side of justice! You would have let me plead that Hurd's sin was not against me, but against the community, and that in determining whether to do what you wished or no, I must think of the community and its good before even I thought of pleasing you. If I had possessed no more than Hurd, all this would have been permitted me ; but because of Maxwell Court—because of my *money*,'—she shrank before the accent of the word—' you refused me the commonest moral rights. *My* scruple, *my* feeling, were nothing to you. Your pride was engaged as well as your pity, and I must give way. Marcella ! you talk of justice—you talk of equality—is the only man who can get neither at your hands—the man whom you promised to marry?'

His voice dwelt on that last word, dwelt and broke. He leant over her in his roused strength, and tried to take her hand. But she moved away from him with a cry.

'It is no use ! Oh, don't—don't! It may be all true. I was vain, I dare say, and unjust, and hard. But don't you see—don't you understand—if we *could* take such different views of such a case—if it could divide us so deeply—what chance would there be if we

were married? I ought never—never—to have said "Yes" to
you—even as I was then. But *now*,' she turned to him slowly,
'can't you see it for yourself? I am a changed creature. Certain
things in me are gone—*gone*—and instead there is a fire—something driving, tormenting—which must burn its way out. When I
think of what I liked so much when you asked me to marry you—
being rich, and having beautiful things, and dresses, and jewels,
and servants, and power—social power—above all *that*—I feel
sick and choked. I couldn't breathe now in a house like Maxwell
Court. The poor have come to mean to me the only people who
really *live*, and really *suffer*. I must live with them, work for
them, find out what I can do for them. You must give me up—
you must indeed. Oh! and you will! You will be glad enough,
thankful enough, when—when—*you know what I am!*'

He started at the words. Where was the prophetess? He
saw that she was lying white and breathless, her face hidden
against the arm of the chair.

In an instant he was on his knees beside her.

'Marcella!' he could hardly command his voice, but he held
her struggling hand against his lips. 'You think that suffering
belongs to one class? Have you really no conception of what
you will be dealing to me if you tear yourself away from me?'

She withdrew her hand, sobbing.

'Don't, don't stay near me!' she said; 'there is—more—there
is something else.'

Aldous rose.

'You mean,' he said in an altered voice, after a pause of silence,
'that another influence—another man—has come between us?'

She sat up, and with a strong effort drove back her weeping.

'If I could say to you only this,' she began at last, with long
pauses, '"I mistook myself and my part in life. I did wrong, but
forgive me, and let me go for both our sakes"—that would be—
well!—that would be difficult,—but easier than this! Haven't you
understood at all? When—when Mr. Wharton came, I began to
see things very soon, not in my own way, but in his way. I had
never met anyone like him—not anyone who showed me such possibilities in *myself*—such new ways of using one's life, and not only
one's possessions—of looking at all the great questions. I thought
it was just friendship, but it made me critical, impatient of everything else. I was never myself from the beginning. Then,—
after the ball,'—he stooped over her that he might hear her the
more plainly—'when I came home I was in my room and I heard
steps—there are ghost stories, you know, about that part of the
house—I went out to see. Perhaps, in my heart of hearts—oh, I

can't tell, I can't tell !—any way, he was there.   We went into the
library, and we talked.   He did not want to touch our marriage,—
but he said all sorts of mad things,—and at last—he kissed me.'

The last words were only breathed.   She had often pictured herself confessing these things to him.   But the humiliation in which
she actually found herself before him was more than she had ever
dreamed of, more than she could bear.   All those great words of
pity and mercy—all that implication of a moral atmosphere to
which he could never attain—to end in this story !   The effect of it,
on herself, rather than on him, was what she had not foreseen.

Aldous raised himself slowly.

' And when did this happen ? ' he asked, after a moment.

' I told you—the night of the ball—of the murder,' she said with
a shiver ; ' we saw Hurd cross the avenue.   I meant to have told
you everything at once.'

' And you gave up that intention ? ' he asked her, when he had
waited a little for more, and nothing came.

She turned upon him with a flash of the old defiance.

' How could I think of my own affairs ? '

' Or of mine ? ' he said bitterly.

She made no answer.

Aldous got up and walked to the chimney-piece.   He was very
pale, but his eyes were bright and sparkling.   When she looked
up at him at last she saw that her task was done.   His scorn—his
resentment—were they not the expiation, the penalty she had
looked forward to all along ?—and with that determination to bear
them calmly ?   Yet, now that they were there in front of her, they
stung.

' So that—for all those weeks—while you were letting me write
as I did, while you were letting me conceive you and your action
as I did, you had this on your mind ?   You never gave me a hint ;
you let me plead ; you let me regard you as wrapped up in the
unselfish end ; you sent me those letters of his—those most misleading letters !—and all the time——'

' But I meant to tell you—I always meant to tell you,' she cried
passionately.   ' I would never have gone on with a secret like that
—not for your sake—but for my own.'

' Yet you did go on—so long,' he said steadily ; ' and my agony
of mind during those weeks—my feeling towards you—my——'

He broke off, wrestling with himself.   As for her, she had fallen
back in her chair, physically incapable of anything more.

He walked over to her side and took up his hat.

' You have done me wrong,' he said, gazing down upon her.   ' I
pray God you may not do yourself a greater wrong in the future !

Give me leave to write to you once more, or to send my friend
Edward Hallin to see you. Then I will not trouble you again.'

He waited, but she could give him no answer. Her form as
she lay there in this physical and moral abasement printed itself
upon his heart. Yet he felt no desire whatever to snatch the last
touch—the last kiss—that wounded passion so often craves. Inwardly, and without words, he said farewell to her. She heard his
steps across the room ; the door shut ; she was alone—and free.

BOOK III

'O Neigung, sage, wie hast du so tief
Im Herzen dich verstecket?
Wer hat dich, die verborgen schlief,
Gewecket?'

CHAPTER I

'Don't suppose that I feel enthusiastic or sentimental about the "claims of Labour,"' said Wharton, smiling to the lady beside him. 'You may get that from other people, but not from me. I am not moral enough to be a fanatic. My position is simplicity itself. When things are inevitable, I prefer to be on the right side of them, and not on the wrong. There is not much more in it than that. I would rather be on the back of the "bore," for instance, as it sweeps up the tidal river, than the swimmer caught underneath it.'

'Well, that is intelligible,' said Lady Selina Farrell, looking at her neighbour, as she crumbled her dinner-roll. To crumble your bread at dinner is a sign of nervousness, according to Sydney Smith, who did it with both hands when he sat next an archbishop ; yet no one for a good many years past had ever suspected Lady Selina of nervousness, though her powers had probably been tried before now by the neighbourhood of many Primates, Catholic and Anglican. For Lady Selina went much into society, and had begun it young.

'Still, you know,' she resumed after a moment's pause—'you *play* enthusiasm in public—I suppose you must.'

'Oh! of course,' said Wharton indifferently. 'That is in the game.'

'Why should it be—always? If you are a leader of the people, why don't you educate them? My father says that bringing feeling into politics is like making rhymes in one's account book.'

'Well, when you have taught the masses how *not* to feel,' said Wharton laughing, 'we will follow your advice. Meanwhile it is our brains and their feelings that do the trick. And, by the way, Lady Selina, are *you* always so cool? If you saw the Revolution coming to-morrow into the garden of Alresford House, would you go to the balcony and argue?'

'I devoutly hope there would be somebody ready to do something more to the point,' said Lady Selina hastily. 'But of course *we* have enthusiasms too.'

'What, the Flag—and the Throne—that kind of thing?'

The ironical attention which Wharton began at this moment to devote to the selection of an olive annoyed his companion.

'Yes,' she repeated emphatically, 'the Flag and the Throne—all that has made England great in the past. But we know very well that they are not *your* enthusiasms.'

Wharton's upper lip twitched a little.

'And you are quite sure that Busbridge Towers has nothing to do with it?' he said suddenly, looking round upon her.

Busbridge Towers was the fine ancestral seat which belonged to Lady Selina's father, that very respectable and ancient peer, Lord Alresford, whom an ungrateful party had unaccountably omitted—for the first time—from the latest Conservative administration.

'Of course we perfectly understand,' replied Lady Selina scornfully, 'that your side—and especially your Socialist friends, put down all that *we* do and say to greed and selfishness. It is our misfortune—hardly our fault.'

'Not at all,' said Wharton quietly, 'I was only trying to convince you that it is a little difficult to drive feeling out of politics. Do you suppose our host succeeds? You perceive?—this is a Radical house—and a Radical banquet?'

He pushed the *menu* towards her significantly. Then his eye travelled with its usual keen rapidity over the room, over the splendid dinner-table, with its display of flowers and plate, and over the assembled guests. He and Lady Selina were dining at the hospitable board of a certain rich manufacturer, who drew enormous revenues from the west, had formed part of the Radical contingent of the last Liberal ministry, and had especially distinguished himself by a series of uncompromising attacks on the ground landlords of London.

Lady Selina sighed.

'It is all a horrible tangle,' she said, 'and what the next twenty years will bring forth who can tell? Oh! one moment, Mr. Wharton, before I forget. Are you engaged for Saturday week?'

He drew a little note-book out of his pocket and consulted it. It appeared that he was not engaged.

'Then will you dine with us?' She lightly mentioned the names of four or five distinguished guests, including the Conservative Premier of the day. Wharton made her a little ceremonious bow.

'I shall be delighted. Can you trust me to behave?'

Lady Selina's smile made her his match for the moment.

'Oh! we can defend ourselves!' she said. 'By the way, I think you told me that Mr. Raeburn was not a friend of yours.'

'No,' said Wharton, facing her look with coolness. ' If you have asked Mr. Raeburn for the 23rd, let me crave your leave to cancel that note in my pocket-book. Not for my sake, you understand, at all.'

She had difficulty in concealing her curiosity. But his face betrayed nothing. It always seemed to her that his very dark and straight eyebrows, so obtrusive and unusual as compared with the delicacy of the features, of the fair skin and light brown curls, made it easy for him to wear any mask he pleased. By their mere physical emphasis they drew attention away from the subtler and more revealing things of expression.

' They say,' she went on, 'that he is sure to do well in the House, if only he can be made to take interest enough in the party. But one of his admirers told me that he was not at all anxious to accept this post they have just given him. He only did it to please his grandfather. My father thinks Lord Maxwell much aged this year. He is laid up, now, with a chill of some sort, I believe. Mr. Raeburn will have to make haste if he is to have any career in the Commons. But you can see he cares very little about it. All his friends tell me they find him changed since that unlucky affair last year. By the way, did you ever see that girl?'

'Certainly. I was staying in her father's house while the engagement was going on.'

'Were you?' said Lady Selina eagerly. 'And what did you think of her?'

' Well, in the first place,' said Wharton slowly, ' she is beautiful —you knew that?'

Lady Selina nodded.

'Yes. Miss Raeburn, who has told me most of what I know, always throws in a shrug and a "but" when you ask about her looks. However, I have seen a photograph of her, so I can judge for myself. It seemed to me a beauty that men perhaps would admire more than women.'

Wharton devoted himself to his green peas, and made no reply. Lady Selina glanced at him sharply. She herself was by no means a beauty. But neither was she plain. She had a long, rather distinguished face, with a marked nose and a wide thin-lipped mouth. Her plentiful fair hair, a little dull and ashy in colour, was heaped up above her forehead in infinitesimal curls and rolls which did great credit to her maid, and gave additional height to the head and length to a thin white neck. Her light blue eyes were very direct and observant. Their expression implied both considerable knowledge of the world, and a natural inquisitiveness. Many persons indeed were of opinion that Lady Selina wished to know too much about you and were on their guard when she approached.

'You admired her very much, I see,' she resumed, as Wharton still remained silent.

'Oh, yes. We talked Socialism, and then I defended her poacher for her.'

'Oh, I remember. And it is really true, as Miss Raeburn says, that she broke it off because she could not get Lord Maxwell and Mr. Raeburn to sign the petition for the poacher?'

'Somewhere about true,' said Wharton carelessly.

'Miss Raeburn always gives the same account ; you can never get anything else out of her. But I sometimes wonder whether it is the *whole* truth. *You* think she was sincere?'

'Well, she gave up Maxwell Court and thirty thousand a year,' he replied drily. 'I should say she had at least earned the benefit of the doubt.'

'I mean,' said Lady Selina, 'was she in love with anybody else, and was the poacher an excuse?'

She turned upon him as she spoke—a smiling, self-possessed person—a little spoilt by those hard, inquisitive eyes.

'No, I think not,' said Wharton, throwing his head back to meet her scrutiny. 'If so, nothing has been heard of him yet. Miss Boyce has been at St. Edward's Hospital for the last year.'

'To learn nursing? It is what all the women do nowadays, they tell me, who can't get on with their relations or their lovers. Do you suppose it is such a very hard life?'

'I don't want to try!' said Wharton. 'Do you?'

She evaded his smile.

'What is she going to do when she has done her training?'

'Settle down and nurse among the poor, I believe.'

'Magnificent, no doubt, but hardly business, from her point of view. How much more she might have done for the poor with thirty thousand a year! And any woman could put up with Aldous Raeburn.'

Wharton shrugged his shoulders.

'We come back to those feelings, Lady Selina, you think so badly of.'

She laughed.

'Well, but feelings must be intelligible. And this seems so small a cause. However, were you there when it was broken off?'

'No ; I have never seen her since the day of the poacher's trial.'

'Oh ! So she has gone into complete seclusion from all her friends?'

'That I can't answer for. I can only tell you my own experience.'

Lady Selina bethought herself of a great many more questions to ask, but somehow did not ask them. The talk fell upon politics, which lasted till the hostess gave the signal, and Lady Selina, gathering up her fan and gloves, swept from the room next after the Countess at the head of the table, while a host of elderly ladies, wives of ministers and the like, stood meekly by to let her pass.

As he sat down again, Wharton made the entry of the dinner at Alresford House, to which he had just promised himself, a little plainer. It was the second time in three weeks that Lady Selina had asked him, and he was well aware that several other men at this dinner-table, of about the same standing and prospects as himself, would be very glad to be in his place. Lady Selina, though she was unmarried, and not particularly handsome or particularly charming, was a personage—and knew it. As the mistress of her father's various fine houses, and the kinswoman of half the great families of England, she had ample social opportunities, and made, on the whole, clever use of them. She was not exactly popular, but in her day she had been extremely useful to many, and her invitations were prized. Wharton had been introduced to her at the beginning of this, his second session, had adopted with her the easy, aggressive, 'personal' manner—which, on the whole, was his natural manner towards women—and had found it immediately successful.

When he had replaced his pocket-book he found himself approached by a man on his own side of the table, a member of Parliament like himself, with whom he was on moderately friendly terms.

'Your motion comes on next Friday, I think,' said the new comer.

Wharton nodded.

'It'll be a beastly queer division,' said the other—'a precious lot of cross-voting.'

'That'll be the way with that kind of question for a good while to come—don't you think'—said Wharton smiling, 'till we get a complete reorganisation of parties?'

As he leaned back in his chair, enjoying his cigarette, his half-shut eyes behind the curls of smoke made a good-humoured but contemptuous study of his companion.

Mr. Bateson was a young manufacturer, recently returned to Parliament, and newly married. He had an open ruddy face, spoilt by an expression of chronic perplexity which was almost fretfulness. Not that the countenance was without shrewdness;

but it suggested that the man had ambitions far beyond his powers of performance, and already knew himself to be inadequate.

'Well, I shouldn't wonder if you get a considerable vote,' he resumed, after a pause ; 'it's like women's suffrage. People will go on voting for this kind of thing, till there seems a chance of getting it. *Then* !'

'Ah, well !' said Wharton easily, 'I see we shan't get *you*.'

'I !—vote for an eight-hours day, by local and trade option ! In my opinion I might as well vote for striking the flag on the British Empire at once ! It would be the death-knell of all our prosperity.'

Wharton's artistic ear disliked the mixture of metaphor, and he frowned slightly.

Mr. Bateson hurried on. He was already excited, and had fallen upon Wharton as a prey.

'And you really desire to make it *penal* for us manufacturers— for me in my industry—in spite of all the chances and changes of the market, to work my men more than eight hours a day—*even* if they wish it !'

'We must get our decision, our majority of the adult workers in any given district in favour of an eight-hours day,' said Wharton blandly ; 'then when they have voted for it, the local authority will put the Act in motion.'

'And my men—conceivably—may have voted in the minority, against any such tomfoolery ; yet, when the vote is given, it will be a punishable offence for them, and me, to work overtime ? You *actually* mean that ; how do you propose to punish us ?'

'Well,' said Wharton, relighting his cigarette, 'that is a much debated point. Personally, I am in favour of imprisonment rather than fine.'

The other bounded on his chair.

'You would imprison me for working overtime—with *willing men* !'

Wharton eyed him with smiling composure. Two or three other men—an old general, the smart private secretary of a cabinet minister, and a well-known permanent official at the head of one of the great spending departments—who were sitting grouped at the end of the table a few feet away, stopped their conversation to listen.

'Except in cases of emergency, which are provided for under the Act,' said Wharton. 'Yes, I should imprison you, with the greatest pleasure in life. Eight hours *plus* overtime is what we are going to stop, *at all hazards* !'

A flash broke from his blue eyes. Then he tranquilly resumed his smoking.

The young manufacturer flushed with angry agitation.

'But you must know—it is inconceivable that you should not know—that the whole thing is stark staring lunacy. In our business trade is declining, the export falling every year, the imports from France steadily advancing. And you are going to make us fight a country where men work eleven hours a day for lower wages, with our hands tied behind our backs by legislation of this kind? Well, you know'—he threw himself back in his chair with a contemptuous laugh—'there can be only one explanation. You and your friends, of course, have banished political economy to Saturn—and you suppose that by doing so you get rid of it for all the rest of the world. But I imagine it will beat you, all the same!'

He stopped in a heat. As usual, what he found to say was not equal to what he wanted to say, and beneath his anger with Wharton was the familiar fuming at his own lack of impressiveness.

'Well, I dare say,' said Wharton serenely. 'However, let's take your "political economy" a moment, and see if I can understand what you mean by it. There never were two words that meant all things to all men so disreputably!'

And thereupon to the constant accompaniment of his cigarette, and with the utmost composure and good temper, he began to 'heckle' his companion, putting questions, suggesting perfidious illustrations, extracting innocent admissions, with a practised shrewdness and malice which presently left the unfortunate Bateson floundering in a sea of his own contradictions, and totally unable for the moment to attach any rational idea whatever to those great words of his favourite science, wherewith he was generally accustomed to make such triumphant play, both on the platform and in the bosom of the family.

The permanent official round the corner watched the unequal fight with attentive amusement. Once when it was a question of Mill's doctrine of cost of production as compared with that of a leading modern collectivist, he leant forward and supplied a correction of something Wharton had said. Wharton instantly put down his cigarette and addressed him in another tone. A rapid dialogue passed between them, the dialogue of experts, sharp, allusive, elliptical, in the midst of which the host gave the signal for joining the ladies.

'Well, all I know is,' said Bateson, as he got up, 'that these kind of questions, if you and your friends have your way, will *wreck* the Liberal party before long—far more effectually than anything Irish has ever done. On these things some of us will fight, if it must come to that.'

Wharton laughed.

'It would be a national misfortune if you didn't give us a stiff job,' he said, with an airy good-humour which at once made the other's blustering look ridiculous.

'I wonder what that fellow is going to do in the House,' said the permanent official to his companion as they went slowly upstairs, Wharton being some distance ahead. 'People are all beginning to talk of him as a coming man, though nobody quite knows why, as yet. They tell me he frames well in speaking, and will probably make a mark with his speech next Friday. But his future seems to me very doubtful. He can only become a power as the head of a new Labour party. But where is the party? They all want to be kings. The best point in his favour is that they are likely enough to take a gentleman if they must have a leader. But there still remains the question whether he can make anything out of the material.'

'I hope to God he can't!' said the old general grimly; 'it is these town-chatterers of yours that will bring the Empire about our heads before we've done. They've begun it already, wherever they saw a chance.'

In the drawing-room Wharton devoted himself for a few minutes to his hostess, a little pushing woman, who confided to his apparently attentive ear a series of grievances as to the bad manners of the great ladies of their common party, and the general evil plight of Liberalism in London from the social point of view.

'Either they give themselves airs—*rediculous* airs !—or they admit everybody !' she said, with a lavish use of white shoulders and scarlet fan by way of emphasis. 'My husband feels it just as much as I do. It is a real misfortune for the party that its social affairs should be so villainously managed. Oh ! I dare say *you* don't mind, Mr. Wharton, because you are a Socialist. But, I assure you, those of us who still believe in the influence of the best people don't like it.'

A point whence Wharton easily led her through a series of spiteful anecdotes bearing on her own social mishaps and rebuffs, which were none the less illuminating because of the teller's anxious effort to give them a dignified and disinterested air. Then, when neither she nor her plight were any longer amusing, he took his leave, exchanging another skirmishing word or two on the staircase with Lady Selina, who, it appeared, was 'going on' as he was, and to the same house.

In a few minutes his hansom landed him at the door of a great mansion in Berkeley Square, where a huge evening party was proceeding, given by one of those Liberal ladies whom his late hostess had been so freely denouncing. The lady and the house belonged to a man who had held high office in the late Administration.

As he made his way slowly to the top of the crowded stairs, the stately woman in white satin and diamonds who was 'receiving' on the landing marked him, and when his name was announced she came forward a step or two. Nothing could have been more flattering than the smile with which she gave him her gloved hand to touch.

'Have you been out of town all these Sundays?' she said to him, with the slightest air of soft reproach. 'I am always at home, you know—I told you so!'

She spoke with the ease of one who could afford to make whatever social advances she pleased. Wharton excused himself, and they chatted a little in the intervals of her perpetual greetings to the mounting crowd. She and he had met at a famous country house in the Easter recess, and her aristocrat's instinct for all that gives savour and sharpness to the dish of life had marked him at once.

'Sir Hugh wants you to come down and see us in Sussex,' she said, stretching her white neck a little to speak after him, as he was at last carried through the drawing-room door by the pressure behind him. 'Will you?'

He threw back an answer which she rather took for granted than heard, for she nodded and smiled through it—stiffening her delicate face the moment afterwards to meet the timid remarks of one of her husband's constituents—asked by Sir Hugh in the street that afternoon—who happened to present her with the next hand to shake.

Inside, Wharton soon found himself brought up against the ex-Secretary of State himself, who greeted him cordially, and then bantered him a little on his coming motion.

'Oh, I shall be interested to see what you make of it. But, you know, it has no *actuality*—never can have—till you can agree among yourselves. You *say* you want the same thing—I dare say you'll all swear it on Friday—but *really*——'

The statesman shook his head pleasantly.

'The details are a little vague still, I grant you,' said Wharton, smiling.

'And you think the principle matters twopence without the details? I have always found that the difficulty with the Christian command, "Be ye perfect." The principle doesn't trouble me at all!'

The swaying of the entering throng parted the two speakers,

and for a second or two the portly host followed with his eye the
fair profile and lightly-built figure of the younger man as they re-
ceded from him in the crowd. It was in his mind that the next
twenty years, whether this man or that turned out to be important
or no, must see an enormous quickening of the political pace. He
himself was not conscious of any jealousy of the younger men ; but
neither did he see among them any commanding personality. This
young fellow, with his vivacity, his energy, and his Socialist whims,
was interesting enough ; and his problem was interesting—the problem of whether he could make a party out of the heterogeneous
group of which he was turning out to be indisputably the ablest
member. But what was there *certain* or *inevitable* about his future
after all ? And it was the same with all the rest. Whereas the
leaders of the past had surely announced themselves beyond mistake from the beginning. He was inclined to think, however, that
we were levelling up rather than levelling down. The world grew
too clever, and leadership was more difficult every day.

Meanwhile Wharton found his progress through these stately
rooms extremely pleasant. He was astonished at the multitude of
people he knew, at the numbers of faces that smiled upon him.
Presently, after half an hour of hard small talk, he found himself
for a moment without an acquaintance, leaning against an archway
between two rooms, and free to watch the throng. Self-love,
'that froward presence, like a chattering child within us,' was all
alert and happy. A feeling of surprise, too, which had not yet
worn away. A year before he had told Marcella Boyce, and with
conviction, that he was an outcast from his class. He smiled now
at that past *naïveté* which had allowed him to take the flouts of
his country neighbours and his mother's unpopularity with her
aristocratic relations for an index of the way in which 'society' in
general would be likely to treat him and his opinions. He now
knew, on the contrary, that those opinions had been his best advertisement. Few people, it appeared, were more in demand
among the great than those who gave it out that they would, if
they could, abolish the great.

'It's because they're not enough afraid of us—yet,' he said to
himself, not without spleen. 'When we really get to business—if
we ever do—I shall not be coming to Lady Cradock's parties.'

'Mr. Wharton, do you ever do such a frivolous thing as go to
the theatre ?' said a pretty, languishing creature at his elbow, the
wife of a London theatrical manager. 'Suppose you come and see
us in "The Minister's Wooing," first night next Saturday. I've
got *one* seat in my box, for somebody *very* agreeable. Only it
must be somebody who can appreciate my frocks !'

'I should be charmed,' said Wharton. 'Are the frocks so adorable?'

'Adorable! Then I may write you a note? You don't have your horrid Parliament that night, do you?' and she fluttered on.

'I think you don't know my younger daughter, Mr. Wharton?' said a severe voice at his elbow.

He turned and saw an elderly matron with the usual matronly cap and careworn countenance putting forward a young thing in white, to whom he bowed with great ceremony. The lady was the wife of a north-country magnate of very old family, and one of the most exclusive of her kind in London. The daughter, a vision of young shyness and bloom, looked at him with frightened eyes as he leant against the wall beside her and began to talk. She wished he would go away and let her get to the girl-friend who was waiting for her and signalling to her across the room. But in a minute or two she had forgotten to wish anything of the kind. The mixture of audacity with a perfect self-command in the manner of her new acquaintance, that searching, half-mocking look, which saw everything in detail, and was always pressing beyond the generalisations of talk and manners, the lightness and brightness of the whole aspect, of the curls, the eyes, the flexible determined mouth, these things arrested her. She began to open her virgin heart, first in protesting against attack, then in confession, till in ten minutes her white breast was heaving under the excitement of her own temerity, and Wharton knew practically all about her, her mingled pleasure and remorse in 'going out,' her astonishment at the difference between the world as it was this year, and the world as it had been last, when she was still in the schoolroom—her Sunday-school—her brothers—her ideals—for she was a little nun at heart—her favourite clergyman—and all the rest of it.

'I say, Wharton, come and dine, will you, Thursday, at the House—small party—meet in my room?'

So said one of the party whips, from behind into his ear. The speaker was a popular young aristocrat, who in the preceding year had treated the member for West Brookshire with chilliness. Wharton turned—to consider a moment—then gave a smiling assent.

'All right!' said the other, withdrawing his hand from Wharton's shoulder—'good-night! Two more of these beastly crushes to fight through till I can get to my bed, worse luck! Are any of your fellows here to-night?'

Wharton shook his head.

'Too austere, I suppose?'

'A question of dress coats. I should think,' said Wharton drily.

The other shrugged his shoulders.

'And this calls itself a party gathering—in a Radical and democratic house—what a farce it all is !'

'Agreed ! good-night !'

And Wharton moved on, just catching as he did so the eyes of his new girl-acquaintance looking back at him from a distant door. Their shy owner withdrew them instantly, coloured, and passed out of sight.

At the same moment a guest entered by the same door, a tall grave man in the prime of life, but already grey-haired. Wharton, to his surprise, recognised Aldous Raeburn and saw also that the master of the house had him by the arm. They came towards him, talking. The crowd prevented him from getting effectually out of their way, but he turned aside and took up a magazine lying on a bookcase near.

'And you really think him a trifle better ?' said the ex-minister.

'Oh yes, better—certainly better—but I am afraid he will hardly get back to work this session—the doctors talk of sending him away at once.'

'Ah well,' said the other, smiling, 'we don't intend, it seems, to let you send anything important up to the Lords yet awhile, so there will be time for him to recruit.'

'I wish I was confident about the recruiting,' said Raeburn sadly. 'He has lost much strength. I shall go with them to the Italian lakes at the end of next week, see them settled, and come back at once.'

'Shall you miss a sitting of the Commission ?' asked his host. Both he and Raeburn were members of an important Labour Commission appointed the year before by the new Conservative Government.

'Hardly, I think,' said Raeburn. 'I am particularly anxious not to miss D——'s evidence.'

And they fell talking a little about the Commission and the witnesses recently examined before it. Wharton, who was wedged in by a group of ladies, and could not for the moment move, heard most of what they were saying, much against his will. Moreover Raeburn's tone of quiet and masterly familiarity with what he and his companion were discussing annoyed him. There was nothing in the world that he himself would more eagerly have accepted than a seat on that Commission.

'Ah ! there is Lady Cradock !' said Raeburn, perceiving his hostess across a sea of intervening. faces, and responding to her little wave of the hand. 'I must go and get a few words with her and then take my aunt away.'

As he made his way towards her, he suddenly brushed against Wharton, who could not escape. Raeburn looked up, recognised the man he had touched, flushed slightly and passed on. A bystander would have supposed them strangers to each other.

CHAPTER II

TWO or three minutes later, Wharton was walking down a side street towards Piccadilly. After all the flattering incidents of the evening, the chance meeting with which it concluded had jarred unpleasantly. Confound the fellow! Was he the first man in the world who had been thrown over by a girl because he had been discovered to be a tiresome pedant? For even supposing Miss Boyce had described that little scene in the library at Mellor to her *fiancé* at the moment of giving him his dismissal—and the year before, by the help of all the news that reached him about the broken engagement, by the help still more of the look, or rather the entire absence of look wherewith Raeburn had walked past his greeting and his outstretched hand in a corridor of the House, on the first occasion of their meeting after the news had become public property, Wharton was inclined to think she *had*—what then? No doubt the stern moralist might have something to say on the subject of taking advantage of a guest's position to tamper with another man's betrothed. If so, the stern moralist would only show his usual incapacity to grasp the actual facts of flesh and blood. What chance would he or anyone else have had with Marcella Boyce, if she had happened to be in love with the man she had promised to marry? That little trifle had been left out in the arrangement. It might have worked through perfectly well without; as it happened it had broken down. *Realities* had broken it down. Small blame to them!

'I stood for *truth*!' he said to himself with a kind of rage— 'that moment when I held her in the library, she *lived*.—Raeburn offered her a platform, a position; *I* made her think, and feel. I helped her to know herself. Our relation was not passion; it stood on the threshold—but it was real—a true relation so far as it went. That it went no farther was due again to circumstances— realities—of another kind. That *he* should scorn and resent my performance at Mellor is natural enough. If we were in France he would call me out, and I should give him satisfaction with all the pleasure in life. But what am *I* about? Are his ways mine? I should have nothing left but to shoot myself to-morrow if they were!'

He walked on swiftly, angrily rating himself for those symptoms of a merely false and conventional conscience which were apt to be roused in him by contact with Aldous Raeburn.

'Has he not interfered with my freedom—stamped his pedantic foot on me—ever since we were boys together? I have owed him one for many years—now I have paid it. Let him take the chances of war!'

Then, driven on by an irritation not to be quieted, he began against his will to think of those various occasions on which he and Aldous Raeburn had crossed each other in the past—of that incident in particular which Miss Raeburn had roughly recalled to Lady Winterbourne's reluctant memory.

Well, and what of it? It had occurred when Wharton was a lad of twenty-one, and during an interval of some months when Aldous Raeburn, who had left Cambridge some three years before, and was already the man of importance, had shown a decided disposition to take up the brilliant, unmanageable boy, whom the Levens, among other relations, had already washed their hands of.

'What did he do it for?' thought Wharton. 'Philanthropic motives of course. He is one of the men who must always be saving souls, and the black sheep of the world come in handy for the purpose. I remember I was flattered then. It takes one some time to understand the workings of the Hebraistic conscience!'

Yes—as it galled him to recollect—he had shown great plasticity for a time. He was then in the middle of his Oxford years, and Raeburn's letters and Raeburn's influence had certainly pulled him through various scrapes that might have been disastrous. Then— a little later—he could see the shooting-lodge on the moors above Loch Etive, where he and Raeburn, Lord Maxwell, Miss Raeburn, and a small party had spent the August of his twenty-first birthday. Well—that surly keeper, and his pretty wife who had been Miss Raeburn's maid—could anything be more inevitable? A hard and jealous husband, and one of the softest, most sensuous natures that ever idleness made love to. The thing was in the air!—in the summer, in the blood—as little to be resisted as the impulse to eat when you are hungry, or drink when you thirst. Besides, what particular harm had been done, what particular harm *could* have been done with such a Cerberus of a husband? As to the outcry which had followed one special incident, nothing could have been more uncalled for, more superfluous. Aldous had demanded contrition, had said strong things with the flashing eyes, the set mouth of a Cato. And the culprit had turned obstinate—would repent nothing—not for the asking. Everything was arguable, and Renan's doubt as to whether he or Théophile Gautier were in the right of it, would remain a doubt to all time—that was all Raeburn could get out of him. After which the Hebraist friend of course had turned his back on the offender, and there was an end of it.

That incident, however, had belonged to a stage in his past life, a stage marked by a certain prolonged tumult of the senses, on which he now looked back with great composure. That tumult had found vent in other adventures more emphatic a good deal than the adventure of the keeper's wife. He believed that one or two of them had been not unknown to Raeburn.

Well, that was done with! His mother's death—that wanton stupidity on the part of fate—and the shock it had somehow caused him, had first drawn him out of the slough of a cheap and facile pleasure on which he now looked back with contempt. Afterwards, his two years of travel, and the joys at once virile and pure they had brought with them, joys of adventure, bodily endurance, discovery, together with the intellectual stimulus which comes of perpetual change, of new heavens, new seas, new societies, had loosened the yoke of the flesh and saved him from himself. The deliverance so begun had been completed at home, by the various chances and opportunities which had since opened to him a solid and tempting career in that Labour movement his mother had linked him with, without indeed ever understanding either its objects or its men. The attack on capital now developing on all sides, the planning of the vast campaign, and the handling of its industrial troops, these things had made the pursuit of women look insipid, coupled as they were with the thrill of increasing personal success. Passion would require to present itself in new forms, if it was now to take possession of him again.

As to his relation to Raeburn, he well remembered that when, after that long break in his life, he and Aldous had met casually again, in London or elsewhere, Aldous had shown a certain disposition to forget the old quarrel, and to behave with civility, though not with friendliness. As to Wharton he was quite willing, though at the same time he had gone down to contest West Brookshire, and, above all, had found himself in the same house as Aldous Raeburn's betrothed, with an even livelier sense than usual of the excitement to be got out of mere living.

No doubt when Raeburn heard that story of the library—if he

had heard it—he recognised in it the man and the character he had known of old, and had shrunk from the connection of both with Marcella Boyce in bitter and insurmountable disgust. A mere Hebraist's mistake !

'That girl's attraction for me was not an attraction of the senses—except so far that for every normal man and woman charm is charm, and ginger is hot in the mouth, and always will be ! What I played for with her was *power*—power over a nature that piqued and yet by natural affinity belonged to me. I could not have retained that power, as it happened, by any bait of passion. Even without the Hurd affair, if I had gone on to approach her so, her whole moral nature would have risen against me and her own treachery. I knew that perfectly well, and took the line I did because for the moment the game was too exciting, too interesting, to give up. For the moment ! then a few days,—a few weeks later—Good Lord ! what stuff we mortals be !'

And he raised his shoulders, mocking, yet by no means disliking his own idiosyncrasies. It had been strange, indeed, that complete change of mental emphasis, that alteration of spiritual axis that had befallen him within the first weeks of his parliamentary life, nay, even before the Hurd agitation was over. That agitation had brought him vigorously and profitably into public notice at a convenient moment. But what had originally sprung from the impulse to retain a hold over a woman, became in the end the instrument of a new and quite other situation. Wharton had no sooner entered the House of Commons than he felt himself strangely at home there. He had the instinct for debate : the instinct for management : together with a sensitive and contriving ambition. He found himself possessed for the moment of powers of nervous endurance that astonished him—a patience of boredom besides, a capacity for drudgery, and for making the best of dull men. The omens were all favourable, sometimes startlingly so. He was no longer hampered by the ill-will of a county or a family connection. Here, in this new world, every man counted strictly for what, in the parliamentary sense, he was worth. Wharton saw that, owing to his public appearances during the two preceding years, he was noticed, listened to, talked about in the House, from the first ; and that his position in the newly-formed though still loosely-bound Labour party was one of indefinite promise. The anxieties and pitfalls of the position only made it the more absorbing.

The quick, elastic nature adjusted itself at once. To some kinds of success, nothing is so important as the ability to forget— to sweep the mind free of everything irrelevant and superfluous. Marcella Boyce, and all connected with her passed clean out of

Wharton's consciousness. Except that once or twice he said to himself with a passing smile that it was a good thing he had not got himself into a worse scrape at Mellor. Good heavens! in what plight would a man stand—a man with his career to make—who had given Marcella Boyce claims upon him! As well entangle oneself with the Tragic Muse at once as with that stormy, unmanageable soul !

So much for a year ago. To-night, however, the past had been thrust back upon him, both by Lady Selina's talk and by the meeting with Raeburn. To smart indeed once more under that old ascendency of Raeburn's, was to be provoked into thinking of Raeburn's old love.

Where was Miss Boyce? Surely her year of hospital training must be up by now?

He turned into St. James's Street, stopped at a door not far from the Palace end, let himself in, and groped his way to the second floor. A sleepy manservant turned out of his room, and finding that his master was not inclined to go to bed, brought lights and mineral water. Wharton was practically a teetotaller. He had taken a whim that way as a boy, and a few experiments in drunkenness which he had made at college had only confirmed what had been originally perhaps a piece of notoriety-hunting. He had, as a rule, flawless health, and the unaccustomed headaches and nausea which followed these occasional excesses had disgusted and deterred him. He shook himself easily free of a habit which had never gained a hold upon him, and had ever since found his abstinence a source both of vanity and of distinction. Nothing annoyed him more than to hear it put down to any ethical motive. 'If I liked the beastly stuff, I should swim in it to-morrow,' he would say with an angry eye when certain acquaintance—not those he made at Labour Congresses—goaded him on the point. 'As it is, why should I make it, or chloral, or morphia, or any other poison, my master? What's the inducement—eh, you fellows?'

En revanche he smoked inordinately.

'Is that all, sir?' said his servant, pausing behind his chair, after candles, matches, cigarettes, and Apollinaris had been supplied in abundance.

'Yes ; go to bed, Williams, but don't lock up. Good-night.'

The man departed, and Wharton, going to the window which opened on a balcony looking over St. James's Street, threw it wide, and smoked a cigarette leaning against the wall. It was on the whole a fine night and warm, though the nip of the east wind was not yet out of the air. In the street below there was still a good deal of movement, for it was only just past midnight and the clubs were not yet empty. To his right the turreted gate-house of the Palace with its clock rose dark against a sky covered with light, windy cloud. Beyond it his eye sought instinctively for the Clock Tower, which stood to-night dull and beaconless—like someone in a stupid silence. That light of the sitting House had become to him one of the standing pleasures of life. He had never yet been honestly glad of its extinction.

'I'm a precious raw hand,' he confessed to himself with a shake of the head as he stood there smoking. 'And it can't last —nothing does.'

Presently he laid down his cigarette a moment on the edge of the balcony, and, coming back into the room, opened a drawer, searched a little, and finally took out a letter. He stooped over the lamp to read it. It was the letter which Marcella Boyce had written him some two or three days after the breach of her engagement. That fact was barely mentioned at the beginning of it, without explanation or comment of any kind. Then the letter continued :—

'I have never yet thanked you as I ought for all that you have done and attempted through these many weeks. But for them it must have been plain to us both that we could never rightly meet again. I am very destitute just now—and I cling to self-respect as though it were the only thing left me. But that scene in the past, which put us both wrong with honour and conscience, has surely been wiped out—*thought*—*suffered* away. I feel that I dare now say to you, as I would to any other co-worker and co-thinker—if in the future you ever want my work, if you can set me, with others, to any task that wants doing and that I could do—ask me, and I am not likely to refuse.

'But for the present I am going quite away into another world. I have been more ill than I have ever been in my life this last few days, and they are all, even my father, ready to agree with me that I must go. As soon as I am a little stronger I am to have a year's training at a London hospital, and then I shall probably live for a while in town and nurse. This scheme occurred to me as I came back with the wife from seeing Hurd the day before the execution. I knew then that all was over for me at Mellor.

'As for the wretched break-down of everything—of all my schemes and friendships here—I had better not speak of it. I feel that I have given these village-folk, whom I had promised to help, one more reason to despair of life. It is not pleasant to carry such a thought away with one. But if the tool breaks and blunts, how can the task be done? It can be of no use till it has been re-set.

'I should like to know how your plans prosper. But I shall see your paper and follow what goes on in Parliament. For the present I want neither to write nor get letters. They tell me that as a probationer I shall spend my time at first in washing glasses, and polishing bath-taps, on which my mind rests !

'If you come across my friends of whom I have spoken to you —Louis, Anthony, and Edith Craven—and could make any use of Louis for the *Labour Clarion*, I should be grateful. I hear they have had bad times of late, and Louis has engaged himself, and wants to be married. You remember I told you how we worked at the South Kensington classes together, and how they made me a Venturist?

'Yours very truly,
'MARCELLA BOYCE.'

Wharton laid down the letter, making a wry mouth over some of its phrases.

'"*Put us both wrong with honour and conscience.*" "*One more reason for despair of life*"—"*All was over for me at Mellor*" —dear ! dear !—how women like the big words—the emphatic pose. All those little odds and ends of charities—that absurd straw-plaiting scheme ! Well, perhaps one could hardly expect her to show a sense of humour just then. But why does nature so often leave it out in these splendid creatures?'

'Hullo !' he added, as he bent over the table to look for a pen ; 'why didn't that idiot give me these?'

For there, under an evening paper which he had not touched, lay a pile of unopened letters. His servant had forgotten to point them out to him. On the top was a letter on which Wharton pounced at once. It was addressed in a bold inky hand, and he took it to be from Nehemiah Wilkins, M.P., his former colleague at the Birmingham Labour Congress, of late a member of the *Labour Clarion* staff, and as such a daily increasing plague and anxiety to the *Clarion's* proprietor.

However, the letter was not from Wilkins. It was from the secretary of a Midland trades-union, with whom Wharton had already been in communication. The union was recent, and represented the as yet feeble organisation of a metal industry in process of transition from the home-workshop to the full factory, or Great Industry stage. The conditions of work were extremely bad, and grievances many ; wages were low, and local distress very great. The secretary, a young man of ability and enthusiasm, wrote to Wharton to say that certain alterations in the local 'payment lists' lately made by the employers amounted to a reduction

of wages ; that the workers, beginning to feel the heartening effects
of their union, were determined not to submit ; that bitter and even
desperate agitation was spreading fast, and that a far-reaching
strike was imminent.   Could they count on the support of the
Clarion?   The *Clarion* had already published certain letters on
the industry from a Special Commissioner—letters which had
drawn public attention, and had been eagerly read in the district
itself.   Would the *Clarion* now 'go in' for them?   Would Mr.
Wharton personally support them, in or out of Parliament, and get
his friends to do the same?   To which questions, couched in terms
extremely flattering to the power of the *Clarion* and its owner, the
secretary appended a long and technical statement of the situation.

Wharton looked up from the letter with a kindling eye.   He
foresaw an extremely effective case, both for the newspaper and
the House of Commons.   One of the chief capitalists involved was
a man called Denny, who had been long in the House, for whom
the owner of the *Clarion* entertained a strong personal dislike.
Denny had thwarted him vexatiously—had perhaps even made him
ridiculous—on one or two occasions ; and Wharton saw no reason
whatever for forgiving one's enemies until, like Narvaez, one had
'shot them all.'   There would be much satisfaction in making
Denny understand who were his masters.   And with these motives
there mingled a perfectly genuine sympathy with the 'poor devils'
in question, and a desire to see them righted.

'Somebody must be sent down at once,' he said to himself.   'I
suppose,' he added, with discontent, 'it must be Wilkins.'

For the man who had written the articles for the *Labour
Clarion*, as Special Commissioner, had some three weeks before
left England to take command of a colonial newspaper.

Still pondering, he took up the other letters, turned them over
—childishly pleased for the thousandth time by the M.P. on each
envelope and the number and variety of his correspondence—and
eagerly chose out three—one from his bankers, one from his
Lincolnshire agent, and one from the *Clarion* office, undoubtedly
this time in Wilkins's hand.

He read them, grew a little pale, swore under his breath, and
angrily flinging the letters away from him, he took up his cigarette
again and thought.

The letter from his bankers asked his attention in stiff terms to a
largely overdrawn account, and entirely declined to advance a sum
of money for which he had applied to them without the guarantee
of two substantial names in addition to his own.   The letter from
his agent warned him that the extraordinary drought of the past
six weeks, together with the general agricultural depression, would

certainly mean a large remission of rents at the June quarter day, and also informed him that the holders of his co-operative farm would not be able to pay their half-yearly interest on the capital advanced to them by the landlord.

As to the third letter, it was in truth much more serious than the two others. Wilkins, the passionate and suspicious workman, of great natural ability, who had been in many ways a thorn in Wharton's side since the beginning of his public career, was now member for a mining constituency. His means of support were extremely scanty, and at the opening of the new Parliament Wharton had offered him well-paid work on the *Clarion* news-paper. It had seemed to the proprietor of the *Clarion* a way of attaching a dangerous man to himself, perhaps also of controlling him. Wilkins had grudgingly accepted, understanding perfectly well what was meant.

Since then the relation between the two men had been one of perpetual friction. Wilkins's irritable pride would yield nothing, either in the House or in the *Clarion* office, to Wharton's university education and class advantages, while Wharton watched with alarm the growing influence of this insubordinate and hostile member of his own staff on those labour circles from which the *Clarion* drew its chief support.

In the letter he had just read Wilkins announced to the pro-prietor of the *Clarion*, that in consequence of the 'scandalous mismanagement' of that paper's handling of a certain trade arbitration which had just closed, he, Wilkins, could no longer continue to write for it, and begged to terminate his engagement at once, there being no formal agreement between himself and Wharton as to length of notice on either side. A lively attack on the present management and future prospects of the *Clarion* followed, together with the threat that the writer would do what in him lay henceforward to promote the cause of a certain rival organ lately started, among such working men as he might be able to influence.

'*Brute* ! jealous, impracticable brute !' exclaimed Wharton aloud, as he stood chafing and smoking by the window. All the difficulties which this open breach was likely to sow in his path stood out before him in clear relief.

'*Personal* leadership, there is the whole problem,' he said to himself in moody despair. 'Can I—like Parnell—make a party and keep it together ? Can I through the *Clarion*—and through influence *outside* the House—coerce the men *in* the House ? If so, we can do something, and Lady Cradock will no longer throw me her smiles. If not, the game is up ; both for me and for them.

They have no cohesion, no common information, no real power. Without leaders they are a mere set of half-educated firebrands whom the trained mind of the country humours because it must, and so far as they have brute force behind them. Without *leadership*, *I* am a mere unit of the weakest group in the House. Yet, by Jove ! it looks as though I had not the gifts.'

And he looked back with passionate chagrin on the whole course of his connection with Wilkins, his unavailing concessions and small humiliations, his belief in his own tact and success, all the time that the man 'dealt with was really slipping out of his hands.

'Damn the fellow !' he said at last, flinging his cigarette away. 'Well, that's done with. All the same, he would have liked that Midland job ! He has been hankering after a strike there for some time, and might have ranted as he pleased. I shall have the satisfaction of informing him he has lost his opportunity. Now then—whom to send ? By Jove ! what about Miss Boyce's friend ?'

He stood a moment twisting the quill-pen he had taken up, then he hastily found a sheet of paper and wrote :—

'Dear Miss Boyce,—It is more than a year since I have heard of you, and I have been wondering with much interest lately whether you have really taken up a nursing life. You remember speaking to me of your friends the Cravens? I come across them sometimes at the Venturist meetings, and have always admired their ability. Last year I could do nothing practical to meet your wishes. This year, however, there is an opening on the *Clarion*, and I should like to discuss it with you. Are you in town or to be found? I could come any afternoon next week, *early*—I go down to the House at four—or on Saturdays. But I should like it to be Tuesday or Wednesday, that I might try and persuade you to come to our Eight Hours debate on Friday night. It would interest you, and I think I could get you a seat. We Labour members are like the Irishmen—we can always get our friends in.

'I must send this round by Mellor, so it may not reach you till Tuesday. Perhaps you will kindly telegraph. The *Clarion* matter is pressing.

'Yours sincerely,
'H. S. WHARTON.'

When he had finished he lingered a moment over the letter, the play of conflicting motives and memories bringing a vague smile to the lips.

Reverie, however, was soon dispersed. He recollected his other correspondents, and springing up he began to pace his room, gloomily thinking over his money difficulties, which were many. He and his mother had always been in want of money ever since he could remember. Lady Mildred would spend huge sums on her various crotchets and campaigns, and then subside for six months into wretched lodgings in a back street of Southsea or Worthing, while the Suffolk house was let, and her son mostly went abroad. This perpetual worry of needy circumstances had always, indeed, sat lightly on Wharton. He was unmarried, and so far scarcity had generally passed into temporary comfort before he had time to find it intolerable. But now the whole situation was becoming more serious. In the first place, his subscriptions and obligations as a member of Parliament, and as one of the few propertied persons in a moneyless movement, were considerable. Whatever Socialism might make of money in the future, he was well aware that money in the present was no less useful to a Socialist politician than to anyone else. In the next place, the starting and pushing of the *Clarion* newspaper—originally purchased by the help of a small legacy from an uncle—had enormously increased the scale of his money transactions and the risks of life.

How was it that, with all his efforts, the *Clarion* was not making, but losing money? During the three years he had possessed it he had raised it from the position of a small and foul-mouthed print, indifferently nourished on a series of small scandals, to that of a Labour organ of some importance. He had written a weekly signed article for it, which had served from the beginning to bring both him and the paper into notice ; he had taken pains with the organisation and improvement of the staff; above all, he had spent a great deal more money upon it, in the way of premises and appliances, than he had been, as it turned out, in any way justified in spending.

Hence, indeed, these tears. Rather more than a year before, while the *Clarion* was still enjoying a first spurt of success and notoriety, he had, with a certain recklessness which belonged to his character, invested in new and costly machinery, and had transferred the paper to larger offices. All this had been done on borrowed money.

Then, for some reason or other, the *Clarion* had ceased to answer to the spur—had, indeed, during the past eight months been flagging heavily. The outside world was beginning to regard the *Clarion* as an important paper. Wharton knew all the time that its advertisements were falling off, and its circulation declining. Why? Who can say? If it is true that books have their fates, it is still more true of newspapers. Was it that a collectivist paper—the rival organ mentioned by Wilkins—recently

started by a group of young and outrageously clever Venturists
and more closely in touch than the *Clarion* with two or three of
the great unions, had filched the *Clarion's* ground? Or was it
simply that, as Wharton put it to himself in moments of rage and
despondency, the majority of working men 'are either sots or
blockheads, and will read and support *nothing* but the low racing
or police-court news, which is all their intelligences deserve'?
Few people had at the bottom of their souls a more scornful distrust of the 'masses' than the man whose one ambition at the
present moment was to be the accepted leader of English labour.

Finally, his private expenditure had always been luxurious ;
and he was liable, it will be seen, to a kind of debt that is not
easily kept waiting. On the whole, his bankers had behaved to
him with great indulgence.

He fretted and fumed, turning over plan after plan as he
walked, his curly head sunk in his shoulders, his hands behind his
back. Presently he stopped—absently—in front of the inner wall
of the room, where, above a heavy rosewood bookcase, brought
from his Lincolnshire house, a number of large framed photographs
were hung close together.

His eye caught one and brightened. With an impatient
gesture, like that of a reckless boy, he flung his thoughts away
from him.

'If ever the game becomes too tiresome here, why, the next
steamer will take me out of it ! What a *gorgeous* time we had on
that glacier !'

He stood looking at a splendid photograph of a glacier in the
Thibetan Himalayas, where, in the year following his mother's
death, he had spent four months with an exploring party. The
plate had caught the very grain and glisten of the snow, the very
sheen and tint of the ice. He could *feel* the azure of the sky, the
breath of the mountain wind. The man seated on the ladder over
that bottomless crevasse was himself. And there were the guides,
two from Chamounix, one from Grindelwald, and that fine young
fellow, the son of the elder Chamounix guide, whom they had lost
by a stone-shower on that nameless peak towering to the left of
the glacier. Ah, those had been years of *life*, those *Wanderjahre* !
He ran over the photographs with a kind of greed, his mind meanwhile losing itself in covetous memories of foamy seas, of long,
low, tropical shores with their scattered palms, of superb rivers
sweeping with sound and fury round innumerable islands, of great
buildings ivory-white amid the wealth of creepers which had pulled
them into ruin, vacant now for ever of the voice of man, and ringed
by untrodden forests.

' " Better fifty years of Europe than a cycle of Cathay," ' he thought. 'Ah ! but how much did the man who wrote that know about Cathay ?'

And with his hands thrust into his pockets, he stood lost awhile in a flying dream that defied civilisation and its cares. How well, how indispensable to remember, that beyond these sweltering streets where we choke and swarm, Cathay stands always waiting ! *Somewhere*, while we toil in the gloom and the crowd, there is *air*, there is *sea*, the joy of the sun, the life of the body, so good, so satisfying ! This interminable ethical or econo-mical battle, these struggles selfish or altruistic, in which we shout ourselves hoarse to no purpose—why ! they could be shaken off at a moment's notice !

'However'—he turned on his heel—'suppose we try a few other trifles first. What time ? those fellows won't have gone to bed yet !'

He took out his watch, then extinguished his candles, and made his way to the street. A hundred yards or so away from his own door he stopped before a well-known fashionable club, extremely small and extremely select, where his mother's brother, the peer of the family, had introduced him when he was young and tender, and his mother's relations still cherished hopes of snatch-ing him as a brand from the burning.

The front rooms of the club were tolerably full still. He passed on to the back. A door-keeper stationed in the passage stepped back and silently opened a door. It closed instantly behind him, and Wharton found himself in a room with some twenty other young fellows playing baccarat, piles of shining money on the tables, the electric lamps hung over each, lighting every detail of the scene with the same searching disenchanting glare.

'I say !' cried a young dark-haired fellow, like a dishevelled Lord Byron. 'Here comes the Labour leader—make room !'

And amid laughter and chaffing, he was drawn down to the baccarat table where a new deal was just beginning. He felt in his pockets for money ; his eyes, intent and shining, followed every motion of the dealer's hand. For three years now, ever since his return from his travels, the gambler's passion had been stealing on him. Already this season he had lost and won—on the whole lost —large sums. And the fact was—so far—absolutely unknown except to the men with whom he played in this room.

CHAPTER III

'IF yer goin downstairs, Nuss, you'd better take that there scuttle with yer, for the coals is gittin low an' it ull save yer a journey !'

Marcella looked with amusement at her adviser—a small bandy-legged boy in shirt and knickerbockers, with black Jewish eyes in a strongly featured face. He stood leaning on the broom he had just been wielding, his sleeves rolled up to the shoulder showing his tiny arms ; his expression sharp and keen as a hawk's.

'Well, Benny, then you look after your mother while I'm gone, and don't let anyone in but the doctor.'

And Marcella turned for an instant towards the bed whereon lay a sick woman too feeble apparently to speak or move.

'I ain't a goin ter,' said the boy shortly, beginning to sweep again with energy, 'an' if this ere baby cries, give it the bottle, I spose?'

'No, certainly not,' said Marcella firmly ; 'it has just had one. You sweep away, Benny, and let the baby alone.'

Benny looked a trifle wounded, but recovered himself imme-diately, and ran a general's eye over Marcella, who was just about to leave the room.

'Now look ere, Nuss,' he said in a tone of pitying remonstrance, 'yer never a goin down to that ere coal cellar without a light. Yer'll 'ave to come runnin up all them stairs again—sure as I'm alive yer will !'

And darting to a cupboard he pulled out a grimy candlestick with an end of dip and some matches, disposed of them at the bottom of the coal-scuttle that Marcella carried over her left arm, and then, still masterfully considering her, let her go.

Marcella groped her way downstairs. The house was one of a type familiar all over the poorer parts of West Central London— the eighteenth-century house inhabited by law or fashion in the days of Dr. Johnson, now parcelled out into insanitary tenements, miserably provided with air, water, and all the necessaries of life, but still showing in its chimney-piece or its decaying staircase signs of the graceful domestic art which had ruled at the building and fitting of it.

Marcella, however, had no eye whatever at the moment for the panelling on the staircase, or the delicate ironwork of the broken balustrade. Rather it seemed to her, as she looked into some of the half-open doors of the swarming rooms she passed, or noticed with disgust the dirt and dilapidation of the stairs, and the evil smells of the basement, that the house added one more to the

standing shames of the district—an opinion doubly strong in her
when at last she emerged from her gropings among the dens of the
lower regions, and began to toil upstairs again with her filled kettle
and coal-scuttle.

The load was heavy, even for her young strength, and she had
just passed a sleepless night. The evening before she had been
sent for in haste to a woman in desperate illness. She came, and
found a young Jewess, with a ten-days-old child beside her, struggling with her husband and two women friends in a state of raging
delirium. The room was full to suffocation of loud-tongued, large-
eyed Jewesses, all taking turns at holding the patient, and chattering
or quarrelling between their turns. It had been Marcella's first
and arduous duty to get the place cleared, and she had done it
without ever raising her voice or losing her temper for an instant.
The noisy pack had been turned out ; the most competent woman
among them chosen to guard the door and fetch and carry for the
nurse ; while Marcella set to work to wash her patient and remake
the bed as best she could, in the midst of the poor thing's wild
shrieks and wrestlings.

It was a task to test both muscular strength and moral force to
their utmost. After her year's training Marcella took it simply in
the day's work. Some hours of intense effort and strain ; then she
and the husband looked down upon the patient, a woman of about
six-and-twenty, plunged suddenly in narcotic sleep, her matted
black hair, which Marcella had not dared to touch, lying in wild
waves on the clean bedclothes and night-gear that her nurse had
extracted from this neighbour and that—she could hardly have told
how.

'Ach, mein Gott, mein Gott !' said the husband, rising and
shaking himself. He was a Jew from German Poland, and, unlike
most of his race, a huge man, with the make and the muscles of a
prize-fighter. Yet, after the struggle of the last two hours he was
in a bath of perspiration.

'You will have to send her to the infirmary if this comes on
again,' said Marcella.

The husband stared in helpless misery, first at his wife, then at
the nurse.

'You will not go away, mees,' he implored ; 'you will not leaf
me alone ?'

Wearied as she was, Marcella could have smiled at the abject
giant.

'No, I will stay with her till the morning and till the doctor
comes. You had better go to bed.'

It was close on three o'clock. The man demurred a little, but he was in truth too worn out to resist. He went into the back room and lay down with the children.

Then Marcella was left through the long summer dawn alone with her patient. Her quick ear caught every sound about her—the heavy breaths of the father and children in the back room, the twittering of the sparrows, the first cries about the streets, the first movements in the crowded house. Her mind all the time was running partly on contrivances for pulling the woman through—for it was what a nurse calls 'a good case,' one that rouses all her nursing skill and faculty—partly on the extraordinary miscon-duct of the doctor, to whose criminal neglect and mismanagement of the case she hotly attributed the whole of the woman's illness.; and partly—in deep, swift sinkings of meditative thought—on the strangeness of the fact that she should be there at all, sitting in this chair in this miserable room, keeping guard over this Jewish mother and her child !

The year in hospital had *rushed*—dreamless sleep by night, exhausting fatigue of mind and body by day. A hospital nurse, if her work *seizes* her, as it had seized Marcella, never thinks of her-self. Now, for some six or seven weeks, she had been living in rooms, as a district nurse, under the control of a central office and superintendent. Her work lay in the homes of the poor, and was of the most varied kind. The life was freer, more elastic ; allowed room at last to self-consciousness.

But now the night was over. The husband had gone off to work at a factory near, whence he could be summoned at any moment ; the children had been disposed of to Mrs. Levi, the helpful neigh-bour ; she herself had been home for an hour to breakfast and dress, had sent to the office asking that her other cases might be attended to, and was at present in sole charge, with Benny to help her, waiting for the doctor.

When she reached the sick-room again with her burdens, she found Benjamin sitting pensive, with the broom across his knees.

'Well, Benny !' she said as she entered, 'how have you got on ?'

'Yer can't move the dirt on them poards with sweepin,' said Benny, looking at them with disgust ; 'an' I ain't a goin to try it no more.'

'You're about right there, Benny,' said Marcella mournfully as she inspected them. 'Well, we'll get Mrs. Levi to come in and scrub—as soon as your mother can bear it.'

She stepped up to the bed and looked at her patient, who seemed to be passing into a state of restless prostration, more or

less under the influence of morphia. Marcella fed her with strong
beef-tea made by herself during the night, and debated whether
she should give brandy. No—either the doctor would come
directly, or she would send for him. She had not seen him yet,
and her lip curled at the thought of him. He had ordered a nurse
the night before, but had not stayed to meet her, and Marcella had
been obliged to make out his instructions from the husband as best
she could.

Benny looked up at her with a wink as she went back to
the fire.

' I didn't let none o' *them* in,' he said, jerking his thumb over
his shoulder. ' They come a whisperin at the door, an' a rattlin
ov the handle as soon as ever you gone downstairs. But I tole
'em just to take theirselves off, an' as ow you didn't want 'em.
Sillies !'

And taking a crust smeared with treacle out of his pocket,
Benny returned with a severe air to the sucking of it.

Marcella laughed.

' Clever Benny,' she said, patting his head ; ' but why aren't you
at school, sir ? '

Benjamin grinned.

' Ow d'yer spose my ma's goin to git along without me to do
for 'er and the babby ? ' he replied slily.

' Well, Benny, you'll have the Board officer down on you.'

At this the urchin laughed out.

' Why, 'e wor here last week ! Ee can't be troublin 'isself
about this 'ere bloomin street *ev*ery day in the week.'

There was a sharp knock at the door.

' The doctor,' she said, as her face dismissed the frolic
brightness which had stolen upon it for a moment. ' Run away,
Benny.'

Benny opened the door, looked the doctor coolly up and down,
and then withdrew to the landing, where his sisters were waiting
to play with him.

The doctor, a tall man of thirty, with a red, blurred face and a
fair moustache, walked in hurriedly, and stared at the nurse standing
by the fire.

' You come from the St. Martin's Association ? '

Marcella stiffly replied. He took her temperature-chart from
her hand and asked her some questions about the night, staring at
her from time to time with eyes that displeased her. Presently
she came to an account of the condition in which she had found
her patient. The edge on the words, for all their professional
quiet, was unmistakable. She saw him flush.

He moved towards the bed, and she went with him. The woman moaned as he approached her. He set about his business with hands that shook. Marcella decided at once that he was not sober, and watched his proceedings with increasing disgust and amazement. Presently she could bear it no longer.

'I think,' she said, touching his arm, 'that you had better leave it to me—and—go away !'

He drew himself up with a start which sent the things he held flying, and faced her fiercely.

'What do you mean ?' he said. 'Don't you know your place ?'

The girl was very white, but her eyes were scornfully steady.

'Yes—I know my place !'

Then with a composure as fearless as it was scathing she said what she had to say. She knew—and he could not deny—that he had endangered his patient's life. She pointed out that he was in a fair way to endanger it again. Every word she said lay absolutely within her sphere as a nurse. His cloudy brain cleared under the stress of it.

Then his eyes flamed, his cheeks became purple, and Marcella thought for an instant he would have struck her. Finally he turned down his shirt-cuffs and walked away.

'You understand,' he said thickly, turning upon her, with his hat in his hand, 'that I shall not attend this case again till your Association can send me a nurse that will do as she is told without insolence to the doctor. I shall now write a report to your superintendent.'

'As you please,' said Marcella quietly. And she went to the door and opened it.

He passed her sneering.

'A precious superior lot you lady-nurses think yourselves, I dare say. I'd sooner have one old Gamp than the whole boiling of you !'

Marcella eyed him sternly, her nostrils tightening. 'Will you go ?' she said.

He gave her a furious glance, and plunged down the stairs outside, breathing threats.

Marcella put her hand to her head a moment, and drew a long breath. There was a certain piteousness in the action, a consciousness of youth and strain.

Then she saw that the landing and the stairs above were beginning to fill with dark-haired Jewesses, eagerly peering and talking. In another minute or two she would be besieged by them. She called sharply, 'Benny !'

Instantly Benny appeared from the landing above, elbowing the Jewesses to right and left.

'What is it you want, Nuss? No, she don't want none o' *you* --*there* !'

And Benjamin darted into the room, and would have slammed the door in all their faces, but that Marcella said to him—

'Let in Mrs. Levi, please.'

The kind neighbour, who had been taking care of the children, was admitted, and then the key was turned. Marcella scribbled a line on a half-sheet of paper, and, with careful directions, de‑spatched Benny with it.

'I have sent for a new doctor,' she explained, still frowning and white, to Mrs. Levi. 'That one was not fit.'

The woman's olive-skinned face lightened all over. 'Thanks to the Lord !' she said, throwing up her hands. 'But how in the world did you do 't, miss ? There isn't a single soul in this house that doesn't go all of a tremble at the sight of 'im. Yet all the women has 'im when they're ill—bound to. They thinks he must be clever, 'cos he's such a brute. I do believe sometimes it's that. He *is* a brute !'

Marcella was bending over her patient, trying so far as she could to set her straight and comfortable again. But the woman had begun to mutter once more words in a strange dialect that Marcella did not understand, and could no longer be kept still. The temperature was rising again, and another fit of delirium was imminent. Marcella could only hope that she and Mrs. Levi between them would be able to hold her till the doctor came. When she had done all that was in her power, she sat beside the poor tossing creature, controlling and calming her as best she could, while Mrs. Levi poured into her shrinking ear the story of the woman's illness and of Dr. Blank's conduct of it. Marcella's feeling, as she listened, was made up of that old agony of rage and pity ! The sufferings of the poor, *because* they were poor—these things often, still, darkened earth and heaven for her. That wretch would have been quite capable, no doubt, of conducting himself decently and even competently, if he had been called to some supposed lady in one of the well-to-do squares which made the centre of this poor and crowded district.

'Hullo, nurse !' said a cheery voice ; 'you seem to have got a bad case.'

The sound was as music in Marcella's ears. The woman she held was fast becoming unmanageable—had just shrieked, first for 'poison,' then for a 'knife,' to kill herself with, and could hardly be prevented, by the combined strength of her nurse and Mrs. Levi,

now from throwing herself madly out of bed, and now from tearing
out her black hair in handfuls.   The doctor—a young Scotchman
with spectacles, and stubbly red beard—came quickly up to the
bed, asked Marcella a few short questions, shrugged his shoulders
over her dry report of Dr. Blank's proceedings, then took out a
black case from his pocket, and put his morphia syringe together.

For a long time no result whatever could be obtained by any
treatment.   The husband was sent for, and came trembling, imploring doctor and nurse, in the intervals of his wife's paroxysms,
not to leave him alone.

Marcella, absorbed in the tragic horror of the case, took no
note of the passage of time.   Everything that the doctor suggested
she carried out with a deftness, a tenderness, a power of mind,
which keenly affected his professional sense.   Once, the poor
mother, left unguarded for an instant, struck out with a wild right
hand.   The blow caught Marcella on the cheek, and she drew
back with a slight involuntary cry.

'You are hurt,' said Dr. Angus, running up to her.

'No, no,' she said, smiling through the tears that the shock
had called into her eyes, and putting him rather impatiently aside ;
' it is nothing.   You said you wanted some fresh ice.'

And she went into the back room to get it.

The doctor stood with his hands in his pockets, studying the
patient.

'You will have to send her to the infirmary,' he said to the
husband ; 'there is nothing else for it.'

Marcella came back with the ice, and was able to apply it to
the head.   The patient was quieter—was, in fact, now groaning
herself into a fresh period of exhaustion.

The doctor's sharp eyes took note of the two figures, the huddled
creature on the pillows and the stately head bending over her, with
the delicately hollowed cheek, whereon the marks of those mad
fingers stood out red and angry.   He had already had experience
of this girl in one or two other cases.

'Well,' he said, taking up his hat, ' it is no good shilly-shallying.
I will go and find Dr. Swift.'   Dr. Swift was the parish doctor.

When he had gone, the big husband broke down and cried,
with his head against the iron of the bed close to his wife.   He
put his great hand on hers, and talked to her brokenly in their own
patois.   They had been eight years married, and she had never
had a day's serious illness till now.   Marcella's eyes filled with
tears as she moved about the room, doing various little tasks.

At last she went up to him.

'Won't you go and have some dinner?' she said to him kindly.

'There's Benjamin calling you,' and she pointed to the door of the back room where stood Benny, his face puckered with weeping, forlornly holding out a plate of fried fish in the hope of attracting his father's attention.

The man, who in spite of his size and strength was in truth childishly soft and ductile, went as he was bid, and Marcella and Mrs. Levi set about doing what they could to prepare the wife for her removal.

Presently parish doctor and sanitary inspector appeared, strange and peremptory invaders who did but add to the terror and misery of the husband. Then at last came the ambulance, and Dr. Angus with it. The patient, now once more plunged in narcotic stupor, was carried downstairs by two male nurses, Dr. Angus presiding. Marcella stood in the doorway and watched the scene ; the gradual disappearance of the helpless form on the stretcher, with its fevered face under the dark mat of hair ; the figures of the straining men heavily descending step by step, their heads and shoulders thrown out against the dirty drabs and browns of the staircase ; the crowd of Jewesses on the stairs and landing, craning their necks, gesticulating and talking, so that Dr. Angus could hardly make his directions heard, angrily as he bade them stand back ; and on the top stair, the big husband, following the form of his departing and unconscious wife with his eyes, his face convulsed with weeping, the whimpering children clinging about his knees.

How hot it was !—how stifling the staircase smelt, and how the sun beat down from that upper window on the towzled unkempt women with their large-eyed children !

CHAPTER IV

MARCELLA on her way home turned into a little street leading to a great block of model dwellings, which rose on the right-hand side and made everything else, the mews entrance opposite, the lines of squalid shops on either side, look particularly small and dirty. The sun was beating fiercely down, and she was sick and tired.

As she entered the iron gate of the dwellings, and saw before her the large asphalted court round which they ran—blazing heat on one side of it, and on the other some children playing cricket against the wall with chalk-marks for wickets—she was seized with depression. The tall yet mean buildings, the smell of dust and heat, the general impression of packed and crowded humanity—

these things, instead of offering her rest, only continued and accented the sense of strain, called for more endurance, more making the best of it.

But she found a tired smile for some of the children who ran up to her, and then she climbed the stairs of the E. block, and opened the door of her own tenement, number 10. In number 9 lived Minta Hurd and her children, who had joined Marcella in London some two months before. In sets 7 and 8, on either side of Marcella and the Hurds, lived two widows, each with a family, who were mostly out charing during the day.

Marcella's Association allowed its District Nurses to live outside the 'home' of the district on certain conditions, which had been fulfilled in Marcella's case by her settlement next door to her old friends in these buildings which were inhabited by a very respectable though poor class. Meanwhile the trustees of the buildings had allowed her to make a temporary communication between her room and the Hurds', so that she could either live her own solitary and independent life, or call for their companionship, as she pleased.

As she shut her door behind her she found herself in a little passage or entry. To the left was her bedroom. Straight in front of her was the living room with a small close range in it, and behind it a little back kitchen.

The living room was cheerful and even pretty. Her artstudent's training showed itself. The cheap blue and white paper, the couple of oak flap tables from a broker's shop in Marchmont Street, the two or three cane chairs with their bright chintz cushions, the Indian rug or two on the varnished boards, the photographs and etchings on the walls, the books on the tables—there was not one of these things that was not in its degree a pleasure to her young senses, that did not help her to live her life. This afternoon, as she opened the door and looked in, the pretty colours and forms in the tiny room were as water to the thirsty. Her mother had sent her some flowers the day before. There they were on the tables, great bunches of honeysuckles, of blue-bells, and Banksia roses. And over the mantelpiece was a photograph of the place where such flowers as Mellor possessed mostly grew—the unkempt lawn, the old fountain and grey walls of the Cedar Garden.

The green blind over the one window which looked into the court had been drawn down against the glare of the sun, as though by a careful hand. Beside a light wooden rocking-chair, which was Marcella's favourite seat, a tray of tea-things had been put out. Marcella drew a long breath of comfort as she put down her bag.

'Now, *can* I wait for my tea till I have washed and dressed?'

She argued with herself an instant as though she had been a greedy child ; then, going swiftly into the back kitchen, she opened the door between her rooms and the Hurds'.

'Minta!'

A voice responded.

'Minta, make me some tea and boil an egg! there's a good soul! I will be back directly.'

And in ten minutes or so she came back again into the sitting-room, daintily fresh and clean but very pale. She had taken off her nurse's dress and apron, and had put on something loose and white that hung about her in cool folds.

But Minta Hurd, who had just brought in the tea, looked at her disapprovingly.

'Whatever are you so late for?' she asked a little peevishly. 'You'll get ill if you go missing your dinner.'

'I couldn't help it, Minta, it was such a bad case.'

Mrs. Hurd poured out the tea in silence, unappeased. Her mind was constantly full of protest against this nursing. Why should Miss Boyce do such 'funny things'—why should she live as she did, at all?

Their relation to each other was a curious one. Marcella, knowing that the life of Hurd's widow at Mellor was gall and bitterness, had sent for her at the moment that she herself was leaving the hospital, offering her a weekly sum in return for a little cooking and house service. Minta already possessed a weekly pension, coming from a giver unknown to her. It was regularly handed to her by Mr. Harden, and she could only imagine that one of the 'gentlemen' who had belonged to the Hurd Reprieve Committee, and had worked so hard for Jim, was responsible for it, out of pity for her and her children. The payment offered her by Miss Boyce would defray the expense of London house-rent, the children's schooling, and leave a trifle over. Moreover she was pining to get away from Mellor. Her first instinct after her husband's execution had been to hide herself from all the world. But for a long time her precarious state of health, and her dependence first on Marcella, then on Mary Harden, made it impossible for her to leave the village. It was not till Marcella's proposal came that her way was clear. She sold her bits of things at once, took her children, and went up to Brown's Buildings.

Marcella met her with the tenderness, the tragic tremor of feeling from which the peasant's wife shrank anew, bewildered, as she had often shrunk from it in the past. Jim's fate had made her an old woman at thirty-two She was now a little shrivelled consumptive creature with almost white hair, and a face from which youth had gone, unless perhaps there were some traces of it in the still charming eyes, and small open mouth. But these changes had come upon her she knew not why, as the result of blows she felt but had never reasoned about. Marcella's fixed mode of conceiving her and her story caused her from the beginning of their fresh acquaintance a dumb irritation and trouble she could never have explained. It was so tragic, reflective, exacting. It seemed to ask of her feelings that she could not have, to expect from her expression that was impossible. And it stood also between her and the friends and distractions that she would like to have. Why shouldn't that queer man, Mr. Strozzi, who lived down below, and whose name she could not pronounce, come and sit sometimes of an evening, and amuse her and the children? He was a 'Professor of Elocution,' and said and sung comic pieces. He was very civil and obliging too ; she liked him. Yet Miss Boyce was evidently astonished that she could make friends with him, and Minta perfectly understood the lift of her dark eyebrows whenever she came in and found him sitting there.

Meanwhile Marcella had expected her with emotion, and had meant through this experiment to bring herself truly near to the poor. Minta must not call her Miss Boyce, but by her name ; which, however, Minta, reddening, had declared she could never do. Her relation to Marcella was not to be that of servant in any sense, but of friend and sister ; and on her and her children Marcella had spent from the beginning a number of new womanish wiles which, strangely enough, this hard, strenuous life had been developing in her. She would come and help put the children to bed ; she would romp with them in their night-gowns ; she would bend her imperious head over the anxious endeavour to hem a pink cotton pinafore for Daisy, or dress a doll for the baby. But the relation jarred and limped perpetually, and Marcella wistfully thought it her fault.

Just now, however, as she sat gently swaying backwards and forwards in the rocking-chair, enjoying her tea, her mood was one of nothing but content.

'Oh, Minta, give me another cup. I want to have a sleep so badly, and then I am going to see Miss Hallin, and stay to supper with them.'

'Well, you mustn't go out in them nursin things again,' said Minta quickly ; 'I've put you in some lace in your black dress, an' it looks beautiful.'

'Oh, thank you, Minta ; but that black dress always seems to me too smart to walk about these streets in.'

'It's just *nice*,' said Minta with decision. 'It's just what everybody that knows you—what your mamma—would like to see you in. I can't abide them nursin clothes—nasty things!'

'I declare!' cried Marcella, laughing, but outraged; 'I never like myself so well in anything.'

Minta was silent, but her small mouth took an obstinate look. What she really felt was that it was absurd for ladies to wear caps and aprons and plain black bonnets, when there was no need for them to do anything of the kind.

'Whatever have you been doing to your cheek?' she exclaimed suddenly, as Marcella handed her the empty cup to take away.

Marcella explained shortly, and Minta looked more discontented than ever. 'A lot of low people as ought to look after themselves,' that was how in her inmost mind she generally defined Marcella's patients. She had been often kind and soft to her neighbours at Mellor, but these dirty, crowded Londoners were another matter.

'Where is Daisy?' asked Marcella as Minta was going away with the tea; 'she must have come back from school.'

'Here I am,' said Daisy with a grin, peeping in through the door of the back kitchen. 'Mother, baby's woke up.'

'Come here, you monkey,' said Marcella; 'come and go to sleep with me. Have you had your tea?'

'Yes, lots,' said Daisy, climbing up into Marcella's lap. 'Are you going to be asleep a long time?'

'No—only a nap. Oh! Daisy, I'm so tired. Come and cuddlie a bit! If you don't go to sleep you know you can slip away—I shan't wake.'

The child, a slight, red-haired thing, with something of the ethereal charm that her dead brother had possessed, settled herself on Marcella's knees, slipped her left thumb into her mouth, and flung her other arm round Marcella's neck. They had often gone to sleep so. Mrs. Hurd came back, drew down the blind further, threw a light shawl over them both, and left them.

An hour and a half later Minta came in again as she had been told. Daisy had slipped away, but Marcella was still lying in the perfect gentleness and relaxation of sleep.

'You said I was to come and wake you,' said Minta, drawing up the blind; 'but I don't believe you're a bit fit to be going about. Here's some hot water, and there's a letter just come.'

Marcella woke with a start, Minta put the letter on her knee, and dream and reality flowed together as she saw her own name in Wharton's handwriting.

She read the letter, then sat flushed and thinking for a while with her hands on her knees.

A little while later she opened the Hurds' front door.

' Minta, I am going now. I shall be back early after supper, for I haven't written my report.'

'There—now you look something like !' said Minta, scanning her approvingly—the wide hat and pretty black dress. 'Shall Daisy run out with that telegram ?'

' No, thanks. I shall pass the post. Good-bye.'

And she stooped and kissed the little withered woman. She wished, ardently wished, that Minta would be more truly friends with her !

After a brisk walk through the June evening she stopped—still within the same district—at the door of a house in a long, old-fashioned street, wherein the builder was busy on either hand, since most of the long leases had just fallen in. But the house she entered was still untouched. She climbed a last-century staircase, adorned with panels of stucco work—slender Italianate reliefs of wreaths, ribbons, and medallions on a pale green ground. The decoration was clean and cared for, the house in good order. Eighty years ago it was the home of a famous judge, who entertained in its rooms the legal and literary celebrities of his day. Now it was let out to professional people in lodgings or unfurnished rooms. Edward Hallin and his sister occupied the top floor.

Miss Hallin, a pleasant-looking, plain woman of about thirty-five, came at once in answer to Marcella's knock, and greeted her affectionately. Edward Hallin sprang up from a table at the further end of the room.

' You are so late ! Susy and I had made up our minds you had forgotten us !'

' I didn't get home till four, and then I had to have a sleep,' she explained, half shyly.

'What ! you haven't been night-nursing ?'

' Yes, for once.'

' Susy, tell them to bring up supper, and let's look after her.'

He wheeled round a comfortable chair to the open window—the charming circular bow of last-century design, which filled up the end of the room and gave it character. The window looked out on a quiet line of back gardens, such as may still be seen in Bloomsbury, with fine plane trees here and there just coming into full leaf ; and beyond them the backs of another line of houses in a distant square, with pleasant irregularities of old brickwork and tiled roof. The mottled trunks of the planes, their blackened twigs and branches, their thin, beautiful leaves, the forms of the houses beyond, rose in a charming medley of line against the blue and peaceful sky. No near sound was to be heard, only the distant murmur that no Londoner escapes; and some of the British Museum pigeons were sunning themselves on the garden-wall below.

Within, the Hallins' room was spacious and barely furnished. The walls, indeed, were crowded with books, and broken, where the books ceased, by photographs of Italy and Greece; but of furniture proper there seemed to be little beside Hallin's large writing-table facing the window, and a few chairs, placed on the blue drugget which brother and sister had chosen with a certain anxiety, dreading secretly lest it should be a piece of self-indulgence to buy what pleased them both so much. On one side of the fireplace was Miss Hallin's particular corner; her chair, the table that held her few special books, her work-basket, with its knitting, her accounts. There, in the intervals of many activities, she sat and worked or read, always cheerful and busy, and always watching over her brother.

'I wish,' said Hallin, with some discontent, when Marcella had settled herself, 'that we were going to be alone to-night; that would have rested you more.'

'Why, who is coming?' said Marcella, a little flatly. She had certainly hoped to find them alone.

'Your old friend, Frank Leven, is coming to supper. When he heard you were to be here he vowed that nothing could or should keep him away. Then, after supper, one or two people asked if they might come in. There are some anxious things going on.'

He leant his head on his hand for a moment with a sigh, then forcibly wrenched himself from what were evidently recurrent thoughts.

'Do tell me some more of what you are doing!' he said, bending forward to her. 'You don't know how much I have thought of what you have told me already.'

'I'm doing just the same,' she said, laughing. 'Don't take so much interest in it. It's the fashion just now to admire nurses; but it's ridiculous. We do our work like other people—sometimes badly, sometimes well. And some of us wouldn't do it if we could help it.'

She threw out the last words with a certain vehemence, as though eager to get away from any sentimentalism about herself. Hallin studied her kindly.

'Is this miscellaneous work a relief to you after hospital?' he asked.

'For the present. It is more exciting, and one sees more character. But there are drawbacks. In hospital everything was settled for you—every hour was full, and there were always orders to follow. And the "off" times were no trouble—I never did anything else but walk up and down the Embankment if it was fine, or go to the National Gallery if it was wet.'

'And it was the monotony you liked?'

She made a sign of assent.

'Strange!' said Hallin. 'Who could ever have foreseen it?'

She flushed.

'You might have foreseen it, I think,' she said, not without a little impatience. 'But I didn't like it all at once. I hated a great deal of it. If they had let me alone all the time to scrub and polish and wash—the things they set me to at first—I thought I should have been quite happy. To see my table full of glasses without a spot, and my brass taps shining, made me as proud as a peacock! But then of course I had to learn the real work, and that was very odd at first.'

'How? Morally?'

She nodded, laughing at her own remembrances. 'Yes—it seemed to me all topsy-turvy. I thought the Sister at the head of the ward rather a stupid person. If I had seen her at Mellor I shouldn't have spoken two words to her. And here she was ordering me about—rating me as I had never rated a housemaid—laughing at me for not knowing this or that, and generally making me feel that a raw probationer was one of the things of least account in the whole universe. I knew perfectly well that she had said to herself, "Now then I must take that proud girl down a peg, or she will be no use to anybody;" and I had somehow to put up with it.'

'Drastic!' said Hallin, laughing. 'Did you comfort yourself by reflecting that it was everybody's fate?'

Her lip twitched with amusement.

'Not for a long time. I used to have the most absurd ideas!—sometimes looking back I can hardly believe it—perhaps it was partly a queer state of nerves. When I was at school and got in a passion I used to try and overawe the girls by shaking my Speaker great-uncle in their faces. And so in hospital; it would flash across me sometimes in a plaintive sort of way that they *couldn't* know that I was Miss Boyce of Mellor, and had been mothering and ruling the whole of my father's village—or they wouldn't treat me so. Mercifully I held my tongue. But one day it came to a crisis. I had had to get things ready for an operation, and had done very well. Dr. Marshall had paid me even a little compliment all to myself. But then afterwards the patient was some time in coming to, and there had to be hot-water bottles. I had them ready of course ; but they were too hot, and in my zeal and nervousness I burnt the patient's elbow in two places. Oh ! the *fuss*, and the scolding, and the humiliation ! When I left the ward that evening I thought I would go home next day.'

' But you didn't ? '

' If I could have sat down and thought it out, I should probably have gone. But I couldn't think it out—I was too *dead* tired. That is the chief feature of your first months in hospital—the utter helpless fatigue at night. You go to bed aching and you wake up aching. If you are healthy as I was, it doesn't hurt you ; but, when your time comes to sleep, sleep you *must*. Even that miserable night my head was no sooner on the pillow than I was asleep ; and next morning there was all the routine as usual, and the dread of being a minute late on duty. Then when I got into the ward the Sister looked at me rather queerly and went out of her way to be kind to me. Oh! I was so grateful to her ! I could have brushed her boots or done any other menial service for her with delight. And—then—somehow I pulled through. The enormous interest of the work seized me—I grew ambitious—they pushed me on rapidly—everybody seemed suddenly to become my friend instead of my enemy—and I ended by thinking the hospital the most fascinating and engrossing place in the whole world.'

' A curious experience,' said Hallin. ' I suppose you had never obeyed anyone in your life before ? '

' Not since I was at school—and then—not much ! '

Hallin glanced at her as she lay back in her chair. How richly human the face had grown ! It was as forcible as ever in expression and colour, but that look which had often repelled him in his first acquaintance with her, as of a hard speculative eagerness more like the ardent boy than the woman, had very much disappeared. It seemed to him absorbed in something new—something sad and yet benignant, informed with all the pathos and the pain of growth.

' How long have you been at work to-day ? ' he asked her.

' I went at eleven last night. I came away at four this afternoon.'

Hallin exclaimed, ' You had food ? '

'.Do you think I should let myself starve with my work to do ? ' she asked him, with a shade of scorn and her most professional air. ' And don't suppose that such a case occurs often. It is a very rare thing for us to undertake night-nursing at all.'

' Can you tell me what the case was ? '

She told him vaguely, describing also in a few words her encounter with Dr. Blank.

'I suppose he will make a fuss,' she said, with a restless look, 'and that I shall be blamed.'

'I should think your second doctor will take care of that!' said Hallin.

'I don't know. I couldn't help it. But it is one of our first principles not to question a doctor. And last week too I got the Association into trouble. A patient I had been nursing for weeks and got quite fond of had to be removed to hospital. She asked me to cut her hair. It was matted dreadfully, and would have been cut off directly she got to the ward. So I cut it, left her all comfortable, and was to come back at one to meet the doctor and help get her off. When I came, I found the whole court in an uproar. The sister of the woman, who had been watching for me, stood on the doorstep, and implored me to go away. The husband had gone out of his senses with rage because I had cut his wife's hair without his consent. "He'll murder you, Nuss!" said the sister, "if he sees you! Don't come in!—he's mad—he's *been going round on 'is 'ands and knees on the floor!*"'

Hallin interrupted with a shout of laughter. Marcella laughed too; but to his amazement he saw that her hand shook, and that there were tears in her eyes.

'It's all very well,' she said with a sigh, 'but I had to come away in disgrace, all the street looking on. And he made such a fuss at the office as never was. It was unfortunate—we don't want the people set against the nurses. And now Dr. Blank!—I seem to be always getting into scrapes. It is different from hospital, where everything is settled for one.'

Hallin could hardly believe his ears. Such womanish terrors and depressions from Marcella Boyce! Was she, after all, too young for the work, or was there some fret of the soul reducing her natural force? He felt an unwonted impulse of tenderness towards her—such as one might feel towards a tired child—and set himself to cheer and rest her.

He had succeeded to some extent, when he saw her give a little start, and following her eyes he perceived that unconsciously his arm, which was resting on the table, had pushed into her view a photograph in a little frame, which had been hitherto concealed from her by a glass of flowers. He would have quietly put it out of sight again, but she sat up in her chair.

'Will you give it me?' she said, putting out her hand.

He gave it her at once.

'Susy brought it home from Miss Raeburn the other day. His

aunt made him sit to one of the photographers who are always besieging public men. We thought it good.'

'It is very good,' she said, after a pause. 'Is the hair really—as grey as that?' She pointed to it.

'Quite. I am very glad that he is going off with Lord Maxwell to Italy. It will be ten days' break for him at any rate. His work this last year has been very heavy. He has had his grandfather's to do really, as well as his own ; and this Commission has been a stiff job too. I am rather sorry that he has taken this new post.'

'What post?'

'Didn't you hear? They have made him Under-Secretary to the Home Department. So that he is now in the Government.'

She put back the photograph, and moved her chair a little so as to see more of the plane trees and the strips of sunset cloud.

'How is Lord Maxwell?' she asked presently.

'Much changed. It might end in a sudden break-up at any time.'

Hallin saw a slight contraction pass over her face. He knew that she had always felt an affection for Lord Maxwell. Suddenly Marcella looked hastily round her. Miss Hallin was busy with a little servant at the other end of the room making arrangements for supper.

'Tell me,' she said, bending over the arm of her chair and speaking in a low, eager voice, 'he is beginning to forget it?'

Hallin looked at her in silence, but his half sad, half ironic smile suggested an answer from which she turned away.

'If he only would!' she said, speaking almost to herself, with a kind of impatience. 'He ought to marry, for everybody's sake.'

'I see no sign of his marrying—at present,' said Hallin drily.

He began to put some papers under his hand in order. There was a cold dignity in his manner which she perfectly understood. Ever since that day—that never-forgotten day—when he had come to her the morning after her last interview with Aldous Raeburn—come with reluctance and dislike, because Aldous had asked it of him—and had gone away her friend, more drawn to her, more touched by her than he had ever been in the days of the engagement, their relation on this subject had been the same. His sweetness and kindness to her, his influence over her life during the past eighteen months, had been very great. In that first interview, the object of which had been to convey to her a warning on the subject of the man it was thought she might allow herself to marry, something in the manner with which he had attempted his incredibly difficult task—its simplicity, its delicate respect for her personality, its suggestion of a character richer and saintlier than anything she had yet known, and unconsciously revealing itself under the stress of emotion—this something had suddenly broken down his pale, proud companion, had to his own great dismay brought her to tears, and to such confidences, such indirect askings for help and understanding as amazed them both.

Experiences of this kind were not new to him. His life consecrated to ideas, devoted to the wresting of the maximum of human service from a crippling physical weakness ; the precarious health itself which cut him off from a hundred ordinary amuse. ments and occupations, and especially cut him off from marriage— together with the ardent temperament, the charm, the imaginative insight which had been his cradle-gifts—these things ever since he was a lad had made him again and again the guide and prop of natures stronger and stormier than his own. Often the unwilling guide ; for he had the half-impatient, breathless instincts of the man who has set himself a task, and painfully doubts whether he will have power and time to finish it. The claims made upon him seemed to him often to cost him physical and brain energy he could ill spare.

But his quick tremulous sympathy rendered him really a defenceless prey in such matters. Marcella threw herself upon him as others had done ; and there was no help for it. Since their first memorable interview, at long intervals, he had written to her and she to him. Of her hospital life, till to-night, she had never told him much. Her letters had been the passionate outpourings of a nature sick of itself, and for the moment of living ; full of explanations which really explained little ; full too of the untaught pangs and questionings of a mind which had never given any sustained or exhaustive effort to any philosophical or social question, and yet was in a sense tortured by them all—athirst for an impossible justice, and aflame for ideals mocked first and above all by the writer's own weakness and defect. Hallin had felt them interesting, sad, and, in a sense, fine ; but he had never braced himself to answer them without groans. There were so many other people in the world in the same plight !

Nevertheless, all through the growth of friendship one thing had never altered between them from the beginning—Hallin's irrevocable judgment of the treatment she had bestowed on Aldous Raeburn. Never throughout the whole course of their acquaintance had he expressed that judgment to her in so many words. Notwithstanding, she knew perfectly well both the nature and the force of it. It lay like a rock in the stream of their friendship. The currents of talk might circle round it, imply it, glance off from it ; they left it unchanged. At the root of his mind towards her, at the bottom of his gentle sensitive nature, there was a sternness which he often forgot—she never.

This hard fact in their relation had insensibly influenced her greatly, was constantly indeed working in and upon her, especially since the chances of her nursing career had brought her to settle in this district, within a stone's throw of him and his sister, so that she saw them often and intimately. But it worked in different ways. Sometimes—as to-night—it evoked a kind of defiance.

A minute or two after he had made his remark about Aldous, she said to him suddenly,

'I had a letter from Mr. Wharton to-day. He is coming to tea with me to-morrow, and I shall probably go to the House on Friday with Edith Craven to hear him speak.'

Hallin gave a slight start at the name. Then he said nothing ; but went on sorting some letters of the day into different heaps. His silence roused her irritation.

'Do you remember,' she said in a low, energetic voice, 'that I told you I could never be ungrateful, never forget what he had done ?'

'Yes, I remember,' he said, not without a certain sharpness of tone. 'You spoke of giving him help if he ever asked it of you— has he asked it ?'

She explained that what he seemed to be asking was Louis Craven's help, and that his overtures with regard to the *Labour Clarion* were particularly opportune, seeing that Louis was pining to be able to marry, and was losing heart, hope, and health for want of some fixed employment. She spoke warmly of her friends and their troubles, and Hallin's inward distaste had to admit that all she said was plausible. Since the moment in that strange talk which had drawn them together, when she had turned upon him with the passionate cry—'I see what you mean, perfectly ! but I am not going to marry Mr. Wharton, so don't trouble to warn me —for the matter of that he has warned me himself :—but my *gratitude* he *has* earned, and if he asks for it I will *never* deny it him '—since that moment there had been no word of Wharton between them. At the bottom of his heart Hallin distrusted her, and was ashamed of himself because of it. His soreness and jealousy for his friend knew no bounds. 'If that were to come on again '—he was saying to himself now, as she talked to him—' I could not bear it, I could not forgive her !'

He only wished that she would give up talking about Wharton altogether. But, on the contrary, she would talk of him—and with a curious persistence. She must needs know what Hallin thought of his career in Parliament, of his prospects, of his powers as a speaker. Hallin answered shortly, like someone approached on a subject for which he cares nothing.

'Yet, of course, it is not that; it is injustice!' she said to herself, with vehemence. 'He *must* care; they are his subjects, his interests too. But he will not look at it dispassionately, because——'

So they fell out with each other a little, and the talk dragged. Yet, all the while, Marcella's inner mind was conscious of quite different thoughts. How good it was to be here, in this room, beside these two people! She must show herself fractious and difficult with Hallin sometimes; it was her nature. But in reality, that slight and fragile form, that spiritual presence were now shrined in the girl's eager reverence and affection. She felt towards him as many a Catholic has felt towards his director; though the hidden yearning to be led by him was often oddly covered, as now, by an outer self-assertion. Perhaps her quarrel with him was that he would not lead her enough—would not tell her precisely enough what she was to do with herself.

CHAPTER V

WHILE she and Hallin were sitting thus, momentarily out of tune with each other, the silence was suddenly broken by a familiar voice.

'I say, Hallin—is this all right?'

The words came from a young man who, having knocked unheeded, opened the door, and cautiously put in a curly head.

'Frank!—is that you? Come in,' cried Hallin, springing up.

Frank Leven came in, and at once perceived the lady sitting in the window.

'Well, I *am* glad!' he cried, striding across the room and shaking Hallin's hand by the way. 'Miss Boyce! I thought none of your friends were ever going to get a sight of you again! Why, what——'

He drew back, scanning her, a gay look of quizzing surprise on his fair boy's face.

'He expected me in cap and apron,' said Marcella, laughing; 'or means to pretend he did.'

'I expected a sensation! And here you are, just as you were, only twice as—— I say, Hallin, doesn't she look well!'—this in a stage aside to Hallin, while the speaker was drawing off his gloves, and still studying Marcella.

'Well, *I* think she looks tired,' said Hallin, with a little attempt
at a smile, but turning away. Everybody felt a certain tension,
a certain danger, even in the simplest words, and Miss Hallin's
call to supper was very welcome.

The frugal meal went gaily. The chattering Christchurch boy
brought to it a breath of happy careless life, to which the three
others—overdriven and overpressed, all of them—responded with
a kind of eagerness. Hallin especially delighted in him, and
would have out all his budget—his peacock's pride at having been
just put into the 'Varsity eleven, his cricket engagements for the
summer, his rows with his dons, above all his lasting amazement
that he should have just scraped through his Mods.

'I thought those Roman emperors would have done for me !'
he declared, with a child's complacency. '*Brutes* ! I couldn't
remember them. I learnt them up and down, backwards and
forwards—but it was no good ; they nearly dished me !'

'Yet it comes back to me,' said Hallin slyly, 'that when a
certain person was once asked to name the winner of the Derby
in some obscure year, he began at the beginning, and gave us all
of them, from first to last, without a hitch.'

'The winner of the *Derby* !' said the lad eagerly, bending forward with his hands on his knees ; 'why I should rather think so !
That isn't memory ; that's *knowledge* !—Goodness ! who's this ?'

The last remark was addressed *sotto voce* to Marcella. Supper
was just over, and the two guests, with Hallin, had returned to
the window, while Miss Hallin, stoutly refusing their help, herself
cleared the table and set all straight.

Hallin, hearing a knock, had gone to the door while Leven
was speaking. Four men came crowding in, all of them apparently
well known both to Hallin and his sister. The last two seemed
to be workmen ; the others were Bennett, Hallin's old and tried
friend among the Labour leaders, and Nehemiah Wilkins, M.P.
Hallin introduced them all to Marcella and Leven ; but the new-
comers took little notice of anyone but their host, and were soon
seated about him discussing a matter already apparently familiar
to them, and into which Hallin had thrown himself at once with
that passionate directness which, in the social and speculative
field, replaced his ordinary gentleness of manner. He seemed to
be in strong disagreement with the rest—a disagreement which
troubled himself and irritated them.

Marcella watched them with quick curiosity from the window
where she was sitting, and would have liked to go forward to
listen. But Frank Leven turned suddenly round upon her with
sparkling eyes.

'Oh, I say! don't go. Do come and sit here with me a bit. Oh, isn't it rum! isn't it *rum*! Look at Hallin,—those are the people whom he *cares* to talk to. That's a shoemaker, that man to the left—really an awfully cute fellow ; and this man in front, I think he told me he was a mason, a Socialist of course—would like to string *me* up to-morrow. Did you ever see such a countenance? Whenever that man begins, I think we must be precious near to shooting. And he's pious too, would pray over us first and shoot us afterwards—which isn't the case I understand with many of 'em. Then the others—you know them? That's Bennett —regular good fellow—always telling his pals not to make fools of themselves—for which of course they love him no more than they are obliged.—And Wilkins—oh! *Wilkins'*—he chuckled— 'they say it'll come to a beautiful row in the House before they've done, between him and my charming cousin, Harry Wharton. My father says he backs Wilkins.'

Then suddenly the lad recollected himself and his clear cheek coloured a little after a hasty glance at his companion. He fell to silence and looking at his boots. Marcella wondered what was the matter with him. Since her flight from Mellor she had lived, so to speak, with her head in the sand. She herself had never talked directly of her own affairs to anybody. Her sensitive pride did not let her realise that, notwithstanding, all the world was aware of them.

'I don't suppose you know much about your cousin!' she said to him with a little scorn.

'Well, I don't want to!' said the lad, 'that's one comfort! But I don't know anything about anything!—Miss Boyce!'

He plunged his head in his hands, and Marcella, looking at him, saw at once that she was meant to understand she had woe and lamentation beside her.

Her black eyes danced with laughter. At Mellor she had been several times his confidante. The handsome lad was not apparently very fond of his sisters and had taken to her from the beginning. To-night she recognised the old symptoms.

'What, you have been getting into scrapes again?' she said. 'How many since we met last?'

'There! you make fun of it!' he said indignantly from behind his fingers. 'You're like all the rest.'

Marcella teased him a little more till at last she was astonished by a flash of genuine wrath from the hastily uncovered eyes.

'If you're only going to chaff a fellow let's go over there and talk! And yet I did want to tell you about it—you were awfully kind to me down at home. I want to tell you—and I don't want to tell you— perhaps I *oughtn't* to tell you—you'll think me a brute, I dare say, an ungentlemanly brute for speaking of it at all—and yet somehow——'

The boy, crimson, bit his lips. Marcella, arrested and puzzled, laid a hand on his arm. She had been used to these motherly ways with him at Mellor, on the strength of her seniority, so inadequately measured by its two years or so of time !

' I won't laugh,' she said ; ' tell me.'

' No—really ?—shall I ?'

Whereupon there burst forth a history precisely similar it seemed to some half-dozen others she had already heard from the same lips. A pretty girl—or rather ' an *ex*quisite creature !' met at the house of some relation in Scotland, met again at the ' Boats' at Oxford, and yet again at Commemoration balls, Nuneham picnics, and the rest ; adored and adorable ; yet, of course, a sphinx born for the torment of men, taking her haughty way over a prostrate sex, kind to-day, cruel to-morrow ; not to be won by money, yet, naturally, not to be won without it ; possessed like Rose Aylmer of ' every virtue, every grace,' whether of form or family ; yet making nothing but a devastating and death-dealing use of them—how familiar it all was !—and how many more of them there seemed to be in the world, on a man's reckoning, than on a woman's !

And you know,' said the lad eagerly, ' though she's so *frightfully* pretty— well, frightfully fetching, rather—and well dressed and all the rest of it, she isn't a bit silly, not one of your emptyheaded girls—not she. She's read a *lot* of things—a lot ! I'm sure, Miss Boyce,' he looked at her confidently, ' if *you* were to see her you'd think her awfully clever. And yet she's so little—and so dainty—and she dances—my goodness ! you should see her dance, skirt-dance I mean—Letty Lind isn't in it ! She's good too, awfully good. I think her mother's a most dreadful old bore —well, no, I didn't mean that—of course I didn't mean that !— but she's fussy, you know, and invalidy, and has to be wrapped up in shawls, and dragged about in bath chairs, and Betty's an angel to her—she is really—though her mother's always snapping her head off. And as to the *poor*——'

Something in his tone, in the way he had of fishing for her approval, sent Marcella into a sudden fit of laughter. Then she put out a hand to restrain this plunging lover.

' Look here—do come to the point—have you proposed to her ?'

' I should rather think I have !' said the boy fervently. 'About once a week since Christmas. Of course she's played with me—that sort always does—but I think I might really have a chance with her, if it weren't for her mother—horrible old—no, of *course* I don't mean that! But now it comes in—what I oughtn't to tell you—I *know* I oughtn't to tell you! I'm always making a beastly mess of it. It's because I can't help talking of it!'

And shaking his curly head in despair, he once more plunged his red cheeks into his hands and fell abruptly silent.

Marcella coloured for sympathy. 'I really wish you wouldn't talk in riddles,' she said. 'What *is* the matter with you?—of course you must tell me.'

'Well, I know you won't mind!' cried the lad, emerging. 'As if you could mind! But it sounds like my impudence somehow to be talking to you about—about—— You see,' he blurted out, 'she going to Italy with the Raeburns. She's a connection of theirs, somehow, and Miss Raeburn's taken a fancy to her lately—and her mother's treated me like dirt ever since they asked her to go to Italy—and naturally a fellow sees what *that* means—and what her mother's after. I don't believe Betty *would*; he's too old for her, isn't he? Oh my goodness!'—this time he smote his knee in real desperation—'now I *have* done it. I'm simply *bursting* always with the thing I'd rather cut my head off than say. Why they make 'em like me I don't know!'

'You mean,' said Marcella with impatience—'that her mother wants her to marry Mr. Raeburn?'

He looked round at his companion. She was lying back in a deep chair, her hands lightly clasped on her knee. Something in her attitude, in the pose of the tragic head, in the expression of the face stamped to-night with a fatigue which was also a dignity, struck a real compunction into his mood of vanity and excitement. He had simply not been able to resist the temptation to talk to her. She reminded him of the Raeburns, and the Raeburns were in his mind at the present moment by day and by night. He knew that he was probably doing an indelicate and indiscreet thing, but all the same his boyish egotism would not be restrained from the headlong pursuit of his own emotions. There was in him too such a burning curiosity as to how she would take it—what she would say.

Now however he felt a genuine shrinking. His look changed. Drawing his chair close up to her, he began a series of penitent and self-contradictory excuses which Marcella soon broke in upon.

'I don't know why you talk like that,' she said, looking at him steadily. 'Do you suppose I can go on all my life without hearing Mr. Raeburn's name mentioned? And don't apologise so much!

It really doesn't matter what I suppose—that *you* think—about my present state of mind. It is very simple. I ought never to have accepted Mr. Raeburn. I behaved badly. I know it—and everybody knows it. Still one has to go on living one's life somehow. The point is that I am rather the wrong person for you to come to just now, for if there is one thing I ardently wish about Mr. Raeburn, it is that he should get himself married.'

Frank Leven looked at her in bewildered dismay.

' I never thought of that,' he said.

' Well, you might, mightn't you ?'

For another short space there was silence between them, while the rush of talk in the centre of the room was still loud and unspent.

Then she rated herself for want of sympathy. Frank sat beside her shy and uncomfortable, his confidence chilled away.

' So you think Miss Raeburn has views ?' she asked him, smiling, and in her most ordinary voice.

The boy's eye brightened again with the implied permission to go on chattering.

' I know she has ! Betty's brother as good as told me that she and Mrs. Macdonald—that's Betty's mother—she hasn't got a father—had talked it over. And now Betty's going with them to Italy, and Aldous is going too for ten days—and when I go to the Macdonalds Mrs. Macdonald treats me as if I were a little chap in jackets, and Betty worries me to death. It's sickening !'

' And how about Mr. Raeburn ?'

' Oh, Aldous seems to like her very much,' he said despondently. ' She's always teasing and amusing him. When she's there she never lets him alone. She harries him out. She makes him read to her and ride with her. She makes him discuss all sorts of things with her you'd *never* think Aldous would discuss—her lovers and her love affairs, and being in love !—it's extraordinary the way she drives him round. At Easter she and her mother were staying at the Court, and one night Betty told me she was bored to death. It was a very smart party, but everything was so flat and everybody was so dull. So she suddenly got up and ran across to Aldous. " Now look here, Mr. Aldous," she said ; " this'll never do ! you've got to come and dance with me, and *push* those chairs and tables aside "—I can fancy the little stamp she'd give—" and make those other people dance too." And she made him—she positively made him. Aldous declared he didn't dance, and she wouldn't have a word of it. And presently she got to all her tricks, skirt-dancing and the rest of it—and of course the evening went like smoke.'

Marcella's eyes, unusually wide open, were somewhat intently fixed on the speaker.

'And Mr. Raeburn liked it?' she asked in a tone that sounded incredulous.

'Didn't he just? She told me they got regular close friends after that, and he told her everything—oh, well,' said the lad embarrassed, and clutching at his usual formula—'of course I didn't mean that. And she's fearfully flattered, you can see she is, and she tells me that she adores him—that he's the only great man she's ever known—that I'm not fit to black his boots, and ought to be grateful whenever he speaks to me—and all that sort of rot. And now she's going off with them. I shall have to shoot myself —I declare I shall!'

'Well, not yet,' said Marcella in a soothing voice; 'the case isn't clear enough. Wait till they come back. Shall we move? I'm going over there to listen to that talk. But—first—come and see me whenever you like—3 to 4.30, Brown's Buildings, Maine Street—and tell me how this goes on.'

She spoke with a careless lightness, laughing at him with a half sisterly freedom. She had risen from her seat, and he, whose thoughts had been wrapped up for months in one of the smallest of the sex, was suddenly struck with her height and stately gesture as she moved away from him.

'By Jove! Why didn't she stick to Aldous?' he said to himself discontentedly as his eyes followed her. 'It was only her cranks, and of course she'll get rid of *them*. Just like my luck!'

Meanwhile Marcella took a seat next to Miss Hallin, who looked up from her knitting to smile at her. The girl fell into the attitude of listening; but for some minutes she was not listening at all. She was reflecting how little men knew of each other!—even the most intimate friends—and trying to imagine what Aldous Raeburn would be like, married to such a charmer as Frank had sketched. His friendship for her meant, of course, the attraction of contraries —one of the most promising of all possible beginnings. On the whole, she thought Frank's chances were poor.

Then, unexpectedly, her ear was caught by Wharton's name, and she discovered that what was going on beside her was a passionate discussion of his present position and prospects in the Labour party—a discussion, however, mainly confined to Wilkins and the two workmen. Bennett had the air of the shrewd and kindly spectator who has his own reasons for treating a situation with reserve; and Hallin was lying back in his chair flushed and worn out. The previous debate, which had now merged in these questions of men and personalities, had made him miserable; he had no heart for anything more. Miss Hallin observed him anxiously, and made restless movements now and then, as though she had it in her mind to send all her guests away.

The two Socialist workmen were talking strongly in favour of an organised and distinct Labour party, and of Wharton's leadership. They referred constantly to Parnell, and what he had done for 'those Irish fellows.' The only way to make Labour formidable in the House was to learn the lesson of Unionism and of Parnellism, to act together and strike together, to make of the party a 'two-handed engine,' ready to smite Tory and Liberal impartially. To this end a separate organisation, separate place in the House, separate Whips—they were ready, nay clamorous, for them all. And they were equally determined on Harry Wharton as a leader. They spoke of the *Clarion* with enthusiasm, and declared that its owner was already an independent power, and was, moreover, as 'straight' as he was sharp.

The contention and the praise lashed Wilkins into fury. After making one or two visible efforts at a sarcastic self-control which came to nothing, he broke out into a flood of invective which left the rest of the room staring. Marcella found herself indignantly wondering who this big man, with his fierce eyes, long, puffy cheeks, coarse black hair, and north-country accent, might be. Why did he talk in this way, with these epithets, this venom? It was intolerable !

Hallin roused himself from his fatigue to play the peace-maker. But some of the things Wilkins had been saying had roused the wrath of the two workmen, and the talk flamed up unmanageably —Wilkins's dialect getting more pronounced with each step of the argument.

'Well, if I'd ever ha' thowt that I war coomin to Lunnon to put myself and my party oonder the heel o' Muster Harry Wharton, I'd ha' stayed at *home*, I tell tha,' cried Wilkins, slapping his knee. ' If it's to be the People's party, why, in the name o' God, must yo put a yoong ripstitch like yon at the head of it ? a man who'll just mak *use* of us all, you and me, an' ivery man Jack of us, for his own advancement, an' ull kick us down when he's done with us ! Why shouldn't he ? What is he ? Is he a man of *us*—bone of our bone ? He's a *landlord*, and an aristocrat, I tell tha ! What have the likes of him ever been but thorns in our side ? When have the landlords ever gone with the people? Have they not been the blight and the curse of the country for hun'erds of years ? And you're goin to tell me that a man bred out o' *them*—living on his rent and interest—grinding the faces of the poor, I'll be bound, if the truth were known, as all the rest of them do—is goin to lead *me*, an' those as'll act with me to the pullin down of the landlords ! Why are we to go lickspittlin to any man of his sort to do our work for us? Let him go to his own class—I'm told Mr. Wharton is mighty fond of countesses, and they of him!—or let him set up as the friend of the working man just as he likes—I'm quite agreeable !— I shan't make any bones about takin his *vote*; but I'm not goin to make him master over me, and give him the right to speak for my mates in the House of Commons. I'd cut my hand off fust !'

Leven grinned in the background. Bennett lay back in his chair with a worried look. Wilkins's crudities were very distasteful to him both in and out of the House. The younger of the Socialist workmen, a mason, with a strong square face, incongruously lit somehow with the eyes of the religious dreamer, looked at Wilkins contemptuously.

'There's none of you in the House will take orders,' he said quickly, 'and that's the ruin of us. We all know that. Where do you think we'd have been in the struggle with the employers, if we'd gone about our business as you're going about yours in the House of Commons?'

'I'm not sayin we shouldn't *organise*,' said Wilkins fiercely. 'What I'm sayin is, get a man of the working class—a man who has the *wants* of the working class—a man whom the working class can get a hold on—to do your business for you, and not any bloodsucking landlord or capitalist. It's a slap i' the face to ivery honest working man i' the coontry, to mak a Labour party and put Harry Wharton at t' head of it !'

The young Socialist looked at him askance. 'Of course you'd like it yourself !' was what he was thinking. 'But they'll take a man as can hold his own with the swells—and quite right too !'

'And if Mr. Wharton *is* a landlord he's a good sort !' exclaimed the shoemaker—a tall, lean man in a well-brushed frock coat. 'There's many on us knows as have been to hear him speak, what he's tried to do about the land, and the co-operative farming. E's *straight* is Mr. Wharton. We 'aven't got Socialism yet—an' it isn't 'is fault bein a landlord. Ee was born it.'

'I tell tha he's playin for his own hand !' said Wilkins doggedly, the red spot deepening on his swarthy cheek—'he's runnin that paper for his own hand—haven't I had experience of him? I know it— And I'll prove it some day ! He's one for featherin his own nest is Mr. Wharton—and when he's doon it by makkin fools of us, he'll leave us to whistle for any good we're iver likely to get out o' *him*. *He* go agen the landlords when it coom to the real toossle,—I know 'em—I tell tha—I know 'em !'

A woman's voice, clear and scornful, broke into the talk.

'It's a little strange to think, isn't it, that while we in London go on groaning and moaning about insanitary houses, and making our small attempts here and there, half of the country poor of England have been re-housed in our generation by these same landlords—no fuss about it—and rents for five-roomed cottages somewhere about one and fourpence a week!'

Hallin swung his chair round and looked at the speaker—amazed!

Wilkins also stared at her under his eyebrows. He did not like women—least of all, ladies.

He gruffly replied that if they had done anything like as much as she said—which, he begged her pardon, but he didn't believe--it was done for the landlords' own purposes, either to buy off public opinion, or just for show and aggrandisement. People who had prize pigs and prize cattle must have prize cottages of course—'with a race of slaves inside 'em!'

Marcella, bright-eyed, erect, her thin right hand hanging over her knee, went avengingly into facts—the difference between landlords' villages and 'open' villages; the agrarian experiments made by different great landlords; the advantage to the community, even from the Socialist point of view, of a system which had preserved the land in great blocks, for the ultimate use of the State, as compared with a system like the French, which had for ever made Socialism impossible.

Hallin's astonishment almost swept away his weariness.

'Where in the world did she get it all from, and is she standing on her head, or am I?'

After an animated little debate, in which Bennett and the two workmen joined, while Wilkins sat for the most part in moody, contemptuous silence, and Marcella, her obstinacy roused, carried through her defence of the landlords with all a woman's love of emphasis and paradox, everybody rose simultaneously to say goodnight.

'You ought to come and lead a debate down at our Limehouse club,' said Bennett pleasantly to Marcella, as she held out her hand to him; 'you'd take a lot of beating.'

'Yet I'm a Venturist, you know,' she said laughing; '*I am*.'

He shook his head, laughed too, and departed.

When the four had gone, Marcella turned upon Hallin.

'Are there many of these Labour members like *that*?'

Her tone was still vibrating and sarcastic.

'He's not much of a talker, our Nehemiah,' said Hallin smiling; 'but he has the most extraordinary power as a speaker over a large popular audience that I have ever seen. The man's honesty is amazing—it's his tempers and his jealousies get in his way. You astonished him ; but, for the matter of that, you astonished Frank and me still more !'

And as he fell back into his chair, Marcella caught a flash of expression, a tone that somehow put her on her defence.

' I was not going to listen to such unjust stuff without a word. Politics is one thing—slanderous abuse is another !' she said, throwing back her head with a gesture which instantly brought back to Hallin the scene in the Mellor drawing-room, when she had denounced the game-laws and Wharton had scored his first point.

He was silent, feeling a certain inner exasperation with women and their ways.

' " She only did it to annoy," ' cried Frank Leven ; ' " because she knows it teases." *We* know very well what she thinks of us. But where did you get it all from, Miss Boyce ? I just wish you'd tell me. There's a horrid Radical in the House I'm always having rows with—and upon my word I didn't know there was half so much to be said for us !'

Marcella flushed.

' Never mind where I got it !' she said.

In reality, of course, it was from those Agricultural Reports she had worked through the year before under Wharton's teaching, with so much angry zest, and to such different purpose.

When the door closed upon her and upon Frank Leven, who was to escort her home, Hallin walked quickly over to the table, and stood looking for a moment in a sort of bitter reverie at Raeburn's photograph.

His sister followed him, and laid her hand on his shoulder.

' Do go to bed, Edward ! I am afraid that talk has tired you dreadfully.'

' It would be no good going to bed, dear,' he said, with a sigh of exhaustion. ' I will sit and read a bit, and see if I can get myself into sleeping trim. But you go, Susy—good-night.'

When she had gone he threw himself into his chair again with the thought—' She must contradict here as she contradicted there ! *She*—and justice ! If she could have been just to a landlord for one hour last year——'

He spent himself for a while in endless chains of recollection, oppressed by the clearness of his own brain, and thirsting for sleep. Then from the affairs of Raeburn and Marcella, he passed with a fresh sense of strain and effort to his own. That discussion with those four men which had filled the first part of the evening weighed upon him in his weakness of nerve, so that suddenly in the phantom silence of the night, all life became an oppression and a terror, and rest, either to-night or in the future, a thing never to be his.

He had come to the moment of difficulty, of tragedy, in a career which so far, in spite of all drawbacks of physical health and cramped activities, had been one of singular happiness and success. Ever since he had discovered his own gifts as a lecturer to working men, content, cheerfulness, nay, a passionate interest in every hour, had been quite compatible for him with all the permanent limitations of his lot. The study of economical and historical questions; the expression through them of such a hunger for the building of a 'city of God' among men, as few are capable of; the evidence not to be ignored even by his modesty, and perpetually forthcoming over a long period of time, that he had the power to be loved, the power to lead, among those toilers of the world on whom all his thoughts centred—these things had been his joy, and had led him easily through much self-denial to the careful husbanding of every hour of strength and time in the service of his ideal end.

And now he had come upon opposition—the first cooling of friendships, the first distrust of friends, that he had ever known.

Early in the spring of this year a book called *To-morrow and the Land* had appeared in London, written by a young London economist of great ability, and dealing with the nationalisation of the land. It did not offer much discussion of the general question, but it took up the question as it affected England specially and London in particular. It showed—or tried to show—in picturesque detail what might be the consequences for English rural or municipal life of throwing all land into a common or national stock, of expropriating the landlords, and transferring all rent to the people, to the effacement of taxation and the indefinite enrichment of the common lot. The book differed from *Progress and Poverty*, which also powerfully and directly affected the English working class, in that it suggested a financial scheme, of great apparent simplicity and ingenuity, for the compensation of the landlords; it was shorter, and more easily to be grasped by the average working man; and it was written in a singularly crisp and taking style, and—by the help of a number of telling illustrations borrowed directly from the circumstances of the larger English towns, especially of London— treated with abundant humour.

The thing had an enormous success—in popular phrase, 'caught on.' Soon Hallin found that all the more active and intelligent spirits in the working-class centres where he was in vogue as a lecturer were touched—nay, possessed—by it. The crowd of more or less socialistic newspapers which had lately sprung up in

London were full of it ; the working men's clubs rang with it. It
seemed to him a madness—and infection ; and it spread like one.
The book had soon reached an immense sale, and was in everyone's hands.

To Hallin, a popular teacher, interested above all in the
mingled problems of ethics and economics, such an incident was
naturally of extreme importance. But he was himself opposed by
deepest conviction, intellectual and moral, to the book and its conclusions. The more its success grew, the more eager and passionate became his own desire to battle with it. His platform, of
course, was secured to him ; his openings many. Hundreds and
thousands of men all over England were keen to know what he
had to say about the new phenomenon.

And he had been saying his say—throwing into it all his energies, all his finest work. With the result that—for the first time
in eleven years—he felt his position in the working-class movement giving beneath his feet, and his influence beginning to drop
from his hand. Coldness in place of enthusiasm ; critical aloofness in place of affection ; readiness to forget and omit him in
matters where he had always hitherto belonged to the inner circle
and the trusted few—these bitter ghosts, with their hard, unfamiliar
looks, had risen of late in his world of idealist effort and joy, and
had brought with them darkness and chill. He could not give
way, for he had a singular unity of soul—it had been the source of
his power—and every economical or social conviction was in some
way bound up with the moral and religious passion which was his
being—his inmost nature. And his sensitive state of nerve and
brain, his anchorite's way of life, did not allow him the distractions
of other men. The spread of these and other similar ideas seemed
to him a question of the future of England ; and he had already
begun to throw himself into the unequal struggle with a martyr's
tenacity, and with some prescience of the martyr's fate.

Even Bennett ! As he sat there alone in the dim lamp-light,
his head bent over his knees, his hands hanging loosely before him,
he thought bitterly of the defection of that old friend who had
stood by him through so many lesser contests. It was *impossible*
that Bennett should think the schemes of that book feasible ! Yet
he was one of the honestest of men, and, within a certain range,
one of the most clear-headed. As for the others, they had been all
against him. Intellectually, their opinion did not matter to him ;
but morally it was so strange to him to find himself on the side of
doubt and dissent, while all his friends were talking language
which was almost the language of a new faith !

He had various lecturing engagements ahead, connected with

this great debate which was now surging throughout the Labour world of London. He had accepted them with eagerness; in these weary night hours he looked forward to them with terror, seeing before him perpetually thousands of hostile faces, living in a nightmare of lost sympathies and broken friendships. Oh, for *sleep*—for the power to rest—to escape this corrosion of an ever active thought, which settled and reconciled nothing !

' *The tragedy of life lies in the conflict between the creative will of man and the hidden wisdom of the world, which seems to thwart it.*' These words, written by one whose thought had penetrated deep into his own, rang in his ears as he sat brooding there. Not the hidden fate, or the hidden evil, but the hidden *wisdom*. Could one die and still believe it? Yet what else was the task of faith ?

CHAPTER VI

' So I understand you wish me to go down at once?' said Louis Craven. ' This is Friday—say Monday ? '

Wharton nodded. He and Craven were sitting in Marcella's little sitting-room. Their hostess and Edith Craven had escaped through the door in the back kitchen communicating with the Hurds' tenement, so that the two men might be left alone a while. The interview between them had gone smoothly, and Louis Craven had accepted immediate employment on the *Labour Clarion*, as the paper's correspondent in the Midlands, with special reference to the important strike just pending. Wharton, whose tendency in matters of business was always to go rather farther than he had meant to go, for the sake generally of making an impression on the man with whom he was dealing, had spoken of a two years' engagement, and had offered two hundred a year. So far as that went, Craven was abundantly satisfied.

' And I understand from you,' he said, ' that the paper *goes in* for the strike, that you will fight it through?'

He fixed his penetrating greenish eyes on his companion. Louis Craven was now a tall man with narrow shoulders, a fine oval head and face, delicate features, and a nervous look of short sight, producing in appearance and manner a general impression of thin grace and of a courtesy which was apt to pass unaccountably into sarcasm. Wharton had never felt himself personally at ease with him, either now, or in the old days of Venturist debates.

'Certainly, we shall fight it through,' Wharton replied, with emphasis—' I have gone through the secretary's statement, which I now hand over to you, and I never saw a clearer case. The poor wretches have been skinned too long; it is high time the public backed them up. There are two of the masters in the House. Denny, I should say, belonged quite to the worst type of employer going.'

He spoke with light venom, buttoning his coat as he spoke with the air of the busy public man who must not linger over an appointment.

'Oh! Denny!' said Craven musing; 'yes, Denny is a hard man, but a just one according to his lights. There are plenty worse than he.'

Wharton was disagreeably reminded of the Venturist habit of never accepting anything that was said quite as it stood—of not, even in small things, 'swearing to the words' of anybody. He was conscious of the quick passing feeling that his judgment, with regard to Denny, ought to have been enough for Craven.

'One thing more,' said Craven suddenly, as Wharton looked for his stick—'you see there is talk of arbitration.'

'Oh yes, I know!' said Wharton impatiently; 'a mere blind. The men have been done by it twice before. They get some big-wig from the neighbourhood—not in the trade, indeed, but next door to it—and, of course, the award goes against the men.'

'Then the paper will not back arbitration?'

Craven took out a note-book.

'No!—The quarrel itself is as plain as a pike-staff. The men are asking for a mere pittance, and must get it if they are to live. It's like all these home industries, abominably ground down. We must go for them! I mean to go for them hot and strong. Poor devils! did you read the evidence in that Blue-book last year? Arbitration? no, indeed! let them live first!'

Craven looked up absently.

'And I think,' he said, 'you gave me Mr. Thorpe's address?' Mr. Thorpe was the secretary.

Again Wharton gulped down his annoyance. If he chose to be expansive, it was not for Craven to take no notice.

Craven, however, except in print, where he could be as vehement as anybody else, never spoke but in the driest way of those work-man's grievances, which in reality burnt at the man's heart. A deep disdain for what had always seemed to him the cheapest form of self-advertisement, held him back. It was this dryness, com-bined with an amazing disinterestedness, which had so far stood in his way.

Wharton repeated the address, following it up by some rather curt directions as to the length and date of articles, to which Craven gave the minutest attention.

'May we come in?' said Marcella's voice.

'By all means,' said Wharton, with a complete change of tone. 'Business is up and I am off!'

He took up his hat as he spoke.

'Not at all! Tea is just coming, without which no guest departs,' said Marcella, taking as she spoke a little tray from the red-haired Daisy who followed her, and motioning to the child to bring the tea-table.

Wharton looked at her irresolute. He had spent half an hour with her tête-à-tête before Louis Craven arrived, and he was really due at the House. But now that she was on the scene again, he did not find it so easy to go away. How astonishingly beautiful she was, even in this disguise! She wore her nurse's dress; for her second daily round began at half-past four, and her cloak, bonnet, and bag were lying ready on a chair beside her. The dress was plain brown holland, with collar and armlets of white linen; but, to Wharton's eye, the dark Italian head and the long slenderness of form had never shown more finely. He hesitated and stayed.

'All well?' said Marcella, in a half whisper, as she passed Louis Craven on her way to get some cake.

He nodded and smiled, and she went back to the tea-table with an eye all gaiety, pleased with herself and everybody else.

The quarter of an hour that followed went agreeably enough. Wharton sat among the little group, far too clever to patronise a cat, let alone a Venturist, but none the less master and conscious master of the occasion because it suited him to take the airs of equality. Craven said little, but as he lounged in Marcella's long cane chair with his arms behind his head, his serene and hazy air showed him contented; and Marcella talked and laughed with the animation that belongs to one whose plots for improving the universe have at least temporarily succeeded. Or did it betray, perhaps, a woman's secret consciousness of some presence beside her, more troubling and magnetic to her than others?

'Well then, Friday,' said Wharton at last, when his time was more than spent. 'You must be there early, for there will be a crush. Miss Craven comes too? Excellent! I will tell the door-keeper to look out for you. Good-bye!—good-bye!'

And with a hasty shake of the hand to the Cravens, and one more keen glance, first at Marcella and then round the little workman's room in which they had been sitting, he went.

He had hardly departed before Anthony Craven, the lame elder brother, who must have passed him on the stairs, appeared.

'Well—any news?' he said, as Marcella found him a chair.

'All right!' said Louis, whose manner had entirely changed since Wharton had left the room. 'I am to go down on Monday to report the Damesley strike that is to be. A month's trial, and then a salary—two hundred a year. Oh ! it'll do.'

He fidgeted and looked away from his brother, as though trying to hide his pleasure. But in spite of him it transformed every line of the pinched and worn face.

'And you and Anna will walk to the Registry Office next week?' said Anthony, sourly, as he took his tea.

'It can't be next week,' said Edith Craven's quiet voice interposing. 'Anna's got to work out her shirt-making time. She only left the tailoresses and began this new business ten days ago. And she was to have a month at each.

Marcella's lifted eyebrows asked for explanations. She had not yet seen Louis's betrothed, but she was understood to be a character, and a better authority on many Labour questions than he.

Louis explained that Anna was exploring various sweated trades for the benefit of an East End newspaper. She had earned fourteen shillings her last week at tailoring, but the feat had exhausted her so much that he had been obliged to insist on two or three days' respite before moving on to shirts. Shirts were now brisk, and the hours appallingly long in this heat.

'It was on shirts they made acquaintance,' said Edith pensively. 'Louis was lodging on the second floor, she in the third floor back, and they used to pass on the stairs. One day she heard him imploring the little slavey to put some buttons on his shirts. The slavey tossed her head, and said she'd see about it. When he'd gone out, Anna came downstairs, calmly demanded his shirts, and, having the slavey under her thumb, got them, walked off with them, and mended them all. When Louis came home he discovered a neat heap reposing on his table. Of course he wept—whatever he may say. But next morning Miss Anna found her shoes outside her door, blacked as they had never been blacked before, with a note inside one of them. Affecting ! wasn't it ? Thenceforward, as long as they remained in those lodgings, Anna mended and Louis blacked. Naturally, Anthony and I drew our conclusions.'

Marcella laughed.

'You must bring her to see me,' she said to Louis.

'I will,' said Louis, with some perplexity; 'if I can get hold of her. But when she isn't stitching she's writing, or trying to set up Unions. She does the work of six. She'll earn nearly as much as I do when we're married. Oh! we shall swim!'

Anthony surveyed his radiant aspect—so unlike the gentle or satirical detachment which made his ordinary manner—with a darkening eye, as though annoyed by his effusion.

'Two hundred a year?' he said slowly; 'about what Mr. Harry Wharton spends on his clothes, I should think. The Labour men tell me he is superb in that line. And for the same sum that he spends on his clothes he is able to buy *you*, Louis, body and soul, and you seem inclined to be grateful.'

'Never mind,' said Louis recklessly. 'He didn't buy someone else—and I *am* grateful!'

'No; by Heaven, you shan't be!' said Anthony, with a fierce change of tone. '*You* the dependent of that charlatan! I don't know how I'm to put up with it. You know very well what I think of him, and of your becoming dependent on him.'

Marcella gave an angry start. Louis protested.

'Nonsense!' said Anthony doggedly; 'you'll have to bear it from me, I tell you—unless you muzzle me too with an Anna.'

'But I don't see why *I* should bear it,' said Marcella, turning upon him. 'I think you know that I owe Mr. Wharton a debt. Please remember it!'

Anthony looked at her an instant in silence. A question crossed his mind concerning her. Then he made her a little clumsy bow.

'I am dumb,' he said. 'My manners, you perceive, are what they always were.'

'What do you mean by such a remark?' cried Marcella, fuming. 'How can a man who has reached the position he has in so short a time—in so many different worlds—be disposed of by calling him an ugly name? It is more than unjust—it is absurd! Besides, what can you know of him?'

'You forget,' said Anthony, as he calmly helped himself to more bread and butter, 'that it is some three years since Master Harry Wharton joined the Venturists and began to be heard of at all. I watched his beginnings, and if I didn't know him well, my friends and Louis's did. And most of them—as he knows!—have pretty strong opinions by now about the man.'

'Come, come, Anthony!' said Louis, 'nobody expects a man of that type to be the pure-eyed patriot. But neither you nor I can deny that he has done some good service. Am I asked to take him to my bosom? Not at all! He proposes a job to me, and offers to pay me. I like the job, and mean to use him and his paper, both to earn some money that I want, and do a bit of decent work.'

' *You*—use Harry Wharton !' said the cripple, with a sarcasm that brought the colour to Louis's thin cheek and made Marcella angrier than before. She saw nothing in his attack on Wharton, except personal prejudice and ill-will. It was natural enough, that a man of Anthony Craven's type—poor, unsuccessful, and embittered—should dislike a popular victorious personality.

'Suppose we leave Mr. Wharton alone?' she said with emphasis, and Anthony making her a little proud gesture of submission, threw himself back in his chair, and was silent.

It had soon become evident to Marcella, upon the renewal of her friendship with the Cravens, that Anthony's temper towards all men, especially towards social reformers and politicians, had developed into a mere impotent bitterness. While Louis had renounced his art, and devoted himself to journalism, unpaid public work and starvation, that he might so throw himself the more directly into the Socialist battle, Anthony had remained an artist, mainly employed as before in decorative design. Yet he was probably the more fierce Venturist and anti-capitalist of the two. Only what with Louis was an intoxication of hope, was on the whole with Anthony a counsel of despair. He loathed wealth more passionately than ever ; but he believed less in the working-man, less in his kind. Rich men must cease to exist ; but the world on any terms would probably remain a sorry spot.

In the few talks that he had had with Marcella since she left the hospital, she had allowed him to gather more or less clearly— though with hardly a mention of Aldous Raeburn's name—what had happened to her at Mellor. Anthony Craven thought out the story for himself, finding it a fit food for a caustic temper. Poor devil—the lover ! To fall a victim to enthusiasms so raw, so unprofitable from any point of view, was hard. And as to this move to London, he thought he foresaw the certain end of it. At any rate he believed in her no more than before. But her beauty was more marked than ever, and would, of course, be the dominant factor in her fate. He was thankful, at any rate, that Louis in this two years' interval had finally transferred his heart elsewhere.

After watching his three companions for a while, he broke in upon their chat with an abrupt

'What *is* this job, Louis ?'

'I told you. I am to investigate, report, and back up the Damesley strike, or rather the strike that begins at Damesley next week.'

'No chance!' said Anthony shortly; 'the masters are too strong. I had a talk with Denny yesterday.'

The Denny he meant, however, was not Wharton's colleague in the House, but his son—a young man who, beginning life as the heir of one of the most stiff-backed and autocratic of capitalists, had developed Socialist opinions, renounced his father's allowance, and was now a member of the 'intellectual proletariat,' as they have been called, the free-lances of the Collectivist movement. He had lately joined the Venturists. Anthony had taken a fancy to him. Louis as yet knew little or nothing of him.

'Ah, well!' he said, in reply to his brother, 'I don't know. I think the *Clarion can* do something. The press grows more and more powerful in these things.'

And he repeated some of the statements that Wharton had made—that Wharton always did make, in talking of the *Clarion* —as to its growth under his hands, and increasing influence in Labour disputes.

'Bunkum!' interrupted Anthony drily; 'pure bunkum! My own belief is that the *Clarion* is a rotten property, and that he knows it!'

At this both Marcella and Louis laughed out. Extravagance after a certain point becomes amusing. They dropped their vexation, and Anthony for the next ten minutes had to submit to the part of the fractious person whom one humours but does not argue with. He accepted the part, saying little, his eager, feverish eyes, full of hostility, glancing from one to the other.

However, at the end, Marcella bade him a perfectly friendly farewell. It was always in her mind that Anthony Craven was lame and solitary, and her pity no less than her respect for him had long since yielded him the right to be rude.

'How are you getting on?' he said to her abruptly as he dropped her hand.

'Oh, very well! my superintendent leaves me almost alone now, which is a compliment. There is a parish doctor who calls me "my good woman," and a sanitary inspector who tells me to go to him whenever I want advice. Those are my chief grievances, I think.'

'And you are as much in love with the poor as ever?'

She stiffened at the note of sarcasm, and a retaliatory impulse made her say,—

'I see a great deal more happiness than I expected.'

He laughed.

'How like a woman! A few ill-housed villagers made you a democrat. A few well-paid London artisans will carry you safely back to your class. Your people were wise to let you take this work.'

'Do you suppose I nurse none but well-paid artisans?' she asked him, mocking. 'And I didn't say "money" or "comfort," did I? but "happiness." As for my "democracy," you are not perhaps the best judge.'

She stood resting both hands on a little table behind her, in an attitude touched with the wild freedom which best became her, a gleam of storm in her great eyes.

'Why are you still a Venturist?' he asked her abruptly.

'Because I have every right to be! I joined a society, pledged to work "for a better future." According to my lights, I do what poor work I can in that spirit.'

'You are not a Socialist. Half the things you say, or imply, show it. And we *are* Socialists.'

She hesitated, looking at him steadily.

'No!—so far as Socialism means a political system—the trampling out of private enterprise and competition, and all the rest of it—I find myself slipping away from it more and more. No!—as I go about among these wage-earners, the emphasis—do what I will—comes to lie less and less on possession—more and more on character. I go to two tenements in the same building. One is Hell—the other Heaven. Why? Both belong to well-paid artisans with equal opportunities. Both, so far as I can see, might have a decent and pleasant life of it. But one is a man; the other, with all his belongings, will soon be a vagabond. That is not all, I know—oh! don't trouble to tell me so!—but it is more than I thought. No!—my sympathies in this district where I work are not so much with the Socialists that I know here—saving your presence! but—with the people, for instance, that slave at Charity Organisation! and get all the abuse from all sides.'

Anthony laughed scornfully.

'It is always the way with a woman,' he said; 'she invariably prefers the tinkers to the reformers.'

'And as to your Socialism,' she went on, unheeding, the thought of many days finding defiant expression—'it seems to me like all other interesting and important things—destined to help something else! Christianity begins with the poor and division of goods—it becomes the great bulwark of property and the feudal state. The Crusades—they set out to recover the tomb of the Lord!—what they did was to increase trade and knowledge. And so with Socialism. It talks of a new order—what it *will* do is to help to make the old sound!'

Anthony clapped her ironically.

'Excellent! When the Liberty and Property Defence people have got hold of you—ask me to come and hear!'

Meanwhile Louis stood behind with his hands on his sides, a smile in his blinking eyes. He really had a contempt for what a handsome, half-taught girl of twenty-three might think. Anthony only pretended or desired to have it.

Nevertheless, Louis said good-bye to his hostess with real, and, for him, rare effusion. Two years before, for the space of some months, he had been in love with her. That she had never responded with anything warmer than liking and comradeship he knew; and his Anna now possessed him wholly. But there was a deep and gentle chivalry at the bottom of all his stern social faiths; and the woman towards whom he had once felt as he had towards Marcella Boyce could never lose the glamour lent her by that moment of passionate youth. And now, so kindly, so eagerly!— she had given him his Anna.

When they were all gone Marcella threw herself into her chair a moment to think. Her wrath with Anthony was soon dismissed. But Louis's thanks had filled her with delicious pleasure. Her cheek, her eye had a child's brightness. The old passion for ruling and influencing was all alive and happy.

'I will see it is all right,' she was saying to herself. 'I will look after them.'

What she meant was, 'I will see that Mr. Wharton looks after them!' and, through the link of thought, memory flew quickly back to that *tête-à-tête* with him which had preceded the Cravens' arrival.

How changed he was, yet how much the same! He had not sat beside her for ten minutes before each was once more vividly, specially conscious of the other. She felt in him the old life and daring, the old imperious claim to confidence, to intimacy—on the other hand a new atmosphere, a new gravity, which suggested growing responsibilities, the difficulties of power, a great position —everything fitted to touch such an imagination as Marcella's, which, whatever its faults, was noble, both in quality and range. The brow beneath the bright chestnut curls had gained lines that pleased her—lines that a woman marks, because she thinks they mean experience and mastery.

Altogether, to have met him again was pleasure, to think of him was pleasure; to look forward to hearing him speak in Parliament was pleasure; so too was his new connection with her old friends. And a pleasure which took nothing from self-respect; which was open, honourable, eager. As for that ugly folly of the past, she frowned at the thought of it, only to thrust the remembrance passionately away. That *he* should remember or allude to it, would put an end to friendship. Otherwise friends they would and should be; and the personal interest in his public career should lift her out of the cramping influences that flow from the perpetual commerce of poverty and suffering. Why not? Such equal friendships between men and women grow more possible every day. While, as for Hallin's distrust, and Anthony Craven's jealous hostility, why should a third person be bound by either of them? Could anyone suppose that such a temperament as Wharton's would be congenial to Hallin or to Craven—or—to yet another person, of whom she did not want to think? Besides, who wished to make a hero of him? It was the very complexity and puzzle of the character that made its force.

So, with a reddened cheek, she lost herself a few minutes in this pleasant sense of a new wealth in life; and was only roused from the dreamy running to and fro of thought by the appearance of Minta, who came to clear away the tea.

'Why, it is close on the half-hour!' cried Marcella, springing up. 'Where are my things?'

She looked down the notes of her cases, satisfied herself that her bag contained all she wanted, and then hastily tied on her bonnet and cloak.

Suddenly—the room was empty, for Minta had just gone away with the tea—by a kind of subtle reaction, the face in that photograph on Hallin's table flashed into her mind—its look—the grizzled hair. With an uncontrollable pang of pain she dropped her hands from the fastenings of her cloak, and wrung them together in front of her—a dumb gesture of contrition and of grief.

She!—she talk of social reform and 'character;' she give her opinion, as of right, on points of speculation and of ethics; she, whose main achievement so far had been to make a good man suffer! Something belittling and withering swept over all her estimate of herself, all her pleasant self-conceit. Quietly, with downcast eyes, she went her way.

CHAPTER VII

HER first case was in Brown's Buildings itself—a woman suffering from bronchitis and heart complaint, and tormented besides by an ulcerated foot which Marcella had now dressed daily for some weeks. She lived on the top floor of one of the easterly blocks, with two daughters and a son of eighteen.

When Marcella entered the little room it was as usual spotlessly clean and smelt of flowers. The windows were open, and a young woman was busy shirt-ironing on a table in the centre of the room. Both she and her mother looked up with smiles as Marcella entered. Then they introduced her with some ceremony to a ' lady,' who was sitting beside the patient, a long-faced melancholy woman employed at the moment in marking linen handkerchiefs, which she did with extraordinary fineness and delicacy. The patient and her daughter spoke of Marcella to their friend as ' the young person,' but all with a natural courtesy and charm that could not have been surpassed.

Marcella knelt to undo the wrappings of the foot. The woman, a pale transparent creature, winced painfully as the dressing was drawn off; but between each half-stifled moan of pain she said something eager and grateful to her nurse. ' I never knew anyone, Nurse, do it as gentle as you—' or—' I *do* take it kind of you, Nurse, to do it so *slow*—oh ! there were a young person before you—' or ' Hasn't she got nice hands, Mrs. Burton ? they don't never seem to *jar* yer.'

' Poor foot ! but I think it is looking better,' said Marcella, getting up at last from her work, when all was clean and comfortable and she had replaced the foot on the upturned wooden box that supported it—for its owner was not in bed, but sitting propped up in an old armchair. ' And how is your cough, Mrs. Jervis ? '

' Oh ! it's very bad, nights,' said Mrs. Jervis mildly—' disturbs Emily dreadful. But I always pray every night, when she lifts me into bed, as I may be took before the morning, an' God ull do it soon.'

' Mother ! ' cried Emily, pausing in her ironing, ' you know you oughtn't to say them things.'

Mrs. Jervis looked at her with a sly cheerfulness. Her emaciated face was paler than usual because of the pain of the dressing, but from the frail form there breathed an indomitable air of *life*, a gay courage indeed which had already struck Marcella with wonder.

' Well, yer not to take 'em to heart, Em'ly. It ull be when it will be—for the Lord likes us to pray, but He'll take his own time —an' she's got troubles enough of her own, Nurse. D'yer see as she's leff off her ring ? '

Marcella looked at Emily's left hand, while the girl flushed all over, and ironed with a more fiery energy than before.

' I've 'eerd such things of 'im, Nurse, this last two days,' she

said with low vehemence—'as I'm *never* goin to wear it again.
It ud burn me ! '

Emily was past twenty. Some eighteen months before this
date she had married a young painter. After nearly a year of incredible misery her baby was born. It died, and she very nearly
died also, owing to the brutal ill-treatment of her husband. As
soon as she could get on her feet again, she tottered home to her
widowed mother, broken for the time in mind and body, and filled
with loathing of her tyrant. He made no effort to recover her,
and her family set to work to mend if they could what he had
done. The younger sister of fourteen was earning seven shillings
a week at paper-bag making ; the brother, a lad of eighteen, had
been apprenticed by his mother, at the cost of heroic efforts some
six years before, to the leather-currying trade, in a highly skilled
branch of it, and was now taking sixteen shillings a week with the
prospect of far better things in the future. He at once put aside
from his earnings enough to teach Emily 'the shirt ironing,' denying
himself every indulgence till her training was over.

Then they had their reward. Emily's colour and spirits came
back ; her earnings made all the difference to the family between
penury and ease ; while she and her little sister kept the three tiny
rooms in which they lived, and waited on their invalid mother, with
exquisite cleanliness and care.

Marcella stood by the ironing-table a moment after the girl's
speech.

'Poor Emily !' she said softly, laying her hand on the ringless
one that held down the shirt on the board.

Emily looked up at her in silence. But the girl's eyes glowed
with things unsaid and inexpressible—the 'eternal passion, eternal
pain,' which in half the human race have no voice.

'He was a very rough man was Em'ly's husband,' said Mrs.
Jervis, in her delicate thoughtful voice—'a very uncultivated man.'

Marcella turned round to her, startled and amused by the
adjective. But the other two listeners took it quite quietly. It
seemed to them apparently to express what had to be said.

'It's a sad thing is want of edication,' Mrs. Jervis went on in
the same tone. 'Now there's that lady there'—with a little courtly
wave of her hand towards Mrs. Burton—'she can't read, yer know,
Nurse, an' I'm that sorry for her ! But I've been reading to her, an'
Emily—just while my cough's quiet—one of my ole tracks.'

She held up a little paper-covered tract worn with use. It was
called 'A Pennorth of Grace, or a Pound of Works?' Marcella
looked at it in respectful silence as she put on her cloak. Such
things were not in her line.

'I do *love* a track!' said Mrs. Jervis pensively. 'That's why I don't like these buildings so well as them others, Em'ly. Here you never get no tracks; and there, what with one person and another, there was a new one most weeks. But'—her voice dropped, and she looked timidly, first at her friend, and then at Marcella— 'she isn't a Christian, Nurse. Isn't it sad?'

Mrs. Burton, a woman of a rich mahogany complexion, with a black 'front,' and a mouth which turned down decisively at the corners, looked up from her embroidery with severe composure.

'No, Nurse, I'm not a Christian,' she said in the tone of one stating a disagreeable fact for which they are noways responsible. 'My brother is—and my sisters—real good Christian people. One of my sisters married a gentleman up in Wales. She 'as two servants, an' fam'ly prayers reg'lar. But I've never felt no "call," and I tell 'em I can't purtend. An' Mrs. Jervis here, she don't seem to make me see it no different.'

She held her head erect, however, as though the unusually high sense of probity involved was, after all, some consolation. Mrs. Jervis looked at her with pathetic eyes. But Emily coloured hotly. Emily was a churchwoman.

'Of course you're a Christian, Mrs. Burton,' she said indignantly. 'What she means, Nurse, is she isn't a "member" of any chapel, like mother. But she's been baptised and confirmed, for I asked her. And of course she's a Christian.'

'Em'ly!' said Mrs. Jervis, with energy.

Emily looked round trembling. The delicate invalid was sitting bolt upright, her eyes sparkling, a spot of red on either hollow cheek. The glances of the two women crossed; there seemed to be a mute struggle between them. Then Emily laid down her iron, stepped quickly across to her mother, and, kneeling beside her, threw her arms around her.

'Have it your own way, mother,' she said, while her lip quivered; 'I wasn't a-goin to cross you.'

Mrs. Jervis laid her waxen cheek against her daughter's tangle of brown hair with a faint smile, while her breathing, which had grown quick and panting, gradually subsided. Emily looked up at Marcella with a terrified self-reproach. They all knew that any sudden excitement might kill out the struggling flame of life.

'You ought to rest a little, Mrs. Jervis,' said Marcella, with gentle authority. 'You know the dressing must tire you, though you won't confess it. Let me put you comfortable. There; aren't the pillows easier so? Now rest—and good-bye.'

But Mrs. Jervis held her, while Emily slipped away.

'I shall rest soon,' she said significantly. 'An' it hurts me when Emily talks like that. It's the only thing that ever comes atween us. She thinks o' forms an' ceremonies; an' *I* think o' *grace*.'

Her old woman's eyes, so clear and vivid under the blanched brow, searched Marcella's face for sympathy. But Marcella stood shy and wondering in the presence of words and emotions she understood so little. So narrow a life, in these poor rooms, under these crippling conditions of disease !—and all this preoccupation with, this passion over, the things not of the flesh, the thwarted cabined flesh, but of the spirit—wonderful !

On coming out from Brown's Buildings she turned her steps reluctantly towards a street some distance from her own immediate neighbourhood, where she had a visit to pay which filled her with repulsion and an unusual sense of helplessness. A clergyman who often availed himself of the help of the St. Martin's nurses had asked the superintendent to undertake for him 'a difficult case.' Would one of their nurses go regularly to visit a certain house, ostensibly for the sake of a little boy of five just come back from hospital who required care at home for a while, *really* for the sake of his young mother, who had suddenly developed drinking habits and was on the road to ruin ?

Marcella happened to be in the office when the letter arrived. She somewhat unwillingly accepted the task, and she had now paid two or three visits, always dressing the child's sore leg, and endeavouring to make acquaintance with the mother. But in this last attempt she had not had much success. Mrs. Vincent was young and pretty, with a flighty restless manner. She was always perfectly civil to Marcella, and grateful to her apparently for the ease she gave the boy. But she offered no confidences ; the rooms she and her husband occupied showed them to be well-to-do ; Marcella had so far found them well-kept ; and though the evil she was sent to investigate was said to be notorious, she had as yet discovered nothing of it for herself. It seemed to her that either she must be stupid, or that there must be something about her which made Mrs. Vincent more secretive with her than with others ; and neither alternative pleased her.

To-day, however, as she stopped at the Vincents' door, she noticed that the doorstep, which was as a rule shining white, was muddy and neglected. Then nobody came to open, though she knocked and rang repeatedly. At last a neighbour, who had been watching the strange nurse through her own parlour window, came out to the street.

' I think, miss,' she said, with an air of polite mystery, ' as you'd better walk in.   Mrs. Vincent 'asn't been enjying very good 'ealth this last few days.'

Marcella turned the handle, found it yielded, and went in.   It was after six o'clock, and the evening sun streamed in through a door at the back of the house.   But in the Vincents' front parlour the blinds were all pulled down, and the only sound to be heard was the fretful wailing of a child.   Marcella timidly opened the sitting-room door.

The room at first seemed to her dark.   Then she perceived Mrs. Vincent sitting by the grate, and the two children on the floor beside her.   The elder, the little invalid, was simply staring at his mother in a wretched silence ; but the younger, the baby of three, was restlessly throwing himself hither and thither, now pulling at the woman's skirts, now crying lustily, now whining in a hungry voice, for ' Máma ! din-din !   Máma ! din-din ! '

Mrs. Vincent neither moved nor spoke, even when Marcella came in.   She sat with her hands hanging over her lap in a desolation incapable of words.   She was dirty and unkempt ; the room was covered with litter ; the breakfast things were still on the table ; and the children were evidently starving.

Marcella, seized with pity, and divining what had happened, tried to rouse and comfort her.   But she got no answer.   Then she asked for matches.   Mrs. Vincent made a mechanical effort to find them, but subsided helpless with a shake of the head.   At last Marcella found them herself, lit a fire of some sticks she discovered in a cupboard, and put on the kettle.   Then she cut a slice of bread and dripping for each of the children—the only eatables she could find—and after she had dressed Bertie's leg she began to wash up the tea things and tidy the room, not knowing very well what to be at, but hoping minute by minute to get Mrs. Vincent to speak to her.

In the midst of her labours, an elderly woman cautiously opened the door and beckoned to her.

Marcella went out into the passage.

' I'm her mother, miss !   I 'eered you were 'ere, an' I follered yer.   Oh ! such a business as we 'ad, 'er 'usband an' me, a gettin of 'er 'ome last night.   There's a neighbour come to me, an' she says : " Mrs. Lucas, there's your daughter a drinkin in that public 'ouse, an' if I was you I'd go and fetch her out ; for she's got a lot o' money, an' she's treatin everybody all round."   An' Charlie—that's 'er 'usband—ee come along too, an' between us we got holt on her.   An' iver sence we brought her 'ome last night, she set there in that cheer, an' niver a word to nobody !   Not to me 't any rate, nor the chillen.   I believe 'er 'usband an' 'er 'ad words this mornin. But she won't tell me nothin. She sits there—just heart-broke '—the woman put up her apron to her eyes and began crying. ' She ain't eaten nothink all day, and I dursen't leave the 'ouse out o' me sight—I lives close by, miss—for fear of 'er doing 'erself a mischief.'

' How long has she been like this ?' said Marcella, drawing the door cautiously to, behind her.

'About fourteen month,' said the woman hopelessly. 'An' none of us knows why. She was such a neat, pretty girl when she mar-ried 'im—an' ee such a steady fellow. An' I've done *my* best. I've talked to 'er, an' I've 'id 'er 'at an' her walking things, an' taken 'er money out of 'er pockets. An', bless yer, she's been all right now for seven weeks—till last night. Oh, deary, deary me ! whatever 'ull become o' them—'er, an' 'im, an' the children ! '

The tears coursed down the mother's wrinkled face.

' Leave her to me a little longer,' said Marcella softly ; 'but come back to me in about half an hour and don't let her be alone.'

The woman nodded, and went away.

Mrs. Vincent turned quickly round as Marcella came back again, and spoke for the first time :

' That was my mother you were talkin to ?'

'Yes,' said Marcella quietly, as she took the kettle off the fire. ' Now I do want you to have a cup of tea, Mrs. Vincent. Will you, if I make it ?'

The poor creature did not speak, but she followed Marcella's movements with her weary eyes. At last when Marcella knelt down beside her holding out a cup of tea and some bread and butter, she gave a sudden cry. Marcella hastily put down what she carried, lest it should be knocked out of her hand.

' He struck me this morning !—Charlie did—the first time in seven years. Look here ! '

She pulled up her sleeve, and on her white, delicate arm she showed a large bruise. As she pointed to it her eyes filled with miserable tears ; her lips quivered ; anguish breathed in every feature. Yet even in this abasement Marcella was struck once more with her slim prettiness, her refined air. This woman drink-ing and treating in a low public-house at midnight !—rescued thence by a decent husband !

She soothed her as best she could, but when she had succeeded in making the wretched soul take food, and so in putting some physical life into her, she found herself the recipient of an outburst of agony before which she quailed. The woman clung to her, moaning about her husband, about the demon instinct that had got hold of her, she hardly knew how—by means it seemed originally of a few weeks of low health and small self-indulgences—and she felt herself powerless to fight; about the wreck she had brought upon her home, the shame upon her husband, who was the respected, well-paid foreman of one of the large shops of the neighbourhood. All through it came back to him.

' We had words, Nurse, this morning, when he went out to his work. He said he'd nearly died of shame last night; that he couldn't bear it no more; that he'd take the children from me. And I was all queer in the head still, and I sauced him—and then —he looked like a devil—and he took me by the arm—and *threw* me down—as if I'd been a sack. An' he never, *never*—touched me—before—in all his life. An' he's never come in all day. An' perhaps I shan't ever see him again. An' last time—but it wasn't so bad as this—he said he'd try an' love me again if I'd behave. An' he did try—an' I tried too. But now it's no good, an' perhaps he'll not come back. Oh, what shall I do? what shall I do?' she flung her arms above her head. ' Won't *anybody* find him? won't *anybody* help me?'

She dropped a hand upon Marcella's arm, clutching it, her wild eyes seeking her companion's.

But at the same moment, with the very extremity of her own emotion, a cloud of impotence fell upon Marcella. She suddenly felt that she could do nothing—that there was nothing in her adequate to such an appeal—nothing strong enough to lift the weight of a human life thus flung upon her.

She was struck with a dryness, a numbness, that appalled her. She tried still to soothe and comfort, but nothing that she said went home—took hold. Between the feeling in her heart which might have reached and touched this despair, and the woman before her, there seemed to be a barrier she could not break. Or was it that she was really barren and poor in soul, and had never realised it before? A strange misery rose in her too, as she still knelt, tending and consoling, but with no efficacy—no power.

At last Mrs. Vincent sank into miserable quiet again. The mother came in, and silently began to put the children to bed. Marcella pressed the wife's cold hand, and went out hanging her head. She had just reached the door when it opened, and a man entered. A thrill passed through her at the sight of his honest, haggard face, and this time she found what to say.

' I have been sitting by your wife, Mr. Vincent. She is very ill and miserable, and very penitent. You will be kind to her?'

The husband looked at her, and then turned away.

' God help us !' he said; and Marcella went without another word, and with that same wild, unaccustomed impulse of prayer filling her being which had first stirred in her at Mellor at the awful moment of Hurd's death.

She was very silent and distracted at tea, and afterwards—saying that she must write some letters and reports—she shut herself up, and bade good-night to Minta and the children.

But she did not write or read. She hung at the window a long time, watching the stars come out, as the summer light died from the sky, and even the walls and roofs and chimneys of this interminable London spread out before her, took a certain dim beauty. And then, slipping down on the floor, with her head against a chair—an attitude of her stormy childhood—she wept with an abandonment and a passion she had not known for years. She thought of Mrs. Jervis—the saint—so near to death, so satisfied with 'grace,' so steeped in the heavenly life ; then of the poor sinner she had just left and of the agony she had no power to stay. Both experiences had this in common—that each had had some part in plunging her deeper into this darkness of self-contempt.

What had come to her? During the past weeks there had been something wrestling in her—some new birth—some 'conviction of sin,' as Mrs. Jervis would have said. As she looked back over all her strenuous youth she hated it. What was wrong with her? Her own word to Anthony Craven returned upon her, mocked her—made now a scourge for her own pride, not a mere measure of blame for others. Aldous Raeburn, her father and mother, her poor—one and all rose against her—plucked at her—reproached her. 'Ay ! what, indeed, are wealth and poverty?' cried a voice, which was the voice of them all ; 'what are opinions—what is influence, beauty, cleverness ?—what is anything worth but *character*—but *soul* ?'

And character—soul—can only be got by self-surrender ; and self-surrender comes not of knowledge but of love.

A number of thoughts and phrases, hitherto of little meaning to her, floated into her mind—sank and pressed there. That strange word 'grace' for instance !

A year ago it would not have smitten or troubled her. After her first inevitable reaction against the evangelical training of her school years, the rebellious cleverness of youth had easily decided that religion was played out, that Socialism and Science were enough for mankind.

But nobody could live in hospital—nobody could go among the poor—nobody could share the thoughts and hopes of people like Edward Hallin and his sister, without understanding that it is still here in the world—this 'grace' that 'sustaineth'—however variously interpreted, still living and working, as it worked of old, among the little Galilean towns, in Jerusalem, in Corinth.   To Edward Hallin it did not mean the same, perhaps, as it meant to the hard-worked clergymen she knew, or to Mrs. Jervis.   But to all it meant the motive power of life—something subduing, transforming, de-livering—something that to-night she envied with a passion and a yearning that amazed herself.

How many things she craved, as an eager child craves them ! First, some moral change, she knew not what—then Aldous Raeburn's pardon and friendship—then, and above all, the power to lose herself—the power to *love*.

Dangerous significant moment in a woman's life—moment at once of despair and of illusion !

CHAPTER VIII

WHARTON was sitting in a secluded corner of the library of the House of Commons.   He had a number of loose sheets of paper on a chair beside him, and others in his hand and on his knee. It was Friday afternoon ; questions were going on in the House ; and he was running rapidly for the last time through the notes of his speech, pencilling here and there, and every now and then taking up a volume of Hansard that lay near that he might verify a quotation.

An old county member, with a rugged face and eye-glasses, who had been in Parliament for a generation, came to the same corner to look up a speech.   He glanced curiously at Wharton, with whom he had a familiar House of Commons acquaintance.

' Nervous, eh ? ' he said, as he put on his eye-glasses to inspect first Wharton, then the dates on the backs of the Reports.

Wharton put his papers finally together, and gave a long stretch.

' Not particularly.'

' Well, it's a beastly audience ! ' said the other, carrying off his book.

Wharton, lost apparently in contemplation of the ceiling, fell into a dreamy attitude.   But his eye saw nothing of the ceiling, and was not at all dreamy.   He was not thinking of his speech, nor of the other man's remark.   He was thinking of Marcella Boyce.

When he left her the other day he had been conscious, only more vividly and intensely, more possessively as it were, than she,

of the same general impression that had been left upon her. A
new opening for pleasure—their meeting presented itself to him,
too, in the same way. What had he been about all this time?
Forget?—such a creature? Why, it was the merest wantonness !
As if such women—with such a brow, such vitality, such a gait—
passed in every street !

What possessed him now was an imperious eagerness to push
the matter, to recover the old intimacy—and as to what might
come out of it, let the Gods decide ! He could have had but a
very raw appreciation of her at Mellor. It seemed to him that
she had never forced him to think of her then in absence, as he
had thought of her since the last meeting.

As for the nursing business, and the settlement in Brown's
Buildings, it was, of course, mere play-acting. No doubt when
she emerged she would be all the more of a personage for having
done it. But she must emerge soon. To rule and shine was as
much her *métier* as it was the *métier* of a bricklayer's labourer to
carry hods. By George ! what would not Lady Selina give for
beauty of such degree and kind as that ! They must be brought
together. He already foresaw that the man who should launch
Marcella Boyce in London would play a stroke for himself as well
as for her. And she must be launched in London. Let other
people nurse, and pitch their tents in little workmen's flats, and
live democracy instead of preaching it. Her fate was fixed for her
by her physique. *Il ne faut pas sortir de son caractère.*

The sight of Bennett approaching distracted him.

Bennett's good face showed obvious vexation.

' He sticks to it,' he said, as Wharton jumped up to meet him.
' Talks of his conscience—and a lot of windy stuff. He seems to
have arranged it with the Whips. I dare say he won't do much
harm.'

' Except to himself,' said Wharton, with dry bitterness. ' Goodness ! let's leave him alone !'

He and Bennett lingered a few minutes discussing points of
tactics. Wilkins had, of course, once more declared himself the
enfant terrible of a party which, though still undefined, was drawing
nearer day by day to organised existence and separate leadership.
The effect of to-night's debate might be of far-reaching importance.
Wharton's Resolution, pledging the House to a Legal Eight Hours
Day for all trades, came at the end of a long and varied agitation,
was at the moment in clear practical relation to labour movements
all over the country, and had in fact gained greatly in significance
and interest since it was first heard of in public, owing to events of
current history. Workable proposals—a moderate tone—and the

appearance, at any rate, of harmony and a united front among the
representatives of labour—if so much at least could be attained to-
night, both Wharton and Bennett believed that not only the cause
itself, but the importance of the Labour party in the House would
be found to have gained enormously.

'I hope I shall get my turn before dinner,' said Bennett, as he
was going ; 'I want badly to get off for an hour or so. The division won't be till half-past ten at earliest.'

Wharton stood for a moment in a brown study, with his hands
in his pockets, after Bennett left him. It was by no means wholly
clear to him what line Bennett would take—with regard to one or
two points. After a long acquaintance with the little man, Wharton
was not always, nor indeed generally, at his ease with him. Bennett had curious reserves. As to his hour off, Wharton felt tolerably certain that he meant to go and hear a famous Revivalist
preacher hold forth at a public hall not far from the House The
streets were full of placards.

Well!—to every man his own excitements ! What time? He
looked first at his watch, then at the marked question paper
Bennett had left behind him. The next minute he was hurrying
along passages and stairs, with his springing, boyish step, to the
Ladies' Gallery.

The magnificent doorkeeper saluted him with particular deference. Wharton was in general a favourite with officials.

'The two ladies are come, sir. You'll find them in the front—
oh ! not very full yet, sir—will be directly.'

Wharton drew aside the curtain of the Gallery, and looked in.
Yes !—there was the dark head bent forward, pressed indeed
against the grating which closes the front of the den into which the
House of Commons puts its ladies—as though its owner were already
absorbed in what was passing before her.

She looked up with an eager start, as she heard his voice in
her ear.

'Oh ! now, come and tell us everything—and who everybody is.
Why don't we see the Speaker?—and which is the Government
side?—Oh yes, I see. And who's this speaking now?'

'Why, I thought you knew everything,' said Wharton as, with
a greeting to Miss Craven, he slipped in beside them and took a
still vacant chair for an instant. 'How shall I instruct a Speaker's
great-niece?'

'Why, of course I feel as if the place belonged to me!' said
Marcella impatiently ; 'but that somehow doesn't seem to help me
to people's names. Where's Mr. Gladstone? Oh, I see. Look,
look, Edith !—he's just come in !—Oh, don't be so superior, though

you *have* been here before—you couldn't tell me heaps of people!'

Her voice had a note of joyous excitement like a child's.

'That's because I'm short-sighted,' said Edith Craven calmly; 'but it's no reason why you should show me Mr. Gladstone.'

'Oh, my dear, my dear!—do be quiet! Now, Mr. Wharton, where are the Irishmen? Oh! I wish we could have an Irish row! And where do you sit?—I see—and there's Mr. Bennett—and that black-faced man, Mr. Wilkins, I met at the Hallins—you don't like him, do you?' she said, drawing back and looking at him sharply.

'Who? Wilkins? Perhaps you'd better ask me that question later on!' said Wharton, with a twist of the lip; 'he's going to do his best to make a fool of himself and us to-night—we shall see! It's kind of you to wish us an Irish row!—considering that if I miss my chance to-night I shall never get another!'

'Then for heaven's sake don't let's wish it!' she said decidedly.

'Oh, that's the Irish Secretary answering now, is it?'—A pause—'Dear me, how civil everybody is. I don't think this is a good place for a Democrat, Mr. Wharton—I find myself terribly in love with the Government. But who's that?'

She craned her neck. Wharton was silent. The next instant she drew hurriedly back.

'I didn't see,' she murmured; 'it's so confusing.'

A tall man had risen from the end of the Government bench, and was giving an answer connected with the Home Secretary's department. For the first time since their parting in the Mellor drawing-room Marcella saw Aldous Raeburn.

She fell very silent, and leant back in her chair. Yet Wharton's quick glance perceived that she both looked and listened intently, so long as the somewhat high-pitched voice was speaking.

'He does those things very well,' he said carelessly, judging it best to take the bull by the horns. 'Never a word too much—they don't get any change out of him. Do you see that old fellow in the white beard under the gallery? He is one of the chartered bores. When he gets up to-night the House will dine. I shall come up and look for you, and hand you over to a friend if I may —a Staffordshire member, who has his wife here—Mrs. Lane. I have engaged a table, and I can start with you. Unfortunately I musn't be long out of the House, as it's my motion; but they will look after you.'

The girls glanced a little shyly at each other. Nothing had been said about dining; but Wharton took it for granted; and they yielded. It was Marcella's 'day off,' and she was a free woman.

'Good-bye, then,' he said, getting up.   'I shall be on in about twenty minutes.   Wish me well through !'

Marcella looked round and smiled.   But her vivacity had been quenched for the moment ; and Wharton departed not quite so well heartened for the fray as he could have wished to be.   It was hard luck that the Raeburn ghost should walk this particular evening.

Marcella bent forward again when he had gone, and remained for long silent, looking down into the rapidly filling House.   Aldous Raeburn was lying back on the Treasury bench, his face up-turned.   She knew very well that it was impossible he should see her ; yet every now and then she shrank a little away as though he must.   The face looked to her older and singularly blanched ; but she supposed that must be the effect of the light ; for she noticed the same pallor in many others.

'*All that my life can do to pour good measure—pressed down—running over—into yours, I vowed you then !*'

The words stole into her memory, throbbing there like points of pain.   Was it indeed this man under her eyes—so listless, so un-conscious—who had said them to her with a passion of devotion it shamed her to think of?

And now—never so much as an ordinary word of friendship between them again?   'On the broad seas of life enisled'—separate, estranged, for ever?   It was like the touch of death—the experience brought with it such a chill—such a sense of irre-parable fact, of limitations never to be broken through.

Then she braced herself.   The 'things that are behind' must be left.   To have married him after all would have been the greatest wrong.   Nor, in one sense, was what she had done irre-parable.   She chose to believe Frank Leven, rather than Edward Hallin.   Of course he must and should marry !   It was absurd to suppose that he should not.   No one had a stronger sense of family than he.   And as for the girl—the little dancing, flirting girl !—why, the thing happened every day.   *His* wife should not be too strenuous, taken up with problems and questions of her own.   She should cheer, amuse, distract him.   Marcella en-deavoured to think of it all with the dry common-sense her mother would have applied to it.   One thing at least was clear to her—the curious recognition that never before had she considered Aldous Raeburn, *in and for himself*, as an independent human being.

'He was just a piece of furniture in my play, last year,' she said to herself with a pang of frank remorse.   'He was well quit of me !'

But she was beginning to recover her spirits, and when at last Raeburn, after a few words with a minister who had just arrived, disappeared suddenly behind the Speaker's chair, the spectacle below her seized her with the same fascination as before.

The House was filling rapidly. Questions were nearly over, and the speech of the evening, on which considerable public expectation both inside and outside Parliament had been for some time concentrated, was fast approaching. Peers were straggling into the gallery ; the reporters were changing just below her : and some 'crack hands' among them, who had been lounging till now, were beginning to pay attention and put their paper in order. The Irish benches, the Opposition, the Government—all were full, and there was a large group of members round the door.

'There he is !' cried Marcella involuntarily, with a pulse of excitement, as Wharton's light young figure made its way through the crowd. He sat down on a corner seat below the gangway and put on his hat.

In five minutes more he was on his feet, speaking to an attentive and crowded House in a voice—clear, a little hard, but capable of the most accomplished and subtle variety—which for the first moment sent a shudder of memory through Marcella.

Then she found herself listening with as much trepidation and anxiety as though some personal interest and reputation depended for her, too, on the success of the speech. Her mind was first invaded by a strong, an *irritable* sense of the difficulty of the audience. How was it possible for anyone, unless he had been trained to it for years, to make any effect upon such a crowd !—so irresponsive, individualist, unfused—so lacking, as it seemed to the raw spectator, in the qualities and excitements that properly belong to multitude ! Half the men down below, under their hats, seemed to her asleep ; the rest indifferent. And were those languid, indistinguishable murmurs what the newspapers call '*cheers*'?

But the voice below flowed on ; point after point came briskly out ; the atmosphere warmed ; and presently this first impression passed into one wholly different—nay, at the opposite pole. Gradually the girl's ardent sense—informed, perhaps, more richly than most women's with the memories of history and literature, for in her impatient way she had been at all times a quick, omnivorous reader—awoke to the peculiar conditions, the special thrill, attaching to the place and its performers. The philosopher derides it ; the man of letters out of the House talks of it with a smile as a 'Ship of Fools' ; both, when occasion offers, passionately desire a seat in it ; each would give his right hand to succeed in it.

Why ? Because here after all is power—here is the central machine. Here are the men who, both by their qualities and their

defects, are to have for their span of life the leading—or the wreck-
ing?—of this great fate-bearing force, this 'weary Titan' we call
our country.   Here things are not only debated, but done—lamely
or badly, perhaps, but still *done*—which will affect our children's
children ; which link us to the Past ; which carry us on safely or
dangerously to a Future only the Gods know.   And in this passage,
this chequered, doubtful passage from thinking to doing, an infinite
savour and passion of life is somehow disengaged.   It penetrates
through the boredom, through all the failure, public and personal ;
it enwraps the spectacle and the actors ; it carries and supports
patriot and adventurer alike.

Ideas, perceptions of this kind—the first chill over—stole upon
and conquered Marcella.   Presently it was as though she had
passed into Wharton's place, was seeing with his eyes, feeling with
his nerves.   It would be a success this speech—it was a success !
The House was gained, was attentive.   A case long familiar to it
in portions and fragments, which had been spoilt by violence and
discredited by ignorance, was being presented to it with all the
resources of a great talent—with brilliancy, moderation, practical
detail—moderation above all !   From the slight historical sketch,
with which the speech opened, of the English 'working day,' the
causes and the results of the Factory Acts—through the general
description of the present situation, of the workman's present hours,
opportunities and demands, the growth of the desire for State
control, the machinery by which it was to be enforced, and the
effects it might be expected to have on the workman himself, on
the great army of the 'unemployed,' on wages, on production, and
on the economic future of England—the speaker carried his thread
of luminous speech, without ever losing his audience for an instant.
At every point he addressed himself to the smoothing of difficulties,
to the propitiation of fears ; and when, after the long and masterly
handling of detail, he came to his peroration, to the bantering of
capitalist terrors, to the vindication of the workman's claim to fix
the conditions of his labour, and to the vision lightly and simply
touched of the regenerate working home of the future, inhabited
by free men, dedicated to something beyond the first brutal necessities of the bodily life, possessed indeed of its proper share of the
human inheritance of leisure, knowledge and delight—the crowded
benches before and behind him grudged him none of it.   The
House of Commons is not tolerant of 'flights,' except from its chartered masters.   But this young man had earned his flight ; and
they heard him patiently.   For the rest, the Government had been
most attractively wooed ; and the Liberal party in the midst of
much plain speaking had been treated on the whole with a deference

and a forbearance that had long been conspicuously lacking in the
utterances of the Labour men.

'"The mildest mannered man" *et cetera*:' said a smiling
member of the late Government to a companion on the front Opposition bench, as Wharton sat down amid the general stir and movement which betoken the break-up of a crowded House, and the
end of a successful speech which people are eager to discuss in the
lobbies. 'A fine performance, eh? Great advance on anything
last year.'

'Bears about as much relation to facts as I do to the angels!'
growled the man addressed.

'What! as bad as that?' said the other laughing. 'Look! they
have put up old Denny. I think I shall stay and hear him.' And
he laid down his hat again which he had taken up.

Meanwhile Marcella in the Ladies' Gallery had thrown herself
back in her chair with a long breath.

'How can one listen to anything else!' she said; and for a
long time she sat staring at the House without hearing a word of
what the very competent, caustic, and well-informed manufacturer
on the Government side was saying. Every dramatic and æsthetic
instinct she possessed—and she was full of them—had been stirred
and satisfied by the speech and the speaker.

But more than that. He had spoken for the toiler and the poor;
his peroration above all had contained tones and accents which
were in fact the products of something perfectly sincere in the
speaker's motley personality; and this girl, who in her wild way
had given herself to the poor, had followed him with all her passionate heart. Yet, at the same time, with an amount of intellectual
dissent every now and then as to measures and methods, a scepticism of detail which astonished herself! A year before she had
been as a babe beside him, whether in matters of pure mind or of
worldly experience. Now she was for the first time conscious of a
curious growth—independence.

But the intellectual revolt, such as it was, was lost again,
as soon as it arose, in the general impression which the speech
had left upon her—in this warm quickening of the pulses, this
romantic interest in the figure, the scene, the young emerging
personality.

Edith Craven looked at her with wondering amusement. She
and her brothers were typical Venturists—a little cynical, therefore,
towards all the world, friend or foe. A Venturist is a Socialist
minus cant, and a cause which cannot exist at all without a passion
of sentiment lays it down—through him—as a first law, that sentiment in public is the abominable thing. Edith Craven thought

that after all Marcella was little less raw and simple now than she had been in the old days.

'There!' said Marcella with relief, 'that's done. Now, who's this? That man *Wilkins!*'

Her tone showed her disgust. Wilkins had sprung up the instant Wharton's Conservative opponent had given the first decisive sign of sitting down. Another man on the same side was also up, but Wilkins, black and frowning, held his own stubbornly, and his rival subsided.

With the first sentences of the new speech the House knew that it was to have an emotion, and men came trooping in again. And certainly the short stormy utterance was dramatic enough. Dissent on the part of an important North-country Union from some of the most vital machinery of the bill which had been sketched by Wharton—personal jealousy and distrust of the mover of the resolution—denial of his representative place, and sneers at his kid-gloved attempts to help a class with which he had nothing to do—the most violent protest against the servility with which he had truckled to the now effete party of free contract and political enfranchisement—and the most passionate assertion that between any Labour party, worthy of the name, and either of the great parties of the past there lay and must lie a gulf of hatred, unfathomable and unquenchable till Labour had got its rights, and landlord, employer, and dividend-hunter were trampled beneath its heel—all these ugly or lurid things emerged with surprising clearness from the torrent of North-country speech. For twenty minutes Nehemiah Wilkins rioted in one of the best 'times' of his life. That he was an orator thousands of working men had borne him witness again and again ; and in his own opinion he had never spoken better.

The House at first enjoyed its sensation. Then, as the hard words rattled on, it passed easily into the stage of amusement Lady Cradock's burly husband bent forward from the front Opposition bench, caught Wharton's eye, and smiled, as though to say 'What!—you haven't even been able to keep up appearances so far !' And Wilkins's final attack upon the Liberals—who, after ruining their own chances and the chances of the country, were now come cap in hand to the working man whining for his support as their only hope of recovery—was delivered to a mocking chorus of laughter and cheers, in the midst of which, with an angry shake of his great shoulders, he flung himself down on his seat.

Meanwhile Wharton, who had spent the first part of Wilkins's speech in a state of restless fidget, his hat over his eyes, was alternately sitting erect with radiant looks, or talking rapidly to Bennett who had come to sit beside him. The Home Secretary got up after Wilkins had sat down, and spent a genial forty minutes in delivering the Government *non possumus*, couched, of course, in the tone of deference to King Labour which the modern statesman learns at his mother's knee, but enlivened with a good deal of ironical and effective perplexity as to which hand to shake and whose voice to follow, and winding up with a tribute of compliment to Wharton, mixed with some neat mock condolence with the Opposition under the ferocities of some others of its nominal friends.

Altogether, the finished performance of the old stager, the *habitué*. While it was going on, Marcella noticed that Aldous Raeburn had come back again to his seat next to the speaker, who was his official chief. Every now and then the Minister turned to him, and Raeburn handed him a volume of Hansard or the copy of some Parliamentary Return whence the great man was to quote. Marcella watched every movement ; then from the Government bench her eye sped across the House to Wharton sitting once more buried in his hat, his arms folded in front of him. A little shiver of excitement ran through her. The two men upon whom her life had so far turned were once more in presence of, pitted against, each other—and she, once more, looking on !

When the Home Secretary sat down, the House was growing restive with thoughts of dinner, and a general movement had begun—when it was seen that Bennett was up. Again men who had gone out came back, and those who were still there resigned themselves. Bennett was a force in the House, a man always listened to and universally respected, and the curiosity felt as to the relations between him and this new star and would-be leader had been for some time considerable.

When Bennett sat down, the importance of the member for West Brookshire, both in the House and in the country, had risen a hundred per cent. A man who over a great part of the north was in labour concerns the unquestioned master of many legions, and whose political position had hitherto been one of conspicuous moderation, even to his own hurt, had given Wharton the warmest possible backing ; had endorsed his proposals, to their most conten- tious and doubtful details, and in a few generous though still perhaps ambiguous words had let the House see what he personally thought of the services rendered to labour as a whole during the past five years, and to the weak and scattered group of Labour members in particular, since his entrance into Parliament, by the young and brilliant man beside him.

Bennett was no orator. He was a plain man, ennobled by the training of religious dissent, at the same time indifferently served

often by an imperfect education. But the very simplicity and home-
liness of its expression gave additional weight to this first avowal
of a strong conviction that the time had come when the Labour party
must have separateness and a leader if it were to rise out of
insignificance ; to this frank renunciation of whatever personal
claims his own past might have given him ; and to the promise of
unqualified support to the policy of the younger man, in both its
energetic and conciliatory aspects. He threw out a little, not
unkindly, indignation, if one may be allowed the phrase, in the
direction of Wilkins—who in the middle of the speech abruptly
walked out—and before he sat down, the close attention, the looks,
the cheers, the evident excitement of the men sitting about him,—
amongst whom were two-thirds of the whole Labour representation
in Parliament—made it clear to the House that the speech marked
an epoch not only in the career of Harry Wharton, but in the
parliamentary history of the great industrial movement.

The white-bearded bore under the gallery, whom Wharton had
pointed out to Marcella, got up as Bennett subsided.   The House
streamed out like one man. Bennett, exhausted by the heat and
the effort, mopped his brow with his red handkerchief, and, in the
tension of fatigue, started as he felt a touch upon his arm.   Wharton was bending over to him—perfectly white, with a lip he in vain
tried to steady.

'I can't thank you,' he said ; 'I should make a fool of myself.'

Bennett nodded pleasantly, and presently both were pressing
into the outgoing crowd, avoiding each other with the ineradicable
instinct of the Englishman.

Wharton did not recover his self-control completely till, after
an ordeal of talk and handshaking in the lobby, he was on his way
to the Ladies' Gallery. Then in a flash he found himself filled
with the spirits, the exhilaration, of a schoolboy. This wonderful
experience behind him !—and upstairs, waiting for him, those eyes,
that face ! How could he get her to himself somehow for a moment—and dispose of that Craven girl ?

'Well !' he said to her joyously, as she turned round in the
darkness of the Gallery.

But she was seized with sudden shyness, and he felt, rather
than saw, the glow of pleasure and excitement which possessed
her.

'Don't let's talk here,' she said. 'Can't we go out ? I am
melted !'

'Yes, of course ! Come on to the terrace. It's a divine
evening, and we shall find our party there. Well, Miss Craven,
were you interested ?'

Edith smiled demurely.

'I thought it a good debate,' she said.

'Confound these Venturist prigs!' was Wharton's inward remark as he led the way.

CHAPTER IX

'HOW enchanting!' cried Marcella, as they emerged on the terrace ; and river, shore and sky opened upon them in all the thousand-tinted light and shade of a still and perfect evening. 'Oh, how hot we were –and how badly you treat us in those dens!'

Those confident eyes of Wharton's shone as they glanced at her.

She wore a pretty white dress of some cotton stuff—it seemed to him he remembered it of old—and on the waving masses of hair lay a little bunch of black lace that called itself a bonnet, with black strings tied demurely under the chin. The abundance of character and dignity in the beauty which yet to-night was so young and glowing—the rich arresting note of the voice—the inimitable carriage of the head—Wharton realised them all at the moment with peculiar vividness, because he felt them in some sort as additions to his own personal wealth. To-night she was in his power, his possession.

The terrace was full of people, and alive with a Babel of talk. Yet, as he carried his companions forward in search of Mrs. Lane, he saw that Marcella was instantly marked. Everyone who passed them, or made way for them, looked and looked again.

The girl, absorbed in her pleasant or agitating impressions, knew nothing of her own effect. She was drinking in the sunset light—the poetic mystery of the river—the lovely line of the bridge —the associations of the place where she stood, of this great building overshadowing her. Every now and then she started in a kind of terror lest some figure in the dusk should be Aldous Raeburn ; then when a stranger showed himself she gave herself up again to her young pleasure in the crowd and the spectacle. But Wharton knew that she was observed ; Wharton caught the whisper that followed her. His vanity, already so well-fed this evening, took the attention given to her as so much fresh homage to itself ; and she had more and more glamour for him in the reflected light of this publicity, this common judgment.

'Ah, here are the Lanes !' he said, detecting at last a short lady in black amid a group of men.

Marcella and Edith were introduced. Then Edith found a friend in a young London member who was to be one of the party, and strolled off with him till dinner should be announced.

'I will just take Miss Boyce to the end of the terrace,' said Wharton to Mr. Lane ; 'we shan't get anything to eat yet awhile. What a crowd !   The Alresfords not come yet, I see.'

Lane shrugged his shoulders as he looked round.

'Raeburn has a party to-night.   And there are at least three or four others besides ourselves.   I should think food and service will be equally scarce !'

Wharton glanced quickly at Marcella.   But she was talking to Mrs. Lane, and had heard nothing.

'Let me just show you the terrace,' he said to her.   'No chance of dinner for another twenty minutes.'

They strolled away together.   As they moved along, a number of men waylaid the speaker of the night with talk and congratulations—glancing the while at the lady on his left.   But presently they were away from the crowd which hung about the main entrance to the terrace, and had reached the comparatively quiet western end, where were only a few pairs and groups walking up and down.

'Shall I see Mr. Bennett?' she asked him eagerly, as they paused by the parapet, looking down upon the grey-brown water swishing under the fast incoming tide.   'I want to.'

'I asked him to dine, but he wouldn't.   He has gone to a prayer-meeting—at least I guess so.   There is a famous American evangelist speaking in Westminster to-night—I am as certain as I ever am of anything that Bennett is there—dining on Moody and Sankey.   Men are a medley, don't you think?—So you liked his speech ?'

'How coolly you ask !' she said laughing.   'Did *you* ?'

He was silent a moment, his smiling gaze fixed on the water. Then he turned to her.

'How much gratitude do you think I owe him?'

'As much as you can pay,' she said with emphasis.   'I never heard anything more complete, more generous.'

'So you were carried away?'

She looked at him with a curious, sudden gravity—a touch of defiance.

'No !—neither by him, nor by you.   I don't believe in your Bill—and I am *sure* you will never carry it !'

Wharton lifted his eyebrows.

'Perhaps you'll tell me where you are,' he said, 'that I may know how to talk? When we last discussed these things at Mellor, I *think*—you were a Socialist?'

'What does it matter what I was last year?' she asked him gaily, yet with a final inflection of the voice which was not gay; 'I was a baby! *Now* perhaps I have earned a few poor, little opinions—but they are a ragged bundle—and I have never any time to sort them.'

'Have you left the Venturists?'

'No!—but I am full of perplexities; and the Cravens, I see, will soon be for turning me out. You understand—I *know* some working folk now!'

'So you did last year.'

'No!'—she insisted, shaking her head—'that was all different. But now I am *in* their world—I live with them—and they talk to me. One evening in the week I am "at home" for all the people I know in our Buildings—men and women. Mrs. Hurd—you know whom I mean?'—her brow contracted a moment—'she comes with her sewing to keep me company; so does Edith Craven; and sometimes the little room is packed. The men smoke—when we can have the windows open!—and I believe I shall soon smoke too—it makes them talk better. We get all sorts—Socialists, Conservatives, Radicals——'

'——And you don't think much of the Socialists?'

'Well! they are the interesting, dreamy fellows,' she said laughing, 'who don't save, and muddle their lives. And as for argument, the Socialist workman doesn't care twopence for facts—that don't suit him. It's superb the way he treats them!'

'I should like to know who does care!' said Wharton with a shrug. Then he turned with his back to the parapet, the better to command her. He had taken off his hat for coolness, and the wind played with the crisp curls of hair. 'But tell me'—he went on—'who has been tampering with you? Is it Hallin? You told me you saw him often.'

'Perhaps. But what if it's everything?—*living*?—saving your presence! A year ago at any rate the world was all black—*or* white—to me. Now I lie awake at night, puzzling my head about the shades between—which makes the difference. A compulsory Eight Hours' Day for all men in all trades!' Her note of scorn startled him. 'You *know* you won't get it! And all the other big exasperating things you talk about—public organisation of labour, and the rest—you won't get them till all the world is a New Jerusalem—and when the world is a New Jerusalem, nobody will want them!'

Wharton made her an ironical bow.

'Nicely said!—though we have heard it before. Upon my word, you have marched!—or Edward Hallin has carried you. So now you think the poor are as well off as possible, in the best of all possible worlds—is that the result of your nursing? You agree with Denny, in fact? the man who got up after me?'

His tone annoyed her. Then suddenly the name suggested to her a recollection that brought a frown.

'That was the man, then, you attacked in the *Clarion* this morning!'

'Ah! you read me!' said Wharton, with sudden pleasure. 'Yes—that opened the campaign. As you know, of course, Craven has gone down, and the strike begins next week. Soon we shall bring two batteries to bear, he letting fly as correspondent, and I from the office. I enjoyed writing that article.'

'So I should think,' she said drily; 'all I know is, it made *one* reader passionately certain that there was another side to the matter! There may not be. I dare say there isn't; but on me at least that was the effect. Why is it'—she broke out with vehemence—'that not a single Labour paper is ever capable of the simplest justice to an opponent?'

'You think any other sort of paper is any better?' he asked her scornfully.

'I dare say not. But that doesn't matter to me! it is *we* who talk of justice, of respect, and sympathy from man to man, and then we go and blacken the men who don't agree with us—whole classes, that is to say, of our fellow-countrymen, not in the old honest slashing style, Tartuffes that we are!—but with all the delicate methods of a new art of slander, pursued almost for its own sake. We know so much better—always—than our opponents, we hardly condescend even to be angry. One is only "sorry"—"obliged to punish"—like the priggish governess of one's childhood!'

In spite of himself, Wharton flushed.

'My best thanks!' he said. 'Anything more? I prefer to take my drubbing all at once.'

She looked at him steadily.

'Why did you write, or allow that article on the West Brookshire landlords two days ago?'

Wharton started.

'Well! wasn't it true?'

'No!' she said with a curling lip: 'and I think you know it wasn't true.'

'What! as to the Raeburns? Upon my word, I should have

imagined,' he said slowly, 'that it represented your views at one time with tolerable accuracy.'

Her nerve suddenly deserted her. She bent over the parapet, and, taking up a tiny stone that lay near, she threw it unsteadily into the river. He saw the hand shake.

'Look here,' he said, turning round so that he too leant over the river, his arms on the parapet, his voice close to her ear. 'Are you always going to quarrel with me like this? Don't you know that there is no one in the world I would sooner please if I could?'

She did not speak.

'In the first place,' he said, laughing, 'as to my speech, do you suppose that I believe in that Bill which I described just now?'

'I don't know,' she said, indignantly, once more playing with the stones on the wall. 'It sounded like it.'

'That is my gift—my little *carillon*, as Renan would say. But do you imagine I want you or anyone else to tell me that we shan't get such a Bill for generations? Of course we shan't!'

'Then why do you make farcical speeches, bamboozling your friends and misleading the House of Commons?'

He saw the old storm-signs with glee—the lightning in the eye, the rose on the cheek. She was never so beautiful as when she was angry.

'Because, my dear lady—*we must generate our force*. Steam must be got up—I am engaged in doing it. We shan't get a compulsory eight hours' day for all trades—but in the course of the agitation for that precious illusion, and by the help of a great deal of beating of tom-toms, and gathering of clans, we shall get a great many other things by the way that we *do* want. Hearten your friends, and frighten your enemies—there is no other way of scoring in politics,—and the particular score doesn't matter. Now don't look at me as if you would like to impeach me!—or I shall turn the tables. *I* am still fighting for my illusions in my own way—*you*, it seems, have given up yours!'

But for once he had underrated her sense of humour. She broke into a low merry laugh which a little disconcerted him.

'You mock me?' he said quickly—'think me insincere, unscrupulous?—Well, I dare say! But you have no right to mock me. Last year, again and again, you promised me guerdon. Now it has come to paying—and I claim!'

His low distinct voice in her ear had a magnetising effect upon her. She slowly turned her face to him, overcome by—yet fighting against—memory. If she had seen in him the smallest sign of reference to that scene she hated to think of, he would have probably lost this hold upon her on the spot. But his tact was perfect. She saw nothing but a look of dignity and friendship, which brought upon her with a rush all those tragic things they had shared and fought through, purifying things of pity and fear, which had so often seemed to her the atonement for, the washing away of that old baseness.

He saw her face tremble a little. Then she said proudly—

'I promised to be grateful. So I am.'

'No, no !' he said, still in the same low tone. 'You promised me a friend. Where is she ?'

She made no answer. Her hands were hanging loosely over the water, and her eyes were fixed on the haze opposite, whence emerged the blocks of the great hospital and the twinkling points of innumerable lamps. But his gaze compelled her at last, and she turned back to him. He saw an expression half hostile, half moved, and pressed on before she could speak.

'Why do you bury yourself in that nursing life ?' he said, drily. 'It is not the life for you ; it does not fit you in the least.'

'You test your friends !' she cried, her cheek flaming again at the provocative change of voice. 'What possible right have you to that remark ?'

'I know you, and I know the causes you want to serve. You can't serve them where you are. Nursing is not for you ; you are wanted among your own class—among your equals—among the people who are changing and shaping England. It is absurd. You are masquerading.'

She gave him a little sarcastic nod.

'Thank you. I am doing a little honest work for the first time in my life.'

He laughed. It was impossible to tell whether he was serious or posing.

'You are just what you were in one respect—terribly in the right ! Be a little humble to-night for a change. Come, condescend to the classes ! Do you see Mr. Lane calling us ?'

And, in fact, Mr. Lane, with his arm in the air, was eagerly beckoning to them from the distance.

'Do you know Lady Selina Farrell ?' he asked her, as they walked quickly back to the dispersing crowd.

'No ; who is she ?'

Wharton laughed.

'Providence should contrive to let Lady Selina overhear that question once a week—in your tone ! Well, she is a personage— Lord Alresford's daughter—unmarried—rich—has a *salon*, or thinks she has—manipulates a great many people's fortunes and lives—or thinks she does, which, after all, is what matters—to Lady Selina. She wants to know you, badly. Do you think you can be kind to her? There she is—you will let me introduce you? She dines with us.'

In another moment Marcella had been introduced to a tall, fair lady in a very fashionable black and pink bonnet, who held out a gracious hand.

'I have heard so much of you!' said Lady Selina, as they walked along the passage to the dining-room together. 'It must be so wonderful, your nursing!'

Marcella laughed, rather restively.

'No, I don't think it is,' she said; 'there are so many of us.'

'Oh, but the things you do—Mr. Wharton told me—so interesting!'

Marcella said nothing, and as to her looks the passage was dark. Lady Selina thought her a very handsome but very *gauche* young woman. Still, *gauche* or no, she had thrown over Aldous Raeburn and thirty thousand a year; an act which, as Lady Selina admitted, put you out of the common run.

'Do you know most of the people dining?' she inquired in her blandest voice. 'But no doubt you do. You are a great friend of Mr. Wharton's, I think?'

'He stayed at our house last year,' said Marcella, abruptly. 'No, I don't know anybody.'

'Then shall I tell you? It makes it more interesting, doesn't it? It ought to be a pleasant little party.'

And the great lady lightly ran over the names. It seemed to Marcella that most of them were very 'smart' or very important. Some of the smart names were vaguely known to her from Miss Raeburn's talk of last year; and, besides, there were a couple of Tory Cabinet ministers and two or three prominent members. It was all rather surprising.

At dinner she found herself between one of the Cabinet ministers and the young and good-looking private secretary of the other. Both men were agreeable, and very willing, besides, to take trouble with this unknown beauty. The minister, who knew the Raeburns very well, was discussing with himself all the time whether this was indeed the Miss Boyce of that story. His suspicion and curiosity were at any rate sufficiently strong to make him give himself much pains to draw her out.

Her own conversation, however, was much distracted by the attention she could not help giving to her host and his surroundings. Wharton had Lady Selina on his right, and the young and distinguished wife of Marcella's minister on his left. At the other

end of the table sat Mrs. Lane, doing her duty spasmodically to
Lord Alresford, who still, in a blind old age, gave himself all the
airs of the current statesman and possible premier. But the talk,
on the whole, was general—a gay and careless give-and-take of
Parliamentary, social, and racing gossip, the ball flying from one
accustomed hand to another.

And Marcella could not get over the astonishment of Wharton's
part in it. She shut her eyes sometimes for an instant and tried
to see him as her girl's fancy had seen him at Mellor—the solitary,
eccentric figure pursued by the hatreds of a renounced Patricianate
—bringing the enmity of his own order as a pledge and offering to
the Plebs he asked to lead. Where even was the speaker of an hour
ago? Chat of Ascot and of Newmarket ; discussion with Lady
Selina or with his left-hand neighbour of country-house 'sets,' with
a patter of names which sounded in her scornful ear like a paragraph from the *World* ; above all, a general air of easy comradeship, which no one at this table, at any rate, seemed inclined to
dispute, with every exclusiveness and every amusement of the
' idle rich,' whereof—in the popular idea—he was held to be one of
the very particular foes !—

No doubt, as the dinner moved on, this first impression changed
somewhat. She began to distinguish notes that had at first been
lost upon her. She caught the mocking, ambiguous tone under
which she herself had so often fumed ; she watched the occasional recoil of the women about him, as though they had been
playing with some soft-pawed animal, and had been suddenly
startled by the gleam of its claws. These things puzzled, partly
propitiated her. But on the whole she was restless and hostile.
How was it possible—from such personal temporising—such a
frittering of the forces and sympathies—to win the single-minded-
ness and the power without which no great career is built ? She
wanted to talk with him—reproach him !

'Well—I must go—worse luck,' said Wharton at last, laying
down his napkin and rising. ' Lane, will you take charge ? I
will join you outside later.'

' If he ever finds us ! ' said her neighbour to Marcella. ' I never
saw the place so crowded. It is odd how people enjoy these
scrambling meals in these very ugly rooms.'

Marcella, smiling, looked down with him over the bare coffee-
tavern place, in which their party occupied a sort of high table
across the end, while two other small gatherings were accommo-
dated in the space below

' Are there any other rooms than this ? ' she asked idly.

' One more,' said a young man across the table, who had been introduced to her in the dusk outside, and had not yet succeeded in getting her to look at him, as he desired. 'But there is another big party there to-night—Raeburn—you know,' he went on innocently, addressing the minister; 'he has got the Winterbournes and the Macdonalds—quite a gathering—rather an unusual thing for him.'

The minister glanced quickly at his companion. But she had turned to answer a question from Lady Selina, and thenceforward, till the party rose, she gave him little opportunity of observing her.

As the outward-moving stream of guests was once more in the corridor leading to the terrace, Marcella hurriedly made her way to Mrs. Lane.

'I think,' she said—'I am afraid—we ought to be going—my friend and I. Perhaps Mr. Lane—perhaps he would just show us the way out—we can easily find a cab.'

There was an imploring, urgent look in her face which struck Mrs. Lane. But Mr. Lane's loud friendly voice broke in from behind.

'My dear Miss Boyce !—we can't possibly allow it—no ! no !—just half an hour—while they bring us our coffee—to do your homage, you know, to the terrace—and the river—and the moon ! —And then—if you don't want to go back to the House for the division—we will see you safely into your cab. Look at the moon !—and the tide'—they had come to the wide door opening on the terrace—'aren't they doing their very best for you ?'

Marcella looked behind her in despair. *Where* was Edith ? Far in the rear !—and fully occupied apparently with two or three pleasant companions. She could not help herself. She was carried on, with Mr. Lane chatting beside her—though the sight of the shining terrace, with its moonlit crowd of figures, breathed into her a terror and pain she could hardly control.

'Come and look at the water,'—she said to Mr. Lane—'I would rather not walk up and down, if you don't mind.'

He thought she was tired, and politely led her through the sitting or promenading groups till once more she was leaning over the parapet, now trying to talk, now to absorb herself in the magic of bridge, river, and sky, but in reality listening all the time with a shrinking heart for the voices and the footfalls that she dreaded. Lady Winterbourne, above all ! How unlucky ! It was only that morning that she had received a forwarded letter from that old friend, asking urgently for news and her address.

'Well, how did you like the speech to-night—*the* speech ?' said

Mr. Lane, a genial Gladstonian member, more heavily weighted with estates than with ideas. ' It was splendid—wasn't it ?—in the way of speaking. Speeches like that are a safety-valve—that's my view of it. Have 'em out—all these ideas—get 'em discussed !'—with a good-humoured shake of the head for emphasis. ' Does nobody any harm and may do good. I can tell you, Miss Boyce, the House of Commons is a capital place for taming these clever young men !—you must give them their head—and they make excellent fellows after a bit. Why—who's this?—My dear Lady Winterbourne !—this *is* a sight for sair een !'

And the portly member with great effusion grasped the hand of a stately lady in black, whose abundant white hair caught the moonlight.

' *Marcella* !' cried a woman's voice.

Yes,—there he was !—close behind Lady Winterbourne. In the soft darkness he and his party had run upon the two persons talking over the wall without an idea—a suspicion.

She hurriedly withdrew herself from Lady Winterbourne, hesitated a second, then held out her hand to him. The light was behind him. She could not see his face in the darkness ; but she was suddenly and strangely conscious of the whole scene—of the great dark building with its lines of fairy-lit gothic windows—the blue gulf of the river crossed by lines of wavering light—the swift passage of a steamer with its illuminated saloon and crowded deck —of the wonderful mixture of moonlight and sunset in the air and sky—of this dark figure in front of her.

Their hands touched. Was there a murmured word from him ? She did not know ; she was too agitated, too unhappy to hear it if there was. She threw herself upon Lady Winterbourne, in whom she divined at once a tremor almost equal to her own.

' Oh ! do come with me—come away !—I want to talk to you !' she said incoherently under her breath, drawing Lady Winter-bourne with a strong hand.

Lady Winterbourne yielded, bewildered, and they moved along the terrace.

' Oh, my dear, my dear !' cried the elder lady—' to think of finding *you* here ! How astonishing—how—how dreadful ! No ! —I don't mean that. Of course you and he must meet—but it was only yesterday he told me he had never seen you again—since— and it gave me a turn. I was very foolish just now. There now —stay here a moment—and tell me about yourself.'

And again they paused by the river, the girl glancing nervously behind her as though she were in a company of ghosts. Lady Winterbourne recovered herself, and Marcella, looking at her,

saw the old tragic severity of feature and mien blurred with the
same softness, the same delicate tremor. Marcella clung to her
with almost a daughter's feeling. She took up the white wrinkled
hand as it lay on the parapet, and kissed it in the dark so that no
one saw.

'I *am* glad to see you again,' she said passionately, 'so glad!'
Lady Winterbourne was surprised and moved.

'But you have never written all these months, you unkind
child! And I have heard so little of you—your mother never
seemed to know. When will you come and see me—or shall I
come to you? I can't stay now, for we were just going; my
daughter, Ermyntrude Welwyn, has to take someone to a ball.
How *strange*'—she broke off—'how very strange that you and he
should have met to-night! He goes off to Italy to-morrow, you
know, with Lord Maxwell.'

'Yes, I had heard,' said Marcella more steadily. 'Will you
come to tea with me next week?—Oh, I will write.—And we must
go too—where *can* my friend be?'

She looked round in dismay, and up and down the terrace for
Edith.

'I will take you back to the Lanes, anyway,' said Lady Winterbourne; 'or shall we look after you?'

'No! no! Take me back to the Lanes.'

'Mamma, are you coming?' said a voice like a softened version
of Lady Winterbourne's. Then something small and thin ran
forward, and a girl's voice said piteously:

'*Dear* Lady Winterbourne, my frock and my hair take *so* long
to do! I shall be cross with my maid, and look like a fiend.
Ermyntrude will be sorry she ever knew me. *Do* come!'

'Don't cry, Betty. I certainly shan't take you if you do!' said
Lady Ermyntrude laughing. 'Mamma, is this Miss Boyce—*your*
Miss Boyce?'

She and Marcella shook hands, and they talked a little, Lady
Ermyntrude under cover of the darkness looking hard and curiously
at the tall stranger whom, as it happened, she had never seen
before. Marcella had little notion of what she was saying. She
was far more conscious of the girlish form hanging on Lady Winterbourne's arm than she was of her own words, of 'Betty's' beautiful soft eyes—also shyly and gravely fixed upon herself—under
that marvellous cloud of fair hair; the long, pointed chin; the
whimsical little face.

'Well, none of *you* are any good!' said Betty at last in a tragic
voice. 'I shall have to walk home my own poor little self, and
"ask a p'leeceman." Mr. Raeburn!'

He disengaged himself from a group behind and came—with no alacrity. Betty ran up to him.

'Mr. Raeburn ! Ermyntrude and Lady Winterbourne are going to sleep here, if you don't mind making arrangements ! But *I* want a hansom.'

At that very moment Marcella caught sight of Edith strolling along towards her with a couple of members, and chatting as though the world had never rolled more evenly.

'Oh ! there she is—there is my friend !' cried Marcella to Lady Winterbourne. 'Good night—good night !'

She was hurrying off when she saw Aldous Raeburn was standing alone a moment. The exasperated Betty had made a dart from his side to 'collect' another straying member of the party.

An impulse she could not master scattered her wretched discomfort—even her chafing sense of being the observed of many eyes. She walked up to him.

'Will you tell me about Lord Maxwell?' she said in a tremulous hurry. 'I am so sorry he is ill—I hadn't heard—I——'

She dared not look up. Was that *his* voice answering?

'Thank you. We have been very anxious about him ; but the doctors to-day give a rather better report. We take him abroad to-morrow.'

'Marcella ! at last !' cried Edith Craven, catching hold of her friend ; 'you lost me ? Oh, nonsense ; it was all the other way. But look, there is Mr. Wharton coming out. I must go—come and say good night—everybody is departing.'

Aldous Raeburn lifted his hat. Marcella felt a sudden rush of humiliation—pain—sore resentment. That cold, strange tone—those unwilling words !—She had gone up to him—as undisciplined in her repentance as she had been in aggression—full of a passionate yearning to make friends—somehow to convey to him that she 'was sorry,' in the old child's phrase which her self-willed childhood had used so little. There could be no misunderstanding possible ! He of all men knew best how irrevocable was the past. But why, when life has brought reflection, and you realise at length that you have vitally hurt, perhaps maimed, another human being, should it not be possible to fling conventions aside, and go to that human being with the frank confession which by all the promises of ethics and religion *ought* to bring peace—peace and a soothed conscience ?

But she had been repulsed—put aside, so she took it—and by one of the kindest and most generous of men ! She moved along the terrace in a maze, seeing nothing, biting her lip to keep back the angry tears. All that obscure need, that new stirring of moral life within her—which had found issue in this little futile advance towards a man who had once loved her and could now, it seemed, only despise and dislike her—was beating and swelling stormlike within her. She had taken being loved so easily, so much as a matter of course! How was it that it hurt her now so much to have lost love, and power, and consideration? She had never felt any passion for Aldous Raeburn—had taken him lightly and shaken him off with a minimum of remorse. Yet to-night a few cold words from him—the proud manner of a moment—had inflicted a smart upon her she could hardly bear. They had made her feel herself so alone, unhappy, uncared for!

But, on the contrary, she *must* be happy!—*must* be loved! To this, and this only, had she been brought by the hard experience of this strenuous year.

'Oh, Mrs. Lane, *be* an angel!' exclaimed Wharton's voice. 'Just one turn—five minutes! The division will be called directly, and then we will all thank our stars and go to bed!'

In another instant he was at Marcella's side, bareheaded, radiant, reckless even, as he was wont to be in moments of excitement. He had seen her speak to Raeburn as he came out on the terrace, but his mind was too full for any perception of other people's situations—even hers. He was absorbed with himself, and with her, as she fitted his present need. The smile of satisfied vanity, of stimulated ambition, was on his lips; and his good-humour inclined him more than ever to Marcella, and the pleasure of a woman's company. He passed with ease from triumph to homage; his talk now audacious, now confiding, offered her a deference, a flattery, to which, as he was fully conscious, the events of the evening had lent a new prestige.

She too, in his eyes, had triumphed—had made her mark. His ears were full of the comments made upon her to-night by the little world on the terrace. If it were not for money—*hateful* money!—what more brilliant wife could be desired for any rising man?

So the five minutes lengthened into ten, and by the time the division was called, and Wharton hurried off, Marcella, soothed, taken out of herself, rescued from the emptiness and forlornness of a tragic moment, had given him more conscious cause than she had ever given him yet to think her kind and fair.

CHAPTER X

'My dear Ned, do be reasonable ! Your sister is in despair, and so am I. Why do you torment us by staying on here in the heat, and taking all these engagements, which you know you are no more fit for than——'

'A sick grasshopper,' laughed Hallin. 'Healthy wretch ! Did Heaven give you that sun-burn only that you might come home from Italy and twit us weaklings ? Do you think I *want* to look as rumbustious as you ? "Nothing too much," my good friend !'

Aldous looked down upon the speaker with an anxiety quite untouched by Hallin's 'chaff.'

'Miss Hallin tells me,' he persisted, 'that you are wearing yourself out with this lecturing campaign, that you don't sleep, and that she is more unhappy about you than she has been for months. Why not give it up now, rest, and begin again in the winter ?'

Hallin smiled a little as he sat with the tips of his fingers lightly joined in front of him.

'I doubt whether I shall live through the winter,' he said quietly.

Raeburn started. Hallin in general spoke of his health, when he allowed it to be mentioned at all, in the most cheerful terms.

'Why you should behave as though you *wished* to make such a prophecy true I can't conceive !' he said in impatient pain.

Hallin offered no immediate answer, and Raeburn, who was standing in front of him, leaning against the wood-work of the open window, looked unhappily at the face and form of his friend. In youth that face had possessed a Greek serenity and blitheness, dependent perhaps on its clear aquiline feature, the steady transparent eyes—*cœli lucida templa*—the fresh fairness of the complexion, and the boyish brow under its arch of pale brown hair. And to stronger men there had always been something peculiarly winning in the fragile grace of figure and movements, suggesting, as they did, sad and perpetual compromise between the spirit's eagerness and the body's weakness.

'Don't make yourself unhappy, my dear boy,' said Hallin at last, putting up a thin hand and touching his friend—'I *shall* give up soon. Moreover, it will give me up. Workmen want to do something else with their evenings in July than spend them in listening to stuffy lectures. I shall go to the Lakes. But there are a few engagements still ahead, and—I confess I am more restless than I used to be. The night cometh when no man can work.'

They fell into a certain amount of discursive talk—of the political situation, working-class opinion, and the rest. Raeburn had been alive now for some time to a curious change of balance in his friend's mind. Hallin's buoyant youth had concerned itself almost entirely with positive crusades and enthusiasms. Of late he seemed rather to have passed into a period of negations, of strong opposition to certain current *isms* and faiths; and the happy boyish tone of earlier years had become the 'stormy note of men contention-tost,' which belongs, indeed, as truly to such a character as the joy of young ideals.

He had always been to some extent divided from Raeburn and others of his early friends by his passionate democracy—his belief in, and trust of, the multitude. For Hallin, the divine originating life was realised and manifested through the common humanity and its struggle, as a whole ; for Raeburn, only in the best of it, morally or intellectually ; the rest remaining an inscrutable problem, which did not, indeed, prevent faith, but hung upon it like a dead weight. Such divisions, however, are among the common divisions of thinking men, and had never interfered with the friendship of these two in the least.

But the developing alienation between Hallin and hundreds of his working-men friends was of an infinitely keener and sorer kind. Since he had begun his lecturing and propagandist life, Socialist ideas of all kinds had made great way in England. And, on the whole, as the prevailing type of them grew stronger, Hallin's sympathy with them had grown weaker and weaker. Property to him meant 'self-realisation'; and the abuse of property was no more just ground for a crusade which logically aimed at doing away with it, than the abuse of other human powers or instincts would make it reasonable to try and do away with—say love, or religion. To give property, and therewith the fuller human opportunity, to those that have none, was the inmost desire of his life. And not merely common property—though like all true soldiers of the human cause he believed that common property will be in the future enormously extended—but in the first place, and above all, to distribute the discipline and the trust of personal and private possession among an infinitely greater number of hands than possess them already. And that not for wealth's sake—though a more equal distribution of property, and therewith of capacity, must inevitably tend to wealth—but for the soul's sake, and for the sake of that continuous appropriation by the race of its moral and spiritual heritage.

How is it to be done ? Hallin, like many others, would have answered—'For England—mainly by a fresh distribution of the land.' Not, of course, by violence—which only means the worst form of waste known to history—but by the continuous pressure of an emancipating legislation, relieving land from shackles long since struck off other kinds of property—by the assertion, within a certain limited range, of communal initiative and control—and above all by the continuous private effort in all sorts of ways and spheres of 'men of good will.' For all sweeping uniform schemes he had the natural contempt of the student—or the moralist. To imagine that by nationalising sixty annual millions of rent, for instance, you could make England a city of God, was not only a vain dream, but a belittling of England's history and England's task. A nation is not saved so cheaply !—and to see those energies turned to land nationalisation or the scheming of a collectivist millennium, which might have gone to the housing, educating and refining of English men, women, and children of to-day, to moralising the employer's view of his profit, and the landlord's conception of his estate—filled him with a growing despair.

The relation of such a habit of life and mind to the Collectivist and Socialist ideas now coming to the front in England, as in every other European country, is obvious enough. To Hallin the social life, the community, was everything—yet to be a 'Socialist' seemed to him more and more to be a traitor ! He would have built his state on the purified will of the individual man, and could conceive no other foundation for a state worth having. But for purification there must be effort, and for effort there must be freedom. Socialism, as he read it, despised and decried freedom, and placed the good of man wholly in certain external conditions. It was aiming at a state of things under which the joys and pains, the teaching and the risks of true possession, were to be for ever shut off from the poor human will, which yet, according to him, could never do without them, if man was to be man.

So that he saw it all *sub specie æternitatis*, as a matter not of economic theory, but rather of religion. Raeburn, as they talked, shrank in dismay from the burning intensity of mood underlying his controlled speech. He spoke, for instance, of Bennett's conversion to Harry Wharton's proposed Bill, or of the land nationalising scheme he was spending all his slender stores of breath and strength in attacking, not with anger or contempt, but with a passionate sorrow which seemed to Raeburn preposterous ! intolerable! —to be exhausting in him the very springs and sources of a too precarious life. There rose in Aldous at last an indignant protest which yet could hardly find itself words. What help to have softened the edge and fury of religious war, only to discover new antagonisms of opinion as capable of devastating heart and affections as any *homoousion* of old? Had they not already cost

him love ? Were they also, in another fashion, to cost him his
friend ?

'Ah, dear old fellow—enough !' said Hallin at last— take me
back to Italy !   You have told me so little—such a niggardly little !'
'I told you that we went and I came back in a water-spout,'
said Aldous ; 'the first rain in Northern Italy for four months—
worse luck ! " Rain at Reggio, rain at Parma.—At Lodi rain, Pia-
cenza rain !"—that might about stand for my diary, except for one
radiant day when my aunt, Betty Macdonald, and I descended on
Milan, and climbed the Duomo.'
'Did Miss Betty amuse you ? '
Aldous laughed.
'Well, at least she varied the programme.   The greater part
of our day in Milan Aunt Neta and I spent in rushing after her
like its tail after a kite.   First of all, she left us in the Duomo
Square, running like a deer, and presently, to Aunt Neta's horror,
we discovered that she was pursuing a young Italian officer in a
blue cloak.   When we came up with the pair she was inquiring, in
her best Italian, where the " Signor " got his cloak, because positively she must have one like it, and he, cap in hand, was explaining to the Signorina that if she would but follow him round the
corner to his military tailor's, she could be supplied on the spot.
So there we all went, Miss Betty insisting.   You can imagine
Aunt Neta.   She bought a small shipload of stuff—and then positively skipped for joy in the street outside—the amazed officer looking on.   And as for her career over the roof of the Duomo—the
agitation of it nearly brought my aunt to destruction—and even I
heaved a sigh of relief when I got them both down safe.'
'Is the creature all tricks ? ' said Hallin with a smile.   'As you
talk of her to me I get the notion of a little monkey just cut loose
from a barrel organ.'
'Oh ! but the monkey has so much heart,' said Aldous, laughing again, as everyone was apt to laugh who talked about Betty
Macdonald, 'and it makes friends with every sick and sorry creature it comes across, especially with old maids !   It amounts to
genius, Betty's way with old maids.   You should see her in the
middle of them in the hotel *salon* at night—a perfect ring of them
—and the men outside, totally neglected, and out of temper.   I
have never seen Betty yet in a room with somebody she thought
ill at ease, or put in the shade—a governess, or a schoolgirl, or a
lumpish boy—that she did not devote herself to that somebody.   It
is a pretty instinct ; I have often wondered whether it is nature or art.'
He fell silent, still smiling.   Hallin watched him closely.   Per-

haps the thought which had risen in his mind revealed itself by some subtle sign or other to Aldous. For suddenly Raeburn's expression changed ; the over-strenuous, harassed look, which of late had somewhat taken the place of his old philosopher's quiet, reappeared.

'I did not tell you, Hallin,' he began, in a low voice, raising his eyes to his friend, 'that I had seen her again.'

Hallin paused a moment. Then he said :

'No. I knew she went to the House to hear Wharton's speech, and that she dined there. I supposed she might just have come across you—but she said nothing.'

'Of course, I had no idea,' said Aldous ; 'suddenly Lady Winterbourne and I came across her on the terrace. Then I saw she was with that man's party. She spoke to me afterwards—I believe now—she meant to be kind '—his voice showed the difficulty he had in speaking at all—'but I saw him coming up to talk to her. I am ashamed to think of my own manner, but I could not help myself.'

His face and eye took, as he spoke, a peculiar vividness and glow. Raeburn had not for months mentioned to him the name of Marcella Boyce, but Hallin had all along held two faiths about the matter : first, that Aldous was still possessed by a passion which had become part of his life ; secondly, that the events of the preceding year had produced in him an exceedingly bitter sense of ill-usage, of a type which Hallin had not perhaps expected.

'Did you see anything to make you suppose,' he asked quietly after a pause, 'that she is going to marry him ?'

'No—no,' Aldous repeated slowly ; 'but she is clearly on friendly, perhaps intimate, terms with him. And just now, of course, she is more likely to be influenced by him than ever. He made a great success—of a kind—in the House a fortnight ago. People seem to think he may come rapidly to the front.'

'So I understand. I don't believe it. The jealousies that divide that group are too unmanageable. If he *were* a Parnell ! But he lacks just the qualities that matter—the reticence, the power of holding himself aloof from irrelevant things and interests, the hard self-concentration.'

Aldous raised his shoulders.

'I don't imagine there is any lack of that ! But certainly he holds himself aloof from nothing and nobody ! I hear of him everywhere.'

'What !—among the smart people ?'

Aldous nodded.

'A change of policy by all accounts,' said Hallin, musing. 'He

must do it with intention. He is not the man to let himself be
be-Capua-ed all at once.'

'Oh dear, no!' said Aldous drily. 'He does it with intention.
Nobody supposes him to be the mere toady. All the same I think
he may very well overrate the importance of the class he is trying
to make use of, and its influence. Have you been following the
strike "leaders" in the *Clarion*?'

'No!' cried Hallin, flushing. 'I would not read them for the
world! I might not be able to go on giving to the strike.'

Aldous fell silent, and Hallin presently saw that his mind had
harked back to the one subject that really held the depths of it.
The truest friendship, Hallin believed, would be never to speak to
him of Marcella Boyce—never to encourage him to dwell upon her,
or upon anything connected with her. But his yearning, sympathetic instinct would not let him follow his own conviction.

'Miss Boyce, you know, has been here two or three times while
you have been away,' he said quickly, as he got up to post a letter.

Aldous hesitated ; then he said—

'Do you gather that her nursing life satisfies her?'

Hallin made a little face.

'Since when has she become a person likely to be " satisfied"
with anything? She devotes to it a splendid and wonderful energy.
When she comes here I admire her with all my heart, and pity her
so much that I could cry over her !'

Aldous started.

'I don't know what you mean,' he said, as he too rose and laid
his hand on Hallin's for a moment. 'But don't tell me! It's best
for me not to talk of her. If she were associated in my mind with
any other man than Wharton, I think somehow I could throw the
whole thing off. But this—this——' He broke off ; then resumed,
while he pretended to look for a parcel he had brought with him,
by way of covering an agitation he could not suppress. 'A person
you and I know said to me the other day, " It may sound un-
romantic, but I could never think of a woman who had thrown me
over except *with ill-will*." The word astonished me, but sometimes I understand it. I find myself full of *anger* to the most futile,
the most ridiculous degree !'

He drew himself up nervously, already scorning his own
absurdity, his own breach of reticence. Hallin laid his hands on
the taller man's shoulders, and there was a short pause.

'Never mind, old fellow,' said Hallin simply, at last, as his
hands dropped ; 'let's go and do our work. What is it you're
after?—I forget.'

Aldous found his packet and his hat, explaining himself again, meanwhile, in his usual voice. He had dropped in on Hallin for a morning visit, meaning to spend some hours before the House met in the investigation of some small workshops in the neighbourhood of Drury Lane. The Home Office had been called upon for increased inspection and regulation ; there had been a great conflict of evidence, and Aldous had finally resolved in his student's way to see for himself the state of things in two or three selected streets.

It was a matter on which Hallin was also well-informed, and felt strongly. They stayed talking about it a few minutes, Hallin eagerly directing Raeburn's attention to the two or three points where he thought the Government could really do good.

Then Raeburn turned to go.

'I shall come and drag you out to-morrow afternoon,' he said, as he opened the door.

'You needn't,' said Hallin with a smile ; 'in fact, don't; I shall have my jaunt.'

Whereby Aldous understood that he would be engaged in his common Saturday practice of taking out a batch of elder boys or girls from one or other of the schools of which he was manager, for a walk or to see some sight.

'If it's your boys,' he said protesting, 'you're not fit for it. Hand them over to me.'

'Nothing of the sort,' said Hallin gaily, and turned him out of the room.

Raeburn found the walk from Hallin's Bloomsbury quarters to Drury Lane hot and airless. The planes were already drooping and yellowing in the squares, the streets were at their closest and dirtiest, and the traffic of Holborn and its approaches had never seemed to him more bewildering in its roar and volume. July was in, and all freshness had already disappeared from the too short London summer.

For Raeburn on this particular afternoon there was a curious forlornness in the dry and tainted air. His slack mood found no bracing in the sun or the breeze. Everything was or seemed distasteful to a mind out of tune—whether this work he was upon, which only yesterday had interested him considerably, or his Parliamentary occupations, or some tiresome estate business which would have to be looked into when he got home. He was oppressed, too, by the last news of his grandfather. The certainty that this dear and honoured life, with which his own had been so closely intertwined since his boyhood, was drawing to its close weighed upon him now heavily and constantly. The loss itself would take from him an object on which affection—checked and thwarted elsewhere—was still free to spend itself in ways peculiarly noble and tender ; and as for those other changes to which the first great change must lead—his transference to the Upper House, and the extension for himself of all the ceremonial side of life—he looked forward to them with an intense and resentful repugnance, as to aggravations, perversely thrust on him from without, of a great and necessary grief. Few men believed less happily in democracy than Aldous Raeburn ; on the other hand, few men felt a more steady distaste for certain kinds of inequality.

He was to meet a young inspector at the corner of Little Queen Street, and they were to visit together a series of small brush-draw-ing and box-making workshops in the Drury Lane district, to which the attention of the Department had lately been specially drawn. Aldous had no sooner crossed Holborn than he saw his man wait-ing for him, a tall strip of a fellow, with a dark bearded face, and a manner which shyness had made a trifle morose. Aldous, however, knew him to be not only a capital worker, but a man of parts, and had got much information and some ideas out of him already. Mr. Peabody gave the Under-secretary a slight preoccupied smile in re-turn for his friendly greeting, and the two walked on together talking.

The inspector announced that he proposed to take his com-panion first of all to a street behind Drury Lane, of which many of the houses were already marked for demolition—a 'black street,' bearing a peculiarly vile reputation in the neighbourhood. It con-tained on the whole the worst of the small workshops which he desired to bring to Raeburn's notice, besides a variety of other horrors, social and sanitary.

After ten minutes' walking they turned into the street. With its condemned houses, many of them shored up and windowless, its narrow roadway strewn with costers' refuse—it was largely in-habited by costers frequenting Covent Garden Market—its filthy gutters and broken pavements, it touched, indeed, a depth of sinis-ter squalor beyond most of its fellows. The air was heavy with odours which, in this July heat, seemed to bear with them the inmost essences of things sickening and decaying ; and the chil-dren, squatting or playing amid the garbage of the street, were further than most of their kind from any tolerable human type.

A policeman was stationed near the entrance of the street. After they had passed him, Mr. Peabody ran back and said a word in his ear.

' I gave him your name,' he said briefly, in answer to Raeburn's interrogative look, when he returned, 'and told him what we were after. The street is not quite as bad as it was ; and there are little oases of respectability in it you would never expect. But there is plenty of the worst thieving and brutality left in it still. Of course, now you see it at its dull moment. To-night the place will swarm with barrows and stalls, all the people will be in the street, and after dark it will be as near pandemonium as may be. I happen to know the School Board visitor of these parts ; and a City Missionary, too, who is afraid of nothing.'

And standing still a moment, pointing imperceptibly to right and left, he began in his shy, monotonous voice to run through the inhabitants of some of the houses and a few typical histories. This group was mainly peopled by women of the very lowest class and their ' bullies '—that is to say, the men who aided them in plundering, sometimes in murdering, the stranger who fell into their claws ; in that house a woman had been slowly done to death by her husband and his brutal brothers under every circumstance of tragic horror ; in the next a case of flagrant and revolting cruelty to a pair of infant children had just been brought to light. In addition to its vice and its thievery, the wretched place was, of course, steeped in drink. There were gin-palaces at all the corners ; the women drank, in proportion to their resources, as badly as the men, and the children were fed with the stuff in infancy, and began for themselves as early as they could beg or steal a copper of their own.

When the dismal catalogue was done they moved on towards the further end of the street, and a house on the right-hand side. Behind the veil of his official manner Aldous's shrinking sense took all it saw and heard as fresh food for a darkness and despondency of soul already great enough. But his companion—a young enthusiast, secretly very critical of ' big-wigs '—was conscious only of the trained man of affairs, courteous, methodical, and well-informed, putting a series of preliminary questions with unusual point and rapidity.

Suddenly, under the influence of a common impression, both men stood still and looked about them. There was a stir in the street. Windows had been thrown open, and scores of heads were looking out. People emerged from all quarters, seemed to spring from the ground or drop from the skies, and in a few seconds, as it were, the street, so dead-alive before, was full of a running and shouting crowd.

' It is a fight !' said Peabody, as the crowd came up with them. ' Listen !'

Shrieks—of the most ghastly and piercing note, rang through the air. The men and women who rushed past the two strangers —hustling them, yet too excited to notice them—were all making for a house some ten or twelve yards in front of them, to their left. Aldous had turned white.

' It is a woman !' he said, after an instant's listening, ' and it sounds like murder. You go back for that policeman !'

And without another word he threw himself on the crowd, forcing his way through it by the help of arms and shoulders which, in years gone by, had done good service for the Trinity Eight. Drink-sodden men and screaming women gave way before him. He found himself at the door of the house, hammering upon it with two or three other men who were there before him. The noise from within was appalling—cries, groans, uproar—all the sounds of a deadly struggle proceeding apparently on the second floor of the house. Then came a heavy fall—then the sound of a voice, different in quality and accent from any that had gone before, crying piteously and as though in exhaustion—' Help ! '

Almost at the same moment the door which Aldous and his companions were trying to force was burst open from within, and three men seemed to be shot out from the dark passage inside— two wrestling with the third, a wild beast in human shape, maddened apparently with drink, and splashed with blood.

' Ee's done for her ! ' shouted one of the captors ; ' an' for the Sister too ! '

' The Sister ! ' shrieked a woman behind Aldous—' it's the nuss he means ! I sor her go in when I wor at my window half an hour ago. Oh ! yer *blackguard*, you ! '—and she would have fallen upon the wretch, in a frenzy, had not the bystanders caught hold of her.

' Stand back ! ' cried a policeman. Three of them had come up at Peabody's call. The man was instantly secured, and the crowd pushed back.

Aldous was already upstairs.

' Which room ? ' he asked of a group of women crying and cowering on the first landing—for all sounds from above had ceased.

' Third floor front,' cried one of them. ' We all of us *begged* and *implored* of that young person, sir, not to go a-near him ! Didn't we, Betsy ?—didn't we, Doll ? '

Aldous ran up.

On the third floor, the door of the front room was open. A woman lay on the ground, apparently beaten to death.

By her side, torn, dishevelled, and gasping, knelt Marcella Boyce. Two or three other women were standing by in helpless terror and curiosity. Marcella was bending over the bleeding victim before her. Her own left arm hung as though disabled by her side ; but with the right hand she was doing her best to staunch some of the bleeding from the head. Her bag stood open beside her, and one of the chattering women was handing her what she asked for. The sight stamped itself in lines of horror on Raeburn's heart.

In such an exaltation of nerve *she* could be surprised at

nothing. When she saw Raeburn enter the room, she did not even start.

'I think,' she said, as he stooped down to her—speaking with pauses, as though to get her breath—'he has—killed her. But there—is a chance. Are the—police there—and a stretcher?'

Two constables entered as she spoke, and the first of them instantly sent his companion back for a stretcher. Then, noticing Marcella's nursing dress and cloak, he came up to her respectfully.

'Did you see it, miss?'

'I—I tried to separate them,' she replied, still speaking with the same difficulty, while she silently motioned to Aldous, who was on the other side of the unconscious and apparently dying woman, to help her with the bandage she was applying. 'But he was—such a great—powerful brute.'

Aldous, hating the clumsiness of his man's fingers, knelt down and tried to help her. Her trembling hand touched, mingled with his.

'I was downstairs,' she went on, while the constable took out his note-book, 'attending a child—that's ill—when I heard the screams. They were on the landing; he had turned her out of the room—then rushed after her—I *think*—to throw her downstairs—I stopped that. Then he took up something—oh! there it is!' She shuddered, pointing to a broken piece of a chair which lay on the floor. 'He was quite mad with drink—I couldn't—do much.'

Her voice slipped into a weak, piteous note.

'Isn't your arm hurt?' said Aldous, pointing to it.

'It's not broken—it's wrenched; I can't use it. There—that's all we can do—till she gets—to hospital.'

Then she stood up, pale and staggering, and asked the policeman if he could put on a bandage. The man had got his ambulance certificate, and was proud to say that he could. She took a roll out of her bag, and quietly pointed to her arm. He did his best, not without skill, and the deep line of pain furrowing the centre of the brow relaxed a little. Then she sank down on the floor again beside her patient, gazing at the woman's marred face —indescribably patient in its deep unconsciousness—at the gnarled and bloodstained hands, with their wedding-ring; at the thin locks of torn grey hair—with tears that ran unheeded down her cheeks, in a passion of anguished pity, which touched a chord of memory in Raeburn's mind. He had seen her look so once before—beside Minta Hurd, on the day of Hurd's capture.

At the same moment he saw that they were alone. The policeman had cleared the room, and was spending the few minutes that must elapse before his companion returned with the stretcher, in taking the names and evidence of some of the inmates of the house, on the stairs outside.

'You can't do anything more,' said Aldous gently, bending over her. 'Won't you let me take you home?—you want it sorely. The police are trained to these things, and I have a friend here who will help. They will remove her with every care —he will see to it.'

Then for the first time her absorption gave way. . She remembered who he was—where they were—how they had met last. And with the remembrance came an extraordinary leap of joy, flashing through pain and faintness. She had the childish feeling that he could not look unkindly at her any more—after this! When at the White House she had got herself into disgrace, and could not bring her pride to ask pardon, she would silently set up a headache or a cut finger that she might be pitied, and so, perforce, forgiven. The same tacit thought was in her mind now. No !—after this he *must* be friends with her.

'I will just help to get her downstairs,' she said, but with a quivering, appealing accent—and so they fell silent.

Aldous looked round the room—at the miserable filthy garret with its begrimed and peeling wall-paper, its two or three broken chairs, its heap of rags across two boxes that served for a bed, its empty gin-bottles here and there—all the familiar, one might almost say conventionalised, signs of human ruin and damnation —then at this breathing death between himself and her. Perhaps his strongest feeling was one of fierce and natural protest against circumstance—against her mother !—against a reckless philanthropy that could thus throw the finest and fragilest things of a poorly furnished world into such a hopeless struggle with devildom.

'I have been here several times before,' she said presently, in a faint voice, 'and there has never been any trouble. By day the street is not much worse than others—though, of course, it has a bad name. There is a little boy on the next floor very ill with typhoid. Many of the women in the house are very good to him and his mother. This poor thing—used to come in and out— when I was nursing him.—Oh, I wish—I *wish* they would come !' she broke off in impatience, looking at the deathly form—'every moment is of importance !'

As Aldous went to the door to see if the stretcher were in sight, it opened, and the police came in. Marcella, herself helpless, directed the lifting of the bloodstained head ; the police obeyed her with care and skill. Then Raeburn assisted in the carrying downstairs, and presently the police with their burden, and accompanied apparently by the whole street, were on their way to the nearest hospital.

Then Aldous, to his despair and wrath, saw that an inspector of police, who had just come up, was talking to Marcella, no doubt instructing her as to how and where she was to give her evidence. She was leaning against the passage wall, supporting her injured arm with her hand, and seemed to him on the point of fainting.

'Get a cab at once, will you !' he said peremptorily to Peabody ; then going up to the inspector he drew him forward. They exchanged a few words, the inspector lifted his cap, and Aldous went back to Marcella.

'There is a cab here,' he said to her. 'Come, please, directly. They will not trouble you any more for the present.'

He led her out through the still lingering crowd and put her into the cab. As they drove along, he felt every jolt and roughness of the street as though he were himself in anguish. She was some time before she recovered the jar of pain caused her by the act of getting into the cab. Her breath came fast, and he could see that she was trying hard to control herself and not to faint.

He, too, restrained himself so far as not to talk to her. But the exasperation, the revolt within, was in truth growing unmanageably. Was this what her new career—her enthusiasms—meant, or might mean ! Twenty-three !—in the prime of youth, of charm ! Horrible, unpardonable waste ! He could not bear it, could not submit himself to it.

Oh ! let her marry Wharton, or anyone else, so long as it were made impossible for her to bruise and exhaust her young bloom amid such scenes—such gross physical abominations. Amazing ! —how meanly, passionately timorous the man of Raeburn's type can be for the woman ! He himself may be morally 'ever a fighter,' and feel the glow, the stern joy of the fight. But she !— let her leave the human brute and his unsavoury struggle alone ! It cannot be borne—it was never meant—that she should dip her delicate wings, of her own free will at least, in such a mire of blood and tears. It was the feeling that had possessed him when Mrs. Boyce told him of the visit to the prison, the night in the cottage.

In her whirl of feverish thought, she divined him very closely. Presently, as he watched her—hating the man for driving and the cab for shaking—he saw her white lips suddenly smile.

' I know,' she said, rousing herself to look at him ; 'you think nursing is all like that !'

' I hope not !' he said, with effort, trying to smile too.

'I never saw a fight before,' she said, shutting her eyes again. 'Nobody is ever rude to us—I often pine for experiences!'

How like her old, wild tone! His rigid look softened involuntarily.

'Well, you have got one now,' he said, bending over to her. 'Does your arm hurt you much?'

'Yes—but I can bear it. What vexes me is that I shall have to give up work for a bit.—Mr. Raeburn!'

'Yes.' His heart beat.

'We may meet often—mayn't we?—at Lady Winterbourne's—or in the country? Couldn't we be friends? You don't know how often——' She turned away her weary head a moment—gathered strength to begin again—'—how often I have regretted—last year. I see now—that I behaved—more unkindly'—her voice was almost a whisper—'than I thought then. But it is all done with—couldn't we just be good friends—understand each other, perhaps, better than we ever did?'

She kept her eyes closed, shaken with alternate shame and daring.

As for him, he was seized with overpowering dumbness and chill. What was really in his mind was the Terrace—was Wharton's advancing figure. But her state—the moment—coerced him.

'We could not be anything but friends,' he said gently, but with astonishing difficulty; and then could find nothing more to say. She knew his reserve, however, and would not this time be repelled

She put out her hand.

'No!' she said, looking at it and withdrawing it with a shudder; 'oh no!'

Then suddenly a passion of tears and trembling overcame her. She leant against the side of the cab, struggling in vain to regain her self-control, gasping incoherent things about the woman she had not been able to save. He tried to soothe and calm her, his own heart wrung. But she hardly heard him.

At last they turned into Maine Street, and she saw the gateway of Brown's Buildings.

'Here we are,' she said faintly, summoning all her will; 'do you know you will have to help me across that court, and upstairs —then I shan't be any more trouble.'

So, leaning on Raeburn's arm, Marcella made her slow progress across the court of Brown's Buildings and through the gaping groups of children. Then at the top of her flight of steps she withdrew herself from him with a wan smile.

'Now I am home,' she said. 'Good-bye!'

Aldous looked round him well at Brown's Buildings as he de-

parted. Then he got in a hansom, and drove to Lady Winterbourne's house, and implored her to fetch and nurse Marcella
Boyce, using her best cleverness to hide all motion of his in the
matter.

After which he spent—poor Aldous !—one of the most restless
and miserable nights of his life.

CHAPTER XI

MARCELLA was sitting in a deep and comfortable chair at the
open window of Lady Winterbourne's drawing-room. The house
—in James Street, Buckingham Gate—looked out over the exer-
cising ground of the great barracks in front, and commanded the
greenery of St. James's Park to the left. The planes lining the
barrack railings were poor, wilted things, and London was as hot
as ever. Still the charm of these open spaces of sky and park, after
the high walls and innumerable windows of Brown's Buildings,
was very great ; Marcella wanted nothing more but to lie still, to
dally with a book, to dream as she pleased, and to be let alone.

Lady Winterbourne and her married daughter, Lady Ermyntrude, were still out, engaged in the innumerable nothings of the
fashionable afternoon. Marcella had her thoughts to herself.

But they were not of a kind that anyone need have wished to
share. In the first place, she was tired of idleness. In the early
days after Lady Winterbourne had carried her off, the soft beds
and sofas, the trained service and delicate food of this small but
luxurious house had been so pleasant to her that she had scorned
herself for a greedy Sybaritic temper, delighted by any means to
escape from plain living. But she had been here a fortnight, and
was now pining to go back to work. Her mood was too restless
and transitional to leave her long in love with comfort and folded
hands. She told herself that she had no longer any place among
the rich and important people of this world ; far away beyond
these parks and palaces, in the little network of dark streets she
knew, lay the problems and the cares that were really hers,
through which her heart was somehow wrestling—must somehow
wrestle—its passionate way. But her wrenched arm was still in a
sling, and was, moreover, undergoing treatment at the hands of a
clever specialist ; and she could neither go home, as her mother
had wished her to do, nor return to her nursing—a state of affairs
which of late had made her a little silent and moody.

On the whole she found her chief pleasure in the two weekly
visits she paid to the woman whose life, it now appeared, she *had*
saved—probably at some risk of her own.   The poor victim would
go scarred and maimed through what remained to her of existence.
But she lived; and—as Marcella and Lady Winterbourne and
Raeburn had abundantly made up their minds—would be perma-
nently cared for and comforted in the future.

Alas ! there were many things that stood between Marcella and
true rest.   She had been woefully disappointed, nay wounded, as
to the results of that tragic half-hour which for the moment had
seemed to throw a bridge of friendship over those painful, estranging
memories lying between her and Aldous Raeburn.   He had called
two or three times since she had been with Lady Winterbourne ;
he had done his best to make her inevitable appearance as a witness in the police-court as easy to her as possible ; the man who
had stood by her through such a scene could do no less, in common
politeness and humanity.   But each time they met his manner had
been formal and constrained ; there had been little conversation ;
and she had been left to the bitterness of feeling that she had made
a strange if not unseemly advance, of which he must think unkindly,
since he had let it count with him so little.

Childishly, angrily—*she wanted him to be friends*.   Why
shouldn't he ?   He would certainly marry Betty Macdonald in
time, whatever Mr. Hallin might say.   Then why not put his pride
away and be generous ?   Their future lives must of necessity touch
each other, for they were bound to the same neighbourhood, the
same spot of earth.   She knew herself to be her father's heiress.
Mellor must be hers some day ; and before that day, whenever her
father's illness, of which she now understood the incurable though
probably tedious nature, should reach a certain stage, she must go
home and take up her life there again.   Why embitter such a
situation ?—make it more difficult for everybody concerned ?   Why
not simply bury the past and begin again ?   In her restlessness she
was inclined to think herself much wiser and more magnanimous
than he.

Meanwhile in the Winterbourne household she was living
among people to whom Aldous Raeburn was a dear and familiar
companion, who admired him with all their hearts, and felt a sympathetic interest alike in his private life and his public career.
Their circle, too, was his circle ; and by means of it she now saw
Aldous in his relations to his equals and colleagues, whether in the
Ministry or the House.   The result was a number of new impressions which she half resented, as we may resent the information
that some stranger will give us upon a subject we imagined our-

selves better acquainted with than anybody else. The promise of Raeburn's political position struck her quick mind with a curious surprise. She could not explain it as she had so often tacitly explained his place in Brookshire—by the mere accidents of birth. After all, aristocratic as we still are, no party can now afford to choose its men by any other criterion than personal profitableness. And a man nowadays is in the long run personally profitable, far more by what he is than by what he has—so far at least has 'progress' brought us.

She saw then that this quiet, strong man, with his obvious defects of temperament and manner, had already gained a remarkable degree of 'consideration,' using the word in its French sense, among his political contemporaries. He was beginning to be reckoned upon as a man of the future by an inner circle of persons whose word counted and carried; while yet his name was comparatively little known to the public. Marcella, indeed, had gathered her impression from the most slight and various sources —mostly from the phrases, the hints, the manner of men already themselves charged with the most difficult and responsible work of England. Above all things did she love and admire power—the power of personal capacity. It had been the secret, it was still half the secret, of Wharton's influence with her. She saw it here under wholly different conditions and accessories. She gave it recognition with a kind of unwillingness. All the same, Raeburn took a new place in her imagination.

Then—apart from the political world and its judgments—the intimacy between him and the Winterbourne family showed her to him in many new aspects. To Lady Winterbourne, his mother's dear and close friend, he was almost a son ; and nothing could be more charming than the affectionate and playful tolerance with which he treated her little oddities and weaknesses. And to all her children he was bound by the memories and kindnesses of many years. He was the godfather of Lady Ermyntrude's child ; the hero and counsellor of the two sons, who were both in Parliament, and took his lead in many things ; while there was no one with whom Lord Winterbourne could more comfortably discuss county or agricultural affairs. In the old days Marcella had somehow tended to regard him as a man of few friends. And in a sense it was so. He did not easily yield himself ; and was often thought dull and apathetic by strangers. But here, amid these old companions, his delicacy and sweetness of disposition had full play ; and although, now that Marcella was in their house, he came less often, and was less free with them than usual, she saw enough to make her wonder a little that they were all so kind and indulgent to *her*, seeing that they cared so much for him and all that affected him.

Well! she was often judged, humbled, reproached. Yet there was a certain irritation in it. Was it all her own fault that in her brief engagement she had realised him so little? Her heart was sometimes oddly sore; her conscience full of smart; but there were moments when she was as combative as ever.

Nor had certain other experiences of this past fortnight been any more soothing to this sore craving sense of hers. It appeared very soon that nothing would have been easier for her had she chosen than to become the lion of the later season. The story of the Batton Street tragedy had, of course, got into the papers, and had been treated there with the usual adornments of the ' New Journalism.'

The world which knew the Raeburns or knew of them—comparatively a large world—fell with avidity on the romantic juxtaposition of names. To lose your betrothed as Aldous Raeburn had lost his, and then to come across her again in this manner and in these circumstances—there was a dramatic neatness about it to which the careless Fate that governs us too seldom attains. London discussed the story a good deal ; and would have liked dearly to see and to exhibit the heroine. Mrs. Lane in particular, the hostess of the House of Commons dinner, felt that she had claims, and was one of the first to call at Lady Winterbourne's and see her guest. She soon discovered that Marcella had no intention whatever of playing the lion ; and must, in fact, avoid excitement and fatigue. But she had succeeded in getting the girl to come to her once or twice of an afternoon to meet two or three people. It was better for the wounded arm that its owner should walk than drive ; and Mrs. Lane lived at a convenient distance, at a house in Piccadilly, just across the Green Park.

Here then, as in James Street, Marcella had met in discreet succession a few admiring and curious persons, and had tasted some of the smaller sweets of fame. But the magnet that drew her to the Lanes' house had been no craving for notoriety ; at the present moment she was totally indifferent to what perhaps constitutionally she might have liked ; the attraction had been simply the occasional presence there of Harry Wharton. He excited, puzzled, angered, and commanded her more than ever. She could not keep herself away from the chance of meeting him. And Lady Winterbourne neither knew him, nor apparently wished to know him—a fact which probably tended to make Marcella obstinate.

Yet what pleasure had there been after all in these meetings !

Again and again she had seen him surrounded there by pretty and fashionable women, with some of whom he was on amazingly easy terms, while with all of them he talked their language, and so far as she could see to a great extent lived their life. The contradiction of the House of Commons evening returned upon her perpetually. She thought she saw in many of his new friends a certain malicious triumph in the readiness with which the young demagogue had yielded to their baits. No doubt they were at least as much duped as he. Like Hallin, she did not believe that at bottom he was the man to let himself be held by silken bonds if it should be to his interest to break them. But, meanwhile, his bearing among these people—the claims they and their amusements made upon his time and his mind—seemed to this girl, who watched them with her dark, astonished eyes, a kind of treachery to his place and his cause. It was something she had never dreamed of; and it roused her contempt and irritation.

Then as to herself. He had been all eagerness in his inquiries after her from Mrs. Lane; and he never saw her in the Piccadilly drawing-room that he did not pay her homage, often with a certain extravagance, a kind of appropriation, which Mrs. Lane secretly thought in bad taste, and Marcella sometimes resented. On the other hand, things jarred between them frequently. From day to day he varied. She had dreamt of a great friendship; but instead, it was hardly possible to carry on the thread of their relation from meeting to meeting with simplicity and trust. On the Terrace he had behaved, or would have behaved, if she had allowed him, as a lover. When they met again at Mrs. Lane's he would be sometimes devoted in his old paradoxical, flattering vein; sometimes, she thought, even cool. Nay, once or twice he was guilty of curious little neglects towards her, generally in the presence of some great lady or other. On one of these occasions she suddenly felt herself flushing from brow to chin at the thought—'He does not want anyone to suppose for a moment that he wishes to marry me!'

It had taken Wharton some difficult hours to subdue in her the effects of that one moment's fancy. Till then it is the simple truth to say that she had never seriously considered the possibility of marrying him. When it *did* enter her mind, she saw that it had already entered his—and that he was full of doubts! The perception had given to her manner an increasing aloofness and pride which had of late piqued Wharton into efforts from which vanity, and, indeed, something else, could not refrain, if he was to preserve his power.

So she was sitting by the window this afternoon, in a mood which had in it neither simplicity nor joy. She was conscious of a certain dull and baffled feeling—a sense of humiliation—which hurt.   Moreover, the scene of sordid horror she had gone through haunted her imagination perpetually.   She was unstrung, and the world weighed upon her—the pity, the ugliness, the confusion of it.

The muslin curtain beside her suddenly swelled out in a draught of air, and she put out her hand quickly to catch the French window lest it should swing to.   Someone had opened the door of the room.

'*Did* I blow you out of window?' said a girl's voice; and there behind her, in a half-timid attitude, stood Betty Macdonald, a vision of white muslin, its frills and capes a little tossed by the wind, the pointed face and golden hair showing small and elf-like under the big shady hat.

'Oh, do come in!' said Marcella shyly.   'Lady Winterbourne will be in directly.'

'So Panton told me,' said Betty, sinking down on a high stool beside Marcella's chair, and taking off her hat; 'and Panton doesn't tell *me* any stories *now*—I've trained him.   I wonder how many he tells in the day?   Don't you think there will be a special little corner of purgatory for London butlers?   I hope Panton will get off easy!'

Then she laid her sharp chin on her tiny hand, and studied Marcella.   Miss Boyce was in the light black dress that Minta approved; her pale face and delicate hands stood out from it with a sort of noble emphasis.   When Betty had first heard of Marcella Boyce as the heroine of a certain story, she had thought of her as a girl one would like to meet, if only to prick her somehow for breaking the heart of a good man.   Now that she saw her close she felt herself nearly falling in love with her.   Moreover, the incident of the fight and of Miss Boyce's share in it had thrilled a creature all susceptibility and curiosity; and the little merry thing would sit hushed, looking at the heroine of it, awed by the thought of what a girl only two years older than herself must have already seen of sin and tragedy, envying her with all her heart, and by contrast honestly despising—for the moment—that very happy and popular person, Betty Macdonald!

'Do you like being alone?' she asked Marcella abruptly.

Marcella coloured.

'Well, I was just getting very tired of my own company,' she said.   'I was very glad to see you come in.'

'Were you?' said Betty joyously, with a little gleam in her pretty eyes.   Then suddenly the golden head bent forward.   'May I kiss you?' she said, in the wistfullest, eagerest voice.

Marcella smiled, and, laying her hand on Betty's, shyly drew her.

'That's better!' said Betty, with a long breath. 'That's the second milestone : the first was when I saw you on the Terrace. Couldn't you mark all your friendships by little white stones? I could. But the horrid thing is when you have to mark them back again ! Nobody ever did that with you !'

'Because I have no friends,' said Marcella quickly. Then, when Betty clapped her hands in amazement at such a speech, she added quickly with a smile, 'except a few I make poultices for.'

'There !' said Betty enviously, 'to think of being really *wanted*—for poultices—or anything ! I never was wanted in my life ! When I die they'll put on my poor little grave—

> She's buried here—that hizzie Betty ;
> She did na gude—so don't ee fret ye !

—Oh, there they are !'—she ran to the window—' Lady Winter-bourne and Ermyntrude. Doesn't it make you laugh to see Lady Winterbourne doing her duties? She gets into her carriage after lunch as one might mount a tumbril. I expect to hear her tell the coachman to drive to "the scaffold at Hyde Park Corner." She looks the unhappiest woman in England—and all the time Ermyntrude declares she likes it, and wouldn't do without her season for the world ! She gives Ermyntrude a lot of trouble, but she *is* a dear—a naughty dear—and mothers are *such* a chance! Ermyntrude ! *where* did you get that bonnet? You got it without me—and my feelings won't stand it !'

Lady Ermyntrude and Betty threw themselves on a sofa together, chattering and laughing. Lady Winterbourne came up to Marcella and inquired after her. She was still slowly drawing off her gloves, when the drawing-room door opened again.

'Tea, Panton !' said Lady Winterbourne, without turning her head, and in the tone of Lady Macbeth. But the magnificent butler took no notice.

'Lady Selina Farrell !' he announced in a firm voice.

Lady Winterbourne gave a nervous start ; then, with the air of a person cut out of wood, made a slight advance, and held out a limp hand to her visitor.

'Won't you sit down ?' she said.

Anybody who did not know her would have supposed that she had never seen Lady Selina before. In reality she and the Alres-fords were cousins. But she did not like Lady Selina, and never took any pains to conceal it—a fact which did not in the smallest degree interfere with the younger lady's performance of her family duties.

Lady Selina found a seat with easy aplomb, put up her bejewelled fingers to draw off her veil, and smilingly prepared herself for tea. She inquired of Betty how she was enjoying herself, and of Lady Ermyntrude how her husband and baby in the country were getting on without her. The tone of this last question made the person addressed flush and draw herself up. It was put as banter, but certainly conveyed that Lady Ermyntrude was neglecting her family for the sake of dissipations. Betty meanwhile curled herself up in a corner of the sofa, letting one pretty foot swing over the other, and watching the new comer with a malicious eye, which instantly and gleefully perceived that Lady Selina thought her attitude ungraceful.

Marcella, of course, was greeted and condoled with—Lady Selina, however, had seen her since the tragedy—and then Lady Winterbourne, after every item of her family news, and every symptom of her own and her husband's health had been rigorously inquired into, began to attempt some feeble questions of her own —how, for instance, was Lord Alresford's gout ?

Lady Selina replied that he was well, but much depressed by the political situation. No doubt Ministers had done their best, but he thought two or three foolish mistakes had been made during the session. Certain blunders ought at all hazards to have been avoided. He feared that the party and the country might have to pay dearly for them. But *he* had done his best.

Lady Winterbourne, whose eldest son was a junior whip, had been the recipient, since the advent of the new Cabinet, of so much rejoicing over the final exclusion of ' that vain old idiot, Alresford,' from any further chances of muddling a public department, that Lady Selina's talk made her at once nervous and irritable. She was afraid of being indiscreet ; yet she longed to put her visitor down. In her odd disjointed way, too, she took a real interest in politics. Her craving idealist nature—mated with a cheery sportsman husband who laughed at her, yet had made her happy —was always trying to reconcile the ends of eternal justice with the measures of the Tory party. It was a task of Sisyphus ; but she would not let it alone.

' I do not agree with you,' she said with cold shyness in answer to Lady Selina's concluding laments—' I am told—our people say —we are doing very well—except that the session is likely to be dreadfully long.'

Lady Selina raised both her eyebrows and her shoulders.

'*Dear* Lady Winterbourne ! you really mean it ?' she said with the indulgent incredulity one shows to the simple-minded—'But just think ! The session will go on, everyone says, till *quite* the end of September. Isn't that enough of itself to make a party discontented? *All* our big measures are in dreadful arrears. And my father believes so *much* of the friction might have been avoided. He is all in favour of doing more for Labour. He thinks these Labour men might have been easily propitiated without anything revolutionary. It's no good supposing that these poor starving people will wait for ever!'

'Oh!' said Lady Winterbourne, and sat staring at her visitor. To those who knew its author well, the monosyllable could not have been more expressive. Lady Winterbourne's sense of humour had no voice, but inwardly it was busy with Lord Alresford as the 'friend of the poor.' *Alresford* !—the narrowest and niggardliest tyrant alive, so far as his own servants and estate were concerned. And as to Lady Selina, it was well known to the Winterbourne cousinship that she could never get a maid to stay with her six months.

'What did *you* think of Mr. Wharton's speech the other night?' said Lady Selina, bending suavely across the tea-table to Marcella.

'It was very interesting,' said Marcella stiffly—perfectly conscious that the name had pricked the attention of everybody in the room, and angry with her cheeks for reddening.

'Wasn't it ?' said Lady Selina heartily. 'You can't *do* those things, of course ! But you should show every sympathy to the clever enthusiastic young men—the men like that—shouldn't you ? That's what my father says. He says we've got to win them. We've got somehow to make them feel us their friends—or we shall *all* go to ruin ! They have the voting power—and we are the party of education, of refinement. If we can only lead that kind of man to see the essential justice of our cause—and at the same time give them our help—in reason—show them we want to be their friends—wouldn't it be best ? I don't know whether I put it rightly—you know so much about these things ! But we can't undo '67—can we ? We must get round it somehow—mustn't we ? And my father thinks Ministers so unwise ! But perhaps'—and Lady Selina drew herself back with a more gracious smile than ever—'I ought not to be saying these things to you—of course I know you *used* to think us Conservatives very bad people—but Mr. Wharton tells me, perhaps you don't think *quite* so hardly of us as you used ?'

Lady Selina's head in its Paris bonnet fell to one side in a gentle interrogative sort of way

Something roused in Marcella.

'Our cause?' she repeated, while the dark eye dilated—'I wonder what you mean?'

'Well, I mean—,' said Lady Selina, seeking for the harmless word, in the face of this unknown explosive-looking girl—'I mean, of course, the cause of the educated—of the people who have made the country.'

'I think,' said Marcella quietly, 'you mean the cause of the rich!—don't you?'

'Marcella!' cried Lady Winterbourne, catching at the tone rather than words—'I thought you didn't feel like that any more —not about the distance between the poor and the rich—and our tyranny—and its being hopeless—and the poor always hating us— I thought you'd changed.'

And forgetting Lady Selina, remembering only the old talks at Mellor, Lady Winterbourne bent forward and laid an appealing hand on Marcella's arm.

Marcella turned to her with an odd look.

'If you only knew,' she said, 'how much more possible it is to think well of the rich, when you are living amongst the poor!'

'Ah! you must be at a distance from us to do us justice?' inquired Lady Selina, setting her bracelets with a sarcastic lip.

'*I* must,' said Marcella, looking, however, not at her, but at Lady Winterbourne. 'But then, you see,'—she caressed her friend's hand with a smile—'it is so easy to throw some people into opposition!'

'Dreadfully easy!' sighed Lady Winterbourne.

The flush mounted again in the girl's cheek. She hesitated, then felt driven to explanations.

'You see—oddly enough'—she pointed away for an instant to the north-east through the open window—'it's when I'm over there—among the people who have nothing—that it does me good to remember that there are persons who live in James Street, Buckingham Gate!'

'My dear! I don't understand, said Lady Winterbourne, studying her with her most perplexed and tragic air.

'Well, isn't it simple?' said Marcella, still holding her hand and looking up at her. 'It comes, I suppose, of going about all day in those streets and houses, among people who live in one room—with not a bit of prettiness anywhere—and no place to be alone in, or to rest in. I come home and *gloat* over all the beautiful dresses and houses and gardens I can think of!'

'But don't you *hate* the people that have them?' said Betty, again on her stool, chin in hand.

'No! it doesn't seem to matter to me then what kind of people they are. And I don't so much want to take from them and give to the others. I only want to be sure that the beauty, and the leisure, and the freshness are *some*where—not lost out of the world.'

'How strange!—in a life like yours—that one should think so much of the *ugliness* of being poor—more than of suffering or pain,' said Betty, musing.

'Well—in some moods—you do—*I* do!' said Marcella; 'and it is in those moods that I feel least resentful of wealth. If I say to myself that the people who have all the beauty and the leisure are often selfish and cruel—after all they die out of their houses and their parks, and their pictures, in time, like the shell-fish out of its shell. The beauty and the grace which they created or inherited remain. And why should one be envious of *them* personally? They have had the best chances in the world and thrown them away—are but poor animals at the end! At any rate I can't hate them—they seem to have a function—when I am moving about Drury Lane!' she added with a smile.

'But how can one help being ashamed?' said Lady Winterbourne, as her eyes wandered over her pretty room, and she felt herself driven somehow into playing devil's advocate.

'No! no!' said Marcella eagerly, 'don't be ashamed! As to the people who make beauty more beautiful—who share it and give it—I often feel as if I could say to them on my knees, Never, *never* be ashamed merely of being rich—of living with beautiful things, and having time to enjoy them! One might as well be ashamed of being strong rather than a cripple, or having two eyes rather than one!'

'Oh, but, my dear!' cried Lady Winterbourne, piteous and bewildered, 'when one has all the beauty and the freedom—and other people must *die* without any——'

'Oh, I know, I *know*!' said Marcella, with a quick gesture of despair; 'that's what makes the world the world. And one begins with thinking it can be changed—that it *must* and *shall* be changed!—that everybody could have wealth—could have beauty and rest, and time to think, that is to say—if things were different—if one could get Socialism—if one could beat down the capitalist —if one could level down, and level up, till everybody had 200*l.* a year. One turns and fingers the puzzle all day long. It seems so *near* coming right—one guesses a hundred ways in which it might be done! Then after a while one stumbles upon doubt—one begins to see that it never *will*, never *can* come right—not in any mechanical way of that sort—that *that* isn't what was meant!'

Her voice dropped drearily. Betty Macdonald gazed at her

with a girl's nascent adoration. Lady Winterbourne was looking
puzzled and unhappy, but absorbed like Betty in Marcella. Lady
Selina, studying the three with smiling composure, was putting on
her veil, with the most careful attention to fringe and hairpins. As
for Ermyntrude, she was no longer on the sofa ; she had risen
noiselessly, finger on lip, almost at the beginning of Marcella's
talk, to greet a visitor. She and he were standing at the back of
the room, in the opening of the conservatory, unnoticed by any of
the group in the bow window.

'Don't you think,' said Lady Selina airily, her white fingers
still busy with her bonnet, 'that it would be a very good thing to
send all the Radicals—the well-to-do Radicals I mean—to live
among the poor ? It seems to teach people such extremely useful
things !'

Marcella straightened herself as though someone had touched
her impertinently. She looked round quickly.

'I wonder what you suppose it teaches ?'

'Well,' said Lady Selina, a little taken aback and hesitating;
'well ! I suppose it teaches a person to be content—and not to
cry for the moon !'

'You *think*,' said Marcella slowly, 'that to live among the poor
can teach anyone—anyone that's *human*—to be *content* !'

Her manner had the unconscious intensity of emphasis, the
dramatic force that came to her from another blood than ours.
Another woman could hardly have fallen into such a tone without
affectation—without pose. At this moment certainly Betty, who
was watching her, acquitted her of either, and warmly thought her
a magnificent creature.

Lady Selina's feeling simply was that she had been roughly
addressed by her social inferior. She drew herself up.

'As I understand you,' she said stiffly, 'you yourself confessed
that to live with poverty had led you to think more reasonably of
wealth.'

Suddenly a movement of Lady Ermyntrude's made the speaker
turn her head. She saw the pair at the end of the room, looked
astonished, then smiled.

'Why, Mr. Raeburn ! where have you been hiding yourself
during this great discussion ? Most consoling, wasn't it—on the
whole—to us West End people ?'

She threw back a keen glance at Marcella. Lady Ermyntrude
and Raeburn came forward.

'I made him be quiet,' said Ermyntrude, not looking, however,
quite at her ease ; 'it would have been a shame to interrupt.'

'I think so, indeed !' said Lady Selina with emphasis. 'Good-bye, dear Lady Winterbourne ; good-bye, Miss Boyce ! You have comforted me very much ! Of *course* one is sorry for the poor ; but it is a great thing to hear from anybody who knows as much about it as *you* do, that—after all—it is no crime—to possess a little !'

She stood smiling—looking from the girl to the man—then, escorted by Raeburn in his very stiffest manner, she swept out of the room.

When Aldous came back—with a somewhat slow and hesitating step—he approached Marcella, who was standing silent by the window, and asked after the lame arm. He was sorry, he said, to see that it was still in its sling. His tone was a little abrupt. Only Lady Winterbourne saw the quick nervousness of the eyes.

' Oh ! thank you,' said Marcella coldly, ' I shall get back to work next week.'

She stooped and took up her book.

' I must please go and write some letters,' she said, in answer to Lady Winterbourne's flurried look.

And she walked away. Betty and Lady Ermyntrude also went to take off their things.

'Aldous !' said Lady Winterbourne, holding out her hand to him.

He took it, glanced unwillingly at her wistful, agitated face, pressed the hand, and let it go.

' Isn't it sad,' said his old friend, unable to help herself, ' to see her battling like this with life—with thought—all alone ? Isn't it sad, Aldous ? '

' Yes,' he said. Then, after a pause. ' Why *doesn't* she go home ? My patience gives out when I think of Mrs. Boyce.'

' Oh ! it isn't Mrs. Boyce's fault,' said Lady Winterbourne hopelessly. ' And I don't know why one should be sorry for her particularly—why one should want her to change her life again. She does it splendidly. Only I never, *never* feel that she is a bit happy in it.'

It was Hallin's cry over again.

He said nothing for a moment ; then he forced a smile.

' Well ! neither you nor I can help it, can we ? ' he said. The grey eyes looked at her steadily—bitterly. Lady Winterbourne, with the sensation of one who, looking for softness, has lit on granite, changed the subject.

Meanwhile, Marcella upstairs was walking restlessly up and down. She could hardly keep herself from rushing off—back to Brown's Buildings at once. *He* in the room while she was saying those things ! Lady Selina's words burnt in her ears. Her

morbid, irritable sense was all one vibration of pride and revolt.
Apology—appeal—under the neatest comedy guise ! Of course !
—now that Lord Maxwell was dying, and the ill-used suitor was so
much the nearer to his peerage. A foolish girl had repented her of
her folly—was anxious to make those concerned understand—what
more simple ?

Her nerves were strained and out of gear. Tears came in a
proud, passionate gush ; and she must needs allow herself the relief
of them.

Meanwhile, Lady Selina had gone home full of new and uncomfortable feelings. She could not get Marcella Boyce out of her
head—neither as she had just seen her, under the wing of 'that
foolish woman, Adelaide Winterbourne,' nor as she had seen her
first, on the Terrace with Harry Wharton. It did not please Lady
Selina to feel herself in any way eclipsed, or even rivalled, by such
an unimportant person as this strange and ridiculous girl. Yet it
crossed her mind with a stab, as she lay resting on the sofa in her
bedroom before dinner, that never in all her thirty-five years had
any human being looked into *her* face with the same alternations of
eagerness and satisfied pleasure she had seen on Harry Wharton's,
as he and Miss Boyce strolled the Terrace together—nor even with
such a look as that silly baby Betty Macdonald had put on as she
sat on the stool at the heroine's feet.

There was to be a small dinner-party at Alresford House that
night. Wharton was to be among the guests. He was fast becoming one of the *habitués* of the house, and would often stay
behind to talk to Lady Selina when the guests were gone, and
Lord Alresford was dozing peacefully in a deep arm-chair.

Lady Selina lay still in the evening light, and let her mind,
which worked with extraordinary shrewdness and force in the
grooves congenial to it, run over some possibilities of the future.

She was interrupted by the entrance of her maid, who, with
the quickened breath and heightened colour she could not repress
when speaking to her formidable mistress, told her that one of the
younger housemaids was very ill. Lady Selina inquired, found
that the doctor who always attended the servants had been sent
for, and thought that the illness *might* turn to rheumatic fever.

'Oh, send her off to the hospital at once !' said Lady Selina.
'Let Mrs. Stewart see Dr. Briggs first thing in the morning, and
make arrangements. You understand ?'

The girl hesitated, and the candles she was lighting showed
that she had been crying.

'If your ladyship would but let her stay,' she said timidly, 'we'd all take our turns at nursing her. She comes from Ireland, perhaps you'll remember, my lady. She's no friends in London, and she's frightened to death of going to the hospital.'

'That's nonsense!' said Lady Selina sternly. 'Do you think I can have all the work of the house put out because someone is ill? She might die even—one never knows. Just tell Mrs Stewart to arrange with her about her wages, and to look out for somebody else at once.'

The girl's mouth set sullenly as she went about her work—put out the shining satin dress, the jewels, the hairpins, the curling-irons, the various powders and cosmetics that were wanted for Lady Selina's toilette, and all the time there was ringing in her ears the piteous cry of a little Irish girl, clinging like a child to her only friend : 'Oh, Marie ! dear Marie ! do get her to let me stay— I'll do everything the doctor tells me—I'll make *haste* and get well —I'll give no trouble. And it's all along of the work—and the damp up in these rooms—the doctor said so.'

An hour later Lady Selina was in the stately drawing-room of Alresford House, receiving her guests. She was out of sorts and temper, and though Wharton arrived in due time, and she had the prospect to enliven her during dinner—when he was of necessity parted from her by people of higher rank—of a *tête-à-tête* with him before the evening was over, the dinner went heavily. The Duke on her right hand, and the Dean on her left, were equally distasteful to her. Neither food nor wine had savour ; and once, when in an interval of talk she caught sight of her father's face and form at the further end, growing more vacant and decrepit week by week, she was seized with a sudden angry pang of revolt and repulsion. Her father wearied and disgusted her. Life was often triste and dull in the great house. Yet, when the old man should have found his grave, she would be a much smaller person than she was now, and the days would be so much the more tedious.

Wharton, too, showed less than his usual animation. She said to herself at dinner that he had the face of a man in want of sleep. His young brilliant look was somewhat tarnished, and there was worry in the restless eye. And, indeed, she knew that things had not been going so favourably for him in the House of late—that the stubborn opposition of the little group of men led by Wilkins was still hindering that concentration of the party and definition of his own foremost place in it which had looked so close and probable a few weeks before. She supposed he had been exhausting himself, too, over that shocking Midland strike. The *Clarion* had been throwing itself into the battle of the men with a monstrous violence, for which she had several times reproached him.

When all the guests had gone but Wharton, and Lord Alresford, duly placed for the sake of propriety in his accustomed chair, was safely asleep, Lady Selina asked what was the matter.

'Oh, the usual thing!' he said, as he leant against the mantelpiece beside her. 'The world's a poor place, and my doll's stuffed with sawdust. Did you ever know any doll that wasn't?'

She looked up at him a moment without speaking.

'Which means,' she said, 'that you can't get your way in the House?'

'No,' said Wharton meditatively, looking down at his boots. 'No—not yet.'

'You think you will get it some day?'

He raised his eyes.

'Oh yes!' he said; 'oh dear, yes!—some day.'

She laughed.

'You had better come over to us.'

'Well, there is always that to think of, isn't there? You can't deny you want all the new blood you can get!'

'If you only understood your moment and your chance,' she said quickly, 'you would make the opportunity and do it at once.'

He looked at her aggressively.

'How easy it comes to you Tories to rat!' he said.

'Thank you! it only means that we are the party of common sense. Well, I have been talking to your Miss Boyce.'

He started.

'Where?'

'At Lady Winterbourne's. Aldous Raeburn was there. Your beautiful Socialist was very interesting—and rather surprising. She talked of the advantages of wealth; said she had been converted —by living among the poor—had changed her mind, in fact, on many things. We were all much edified—including Mr. Raeburn. How long do you suppose that business will remain "off"? To my mind, I never saw a young woman more eager to undo a mistake.' Then she added slowly, 'The accounts of Lord Maxwell get more and more unsatisfactory.'

Wharton stared at her with sparkling eyes. 'How little you know her!' he said, not without a tone of contempt.

'Oh! very well,' said Lady Selina, with the slightest shrug of her white shoulders.

He turned to the mantelpiece and began to play with some ornaments upon it.

'Tell me what she said,' he inquired presently.

Lady Selina gave her own account of the conversation. Wharton recovered himself.

'Dear me !' he said, when she stopped. 'Yes—well—we may see another act. Who knows ? Well, good-night, Lady Selina.'

She gave him her hand with her usual aristocrat's passivity, and he went. But it was late indeed that night before she ceased to speculate on what the real effect of her words had been upon him.

As for Wharton, on his walk home he thought of Marcella Boyce and of Raeburn with a certain fever of jealous vanity which was coming, he told himself, dangerously near to passion. He did not believe Lady Selina, but nevertheless he felt that her news might drive him into rash steps he could ill afford, and had indeed been doing his best to avoid. Meanwhile it was clear to him that the mistress of Alresford House had taken an envious dislike to Marcella. How plain she had looked to-night in spite of her gorgeous dress ! and how intolerable Lord Alresford grew !

CHAPTER XII

BUT what right had Wharton to be thinking of such irrelevant matters as women and love-making at all ? He had spoken of public worries to Lady Selina. In reality his public prospects in themselves were, if anything, improved. It was his private affairs that were rushing fast on catastrophe, and threatening to drag the rest with them.

He had never been so hard pressed for money in his life. In the first place his gambling debts had mounted up prodigiously of late. His friends were tolerant and easy-going. But the more tolerant they were the more he was bound to frequent them. And his luck for some time had been monotonously bad. Before long these debts must be paid, and some of them—to a figure he shrank from dwelling upon—were already urgent.

Then as to the *Clarion*, it became every week a heavier burden. The expenses of it were enormous ; the returns totally inadequate. Advertisements were falling off steadily ; and whether the working cost were cut down, or whether a new and good man like Louis Craven, whose letters from the strike district were being now universally read, were put on, the result financially seemed to be precisely the same. It was becoming even a desperate question how the weekly expenses were to be met ; so that Wharton's usual good temper now deserted him entirely as soon as he had crossed

the *Clarion* threshold ; bitterness had become the portion of the
staff, and even the office boys walked in gloom.

Yet, at the same time, withdrawing from the business was
almost as difficult as carrying it on. There were rumours in the
air which had already seriously damaged the paper as a saleable
concern. Wharton, indeed, saw no prospect whatever of selling
except at ruinous loss. Meanwhile, to bring the paper to an
abrupt end would have not only precipitated a number of his
financial obligations ; it would have been, politically, a dangerous
confession of failure made at a very critical moment. For what
made the whole thing the more annoying was that the *Clarion*
had never been so important politically, never so much read by
the persons on whom Wharton's parliamentary future depended,
as it was at this moment. The advocacy of the Damesley strike
had been so far a stroke of business for Wharton as a Labour
Member.

It was now the seventh week of the strike, and Wharton's
'leaders,' Craven's letters from the seat of war, and the *Clarion*
strike fund, which articles and letters had called into existence,
were as vigorous as ever. The struggle itself had fallen into two
chapters. In the first the metal-workers concerned, both men and
women, had stood out for the old wages unconditionally and had
stoutly rejected all idea of arbitration. At the end of three or four
weeks, however, when grave suffering had declared itself among
an already half-starved population, the workers had consented to
take part in the appointment of a board of conciliation. This
board, including the workmen's delegates, overawed by the facts
of foreign competition as they were disclosed by the masters,
recommended terms which would have amounted to a victory for
the employers.

The award was no sooner known in the district than the
passionate indignation of the great majority of the workers knew
no bounds. Meetings were held everywhere ; the men's delegates
at the board were thrown over, and Craven who with his new wife
was travelling incessantly over the whole strike area, wrote a letter
to the *Clarion* on the award which stated the men's case with
extreme ability, was immediately backed up by Wharton in a
tremendous 'leader,' and was received among the strikers with
tears almost of gratitude and enthusiasm.

Since then all negotiations had been broken off. The *Clarion*
had gone steadily against the masters, against the award, against
further arbitration. The theory of the 'living wage,' of which
more recent days have heard so much, was preached in other
terms, but with equal vigour ; and the columns of the *Clarion*

bore witness day by day in the long lists of subscriptions to the strike fund, to the effects of its eloquence on the hearts and pockets of Englishmen.

Meanwhile there were strange rumours abroad. It was said that the trade was really on the eve of a complete and striking revolution in its whole conditions—could this labour war be only cleared out of the way. The smaller employers had been for long on the verge of ruin ; and the larger men, so report had it, were scheming a syndicate on the American plan to embrace the whole industry, cut down the costs of production, and regulate the output.

But for this large capital would be wanted. Could capital be got ? The state of things in the trade, according to the employers, had been deplorable for years ; a large part of the market had been definitely forfeited, so they declared, for good, to Germany and Belgium. It would take years before even a powerful syndicate could work itself into a thoroughly sound condition. Let the men accept the award of the conciliation board ; let there be some stable and reasonable prospect of peace between masters and men, say, for a couple of years ; and a certain group of bankers would come forward ; and all would be well. The men under the syndicate would in time get more than their old wage. *But the award first* ; otherwise the plan dropped, and the industry must go its own way to perdition.

' " Will you walk into my parlour ? " ' said Wharton scornfully to the young Conservative member who, with a purpose, was explaining these things to him in the library of the House of Commons, ' the merest trap ! and, of course, the men will see it so. Who is to guarantee them even the carrying through, much less the success, of your precious syndicate ? And, in return for your misty millennium two years hence, the men are to join at once in putting the employers in a stronger position than ever ? Thank you ! the "rent of ability" in the present state of things is, no doubt, large. But in this particular case the *Clarion* will go on doing its best—I promise you—to nibble some of it away ! '

The Conservative member rose in indignation.

' I should be sorry to have as many starving people on my conscience as you'll have before long ! ' he said as he took up his papers.

At that moment Denny's rotund and square-headed figure passed along the corridor, to which the library door stood open.

' Well, if I thrive upon it as well as Denny does, I shall do ! ' returned Wharton with his usual caustic good-humour as his companion departed.

And it delighted him to think as he walked home that Denny, who had again of late made himself particularly obnoxious in the House of Commons, on two or three occasions, to the owner of the *Clarion*, had probably instigated the quasi-overtures he had just rejected, and must be by now aware of their result.

Then he sent for Craven to come and confer with him.

Craven accordingly came up from the Midlands, pale, thin, and exhausted with the exertions and emotions of seven weeks' incessant labour. Yet personally Wharton found him as before dry and unsympathetic; and disliked him, and his cool ambiguous manner, more than ever. As to the strike, however, they came to a complete understanding. The *Clarion*, or rather the *Clarion* fund, which was doing better and better, held the key of the whole situation. If that fund could be maintained, the men could hold out. In view of the possible formation of the syndicate, Craven denounced the award with more fierceness than ever; maintaining the redoubled importance of securing the men's terms before the syndicate was launched. Wharton promised him with glee that he should be supported to the bitter end.

If, that is to say—a proviso he did not discuss with Craven—the *Clarion* itself could be kept going. In August a large sum, obtained two years before on the security of new 'plant,' would fall due. The time for repayment had already been extended; and Wharton had ascertained that no further extension was possible.

Well! bankruptcy would be a piquant interlude in his various social and political enterprises! How was it to be avoided? He had by now plenty of rich friends in the City or elsewhere, but none, as he finally decided, likely to be useful to him at the present moment. For the amount of money that he required was large—larger, indeed, than he cared to verify with any strictness, and the security that he could offer almost nil.

As to friends in the City, indeed, the only excursion of a business kind that he had made into those regions since his election was now adding seriously to his anxieties—might very well turn out, unless the matter were skilfully managed, to be one of the blackest spots on his horizon.

In the early days of his parliamentary life, when, again, mostly for the *Clarion's* sake, money happened to be much wanted, he had become director of what promised to be an important company, through the interest and good nature of a new and rich acquaintance who had taken a liking to the young member. The company had been largely 'boomed,' and there had been some very profitable dealing in the original shares. Wharton had made two or three thousand pounds, and contributed both point and finish to some of the early prospectuses.

Then, after six months, he had withdrawn from the Board, under apprehensions that had been gradually realised with alarming accuracy. Things, indeed, had been going as wrong as possible ; there were a number of small investors ; and the annual meeting of the company to be held now in some ten days promised a storm. Wharton discovered, partly to his own amazement, for he was a man who quickly forgot, that during his directorate he had devised or sanctioned matters that were not at all likely to commend themselves to the shareholders, supposing the past were really sifted. The ill-luck of it was truly stupendous ; for on the whole he had kept himself financially very clean since he had become a Member ; having all through a jealous eye to his political success.

As to the political situation, nothing could be at once more promising or more anxious !

An important meeting of the whole Labour group had been fixed for August 10, by which time it was expected that a great measure concerning Labour would be returned from the House of Lords with highly disputable amendments. The last six weeks of the session would be in many ways more critical for Labour than its earlier months had been ; and it would be proposed by Bennett, at the meeting on the 10th, to appoint a general chairman of the party, in view of a campaign which would fill the remainder of the session and strenuously occupy the recess.

That Bennett would propose the name of the Member for West Brookshire was perfectly well known to Wharton and his friends. That the nomination would meet with the warmest hostility from Wilkins and a small group of followers was also accurately forecast.

To this day, then, Wharton looked forward as to the crisis of his parliamentary fortunes. All his chances, financial or social, must now be calculated with reference to it. Every power, whether of combat or finesse, that he commanded must be brought to bear upon the issue.

What was, however, most remarkable in the man and the situation at the moment was that, through all these gathering necessities, he was by no means continuously anxious or troubled in his mind. During these days of July he gave himself, indeed, whenever he could, to a fatalist oblivion of the annoyances of life, coupled with a passionate pursuit of all those interests where his chances were still good and the omens still with him.

Especially—during the intervals of ambition, intrigue, journalism, and unsuccessful attempts to raise money—had he meditated the beauty of Marcella Boyce and the chances and difficulties of his relation to her. As he saw her less, he thought of her more, instinctively looking to her for the pleasure and distraction that life was temporarily denying him elsewhere.

At the same time, curiously enough, the stress of his financial position was reflected even in what, to himself, at any rate, he was boldly beginning to call his ' passion' for her. It had come to his knowledge that Mr. Boyce had during the past year succeeded beyond all expectation in clearing the Mellor estate. He had made skilful use of a railway lately opened on the edge of his property ; had sold building land in the neighbourhood of a small country town on the line, within a convenient distance of London ; had consolidated and improved several of his farms and relet them at higher rents ; was, in fact, according to Wharton's local informant, in a fair way to be some day, if he lived, quite as prosperous as his grandfather, in spite of old scandals and invalidism. Wharton knew, or thought he knew, that he would not live, and that Marcella would be his heiress. The prospect was not perhaps brilliant, but it was something ; it affected the outlook.

Although, however, this consideration counted, it was, to do him justice, *Marcella*, the creature herself, that he desired. But for her presence in his life he would probably have gone heiress-hunting with the least possible delay. As it was, his growing determination to win her, together with his advocacy of the Damesley workers—amply sufficed, during the days that followed his evening talk with Lady Selina, to maintain his own illusions about himself and so to keep up the zest of life.

Yes !—to master and breathe passion into Marcella Boyce might safely be reckoned on, he thought, to hurry a man's blood. And after it had gone so far between them—after he had satisfied himself that her fancy, her temper, her heart, were all more or less occupied with him—was he to see her tamely recovered by Aldous Raeburn—by the man whose advancing parliamentary position was now adding fresh offence to the old grievance and dislike? No ! not without a dash—a throw for it !

For a while, after Lady Selina's confidences, jealous annoyance, together with a certain reckless state of nerves, turned him almost into the pining lover. For he could not see Marcella. She came no more to Mrs. Lane ; and the house in James Street was not open to him. He perfectly understood that the Winterbournes did not want to know him.

At last Mrs. Lane, a shrewd little woman with a half contemptuous liking for Wharton, let him know—on the strength of a chance meeting with Lady Ermyntrude—that the Winterbournes would be at the Masterton party on the 25th. They had persuaded Miss Boyce to stay for it, and she would go back to her work the Monday after. Wharton carelessly replied that he did not know whether he would be able to put in an appearance at the Mastertons'. He might be going out of town.

Mrs. Lane looked at him and said, 'Oh, really!' with a little laugh.

Lady Masterton was the wife of the Colonial Secretary, and her vast mansion in Grosvenor Square was the principal rival to Alresford House in the hospitalities of the party. Her reception on July 25 was to be the last considerable event of a protracted but now dying season. Marcella, detained in James Street day after day against her will by the weakness of the injured arm and the counsels of her doctor, had at last extracted permission to go back to work on the 27th ; and to please Betty Macdonald she had promised to go with the Winterbournes to the Masterton party on the Saturday. Betty's devotion, shyly as she had opened her proud heart to it, had begun to mean a good deal to her. There was balm in it for many a wounded feeling ; and, besides, there was the constant, half-eager, half-painful interest of watching Betty's free and childish ways with Aldous Raeburn, and of speculating upon what would ultimately come out of them.

So, when Betty first demanded to know what she was going to wear, and then pouted over the dress shown her, Marcella submitted humbly to being 'freshened up' at the hands of Lady Ermyntrude's maid, bought what Betty told her, and stood still while Betty, who had a genius for such things, chattered, and draped, and suggested.

'I wouldn't make you fashionable for the world!' cried Betty, with a mouthful of pins, laying down masterly folds of lace and chiffon the while over the white satin with which Marcella had provided her. 'What was it Worth said to me the other day?— "Ce qu'on porte, mademoiselle? O, pas grand'chose !—presque pas de corsage, et pas du tout de manches !"—No, that kind of thing wouldn't suit you. But *distinguished* you shall be, if I sit up all night to think it out !'

In the end Betty was satisfied, and could hardly be prevented from hugging Marcella there and then, out of sheer delight in her own handiwork, when at last the party emerged from the cloakroom into the Mastertons' crowded hall. Marcella too felt pleasure in the reflections of herself as they passed up the lavishly be-mirrored staircase. The chatter about dress in which she had been living for some days had amused and distracted her; for there were great feminine potentialities in her; though for eighteen months she had scarcely given what she wore a thought, and in her pre-nursing days had been wont to waver between a kind of proud neglect, which implied the secret consciousness of beauty, and an occasional passionate desire to look well. So that she played her part to-night very fairly; pinched Betty's arm to silence the elf's tongue; and held herself up as she was told, that Betty's handiwork might look its best. But inwardly the girl's mood was very tired and flat. She was pining for her work; pining even for Minta Hurd's peevish look, and the children to whom she was so easily an earthly providence.

In spite of the gradual emptying of London, Lady Masterton's rooms were very full. Marcella found acquaintances. Many of the people whom she had met at Mrs. Lane's, the two Cabinet Ministers of the House of Commons dinner, Mr. Lane himself—all were glad or eager to recall themselves to her as she stood by Lady Winterbourne, or made her way half absently through the press. She talked, without shyness—she had never been shy, and was perhaps nearer now to knowing what it might mean than she had been as a schoolgirl—but without heart; her black eye wandering meanwhile, as though in quest. There was a gay sprinkling of uniforms in the crowd, for the Speaker was holding a *levée*, and as it grew late his guests began to set towards Lady Masterton. Betty, who had been turning up her nose at the men she had so far smiled upon, all of whom she declared were either bald or seventy, was a little propitiated by the uniforms; otherwise, she pronounced the party very dull.

'Well, upon my word!' she cried suddenly, in a tone that made Marcella turn upon her. The child was looking very red and very upright—was using her fan with great vehemence, and Frank Leven was humbly holding out his hand to her.

'I don't like being startled,' said Betty pettishly. 'Yes, you *did* startle me—you did—you did! And then you begin to con-tradict before I've said a word! I'm sure you've been contradicting all the way upstairs—and why don't you say "How do you do?" to Miss Boyce?'

Frank, looking very happy but very nervous, paid his respects rather bashfully to Marcella—she laughed to see how Betty's presence subdued him—and then gave himself up wholly to Betty's tender mercies.

Marcella observed them with an eager interest she could not

wholly explain to herself. It was clear that all thought of anything or anybody else had vanished for Frank Leven at the sight of Betty. Marcella guessed, indeed knew, that they had not met for some little time; and she was touched by the agitation and happiness on the boy's handsome face. But Betty? what was the secret of her kittenish, teasing ways—or was there any secret? She held her little head very high and chattered very fast—but it was not the same chatter that she gave to Marcella, nor, so far as Marcella could judge, to Aldous Raeburn. New elements of character came out in it. It was self-confident, wilful, imperious. Frank was never allowed to have an opinion; was laughed at before his words were out of his mouth; was generally heckled, played with and shaken in a way which seemed alternately to enrage and enchant him. In the case of most girls, such a manner would have meant encouragement; but, as it was Betty, no one could be sure. The little thing was a great puzzle to Marcella, who had found unexpected reserves in her. She might talk of her love affairs to Aldous Raeburn; she had done nothing of the sort with her new friend. And in such matters Marcella herself was far more reserved than most modern women.

'Betty!' cried Lady Winterbourne, 'I am going on into the next room.'

Then in a lower tone she said helplessly to Marcella:

'Do make her come on!'

Marcella perceived that her old friend was in a fidget. Stooping her tall head, she said with a smile:

'But look how she is amusing herself!'

'My dear!—that's just it! If you only knew how her mother —tiresome woman—has talked to me! And the young man has behaved so beautifully till now—has given neither Ermyntrude nor me any trouble.'

Was that why Betty was leading him such a life? Marcella wondered,—then—suddenly—was seized with a sick distaste for the whole scene—for Betty's love affairs—for her own interest in them—for her own self and personality above all. Her great black eyes gazed straight before them, unseeing, over the crowd, the diamonds, the lights; her whole being gave itself to a quick, blind wrestle with some vague overmastering pain, some despair of life and joy to which she could give no name.

She was roused by Betty's voice.

'Mr. Raeburn! will *you* tell me who people are? Mr. Leven's no more use than my fan. Just imagine—I asked him who that lady in the tiara is—and he vows he doesn't know! Why, it just seems that when you go to Oxford, you leave the wits you had before, behind ! And then—of course'—Betty affected a delicate hesitation—'there's the difficulty of being quite sure that you'll ever get any new ones !—But there—look !—I'm in despair !—she's vanished—and I shall *never* know !'

' One moment ! ' said Raeburn, smiling, 'and I will take you in pursuit. She has only gone into the tea-room.'

His hand touched Marcella's.

' Just a *little* better,' he said, with a sudden change of look, in answer to Lady Winterbourne's question. ' The account to-night is certainly brighter. They begged me not to come, or I should have been off some days ago. And next week, I am thankful to say, they will be home.'

Why should she be standing there, so inhumanly still and silent?—Marcella asked herself. Why not take courage again— join in—talk—show sympathy ? But the words died on her lips. After to-night—thank heaven !—she need hardly see him again.

He asked after herself as usual. Then, just as he was turning away with Betty, he came back to her, unexpectedly.

' I should like to tell you about Hallin,' he said gently. ' His sister writes to me that she is happier about him, and that she hopes to be able to keep him away another fortnight. They are at Keswick.'

For an instant there was pleasure in the implication of common ground, a common interest—here if nowhere else. Then the pleasure was lost in the smart of her own strange lack of self-government as she made a rather stupid and awkward reply.

Raeburn's eyes rested on her for a moment. There was in them a flash of involuntary expression, which she did not notice— for she had turned away—which no one saw—except Betty. Then the child followed him to the tea-room, a little pale and pensive.

Marcella looked after them.

In the midst of the uproar about her, the babel of talk fighting against the Hungarian band, which was playing its wildest and loudest in the tea-room, she was overcome by a sudden rush of memory. Her eyes were tracing the passage of those two figures through the crowd ; the man in his black court suit, stooping his refined and grizzled head to the girl beside him, or turning every now and then to greet an acquaintance, with the manner—cordial and pleasant, yet never quite gay even when he smiled—that she, Marcella, had begun to notice of late as a new thing ; the girl lifting her small face to him, the gold of her hair showing against his velvet sleeve. But the inward sense was busy with a number of other impressions, past, and, as it now seemed, incredible.

The little scene when Aldous had given her the pearls, returned so long ago—-why! she could see the fire blazing in the Stone Parlour, feel his arm about her !—the drive home after the Gairsley meeting—that poignant moment in his sitting-room the night of the ball—-his face, his anxious, tender face, as she came down the wide stairs of the Court towards him on that terrible evening when she pleaded with him and his grandfather in vain :—had these things, incidents, relations, been ever a real part of the living world? Impossible! Why, there he was—not ten yards from her—and yet more irrevocably separate from her than if the Sahara stretched between them. The note of cold distance in his courteous manner put her further from him than the merest stranger.

Marcella felt a sudden terror rush through her as she blindly followed Lady Winterbourne ; her limbs trembled under her ; she took advantage of a conversation between her companion and the master of the house to sink down for a moment on a settee, where she felt out of sight and notice.

What was this intolerable sense of loss and folly, this smarting emptiness, this rage with herself and her life? She only knew that whereas the touch, the eye of Aldous Raeburn had neither compelled nor thrilled her, so long as she possessed his whole heart and life—*now*—that she had no right to either look or caress ; now that he had ceased even to regard her as a friend, and was already perhaps making up that loyal and serious mind of his to ask from another woman the happiness she had denied him ; now, when it was absurdly too late, she could——

Could what? Passionate, wilful creature that she was !—with that breath of something wild and incalculable surging through the inmost places of the soul, she went through a moment of suffering as she sat pale and erect in her corner—brushed against by silks and satins, chattered across by this person and that—such as seemed to bruise all the remaining joy and ease out of life.

But only a moment ! Flesh and blood rebelled. She sprang up from her seat ; told herself that she was mad or ill ; caught sight of Mr. Lane coming towards them, and did her best by smile and greeting to attract him to her.

'You look very white, my dear Miss Boyce,' said that cheerful and fatherly person. 'Is it that tiresome arm still? Now, don't please go and be a heroine any more !'

CHAPTER XIII

MEANWHILE, in the tea-room, Betty was daintily sipping her ciaret-cup, while Aldous stood by her.

'No,' said Betty calmly, looking straight at the lady in the tiara who was standing by the buffet, 'she's not beautiful, and I've torn my dress running after her. There's only one beautiful person here to-night !'

Aldous found her a seat, and took one himself beside her, in a corner out of the press. But he did not answer her remark.

'Don't you think so, Mr. Aldous?' said Betty, persisting, but with a little flutter of the pulse.

'You mean Miss Boyce?' he said quietly, as he turned to her.

'Of course !' cried Betty, with a sparkle in her charming eyes ; 'what *is* it in her face? It excites me to be near her. One feels that she will just have lived *twice* as much as the rest of us by the time she comes to the end. You don't mind my talking of her, Mr. Aldous?'

There was an instant's silence on his part. Then he said in a constrained voice, looking away from his companion, 'I don't *mind* it, but I am not going to pretend to you that I find it easy to talk of her.'

'It would be a shame of you to pretend anything,' said Betty fervently, 'after all I've told you ! I confessed all my scrapes to you, turned out all my rubbish bag of a heart—well, nearly all'— she checked herself with a sudden flush—'and you've been as kind to me as any big brother could be. But you're dreadfully lofty, Mr. Aldous ! You keep yourself to yourself. I don't think it's fair !'

Aldous laughed.

'My dear Miss Betty, haven't you found out by now that I am a good listener and a bad talker? I don't talk of myself or'—he hesitated—'the things that have mattered most to me—because, in the first place, it doesn't come easy to me—and, in the next, I can't, you see, discuss my own concerns without discussing other people's.'

'Oh, good gracious !' said Betty, 'what you must have been thinking about me ! I declare I'll never tell you anything again !' —and, beating her tiny foot upon the ground, she sat, scarlet, looking down at it.

Aldous made all the smiling excuses he could muster. He had found Betty a most beguiling and attaching little companion, both at the Court in the Easter recess, and during the Italian journey. Her total lack of reserve, or what appeared so, had been first an amazement to him, and then a positive pleasure and entertainment. To make a friend of him—difficult and scrupulous as he was, and now more than ever—a woman must be at the cost of most of the advances. But, after the first evening with him, Betty had made them in profusion, without the smallest demur, though perfectly well aware of her mother's ambitions. There was a tie of cousin-ship between them, and a considerable difference of age. Betty had decided at once that a mother was a dear old goose, and that great friends she and Aldous Raeburn should be—and, in a sense, great friends they were.

Aldous was still propitiating her, when Lady Winterbourne came into the tea-room, followed by Marcella. The elder lady threw a hurried and not very happy glance at the pair in the corner. Marcella appeared to be in animated talk with a young journalist whom Raeburn knew, and did not look their way.

'Just *one* thing !' said Betty, bending forward and speaking eagerly in Aldous's ear. 'It was all a mistake—wasn't it? Now I know her I feel sure it was. You don't—you don't—really think badly of her ?'

Aldous heard her unwillingly. He was looking away from her towards the buffet, when she saw a change in the eyes—a tighten-ing of the lip—a something keen and hostile in the whole face.

'Perhaps Miss Boyce will be less of a riddle to all of us before long !' he said hastily, as though the words escaped him. 'Shall we get out of this very uncomfortable corner ?'

Betty looked where he had looked, and saw a young man greeting Marcella with a manner so emphatic and intimate, that the journalist had instantly moved out of his way. The young man had a noticeable pile of fair curls above a very white and rounded forehead.

'Who is that talking to Miss Boyce ?' she asked of Aldous ; 'I have seen him, but I can't remember the name.'

'That is Mr. Wharton, the member for one of our divisions,' said Aldous, as he rose from his chair.

Betty gave a little start, and her brow puckered into a frown. As she too rose, she said resentfully to Aldous :

'Well, you *have* snubbed me !'

As usual, he could not find the effective or clever thing to say.

'I did not mean to,' he replied simply ; but Betty, glancing at him, saw something in his face which gripped her heart. A lump rose in her throat.

'Do let's go and find Ermyntrude !' she said.

But Wharton had barely begun his talk with Marcella when a gentleman, on his way to the buffet with a cup to set down, touched him on the arm. Wharton turned in some astonishment and annoyance. He saw a youngish, good-looking man, well known to him as already one of the most important solicitors in London, largely trusted by many rich or eminent persons.

'May I have a word with you presently?' said Mr. Pearson, in a pleasant undertone. 'I have something of interest to say to you, and it occurred to me that I might meet you to-night. Excuse my interrupting you.'

He glanced with admiration at Marcella, who had turned away.

Wharton had a momentary qualm. Then it struck him that Mr. Pearson's manner was decidedly friendly.

'In a moment,' he said. 'We might find a corner, I think, in that further room.'

He made a motion of the head towards a little boudoir which lay beyond the tea-room.

Mr. Pearson nodded and passed on.

Wharton returned to Marcella, who had fallen back on Frank Leven. At the approach of the member for West Brookshire, Lady Winterbourne and her daughter had moved severely away to the further end of the buffet.

'A tiresome man wants me on business for a moment,' he said; then he dropped his voice a little; 'but I have been looking forward to this evening, this chance, for days—shall I find you here again in five minutes?'

Marcella, who had flushed brightly, said that would depend on the time and Lady Winterbourne. He hurried away with a little gesture of despair. Frank followed him with a sarcastic eye.

'Anyone would think he was prime minister already! I never met him yet anywhere that he hadn't some business on hand. Why does he behave as though he had the world on his shoulders? Your *real* swells always seem to have nothing to do.'

'Do you know so many busy people?' Marcella asked him sweetly.

'Oh, you shan't put me down, Miss Boyce!' said the boy, sulkily thrusting his hands into his pockets. 'I am going to work like blazes this winter, if only my dons will let a fellow alone. I say, isn't she *ripping* to-night—Betty?'

And, pulling his moustache in helpless jealousy and annoyance, he stared at the Winterbourne group across the room, which had been now joined by Aldous Raeburn and Betty, standing side by side.

'What do you want me to say?' said Marcella with a little cold laugh. ' I shall make you worse if I praise her. Please put my cup down.'

At the same moment she saw Wharton coming back to her— Mr. Pearson behind him, smiling, and gently twirling the seals of his watch-chain. She was instantly struck by Wharton's look of excitement, and by the manner in which—with a momentary glance aside at the Winterbourne party—he approached her.

' There is such a charming little room in there,' he said, stooping his head to her, ' and so cool after this heat. Won't you try it?'

The energy of his bright eye took possession of her. He led the way ; she followed. Her dress almost brushed Aldous Raeburn as she passed.

He took her into a tiny room. There was no one else there, and he found a seat for her by an open window, where they were almost hidden from view by a stand of flowers.

As he sat down again by her, she saw that a decisive moment had come, and blanched almost to the colour of her dress. Oh ! what to do ! Her heart cried out vaguely to some power beyond itself for guidance, then gave itself up again to the wayward thirst for happiness.

He took her hand strongly in both his own, and bending towards her as she sat bowered among the scent and colours of the flowers, he made her a passionate declaration. From the first moment that he had seen her under the Chiltern beeches, so he vowed, he had felt in her the supreme, incomparable attraction which binds a man to one woman, and one only. His six weeks under her father's roof had produced in him feelings which he knew to be a wrong, without thereby finding in himself any power to check them. They had betrayed him into a mad moment, which he had regretted bitterly because it had given her pain. Otherwise—his voice dropped and shook, his hand pressed hers—' I lived for months on the memory of that one instant.' But he had respected her suffering, her struggle, her need for rest of mind and body. For her sake he had gone away into silence ; he had put a force upon himself which had alone enabled him to get through his parliamentary work.

Then, with his first sight of her in that little homely room and dress—so changed, but so lovely !—everything—admiration, passion—had revived with double strength. Since that meeting he must have often puzzled her, as he had puzzled himself. His life had been a series of perplexities. He was not his own master ; he was the servant of a cause, in which—however foolishly a mocking habit might have led him at times to belittle his own enthusiasms and hers—his life and honour were engaged ; and this cause and his part in it had been for long hampered, and all his clearness of vision and judgment dimmed by the pressure of a number of difficulties and worries he could not have discussed with her—worries practical and financial, connected with the *Clarion*, with the experiments he had been carrying out on his estate, and with other troublesome matters. He had felt a thousand times that his fortunes, political or private, were too doubtful and perilous to allow him to ask any woman to share them.—Then, again, he had seen her—and his resolution, his scruple, had melted in his breast !

Well ! there were still troubles in front ! But he was no longer cowed by them. In spite of them, he dared now to throw himself at her feet, to ask her to come and share a life of combat and of labour, to bring her beauty and her mind to the joint conduct of a great enterprise. To *her* a man might show his effort and his toil, —from *her* he might claim a sympathy it would be vain to ask of any smaller woman.

Then suddenly he broke down. Speech seemed to fail him. Only his eyes—more intense and piercing under their straight brows than she had ever known them—beseeched her—his hand sought hers.

She meanwhile sat in a trance of agitation, mistress neither of reason nor of feeling. She felt his spell, as she had always done. The woman in her thrilled at last to the mere name and neighbourhood of love. The heart in her cried out that pain and loss could only be deadened so—the past could only be silenced by filling the present with movement and warm life.

Yet what tremors of conscience—what radical distrust of herself and him ! And the first articulate words she found to say to him were very much what she had said to Aldous so long ago—only filled with a bitterer and more realised content.

'After all, what do we know of each other ! You don't know me—not as I am. And I feel——'

' Doubts ?' he said, smiling. ' Do you imagine that that seems anything but natural to me ? *I* can have none ; but *you*—— After all, we are not quite boy and girl, you and I ; we have lived, both of us ! But ask yourself—has not destiny brought us together? Think of it all !'

Their eyes met again. Hers sank under the penetration, the flame of his. Yet, throughout, he was conscious of the doorway to his right, of the figures incessantly moving across it. His own eloquence had convinced and moved himself abundantly. Yet, as he saw her yielding, he was filled with the strangest mixture of passion—and a sort of disillusion—almost contempt ! If she had

turned from him with the dignity worthy of that head and brow,
it flashed across him that he could have tasted more of the *abandonment* of love—have explored his own emotion more perfectly.

Still, the situation was poignant enough—in one sense complete.
Was Raeburn still there—in that next room ?

' My answer ?' he said to her, pressing her hand as they sat in
the shelter of the flowers.   For *he* was aware of the practical facts
—the hour, the place—if she was not.

She roused herself.

' I can't,' she said, making a movement to rise, which his strong
grasp, however, prevented. ' I *can't* answer you to-night, Mr. Wharton. I should have much to think over—so much ! It might all look
quite different to me.   You must give me time.'

' To-morrow ?' he said quietly.

' No !' she said impetuously, ' not to-morrow ; I go back to my
work, and I must have quiet and time. In a fortnight—not before.
I will write.'

' Oh, impossible !' he said, with a little frown.

And still holding her, he drew her towards him. His gaze
ran over the face, the warm whiteness under the lace of the dress,
the beautiful arms.   She shrank from it—feeling a sudden movement of dislike and fear ; but before she could disengage herself he
had pressed his lips on the arm nearest to him.

' I gave you no leave !' she said passionately, under her breath,
as he let her go.

He met her flashing look with tender humbleness.

' *Marcella !*'

The word was just breathed into the air.   She wavered—yet a
chill had passed over her.   She could not recover the moment of
magic.

' *Not* to-morrow,' she repeated steadily, though dreading lest
she should burst into tears, ' and not till I see clearly—till I
can——' She caught her breath. ' Now I am going back to Lady
Winterbourne.'

CHAPTER XIV

FOR some hours after he reached his own room, Wharton sat in
front of his open window, sunk in the swift rushing of thought, as
a bramble sways in a river. The July night first paled, then flushed
into morning ; the sun rose above the empty street and the light
mists enwrapping the great city, before he threw himself on his
bed, exhausted enough at last to fall into a restless sleep.

The speculation of those quick-pulsed hours was in the end about equally divided between Marcella and the phrases and turns of his interview with Mr. Pearson. It was the sudden leap of troubled excitement stirred in him by that interview—heightened by the sight of Raeburn—that had driven him past recall by the most natural of transitions, into his declaration to Marcella.

But he had no sooner reached his room than, at first with iron will, he put the thought of Marcella, of the scene which had just passed, away from him. His pulses were still quivering. No matter! It was the brain he had need of. He set it coolly and keenly to work.

Mr. Pearson? Well!—Mr. Pearson had offered him a *bribe*; there could be no question as to that. His clear sense never blinked the matter for an instant. Nor had he any illusions as to his own behaviour. Even now he had no further right to the sleep of the honest man.

Let him realise, however, what had happened. He had gone to Lady Masterton's party, in the temper of a man who knows that ruin is upon him, and determined, like the French criminal, to exact his cigar and *eau de vie* before the knife falls. Never had things looked so desperate; never had all resource seemed to him so completely exhausted. Bankruptcy must come in the course of a few weeks; his entailed property would pass into the hands of a receiver; and whatever recovery might be ultimately possible, by the end of August he would be, for the moment, socially and politically undone.

There could be no question of his proposing seriously to Marcella Boyce. Nevertheless, he had gone to Lady Masterton's on purpose to meet her; and his manner on seeing her had asserted precisely the same intimate claim upon her which, during the past six weeks, had alternately attracted and repelled her.

Then Mr. Pearson had interrupted.

Wharton, shutting his eyes, could see the great man lean against the window-frame close to the spot where, a quarter of an hour later, Marcella had sat among the flowers—the dapper figure, the long, fair moustaches, the hand playing with the eye-glass.

'I have been asked—er—er——' What a conceited manner the fellow had!—'to get some conversation with you, Mr. Wharton, on the subject of the Damesley strike. You give me leave?'

Whereupon, in less than ten minutes, the speaker had executed an important commission, and, in offering Wharton a bribe of the most barefaced kind, had also found time for supplying him with a number of the most delicate and sufficient excuses for taking it.

The masters, in fact, sent an embassy. They fully admitted the power of the *Clarion* and its owner. No doubt, it would not be possible for the paper to keep up its strike fund indefinitely ; there were perhaps already signs of slackening. Still it had been maintained for a considerable time; and so long as it was reckoned on, in spite of the wide-spread misery and suffering now prevailing, the men would probably hold out.

In these circumstances, the principal employers concerned had thought it best to approach so formidable an opponent and to put before him information which might possibly modify his action. They had authorised Mr. Pearson to give him a full account of what was proposed in the way of re-organisation of the trade, including the probable advantages which the work-people themselves would be likely to reap from it in the future.

Mr. Pearson ran in a few sentences through the points of the scheme. Wharton stood about a yard away from him, his hands in his pockets, a little pale and frowning—looking intently at the speaker.

Then Mr. Pearson paused and cleared his throat.

Well !—that was the scheme. His principals believed that, when both it and the employers' determination to transfer their business to the Continent rather than be beaten by the men were made fully known to the owner of the *Clarion*, it must affect his point of view. Mr. Pearson was empowered to give him any details he might desire. Meanwhile—so confident were they in the reasonableness of the case that they even suggested that the owner of the *Clarion* himself should take part in the new Syndicate. On condition of his future co-operation—it being understood that the masters took their stand irrevocably on the award—the men at present responsible for the formation of the Syndicate proposed to allot Mr. Wharton ten Founders' Shares in the new undertaking.

Wharton, sitting alone, recalling these things, was conscious again of that start in every limb, that sudden rush of blood to the face, as though a lash had struck him.

For in a few seconds his mind took in the situation. Only the day before, a City acquaintance had said to him, ' If you and your confounded paper were out of the way, and this thing could be placed properly on the market, there would be a boom in it at once. I am told that in twenty-four hours the Founders' Shares would be worth two thousand pounds apiece !'

There was a pause of silence. Then Wharton threw a queer dark look at the solicitor, and was conscious that his pulse was thumping.

'There can be no question I think, Mr Pearson—between you and me—as to the nature of such a proposal as that !'

'My dear sir,' Mr. Pearson had interrupted hastily, 'let me, above all, ask you to take *time*—time enough, at any rate, to turn the matter well over in your mind. The interests of a great many people, besides yourself, are concerned. Don't give me an answer to-night ; it is the last thing I desire. I have thrown out my suggestion. Consider it. To-morrow is Sunday. If you are disposed to carry it further, come and see me Monday morning—that's all. I will be at your service at any hour, and I can then give you a much more complete outline of the intentions of the Company. Now I really must go and look for Mrs. Pearson's carriage.'

Wharton followed the great man half mechanically across the little room, his mind in a whirl of mingled rage and desire. Then suddenly he stopped his companion.

'Has George Denny anything to do with this proposal, Mr. Pearson ?'

Mr. Pearson paused, with a little air of vague cogitation.

'George Denny? Mr. George Denny, the Member for Westropp? I have had no dealings whatever with that gentleman in the matter.'

Wharton let him pass.

Then as he himself entered the tea-room, he perceived the bending form of Aldous Raeburn chatting to Lady Winterbourne on his right, and that tall whiteness close in front, waiting for him.

His brain cleared in a flash. He was perfectly conscious that a bribe had just been offered him, of the most daring and cynical kind, and that he had received the offer in the tamest way. An insult had been put upon him which had for ever revealed the estimate held of him by certain shrewd people, for ever degraded him in his own eyes.

Nevertheless, he was also conscious that the thing was done. The bribe would be accepted, the risk taken. So far as his money matters were concerned he was once more a free man. The mind had adjusted itself, reached its decision in a few minutes.

And the first effect of the mingled excitement and self-contempt which the decision brought with it had been to drive him into the scene with Marcella. Instinctively he asked of passion to deliver him quickly from the smart of a new and very disagreeable experience.

Well ! why should he not take these men's offer ?

He was as much convinced as they that this whole matter of the strike had of late come to a deadlock. So long as the public would give, the workers, passionately certain of the justice of their own cause, and filled with new ambitions after more decent living, would hold out. On the other hand, he perfectly understood that the masters had also in many ways a strong case, that they had been very hard hit by the strike, and that many of them would rather close their works or transfer them bodily to the Continent than give way. Some of the facts Pearson had found time to mention had been certainly new and striking.

At the same time he never disguised from himself for an instant that but for a prospective 20,000*l.* the facts concerned would not have affected him in the least. Till to-night it had been to his interest to back the strike, and to harass the employers. Now things were changed ; and he took a curious satisfaction in the quick movements of his own intelligence, as his thought rapidly sketched the ' curve ' the *Clarion* would have to take, and the arguments by which he would commend it.

As to his shares, they would be convertible of course into immediate cash. Some man of straw would be forthcoming to buy what he would possess in the name of another man of straw. It was not supposed—he took for granted—by the men who had dared to tempt him, that he would risk his whole political reputation and career for anything less than a bird in the hand.

Well ! what were the chances of secrecy ?

Naturally *they* stood to lose less by disclosure, a good deal, than he did. And Denny, one of the principal employers, was his personal enemy. He would be likely enough for the present to keep his name out of the affair. But no man of the world could suppose that the transaction would pass without his knowledge. Wharton's own hasty question to Mr. Pearson on the subject seemed to himself now, in cold blood, a remarkably foolish one.

He walked up and down thinking this point out. It was the bitter pill of the whole affair.

In the end, with a sudden recklessness of youth and resource, he resolved to dare it. There would *not* be much risk. Men of business do not as a rule blazon their own dirty work, and public opinion would be important to the new Syndicate.

Some risk, of course, there would be. Well ! his risks, as they stood, were pretty considerable. He chose the lesser. Not without something of a struggle—some keen personal smart. He had done a good many mean and questionable things in his time, but never anything as gross as this. The thought of what his relation to a certain group of men—to Denny especially—would be in the future, stung sharply. But it is the part of the man of action to put both scruple and fear behind him on occasion. His career was in question.

Craven ? Well, Craven would be a difficulty. He would telegraph to him first thing in the morning before the offices closed, and see him on Monday. For Marcella's sake the man must be managed—somehow.

And—Marcella! How should she ever know, ever suspect! She already disliked the violence with which the paper had supported the strike. He would find no difficulty whatever in justifying all that she or the public would see, to her.

Then insensibly he let his thoughts glide into thinking of the money. Presently he drew a sheet of paper towards him and covered it with calculations as to his liabilities. By George! how well it worked out! By the time he threw it aside, and walked to the window for air, he already felt himself a *bonâ fide* supporter of the Syndicate—the promoter in the public interest of a just and well-considered scheme.

Finally, with a little joyous energetic movement which betrayed the inner man, he flung down his cigarette, and turned to write an ardent letter to Marcella, while the morning sun stole into the dusty room.

Difficult? of course! Both now and in the future. It would take him half his time yet—and he could ill afford it—to bring her bound and captive. He recognised in her the southern element, so strangely mated with the moral English temper. Yet he smiled over it. The subtleties of the struggle he foresaw enchanted him.

And she would be mastered! In this heightened state of nerve his man's resolution only rose the more fiercely to the challenge of her resistance.

Nor should she cheat him with long delays. His income would be his own again, and life decently easy. He already felt himself the vain showman of her beauty.

A thought of Lady Selina crossed his mind, producing amusement and compassion—indulgent amusement, such as the young man is apt to feel towards the spinster of thirty-five who pays him attention. A certain sense of rehabilitation, too, which at the moment was particularly welcome. For, no doubt, he might have married her and her fortune had he so chosen. As it was, why didn't she find some needy boy to take pity on her? There were plenty going, and she must have abundance of money. Old Alresford, too, was fast doddering off the stage, and then where would she be—without Alresford House, or Busbridge, or those various other pedestals which had hitherto held her aloft?

Early on Sunday morning Wharton telegraphed to Craven, directing him to 'come up at once for consultation.' The rest of the day the owner of the *Clarion* spent pleasantly on the river with Mrs. Lane and a party of ladies, including a young Duchess, who was pretty, literary, and socialistic. At night he went down to the *Clarion* office, and produced a leader on the position of affairs at Damesley which, to the practised eye, contained one paragraph—but one only—wherein the dawn of a new policy might have been discerned.

Naturally the juxtaposition of events at the moment gave him considerable anxiety. He knew very well that the Damesley bargain could not be kept waiting. The masters were losing heavily every day, and were not likely to let him postpone the execution of his part of the contract for a fortnight or so to suit his own convenience. It was like the sale of an 'old master.' His influence must be sold now—at the ripe moment—or not at all.

At the same time it was very awkward. In one short fortnight the meeting of the party would be upon him. Surrender on the Damesley question would give great offence to many of the Labour members. It would have to be very carefully managed—very care fully thought out.

By eleven o'clock on Monday he was in Mr. Pearson's office. After the first involuntary smile, concealed by the fair moustaches, and instantly dismissed, with which the eminent lawyer greeted the announcement of his visitor's name, the two augurs carried through their affairs with perfect decorum. Wharton realised, indeed, that he was being firmly handled. Mr. Pearson gave the *Clarion* a week in which to accomplish its retreat and drop its strike fund. And the fund was to be 'checked' as soon as possible.

A little later, when Wharton abruptly demanded a guarantee of secrecy, Mr. Pearson allowed himself his first—visible—smile.

'My dear sir, are such things generally made public property? I can give you no better assurance than you can extract yourself from the circumstances. As to writing—well!—I should advise you very strongly against anything of the sort. A long experience has convinced me that in any delicate negotiation the less that is *written* the better.'

Towards the end Wharton turned upon his companion sharply, and asked:

'How did you discover that I wanted money?'

Mr. Pearson lifted his eyebrows pleasantly.

'Most of the things in this world, Mr. Wharton, that one wants to know, can be found out. Now—I have no wish to hurry you not in the least—but I may perhaps mention that I have an important appointment directly. Don't you think—we might settle our business?'

Wharton was half-humorously conscious of an inward leap of
fury with the necessities which had given this man—to whom he
had taken an instantaneous dislike—the power of dealing thus
summarily with the member for West Brookshire. However, there
was no help for it ; he submitted, and twenty minutes afterwards
he left Lincoln's Inn carrying documents in the breast-pocket of
his coat which, when brought under his bankers' notice, would be
worth to him an immediate advance of some eight thousand pounds.
The remainder of the purchase-money for his ' shares' would be
paid over to him as soon as his part of the contract had been
carried out.

He did not, however, go to his bank, but straight to the *Clarion*
office, where he had a mid-day appointment with Louis Craven.

At first sight of the tall, narrow-shouldered form and anxious
face waiting for him in his private room, Wharton felt a movement
of ill-humour.

Craven had the morning's *Clarion* in his hand.

' This *cannot* mean '—he said, when they had exchanged a brief
salutation—' that the paper is backing out ? '

He pointed to the suspicious paragraph in Wharton's leader,
his delicate features quivering with an excitement he could ill
repress.

' Well, let us sit down and discuss the thing '—said Wharton,
closing the door—' that's what I wired to you for.'

He offered Craven a cigarette, which was refused, took one
himself, and the two men sat confronting each other with a writing-
table between them. Wharton was disagreeably conscious at times
of the stiff papers in his coat-pocket, and was perhaps a little paler
than usual. Otherwise he showed no trace of mental disturbance ;
and Craven, himself jaded and sleepless, was struck with a momentary perception of his companion's boyish good looks—the tumbling
curls, that Wharton straightened now and then, the charming blue
eyes, the athlete's frame. Any stranger would have taken Craven
for the older man ; in reality it was the other way.

The conversation lasted nearly an hour. Craven exhausted
both argument and entreaty, though when the completeness of the
retreat resolved upon had been disclosed to him, the feeling roused
in him was so fierce that he could barely maintain his composure.
He had been living among scenes of starvation and endurance,
which, to his mind, had all the character of martyrdom. These
men and women were struggling for two objects—the power to
live more humanly, and the free right of combination—to both of
which, if need were, he would have given his own life to help them
without an instant's hesitation. Behind his blinking manner he

saw everything with the idealist's intensity, the reformer's passion.
To be fair to an employer was not in his power. To spend his last
breath, were it called for, in the attempt to succour the working
man against his capitalist oppressors, would have seemed to him
the merest matter of course.

And his mental acuteness was quite equal to his enthusiasm,
and far more evident. In his talk with Wharton, he for a long
time avoided, as before—out of a certain inner disdain—the
smallest touch of sentiment. He pointed out—what, indeed,
Wharton well knew—that the next two or three weeks of the strike
would be the most critical period in its history ; that, if the work-
people could only be carried through them, they were almost sure
of victory. He gave his own reasons for believing that the employers could ultimately be coerced, he offered proof of yielding
among them, proof also that the better men in their ranks were
fully alive to and ashamed of the condition of the workers. As
to the Syndicate, he saw no objection to it, *provided* the workers'
claims were first admitted. Otherwise it would only prove a more
powerful engine of oppression.

Wharton's arguments may perhaps be left to the imagination.
He would have liked simply to play the proprietor and the master
—to say, ' This is my decision, those are my terms—take my work
or leave it.' But Craven was Miss Boyce's friend ; he was also a
Venturist. Chafing under both facts, Wharton found that he must
state his case.

And he did state it with his usual ability. He laid great stress
on ' information from a private source which I cannot disregard,'
to the effect that, if the resistance went on, the trade would be
broken up ; that several of the largest employers were on the point
of making arrangements for Italian factories.

' I know,' he said finally, ' that but for the *Clarion* the strike
would drop. Well ! I have come to the conclusion that the responsibility is too heavy. I shall be doing the men themselves more
harm than good. There is the case in a nutshell. We differ—I
can't help that. The responsibility is mine.'

Craven rose with a quick, nervous movement. The prophet
spoke at last.

' You understand,' he said, laying a thin hand on the table,
' that the condition of the workers in this trade is *infamous* !—
that the award and your action together plunge them back into a
state of things which is a *shame* and a *curse* to England ! '

Wharton made no answer. He, too, had risen, and was putting
away some papers in a drawer. A tremor ran through Craven's
tall frame ; and for an instant, as his eye rested on his companion,

the idea of foul play crossed his mind. He cast it out, that he might deal calmly with his own position.

'Of course, you perceive,' he said, as he took up his hat, 'that I can no longer on these terms remain the *Clarion's* correspondent. Somebody else must be found to do this business.'

'I regret your decision, immensely,' said Wharton with perfect suavity, 'but of course I understand it. I trust, however, that you will not leave us altogether. I can give you plenty of work that will suit you. Here, for instance'—he pointed to a pile of Blue Books from the Labour Commission lying on the table—'are a number of reports that want analysing and putting before the public. You could do them in town at your leisure.'

Craven struggled with himself. His first instinct was to fling the offer in Wharton's face. Then he thought of his wife; of the tiny new household just started with such small, happy, self-denying shifts; of the woman's inevitable lot, of the hope of a child.

'Thank you,' he said, in a husky voice; 'I will consider, I will write.'

Wharton nodded to him pleasantly and he went.

The owner of the *Clarion* drew a long breath.

'Now, I think on the whole it would serve my purpose best to sit down and write to *her*—after that. It would be well that *my* account should come first.'

A few hours later, after an interview with his bankers and a further spell of letter-writing, Wharton descended the steps of his club, in a curious restless state. The mortgage on the *Clarion* had been arranged for, his gambling debts settled, and all his other money matters were successfully in train. Nevertheless the exhilaration of the morning had passed into misgiving and depression.

Vague presentiments hung about him all day, whether in the House of Commons or elsewhere, and it was not till he found himself on his legs at a crowded meeting at Rotherhithe, violently attacking the Government Bill and the House of Lords, that he recovered that easy confidence in the general favourableness of the universe to Harry Wharton and Harry Wharton's plans which lent him so much of his power.

A letter from Marcella—written before she had received either of his—reached him at the House just before he started for his meeting. A touching letter!—yet with a certain resolution in it which disconcerted him.

'Forget, if you will, everything that you said to me last night. It might be—I believe it would be—best for us both. But if you will not—if I must give my answer, then, as I said, I must have

time. It is only quite recently that I have *realised* the enormity
of what I did last year. I must run no risks of so wrenching my
own life—or another's—a second time. Not to be *sure* is for me
torment. Why perfect simplicity of feeling—which would scorn
the very notion of questioning itself—seems to be beyond me, I do
not know. That it is so fills me with a sort of shame and bitterness. But I must follow my nature.

'So let me think it out. I believe you know, for one thing,
that your "cause," your life-work, attracts me strongly. I should
not any longer accept all you say, as I did last year. But mere
opinion matters infinitely less to me than it did. I can imagine
now agreeing with a friend "in everything except opinion." All
that would matter to me now would be to feel that *your* heart was
wholly in your work, in your public acts, so that I might still
admire and love all that I might differ from. But there—for we
must be frank with each other—is just my difficulty. *Why* do you
do so many contradictory things? Why do you talk of the poor,
of labour, of self-denial, and live whenever you can with the idle
rich people, who hate all three in their hearts? You talk their
language ; you scorn what they scorn, or so it seems ; you accept
their standards. Oh !—to the really "consecrate" in heart and
thought I could give my life so easily, so slavishly even ! There
is no one weaker than I in the world. I must have strength to
lean upon—and a strength, pure at the core, that I can respect and
follow.

'Here in this nursing life of mine, I go in and out among
people to the best of whom life is very real and simple—and often,
of course, very sad. And I am another being in it from what I
was at Lady Winterbourne's. Everything looks differently to me.
No, no ! you must please wait till the inner voice speaks so that I
can hear it plainly—for your sake at least as much as for mine. If
you persisted in coming to see me now, I should have to put an
end to it all.'

'Strange is the modern woman !' thought Wharton to himself,
not without sharp pique, as he pondered that letter in the course
of his drive home from the meeting. ' I talk to her of passion, and
she asks me in return why I do things inconsistent with my
political opinions ! puts me through a moral catechism, in fact !
What is the meaning of it all—confound it !—her state of mind
and mine? Is the good old *ars amandi* perishing out of the
world? Let some Stendhal come and tell us why !'

But he sat up to answer her, and could not get free from an
inward pleading or wrestle with her, which haunted him through
all the intervals of these rapid days.

Life while they lasted was indeed a gymnast's contest of breath
and endurance. The *Clarion* made its retreat in Wharton's finest
style, and the fact rang through labouring England. The strike
leaders came up from the Midlands; Wharton had to see
them. He was hotly attacked in the House privately, and even
publicly by certain of his colleagues. Bennett showed concern
and annoyance. Meanwhile the Conservative papers talked the
usual employers' political economy; and the Liberal papers, whose
support of the strike had been throughout perfunctory, and of no
particular use to themselves or other people, took a lead they were
glad to get, and went in strongly for the award.

Through it all Wharton showed extraordinary skill. The
columns of the *Clarion* teemed with sympathetic appeals to the
strikers, flanked by long statements of 'hard fact'—the details of
foreign competition and the rest, the plans of the masters—freely
supplied him by Mr. Pearson. With Bennett and his colleagues in
the House he took a bold line; admitted that he had endangered
his popularity both inside Parliament and out of it at a particularly
critical moment; and implied, though he did not say, that some
men were still capable of doing independent things to their own
hurt. Meanwhile he pushed a number of other matters to the
front, both in the paper and in his own daily doings. He made
at least two important speeches in the provinces, in the course of
these days, on the Bill before the House of Lords; he asked questions in Parliament on the subject of the wages paid to Government employés; and he opened an attack on the report of a
certain Conservative Commission which had been rousing the
particular indignation of a large mass of South London working
men.

At the end of ten days the strike was over; the workers, sullen
and enraged, had submitted, and the plans of the Syndicate were
in all the papers. Wharton, looking round him, realised to his own
amazement that his political position had rather gained than
suffered. The general impression produced by his action had
been on the whole that of a man strong enough to take a line of
his own, even at the risk of unpopularity. There was a new tone
of respect among his opponents, and, resentful as some of the
Labour members were, Wharton did not believe that what he had
done would ultimately damage his chances on the 10th at all.
He had vindicated his importance, and he held his head high,
adopting towards his chances of the leadership a strong and careless tone that served him well.

Meanwhile there were, of course, clever people behind the
scenes who looked on and laughed. But they held their tongues,

and Wharton, who had carefully avoided the mention of names during the negotiations with Pearson, did his best to forget them. He felt uncomfortable, indeed, when he passed the portly Denny in the House or in the street.   Denny had a way of looking at the member for West Brookshire out of the corner of a small, slit-like eye.   He did it more than usual during these days, and Wharton had only to say to himself that for all things there is a price—which the gods exact.

Wilkins, since the first disclosure of the *Clarion* change of policy, had been astonishingly quiet.   Wharton had made certain of violent attack from him.   On the contrary, Wilkins wore now in the House a subdued and preoccupied air that escaped notice even with his own party in the general fulness of the public mind.   A few caustic North-countryisms on the subject of the *Clarion* and its master did indeed escape him now and then, and were reported from mouth to mouth ; but on the whole he lay very low.

Still, whether in elation or anxiety, Wharton seemed to him-self throughout the whole period to be a *fighter*, straining every muscle, his back to the wall and his hand against every man. There at the end of the fortnight stood the three goal-posts that must be passed, in victory or defeat ; the meeting that would for the present decide his parliamentary prospects, his interview with Marcella, and—the confounded annual meeting of the ' People's Banking Company,' with all its threatened annoyances.

He became, indeed, more and more occupied with this latter business as the days went on.   But he could see no way of evading it.   He would have to fight it ; luckily, now, he had the money.

The annual meeting took place two days before that fixed for the committee of the Labour party.   Wharton was not present at it, and in spite of ample warning he gave way to certain lively movements of disgust and depression when at his club he first got hold of the evening papers containing the reports.   His name, of course, figured amply in the denunciations heaped upon the directors of all dates ; the sums which he with others was sup-posed to have made out of the first dealings with the shares on the Stock Exchange were freely mentioned ; and the shareholders as a body had shown themselves most uncomfortably violent.   He at once wrote off a letter to the papers disclaiming all responsibility for the worst irregularities which had occurred, and courting full inquiry—a letter which, as usual, both convinced and affected himself.

Then he went, restless and fuming, down to the House. Bennett passed him in the lobby with an uneasy and averted eye.

Whereupon Wharton seized upon him, carried him into the Library, and talked to him, till Bennett, who, in spite of his extraordinary shrewdness and judgment in certain departments, was a babe in matters of company finance, wore a somewhat cheered countenance.

They came out into the lobby together, Wharton holding his head very high.

'I shall deal with the whole thing in my speech on Thursday !' he said aloud, as they parted.

Bennett gave him a friendly nod and smile.

There was in this little man, with his considerable brain and his poet's heart, something of the 'imperishable child.' Like a wholesome child, he did not easily 'think evil'; his temper towards all men—even the owners of 'way-leaves' and mining royalties—was optimist. He had the most naïve admiration for Wharton's ability, and for the academic attainments he himself secretly pined for ; and to the young complex personality itself he had taken from the beginning an unaccountable liking. The bond between the two, though incongruous and recent, was real ; Wharton was as glad of Bennett's farewell kindness as Bennett had been of the younger man's explanations.

So that during that day and the next, Bennett went about contradicting, championing, explaining; while Wharton, laden with Parliamentary business, vivid, unabashed, and resourceful, let it be known to all whom it concerned that in his solicitor's opinion he had a triumphant answer to all charges ; and that meanwhile no one could wonder at the soreness of those poor devils of shareholders.

The hours passed on. Wednesday was mainly spent by Wharton in a series of conferences and intrigues either at the House or at his club ; when he drove home exhausted at night he believed that all was arranged—the train irrevocably laid, and his nomination to the chairmanship of the party certain.

Wilkins and six or seven others would probably prove irreconcilable ; but the vehemence and rancour shown by the great Nehemiah during the summer in the pursuit of his anti-Wharton campaign had to some extent defeated themselves. A personal grudge in the hands of a man of his type is not a formidable weapon. Wharton would have felt perfectly easy on the subject but for some odd bits of manner on Wilkins's part during the last forty-eight hours—whenever, in fact, the two men had run across each other in the House—marked by a sort of new and insolent good humour, that puzzled him. But there is a bravado of defeat. Yes !--he thought Wilkins was disposed of.

From his present point of ease—debts paid, banker propitiated, income assured—it amazed him to look back on his condition of a fortnight before. Had the Prince of Darkness himself offered such a bargain it must have been accepted. After all his luck had held! Once get through this odious company business—as to which, with a pleasing consciousness of turning the tables, he had peremptorily instructed Mr. Pearson himself—and the barque of his fortunes was assured.

Then, with a quick turn of the mind, he threw the burden of affairs from him. His very hopefulness and satisfaction had softened his mood. There stole upon him the murmurs and voices of another world of thought—a world well known to his versatility by report, though he had as a rule small inclination to dwell therein. But he was touched and shaken to-night by his own achievement. The heavenly powers had been unexpectedly kind to him, and he was half moved to offer them something in return.

'Do as you are done by'—that was an ethic he understood. And in moments of feeling he was as ready to apply it to great Zeus himself as to his friends or enemies in the House of Commons. He had done this doubtful thing—but why should it ever be necessary for him to do another? Vague philosophic yearnings after virtue, moderation, patriotism, crossed his mind. The Pagan ideal sometimes smote and fired him, the Christian never. He could still read his Plato and his Cicero, whereas gulfs of unfathomable distaste rolled between him and the New Testament. Perhaps the author of all authors for whom he had most relish was Montaigne. He would have taken him down to-night had there been nothing more kindling to think of.

Marcella!—ah! Marcella! He gave himself to the thought of her with a new and delightful tenderness which had in it elements of compunction. After those disagreeable paragraphs in the evening papers, he had instantly written to her. 'Every public man' —he had said to her, finding instinctively the note of dignity that would appeal to her—'is liable at some period of his career to charges of this sort. They are at once exaggerated and blackened, because he is a public man. To you I owe perfect frankness, and you shall have it. Meanwhile I do not ask—I know—that you will be just to me, and put the matter out of your thoughts till I can discuss it with you. Two days more till I see your face! The time is long!'

To this there had been no answer. Her last letter indeed had rung sadly and coldly. No doubt Louis Craven had something to do with it. It would have alarmed him could he simply have found the time to think about it. Yet she was ready to see him on the

11th ; and his confidence in his own powers of managing fate was tougher than ever. What pleasant lies he had told her at Lady Masterton's ! Well ! What passion ever yet but had its subterfuges ? One more wrestle, and he would have tamed her to his wish, wild falcon that she was. Then—pleasure and brave living ! And she also should have her way. She should breathe into him the language of those great illusions he had found it of late so hard to feign with her ; and they two would walk and rule a yielding world together. Action, passion, affairs—life explored and exploited—and at last—'*que la mort me treuve plantant mes choulx —mais nonchalant d'elle !—et encore plus de mon jardin imparfaict !*'

He declaimed the words of the great Frenchman with something of the same temper in which the devout man would have made an act of faith. Then, with a long breath and a curious emotion, he went to try and sleep himself into the new day.

CHAPTER XV

THE following afternoon about six o'clock Marcella came in from her second round. After a very busy week, work happened to be slack ; and she had been attending one or two cases in and near Brown's Buildings rather because they were near than because they seriously wanted her. She looked to see whether there was any letter or telegram from the office which would have obliged her to go out again. Nothing was to be seen ; and she put down her bag and cloak, childishly glad of the extra hour of rest.

She was, indeed, pale and worn. The moral struggle which had filled the past fortnight from end to end had deepened all the grooves and strained the forces of life ; and the path, though glimmering, was not wholly plain.

A letter lay unfinished in her drawer—if she sent it that night, there would be little necessity or inducement for Wharton to climb those stairs on the morrow. Yet, if he held her to it, she must see him.

As the sunset and the dusk crept on she still sat silent and alone, sunk in a depression which showed itself in every line of the drooping form. She was degraded in her own eyes. The nature of the impulses which had led her to give Wharton the hold upon her she had given him had become plain to her. What lay between them, and the worst impulses that poison the lives of women, but

differences of degree, of expression?   After those wild hours of
sensuous revolt, a kind of moral terror was upon her.

What had worked in her?   What was at the root of this
vehemence of moral reaction, this haunting fear of losing for ever
the *best* in life—self-respect, the comradeship of the good, com-
munion with things noble and unstained—which had conquered at
last the mere *woman*, the weakness of vanity and of sex?   She
hardly knew.   Only there was in her a sort of vague thankfulness
for her daily work.   It did not seem to be possible to see one's own
life solely under the aspects of selfish desire while hands and mind
were busy with the piteous realities of sickness and of death.   From
every act of service—from every contact with the patience and
simplicity of the poor—*something* had spoken to her, that divine
ineffable something for ever 'set in the world,' like beauty, like
charm, for the winning of men to itself.   ' Follow truth !' it said to
her in faint mysterious breathings—'the truth of your own heart.
The sorrow to which it will lead you is the only *joy* that remains to
you.'

Suddenly she looked round her little room with a rush of
tenderness.   The windows were open to the evening and the shouts
of children playing in the courtyard came floating up.   A bowl of
Mellor roses scented the air ; the tray for her simple meal stood
ready, and beside it a volume of ' The Divine Comedy,' one of her
mother's very rare gifts to her, in her motherless youth—for of late
she had turned thirstily to poetry.   There was a great peace and
plainness about it all ; and, besides, touches of beauty—tokens of
the soul.   Her work spoke in it ; called to her ; promised comfort
and ennobling.   She thought with yearning, too, of her parents ;
of the autumn holiday she was soon to spend with them.   Her
heart went out—sorely—to all the primal claims upon it.

Nevertheless, clear as was the inner resolution, the immediate
future filled her with dread.   Her ignorance of herself—her
excitable folly—had given Wharton rights which her conscience
admitted.   He would not let her go without a struggle, and she
must face it.

As to the incidents which had happened during the fortnight—
Louis Craven's return, and the scandal of the ' People's Banking
Company'—they had troubled and distressed her ; but it would
not be true to say that they had had any part in shaping her slow
determination.   Louis Craven was sore and bitter.   She was very
sorry for him ; and his reports of the Damesley strikers made her
miserable.   But she took Wharton's ' leaders ' in the *Clarion* for
another equally competent opinion on the same subject ; and told

herself that she was no judge. As for the Company scandal, she had instantly and proudly responded to the appeal of his letter, and put the matter out of her thoughts, till at least he should give his own account. So much at any rate she owed to the man who had stood by her through the Hurd trial. Marcella Boyce would not readily believe in his dishonour ! She did not in fact believe it. In spite of later misgivings, the impression of his personality, as she had first conceived it, in the early days at Mellor, was still too strong.

No—rather—she had constantly recollected throughout the day what was going on in Parliament. These were for him testing and critical hours, and she felt a wistful sympathy. Let him only rise to his part—take up his great task.

An imperious knocking on her thin outer door roused her. She went to open it and saw Anthony Craven,—the perspiration standing on his brow, his delicate cripple's face white and fierce.

' I want to talk to you,' he said without preface.—' Have you seen the afternoon papers ? '

' No,' she said in astonishment. ' I was just going to send for them. What is wrong ? '

He followed her into the sitting-room without speaking ; and then he unfolded the *Pall Mall* he had in his hand and pointed to a large-print paragraph on the central page with a shaking hand.

Marcella read :

' EXCITING SCENES IN THE HOUSE.— MEETING OF THE LABOUR MEMBERS.—A committee of the Labour representatives in Parliament met this afternoon at two o'clock for the purpose of electing a chairman, and appointing whips to the party, thus con stituting a separate Parliamentary group. Much interest was felt in the proceedings, which it was universally supposed would lead to the appointment of Mr. H. S. Wharton, the Member for West Brookshire, as chairman and leader of the Labour party. The excitement of the meeting and in the House may be imagined when —after a short but very cordial and effective speech from Mr. Bennett, the Member for North Whinwick, in support of Mr. Wharton's candidature—Mr. Wilkins, the miners' Member for Derlingham, rose and made a series of astounding charges against the personal honour of the member for West Brookshire. Put briefly, they amount to this : that during the recent strike at Damesley the support of the *Clarion* newspaper, of which Mr. Wharton is owner and practically editor, was *bought* by the employers in return for certain shares in the new Syndicate ; that the money for these shares—which is put as high as 20,000*l.*—had

already gone into Mr. Wharton's private pocket ; and that the change
of policy on the part of the *Clarion*, which led to the collapse of
the strike, was thus entirely due to what the Labour members can
only regard under the circumstances as a bribe of a most disgrace-
ful kind. The effect produced has been enormous. The debate
is still proceeding, and reporters have been excluded. But I hope
to send a fuller account later.'

Marcella dropped the paper from her hand.

' What does it mean ? ' she said to her companion.

' Precisely what it says,' replied Anthony, with a nervous impatience he could not repress. 'Now,' he added, as his lameness
forced him to sit down, ' will you kindly allow me some conversation with you ? It was you—practically—who introduced Louis to
that man. You meant well to Louis, and Mr. Wharton has been
your friend. We therefore feel that we owe you some explanation.
For that paragraph '—he pointed to the paper—' is, substantially—
Louis's doing, and mine.'

' *Yours* ? ' she said mechanically. ' But Louis has been going
on working for the paper—I persuaded him.'

' I know. It was not we who actually discovered the thing.
But we set a friend to work. Louis has had his suspicions all
along. And at last—by the merest chance—we got the facts.'

Then he told the story, staring at her the while with his
sparkling eyes, his thin invalid's fingers fidgeting with his hat. If
there was in truth any idea in his mind that the relations between
his companion and Harry Wharton were more than those of friendship, it did not avail to make him spare her in the least. He was
absorbed in vindictive feeling, which applied to her also. He might
say for form's sake that she had meant well ; but in fact he regarded
her at this moment as a sort of odious Canidia whose one function
had been to lure Louis to misfortune. Cut off himself, by half a
score of peculiarities, physical and other, from love, pleasure, and
power, Anthony Craven's whole affections and ambitions had for
years centred in his brother. And now Louis was not only violently
thrown out of employment, but compromised by the connection
with the *Clarion* ; was, moreover, saddled with a wife—and in
debt.

So that his explanation was given with all the edge he could put
upon it. Let her stop him, if she pleased !—But she did not stop
him.

The facts were these :—

Louis had, indeed, been persuaded by Marcella, for the sake of
his wife and bread and butter, to go on working for the *Clarion*, as
a reviewer. But his mind was all the time feverishly occupied with

the apostasy of the paper and its causes. Remembering Wharton's sayings and letters throughout the struggle, he grew less and less able to explain the incident by the reasons Wharton had himself supplied, and more and more convinced that there was some mystery behind.

He and Anthony talked the matter over perpetually. One evening Anthony brought home from a meeting of the Venturists that George Denny, the son of one of the principal employers in the Damesley trade, whose name he had mentioned once before in Marcella's ears. Denny was by this time the candidate for a Labour constituency, an ardent Venturist, and the laughing-stock of his capitalist family, with whom, however, he was still on more or less affectionate terms. His father thought him an incorrigible fool, and his mother wailed over him to her friends. But they were still glad to see him whenever he would condescend to visit them ; and all friction on money matters was avoided by the fact that Denny had for long refused to take any pecuniary help from his father, and was nevertheless supporting himself tolerably by lecturing and literature.

Denny was admitted into the brothers' debate, and had indeed puzzled himself a good deal over the matter already. He had taken a lively interest in the strike, and the articles in the *Clarion* which led to its collapse had seemed to him both inexplicable and enraging.

After his talk with the Cravens, he went away, determined to dine at home on the earliest possible opportunity. He announced himself accordingly in Hertford Street, was received with open arms, and then deliberately set himself, at dinner and afterwards, to bait his father on social and political questions, which, as a rule, were avoided between them.

Old Denny fell into the trap, lost his temper and self-control completely, and at a mention of Harry Wharton—skilfully introduced at the precisely right moment—as an authority on some matter connected with the current Labour programme, he threw himself back in his chair with an angry laugh.

'Wharton ? *Wharton* ? You quote that fellow to *me* ?'

'Why shouldn't I ?' said the son, quietly.

'Because, my good sir,—he's a *rogue*,—that's all !—a common rogue, from my point of view even—still more from yours.'

'I know that any vile tale you can believe about a Labour leader you do, father,' said George Denny with dignity.

Whereupon the older man thrust his hand into his coat-pocket, and drawing out a small leather case, in which he was apt to carry important papers about with him, extracted from it a list containing names and figures, and held it with a somewhat tremulous hand under his son's eyes.

'Read it, sir! and hold your tongue! Last week my friends and I *bought* that man—and his precious paper—for a trifle of 20,000*l*. or thereabouts. It paid us to do it, and we did it. I dare say *you* will think the proceeding questionable. In my eyes it was perfectly legitimate, a piece of "bonne guerre." The man was ruining a whole industry. Some of us had taken his measure, had found out too—by good luck!—that he was in sore straits for money—mortgages on the paper, gambling debts, and a host of other things—discovered a shrewd man to play him, and made our bid! He rose to it like a gudgeon—gave us no trouble whatever. I need not say, of course'—he added, looking up at his son—'that I have shown you that paper in the *very strictest confidence*. But it seemed to me it was my duty as a father to warn you of the nature of some of your associates!'

'I understand,' said George Denny, as, after a careful study of the paper—which contained, for the help of the writer's memory, a list of the sums paid and founders' shares allotted to the various 'promoters' of the new Syndicate—he restored it to its owner. 'Well, I, father, have *this* to say in return. I came here to-night in the hope of getting from you this very information, and in the public interest I hold myself not only free but *bound* to make public use of it, at the earliest possible opportunity!'

The family scene may be imagined. But both threats and blandishments were entirely lost upon the son. There was in him an idealist obstinacy which listened to nothing but the cry of a *cause*, and he declared that nothing would or should prevent him from carrying the story of the bribe direct to Nehemiah Wilkins, Wharton's chief rival in the House, and so saving the country and the Labour party from the disaster and disgrace of Wharton's leadership. There was no time to lose, the party meeting in the House was only two days off.

At the end of a long struggle, which exhausted everybody concerned, and was carried on to a late hour of the night, Denny *père*, influenced by a desire to avoid worse things—conscious, too, of the abundant evidence he possessed of Wharton's acceptance and private use of the money—and, probably, when it came to the point, not unwilling,—under compulsion!—to tumble such a hero from his pedestal, actually wrote, under his son's advice, a letter to Wilkins. It was couched in the most cautious language, and professed to be written in the interests of Wharton himself, to put an end 'to certain ugly and unfounded rumours that have been brought to my knowledge.' The negotiation itself was described in the driest business terms. ' Mr. Wharton, upon cause shown, consented to take part in the founding of the Syndicate, and in return for his assistance, was allotted ten founders' shares in the new company. The transaction differed in nothing from those of ordinary business '—a last sentence slyly added by the Socialist son, and innocently accepted by one of the shrewdest of men.

After which, Master George Denny scarcely slept, and by nine o'clock next morning was in a hansom on his way to Wilkins's lodgings in Westminster. The glee of that black-bearded patriot hardly needs description. He flung himself on the letter with a delight and relief so exuberant that George Denny went off to another more phlegmatic member of the anti-Wharton ' cave,' with entreaties that an eye should be kept on the Member for Derling-ham, lest he should do or disclose anything before the dramatic moment.

Then he himself spent the next forty-eight hours in ingenious efforts to put together certain additional information as to the current value of founders' shares in the new company, the nature and amount of Wharton's debts, and so on. Thanks to his father's hints he was able in the end to discover quite enough to furnish forth a supplementary statement. So that, when the 10th arrived, the day rose upon a group of men breathlessly awaiting a play within a play—with all their parts rehearsed, and the prompter ready.

Such in substance was Anthony's story. So carried away was he by the excitement and triumph of it, that he soon ceased to notice what its effect might be upon his pale and quick-breathing companion.

'And now what has happened?' she asked him abruptly, when at last he paused.

'Why, you saw!' he said in astonishment, pointing to the evening paper—'at least the beginning of it. Louis is at the House now. I expect him every moment. He said he would follow me here.'

Marcella pressed her hands upon her eyes a moment as though in pain. Anthony looked at her with a tardy prick of remorse.

'I hear Louis's knock!' he said, springing up. 'May I let him in?' And, without waiting for reply, he hobbled as fast as his crutch would carry him to the outer door. Louis came in. Marcella rose mechanically. He paused on the threshold, his short sight trying to make her out in the dusk. Then his face softened and quivered. He walked forward quickly.

'I know you have something to forgive us,' he said, 'and

that this will distress you. But we could not give you warning. Everything was so rapid, and the public interests involved so crushing.'

He was flushed with vengeance and victory, but as he approached her his look was deprecating—almost timid. Only the night before, Anthony for the first time had suggested to him an idea about her. He did not believe it—had had no time in truth to think of it in the rush of events. But now he saw her, the doubt pulled at his heart. Had ne indeed stabbed the hand that had tried to help him?

Anthony touched him impatiently on the arm. 'What has happened, Louis? I have shown Miss Boyce the first news.'

'It is all over,' said Louis, briefly. 'The meeting was breaking up as I came away. It had lasted nearly five hours. There was a fierce fight, of course, between Wharton and Wilkins. Then Bennett withdrew his resolution, refused to be nominated himself —nearly broke down, in fact, they say; he had always been attached to Wharton, and had set his heart upon making him leader—and finally, after a long wrangle, Molloy was appointed chairman of the party.'

'Good!' cried Anthony, not able to suppress the note of exultation.

Louis did not speak. He looked at Marcella.

'Did he defend himself?' she asked in a low, sharp voice

Louis shrugged his shoulders.

'Oh, yes. He spoke—but it did him no good. Everybody agreed that the speech was curiously ineffective. One would have expected him to do it better. But he seemed to be knocked over. He said, of course, that he had satisfied himself, and given proof in the paper, that the strike could not be maintained, and that being so he was free to join any syndicate he pleased. But he spoke amid dead silence, and there was a general groan when he sat down. Oh, it was not this business only! Wilkins made great play in part of his speech with the company scandal too. It is a complete smash all round.'

'Which he will never get over?' said Marcella quickly.

'Not with our men. What he may do elsewhere is another matter. Anthony has told you how it came out?'

She made a sign of assent. She was sitting erect and cold, her hands round her knees.

'I did not mean to keep anything from you,' he said in a low voice, bending to her. 'I know—you admired him—that he had given you cause. But—my mind has been on *fire*—ever since I came back from those Damesley scenes!'

She offered no reply. Silence fell upon all three for a minute or two ; and in the twilight each could hardly distinguish the others. Every now and then the passionate tears rose in Marcella's eyes ; her heart contracted. That very night when he spoke to her, when he used all those big words to her about his future, those great ends for which he had claimed her woman's help—he had these things in his mind.

'I think,' said Louis Craven presently, touching her gently on the arm—he had tried once in vain to attract her attention—'I think I hear someone asking for you outside on the landing—Mrs. Hurd seems to be bringing them in.'

As he spoke, Anthony suddenly sprang to his feet, and the outer door opened.

'Louis !' cried Anthony, 'it is *he* !'

'Are yer at home, miss ?' said Minta Hurd, putting in her head ; ' I can hardly see, it's so dark. Here's a gentleman wants to see you.'

As she spoke, Wharton passed her, and stood—arrested—by the sight of the three figures. At the same moment Mrs. Hurd lit the gas in the little passage. The light streamed upon his face, and showed him the identity of the two men standing beside Marcella.

Never did Marcella forget that apparition—the young grace and power of the figure—the indefinable note of wreck, of catastrophe—the Lucifer brightness of the eyes in the set face. She moved forward. Anthony stopped her.

'Good night, Miss Boyce !'

She shook hands unconsciously with him and with Louis. The two Cravens turned to the door. Wharton advanced into the room, and let them pass.

'You have been in a hurry to tell your story !' he said, as Louis walked by him.

Contemptuous hate breathed from every feature, but he was perfectly self-controlled.

'Yes—' said Craven calmly.—' Now it is your turn.'

The door was no sooner shut than Wharton strode forward and caught her hand.

'They have told you everything ? Ah !'—

His eye fell upon the evening paper. Letting her go, he felt for a chair and dropped into it. Throwing himself back, his hands behind his head, he drew a long breath and his eyes closed. For the first time in his life or hers she saw him weak and spent like other men. Even his nerve had been worn down by the excitement of these five fighting hours. The eyes were lined and hollow

—the brow contracted; the young roundness of the cheek was lost in the general pallor and patchiness of the skin ; the lower part of the face seemed to have sharpened and lengthened,—and over the whole had passed a breath of something ageing and withering the traces of which sent a shiver through Marcella. She sat down near him, still in her nurse's cloak, one trembling hand upon her lap.

'Will you tell me what made you do this?' she asked, not being able to think of anything else to say.

He opened his eyes with a start.

In that instant's quiet the scene he had just lived through had been rushing before him again—the long table in the panelled committee-room, the keen angry faces gathered about it,—Bennett, in his blue tie and shabby black coat, the clear moist eyes vexed and miserable—Molloy, small and wiry, business-like in the midst of confusion, cool in the midst of tumult—and Wilkins, a black, hectoring leviathan, thundering on the table as he flung his broad Yorkshire across it, or mouthing out Denny's letter in the midst of the sudden electrical silence of some thirty amazed and incredulous hearers.

'*Spies*, yo call us?' with a finger like a dart, threatening the enemy.—'Ay ; an' yo're aboot reet ! I and my friends—we *have* been trackin and spyin for weeks past. We *knew* those men, those starvin women and bairns, were bein *sold*, but we couldn't prove it. Now we've come at the how and the why of it ! And we'll make it harder for men like you *to sell 'em again* ! Yo call it infamy?—Well, *we* call it detection.'

Then rattling on the inner ear came the phrases of the attack which followed on the director of 'The People's Banking Association,' the injured innocent of as mean a job, as unsavoury a bit of vulturous finance, as had cropped into publicity for many a year—and finally the last dramatic cry :

'But it's noa matter, yo say ! Mester Wharton has nobbut played his party an' the workin man a dirty trick or two—*an' yo mun have a gentleman* ! Noa—the workin man isn't fit *himself* to speak wi his own enemies i' th' gate—*yo mun have a gentleman* !—an' Mester Wharton, he says he'll tak the post, an' dea his best for yo—an', remember, *yo mun have a gentleman* ! Soa now—Yes ! or No !—wull yo?—or *woan't yo* ?'

And at that, the precipitation of the great unwieldy form half across the table towards Wharton's seat—the roar of the speaker's immediate supporters thrown up against the dead silence of the rest !

As to his own speech—he thought of it with a soreness, a

disgust which penetrated to bones and marrow. He had been too desperately taken by surprise—had lost his nerve—missed the right tone throughout. Cool defiance, free self-justification, might have carried him through. Instead of which—faugh!

All this was the phantom-show of a few seconds' thought. He roused himself from a miserable reaction of mind and body to attend to Marcella's question.

'Why did I do it?' he repeated; 'why——'

He broke off, pressing both his hands upon his brow. Then he suddenly sat up and pulled himself together.

'Is that tea?' he said, touching the tray. 'Will you give me some?'

Marcella went into the back kitchen and called Minta. While the boiling water was brought and the tea was made, Wharton sat forward with his face on his hands and saw nothing. Marcella whispered a word in Minta's ear as she came in. The woman paused, looked at Wharton, whom she had not recognised before in the dark—grew pale—and Marcella saw her hands shaking as she set the tray in order. Wharton knew nothing and thought nothing of Hurd's widow, but to Marcella the juxtaposition of the two figures brought a wave of complex emotion.

Wharton forced himself to eat and drink, hardly speaking the while. Then, when the tremor of sheer exhaustion had to some extent abated, he suddenly realised who this was that was sitting opposite to him ministering to him.

She felt his hand—his quick powerful hand—on hers.

'To *you* I owe the whole truth—let me tell it!'

She drew herself away instinctively—but so softly that he did not realise it. He threw himself back once more in the chair beside her—one knee over the other, the curly head so much younger to-night than the face beneath it supported on his arms, his eyes closed again for rest—and plunged into the story of the *Clarion*.

It was admirably told. He had probably so rehearsed it to himself several times already. He described his action as the result of a double influence working upon him—the influence of his own debts and necessities—and the influence of his growing conviction that the maintenance of the strike had become a blunder, even a misfortune for the people themselves.

'Then—just as I was at my wits' end, conscious besides that the paper was on a wrong line, and must somehow be got out of it—came the overtures from the Syndicate. I knew perfectly well I ought to have refused them—of *course* my whole career was risked by listening to them. But at the same time they gave me assurances that the workpeople would ultimately gain—they proved to me that I was helping to extinguish the trade. As to the *money* —when a great company has to be launched, the people who help it into being get *paid* for it—it is invariable—it happens every day. I like the system no more than you may do—or Wilkins. But consider. I was in such straits that *bankruptcy* lay between me and my political future. Moreover—I had lost nerve, sleep, balance. I was scarcely master of myself when Pearson first broached the matter to me——'

'Pearson!' cried Marcella involuntarily. She recalled the figure of the solicitor; had heard his name from Frank Leven. She remembered Wharton's impatient words—'There is a tiresome man wants to speak to me on business——'

It was *then* !—that evening ! Something sickened her.

Wharton raised himself in his chair and looked at her attentively with his young haggard eyes. In the faint lamplight she was a pale vision of the purest and noblest beauty. But the lofty sadness of her face filled him with a kind of terror. Desire— impotent pain—violent resolve, swept across him. He had come to her, straight from the scene of his ruin, as to the last bulwark left him against a world bent on his destruction, and bare henceforward of all delights.

'Well, what have you to say to me?' he said, suddenly, in a low changed voice—'as I speak—as I look at you—I see in your face that you distrust—that you have judged me ; those two men, I suppose, have done their work ! Yet from you—*you* of all people—I might look not only for justice—but—I will dare say it —for kindness !'

She trembled. She understood that he appealed to the days at Mellor, and her lips quivered.

'No,' she exclaimed, almost timidly—'I try to think the best. I see the pressure was great.'

'And consider, please,' he said proudly, 'what the reasons were for that pressure.'

She looked at him interrogatively—a sudden softness in her eyes. If at that moment he had confessed himself fully, if he had thrown himself upon her in the frank truth of his mixed character —and he could have done it, with a Rousseau-like completeness— it is difficult to say what the result of this scene might have been. In the midst of shock and repulsion, she was filled with pity ; and there were moments when she was more drawn to his defeat and undoing, than she had ever been to his success.

Yet how question him ? To do so, would be to assume a right, which in turn would imply *his* rights. She thought of that mention of 'gambling debts,' then of his luxurious habits, and extravagant friends. But she was silent. Only, as she sat there opposite to him, one slim hand propping the brow, her look invited him.

He thought he saw his advantage.

'You must remember,' he said, with the same self-assertive bearing, 'that I have never been a rich man; that my mother spent my father's savings on a score of public objects; that she and I started a number of experiments on the estate; that my expenses as a Member of Parliament are very large, and that I spent thousands on building up the *Clarion*. I have been ruined by the *Clarion*, by the cause the *Clarion* supported. I got no help from my party—where was it to come from? They are all poor men. I had to do everything myself, and the struggle has been more than flesh and blood could bear! This year, often, I have not known how to move, to breathe, for anxieties of every sort. Then came the crisis—my work, my usefulness, my career, all threatened. The men who hated me saw their opportunity. I was a fool and gave it them. And my enemies have used it—to the bitter end!'

Tone and gesture were equally insistent and strong. What he was saying to himself was that, with a woman of Marcella's type, one must 'bear it out.' This moment of wreck was also with him the first moment of all-absorbing and desperate desire. To win her—to wrest her from the Cravens' influence—that had been the cry in his mind throughout his dazed drive from the House of Commons. Her hand in his—her strength, her beauty, the romantic reputation that had begun to attach to her, at his command—and he would have taken the first step to recovery, he would see his way to right himself.

Ah! but he had missed his chance! Somehow, every word he had been saying rang false to her. She could have thrown herself as a saving angel on the side of weakness and disaster which had spoken its proper language, and with a reckless and confiding truth had appealed to the largeness of a woman's heart. But this patriot—ruined so nobly—for such disinterested purposes —left her cold! She began to think even—hating herself—of the thousands he was supposed to have made in the gambling over that wretched company—no doubt for the 'cause' too!

But before she could say a word he was kneeling beside her.

'*Marcella*! give me my answer!—I am in trouble and defeat —be a woman, and come to me!'

He had her hands. She tried to recover them.

'No!' she said, with passionate energy, '*that* is impossible. I had written to you before you came, before I had heard a word of this. Please, *please* let me go!'

'Not till you explain !'—he said, still holding her, and roused to a white heat of emotion—' *why* is it impossible ?   You said to me once, with all your heart, that you thanked me, that I had taught you, helped you.   You cannot ignore the bond between us ! And you are free.   I have a right to say to you—you thirst to save, to do good—come and save a man that cries to you !—he confesses to *you*, freely enough, that he has made a hideous mistake —help him to redeem it !'

She rose suddenly with all her strength, freeing herself from him, so that he rose too, and stood glowering and pale.

'When I said that to you.' she cried, ' I was betraying '—her voice failed her in an instant—' we were both false—to the obligation that should have held us—restrained us.   No ! *nc* ! I will never be your wife !   We should hurt each other—poison each other !'

Her eyes shone with wild tears.   As he stood there before her she was seized with a piteous sense of contrast—of the irreparable —of what might have been.

'What do you mean?' he asked her, roughly.

She was silent.

His passion rose.

'Do you remember?' he said, approaching her again, 'that you have given me cause to hope?   It is those two fanatics that have changed you—possessed your mind.'

She looked at him with a pale dignity.

' My letters must have warned you,' she said simply.   ' If you had come to-morrow—in prosperity—you would have got the same answer, at once.   To-day—now—I have had weak moments, because—because I did not know how to add pain to pain.   But they are gone—I see my way !   *I do not love you*—that is the simple, the whole truth—I could not follow you !'

He stared at her an instant in a bitter silence.

' I have been warned,'—he said slowly, but in truth losing con-trol of himself, 'not only by you—and I suppose I understand ! You repent last year.   Your own letter said as much.   You mean to recover the ground—the place you lost.   Ah, well !—most natural !—most fitting !   When the time comes—and my bones are less sore—I suppose I shall have my second congratulations ready !   Meanwhile——'

She gave a low cry and burst suddenly into a passion of weeping, turning her face from him.   But when in pale sudden shame he tried to excuse himself—to appease her—she moved away, with a gesture that overawed him.

' *You* have not confessed yourself'—she said, and his look

wavered under the significance of hers—'but you drive me to it.
Yes, *I repent* !'—her breast heaved, she caught her breath. 'I have
been trying to cheat myself these last few weeks—to run away from
grief—and the other night when you asked me—I would have given
all I have and am to feel like any happy girl, who says "Yes" to
her lover. I tried to feel so. But even then, though I was miserable and reckless, I knew in my heart—it was impossible ! If you
suppose—if you like to suppose—that I—I have hopes or plans—as
mean as they would be silly—you must—of course. But I have
given no one any *right* to think so or say so. Mr. Wharton——'

Gathering all her self-control, she put out her white hand to him.
'Please—please say good-bye to me. It has been hideous vanity
—and mistake—and wretchedness—our knowing each other—from
the beginning. I *am* grateful for all you did : I shall always be
grateful. I hope—oh ! I hope—that—that you will find a way
through this trouble. I don't want to make it worse by a word. If
I could do anything ! But I can't. You must please go. It is late.
I wish to call my friend, Mrs. Hurd.'

Their eyes met—hers full of a certain stern yet quivering power ;
his strained and bloodshot, in his lined young face.

Then, with a violent gesture—as though he swept her out of his
path—he caught up his hat, went to the door, and was gone.

She fell on her chair almost fainting, and sat there for long in
the summer dark, covering her face. But it was not his voice that
haunted her ears.

'*You have done me wrong—I pray God you may not do yourself
a greater wrong in the future !*'

Again and again, amid the whirl of memory, she pressed the sad
remembered words upon the inward wound and fever—tasting,
cherishing the smart of them. And as her trance of exhaustion and
despair gradually left her, it was as though she crept close to some
dim beloved form in whom her heart knew henceforward the secret
and sole companion of its inmost life.

BOOK IV

'You and I—
Why care by what meanders we are here
I' the centre of the labyrinth? Men have died
Trying to find this place which we have found.'

CHAPTER I

AH! how purely, cleanly beautiful was the autumn sunrise! After
her long hardening to the stale noisomeness of London streets, the
taint of London air, Marcella hung out of her window at Mellor in
a thirsty delight, drinking in the scent of dew and earth and trees,
watching the ways of the birds, pouring forth a soul of yearning
and of memory into the pearly silence of the morning.

High up on the distant hill to the left, beyond the avenue, the
pale apricots and golds of the newly-shorn stubbles caught the
mounting light. The beeches of the avenue were turning fast,
and the chestnuts girdling the church on her right hand were
already thin enough to let the tower show through. That was the
bell—the old bell given to the church by Hampden's friend, John
Boyce—striking half-past five; and close upon it came the call of
a pheasant in the avenue. There he was, fine fellow, with his
silly, mincing run, redeemed all at once by the sudden whirr of
towering flight.

To-day Mary Harden and the Rector would be at work in the
church, and to-morrow was to be the Harvest Festival. Was it
two years?—or in an hour or two would she be going with her
basket from the Cedar Garden, to find that figure in the brown
shooting-coat standing with the Hardens on the altar steps?

Alas!—alas!—her head dropped on her hands as she knelt
by the open window. How changed were all the aspects of the
world! Three weeks before, the bell in that little church had
tolled for one who, in the best way and temper of his own generation, had been God's servant and man's friend—who had been
Marcella's friend—and had even, in his last days, on a word from
Edward Hallin, sent her an old man's kindly farewell.

'Tell her,' Lord Maxwell had written with his own hand to
Hallin, 'she has taken up a noble work, and will make, I pray God,
a noble woman. She had, I think, a kindly liking for an old
man, and she will not disdain his blessing.'

He had died at Geneva, Aldous and Miss Raeburn with him.
For instead of coming home in August, he had grown suddenly

worse, and Aldous had gone out to him.   They had brought him
to the Court for burial, and the new Lord Maxwell, leaving his
aunt at the Court, had almost immediately returned to town,—because of Edward Hallin's state of health.

Marcella had seen much of Hallin since he and his sister had
come back to London in the middle of August.   Hallin's apparent
improvement had faded within a week or two of his return to his
rooms ; Aldous was at Geneva ; Miss Hallin was in a panic of
alarm ; and Marcella found herself both nurse and friend.   Day
after day she would go in after her nursing rounds, share their
evening meal, and either write for Hallin, or help the sister—by
the slight extra weight of her professional voice—to keep him from
writing and thinking.

He would not himself admit that he was ill at all, and his
whole energies at the time were devoted to the preparation of a
series of three addresses on the subject of Land Reform, which
were to be delivered in October to the delegates of a large number
of working-men's clubs from all parts of London.   So strong was
Hallin's position among working-men reformers, and so beloved
had been his personality, that as soon as his position towards the
new land nationalising movement, now gathering formidable
strength among the London working men, had come to be widely
understood, a combined challenge had been sent him by some half-
dozen of the leading Socialist and Radical clubs, asking him to give
three weekly addresses in October to a congress of London delegates, time to be allowed after the lecture for questions and debate.

Hallin had accepted the invitation with eagerness, and was
throwing an intensity of labour into the writing of his three lectures
which often seemed to his poor sister to be not only utterly beyond
his physical strength, but to carry with it a note as of a last effort,
a farewell message, such as her devoted affection could ill endure.
For all the time he was struggling with cardiac weakness and
brain irritability which would have overwhelmed anyone less
accustomed to make his account with illness, or to balance against
feebleness of body a marvellous discipline of soul.

Lord Maxwell was still alive, and Hallin, in the midst of his
work, was looking anxiously for the daily reports from Aldous,
living in his friends' life almost as much as his own—handing on
the reports, too, day by day to Marcella, with a manner which had
somehow slipped into expressing a new and sure confidence in her
sympathy—when she one evening found Minta Hurd watching for
her at the door with a telegram from her mother: 'Your father
suddenly worse. Please come at once' She arrived at Mellor
late that same night.

On the same day Lord Maxwell died. Less than a week later he was buried in the little Gairsley church. Mr. Boyce was then alarmingly ill, and Marcella sat in his darkened room or in her own all day, thinking from time to time of what was passing three miles away—of the great house in its mourning—of the figures round the grave. Hallin, of course, would be there. It was a dripping September day, and she passed easily from moments of passionate yearning and clairvoyance to worry herself about the damp and the fatigue that Hallin must be facing.

Since then she had heard occasionally from Miss Hallin. Everything was much as it had been, apparently. Edward was still hard at work, still ill, still serene. ' Aldous '—Miss Hallin could not yet reconcile herself to the new name—was alone in the Curzon Street house, much occupied and harassed apparently by the legal business of the succession, by the election presently to be held in his own constituency, and by the winding-up of his work at the Home Office. He was to resign his under-secretaryship ; but with the new session and a certain re-arrangement of offices it was probable that he would be brought back into the ministry. Meanwhile he was constantly with them ; and she thought that his interest in Edward's work and anxiety about his health were perhaps both good for him as helping to throw off something of his own grief and depression.

Whereby it will be noticed that Miss Hallin, like her brother, had by now come to speak intimately and freely to Marcella of her old lover and their friend.

Now for some days, however, she had received no letter from either brother or sister, and she was particularly anxious to hear. For this was the fourth of October, and on the second he was to have delivered the first of his addresses. How had the frail prophet sped ? She had her fears. For her weekly ' evenings ' in Brown's Buildings had shown her a good deal of the passionate strength of feeling developed during the past year in connection with this particular propaganda. She doubted whether the London working man at the present moment was likely to give even Hallin a fair hearing on the point. However, Louis Craven was to be there. And he had promised to write even if Susie Hallin could find no time. Some report ought to reach Mellor by the evening.

Poor Cravens ! The young wife, who was expecting a baby, had behaved with great spirit through the *Clarion* trouble ; and, selling their bits of furniture to pay their debts, they had gone to lodge near Anthony. Louis had got some odds and ends of designing and artistic work to do through his brother's influence ;

and was writing where he could, here and there. Marcella had introduced them to the Hallins, and Susie Hallin was taking a motherly interest in the coming child. Anthony, in his gloomy way, was doing all he could for them. But the struggle was likely to be a hard one, and Marcella had recognised of late that in Louis as in Anthony there were dangerous possibilities of melancholy and eccentricity. Her heart was often sore over their trouble and her own impotence.

Meantime for some wounds, at any rate, time had brought swift cautery ! Not three days after her final interview with Wharton, while the catastrophe in the Labour party was still in everyone's mouth, and the air was full of bitter speeches and recriminations, Hallin one evening laid down his newspaper with a sudden startled gesture, and then pushed it over to Marcella. There, in the columns devoted to personal news of various sorts, appeared the announcement :

'A marriage has been arranged between Mr. H. S. Wharton, M.P. for West Brookshire, and Lady Selina Farrell, only surviving daughter of Lord Alresford. The ceremony will probably take place somewhere about Easter next. Meanwhile Mr. Wharton, whose health has suffered of late from his exertions in and out of the House, has been ordered to the East for rest by his medical advisers. He and his friend Sir William Ffolliot start for French Cochin China in a few days. Their object is to explore the famous ruined temples of Angkor in Cambodia, and if the season is favourable they may attempt to ascend the Mekong. Mr. Wharton is paired for the remainder of the session.'

'Did you know anything of this ?' said Hallin, with that careful carelessness in which people dress a dubious question.

'Nothing,' she said quietly.

Then an impulse not to be stood against, springing from very mingled depths of feeling, drove her on. She, too, put down the paper and, laying her finger-tips together on her knee, she said with an odd slight laugh :

'But I was the last person to know. About a fortnight ago Mr. Wharton proposed to me.'

Hallin sprang from his chair, almost with a shout. 'And you refused him ?'

She nodded, and then was angrily aware that, totally against her will or consent, and for the most foolish and remote reasons, those two eyes of hers had grown moist.

Hallin went straight over to her.

'Do you mind letting me shake hands with you?' he said, half ashamed of his outburst, a dancing light of pleasure transforming

the thin face. 'There—I am an idiot ! We won't say a word more
—except about Lady Selina. Have you seen her?'

'Three or four times.'

'What is she like?'

Marcella hesitated.

'Is she fat—and forty?' said Hallin fervently.—'Will she beat
him?'

'Not at all. She is very thin—thirty-five, elegant, terribly of
her own opinion—and makes a great parade of "papa."'

She looked round at him, unsteadily, but gaily.

'Oh! I see,' said Hallin with disappointment, 'she will only take
care he doesn't beat her—which I gather from your manner doesn't
matter. And her politics?'

'Lord Alresford was left out of the ministry,' said Marcella slyly.
'He and Lady Selina thought it a pity.'

'Alresford—*Alresford*? Why, of course ! He was Lord Privy
Seal in their last Cabinet—a narrow-minded old stick !—did a heap
of mischief in the Lords. *Well* !'—Hallin pondered a moment—
'Wharton will go over !'

Marcella was silent. The tremor of that wrestler's hour had
not yet passed away. The girl could find no words in which to
discuss Wharton himself, this last amazing act, or its future.

As for Hallin, he sat lost in pleasant dreams of a whitewashed
Wharton, comfortably settled at last below the gangway on the
Conservative side, using all the old catchwords in slightly different
connections, and living gaily on his Lady Selina. Fragments from
the talk of Nehemiah—Nehemiah the happy and truculent, that
new 'scourge of God' upon the parasites of Labour—of poor Bennett, of Molloy, and of various others who had found time to drop
in upon him since the Labour smash, kept whirling in his mind.
The same prediction he had just made to Marcella was to be discerned in several of them. He vowed to himself that he would
write to Raeburn that night, congratulate him and the party on the
possibility of so eminent a recruit—and hint another item of news
by the way. She had trusted her confidence to him without any
pledge—an act for which he paid her well thenceforward, in the
coin of a friendship far more intimate, expansive, and delightful
than anything his sincerity had as yet allowed him to show her.

But these London incidents and memories, near as they were
in time, looked many of them strangely remote to Marcella in this
morning silence. When she drew back from the window, after
darkening the now sun-flooded room in a very thorough business-
like way, in order that she might have four or five hours' sleep,

there was something symbolic in the act. She gave back her mind, her self, to the cares, the anxieties, the remorses of the past three weeks. During the night she had been sitting up with her father that her mother might rest. Now, as she lay down, she thought with the sore tension which had lately become habitual to her, of her father's state, her mother's strange personality, her own shortcomings.

By the middle of the morning she was downstairs again, vigorous and fresh as ever. Mrs. Boyce's maid was for the moment in charge of the patient, who was doing well. Mrs. Boyce was writing some household notes in the drawing-room. Marcella went in search of her.

The bare room, just as it ever was—with its faded antique charm—looked bright and tempting in the sun. But the cheerfulness of it did but sharpen the impression of that thin form writing in the window. Mrs. Boyce looked years older. The figure had shrunk and flattened into that of an old woman; the hair, which two years before had been still young and abundant, was now easily concealed under the close white cap she had adopted very soon after her daughter had left Mellor. The dress was still exquisitely neat, but plainer and coarser. Only the beautiful hands and the delicate stateliness of carriage remained—sole relics of a loveliness which had cost its owner few pangs to part with.

Marcella hovered near her—a little behind her—looking at her from time to time with a yearning compunction—which Mrs. Boyce seemed to be aware of, and to avoid.

'Mamma, can't I do those letters for you? I am quite fresh.'

'No, thank you. They are just done.'

When they were all finished and stamped, Mrs. Boyce made some careful entries in a very methodical account-book, and then got up, locking the drawers of her little writing-table behind her.

'We can keep the London nurse another week, I think,' she said.

'There is no need,' said Marcella quickly. 'Emma and I could divide the nights now and spare you altogether. You see, I can sleep at any time.'

'Your father seems to prefer Nurse Wenlock,' said Mrs. Boyce.

Marcella took the little blow in silence. No doubt it was her due. During the past two years she had spent two separate months at Mellor; she had gone away in opposition to her father's wish; and had found herself on her return more of a stranger to her parents than ever. Mr. Boyce's illness, involving a steady extension of paralytic weakness, with occasional acute fits of pain and danger, had made steady though very gradual progress all the time. But it was not till some days after her return home that Marcella had realised a tenth part of what her mother had undergone since the disastrous spring of the murder.

She passed now from the subject of the nurse with a half-timid remark about 'expense.'

'Oh! the expense doesn't matter!' said Mrs. Boyce, as she stood absently before the lately kindled fire, warming her chilled fingers at the blaze.

'Papa is more at ease in those ways?' Marcella ventured. And kneeling down beside her mother she gently chafed one of the cold hands.

'There seems to be enough for what is wanted,' said Mrs. Boyce, bearing the chafing with patience. 'Your father, I believe, has made great progress this year in freeing the estate. Thank you, my dear. I am not cold now.'

And she gently withdrew her hand.

Marcella, indeed, had already noticed that there were now no weeds on the garden-paths, that instead of one gardener there were three, that the old library had been decently patched and restored, that there was another servant; that William, grown into a very tolerable footman, wore a reputable coat; and that a plain but adequate carriage and horse had met her at the station. Her pity even understood that part of her father's bitter resentment of his ever-advancing disablement came from his feeling that here at last —just as death was in sight—he, that squalid failure, Dick Boyce, was making a success of something.

Presently, as she knelt before the fire, a question escaped her, which, when it was spoken, she half regretted.

'Has papa been able to do anything for the cottages yet?'

'I don't think so,' said Mrs. Boyce calmly. After a minute's pause she added, 'That will be for your reign, my dear.'

Marcella looked up with a sharp thrill of pain.

'Papa is better, mamma, and—and I don't know what you mean. I shall never reign here without you.'

Mrs. Boyce began to fidget with the rings on her thin left hand.

'When Mellor ceases to be your father's it will be yours,' she said, not without a certain sharp decision; 'that was settled long ago. I must be free—and if you are to do anything with this place, you must give your youth and strength to it. And your father is not better—except for the moment. Dr. Clarke exactly foretold the course of his illness to me two years ago, on my urgent request. He may live four months—six, if we can get him to the South. More is impossible.'

There was something ghastly in her dry composure. Marcella caught her hand again and leant her trembling young cheek against it.

'I could not live here without you, mamma!'

Mrs. Boyce could not for once repress the inner fever which in general her will controlled so well.

'I hardly think it would matter to you so much, my dear.'

Marcella shrank.

'I don't wonder you say that!' she said in a low voice. 'Do you think it was all a mistake, mamma, my going away eighteen months ago—a wrong act?'

Mrs. Boyce grew restless.

'I judge nobody, my dear—unless I am obliged. As you know, I am for liberty—above all'—she spoke with emphasis—'for letting the past alone. But I imagine you must certainly have learnt to do without us. Now I ought to go to your father.'

But Marcella held her.

'Do you remember in the *Purgatorio*, mamma, the lines about the loser in the game: "When the game of dice breaks up, he who lost lingers sorrowfully behind, going over the throws, and *learning by his grief*"? Do you remember?'

Mrs. Boyce looked down upon her, involuntarily a little curious, a little nervous, but assenting. It was one of the inconsistencies of her strange character that she had all her life been a persistent Dante student. The taste for the most strenuous and passionate of poets had developed in her happy youth; it had survived through the loneliness of her middle life. Like everything else personal to herself she never spoke of it; but the little worn books on her table had been familiar to Marcella from a child.

'*E tristo impara*?' repeated Marcella, her voice wavering. 'Mamma'—she laid her face against her mother's dress again—'I have lost more throws than you think in the last two years. Won't you believe I may have learnt a little?'

She raised her eyes to her mother's pinched and mask-like face. Mrs. Boyce's lips moved as though she would have asked a question. But she did not ask it. She drew, instead, the stealthy breath Marcella knew well—the breath of one who has measured precisely her own powers of endurance, and will not risk them for a moment by any digression into alien fields of emotion.

'Well, but one expects persons like you to learn,' she said, with a light, cold manner, which made the words mere convention. There was silence an instant; then, probably to release herself, her hand just touched her daughter's hair. 'Now, will you come up in half an hour? That was twelve striking, and Emma is never quite punctual with his food.'

Marcella went to her father at the hour named. She found him in his wheeled chair, beside a window opened to the sun, and overlooking the Cedar Garden. The room in which he sat was the state bedroom of the old house. It had a marvellous paper of branching trees and parrots and red-robed Chinamen, in the taste of the morning room downstairs, a carved four-post bed, a grate adorned with purplish Dutch tiles, an array of family miniatures over the mantelpiece, and on a neighbouring wall a rack of old swords and rapiers. The needlework hangings of the bed were full of holes ; the seats of the Chippendale chairs were frayed or tattered. But, none the less, the inalienable character and dignity of his sleeping-room were a bitter satisfaction to Richard Boyce, even in his sickness. After all said and done, he was king here in his father's and grandfather's place ; ruling where they ruled, and —whether they would or no—dying where they died, with the same family faces to bear him witness from the walls, and the same vault awaiting him.

When his daughter entered, he turned his head, and his eyes, deep and black still as ever, but sunk in a yellow relic of a face, showed a certain agitation. She was disagreeably aware that his thoughts were much occupied with her ; that he was full of grievance towards her, and would probably before long bring the pathos of his situation as well as the weight of his dying authority to bear upon her, for purposes she already suspected with alarm.

'Are you a little easier, papa?' she said, as she came up to him.

'I should think as a nurse you ought to know better, my dear, than to ask,' he said testily. 'When a person is in my condition, inquiries of that sort are a mockery!'

'But one may be in less or more pain, she said gently. 'I hoped Dr. Clarke's treatment yesterday might have given you some relief.'

He did not vouchsafe an answer. She took some work and sat down by him. Mrs. Boyce, who had been tidying a table of food and medicine, came and asked him if he would be wheeled into another room across the gallery, which had been arranged as a sitting-room. He shook his head irritably.

'I am not fit for it. Can't you see? And I want to speak to Marcella.'

Mrs. Boyce went away. Marcella waited, not without tremor. She was sitting in the sun, her head bent over the muslin strings she was hemming for her nurse's bonnet. The window was wide open ; outside, the leaves under a warm breeze were gently drifting down into the Cedar Garden, amid a tangled mass of flowers, mostly yellow or purple. To one side rose the dark layers of the cedars ; to the other, the grey front of the library wing.

Mr. Boyce looked at her with the frown which had now become habitual to him, moved his lips once or twice without speaking ; and at last made his effort.

' I should think, Marcella, you must often regret by now the step you took eighteen months ago ! '

She grew pale.

' How regret it, papa ? ' she said, without looking up.

' Why, good God ! ' he said angrily ; ' I should think the reasons for regret are plain enough. You threw over a man who was de- voted to you, and could have given you the finest position in the county, for the most nonsensical reasons in the world—reasons that by now, I am certain, you are ashamed of.'

He saw her wince, and enjoyed his prerogative of weakness. In his normal health he would never have dared so to speak to her. But of late, during long fits of feverish brooding—intensified by her return home—he had vowed to himself to speak his mind.

' Aren't you ashamed of them ? ' he repeated, as she was silent.

She looked up.

' I am not ashamed of anything I did to save Hurd, if that is what you mean, papa.'

Mr. Boyce's anger grew.

' Of course you know what everybody said ? '

She stooped over her work again, and did not reply.

' It's no good being sullen over it,' he said in exasperation ; ' I'm your father, and I'm dying. I have a right to question you. It's my duty to see something settled, if I can, before I go. Is it *true* that all the time you were attacking Raeburn about politics and the reprieve, and what not, you were really behaving as you never ought to have behaved, with Harry Wharton ? '

He gave out the words with sharp emphasis, and, bending to- wards her, he laid an emaciated hand upon her arm.

' What use is there, papa, in going back to these things ? ' she said, driven to bay, her colour going and coming. ' I may have been wrong in a hundred ways, but you never understood that the real reason for it all was that—that—I never was in love with Mr. Raeburn.'

' Then why did you accept him ? ' He fell back against his pillows with a jerk.

' As to that, I will confess my sins readily enough,' she said, while her lip trembled, and he saw the tears spring into her eyes. 'I accepted him for what you just now called his position in the county, though not quite in that way either.'

He was silent a little, then he began again in a voice which gradually became unsteady from self-pity.

'Well, now look here! I have been thinking about this matter a great deal—and God knows I've time to think and cause to think, considering the state I'm in—and I see no reason whatever why I should not try—before I die—to put this thing *straight*. That man was head over ears in love with you, *madly* in love with you. I used to watch him, and I know. Of course you offended and distressed him greatly. He could never have expected such conduct from you or anyone else. But *he's* not the man to change round easily, or to take up with anyone else. Now, if you regret what you did or the way in which you did it, why shouldn't I—a dying man may be allowed a little licence, I should think!— give him a hint?'

'*Papa!*' cried Marcella, dropping her work, and looking at him with a pale, indignant passion, which a year ago would have quelled him utterly. But he held up his hand.

'Now just let me finish. It would be no good my doing a thing of this kind without saying something to you first, because you'd find it out, and your pride would be the ruin of it. You always had a demoniacal pride, Marcella, even when you were a tiny child; but if you make up your mind now to let me tell him you regret what you did—just that—you'll make him happy, and yourself, for you know very well he's a man of the highest character—and your poor father, who never did *you* much harm anyway!' His voice faltered. 'I'd manage it so that there should be nothing humiliating to you in it whatever. As if there could be anything humiliating in confessing such a mistake as that; besides, what is there to be ashamed of? You're no pauper. I've pulled Mellor out of the mud for you, though you and your mother do give me credit for so precious little!'

He lay back, trembling with fatigue, yet still staring at her with glittering eyes, while his hand on the invalid table fixed to the side of his chair shook piteously. Marcella dreaded the effect the whole scene might have upon him; but, now they were in the midst of it, both feeling for herself and prudence for him drove her into the strongest speech she could devise.

'Papa, if *anything* of that sort were done, I should take care Mr. Raeburn knew I had had nothing to do with it—in such a way that it would be *impossible* for him to carry it further. Dear papa, don't think of such a thing any more. Because I treated Mr.

Raeburn unjustly last year, are we now to harass and persecute him? I would sooner disappear from everybody I know—from you and mamma, from England—and never be heard of again.'

She stopped for a moment—struggling for composure—that she might not excite him too much.

'Besides, it would be absurd! You forget I have seen a good deal of Mr. Raeburn lately—while I have been with the Winterbournes. He has entirely given up all thought of me. Even my vanity could see that plainly enough. His best friends expect him to marry a bright, fascinating little creature of whom I saw a good deal in James Street—a Miss Macdonald.'

'Miss—how—much?' he asked roughly.

She repeated the name, and then dwelt, with a certain amount of confusion and repetition, upon the probabilities of the matter— half conscious all the time that she was playing a part, persuading herself and him of something she was not at all clear about in her own inner mind—but miserably, passionately determined to go through with it all the same.

He bore with what she said to him, half disappointed and depressed, yet also half incredulous. He had always been obstinate, and the approach of death had emphasised his few salient qualities, as decay had emphasised the bodily frame. He said to himself stubbornly that he would find some way yet of testing the matter in spite of her. He would think it out.

Meanwhile, step by step, she brought the conversation to less dangerous things, and she was finally gliding into some chat about the Winterbournes when he interrupted her abruptly—

'And that other fellow—Wharton. Your mother tells me you have seen him in London. Has he been making love to you?'

'Suppose I won't be catechised!' she said gaily, determined to allow no more tragedy of any kind. 'Besides, papa, you can't read your gossip as good people should. Mr. Wharton's engagement to a certain Lady Selina Farrell—a distant cousin of the Winterbournes—was announced in several papers with great plainness three weeks ago.'

At that moment her mother came in, looking anxiously at them both, and half resentfully at Marcella. Marcella, sore and bruised in every moral fibre, got up to go.

Something in the involuntary droop of her beautiful head as she left the room drew her father's eyes after her, and for the time his feeling towards her softened curiously. Well, *she* had not made very much of her life so far! That old strange jealousy of her ability, her beauty, and her social place, he had once felt so hotly, died away. He wished her, indeed, to be Lady Maxwell

Yet for the moment there was a certain balm in the idea that she too—her mother's daughter—with her Merritt blood—could be unlucky.

Marcella went about all day under a vague sense of impending trouble—the result, no doubt, of that intolerable threat of her father's, against which she was, after all, so defenceless.

But whatever it was, it made her all the more nervous and sensitive about the Hallins; about her one true friend, to whom she was slowly revealing herself, even without speech; whose spiritual strength had been guiding and training her; whose physical weakness had drawn to him the maternal, the *spending* instincts which her nursing life had so richly developed.

She strolled down the drive to meet the post. But there were no letters from London, and she came in, inclined to be angry indeed with Louis Craven for deserting her, but saying to herself at the same time that she must have heard if anything had gone wrong.

An hour or so later, just as the October evening was closing in, she was sitting dreaming over a dim wood-fire in the drawing-room. Her father, as might have been expected, had been very tired and comatose all day. Her mother was with him; the London nurse was to sit up, and Marcella felt herself forlorn and superfluous.

Suddenly, in the silence of the house, she heard the front-door bell ring. There was a step in the hall—she sprang up—the door opened, and William, with fluttered emphasis, announced—

' Lord Maxwell !'

In the dusk she could just see his tall form—the short pause as he perceived her—then her hand was in his, and the paralysing astonishment of that first instant had disappeared under the grave emotion of his look.

' Will you excuse me,' he said, ' for coming at this hour? But I am afraid you have heard nothing yet of our bad news—and Hallin himself was anxious I should come and tell you. Miss Hallin could not write, and Mr. Craven, I was to tell you, had been ill for a week with a chill. You haven't then seen any account of the lecture in the papers?'

' No; I have looked yesterday and to-day in our paper, but there was nothing——'

' Some of the Radical papers reported it. I hoped you might have seen it. But when we got down here this afternoon, and there was nothing from you, both Miss Hallin and Edward felt sure you had not heard—and I walked over. It was a most painful, distressing scene, and he—is very ill.'

' But you have brought him to the Court?' she said trembling,

lost in the thought of Hallin, her quick breath coming and going.
' He was able to bear the journey ? Will you tell me ?—will you
sit down ?'

He thanked her hurriedly, and took a seat opposite to her, within the circle of the firelight, so that she saw his deep mourning
and the look of repressed suffering.

' The whole thing was extraordinary—I can hardly now describe it,' he said, holding his hat in his hands and staring into the
fire. ' It began excellently. There was a very full room. Bennett was in the chair—and Edward seemed much as usual. He
had been looking desperately ill, but he declared that he. was
sleeping better, and that his sister and I coddled him. Then,—
directly he was well started !—I felt somehow that the audience
was very hostile. And *he* evidently felt it more and more. There
was a good deal of interruption and hardly any cheers—and I saw
after a little—I was sitting not far behind him—that he was dis-
couraged—that he had lost touch. It was presently clear, indeed,
that the real interest of the meeting lay not in the least in what he
had to say, but in the debate that was to follow. They meant to
let him have his hour—but not a minute more. I watched the
men about me, and I could see them following the clock—thirsting
for their turn. Nothing that he said seemed to penetrate them in
the smallest degree. He was there merely as a ninepin to be
knocked over. I never saw a meeting so *possessed* with a madness
of fanatical conviction—it was amazing ! '

He paused, looking sadly before him. She made a little movement, and he roused himself instantly.

' It was just a few minutes before he was to sit down—I was
thankful !—when suddenly—I heard his voice change. I do not
know now what happened—but I believe he completely lost consciousness of the scene before him—the sense of strain, of exhaustion, of making no way, must have snapped something. He began
a sort of confession—a reverie in public—about himself, his life, his
thoughts his prayers, his hopes—mostly his religious hopes—for
the working man, for England—I *never* heard anything of the kind
from him before—you know his reserve. It was so intimate—so
painful—oh ! so painful ! ' he drew himself together with an involuntary shudder—' before this crowd, this eager hostile crowd which
was only pining for him to sit down—to get out of their way. The
men near me began to look at each other and titter. They wondered what he meant by maundering on like that—" damned canting stuff"—I heard one man near me call it. I tore off a bit of
paper, and passed a line to Bennett asking him to get hold of
Edward, to stop it. But I think Bennett had rather lost his presence

of mind, and I saw him look back at me and shake his head. Then time was up, and they began to shout him down.'

Marcella made an exclamation of horror. He turned to her.

' I think it was the most tragic scene I ever saw,' he said with a feeling as simple as it was intense. ' This crowd so angry and excited —without a particle of understanding or sympathy—laughing, and shouting at him—and he in the midst—white as death—talking this strange nonsense—his voice floating in a high key, quite unlike itself. At last just as I was getting up to go to him, I saw Bennett rise. But we were both too late. He fell at our feet !'

Marcella gave an involuntary sob ! ' What a horror !' she said ; ' what a martyrdom !'

' It was just that,' he answered in a low voice—' it was a martyrdom. And when one thinks of the way in which for years past he has held these big meetings in the hollow of his hand, and now, because he crosses their passion, their whim,—no kindness !—no patience—nothing but a blind hostile fury ! Yet *they* thought him a traitor, no doubt. Oh ! it was all a tragedy !'

There was silence an instant. Then he resumed :

' We got him into the back room. Luckily there was a doctor on the platform. It was heart failure, of course, with brain prostration. We managed to get him home, and Susie Hallin and I sat up. He was delirious all night ; but yesterday he rallied, and last night he begged us to move him out of London if we could. So we got two doctors and an invalid carriage, and by three this afternoon we were all at the Court. My aunt was ready for him—his sister is there—and a nurse. Clarke was there to meet him. He thinks he cannot possibly live more than a few weeks—possibly even a few days. The shock and strain have been irreparable.'

Marcella lay back in her chair, struggling with her grief, her head and face turned away from him, her eyes hidden by her hand-kerchief. Then in some mysterious way she was suddenly con-scious that Aldous was no longer thinking of Hallin, but of her.

' He wants very much to see you,' he said, bending towards her ; ' but I know that you have yourself serious illness to nurse. Forgive me for not having inquired after Mr. Boyce. I trust he is better ?'

She sat up, red-eyed, but mistress of herself. The tone had been all gentleness, but to her quivering sense some slight in-definable change—coldness—had passed into it.

' He *is* better, thank you—for the present. And my mother does not let me do very much. We have a nurse too. When shall I come ?'

He rose.

'Could you—come to-morrow afternoon? There is to be a consultation of doctors in the morning, which will tire him. About six?—that was what he said. He is very weak, but in the day quite conscious and rational. My aunt begged me to say how glad she would be——'

He paused. An invincible awkwardness took possession of both of them. She longed to speak to him of his grandfather but could not find the courage.

When he was gone, she, standing alone in the firelight, gave one passionate thought to the fact that so—in this tragic way—they had met again in this room where he had spoken to her his last words as a lover ; and then, steadily, she put everything out of her mind but her friend—and death.

CHAPTER II

MRS. BOYCE received Marcella's news with more sympathy than her daughter had dared to hope for, and she made no remark upon Aldous himself and his visit, for which Marcella was grateful to her.

As they left the dining-room, after their short evening meal, to go up to Mr. Boyce, Marcella detained her mother an instant.

'Mamma, will you please not tell papa that—that Lord Maxwell came here this afternoon? And will you explain to him why I am going there to-morrow?'

Mrs. Boyce's fair cheek flushed. Marcella saw that she understood.

'If I were you, I should not let your father talk to you any more about those things,' she said with a certain proud impatience.

'If I can help it!' exclaimed Marcella. 'Will you tell him, mamma,—about Mr. Hallin?—and how good he has been to me?'

Then her voice failed her, and, hurriedly leaving her mother at the top of the stairs, she went away by herself to struggle with a grief and smart almost unbearable.

That night passed quietly at the Court. Hallin was at intervals slightly delirious, but less so than the night before ; and in the early morning the young doctor, who had sat up with him, reported him to Aldous as calmer and a little stronger. But the heart mischief was hopeless, and might bring the bruised life to an end at any moment.

He could not, however, be kept in bed, owing to restlessness and difficulty of breathing, and by midday he was in Aldous's sitting-room, drawn close to the window, that he might delight his eyes with the wide range of wood and plain that it commanded. After a very wet September, the October days were now following each other in a settled and sunny peace. The great woods of the Chilterns, just yellowing towards that full golden moment—short, like all perfection,—which only beeches know, rolled down the hill-slopes to the plain, their curving lines cut here and there by straight fir stems, drawn clear and dark on the pale background of sky and lowland. In the park, immediately below the window, groups of wild cherry and of a slender-leaved maple made spots of ' flame and amethyst' on the smooth falling lawns ; the deer wandered and fed, and the squirrels were playing and feasting among the beech nuts.

Since Aldous and his poor sister had brought him home from the Bethnal Green hall in which the Land Reform Conference had been held, Hallin had spoken little, except in delirium, and that little had been marked by deep and painful depression. But this morning, when Aldous was summoned by the nurse, and found him propped up by the window, in front of the great view, he saw gracious signs of change. Death, indeed, already in possession, looked from the blue eyes so plainly that Aldous, on his first entrance, had need of all his own strength of will to keep his composure. But with the certainty of that great release, and with the abandonment of all physical and mental struggle—the struggle of a lifetime—Hallin seemed to-day to have recovered something of his characteristic serenity and blitheness—the temper which had made him the leader of his Cambridge contemporaries, and the dear comrade of his friend's life.

When Aldous came in, Hallin smiled and lifted a feeble hand towards the park and the woods.

' Could it have greeted me more kindly,' he said, in his whispering voice, 'for the end ? '

Aldous sat down beside him, pressing his hand, and there was silence till Hallin spoke again.

'You will keep this sitting-room, Aldous ? '

'Always.'

' I am glad. I have known you in it so long. What good talks we have had here in the old hot days ! I was hot, at least, and you bore with me. Land Reform—Church Reform—Wages Reform—we have threshed them all out in this room. Do you remember that night I kept you up till it was too late to go to bed, talking over my Church plans? How full I was of it !—the Church that was to be the people—reflecting their life, their differences—governed by them—growing with them. You wouldn't join it, Aldous—our poor little Association ! '

Aldous's strong lip quivered.

'Let me think of something I *did* join in,' he said.

Hallin's look shone on him with a wonderful affection.

'Was there anything else you didn't help in? I don't remember it. I've dragged you into most things. You never minded failure. And I have not had so much of it—not till this last. This has been failure—absolute and complete.'

But there was no darkening of expression. He sat quietly smiling.

'Do you suppose anybody who could look beyond the moment would dream of calling it failure?' said Aldous with difficulty.

Hallin shook his head gently, and was silent for a little time, gathering strength and breath again.

'I ought to suffer'—he said, presently. 'Last week I dreaded my own feeling if I should fail or break down—more than the failure itself. But since yesterday—last night—I have no more regrets. I see that my power is gone—that if I were to live I could no longer carry on the battle—or my old life. I am out of touch. Those whom I love and would serve, put me aside. Those who invite me, I do not care to join. So I drop—into the gulf—and the pageant rushes on. But the curious thing is now—I have no suffering. And as to the future—do you remember Jowett in the Introduction to the Phædo——'

He feebly pointed to a book beside him, which Aldous took up. Hallin guided him and he read:

'*Most persons when the last hour comes are resigned to the order of nature and the will of God. They are not thinking of Dante's "Inferno" or "Paradiso," or of the "Pilgrim's Progress." Heaven and Hell are not realities to them, but words or ideas—the outward symbols of some great mystery, they hardly know what.*'

'It is so with me,' said Hallin smiling, as, at his gesture, Aldous laid the book aside; 'yet not quite. To my *mind*, that mystery indeed is all unknown and dark—but to the heart it seems unveiled—with the heart, I see.'

A little later Aldous was startled to hear him say, very clearly and quickly:

'Do you remember that this is the fifth of October?'

Aldous drew his chair closer, that he might not raise his voice.

'Yes, Ned.'

'Two years, wasn't it, to-day? Will you forgive me if I speak of her?'

'You shall say anything you will.'

'Did you notice that piece of news I sent you, in my last letter to Geneva? But of course you did. Did it please you?'

'Yes, I was glad of it,' said Aldous, after a pause, 'extremely glad. I thought she had escaped a great danger.'

Hallin studied his face closely.

'She is free, Aldous—and she is a noble creature—she has learnt from life—and from death—this last two years. And—you still love her. Is it right to make no more effort?'

Aldous saw the perspiration standing on the wasted brow—would have given the world to be able to content or cheer him—yet would not, for the world, at such a moment be false to his own feeling or deceive his questioner.

'I think it is right,' he said, deliberately, '——for a good many reasons, Edward. In the first place, I have not the smallest cause —not the fraction of a cause—to suppose that I could occupy with her now any other ground than that I occupied two years ago. She has been kind and friendly to me—on the whole—since we met in London. She has even expressed regret for last year— meaning, of course, as I understood, for the pain and trouble that may be said to have come from her not knowing her own mind. She wished that we should be friends. And'—he turned his head away—'no doubt I could be, in time. . . . But, you see—in all that, there is nothing whatever to bring me forward again. My fatal mistake last year, I think now, lay in my accepting what she gave me—accepting it so readily, so graspingly even. That was my fault, my blindness, and—it was as unjust to her—as it was hopeless for myself. For hers is a nature'—his eyes came back to his friend; his voice took a new force and energy—'which, in love at any rate, will give all or nothing—and will never be happy itself, or bring happiness, till it gives all. That is what last year taught me. So that even if she—out of kindness or remorse for giving pain—were willing to renew the old tie—I should be her worst enemy and my own if I took a single step towards it. Marriage on such terms as I was thankful for last year would be humiliation to me, and bring no gain to her. It will never serve a man with her'—his voice broke into emotion—'that he should make no claims! Let him claim the uttermost farthing—her whole self. If she gives it, *then* he may know what love means!'

Hallin had listened intently. At Aldous's last words his expression showed pain and perplexity. His mind was full of vague impressions, memories, which seemed to argue with and dispute one of the chief things Aldous had been saying. But they were not definite enough to be put forward. His sensitive, chivalrous sense, even in this extreme weakness, remembered the tragic weight that attaches inevitably to dying words. Let him not do more harm than good.

He rested a little. They brought him food ; and Aldous sat beside him making pretence to read, so that he might be encouraged to rest. His sister came and went ; so did the doctor. But when they were once more alone, Hallin put out his hand and touched his companion.

'What is it, dear Ned ? '

' Only one thing more, before we leave it. Is that *all* that stands between you now—the whole? You spoke to me once in the summer of feeling *angry*, more angry than you could have believed. Of course, I felt the same. But just now you spoke of its all being your fault. Is there anything changed in your mind ? '

Aldous hesitated. It was extraordinarily painful to him to speak of the past, and it troubled him that at such a moment it should trouble Hallin.

' There is nothing changed, Ned, except that perhaps time makes *some* difference always. I don't want now '—he tried to smile—' as I did then, to make anybody else suffer for my suffering. But perhaps I marvel even more than I did at first, that—that—she could have allowed some things to happen as she did ! '

The tone was firm and vibrating ; and, in speaking, the whole face had developed a strong animation most passionate and human.

Hallin sighed.

' I often think,' he said, ' that she was extraordinarily immature —much more immature than most girls of that age—as to feeling. It was really the brain that was alive.'

Aldous silently assented ; so much so that Hallin repented himself.

' But not now,' he said, in his eager dying whisper ; ' not now. The plant is growing full and tall, into the richest life.'

Aldous took the wasted hand tenderly in his own. There was something inexpressibly touching in this final wrestle of Hallin's affection with another's grief. But it filled Aldous with a kind of remorse, and with the longing to free him from that, as from every other burden, in these last precious hours of life. And after a while he succeeded, as he thought, in drawing his mind away from it. They passed to other things. Hallin, indeed, talked very little more during the day. He was very restless and weak, but not in much positive suffering. Aldous read to him at intervals, from Isaiah or Plato, the bright sleepless eyes following every word.

At last the light began to sink. The sunset flooded in from the Berkshire uplands and the far Oxford plain, and lay in gold and purple on the falling woods and the green stretches of the park.

The distant edges of hill were extraordinarily luminous and clear, and Aldous, looking into the west with the eye of one to whom every spot and line were familiar landmarks, could almost fancy he saw beyond the invisible river, the hill, the 'lovely tree against the western sky,' which keep for ever the memory of one with whose destiny it had often seemed to him that Hallin's had something in common. To him, as to Thyrsis, the same early joy, the same 'happy quest,' the same 'fugitive and gracious light' for guide and beacon, that—

> does not come with houses or with gold,
> With place, with honour and a flattering crew ;

and to him, too, the same tasked pipe and tired throat, the same struggle with the 'life of men unblest,' the same impatient tryst with death.

The lovely lines ran dirge-like in his head, as he sat, sunk in grief, beside his friend. Hallin did not speak ; but his eye took note of every change of light, of every darkening tone, as the quiet English scene with its villages, churches, and woods, withdrew itself plane by plane into the evening haze. His soul followed the quiet deer, the homing birds, loosening itself gently the while from pain and from desire, saying farewell to country, to the poor, to the work left undone, and the hopes unrealised—to everything except to love.

It had just struck six when he bent forward to the window beneath which ran the wide front terrace.

'That was her step !' he said, while his face lit up, 'will you bring her here ?'

Marcella rang the bell at the Court with a fast beating heart. The old butler who came gave what her shrinking sense thought a forbidding answer to her shy greeting of him, and led her first into the drawing-room. A small figure in deep black rose from a distant chair and came forward stiffly. Marcella found herself shaking hands with Miss Raeburn.

'Will you sit and rest a little before you go upstairs ?' said that lady with careful politeness, 'or shall I send word at once ? He is hardly worse—but as ill as he can be.'

'I am not the least tired,' said Marcella, and Miss Raeburn rang.

'Tell his lordship, please, that Miss Boyce is here.'

The title jarred and hurt Marcella's ear. But she had scarcely time to catch it before Aldous entered, a little bent, as it seemed to her, from his tall erectness, and speaking with an extreme quietness, even monotony of manner.

'He is waiting for you—will you come at once?'

He led her up the central staircase and along the familiar
passages, walking silently a little in front of her. They passed the
long line of Caroline and Jacobean portraits in the upper gallery, till
just outside his own door Aldous paused.

'He ought not to talk long,' he said, hesitating, 'but you will
know—of course—better than any of us.'

'I will watch him,' she said, almost inaudibly, and he gently
opened the door and let her pass, shutting it behind her.

The nurse, who was sitting beside her patient, got up as Marcella entered, and pointed her to a low chair on his further side.
Susie Hallin rose too, and kissed the new-comer hurriedly, absently,
without a word, lest she should sob. Then she and the nurse disappeared through an inner door. The evening light was still freely
admitted; and there were some candles. By the help of both she
could only see him indistinctly. But in her own mind, as she sat
down, she determined that he had not even days to live.

Yet as she bent over him she saw a playful gleam on the caver-
nous face.

'You won't scold me?' said the changed voice—'you did warn
me—you and Susie—but—I was obstinate. It was best so!'

She pressed her lips to his hand and was answered by a faint
pressure from the cold fingers.

'If I could have been there!' she murmured.

'No—I am thankful you were not. And I must not think of it
—or of any trouble. Aldous is very bitter—but he will take comfort
by and by—he will see it—and them—more justly. They meant
me no unkindness. They were full of an idea as I was. When I
came back to myself—first—all was despair. I was in a blank
horror of myself and life. Now it has gone—I don't know how.
It is not of my own will—some hand has lifted a weight. I seem
to float—without pain.'

He closed his eyes, gathering strength again in the interval, by
a strong effort of will—calling up in the dimming brain what he
had to say. She meanwhile spoke to him in a low voice, mainly
to prevent his talking, telling him of her father, of her mother's
strain of nursing—of herself—she hardly knew what. How grotesque to be giving him these little bits of news about strangers—
to him, this hovering, consecrated soul, on the brink of the great
secret!

In the intervals, while he was still silent, she could not sometimes prevent the pulse of her own life from stirring. Her eye
wandered round the room—Aldous's familiar room. There, on the
writing table with its load of letters and books, stood the photograph

of Hallin ; another, her own, used to stand beside it ; it was solitary now.

Otherwise, all was just as it had been—flowers, books, newspapers—the signs of familiar occupation, the hundred small details
of character and personality which in estrangement take to themselves such a smarting significance for the sad and craving hear:.
The date—the anniversary—echoed in her mind.

Then, with a rush of remorseful pain, her thoughts came back
to the present and to Hallin. At the same moment she saw that
his eyes were open, and fixed upon her with a certain anxiety and
expectancy. He made a movement as though to draw her towards
him ; and she stooped to him.

' I feel,' he said, ' as though my strength were leaving me fast.
Let me ask you one question—because of my love for you—and *him*.
I have fancied—of late—things were changed. Can you tell me—
will you ?—or is it unfair ? '—the words had all their bright, natural
intonation—' Is your heart—still where it was ?—or, could you ever
—undo the past——'

He held her fast, grasping the hand she had given him with
unconscious force. She had looked up startled, her lip trembling
like a child's. Then she dropped her head against the arm of her
chair, as though she could not speak.

He moved restlessly, and sighed.

' I should not,' he said to himself ; ' I should not—it was wrong.
The dying are tyrannous.'

He even began a word of sweet apology. But she shook her
head.

' Don't ! ' she said, struggling with herself ; ' don't say that ! It
would do me good to speak—to you——'

An exquisite smile dawned on Hallin's face.

' Then ! '—he said—' confess ! '

A few minutes later they were still sitting together. She strongly
wished to go ; but he would not yet allow it. His face was full of
a mystical joy—a living faith, which must somehow communicate
itself in one last sacramental effort.

' How strange that you—and I—and he—should have been so
mixed together in this queer life. Now I seem to regret nothing
—I *hope* everything. One more little testimony let me bear !—the
last. We disappear one by one—into the dark—but each may
throw his comrades—a token—before he goes. You have been in
much trouble of mind and spirit—I have seen it. Take my poor
witness. There is one clue, one only—*goodness—the surrendered
will*. Everything is there—all faith—all religion—all hope for rich

or poor.—Whether we feel our way through consciously to the Will
—that asks our will—matters little. Aldous and I have differed
much on this—in words—never at heart! I could use words,
symbols he cannot—and they have given me peace. But half my
best life I owe to him.'

At this he made a long pause—but, still, through that weak
grasp, refusing to let her go—till all was said. Day was almost
gone; the stars had come out over the purple dusk of the park.

'That Will—we reach—through duty and pain,' he whispered
at last, so faintly she could hardly hear him, 'is the root, the
source. It leads us in living—it—carries us in death. But our
weakness and vagueness—want help—want the human life and
voice—to lean on—to drink from. We Christians—are orphans—
without Christ! There again—what does it matter what we think
—*about* him—if only we think—*of* him. In *one* such life are all
mysteries, and all knowledge—and our fathers have chosen for
us——'

The insistent voice sank lower and lower into final silence—
though the lips still moved. The eyelids too fell. Miss Hallin and the
nurse came in. Marcella rose and stood for one passionate instant
looking down upon him. Then, with a pressure of the hand to
the sister beside her, she stole out. Her one prayer was that she
might see and meet no one. So soft was her step that even the
watching Aldous did not hear her. She lifted the heavy latch of
the outer door without the smallest noise, and found herself alone
in the starlight.

After Marcella left him, Hallin remained for some hours in
what seemed to those about him a feverish trance. He did not
sleep, but he showed no sign of responsive consciousness. In
reality his mind all through was full of the most vivid though
incoherent images and sensations. But he could no longer distinguish between them and the figures and movements of the real
people in his room. Each passed into and intermingled with the
other. In some vague, eager way he seemed all the time to be
waiting or seeking for Aldous. There was the haunting impression
of some word to say—some final thing to do—which would not let
him rest. But something seemed always to imprison him, to hold
him back, and the veil between him and the real Aldous watching
beside him grew ever denser.

At night they made no effort to move him from the couch and
the half-sitting posture in which he had passed the day. Death
had come too near. His sister and Aldous and the young doctor
who had brought him from London watched with him. The

curtains were drawn back from both the windows, and in the clearness of the first autumnal frost a crescent moon hung above the
woods, the silvery lawns, the plain.

Not long after midnight Hallin seemed to himself to wake, full
of purpose and of strength.   He spoke, as he thought, to Aldous,
asking to be alone with him.   But Aldous did not move ; that sad
watching gaze of his showed no change.   Then Hallin suffered a
sudden sharp spasm of anguish and of struggle.   Three words to say
—only three words ; but those he *must* say !   He tried again, but
Aldous's dumb grief still sat motionless.   Then the thought leapt in
the ebbing sense, ' Speech is gone ; I shall speak no more ! '

It brought with it a stab, a quick revolt.   But something
checked both, and, in a final offering of the soul, Hallin gave up
his last desire.

What Aldous saw was only that the dying man opened his
hand as though it asked for that of his friend.   He placed his
own within those seeking fingers, and Hallin's latest movement—
which death stopped half-way—was to raise it to his lips.

So Marcella's confession—made in the abandonment, the blind
passionate trust, of a supreme moment—bore no fruit.   It went
with Hallin to the grave.

CHAPTER III

' I THINK I saw the letters arrive,' said Mrs. Boyce to her daughter.   ' And Donna Margherita seems to be signalling to us.'

' Let me go for them, mamma.'

' No, thank you ; I must go in.'

And Mrs. Boyce rose from her seat, and went slowly towards
the hotel.   Marcella watched her widow's cap and black dress as
they passed along the *pergola* of the hotel garden, between bright
masses of geraniums and roses on either side.

They had been sitting in the famous garden of the Cappucini
Hotel at Amalfi.   To Marcella's left, far below the high terrace of
the hotel, the green and azure of the Salernian Gulf shone and
danced in the sun ; to her right, a wood of oak and arbutus
stretched up into a purple cliff—a wood starred above with gold
and scarlet berries, and below with cyclamen and narcissis.
From the earth under the leafy oaks—for the oaks at Amalfi lose
and regain their foliage in winter and spring by imperceptible

gradations—came a moist English smell. The air was damp and warm. A convent bell tolled from invisible heights above the garden ; while the olives and vines close at hand were full of the chattering voices of gardeners and children, and broken here and there by clouds of pink almond-blossom. March had just begun, and the afternoons were fast lengthening. It was little more than a fortnight since Mr. Boyce's death. In the November of the preceding year Mrs. Boyce and Marcella had brought him to Naples by sea, and there, at a little villa on Posilippo, he had drawn sadly to his end. It had been a dreary time, from which Marcella could hardly hope that her mother would ever fully recover. She herself had found in the long months of nursing— nursing of which with quiet tenacity she had gradually claimed and obtained her full share—a deep moral consolation. They had paid certain debts to conscience, and they had for ever enshrined her father's memory in the silence of an unmeasured and loving pity.

But the wife ? Marcella sorely recognised that to her mother these last days had brought none of the soothing, reconciling influences they had involved for herself. Between the husband and wife there had been dumb friction and misery—surely also a passionate affection !—to the end. The invalid's dependence on her had been abject, her devotion wonderful. Yet, in her close contact with them, the daughter had never been able to ignore the existence between them of a wretched though tacit debate—reproach on his side, self-defence or spasmodic effort on hers—which seemed to have its origin deep in the past, yet to be stimulated afresh by a hundred passing incidents of the present. Under the blight of it, as under the physical strain of nursing, Mrs. Boyce had worn and dwindled to a white-haired shadow ; while he had both clung to life and feared death more than would normally have been the case. At the end he had died in her arms, his head on her breast ; she had closed his eyes and performed every last office without a tear ; nor had Marcella ever seen her weep from then till now. The letters she had received, mostly, Marcella believed, from her own family, remained unopened in her travelling-bag. She spoke very little, and was constantly restless, nor could Marcella as yet form any idea of the future.

After the funeral at Naples Mrs. Boyce had written immedi- ately to her husband's solicitor for a copy of his will and a state- ment of affairs. She had then allowed herself to be carried off to Amalfi, and had there, while entirely declining to admit that she was ill, been clearly doing her best to recover health and nerve sufficient to come to some decision, to grapple with some crisis which Marcella also felt to be impending—though as to why it should be impending, or what the nature of it might be, she could only dread and guess.

There was much bitter yearning in the girl's heart as she sat, breathed on by the soft Italian wind blowing from this enchanted sea. The inner cry was that her mother did not love her, had never loved her, and might even now—weird, incredible thought !—be planning to desert her. Hallin was dead—who else was there that cared for her or thought of her ? Betty Macdonald wrote often, —wild, ' *schwärmerisch* ' letters. Marcella looked for them with eagerness, and answered them affectionately. But Betty must soon marry, and then all that would be at an end. Meanwhile Marcella knew well it was Betty's news that made Betty's adoration doubly welcome. Aldous Raeburn—she never did or could think of him under his new name—was apparently in London, much occupied in politics, and constantly, as it seemed, in Betty's society. What likelihood was there that her life and his would ever touch again ? She thought often of her confession to Hallin, but in great perplexity of feeling. She had, of course, said no word of secrecy to him at the time. Such a demand in a man's last hour would have been impossible. She had simply followed a certain mystical love and obedience in telling him what he had asked to know, and in the strong spontaneous impulse had thought of nothing beyond. Afterwards her pride had suffered fresh martyrdom. Could he, with his loving instinct, have failed to give his friend some sign ? If so, it had been unwelcome, for since the day of Hallin's funeral she and Aldous had been more complete strangers than before. Lady Winterbourne, Betty, Frank Leven, had written since her father's death ; but from him, nothing.

By the way, Frank Leven had succeeded at Christmas, by old Sir Charles Leven's unexpected death, to the baronetcy and estates. How would that affect his chances with Betty?—if indeed there were any such chances left.

As to her own immediate future, Marcella knew from many indications that Mellor would be hers at once. But in her general tiredness of mind and body she was far more conscious of the burden of her inheritance than of its opportunities. All that vivid castle-building gift which was specially hers, and would revive, was at present in abeyance. She had pined once for power and freedom, that she might make a Kingdom of Heaven of her own, quickly. Now power and freedom, up to a certain point, were about to be put into her hands ; and instead of plans for acting largely and bountifully on a plastic outer world, she was saying to herself,

hungrily, that unless she had something close to her to love and
live for, she could do nothing. If her mother would end these unnatural doubts, if she would begin to make friends with her own
daughter, and only yield herself to be loved and comforted, why
then it might be possible to think of the village and the straw-plaiting ! Otherwise—the girl's attitude as she sat dreaming in the sun
showed her despondency.

She was roused by her mother's voice calling her from the other
end of the *pergola*.

' Yes, mamma.'

' Will you come in ? There are some letters.'

' It is the will,' thought Marcella, as Mrs. Boyce turned back to
the hotel, and she followed.

Mrs. Boyce shut the door of their sitting-room, and then went up
to her daughter with a manner which suddenly struck and startled
Marcella. There was natural agitation and trouble in it.

' There is something in the will, Marcella, which will, I fear,
annoy and distress you. Your father inserted it without consulting me. I want to know what you think ought to be done. You
will find that Lord Maxwell and I have been appointed joint
executors.'

Marcella turned pale.

' Lord Maxwell !' she said, bewildered. ' *Lord Maxwell—
Aldous* ! What do you mean, mamma ? '

Mrs. Boyce put the will into her hands, and, pointing the way
among the technicalities she had been perusing while Marcella was
still lingering in the garden, showed her the paragraph in question.
The words of the will were merely formal : ' I hereby appoint,' &c.,
and no more ; but in a communication from the family solicitor, Mr.
French, which Mrs. Boyce silently handed to her daughter after
she had read the legal disposition, the ladies were informed that
Mr. Boyce had, before quitting England, written a letter to Lord
Maxwell, duly sealed and addressed, with instructions that it should
be forwarded to its destination immediately after the writer's burial.
' Those instructions,' said Mr. French, ' I have carried out. I
understand that Lord Maxwell was not consulted as to his appointment as executor prior to the drawing up of the will. But you will
no doubt hear from him at once, and as soon as we know that he
consents to act, we can proceed immediately to probate.'

' Mamma, how *could* he ? ' said Marcella in a low, suffocated
voice, letting will and letter fall upon her knee.

' Did he give you no warning in that talk you had with him at
Mellor ? ' said Mrs. Boyce after a minute's silence.

' Not the least,' said Marcella, rising restlessly and beginning to walk up and down. 'He spoke to me about wishing to bring it on again—asked me to let him write. I told him it was all done with—for ever ! As to my own feelings, I felt it was no use to speak of them ; but I thought—I *believed* I had proved to him that Lord Maxwell had absolutely given up all idea of such a thing ; and that it was already probable he would marry someone else. I told him I would rather disappear from everyone I knew than consent to it—he could only humiliate us all by saying a word. And *now*, after that !——'

She stopped in her restless walk, pressing her hands miserably together.

'What *does* he want with us and our affairs?' she broke out. 'He wishes, of course, to have no more to do with me. And now we force him—*force* him into these intimate relations. What can papa have said in that letter to him? What *can* he have said? Oh ! it is unbearable ! Can't we write at once?'

She pressed her hands over her eyes in a passion of humiliation and disgust. Mrs. Boyce watched her closely.

'We must wait, anyway, for his letter,' she said. 'It ought to be here by to-morrow morning.'

Marcella sank on a chair by an open glass door, her eyes wandering, through the straggling roses growing against the wall of the stone balcony outside, to the laughing purples and greens of the sea.

'Of course,' she said, unhappily, 'it is most probable he will consent. It would not be like him to refuse. But, mamma, you must write. *I* must write and beg him not to do it. It is quite simple. We can manage everything for ourselves. Oh ! how *could* papa?' she broke out again in a low wail ; 'how could he?"

Mrs. Boyce's lips tightened sharply. It seemed to her a foolish question. *She*, at least, had had the experience of twenty years out of which to answer it. Death had made no difference. She saw her husband's character and her own seared and broken life with the same tragical clearness ; she felt the same gnawing of an affection not to be plucked out while the heart still beat. This act of indelicacy and injustice was like many that had gone before it ; and there was in it the same evasion and concealment towards herself. No matter. She had made her account with it all twenty years before. What astonished her was, that the force of her strong coercing will had been able to keep him for so long within the limits of the smaller and meaner immoralities of this world.

'Have you read the rest of the will?' she asked, after a long pause.

Marcella lifted it again, and began listlessly to go through it.

'Mamma !' she said presently, looking up, the colour flushing back into her face, 'I find no mention of you in it throughout. There seems to be no provision for you.'

'There is none,' said Mrs. Boyce quietly. 'There was no need. I have my own income. We lived upon it for years before your father succeeded to Mellor. It is therefore amply sufficient for me now.'

'You cannot imagine,' cried Marcella, trembling in every limb, 'that I am going to take the whole of my father's estate, and leave nothing—*nothing* for his wife. It would be impossible—unseemly. It would be to do *me* an injustice, mamma, as well as yourself,' she added proudly.

'No, I think not,' said Mrs. Boyce, with her usual cold absence of emotion. 'You do not yet understand the situation. Your father's misfortunes nearly ruined the estate for a time. Your grandfather went through great trouble, and raised large sums to—' she paused for the right phrase—'to free us from the consequences of your father's actions. I benefited, of course, as much as he did. Those sums crippled all your grandfather's old age. He was a man to whom I was attached—whom I respected. Mellor, I believe, had never been embarrassed before. Well, your uncle did a little towards recovery—but on the whole he was a fool. Your father has done much more, and you, no doubt, will complete it. As for me, I have no claim to anything more from Mellor. The place itself is'—again she stopped for a word of which the energy, when it came, seemed to escape her—'hateful to me. I shall feel freer if I have no tie to it. And at last I persuaded your father to let me have my way.'

Marcella rose from her seat impetuously, walked quickly across the room, and threw herself on her knees beside her mother.

'Mamma, are you still determined—now that we two are alone in the world—to act towards me, to treat me as though I were not your daughter—not your child at all, but a stranger?'

It was a cry of anguish. A sudden slight tremor swept over Mrs. Boyce's thin and withered face. She braced herself to the inevitable.

'Don't let us make a tragedy of it, my dear,' she said, with a light touch on Marcella's hands. 'Let us discuss it reasonably. Won't vou sit down ? I am not proposing anything very dreadful. But, like you, I have some interests of my own, and I should be glad to follow them—now—a little. I wish to spend some of the year in London ; to make that, perhaps, my headquarters, so as to see something of some old friends whom I have had no intercourse with for years—perhaps also of my relations.' She spoke of them with a particular dryness. 'And I should be glad—after this long time—to be somewhat taken out of oneself, to read, to hear what is going on, to feed one's mind a little.'

Marcella, looking at her, saw a kind of feverish light, a sparkling intensity in the pale blue eyes, that filled her with amazement. What, after all, did she know of this strange individuality from which her own being had taken its rise? The same flesh and blood—what an irony of nature!

'Of course,' continued Mrs. Boyce, 'I should go to you, and you would come to me. It would only be for part of the year. Probably we should get more from each other's lives so. As you know, I long to see things as they are, not conventionally. Anyway, whether I were there or no, you would probably want some companion to help you in your work and plans. I am not fit for them. And it would be easy to find someone who could act as chaperon in my absence.'

The hot tears sprang to Marcella's eyes. 'Why did you send me away from you, mamma, all my childhood?' she cried. 'It was wrong—cruel. I have no brother or sister. And you put me out of your life when I had no choice, when I was too young to understand.'

Mrs. Boyce winced, but made no reply. She sat with her delicate hand across her brow. She was the white shadow of her former self; but her fragility had always seemed to Marcella more indomitable than anybody else's strength.

Sobs began to rise in Marcella's throat.

'And now,' she said, in half-coherent despair, 'do you know what you are doing? You are cutting yourself off from me—refusing to have any real bond to me just when I want it most. I suppose you think that I shall be satisfied with the property and the power, and the chance of doing what I like. But,'—she tried her best to gulp back her pain, her outraged feeling, to speak quietly—' I am not like that really any more. I can take it all up, with courage and heart, if you will stay with me, and let me—let me—love you and care for you. But, by myself, I feel as if I could not face it! I am not likely to be happy—for a long time—except in doing what work I can. It is very improbable that I shall marry. I dare say you don't believe me, but it is true. We are both sad and lonely. We have no one but each other. And then you talk in this ghastly way of separating from me—casting me off.'

Her voice trembled and broke; she looked at her mother with a frowning passion.

Mrs. Boyce still sat silent, studying her daughter with a strange, brooding eye. Under her unnatural composure there was in reality a half-mad impatience, the result of physical and moral reaction. This beauty, this youth, talk of sadness, of finality! What folly! Still, she was stirred, undermined in spite of herself.

'There!' she said, with a restless gesture, 'let us, please, talk of it no more. I will come back with you—I will do my best. We will let the matter of my future settlement alone for some months, at any rate, if that will satisfy you or be any help to you.'

She made a movement as though to rise from her low chair. But the great waters swelled in Marcella—swelled and broke. She fell on her knees again by her mother, and before Mrs. Boyce could stop her she had thrown her young arms close round the thin, shrunken form.

'Mother!' she said. 'Mother, be good to me—love me—you are all I have!'

And she kissed the pale brow and cheek with a hungry, almost a violent tenderness that would not be gainsaid, murmuring wild incoherent things.

Mrs. Boyce first tried to put her away, then submitted, being physically unable to resist, and at last escaped from her with a sudden sob that went to the girl's heart. She rose, went to the window, struggled hard for composure, and finally left the room.

But that evening, for the first time, she let Marcella put her on the sofa, tend her, and read to her. More wonderful still, she went to sleep while Marcella was reading. In the lamplight her face looked piteously old and worn. The girl sat for long with her hands clasped round her knees, gazing down upon it, in a trance of pain and longing.

Marcella was awake early next morning, listening to the full voice of the sea as it broke three hundred feet below, against the beach and rocky walls of the little town. She was lying in a tiny white room, one of the cells of the old monastery, and the sun as it rose above the Salernian mountains—the mountains that hold Pæstum in their blue and purple shadows—danced in gold on the white wall. The bell of the cathedral far below tolled the hour. She supposed it must be six o'clock. Two hours more or so, and Lord Maxwell's letter might be looked for.

She lay and thought of it—longed for it, and for the time of answering it, with the same soreness that had marked all the dreams of a restless night. If she could only see her father's letter! It was inconceivable that he should have mentioned *her* name in his plea. He might have appealed to the old friendship between the families. That was possible, and would have, at any

rate, an *appearance* of decency. But who could answer for it—or
for him? She clasped her hands rigidly behind her head, her
brows frowning, bending her mind with an intensity of will to the
best means of assuring Aldous Raeburn that she and her mother
would not encroach upon him. She had a perpetual morbid vision
of herself as the pursuer, attacking him now through his friend, now
through her father. Oh ! when would that letter come, and let
her write her own !

She tried to read, but in reality listened for every sound of
awakening life in the hotel. When at last her mother's maid came
in to call her, she sprang up with a start.

'Deacon, are the letters come ? '

'There are two for your mother, miss ; none for you.'

Marcella threw on her dressing-gown, watched her opportunity,
and slipped in to her mother, who occupied a similar cell next
door.

Mrs. Boyce was sitting up in bed, with a letter before her, her
pale blue eyes fixed absently on the far stretch of sea.

She looked round with a start as Marcella entered. 'The
letter is to me, of course,' she said.

Marcella read it breathlessly.

'Dear Mrs. Boyce,—I have this morning received from your
solicitor, Mr. French, a letter written by Mr. Boyce to myself in
November of last year. In it he asks me to undertake the office
of executor, to which, I hear from Mr. French, he has named me
in his will. Mr. French also inquires whether I shall be willing to
act, and asks me to communicate with you.

'May I, then, venture to intrude upon you with these few
words ? Mr. Boyce refers in his touching letter to the old friendship between our families, and to the fact that similar offices have
often been performed by his relations for mine, or *vice versâ*. But no
reminder of the kind was in the least needed. If I can be of any
service to yourself and to Miss Boyce, neither your poor husband
nor you could do me any greater kindness than to command me.

'I feel naturally some diffidence in the matter. I gather from
Mr. French that Miss Boyce is her father's heiress, and comes at
once into the possession of Mellor. She may not, of course, wish
me to act, in which case I should withdraw immediately ; but I
sincerely trust that she will not forbid me the very small service I
could so easily and gladly render.

'I cannot close my letter without venturing to express the deep
sympathy I have felt for you and yours during the past six months.
I have been far from forgetful of all that you have been going

through, though I may have seemed so. I trust that you and
your daughter will not hurry home for any business cause, if it is
still best for your health to stay in Italy. With your instructions
Mr. French and I could arrange everything.

'Believe me,

'Yours most sincerely,

'MAXWELL.'

'You will find it difficult, my dear, to write a snub in answer
to that letter,' said Mrs. Boyce drily, as Marcella laid it down.

Marcella's face was, indeed, crimson with perplexity and feeling.

'Well, we can think it over,' she said as she went away.

Mrs. Boyce pondered the matter a good deal when she was
left alone. The signs of reaction and change in Marcella were
plain enough. What they precisely meant, and how much, was
another matter. As to him, Marcella's idea of another attachment
might be true, or might be merely the creation of her own irritable
pride. Anyway, he was in the mood to write a charming letter.
Mrs. Boyce's blanched lip had all its natural irony as she thought
it over. To her mind Aldous Raeburn's manners had always been a
trifle too good, whether for his own interests or for this wicked world.
And if he had any idea now of trying again, let him, for Heaven's
sake, not be too yielding or too eager ! 'It was always the way,'
thought Mrs. Boyce, remembering a child in white frock and baby
shoes—'if you wished to make her want anything, you had to take
it away from her.'

Meanwhile the mere thought that matters might even yet so
settle themselves drew from the mother a long breath of relief.
She had spent an all but sleepless night, tormented by Marcella's
claim upon her. After twenty years of self-suppression this woman
of forty-five, naturally able, original, and independent, had seen a
glimpse of liberty. In her first youth she had been betrayed as a
wife, degraded as a member of society. A passion she could not
kill, combined with some stoical sense of inalienable obligation,
had combined to make her both the slave and guardian of her
husband up to middle life ; and her family and personal pride, so
strong in her as a girl, had found its only outlet in this singular
estrangement she had achieved between herself and every other
living being, including her own daughter. Now her husband was
dead, and all sorts of crushed powers and desires, mostly of the
intellectual sort, had been strangely reviving within her. Just
emerged, as she was, from the long gloom of nursing, she already
wished to throw it all behind her—to travel, to read, to make
acquaintances—she who had lived as a recluse for twenty years !

There was in it a last clutch at youth, at life. And she had no desire to enter upon this new existence—in comradeship with Marcella. They were independent and very different human beings. That they were mother and daughter was a mere physical accident.

Moreover, though she was amply conscious of the fine development in Marcella during the past two years, it is probable that she felt her daughter even less congenial to her now than of old. For the rich, emotional nature had, as we have seen, 'suffered conviction,' had turned in the broad sense to 'religion,' was more and more sensitive, especially since Hallin's death, to the spiritual things and symbols in the world. At Naples she had haunted churches ; had read, as her mother knew, many religious books:

Now Mrs. Boyce in these matters had a curious history. She had begun life as an ardent Christian, under Evangelical influences. Her husband, on the other hand, at the time she married him was a man of purely sceptical opinions, a superficial disciple of Mill and Comte, and fond of an easy profanity which seemed to place him indisputably with the superior persons of this world. To the amazement and scandal of her friends, Evelyn Merritt had not been three months his wife before she had adopted his opinions *en bloc*, and was carrying them out to their logical ends with a sincerity and devotion quite unknown to her teacher. Thenceforward her conception of things—of which, however, she seldom spoke—had been actively and even vehemently rationalist ; and it had been one of the chief sorenesses and shames of her life at Mellor that, in order to suit his position as country squire, Richard Boyce had sunk to what, in her eyes, were a hundred mean compliances with things orthodox and established.

Then, in his last illness, he had finally broken away from her, and his own past. ' Evelyn, I should like to see a clergyman,' he had said to her in his piteous voice, ' and I shall ask him to give me the Sacrament.' She had made every arrangement accordingly ; but her bitter soul could see nothing in the step but fear and hypocrisy ; and he knew it. And as he lay talking alone with the man whom they had summoned, two or three nights before the end, she, sitting in the next room, had been conscious of a deep and smarting jealousy. Had not the hard devotion of twenty years made him at least her own ? And here was this black-coated reciter of incredible things stepping into her place. Only in death she recovered him wholly. No priest interfered while he drew his last breath upon her bosom.

And now Marcella ! Yet the girl's voice and plea tugged at her withered heart. She felt a dread of unknown softnesses—of

being invaded and weakened by things in her akin to her daughter,
and so captured afresh. Her mind fell upon the bare idea of a
revival of the Maxwell engagement, and caressed it.

Meanwhile Marcella stood dressing by the open window in the
sunlight, which filled the room with wavy reflections caught from
the sea. Fishing-boats were putting off from the beach, three
hundred feet below her; she could hear the grating of the keels,
the songs of the boatmen. On the little breakwater to the right
an artist's white umbrella shone in the sun; and a half-naked boy,
poised on the bows of a boat moored beside the painter, stood
bent in the eager attitude of one about to drop the bait into the
blue wave below. His brown back burnt against the water.
Cliff, houses, sea, glowed in warmth and light; the air was full of
roses and orange-blossom; and to an English sense had already
the magic of summer.

And Marcella's hands, as she coiled and plaited her black hair,
moved with a new lightness; for the first time since her father's
death her look had its normal fire, crossed every now and then by
something that made her all softness and all woman. No! as her
mother said, one could not snub that letter or its writer. But how
to answer it! In imagination she had already penned twenty different replies. How not to be grasping or effusive, and yet to
show that you could feel and repay kindness—there was the
problem!

Meanwhile, from that letter, or rather in subtle connection with
it, her thoughts at last went wandering off with a natural zest to
her new realm of Mellor, and to all that she would and could do
for the dwellers therein.

CHAPTER IV

IT was a bleak east-wind day towards the end of March. Aldous
was at work in the library at the Court, writing at his grandfather's
table, where in general he got through his estate and county affairs,
keeping his old sitting-room upstairs for the pursuits that were
more particularly his own.

All the morning he had been occupied with a tedious piece of
local business, wading through endless documents concerning a
dispute between the head-master of a neighbouring grammar-school
and his governing body, of which Aldous was one. The affair was
difficult, personal, odious. To have wasted nearly three hours

upon it was, to a man of Aldous's type, to have lost a day. Besides, he had not his grandfather's knack in such things, and was abundantly conscious of it.

However, there it was, a duty which none but he apparently could or would do, and he had been wrestling with it. With more philosophy than usual, too, since every tick of the clock behind him bore him nearer to an appointment which, whatever it might be, would not be tedious.

At last he got up and went to the window to look at the weather. A cutting wind, clearly, but no rain. Then he walked into the drawing-room, calling for his aunt. No one was to be seen, either there or in the conservatory, and he came back to the library and rang.

'Roberts, has Miss Raeburn gone out?'

'Yes, my lord,' said the old butler addressed. 'She and Miss Macdonald have gone out driving, and I was to tell your lordship that Miss Raeburn would drop Miss Macdonald at Mellor on her way home.'

'Is Sir Frank anywhere about?'

'He was in the smoking-room a little while ago, my lord.'

'Will you please try and find him?'

'Yes, my lord.'

Aldous's mouth twitched with impatience as the old servant shut the door.

'How many times did Roberts manage to be-lord me in a minute?' he asked himself; 'yet if I were to remonstrate, I suppose I should only make him unhappy.'

And walking again to the window, he thrust his hands into his pockets and stood looking out with a far from cheerful countenance.

One of the things that most tormented him indeed in this recent existence was a perpetual pricking sense of the contrast between this small world of his ancestral possessions and traditions, with all its ceremonial and feudal usage, and the great rushing world outside it of action and of thought. Do what he would, he could not un-king himself within the limits of the Maxwell estate. To the people living upon it he was the man of most importance within their ken, was inevitably their potentate and earthly providence. He confessed that there was a real need of him, if he did his duty. But on this need the class-practice of generations had built up a deference, a sharpness of class-distinction, which any modern must find more and more irksome in proportion to his modernness. What was in Aldous's mind, as he stood with drawn brows looking out over the view which showed him most of his domain, was a sort of hot impatience of being made day by day, in a hundred foolish ways, to play at greatness.

Yet, as we know, he was no democrat by conviction, had no comforting faith in what seemed to him the rule of a multitudinous ignorance. Still every sane man of to-day knows, at any rate, that the world has taken the road of democracy, and that the key to the future, for good or ill, lies not in the revolts and speculations of the cultivated few, but in the men and movements that can seize the many. Aldous's temper was despondently critical towards the majority of these, perhaps ; he had, constitutionally, little of that poet's sympathy with the crowd, as such, which had given Hallin his power. But, at any rate, they filled the human stage—these men and movements—and his mind as a beholder. Beside the great world-spectacle perpetually in his eye and thought, the small old-world pomps and feudalisms of his own existence had a way of looking ridiculous to him. He constantly felt himself absurd. It was ludicrously clear to him, for instance, that in this kingdom he had inherited it would be thought a huge condescension on his part if he were to ask the secretary of a trades-union to dine with him at the Court. Whereas, in his own honest opinion, the secretary had a far more important and interesting post in the universe than he.

So that, in spite of a strong love of family, rigidly kept to himself, he had very few of the illusions which make rank and wealth delightful. On the other hand, he had a tyrannous sense of obligation, which kept him tied to his place and his work—to such work as he had been spending the morning on. This sense of obligation had for the present withdrawn him from any very active share in politics. He had come to the conclusion early in the year, just about the time when, owing to some rearrangements in the *personnel* of the Government, the Premier had made him some extremely flattering overtures, that he must for the present devote himself to the Court. There were extensive changes and reforms going on in different parts of the estate : some of the schools which he owned and mainly supported were being rebuilt and enlarged ; and he had a somewhat original scheme for the extension of adult education throughout the property very much on his mind —a scheme which must be organised and carried through by himself apparently, if it was to thrive at all.

Much of this business was very dreary to him, some of it altogether distasteful. Since the day of his parting with Marcella Boyce his only real *pleasures* had lain in politics or books. Politics, just as they were growing absorbing to him, must, for a while at any rate, be put aside ; and even books had not fared as well as they might have been expected to do in the country quiet. Day after day he walked or rode about the muddy lanes of the estate, doing the work that seemed to him to be his, as best he could, yet never very certain of its value; rather, spending his thoughts more and more, with regard to his own place and function in the world, on a sort of mental apologetic which was far from stimulating; sorely conscious the while of the unmatched charm and effectiveness with which his grandfather had gone about the same business; and as lonely at heart as a man can well be—the wound of love unhealed, the wound of friendship still deep and unconsoled. To bring social peace and progress, as he understood them, to this bit of Midland England a man of first-rate capacities was perhaps sacrificing what ambition would have called his opportunities. Yet neither was he a hero to himself nor to the Buckinghamshire farmers and yokels who depended on him. They had liked the grandfather better, and had become stolidly accustomed to the grandson's virtues.

The only gleam in the grey of his life since he had determined about Christmas-time to settle down at the Court had come from Mr. French's letter. That letter, together with Mr. Boyce's post-humous note, which contained nothing, indeed, but a skilful appeal to neighbourliness and old family friendship, written in the best style of the ex-Balkan Commissioner, had naturally astonished him greatly. He saw at once what *she* would perceive in it, and turned impatiently from speculation as to what Mr. Boyce might actually have meant, to the infinitely more important matter, how she would take her father's act. Never had he written anything with greater anxiety than he devoted to his letter to Mrs. Boyce. There was in him now a craving he could not stay, to be brought near to her again, to know how her life was going. It had first raised its head in him since he knew that her existence and Wharton's were finally parted, and had but gathered strength from the self-critical loneliness and tedium of these later months.

Mrs. Boyce's reply, couched in terms at once stately and grateful, which accepted his offer of service on her own and her daughter's behalf, had given him extraordinary pleasure. He turned it over again and again, wondering what part or lot Marcella might have had in it, attributing to her this cordiality or that reticence; picturing the two women together in their black dresses—the hotel, the *pergola*, the cliff—all of which he himself knew well. Finally, he went up to town, saw Mr. French, and acquainted himself with the position and prospects of the Mellor estate, feeling himself a sort of intruder, yet curiously happy in the business. It was wonderful what that poor sickly fellow had been able to do in the last two years ; yet his thoughts fell rather into amused surmise as to what *she* would find it in her restless mind to do in the *next* two years.

Nevertheless, all the time, the resolution of which he had spoken to Hallin seemed to himself unshaken. He recognised and adored the womanly growth and deepening which had taken place in her ; he saw that she wished to show him kindness. But he thought he could trust himself now and henceforward not to force upon her a renewed suit for which there was in his eyes no real or abiding promise of happiness.

Marcella and her mother had now been at home some three or four days, and he was just about to walk over to Mellor for his first interview with them. A great deal of the merely formal business consequent on Mr. Boyce's death had been already arranged by himself and Mr. French. Yet he had to consult Marcella as to certain investments, and in a pleasant though quite formal little note he had that morning received from her she had spoken of asking his advice as to some new plans for the estate. It was the first letter she herself had as yet written to him ; hitherto all his correspondence had been carried on with Mrs. Boyce. It had struck him, by the way, as remarkable that there was no mention of the wife in the will. He could only suppose that she was otherwise provided for. But there had been some curious expressions in her letters.

Where was Frank ? Aldous looked impatiently at the clock, as Roberts did not reappear. He had invited Leven to walk with him to Mellor, and the tiresome boy was apparently not to be found. Aldous vowed he would not wait a minute and, going into the hall, put on coat and hat with most business-like rapidity.

He was just equipped when Roberts, somewhat breathless with long searching, arrived in time to say that Sir Frank was on the front terrace.

And there Aldous caught sight of the straight though somewhat heavily built figure, in its grey suit with the broad band of black across the arm.

'Hullo, Frank ! I thought you were to look me up in the library. Roberts has been searching the house for you.'

'You said nothing about the library,' said the boy rather sulkily, 'and Roberts hadn't far to search. I have been in the smoking-room till this minute.'

Aldous did not argue the point, and they set out. It was presently clear to the elder man that his companion was not in the best of tempers. The widowed Lady Leven had sent her first-born over to the Court for a few days that Aldous might have some discussion as to his immediate future with the young man. She was a silly, frivolous woman ; but it was clear, even to her, that Frank was not doing very well for himself in the world ; and advice she would not have taken from her son's Oxford tutor seemed cogent to her when it came from a Raeburn. 'Do at least, for goodness' sake, get him to give up his absurd plan of going to America !' she wrote to Aldous ; 'if he can't take his degree at Oxford, I suppose he must get on without it, and certainly his dons seem very unpleasant. But at least he might stay at home and do his duty to me and his sisters till he marries, instead of going off to the "Rockies" or some other ridiculous place. He really never seems to think of Fanny and Rachel, or what he might do to help me to get them settled now that his poor father is gone.'

No ; certainly the young man was not much occupied with 'Fanny and Rachel'! He spoke with ill-concealed impatience, indeed, of both his sisters and his mother. If his people would get in the way of everything he wanted to do, they needn't wonder if he cut up rough at home. For the present it was settled that he should at any rate go back to Oxford till the end of the summer term—Aldous heartily pitying the unfortunate dons who might have to do with him—but after that he entirely declined to be bound. He swore he would not be tied at home like a girl ; he must and would see the world. This in itself, from a lad who had been accustomed to regard his home as the centre of all delights, and had on two occasions stoutly refused to go with his family to Rome, lest he should miss the best month for his father's trout-stream, was sufficiently surprising.

However, of late some tardy light had been dawning upon Aldous ! The night after Frank's arrival at the Court Betty Macdonald came down to spend a few weeks with Miss Raeburn, being for the moment that lady's particular pet and *protégée*. Frank, whose sulkiness during the twenty-four hours before she appeared had been the despair of both his host and hostess, brightened up spasmodically when he heard she was expected, and went fishing with one of the keepers, on the morning before her arrival, with a fair imitation of his usual spirits. But somehow, since that first evening, though Betty had chattered, and danced, and frolicked her best, though her little figure running up and down the big house gave a new zest to life in it, Frank's manners had gone from bad to worse. And at last Aldous, who had not as yet seen the two much together, and was never an observant man in such matters, had begun to have an inkling. Was it *possible* that the boy was in love, and with Betty ? He sounded Miss Raeburn ; found that she did not rise to his suggestion at all—was, in fact, annoyed by it—and with the usual stupidity of the clever man failed to draw any reasonable inference from the queerness of his aunt's looks and sighs.

As to the little minx herself, she was inscrutable. She teased them all in turns, Frank, perhaps, less than the others. Aldous, as usual, found her a delightful companion. She would walk all over the estate with him in the most mannish garments and boots conceivable, which only made her childish grace more feminine and more provocative than ever. She took an interest in all his tenants; she dived into all his affairs; she insisted on copying his letters. And meanwhile, on either side were Miss Raeburn, visibly recovering day by day her old cheeriness and bustle; and Frank—Frank, who ate nothing, or nothing commensurate to his bulk, and, if possible, said less.

Aldous had begun to feel that the situation must be probed somehow, and had devised this walk, indeed, with some vague intention of plying remonstrances and inquiries. He had an old affection for the boy, which Lady Leven had reckoned upon.

The first difficulty, of course, was to make him talk at all. Aldous tried various sporting 'gambits' with very small success. At last, by good-luck, the boy rose to something like animation in describing an encounter he had had the week before with a piebald weasel in the course of a morning's ferreting.

'All at once we saw the creature's head poke out of the hole—*pure white*, with a brown patch on it. When it saw us, back it scooted!—and we sent in another ferret after the one that was there already. My goodness! there *was* a shindy down in the earth—you could hear them rolling and kicking like anything. We had our guns ready,—but all of a sudden everything stopped—not a sound or a sign of anything! We threw down our guns and dug away like blazes. Presently we came on the two ferrets gorging away at a dead rabbit,—nasty little beasts!—that accounted for *them*; but where on earth was the weasel? I really began to think we had imagined the creature, when, whish! came a flash of white lightning, and out the thing bolted—pure white with a splash of brown—its winter coat, of course. I shot at it, but it was no go. If I'd only put a bag over the hole, and not been an idiot, I should have caught it.'

The boy swung along, busily ruminating for a minute or two, and forgetting his trouble.

'I've seen one something like it before,' he went on—'ages ago, when I was a little chap, and Harry Wharton and I were out rabbiting. By the way—' he stopped short—'do you see that that fellow's come back?'

'I saw the paragraph in the *Times* this morning,' said Aldous drily.

'And I've got a letter from Fanny this morning, to say that he and Lady Selina are to be married in July, and that she's going about making a martyr and a saint of him, talking of the " persecution" he's had to put up with, and the vulgar fellows who couldn't appreciate him, and generally making an ass of herself. Oh ! he won't ask any of us to his wedding—trust him. It *is* a rum business. You know Willie Ffolliot—that queer dark fellow—that used to be in the 10th Hussars—did all those wild things in the Soudan ? '

' Yes—slightly.'

' I heard all about it from him.   He was one of that gambling set at Harry's club there's been all that talk about, you know, since Harry came to grief.   Well !—he was going along Piccadilly one night last summer, quite late, between eleven and twelve, when Harry caught hold of him from behind.   Willie thought he was out of his mind, or drunk.   He told me he never saw anybody in such a queer state in his life.   " You come along with me," said Harry, "come and talk to me, or I shall shoot myself !"   So Willie asked him what was up.   " I'm engaged to be married," said Harry. Whereupon Willie remarked that, considering his manner and his appearance, he was sorry for the young lady.   " *Young* !" said Harry as though he would have knocked him down.   And then it came out that he had just—that moment !—engaged himself to Lady Selina.   And it was the very same day that he got into that precious mess in the House—the *very same night* !   I suppose he went to her to be comforted, and thought he'd pull something off, anyway !   Why she took him !   But of course she's no chicken, and old Alresford may die any day.   And about the bribery business—I suppose he made her think him an injured innocent. Anyway, he talked to Willie, when they got to his rooms, like a raving lunatic, and you know he was always such a cool hand. " Ffolliot," he said, "can you come with me to Siam next week ? " " How much ? " said Will.   " I thought you were engaged to Lady Selina."   Then he swore little oaths, and vowed he had told her he must have a year.   " We'll go and explore those temples in Siam,' he said, and then he muttered something about " Why should I ever come back ? "   Presently he began to talk of the strike—and the paper—and the bribe, and all the rest of it, making out a long rigmarole story.   Oh ! of course he'd done everything for the best —trust him !—and everybody else was a cur and a slanderer.   And Ffolliot declared he felt quite pulpy—the man was such a wreck ; and he said he'd go with him to Siam, or anywhere else, if he'd only cheer up.   And they got out the maps, and Harry began to

quiet down, and at last Will got him to bed.—Fanny says Ffolliot
reports he had great difficulty in dragging him home. However,
Lady Selina has no luck !—there he is.'

'Oh ! he will be one of the shining lights of our side before
long,' said Aldous, with resignation. 'Since he gave up his seat
here, there has been some talk of finding him one in the Alres-
fords' neighbourhood, I believe. But I don't suppose anybody's
very anxious for him. He is to address a meeting, I see, on the
Tory Labour Programme next week. The *Clarion*, I suppose,
will go round with him.'

'Beastly rag !' said Frank, fervently. 'It's rather a queer
thing, isn't it, that such a clever chap as that should have made
such a mess of his chances. It almost makes one not mind being
a fool.'

He laughed, but bitterly, and at the same moment the cloud
that for some twenty minutes or so seemed to have completely
rolled away descended again on eye and expression.

'Well, there are worse things than being a fool,' said Aldous,
with insidious emphasis—'sulking, and shutting up with your best
friends, for instance.'

Frank flushed deeply. and turned upon him with a sort of
uncertain fury.

'I don't know what you mean.'

Whereupon Aldous slipped his arm inside the boy's, and prepared himself with resignation for the scene that had to be got
through somehow, when Frank suddenly exclaimed :

'I say, there's Miss Boyce !'

Never was a man more quickly and completely recalled from
altruism to his own affairs. Aldous dropped his companion's
arm, straightened himself with a thrill of the whole being, and saw
Marcella some distance ahead of them in the Mellor drive, which
they had just entered. She was stooping over something on the
ground, and was not apparently aware of their approach. A ray
of cold sun came out at the moment, touched the bending figure
and the grass at her feet—grass starred with primroses, which she
was gathering.

'I didn't know you were going to call,' said Frank, bewildered.
'Isn't it too soon ?'

And he looked at his companion in astonishment.

'I came to speak to Miss Boyce and her mother on business,'
said Aldous with all his habitual reserve. 'I thought you wouldn't
mind the walk back by yourself.'

'Business ?' the boy echoed involuntarily.

Aldous hesitated. then said quietly :

' Mr. Boyce appointed me executor under his will.'

Frank lifted his eyebrows, and allowed himself at least an inward ' By Jove ! '

By this time Marcella had caught sight of them, and was advancing. She was in deep mourning, but her hands were full of primroses, which shone against the black ; and the sun, penetrating the thin green of some larches to her left, danced in her eyes and on a face full of sensitive and beautiful expression.

They had not met since they stood together beside Hallin's grave. This fact was in both their minds. Aldous felt it, as it were, in the touch of her hand. What he could not know was, that she was thinking quite as much of his letter to her mother and its phrases.

They stood talking a little in the sunshine. Then, as Frank was taking his leave, Marcella said :

' Won't you wait for—for Lord Maxwell, in the old library? We can get at it from the garden, and I have made it quite habitable. My mother, of course, does not wish to see anybody.'

Frank hesitated ; then, pushed by a certain boyish curiosity, and by the angry belief that Betty had been carried off by Miss Raeburn, and was out of his reach till luncheon-time, said he would wait. Marcella led the way, opened the garden-door of the lower corridor, close to the spot where she had seen Wharton standing in the moonlight on a never-to-be-forgotten night, and then ushered them into the library. The beautiful old place had been decently repaired, though in no sense modernised. The roof had no holes, and its delicate stucco-work, formerly stained and defaced by damp, had been whitened, so that the brown and golden tones of the books in the latticed cases told against it with delightful effect. The floor was covered with a cheap matting, and there were a few simple chairs and tables. A wood fire burnt on the old hearth. Marcella's books and work lay about, and some shallow earthenware pans filled with home-grown hyacinths scented the air. What with the lovely architecture of the room itself, its size, its books and old portraits, and the signs it bore of simple yet refined use, it would have been difficult to find a gentler, mellower place. Aldous looked round him with delight.

' I hope to make a village drawing-room of it in time,' she said casually to Frank as she stooped to put a log on the fire. ' I think we shall get them to come, as it has a separate door, and scraper, and mat all to itself.'

' Goodness ! ' said Frank, ' they won't come. It's too far from the village.'

'Don't you be so sure,' said Marcella, laughing. 'Mr. Craven has all sorts of ideas.'

'Who's Mr. Craven?'

'Didn't you meet him at my rooms?'

'Oh! I remember,' ejaculated the boy—'a frightful Socialist!'

'And his wife's worse,' said Marcella merrily. 'They've come down to settle here. They're going to help me.'

'Then for mercy's sake keep them to yourself,' cried Frank, 'and don't let them go loose over the county. We don't want them at our place.'

'Oh! your turn will come. Lord Maxwell'—her tone changed —became shy and a little grave. 'Shall we go into the Stone Parlour? My mother will come down if you wish to see her, but she thought that—that—perhaps we could settle things.'

Aldous had been standing by, hat in hand, watching her, as she chattered to Frank. As she addressed him he gave a little start.

'Oh! I think we can settle everything,' he said.

'Well, this is rum!' said Frank to himself, as the door closed behind them, and instead of betaking himself to the chair and the newspaper with which Marcella had provided him, he began to walk excitedly up and down. 'Her father makes him executor— he manages her property for her—and they behave nicely to each other, as though nothing had ever happened at all. What the deuce does it mean? And all the time Betty—why, Betty's devoted to him!—and it's as plain as a pikestaff what that old cat, Miss Raeburn, is thinking of from morning till night! Well, I'm beat!'

And throwing himself down on a stool by the fire, his chin between his hands, he stared dejectedly at the burning logs.

CHAPTER V

MEANWHILE Marcella and her companion were sitting in the Stone Parlour side by side, save for a small table between them, which held the various papers Aldous had brought with him. At first, there had been on her side—as soon as they were alone—a feeling of stifling embarrassment. All the painful, proud sensations with which she had received the news of her father's action returned upon her; she would have liked to escape; she shrank from what once more seemed an encroachment, a situation as strange as it was embarrassing.

But his manner very soon made it impossible, indeed ridiculous, to maintain such an attitude of mind. He ran through his business with his usual clearness and rapidity. It was not complicated ; her views proved to be the same as his ; and she was empowered to decide for her mother. Aldous took notes of one or two of her wishes, left some papers with her for her mother's signature, and then his work was practically done. Nothing, throughout, could have been more reassuring or more everyday than his demeanour.

Then, indeed, when the end of their business interview approached, and with it the opportunity for conversation of a different kind, both were conscious of a certain tremor. To him this old parlour was torturingly full of memories. In this very place where they sat he had given her his mother's pearls, and taken a kiss in return from the cheek that was once more so near to him. With what free and exquisite curves the hair set about the white brow ! How beautiful was the neck—the hand ! What ripened, softened charm in every movement ! The touching and rebuking thought rose in his mind that from her nursing experience, and its frank contact with the ugliest truths of the physical life—a contact he had often shrunk from realising—there had come to her, not so much added strength, as a new subtlety and sweetness, some delicate, vibrating quality, that had been entirely lacking to her first splendid youth.

Suddenly she said to him, with a certain hesitation :

'There was one more point I wanted to speak to you about. Can you advise me about selling some of those railway shares ?'

She pointed to an item in a short list of investments that lay beside them.

'But why ?' said Aldous, surprised. 'They are excellent property already, and are going up in value.'

'Yes, I know. But I want some ready money immediately— more than we have—to spend on cottage-building in the village. I saw a builder yesterday, and came to a first understanding with him. We are altering the water-supply too. They have begun upon it already, and it will cost a good deal.'

Aldous was still puzzled.

'I see,' he said. 'But—don't you suppose that the income of the estate, now that your father has done so much to free it, will be enough to meet expenses of that kind, without trenching on investments ? A certain amount, of course, should be systematically laid aside every year for rebuilding, and estate improvements generally.'

'Yes ; but you see I only regard half of the income as mine.'

She looked up with a little smile.

He was now standing in front of her, against the fire, his grey eyes, which could be, as she well knew, so cold and inexpressive, bent upon her with eager interest.

'Only half the income?' he repeated. 'Ah!'—he smiled kindly—'is that an arrangement between you and your mother?'

Marcella let her hand fall with a little despairing gesture.

'Oh no!' she said—'oh no! Mamma—mamma will take nothing from me or from the estate. She has her own money, and she will live with me part of the year.'

The intonation in the words touched Aldous profoundly.

'Part of the year?' he said, astonished, yet not knowing how to question her. 'Mrs. Boyce will not make Mellor her home?'

'She would be thankful if she had never seen it,' said Marcella quickly—'and she would never see it again if it weren't for me. It's dreadful what she went through last year, when—when I was in London.'

Her voice fell. Glancing up at him involuntarily, her eye looked with dread for some chill, some stiffening in him. Probably he condemned her, had always condemned her for deserting her home and her parents. But instead she saw nothing but sympathy.

'Mrs. Boyce has had a hard life,' he said, with grave feeling.

Marcella felt a tear leap, and furtively raised her handkerchief to brush it away. Then, with a natural selfishness, her quick thought took another turn. A wild yearning rose in her mind to tell him much more than she had ever done in old days of the miserable home-circumstances of her early youth; to lay stress on the mean unhappiness which had depressed her own child-nature whenever she was with her parents, and had withered her mother's character. Secretly, passionately, she often made the past an excuse. Excuse for what? For the lack of delicacy and loyalty, of the best sort of breeding, which had marked the days of her engagement?

Never—*never* to speak of it with him!—to pour out everything —to ask him to judge, to understand, to forgive!—

She pulled herself together by a strong effort, reminding herself in a flash of all that divided them :—of womanly pride—of Betty Macdonald's presence at the Court—of that vain confidence to Hallin, of which her inmost being must have been ashamed, but that something calming and sacred stole upon her whenever she thought of Hallin, lifting everything concerned with him into a category of its own.

No; let her selfish weakness make no fettering claim upon the

man before her.   Let her be content with the friendship she had,
after all, achieved, that was now doing its kindly best for her.

All these images, like a tumultuous procession, ran through the
mind in a moment. He thought, as she sat there with her bent
head, the hands clasped round the knee in the way he knew so
well, that she was full of her mother, and found it difficult to put
what she felt into words.

'But tell me about your plan,' he said gently, 'if you will.'

'Oh! it is nothing,' she said hurriedly. 'I am afraid you will
think it impracticable—perhaps wrong. It's only this : you see,
as there is no one depending on me—as I am practically alone—
it seemed to me I might make an experiment. Four thousand a
year is a great deal more than I need ever spend—than I *ought*, of
course, to spend on myself. I don't think altogether what I used
to think. I mean to keep up this house—to make it beautiful, to
hand it on, perhaps *more* beautiful than I found it, to those that
come after. And I mean to maintain enough service in it both to
keep it in order and to make it a social centre for all the people
about—for everybody of all classes, so far as I can. I want it to
be a place of amusement and delight and talk to us all—especially
to the very poor.   After all'—her cheek flushed under the quickening of her thought—'*everybody* on the estate, in his different
degree, has contributed to this house, in some sense, for generations. I want it to come into their lives—to make it *their* possession, *their* pride,—as well as mine.   But then that isn't all.   The
people here can enjoy nothing, use nothing, till they have a
worthier life of their own. Wages here, you know, are terribly
low, much lower'—she added timidly—'than with you. They
are, as a rule, eleven or twelve shillings a week. Now there seem
to be about one hundred and sixty labourers on the estate
altogether, in the farmers' employment and in our own. Some, of
course, are boys, and some old men earning a half-wage. Mr.
Craven and I have worked it out, and we find that an average
weekly increase of five shillings per head—which would give the
men of full age and in full work about a pound a week--would
work out at about two thousand a year.'

She paused a moment, trying to put her further statement into
its best order.

'Your farmers, you know,' he said, smiling, after a pause, 'will
be your chief difficulty.'

'Of course !   But I thought of calling a meeting of them.   I
have discussed it with Mr. French—of course he thinks me mad !
—but he gave me some advice. I should propose to them all fresh
leases, with certain small advantages that Louis Craven thinks

would tempt them, at a reduced rental exactly answering to the rise in wages. Then, in return, they must accept a sort of fair-wage clause, binding them to pay henceforward the standard wage of the estate.'

She looked up, her face expressing urgent though silent interrogation.

'You must remember,' he said quickly, 'that though the estate is recovering, and rents have been fairly paid about here during the last eighteen months, you may be called upon at any moment to make the reductions which hampered your uncle. These reductions will, of course, fall upon you as before, seeing that the farmers, in a different way, will be paying as much as before. Have you left margin enough?'

'I think so,' she said eagerly. 'I shall live here very simply, and accumulate all the reserve fund I can. I have set all my heart upon it. I know there are not many people *could* do such a thing—other obligations would, must, come first. And it may turn out a mistake. But—whatever happens—whatever any of us, Socialists or not, may hope for in the future—here one *is* with one's conscience, and one's money, and these people, who like oneself have but the one life! In all labour, it is the modern question, isn't it?—*how much* of the product of labour the workman can extract from the employer? About here there is no union to act for the labourers—they have practically no power. But *in the future*, we must surely *hope* they will combine, that they will be stronger —strong enough to *force* a decent wage. What ought to prevent my free will anticipating a moment—since I *can* do it—that we all want to see?'

She spoke with strong feeling; but his ear detected a new note —something deeper and wistfuller than of old.

'Well—as you say, you are for experiments!' he replied, not finding it easy to produce his own judgment quickly. Then, in another tone—'it was always Hallin's cry.'

She glanced up at him, her lips trembling.

'I know. Do you remember how he used to say—"the big changes may come—the big Collectivist changes. But neither you nor I will see them. I pray *not* to see them. Meanwhile—all still hangs upon, comes back to, the individual. Here are you with your money and power; there are those men and women whom you can share with—in new and honourable ways—*to-day*."'

Then she checked herself suddenly.

'But now I want you to tell me—will you tell me?—all the objections you see. You must often have thought such things over.'

She was looking nervously straight before her. She did not
see the flash of half-bitter, half-tender irony that crossed his face.
Her tone of humility, of appeal, was so strange to him, remembering the past.

'Yes, very often,' he answered. 'Well, I think these are the
kind of arguments you will have to meet.'

He went through the objections that any economist would be
sure to weigh against a proposal of the kind, as clearly as he could,
and at some length—but without zest. What affected Marcella all
through was not so much the matter of what he said, as the manner
of it. It was so characteristic of the two voices in him—the voice
of the idealist checked and mocked always by the voice of the observer and the student. A year before, the little harangue would
have set her aflame with impatience and wrath. Now, beneath
the speaker, she felt and yearned towards the man.

Yet, as to the scheme, when all demurs were made, she was 'of
the same opinion still' ! His arguments were not new to her ; the
inward eagerness overrode them.

'In my own case '—he said at last, the tone passing instantly
into reserve and shyness, as always happened when he spoke of
himself—' my own wages are two or three shillings higher than
those paid generally by the farmers on the estate ; and we have a
pension fund. But, so far, I have felt the risks of any wholesale
disturbance of labour on the estate, depending, as it must entirely
in my case, on the individual life and will, to be too great to let me
go further. I sometimes believe that it is the farmers who would
really benefit most by experiments of the kind !'

She protested vehemently, being at the moment, of course, not
at all in love with mankind in general, but only with those members
of mankind who came within the eye of imagination. He was
enchanted to see the old self come out again—positive, obstinate,
generous ; to see the old confident pose of the head, the dramatic
ease of gesture.

Meanwhile something that had to be said, that must, indeed, be
said, if he were to give her serious and official advice, pressed uncomfortably on his tongue.

'You know,' he said, not looking at her, when at last she had
for the moment exhausted argument and prophecy, 'you have to
think of those who will succeed you here ; still more you have to
think—of marriage—before you pledge yourself to the halving of
your income.'

Now he must needs look at her intently, out of sheer nervousness. The difficulty he had had in compelling himself to make the
speech at all had given a certain hardness and stiffness to his

voice. She felt a sudden shock and chill—resented what he had dismally felt to be an imperative duty.

' I do not think I have any need to think of it—in this connection,' she said proudly. And getting up, she began to gather her papers together.

The spell was broken, the charm gone. He felt that he was dismissed.

With a new formality and silence, she led the way into the hall, he following. As they neared the library there was a sound of voices.

Marcella opened the door in surprise, and there, on either side of the fire, sat Betty Macdonald and Frank Leven.

' *That's* a mercy ! ' cried Betty, running forward to Marcella and kissing her. ' I really don't know what would have happened if Sir Frank and I had been left alone any longer. As for the Kilkenny cats, my dear, don't mention them ! '

The child was flushed and agitated, and there was an angry light in her blue eyes. Frank looked simply lumpish and miserable.

' Yes, here I am,' said Betty, holding Marcella, and chattering as fast as possible. ' I made Miss Raeburn bring me over, that I might *just* catch a sight of you. She would walk home, and leave the carriage for me. Isn't it like all the topsy-turvy things nowadays? When *I'm* her age I suppose I shall have gone back to dolls. Please to look at those ponies !—they're pawing your gravel to bits. And as for my watch, just inspect it ! '—She thrust it reproachfully under Marcella's eyes. ' You've been such a time in there talking, that Sir Frank and I have had time to quarrel for life, and there isn't a minute left for anything rational. Oh ! good-bye, my dear, good-bye. I never kept Miss Raeburn waiting for lunch yet, did I, Aldous? and I musn't begin now. Come along, Aldous ! You'll have to come home with me. I'm frightened to death of those ponies. You shan't drive, but if they bolt, I'll give them to you to pull in. Dear, *dear* Marcella, let me come again—soon—directly ! '

A few more sallies and kisses, a few more angry looks at Frank and appeals to Aldous, who was much less responsive than usual, and the child was seated, very erect and rosy, on the driving-seat of the little pony-carriage, with Aldous beside her.

' Are you coming, Frank? ' said Aldous ; ' there's plenty of room.'

His strong brow had a pucker of annoyance. As he spoke, he looked, not at Frank, but at Marcella. She was standing a trifle back, among the shadows of the doorway, and her attitude conveyed to him an impression of proud aloofness. A sigh that was half pain, half resignation, passed his lips unconsciously.

'Thank you, I'll walk,' said Frank, fiercely.

'Now, will you please explain to me why you look like that, and talk like that?' said Marcella, with cutting composure, when she was once more in the library, and Frank, crimson to the roots of his hair, and saying incoherent things, had followed her there.

'I should think you might guess,' said Frank, in reproachful misery, as he hung over the fire.

'Not at all!' said Marcella; 'you are rude to Betty, and dis· agreeable to me, by which I suppose that you are unhappy. But why should *you* be allowed to show your feelings, when other people don't?'

Frank fairly groaned.

'Well,' he said, making efforts at a tragic calm, and looking for his hat, 'you will, none of you, be troubled with me long. I shall go home to-morrow, and take my ticket for California the day after.'

'*You*,' said Marcella, 'go to California! What right have you to go to California?'

'What right?' Frank stared, then he went on impetuously. 'If a girl torments a man, as Betty has been tormenting me, there is nothing for it, I should think, but to clear out of the way, I am going to clear out of the way, whatever anybody says.'

'And shoot big game, I suppose—amuse yourself somehow?'

Frank hesitated.

· Well, a fellow can't do nothing,' he said, helplessly. ' I suppose I shall shoot.'

'And what right have you to do it? Have you any more right than a public official would have to spend public money in neglecting his duties?'

Frank stared at her.

'Well, I don't know what you mean,' he said at last, angrily; 'give it up.'

'It's quite simple what I mean. You have inherited your father's property. Your tenants pay you rent, that comes from their labour. Are you going to make no return for your income, and your house, and your leisure?'

'Ah! that's your Socialism!' cried the young fellow, roused by her tone. 'No return? Why, they have the land.'

'If I were a thoroughgoing Socialist,' said Marcella, steadily, 'I should say to you, Go! The sooner you throw off all ties to your property, the sooner you prove to the world that you and your class are mere useless parasites, the sooner we shall be rid of you. But unfortunately *I* am not such a good Socialist as that. I waver—I am not sure of what I wish. But one thing I *am* sure of, that unless people like you are going to treat their lives as a profession, to take their calling seriously, there are no more superfluous drones, no more idle plunderers than you, in all civilised society ! '

Was she pelting him in this way that she might so get rid of some of her own inner smart and restlessness ? If so, the unlucky Frank could not guess it. He could only feel himself intolerably ill-used. He had meant to pour himself out to her on the subject of Betty and his woes, and here she was rating him as to his *duties*, of which he had hardly as yet troubled himself to think, being entirely taken up either with his grievances or his enjoyments.

' I'm sure you know you're talking nonsense,' he said sulkily, though he shrank from meeting her fiery look. ' And if I *am* idle, there are plenty of people idler than me—people who live on their money, with no land to bother about, and nothing to do for it at all.'

' On the contrary, it is they who have an excuse. They have no natural opening, perhaps—no plain call. You have both, and, as I said before, you have no *right* to take holidays before you have earned them. You have got to learn your business first, and then do it. Give your eight-hours day like other people ! Who are you, that you should have all the cake of the world, and other people the crusts ? '

Frank walked to the window, and stood staring out, with his back turned to her. Her words stung and tingled ; and he was too miserable to fight.

' I shouldn't care whether it were cake or crusts,' he said at last, in a low voice, turning round to her, ' if only Betty would have me.'

' Do you think she is any the more likely to have you,' said Marcella, unrelenting, ' if you behave as a loafer and a runaway ? Don't you suppose that Betty has good reasons for hesitating when she sees the difference between you—and—and other people ? '

Frank looked at her sombrely—a queer mixture of expressions on the face, in which the maturer man was already to be discerned at war with the powerful young animal.

' I suppose you mean Lord Maxwell ? '

There was a pause.

' You may take what I said,' she said at last, looking into the fire, ' as meaning anybody who pays honestly with work and brains for what society has given him—as far as he can pay, at any rate.'

' Now look here,' said Frank, coming dolefully to sit down beside her ; ' don't slate me any more. I'm a bad lot, I know—

well, an idle lot—I don't think I am a *bad* lot.—But it's no good your preaching to me while Betty's sticking pins into me like this. Now just let me tell you how she's been behaving.'

Marcella succumbed, and heard him. He glanced at her surreptitiously from time to time, but he could make nothing of her. She sat very quiet while he described the constant companionship between Aldous and Betty, and the evident designs of Miss Raeburn. Just as when he made his first confidences to her in London, he was vaguely conscious that he was doing a not very gentlemanly thing. But, again, he was too unhappy to restrain himself, and he longed somehow to make an ally of her.

' Well, I have only one thing to say,' she said at last, with an odd nervous impatience—' go and ask her, and have done with it ! She might have some respect for you then. No, 1 won't help you ; but if you don't succeed, I'll pity you—I promise you that. And now you must go away.'

He went, feeling himself hardly treated, yet conscious never-theless of a certain stirring of the moral waters which had both stimulus and balm in it.

She, left behind, sat quiet in the old library for a few lonely minutes. The boy's plight made her alternately scornful and repentant of her sharpness to him. As to his report, one moment it plunged her in an anguish which she dared not fathom ; the next she was incredulous—could not simply make herself take the thing as real.

But one thing had been real—that word from Aldous to her of ' *marriage*' ! The nostril dilated, the breast heaved, as she lost all thought of Frank in a resentful passion that could neither justify nor calm itself. It seemed still as though he had struck her. Yet she knew well that she had nothing to forgive.

Next morning she went down to the village meaning to satisfy herself on two or three points connected with the new cottages. On the way she knocked at the Rectory garden-door, in the hope of finding Mary Harden and persuading her to come with her.

She had not seen much of Mary since their return. Still, she had had time to be painfully struck once or twice with the white and bloodless look of the rector's sister, and with a certain patient silence about her which seemed to Marcella new. Was it the monotony of the life ? or had both of them been overworking and underfeeding as usual ? The rector had received Marcella with his old gentle but rather distant kindness. Two years be-fore he had felt strongly about many of her proceedings, and had expressed himself frankly enough, at least to Mary. Now he had put his former disapprovals out of his mind, and was only anxious to work smoothly with the owner of Mellor. He had a great respect for ' dignities,' and she, as far as the village was concerned, was to be his ' dignity' henceforward. Moreover, he humbly and truly hoped that she might be able to enlighten him as to a good many modern conceptions and ideas about the poor, for which, absorbed as he was, either in almsgiving of the traditional type, or spiritual ministration, or sacramental theory, he had little time, and, if the truth were known, little affinity.

In answer to her knock Marcella heard a faint ' Come in ' from the interior of the house. She walked into the dining-room, and found Mary sitting by the little table in tears. There were some letters before her, which she pushed away as Marcella entered, but she did not attempt to disguise her agitation.

' What is it, dear ? Tell me,' said Marcella, sitting down beside her, and kissing one of the hands she held.

And Mary told her. It was the story of her life—a simple tale of ordinary things, such as wring the quiet hearts and train the unnoticed saints of this world. In her first youth, when Charles Harden was for a time doing some divinity lecturing in his Oxford college, Mary had gone up to spend a year with him in lodgings. Their Sunday teas and other small festivities were frequented by her brother's friends, men of like type with himself, and most of them either clergymen or about to be ordained. Between one of them, a young fellow looking out for his first curacy, and Mary an attachment had sprung up, which Mary could not even now speak of. She hurried over it, with a trembling voice, to the tragedy beyond. Mr. Shelton got his curacy, went off to a parish in the Lincolnshire Fens, and there was talk of their being married in a year or so. But the exposure of a bitter winter's night, risked in the struggle across one of the bleakest flats of the district to carry the Sacrament to a dying parishioner, had brought on a peculiar and agonising form of neuralgia. And from this pain, so nobly earned, had sprung—oh ! mystery of human fate !—a morphia-habit, with all that such a habit means for mind and body. It was discovered by the poor fellow's brother, who brought him up to London and tried to cure him. Meanwhile he himself had written to Mary to give her up. ' I have no will left, and am no longer a man,' he wrote to her. ' It would be an outrage on my part, and a sin on yours, if we did not cancel our promise.' Charles, who took a hard, ascetic view, held much the same language, and Mary submitted, heartbroken.

Then came a gleam of hope. The brother's care and affection prevailed ; there were rumours of great improvement, of a resump tion of work. 'Just two years ago, when you first came here, I was beginning to believe'—she turned away her head to hide the rise of tears—'that it might still come right.' But after some six or eight months of clerical work in London fresh trouble developed, lung mischief showed itself, and the system, undermined by long and deep depression, seemed to capitulate at once.

'He died last December, at Madeira,' said Mary quietly. 'I saw him before he left England. We wrote to each other almost to the end. He was quite at peace. This letter here was from the chaplain at Madeira, who was kind to him, to tell me about his grave.'

That was all. It was the sort of story that somehow might have been expected to belong to Mary Harden—to her round, plaintive face, to her narrow, refined experience ; and she told it in a way eminently characteristic of her modes of thinking, religious or social, with old-fashioned or conventional phrases which, whatever might be the case with other people, had lost none of their bloom or meaning for her.

Marcella's face showed her sympathy. They talked for half an hour, and at the end of it Mary flung her arms round her companion's neck.

'There !' she said, 'now we must not talk any more about it. I am glad I told you. It was a comfort. And somehow—I don't mean to be unkind ; but I couldn't have told you in the old days— it's wonderful how much better I like you now than I used to do, though perhaps we don't agree much better.'

Both laughed, though the eyes of both were full of tears.

Presently they were in the village together. As they neared the Hurds' old cottage, which was now empty and to be pulled down, a sudden look of disgust crossed Marcella's face.

'Did I tell you my news of Minta Hurd?' she said.

No ; Mary had heard nothing. So Marcella told the grotesque and ugly news, as it seemed to her, which had reached her at Amalfi. Jim Hurd's widow was to be married again, to the queer lanky 'professor of elocution,' with the Italian name and shifty eye, who lodged on the floor beneath her in Brown's Buildings, and had been wont to come in of an evening and play comic songs to her and the children. Marcella was vehemently sure that he was a charlatan—that he got his living by a number of small dishonesties, that he had scented Minta's pension. But apart from the question whether he would make Minta a decent husband, or live upon her and beat her, was the fact itself of her re-marriage, in itself hideous to the girl.

'*Marry* him!' she said. 'Marry anyone! Isn't it incredible?'

They were in front of the cottage. Marcella paused a moment and looked at it. She saw again in sharp vision the miserable woman fainting on the settle, the dwarf sitting, handcuffed, under the eye of his captors; she felt again the rush of that whirlwind of agony through which she had borne the wife's helpless soul in that awful dawn.

And after that—exit!—with her 'professor of elocution.' It made the girl sick to think of. And Mary, out of a Puseyite dislike of second marriage, felt and expressed much the same repulsion.

Well—Minta Hurd was far away, and if she had been there to defend herself her powers of expression would have been no match for theirs. Nor does youth understand such pleas as she might have urged.

'Will Lord Maxwell continue the pension?' said Mary.

Marcella stopped again, involuntarily.

'So that was his doing?' she said. 'I supposed as much.'

'You did not know?' cried Mary, in distress. 'Oh! I believe I ought not to have said anything about it.'

'I always guessed it,' said Marcella shortly, and they walked on in silence.

Presently they found themselves in front of Mrs. Jellison's very trim and pleasant cottage, which lay farther along the common, to the left of the road to the Court. There was an early pear-tree in blossom over the porch, and a swelling greenery of buds in the little garden.

'Will you come in?' said Mary. 'I should like to see Isabella Westall.'

Marcella started at the name.

'How is she?' she asked.

'Just the same. She has never been in her right mind since. But she is quite harmless and quiet.'

They found Mrs. Jellison on one side of the fire, with her daughter on the other, and the little six-year-old Johnnie playing between them. Mrs. Jellison was straw-plaiting, twisting the straws with amazing rapidity, her fingers stained with red from the dye of them. Isabella was, as usual, doing nothing. She stared when Marcella and Mary came in, but she took no other notice of them. Her powerful and tragic face had the look of something originally full of intention, from which spirit and meaning had long departed, leaving a fine but lifeless outline. Marcella had seen it last on the night of the execution, in ghastly apparition at Minta Hurd's window, when it might have been caught by some sculptor in quest of the secrets of violent expression, fixed in clay or marble, and labelled 'Revenge,' or 'Passion.'

Its passionless emptiness now filled her with pity and horror. She sat down beside the widow and took her hand. Mrs. Westail allowed it for a moment, then drew her own away suddenly, and Marcella saw a curious and sinister contraction of the eyes.

'Ah! yo never know how much Isabella unnerstans, an' how much she don't,' Mrs. Jellison was saying to Mary. ' I can't allus make her out, but she don't give no trouble. An' as for that boy, he's a chirruper, he is. He gives 'em fine times at school, he do. Miss Barton, she ast him in class, Thursday, 'bout Ananias and Sapphira. "Johnnie," says she, "whatever made 'em do sich a wicked thing?" "Well, *I* do'n know," says he; "it was jus' their nassty good-for-nothink," says he; "but they was great sillies," says he. Oh! he don't mean no harm!—lor, bless yer, the men is all born contrary, and they can't help themselves. Oh! thank yer, miss, my 'ealth is pretty tidy, though I 'ave been plagued this winter with a something they call the 'flenzy. I wor very bad! "Yo go to bed, Mrs. Jellison," says Doctor Clarke, " or yo'll know of it." But I worn't goin to be talked to by 'im. Why, I knowed 'im when he wor no 'igher nor Johnnie. An' I kep puddlin along, an' one mornin I wor fairly choked, an' I just crawled into that parlour, an' I took a sup o' brandy out o' the bottle'—she looked complacently at Mary, quite conscious that the rector's sister must be listening to her with disapproving ears—'an', lor bless yer, it cut the phlegm, it did, that very moment. My! I did cough. I drawed it up by the yard, I did—an' I crep back along the wall, an' yo cud ha knocked me down wi' one o' my own straws. But I've been better iver since, an' beginnin to eat my vittles too, though I'm never no great pecker—I ain't—not at no time.'

Mary managed to smother her emotions on the subject of the brandy, and the old woman chattered on, throwing out the news of the village in a series of humorous fragments, tinged in general with the lowest opinion of human nature.

When the girls took leave of her, she said slyly to Marcella:

'An' 'ow about your plaitin, miss?—though I dessay I'm a bold 'un for astin.'

Marcella coloured.

'Well, I've got it to think about, Mrs. Jellison. We must have a meeting in the village and talk it over one of these days.'

The old woman nodded in a shrewd silence, and watched them depart.

'Wull, I reckon Jimmy Gedge ull lasst my time,' she said to herself with a chuckle.

If Mrs. Jellison had this small belief in the powers of the new mistress of Mellor over matters which, according to her, had been settled generations ago by 'the Lord and natur,' Marcella certainly was in no mood to contradict her. She walked through the village on her return, scanning everything about her—the slatternly girls plaiting on the doorsteps, the children in the lane, the loungers round the various 'publics,' the labourers, old and young, who touched their caps to her—with a moody and passionate eye.

'Mary!' she broke out as they neared the Rectory, 'I shall be twenty-four directly. How much harm do you think I shall have done here by the time I am sixty-four?'

Mary laughed at her, and tried to cheer her. But Marcella was in the depths of self-disgust.

'What is wanted, really wanted,' she said with intensity, 'is not *my* help, but *their* growth. How can I make them *take for themselves*—take, roughly and selfishly even, if they will only take! As for my giving, what relation has it to anything real or lasting?'

Mary was scandalised.

'I declare you are as bad as Mr. Craven,' she said. 'He told Charles yesterday that the curtseys of the old women in the village to him and Charles—women old enough to be their grandmothers —sickened him of the whole place, and that he should regard it as the chief object of his work here to make such things impossible in the future. Or perhaps you're still of Mr.—Mr. Wharton's opinion—you'll be expecting Charles and me to give up charity. But it's no good, my dear. We're not "advanced," and we never shall be.'

At the mention of Wharton, Marcella threw her proud head back; wave after wave of changing expression passed over the face.

'I often remember the things Mr. Wharton said in this village,' she said at last. 'There was life and salt and power in many of them. It's not what he said, but what he was, that one wants to forget.'

They parted presently, and Marcella went heavily home. The rising of the spring, the breath of the April air, had never yet been sad and oppressive to her as they were to-day.

CHAPTER VI

'OH ! Miss Boyce, may I come in?'

The voice was Frank Leven's. Marcella was sitting in the old library alone late on the following afternoon. Louis Craven, who was now her paid agent and adviser, had been with her, and she had accounts and estimates before her.

'Come in,' she said, startled a little by Frank's tone and manner, and looking at him interrogatively.

Frank shut the heavy old door carefully behind him. Then, as he advanced to her she saw that his flushed face wore an expression unlike anything she had yet seen there—of mingled joy and fear.

She drew back involuntarily.

'Is there anything—anything wrong?'

'No,' he said impetuously, 'no! But I have something to tell you, and I don't know how. I don't know whether I ought. I have run almost all the way from the Court.'

And indeed he could hardly get his breath. He took a stool she pushed to him, and tried to collect himself. She heard her heart beat as she waited for him to speak.

'It's about Lord Maxwell,' he said at last, huskily, turning his head away from her to the fire. 'I've just had a long walk with him. Then he left me; he had no idea I came on here. But something drove me; I felt I must come, I must tell. Will you promise not to be angry with me—to believe that I've thought about it—that I'm doing it for the best?'

He looked at her nervously.

'If you wouldn't keep me waiting so long,' she said faintly, while her cheeks and lips grew white.

' Well,—I was mad this morning! Betty hasn't spoken to me since yesterday. She's been always about with him, and Miss Raeburn let me see once or twice last night that she thought I was in the way. I never slept a wink last night, and I kept out of their sight all the morning. Then, after lunch, I went up to him, and I asked him to come for a walk with me. He looked at me rather queerly—I suppose I was pretty savage. Then he said he'd come. And off we went, ever so far across the park. And I let out. I don't know what I said; I suppose I made a beast of myself. But any way, I asked him to tell me what he meant, and to tell me, if he could, what Betty meant. I said I knew I was a cool hand, and he might turn me out of the house, and refuse to have anything more to do with me if he liked. But I was going to rack and ruin, and should never be any good till I knew where I stood —and Betty would never be serious—and, in short, was he in love with her himself? for anyone could see what Miss Raeburn was thinking of.'

The boy gulped down something like a sob, and tried to give himself time to be coherent again. Marcella sat like a stone.

'When he heard me say that—"in love with her yourself," he stopped dead. I saw that I had made him angry. "What right have you or anyone else," he said, very short, "to ask me such a question?" Then I just lost my head, and said anything that came handy. I told him everybody talked about it—which, of course, was rubbish—and at last I said, "Ask anybody; ask the Winterbournes, ask Miss Boyce—they all think it as much as I do." "*Miss Boyce*!" he said—"Miss Boyce thinks I want to marry Betty Macdonald?" Then I didn't know what to say—for, of course, I knew I'd taken your name in vain; and he sat down on the grass beside a little stream there is in the park, and he didn't speak to me for a long time—I could see him throwing little stones into the water. And at last he called me. "Frank!" he said; and I went up to him. And then——'

The lad seemed to tremble all over. He bent forward and laid his hand on Marcella's knee, touching her cold ones.

'And then he said, "I can't understand yet, Frank, how you or anybody else can have mistaken my friendship for Betty Macdonald. At any rate, I know there's been no mistake on her part. And if you take my advice, you'll go and speak to her like a man, with all your heart, and see what she says. You don't deserve her yet, that I can tell you. As for me"—I can't describe the look of his face; I only know I wanted to go away—"you and I will be friends for many years, I hope, so perhaps you may just understand this, once for all. For me there never has been, and there never will be, but one woman in the world—to love. And you know," he said after a bit, "or you ought to know, very well, who that woman is." And then he got up and walked away. He did not ask me to come, and I felt I dared not go after him. And then I lay and thought. I remembered being here; I thought of what I had said to you—of what I had fancied now and then about—about you. I felt myself a brute all round; for what right had I to come and tell you what he told me? And yet, there it was—-I had to come. And if it was no good my coming, why, we needn't say anything about it ever—need we? But—but—just look here, Miss Boyce; if you—if you could begin over again, and make Aldous happy, then there'd be a good many other people happy too—I can tell you that.'

He could hardly speak plainly. Evidently there was on him an overmastering impulse of personal devotion, gratitude, remorse, which for the moment even eclipsed his young passion. It was but vaguely explained by anything he had said; it rested clearly on the whole of his afternoon's experience.

But neither could Marcella speak, and her pallor began to alarm him.

' I say !' he cried; 'you're not angry with me?'

She moved away from him, and with her shaking finger began to cut the pages of a book that lay open on the mantelpiece. The little mechanical action seemed gradually to restore her to self-control.

'I don't think I can talk about it,' she said at last, with an effort; 'not now.'

'Oh! I know,' said Frank, in penitence, looking at her black dress; 'you've been upset, and had such a lot of trouble. But I——'

She laid her hand on his shoulder. He thought he had never seen her so beautiful, pale as she was.

'I'm not the least angry. I'll tell you so—another day. Now, are you going to Betty?'

The young fellow sprang up, all his expression changing, answering to the stimulus of the word.

'They'll be home directly, Miss Raeburn and Betty,' he said steadily, buttoning his coat; 'they'd gone out calling somewhere. Oh! she'll lead me a wretched life, will Betty, before she's done !'

A charming little ghost of a smile crossed Marcella's white lips.

' Probably Betty knows her business,' she said; ' if she's quite unmanageable, send her to me.'

In his general turmoil of spirits the boy caught her hand and kissed it—would have liked, indeed, to kiss her and all the world. But she laughed, and sent him away, and with a sly, lingering look at her he departed.

She sank into her chair and never moved for long. The April sun was just sinking behind the cedars, and through the open south window of the library came little spring airs and scents of spring flowers. There was an endless twitter of birds, and beside her the soft chatter of the wood fire. An hour before, her mood had been at open war with the spring, and with all those impulses and yearnings in herself which answered to it. Now it seemed to her that a wonderful and buoyant life, akin to all the vast stir, the sweet revivals of Nature, was flooding her whole being.

She gave herself up to it, in a trance interwoven with all the loveliest and deepest things she had ever felt—with her memory of Hallin, with her new gropings after God. Just as the light was going she got up hurriedly and went to her writing-table. She wrote a little note, sat over it a while, with her face hidden in her hands, then sealed, addressed, and stamped it. She went out herself to the hall to put it in the letter-box. For the rest of the evening she went about in a state of dream, overcome some- times by rushes of joy, which yet had in them exquisite elements of pain ; hungering for the passage of the hours, for sleep that might cancel some of them ; picturing the road to the Court and Widrington, along which the old postman had by now carried her letter—the bands of moonlight and shade lying across it, the quiet of the budding woods, and the spot on the hillside where he had spoken to her in that glowing October. It must lie all night in a dull office—her letter ; she was impatient and sorry for it. And when he got it, it would tell him nothing, though she thought it would rather surprise him. It was the merest formal request that he would, if he could, come and see her again the following morn- ing on business.

During the evening Mrs. Boyce lay on the sofa and read. It always still gave the daughter a certain shock of surprise when she saw the slight form resting in this way. In words Mrs. Boyce would allow nothing, and her calm composure had been unbroken from the moment of their return home, though it was not yet two months since her husband's death. In these days she read enormously, which again was a new trait. Especially novels. She read each through rapidly, laid it down without a word of comment, and took up another. Once or twice, but very rarely, Marcella surprised her in absent meditation, her hand covering the page. From the hard, satiric brightness of her look on these occasions it seemed probable that she was speculating on the discrepancies between fiction and real life, and on the falsity of most literary sentiment.

To-night Marcella sat almost silent—she was making a frock for a village child she had carried off from its mother, who was very ill—and Mrs. Boyce read. But as the clock approached ten, the time when they generally went upstairs, Marcella made a few uncertain movements, and finally got up, took a stool, and sat down beside the sofa.

An hour later Marcella entered her own room. As she closed the door behind her she gave an involuntary sob, put down her light, and, hurrying up to the bed, fell on her knees beside it and wept long. Yet her mother had not been unkind to her. Far from it. Mrs. Boyce had praised her—in few words, but with evident sincerity—for the courage that could, if necessary, put convention aside ; had spoken of her own relief; had said pleasant things of Lord Maxwell; had bantered Marcella a little on her social schemes, and wished her the independence to stick to them. Finally, as they got up to go to bed, she kissed Marcella twice instead of once, and said :

'Well, my dear, I shall not be in your way to-morrow morning ; I promise you that.'

The speaker's satisfaction was plain ; yet nothing could have been less maternal. The girl's heart, when she found herself alone, was very sore, and the depression of a past which had been so much of a failure, so lacking in any satisfied emotion and the sweet preludes of family affection, darkened for a while even the present and the future.

After a time she got up, and, leaving her room, went to sit in a passage outside it. It was the piece of wide upper corridor leading to the winding stairs she had descended on the night of the ball. It was one of the loneliest and oddest places in the house, for it communicated only with her room and the little stair-case, which was hardly ever used. It was, indeed, a small room in itself, and was furnished with a few huge old chairs with moth-eaten frames and tattered seats. A flowery paper of last-century date sprawled over the walls, the carpet had many holes in it, and the shallow, traceried windows, set almost flush in the outer surface of the wall, were curtainless now, as they had been two years before.

She drew one of the old chairs to a window, and softly opened it. There was a young moon, and many stars, seen uncertainly through the rush of April cloud. Every now and then a splash of rain moved the creepers and swept across the lawn, to be followed by a spell of growing and breathing silence. The scent of hya-cinths and tulips mounted through the wet air. She could see a long gnostly line of primroses, from which rose the grey base of the Tudor front, checkered with a dim light and shade. Beyond the garden, with its vague forms of fountain and sundial, the cedars stood watching ; the little church slept to her left.

So, face to face with Nature, the old house, and the night, she took passionate counsel with herself. After to-night, surely, she would be no more lonely ! She was going for ever from her own keeping to that of another. For she never, from the moment she wrote her letter, had the smallest doubt as to what his answer to her would be ; never the smallest dread that he would, even in

the lightest passing impression, connect what she was going to do
with any thought of blame or wonder. Her pride and fear were
gone out of her ; only, she dared not think of how he would look
and speak when the moment came, because it made her sick and
faint with feeling.

How strange to imagine what, no doubt, would be said and
thought about her return to him by the outside world ! His great
place in society, his wealth, would be the obvious solution of it for
many—too obvious even to be debated. Looking back upon her
thoughts of this night in after-years, she could not remember that
the practical certainty of such an interpretation had even given her
a moment's pain. It was too remote from all her now familiar
ways of thinking—and his. In her early Mellor days the enormous
importance that her feverish youth attached to wealth and birth
might have been seen in her very attacks upon them. Now all
her standards were spiritualised. She had come to know what
happiness and affection are possible in three rooms, or two, on
twenty-eight shillings a week ; and, on the other hand, her knowledge of Aldous—a man of stoical and simple habit, thrust, with a
student's tastes, into the position of a great landowner—had shown
her, in the case at least of one member of the rich class, how
wealth may be a true moral burden and test, the source of half the
difficulties and pains—of half the nobleness also—of a man's life.
Not in mere wealth and poverty, she thought, but in things of
quite another order—things of social sympathy and relation—
alterable at every turn, even under existing conditions, by the
human will, lie the real barriers that divide us man from man.

Had they ever really formed a part of historical time, those
eight months of their engagement ? Looking back upon them,
she saw herself moving about in them like a creature without eyes,
worked, blindfold, by a crude inner mechanism that took no account
really of impressions from without. Yet that passionate sympathy
with the poor—that hatred of oppression? Even these seemed to
her to-night the blind, spasmodic efforts of a mind that all through
saw nothing—mistook its own violences and self-wills for eternal
right, and was but traitor to what should have been its own first
loyalties, in seeking to save and reform.

Was *true* love now to deliver her from that sympathy, to deaden
in her that hatred ? Her whole soul cried out in denial. By daily
life in natural relations with the poor, by a fruitful contact with
fact, by the clash of opinion in London, by the influence of a noble
friendship, by the education of awakening passion—what had once
been mere tawdry and violent hearsay had passed into a true
devotion, a true thirst for social good. She had ceased to take a

system cut and dried from the Venturists, or anyone else; she had ceased to think of whole classes of civilised society with abhorrence and contempt; and there had dawned in her that temper which is in truth implied in all the more majestic conceptions of the State—the temper that regards the main institutions of every great civilisation, whether it be property, or law, or religious custom, as necessarily, in some degree, divine and sacred. For man has not been their sole artificer! Throughout there has been working with him 'the spark that fires our clay.'

Yes!—but modification, progress, change, there must be, for us as for our fathers! Would marriage fetter her? It was not the least probable that he and she, with their differing temperaments, would think alike in the future, any more than in the past. She would always be for experiments, for risks, which his critical temper, his larger brain, would of themselves be slow to enter upon. Yet she knew well enough that in her hands they would become bearable and even welcome to him. And for himself, she thought with a craving, remorseful tenderness of that pessimist temper of his towards his own work and function that she knew so well. In old days it had merely seemed to her inadequate, if not hypocritical. She would have liked to drive the dart deeper, to make him still unhappier! Now, would not a wife's chief function be to reconcile him with himself and life, to cheer him forward on the lines of his own nature—to believe, understand, help?

Yet always in the full liberty to make her own sacrifices, to realise her own dreamlands! She thought with mingled smiles and tears of her plans for this bit of earth that fate had brought under her hand; she pledged herself to every man, woman and child on it so to live her life that each one of theirs should be the richer for it; she set out, so far as in her lay, to 'choose equality.' And beyond Mellor, in the great changing world of social speculation and endeavour, she prayed always for the open mind, the listening heart.

'There is one conclusion, one cry, I always come back to at last,' she remembered hearing Hallin say to a young Conservative with whom he had been having a long economic and social argument. '*Never resign yourself!*—that seems to be the main note of it. Say, if you will—believe, if you will—that human nature, being what it is, and what, so far as we can see, it always must be, the motives which work the present social and industrial system can never be largely superseded; that property and saving—luck, too!—struggle, success, and failure, must go on. That is one's intellectual conclusion; and one has a right to it—you and I are at one in it. But then—on the heels of it comes the moral

imperative! "Hold what you please about systems and movements, and fight for what you hold; only, as an individual—*never
say—never think !*—that it is in the order of things, in the purpose
of God, that one of these little ones—this Board School child, this
man honestly out of work, this woman 'sweated' out of her life—
should perish!" A contradiction, or a commonplace, you say?
Well and good. The only truths that burn themselves into the
conscience, that work themselves out through the slow and mani-
fold processes of the personal will into a pattern of social improvement, are the contradictions and the commonplaces!'

So here, in the dark, alone with the haunting uplifting pre-
sences of 'admiration, hope, and love,' Marcella vowed, within
the limits of her personal scope and power, never to give up the
struggle for a nobler human fellowship, the lifelong toil to understand, the passionate effort to bring honour and independence and
joy to those who had them not. But not alone; only, not alone!
She had learnt something of the dark aspects, the crushing complexity of the world. She turned from them to-night, at last, with
a natural human terror, to hide herself in her own passion, to
make of love her guide and shelter. Her whole rich being was
wrought to an intoxication of self-giving. Oh! let the night go
faster! faster! and bring his step upon the road, her cry of repentance to his ear.

'I trust I am not late. Your clocks, I think, are ahead of ours.
You said eleven?'

Aldous advanced into the room with hand outstretched. He
had been ushered into the drawing-room, somewhat to his surprise.

Marcella came forward. She was in black as before, and pale,
but there was a knot of pink anemones fastened at her throat,
which, in the play they made with her face and hair, gave him a
start of pleasure.

'I wanted,' she said, 'to ask you again about those shares—
how to manage the sale of them. Could you—could you give me
the name of someone in the City you trust?'

He was conscious of some astonishment.

'Certainly,' he said. 'If you would rather not entrust it to
Mr. French, I can give you the name of the firm my grandfather
and I have always employed; or I could manage it for you if you
would allow me. You have quite decided?'

'Yes,' she said, mechanically,—'quite. And—and I think I
could do it myself. Would you mind writing the address for me,
and will you read what I have written there?'

She pointed to the little writing-table and the writing materials upon it, then turned away to the window. He looked at her an instant with uneasy amazement.

He walked up to the table, put down his hat and gloves beside it, and stooped to read what was written.

'*It was in this room you told me I had done you a great wrong. But wrongdoers may be pardoned sometimes, if they ask it. Let me know by a sign, a look, if I may ask it. If not, it would be kind to go away without a word.*'

She heard a cry. But she did not look up. She only knew that he had crossed the room, that his arms were round her, her head upon his breast.

'Marcella !—wife !' was all he said, and that in a voice so low, so choked, that she could hardly hear it.

He held her so for a minute or more, she weeping, his own eyes dim with tears, her cheek laid against the stormy beating of his heart.

At last he raised her face, so that he could see it.

'So this—this was what you had in your mind towards me, while I have been despairing—fighting with myself, walking in darkness. Oh, my darling ! explain it. How can it be? Am I real? Is this face—are these lips real?'—he kissed both, trembling. 'Oh! when a man is raised thus—in a moment—from torture and hunger to full joy, there are no words——'

His head sank on hers, and there was silence again, while he wrestled with himself.

At last she looked up, smiling.

'You are to please come over here,' she said, and, leading him by the hand, she took him to the other side of the room. 'That is the chair you sat in that morning. Sit down !'

He sat down, wondering, and, before he could guess what she was going to do, she had sunk on her knees beside him.

'I am going to tell you,' she said, 'a hundred things I never told you before. You are to hear me confess ; you are to give me penance ; you are to say the hardest things possible to me. If you don't, I shall distrust you.'

She smiled at him again through her tears. 'Marcella,' he cried in distress, trying to lift her, to rise himself, 'you can't imagine that I should let *you* kneel to *me* !'

'You must,' she said steadily. 'Well, if it will make you happier, I will take a stool and sit by you. But you are there above me—I am at your feet—it is the same chair, and you shall not move '—she stooped in a hasty passion, as though atoning for her 'shall,' and kissed his hand—'till I have said it all—every word !'

So she began it—her long confession, from the earliest days. He winced often—she never wavered. She carried through the sharpest analysis of her whole mind with regard to him; of her relations to him and Wharton in the old days; of the disloyalty and lightness with which she had treated the bond, that yet she had never, till quite the end, thought seriously of breaking; of her selfish indifference to, even contempt for, his life, his interest, his ideals; of her calm forecasts of a married state in which she was always to take the lead and always to be in the right—then of the real misery and struggle of the Hurd trial.

'That was my first true *experience*,' she said; 'it made me wild and hard, but it burnt, it purified. I began to live. Then came the day when—when we parted—the time in hospital—the nursing—the evening on the terrace. I had been thinking of you —because remorse made me think of you—solitude—Mr. Hallin— everything. I wanted you to be kind to me, to behave as though you had forgotten everything, because it would have made me comfortable and happy; or I thought it would. And then, that night you wouldn't be kind, you wouldn't forget—instead, you made me pay my penalty.'

She stared at him an instant, her dark brows drawn together, struggling to keep her tears back, yet lightening from moment to moment into a divine look of happiness. He tried to take possession of her, to stop her, to silence all this self-condemnation on his breast. But she would not have it; she held him away from her.

'That night, though I walked up and down the terrace with Mr. Wharton afterwards, and tried to fancy myself in love with him—that night, for the first time, I began to love you! It was mean and miserable, wasn't it, not to be able to appreciate the gift, only to feel when it was taken away? It was like being good when one is punished, because one must——'

She laid down her head against his chair with a long sigh. He could bear it no longer. He lifted her in his arms, talking to her passionately of the feelings which had been the counterpart to hers, the longings, jealousies, renunciations—above all, the agony of that moment at the Mastertons' party.

'Hallin was the only person who understood,' he said; 'he knew all the time that I should love you to my grave. I could talk to him.'

She gave a little sob of joy, and pushing herself away from him an instant, she laid a hand on his shoulder.

'I told him,' she said—'I told him, that night he was dying. He looked at her with an emotion too deep even for caresses,

'He never spoke—coherently—after you left him. At the end he motioned to me, but there were no words. If I could possibly love you more, it would be because you gave him that joy.'

He held her hand, and there was silence. Hallin stood beside them, living and present again in the life of their hearts.

Then, little by little, delight and youth and love stole again upon their senses.

'Do you suppose,' he exclaimed, 'that I yet understand in the least how it is that I am here, in this chair, with you beside me? You have told me much ancient history !—but all that truly concerns me this morning lies in the dark. The last time I saw you, you were standing at the garden-door, with a look which made me say to myself that I was the same blunderer I had always been, and had far best keep away. Bridge me the gap, please, between that hell and this heaven !'

She held her head high, and changed her look of softness for a frown.

'You had spoken of "*marriage* !"' she said. 'Marriage in the abstract, with a big *M*. You did it in the tone of my guardian giving me away. Could I be expected to stand that?'

He laughed. The joy in the sound almost hurt her.

'So one's few virtues smite one,' he said as he captured her hand again. 'Will you acknowledge that I played my part well? I thought to myself, in the worst of tempers, as I drove away, that I could hardly have been more official. But all this is evasion. What I desire to know, categorically, is, what made you write that letter to me last night, after—after the day before?'

She sat with her chin on her hand, a smile dancing.

'Whom did you walk with yesterday afternoon?' she said slowly.

He looked bewildered.

'There !' she cried, with a sudden wild gesture ; 'when I have told you it will undo it all. Oh ! if Frank had never said a word to me ; if I had had no excuse, no assurance, nothing to go upon, had just called to you in the dark, as it were, there would be some generosity, some atonement in that ! Now you will think I waited to be meanly sure, instead of——'

She dropped her dark head upon his hand again with an abandonment which unnerved him, which he had almost to brace himself against.

'So it was Frank,' he said —'*Frank* ! Two hours ago, from my window, I saw him and Betty down by the river in the park. They were supposed to be fishing. As far as I could see they were sitting or walking hand in hand, in the face of day and the keepers. I prepared wise things to say to them. None of them will be said now, or listened to. As Frank's mentor I am undone.'

He held her, looking at her intently.

'Shall I tell you,' he asked, in a lower voice—'shall I show you something—something that I had on my heart as I was walking here?'

He slipped his hand into the breast-pocket of his coat, and drew out a little plain black leather case. When he opened it she saw that it contained a pen-and-ink sketch of herself that had been done one evening by a young artist staying at the Court, and—a bunch of traveller's joy.

She gazed at it with a mixture of happiness and pain. It reminded her of cold and selfish thoughts, and set them in relief against his constancy. But she had given away all rights—even the right to hate herself. Piteously, childishly, with seeking eyes, she held out her hand to him, as though mutely asking him for the answer to her outpouring—the last word of it all. He caught her whisper.

'Forgive?' he said to her, scorning her for the first and only time in their history. 'Does a man *forgive* the hand that sets him free, the voice that re-creates him? Choose some better word—my wife!'